Aspiring writer Ben Crestfield never wanted to be an African-American statistic: one of too many men who sired children only to run from the responsibilities of fatherhood. Yet his muse led far away from his greatest joy—his daughter Makeba. Acclaim was his reward, but guilt was his penance...and the knowing that his heart could not hide forever behind his words.

Powerful, intelligent, funny, emotionally intense and stylistically brilliant, Alexs D. Pate's *Finding Makeba* explores a sensitive and timely subject—absentee black fathers and the effects of their flight on the families they abandon—and does so in a bold and original manner. Alternating between the autobiographical "novel" that is bringing Ben Crestfield sudden literary recognition and a reemergent teenage daughter's response to the fictional accounting of her father's crimes, Pate's story is neither condemnation nor apology, but rather a poignant appreciation of the forces, internal and external, that direct—and misdirect—a life. It is a story of love, failure, and understanding—of wounds opened and healed; of things forgiven, and things that never can be—and of a long road back that begins at a Philadelphia book signing...when a beautiful young woman with accusing eyes asks an author to inscribe his work "to Makeba Crestfield."

"*Finding Makeba* attempts to sift through the complex layers of a black man's identity...Pate clearly has concerns that go beyond sociology and family dynamics. His work also contemplates the power of language and the limitations of the body."
—*Washington Post Book World*

"A topical but effectively engrossing read by an author with the ability to say things in a new way...Pate [is] a stylistic innovator who can also tell a story."
—*Kirkus Reviews*

Finding Makeba

ALEXS D. PATE

AN AVON BOOK

AVON BOOKS, INC.
1350 Avenue of the Americas
New York, New York 10019

Copyright © 1996 by Alexs D. Pate
Cover illustration by Harry Burman
Published by arrangement with the author
Library of Congress Catalog Card Number: 96-18418
ISBN: 0-380-73152-5
www.avonbooks.com/bard

First Bard Printing: August 1999

BARD TRADEMARK REG U S PAT. OFF AND IN OTHER COUNTRIES, MARCA REGISTRADA, HECHO EN U S.A

Printed in the U.S.A.

OPM 10 9 8 7 6 5 4 3 2 1

FOR
GYANNI, ALEXS
AND CHEKESHA

The secret of fatherhood can only have been revealed to men by the women themselves . . .

THE WOMEN'S ENCYCLOPEDIA OF MYTHS AND SECRETS
by Barbara Walker

Standards for fathers are not so high. Drunkards, adulterers, child-beaters, even criminals are supposed to have a "right" to fatherhood, to say nothing of millions of men who treat their children with a neglectful indifference that would bring down society's wrath on a female parent. Possibly men should be taught to regard fatherhood as a privilege to be earned, not as a right to be abused.

THE WOMEN'S ENCYCLOPEDIA OF MYTHS AND SECRETS

The hearty ringing laugh of a child is sweet music to the ear. There are three most joyous sounds in nature — the hum of a beem, the purr of a cat, and the laugh of a child. They tell of peace, of happiness, and of contentment and make one for a while forget that there is so much misery in the world.

THE COLLEGE OF LIFE OR PRACTICAL SELF-EDUCATOR:
A MANUAL OF SELF-IMPROVEMENT FOR THE COLORED RACE *(1898)*

Finding Makeba

Prologue

Makeba looked across the aisle of the train and found the eyes of a thin-faced man. In the shadowed light of the train he was almost an apparition. His skin was bad, like the gray rocks she used to collect from the railroad beds near Rock Garden, a place of her childhood in North Philadelphia. Her grandmother had called them "funk rock" because if you rubbed them against each other or against cement, they would crumble and emit a nasty odor. The man swam in a shiny blue serge suit. A frayed, dingy white shirt stuck to his body. There were other people on the train, which traveled the Main Line route to downtown Philadelphia, but Makeba could feel only his eyes.

She straightened up. Why was he staring at her like that? Did he know what she was about to do? Could he tell how uneasy she was? She had purposely dressed to avoid the boring gazes of the men who rode trains in the middle of the day. She wore a set of baggy, faded blue denim overalls with a long-underwear top underneath. On her feet were a set of black combat boots. She couldn't be attractive to him.

But he wouldn't turn his head. He seemed to be staring into her chest. Makeba wished she had worn her baseball cap. With that she

1

could have blocked him out. Simply pulled the bill of the cap down over her eyes. But her close-cut hair was no protection; indeed, it was but a frame for her soft, youthful face.

She was already in a steady tremble, a string away from tears. She wasn't even sure she could stand up to get off the train when it arrived at Suburban Station. All morning she had been conscious only of herself. Her thoughts. She had walked past her mother and her stepfather—mindless, oblivious to them, as she left the house. No one had intruded into her consciousness until this man's wild-eyed stare.

Makeba carried a large black shoulder bag. She pulled it onto her lap and looked inside. There was a sixties-style brown suede, fringed purse which held fifty dollars and a loose collection of photographs. Resting against the purse were two books and a small stuffed lion, its frayed cotton fur worn nearly to skin. The face of the lion smiled up at her. It was the kind of encouragement she needed.

With a sigh she leaned back into her seat again. She wasn't afraid of the man across from her. Not today. At best he only symbolized the disconnection that was a part of her life. He could sit there and put his eyes on her and she was powerless to stop him. But he didn't matter. He would eventually get off the train. He would eventually pass into meaninglessness, just as most of the people in her life did.

Makeba took out her journal and a green felt-tip pen. She opened to the first blank page. She did not want to review what she had written the night before. She was afraid that if she turned back to that page, she would not follow through on her mission.

So many things could turn her back. And she had promised herself: Today she would do one of the most difficult things she'd ever done. On this day her life would change. How it would change she had no idea. Maybe there would be no tomorrow. Maybe when she was done doing the thing she had to do, the feelings of fear and dread which had been with her since she was a child would finally be exorcised and she would simply collapse and die.

Makeba felt the rhythmic sway as the cars rocked on their feet. But she had completely missed the moment when the train ducked into the tunnel that led into downtown Philadelphia. Makeba had traveled this route many times and was always fascinated at the moment when daylight became darkness. When the space of suburbia was immediately replaced by the density of the city. The interior lights of the train only heightened the effect. She tried to write but nothing came. She stared at the white pages, trying to block everything else out of her view. Especially the man across from her.

The train stopped briefly at Thirtieth Street Station. As the brakes engaged, the man stood and crossed toward her. The doors opened but he stood staring at her. And then, suddenly, he opened his mouth. "You're a very cute young woman." And then, for the first time, there was a crooked, brown-toothed smile. "Have a nice day." He breathed through his teeth, and stumbled out the door.

Makeba didn't respond. Didn't move a muscle. Wasn't soothed by his good wishes. In fact she wanted to scream at him. To curse him. He was what she hated. Men full of insincerity and lies. He didn't know her. What could he know about her day? What he had said under the guise of cordiality wasn't for her. It rolled off of her. It meant nothing.

She looked again at the empty page and suddenly felt like writing again.

But instead of making her pen put words down, she watched the new passengers board for the short ride from Thirtieth Street to Suburban Station. The train was dotted with businesspeople, more symbols of the lies and exploitation that were all around her. Everyone looked scrubbed and buffed and ready to make more money.

Outside, the May day was bright and warm, one of the first days of the year that hinted at the heat of the coming summer. And then her body was shaking again. Fear came over her, unannounced, like rain. It was a serious journey she was on. And there was no thought which allowed her to escape it. Years of dread were compressed in her thin body. It erupted into anxiety without warning. That was what this trip was about. She was going to the source of everything. The point at which her life, through no fault of her own, had been stuffed full of disappointment.

As a child she had always had flawless cinnamon skin, a shade lighter than her mother's, but now at nineteen, there were the

3

shadows of pimples that had plagued her over the last year. Whenever she became emotionally uncertain, the bumps would rise on her skin like flowers. The small dark spots marked the remnants of the last outbreak.

The train squealed into the station. Makeba closed her journal and replaced it in her bag. She carefully stood up; her heavy combat boots scuffed the floor as she grabbed her bag and slung it over her shoulder.

Makeba found it hard to walk as she left the train and climbed the steps into the station. Her legs felt tired, as if she had run all the way into the city from the suburb of Malvern.

Now, even though she was aware of many more people around her, all of them going somewhere, all of them rushing, she could make out no details.

She wanted to turn around and go back home. What she was doing was crazy. Even though this had been carefully planned, she wasn't sure she could go through with it. Her stomach was lurching. She passed by the concessions and shops of the station like a waif, lost in thought and with increasing fear.

As she emerged from the station, the sunlight surprised her. She had almost forgotten what time of day it was. She pulled out an old pocket watch, given to her by her grandmother. It was nearly two o'clock. Makeba made her way to Chestnut Street. She *wanted* to be late. It would be very dangerous to arrive early and then have too much time to wait. If that happened she might back out. No, actually she wanted to get there just as everything was ending. That would be the right way.

Makeba walked with a loping gait, an imitation of a boy she knew. It was a walk that waded through the center-city crowds in oblivious determination. She waited for no red lights, lumbered through the traffic, weaved her way to her destination.

And then, suddenly, she was standing in front of the bookstore. She froze. Her trembling got worse. Maybe she really *couldn't* do it. And then she saw it. His picture sat in the window like a huckster waving the customers inside. *He* was the reason she had tried so hard in school, only to feel stupid. Had searched so hard for a man to love, only to suffer loneliness. *He* was the reason her speech was subdued and slow, to the point that sometimes even her friends thought she was chronically depressed. *He* was the reason she never felt safe and why nothing ever felt good to her. She had to go in.

Inside the store there was a strong murmur emanating from the back. She moved in that direction. Her mind was blank now. This was what plans were for. They move you even when you cannot think. This was well rehearsed. Instinctive.

She took up a place at the end of the line. She hoped no one would come up behind her. She wanted to be the last. He wouldn't be able to see anyone after her anyway.

The line moved briskly. Makeba was careful to stand behind the woman in front of her so that she could not be seen by the man who sat at a small table, the place where the line ended. And she really didn't want to see him either. Not until she was right in front of him. She heard him laugh. And then others laughed. His voice was complex, soft and compelling at the same time. It was a voice you wanted to listen to.

And then she was one person away. Makeba could now hear the dialogue.

"Do you always write stories about families?"

"It's what I've been thinking most about lately. I've got other stories to tell, but right now, I just believe it's what I have to do." Ben shifted in his chair. "What's your name?"

"Madeline Jones." Madeline was a middle-aged white woman who Makeba thought must have been a teacher. There was a faint hint of chalk sprinkled throughout her navy wool suit with a pleated skirt.

"May I ask you a question, Mr. Crestfield?" Makeba wanted the woman to get her book autographed and keep moving.

"Of course."

Makeba lost her breath again. That voice. She knew that voice even though she had not heard it in so many years. Her knees started to buckle.

"Is this your story? Is this autobiographical in any way?" Makeba stared at the woman's back. That was a dumb question. Of course the story was autobiographical. Someone would have had to live this story. You couldn't make this up.

Ben Crestfield's voice rose in animated laughter. "I get asked that a lot. And I answer it by simply saying that, yes, there are parts that really happened to me and other parts that I made up. But that doesn't mean all of it isn't true."

"I see. Is that why the main character has your name?" Makeba was growing impatient. The woman's questions were so stupid.

"Well, Madeline—it's Madeline, right?" The woman nodded. "Usually, writers change the names and keep the situations true. I just did the opposite."

"I see. Well, after reading your book, I felt like I knew you."

Makeba could feel the air tense a little. Ben Crestfield paused, trying to decide what to say. "Well, Madeline, I take that as a compliment. I hope you feel the same way about my new book, which, by the way, is not about me."

Makeba felt the finality in his comment. Madeline's audience with the author was over. But she made no move to leave. Makeba felt nauseous.

And Madeline *didn't* leave. She leaned over the table, bending at the waist. "Mr. Crestfield, is it possible I could talk with you sometime? Not here, but somewhere else. I think we have a lot in common."

Makeba was instantly frightened. Even though she was trying to keep her head down, she couldn't help but catch a glimpse of the man just beyond Madeline. He was heavier than she remembered. Rounder. He was almost bald, with just a shadow of hair covering his head. Still, even in this subdued atmosphere of books, the smell of dust, paper and ink permeating, the flash in his eyes held her. And just like always, there was somebody between them.

"I'm sorry, Madeline. I'm leaving tomorrow. I don't get to Philadelphia very often. But next time I'm in town maybe we'll run into each other." Makeba looked at the floor. She wasn't sure but she felt like the newly famous writer was trying his best to see over Madeline. Trying to see who his next fan was.

Madeline finally pulled away, leaving Makeba, face pointed

downward, standing in front of the author. She took a deep breath and steeled herself. She knew he was looking at her but she didn't move.

"Yes?" He was speaking to her. "Have you read my book?"

Makeba held each word. She had promised herself that before she spoke a word, she would remember all of the times when she had wished, with all her strength, to hear his voice. And now, those moments were zipping through her head like shards of light. She struggled to hold herself together.

And then, slowly, she reached into her bag. She knew he was watching her. He was silent now. Without looking up, she pulled out a copy of his book. She held it in front of her face and opened it to the page where the dedication was.

Ben looked at the young woman. She was the youngest person who had come in for the book signing. His interest always grew when he came in contact with younger readers. They held the strongest pain. Just the week before in Buffalo he had spent three hours with a young woman who couldn't stop crying. Her father too, gone into the shadows.

But he sensed something about this woman. Some deep signature of pain marked her. And she still hadn't held her head up so he could see her. When he saw the book he smiled.

"Did you like the book?"

"Like it?" Makeba hadn't expected that question.

"Yes, that's what an author asks someone who has read his book." Ben wondered why she wouldn't look at him.

"Well. . ." Makeba stumbled. "Like that woman, I guess I wasn't sure what was real and what wasn't." She paused, uncertain again of her determination. "I just came to the conclusion that it didn't matter, that wasn't the point."

"Yeah, that's the way I wanted it." Ben pulled her copy of the book closer to him so he could sign it. "What's your name? Who should I sign this to?"

"To me." Makeba looked up; now she was a thin light without a body, hovering there. She forced herself to speak. "Make it for Makeba Crestfield." Ben looked into his daughter's eyes and felt his body short-circuit. He leaned back in his chair. Yes. That was his forehead. That was his nose. He knew her soft-featured face. That beautiful brown skin. This was his daughter. He felt his body quaking.

Makeba's eyes were clouding; she knew this would challenge all of her strength, her resolve. She struggled to hold herself back.

Ben was trying to breathe. He was aware he hadn't said anything, and searched inside himself for a voice. But before he could speak, Makeba's hand emerged again from her shoulder bag and offered a second book. This one was black with gold trim embossed on the borders. It was very slim and felt like a hymnbook in his hands.

He opened the cover, a sheet of paper fell out. The script was tight and thin:

Dear Father?

I've been so quiet most of my life. Do you know that? What do you really know about me? You've created this character that is supposed to be me, I guess, but how can you create something you don't really know about? It's not fair. It doesn't really matter if I understand why you left or not. I know I expected you to come back. I know that. And every day, for a while, I thought you would. And then there were months and then, well, to be honest, I stopped thinking about you so much. I could go months without remembering that someone I had loved, my father, was completely gone out of my life. You may have been thinking about me, which I have to say I don't believe, but whether you were or not, I wasn't always thinking about you.

But still, my life has brought me to this moment where I need to talk to you. I need to hear your voice. No matter how hard I have tried to completely push you out of my mind, I have to admit that I still have a hole in me. Maybe I did need to know why it all happened. And maybe I needed to tell you that no matter how you tell this story, it could never adequately explain away the most important fact: You left me. You did. I loved you, yes, but it was more than that. You had a deep effect on me. You thought I was beautiful. You thought I was so smart. You gave me books. (By the way, when a boy buys me a book, he's halfway there.) Anyway, I've changed everything in my life now. I'm going to go to school next year and get myself together. I've been lost for so long. Lost and trapped at the same time. Trapped by something I didn't have anything to do with. But, to be honest, reading your book has made a difference.

I came into town last month and passed by the bookstore with your picture in the window advertising the book. It upset me. I recognized you right away. Until that moment, you were a feeling. Like someone who had died a long time ago. Somebody you might have cared about but who you just had to go on without because they weren't coming back. When I bought the book, finally, I had something—something from you. I carried it around in my bag for almost a week. And when I started reading it, I decided to start writing again. If you could do it, so could I. So I kept a journal. After each chapter, I wrote whatever came into my mind. And now, you are reading it.

Makeba

Ben looked up from the letter into his daughter's eyes. He thought about the agonizing nights he had spent trying to feel her presence. How he had been driven mad by her absence, his absence. How he had slowly taught himself to live without her. It had been like a mythological journey. From safety to terror and back again. He had come the full distance and, like Odysseus, washed up on the shores of sanity again. And he had the golden fleece.

When he wrote the novel she held in her hands, he had used his longing for her as both the reason to tell the truth and the fuel to keep going even when facing her presence in his fiction made him physically ill. He had almost died trying to finish that book. It was truly a letter to her. It held the answer to the question he knew she had to be asking. It held the answer to the question "Why?"

One

Love starts small. In the beginning it is a tiny, nearly invisible blossom. Yet in a short time it can take you over. Overrun you like you were a building and it was ivy. It has its own life. Love grows. Envelops you. Suddenly there is no escape and you are trapped. It becomes so thick you lose control of your own faculties. Finally you are within it.

There, too, is an unseen force. His name is Mates. In the first moments of love, Mates has no substance. But he is there. If you have been in love, especially if that love has ended, as love eventually does, you already know him.

Mates is guilt in waiting. He knows that in every relationship someone will eventually break a promise, or do something which irrevocably destroys that love. He is there to punish that person. He hangs there, waiting—in the space, in the shadows, everywhere.

When called, when things are just so, Mates is able to metamorphose out of the shadows. Some then see him as a wolf, others as a dog. A black dog. At those times his teeth and claws have substance. Then he is able to do his purpose.

His purpose? Well, many, even though they may deny it, have felt his strong jaws clamp down on them. Others, only the sound of his paws forever on their heels. Mates can chase you to the end. To the place where there is only a gasping for breath. The last step before nothing. It has been said that he feeds on the dead, that he eats the hearts of those he pursues and then carries them away into the netherworld.

But you must understand that he is there at the moment when love becomes itself. He knows what we don't. When love dies and one person looks at the other and accuses them of some ugly action, he knows that that guilt has been there all the time, first as air, later as frustration and finally as anger and pain.

Mates was there the day Makeba's parents, Ben and Helen, met. It was at a Saint Valentine's Day party in 1975. Chance. Neither of them knew that on that February night they would begin a falling flight.

As Ben drove his yellow 1970 Volkswagen Bug away from the center of the city on his way to the party, he struggled to keep his eyes focused on the street. A light snow had fallen and he was already high enough to race a cloud to heaven.

He had been with his friend Ramsey, who was still at the Thirteen Bar, eyes glazed and focused on a topless dancer, where Ben had left him. Ben had lied and said he had to go home. Instead, now enfolded in his VW, he was headed to a party in West Oak Lane. And he wanted to go alone.

When Ben and Ramsey were together, they unconsciously stopped each other from approaching women. Together, they sat on the sidelines and exchanged a satiric running commentary as if neither of them were actually interested in the women. Ramsey would find something wrong with every one of them. After all, in the years Ben had known the man, Ramsey had never had a serious girlfriend. He would occasionally meet someone, but after one or two dates she would usually break it off.

Ben suspected that the real problem wasn't Ramsey's weight but his personality. He was rough. Like a chunk of coal. It was just a matter of time before he offended or hurt someone. And, Ben figured, that was why Ramsey always put women down. Ramsey talked about wanting to be in a relationship with a woman, but he wasn't willing to do what that required. Namely, treat women with respect.

Ben went to the go-go bars and he participated in the juvenile banter, but underneath, he did not hate women the way he felt some men, including Ramsey, did. That was the thing, he could feel the hatred that radiated from men toward women. The need to possess, to use, to abuse, to discard. He was aware and he fought those urges whenever they arose in him.

Besides, he was planning to be a writer, at least that's what he was studying in school, and he was becoming more and more consumed with his own identity, his own process of determining the meaning of love. And that was why he had lied to Ramsey about the party. He was tired of going places, being around the social swirl without actually being in it. On the rare occasions when he would break away and try to talk to a woman, Ramsey was always there waiting to make fun of him. He would say things like, "What you want with that girl? I told you, man, they just want your money," or, "Why you want to talk to that bear?" And Ben would stifle his anger, play it off as just another episode of macho ghetto humor.

So he had taken to lying. It was the only way he would ever meet anyone. The only way love could ever come to him. And on this night Ben felt desperate. He knew there was someone out there for him and he wanted to hurry up and meet her.

In the small car, Ben filled all of the space made for the driver. His solid five-foot-nine-inch frame found just enough room to maneuver. He was twenty-two, a recent veteran of the Navy, where he'd met Ramsey, and was laboring through his second year as a part-time English major on the G.I. Bill.

Somehow that night, as he cut through the snow and the cold blowing wind, he found the right block of Sharpnack Street. Ben saw the lights through the frosted window of the house and knew he was in the right place. He parked a half block away. As soon as he opened his car door, he heard the thumping bass twisting through the heavy night air.

Fortified with alcohol, Ben stumbled up the steps to the West

Oak Lane row house. He shivered. He had taken off his leather coat and left it in the car. He never took his leather into parties where he would have to lay it on a mountain of other coats. He wasn't about to give some opportunistic fool the chance to exchange a cheap lightweight London Fog trench for a two-hundred-dollar leather.

The windows of the house were glazed over but he could see the shadows of people dancing inside, defying the cold temperatures outside.

Unlike the house in which he had grown up in North Philadelphia, most West Oak Lane houses had front porches. It was one of the features that the upwardly mobile looked for. And West Oak Lane was the first neighborhood that black folks from North Philly headed for when they got some money.

It was late, a little after midnight and therefore after the proper celebration of Valentine's Day. Ben rang the bell but no one came. Through the haze of the small window on the door, he could see the people dancing. He could hear the music. But none of the dancing bodies was willing to break from the beat and open the door for him. He banged on the door with his fist. Finally, a man dancing closest to the door reluctantly tore himself away from the jam to let Ben in.

Ben quickly pushed through the threshold. It was dark. There was a small lamp sitting on a table at the end of a gray sofa. In it a dark blue light burned. It glowed. It made the room bluedark.

Ben couldn't tell how many people were moving with Earth, Wind and Fire's "Shining Star." You could always count on Earth, Wind and Fire to raise a sweat in the February freeze. The heat that came from the dense layering of bodies rippled in the thick air.

He was struck by the way black folks created heat. They wanted to create heat. That was a part of the process. Dancing without heat was what white people did. And it was hot within the sea of people. It was hard to believe that it could be so cold outside and so smoking inside. From the moment he stepped into the room, he felt the sweat break free and seek the air.

Ben weaved through the crowd. There was a complex odor coursing through the room. A composite smell of individuals. And he could smell each one. Each one a separate celebration of life and energy. The styles and steps formed a raw strength. If dancing were war, African people would rule the world. If dancing ever becomes war, look out. He felt the complex energies of the city. As he passed among the folks, he felt middle-class energy, poor-working-class energy, gang energy, high yellow energy, gospel energy all swirling on the dance floor.

Underneath the blaring stereo a different noise hovered about the dancers. It was like a buzzing whistle that darted between the loud music and the empty space in Ben's head. Like a whirling plastic toy sold at circuses and carnivals. People weren't talking, there was little evidence, even in the cornflower light, of smiling faces. Just serious attention being paid to the rhythm, the beat and the moving body.

He couldn't distinguish faces and so he didn't know if there was anyone there he knew. Ben moved by instinct to the kitchen. In the kitchen he knew he would find the people who wanted to be seen. People who were not afraid to be under the light. Of course he had been to parties where the people in the kitchen were the ones doing the illegal drugs. But that was uncommon. Most people honored kitchens and wouldn't permit foul shit to go on in them. In most houses the kitchen was a respected place.

He worked his way through. As he broke free of the throng of dancers, darkness and sweat, his eyes were unprepared for the bright light of the kitchen.

There he knew he would find Geri and her friends, a small number of women, "girlfriends" they called themselves, who often gave parties or knew where there was one.

Geri was the primary "girlfriend." Every Friday Ben would call Geri and ask what was up. She'd have a list of parties that stretched into the next week. Parties of all sorts. She'd have parties in the serious hoods, in North, South and West Philly. She'd also have another list of parties in Germantown, West Oak Lane and Overbrook. She'd know where they were doing drugs and which party had good food and which one had the best music for dancing. Geri was party central.

But on this night she was having her own set. A Valentine's Day jam. Lovers and folks looking for lovers.

Ben felt the rum running through him. He practically leapt into the kitchen, catching everyone, including Geri, by surprise. The light blinded him. Everything wavered like an underwater image. He could tell there were a lot of people standing around, but suddenly he couldn't see very well.

Geri was breathtaking. Her walnut skin was like velvet. Her penetrating eyes cast a sweet shadow on the sunflower walls of the kitchen. At the time, she had one of the largest Afros he had ever seen. Her body was long and strong. She wore a multicolored tank top and tight white Levi's. Her black platforms set the outfit off.

She was quickly at his side. "Ben? I didn't know you were here yet." She put her fluorescent-red lips on his cheeks. Her face wrinkled. "Are you drunk already?"

Ben didn't feel drunk, but he couldn't explain why he suddenly wrapped his arms around her and pulled her close. So close he could smell the Ambush perfume painting peach on the inside of his mind. So close he felt her breasts against his chest. Lost in the moment, he reduced himself and curled up next to her. Unconscious of everyone around. Unconscious of everything and everyone except his need to be enveloped. He let his fingers meld into the cotton of her tank top.

This is what happens when you are lonely. You find yourself pulled unexplainably into situations you would not normally be pulled into. Like the softness of Geri's body. Ben knew it wasn't right. He could feel Geri tensing up under his clutch. But she felt so good to him. So comfortable. And on this night he felt pliant, malleable.

He should have known better. He knew Geri. He knew she didn't play that. "What's wrong with you?" She gently pushed him an arm's length away.

Ben was instantly shaken back into himself. Whatever traces of him couldn't make it back into his body remained on her. He tried to clear his head. "Nothing. Ah . . . nothing's wrong, Geri. I'm just buzzing a little, that's all. Everything's cool."

She looked at him and laughed. "Cool? You come in here grabbing all over me and you got the nerve to say 'everything's cool'?" She paused. "I ain't your property."

"I know, Geri. I told you, I'm just lunchin', that's all. I didn't mean no harm." As he fumbled with his words, Ben suddenly realized there were three women standing around them. He had obviously interrupted a conversation. Now he became more nervous. Maybe he *was* drunk. He had forgotten for a moment that he was at a party. That people were all around him. He felt them laughing, hiccuping lilts in the yellow kitchen.

Geri smiled, ignoring him with a flourish of her moving hands, simply said, "Ain't no thang, Ben. I was just messing with you. Long as you keep them hands to yourself. I got enough problems tonight without having to fight you off."

Ben knew he'd never have a chance with Geri. She was the first woman the men went after. Somebody was always trying to hit on her. He knew she never considered him as a potential lover. He was too plain. Not flashy enough for Geri. To her, he was a good friend, a brother. Geri would sometimes get mad at him for making simple things complicated. "Damn, Ben," she would say, "I don't know about all that book learning you gettin' at that damn college. You can't make up your mind about shit anymore. Stop making everything so damn hard. Just do what you supposed to do, that's all." That was Geri, fast and to the point.

She introduced him to everyone in the kitchen. He said hello but he couldn't focus on faces. Soon silence surrounded them. The five of them stood there, shifting weight, awkwardly staring at each other. But whoever was controlling the music box was on the money. The Isley Brothers kept the dancers churning.

Finally, to break the silence around him, Ben asked Geri to dance.

"Oh no, Ben. I'm not dancing with you tonight."

"Why not?" Ben's vision had started to work better.

"I've already got a big problem out there. Both of my boyfriends showed up. They're out there waiting to find out which one I'm going to be with tonight."

Geri turned to her friends and made an overly dramatic gesture with her arms as if to say, "I just don't know what to do."

The woman standing next to Ben broke in, "Oh go on with that shit, Geri. You know exactly what you're gonna do. You know who you want." The other two smiled in agreement.

Geri waved them off, her mind moving faster. "I've got an idea." Geri looked at Ben and slowly turned her head in the direction of the woman across from him.

He followed her eyes into the clean caramel picture that was Helen. Standing in her red pumps she was about the same height as Ben. Thin, with a head full of straightened, cascading hair, Helen had a smile that stopped people cold. She would never again be as beautiful to him as she was on that night.

Her eyes gave permission. Ben took her hand.

"Be careful, Helen, Ben's one of them *artistes*, you know," Geri called out as they started for the living room. "He'll be talking 'bout how he wants to invite you home for a poetry reading or some shit."

Helen smiled and Ben quickly ushered her out of the kitchen and into the dining room cum dance floor.

"Are you a writer?" Helen asked as they walked into the darkness.

"I . . . ah . . ." Ben hated that question. He knew what he wanted to be but saying it was difficult. He was just beginning to meet writers at school. He was just beginning to take literature and writing seriously. He thought he wanted to be a writer, but . . .

"Yeah, I guess. I mean, I'm writing a lot of poetry and stuff I . . ."

"That sounds interesting. I've never met a writer. I would never have expected Geri to even know one."

Ben chuckled. "Yeah, I bet that's right." He couldn't help smiling as they took the floor. His head was spinning just a bit and Helen was fine fine fine.

And once they were within the clutch of the steaming, shaking room, they too joined the freed souls. They danced together all night. They spoke without words, only swinging hips and strutting feet. They twisted and skipped. They called the Yoruban spirits. They danced gospel. And finally they swooned into each other.

James Brown, War, Santana, Osibisa, the Spinners, New Birth and Bobby Womack serenaded them. Called them to movement. Ben felt himself slipping into the folds of enchantment. Her softness. Her smell. The way she fit into the groove of his body spoke to him in a language his body understood. It was beyond the intellectual. He wasn't thinking. It was in the energy between them. It was silent and yet it spoke loudly. It told him that she was made to be next to him. So his hands found the places where her skin was exposed and anchored themselves there.

They instantly became the beauty and the curse. When Ben and Helen came together, there was no sky and no ground. Everything around them, above and below them, was only swatches of color. They became eagles, black eagles, entangled in their own wings.

On a slow record he whispered into her ear, "What are you? Are you some kind of spirit? Do you have some sort of magic? Why can't I let you go?"

Helen didn't move her head. "Because I don't want you to. I want you to hold me like this and never let go." The music punctuated her sentence and they danced until the record ended. Then, as someone searched for the next song and there was a hushed murmur throughout the room, Helen said softly, looking directly into his eyes, "If I really got any magic, you can bet I'm gonna try and use it on you."

The entire night was awash in blue lights and soft skin. Eventually they kissed and were swept away by the circumstances of giddiness. They held hands and drank spiked punch. Danced some more. He knew he loved her. He wasn't lonely anymore.

Langston Hughes called it the little spark that danced in the dark. The beginning. The way love starts.

Makeba's Journal

I thought this was supposed to be a novel. But as I flipped ahead I was completely shocked when I saw my real name. And Mom's and Nana's. I thought in fiction you had to make up new names. Now I'm really scared. I didn't think you could do this in a novel. Does it mean that everything I read actually happened? How did you know what she was thinking? How could you write about things you don't know? I don't understand.

What is the truth? That's what I want to know. Who is supposed to tell me the truth? Everybody lies. Everybody is afraid of what happens when you tell the truth. It's strange too, because adults always ask you to trust them. Trust them to do what? is what I want to know. I can trust them to mess up my life. I'm nineteen and I feel like I don't know anything. I always want to know what people don't tell me. I used to ask my teachers about the years that weren't on the history charts. I mean, like what happened to people on an average day. On a day when there wasn't a war or a volcano eruption or something. Do you know what I mean? What is the truth?

Everything happens inside me. I watch other people open their mouths and say things. They just say things. I might have wanted to say the same thing. But I hardly ever talk. I'm one of those silent faces sitting in the back of the room. People thought I was stupid. I know they did.

But, in a strange kind of way, I never got down on myself. I think I wrote poetry to prove that I had stuff to say. Sometimes I would forget that you wanted to be a writer. Occasionally I'd be in my room, trying to write my feelings down, and it would hit me that you might be somewhere doing the same thing.

I had this teacher in the tenth grade that really scared me. His name was Mr. Saunders. He was always bugging me to speak up in class and all that stuff. He was one of those weird white guys. Tall, thin, big glasses that were always sliding down his nose. He tried to act like he was in the know, but he was very lame. Yeah, everyone called him "Spastic Saunders" because he was always bumping his knee on the desk. He was the perfect nerd. Just what you'd expect an English teacher to look like.

Now I should tell you, because you don't know this, I was not a good student. I know you probably imagined that I was smart and all, and maybe I am, but I never tried to show it. In fact, I tried my best to hide it. Why? I don't know. I really don't. My parents—yeah, they are my parents, both of them—would get on my case but I would just stare at them. And later, in my room, I'd find myself crying because I couldn't figure out why I never tried in school. Even when I wanted to. Homework was a big problem. I hardly ever did it. They tried everything: punishment, beatings, everything. But, like, it was my thing to figure out ways to keep from doing what people wanted me to do. Still, I wrote those stupid poems that I thought were so good. And I read. That was the one thing I know you gave me. The books. Can you remember the first book you gave me to read. Can you? It was *The Hobbit*. I still have it. I still read it from time to time.

Anyway, one day, just to shut him up, I gave Mr. Saunders some of my poems to read. He had told me that he was interested in what was going on in my head. He knew I read a lot and I think he thought I was smarter than I acted. And, in a way, he was the first person to pay any special attention to me. Usually when teachers saw I wasn't going to do my homework, they left me alone. Most teachers didn't want the hassle.

God, it took him three or four days to read them. I couldn't believe how upset I got waiting. Then, at the end of class one day he asked me to stay a little later. When I walked up to his desk I could feel my legs shaking. I remember how he smiled at me. At first it was like he was seeing me for the first time. And then he handed the folder to me. When I opened it, all I could see were red marks and notes. Capitalize this, misspelled words circled, punctuation problems. I felt the tears seconds before they rolled up in my eyes. That smile hadn't meant what I first thought. When I looked up at him it was clear to me that it was pity, he felt sorry for me.

I left him sitting there like that. I cut his class so much I think he eventually forgot about me. Got a D in that one. But the grade wasn't the thing. Mr. Saunders took something away from me. Aside from Ka, I had almost no friends. But until that day, I really did believe in myself. He took that and I hated him for it. I hated him and I hated you for making me depend so much on him or anyone, for what you were supposed to give me.

Still, the way you write about meeting Mom is nice. It sounds like love at first sight. Aunt Geri is something else. It's good to know that you loved my mother. That's something.

Mom doesn't even know about this book. I've got a feeling she's not going to like it. But I'm not going to tell her about it until I've finished.

What are you trying to say with this Mates thing? I think it's very cynical to think that every time two people fall in love there will always be someone who messes it up. Just because that happened to you doesn't mean it's true for everybody. Don't get me wrong, I'm cynical too. But it seems to me that the whole idea of it is rotten. People are always looking for someone to take care of them.

Two

As the morning opened its eyes and peeked into the West Oak Lane house, it found Ben and Helen curled up on the floor in a corner against the wall. The music had long since evaporated, as had most of the people. Geri was on the couch with one of the two men who had come there each assuming she was his girlfriend. Her other suitor had quietly left an hour earlier when it became apparent that he had miscalculated his importance.

Helen and Ben sat silent, watching the blur of moving hands as Geri and her chosen lover clutched and kissed and discovered the regions beneath the surface. She moaned loudly as he, eyes closed, moved like a surgeon.

"Do you think they're going to come up for air?" Helen whispered into Ben's ear. He barely heard her words. He felt the heat of her breath. He was already riveted with excitement. He was swimming in his quiet, unprofessed emotion. He wanted her. And if that wasn't possible, he would take what he could get. If tonight all he could do was be close to her, to sit next to her, to watch her red dress grow brighter and more wrinkled in the waxing sunlight, he would accept that.

Helen smiled at him. She didn't feel quiet. She wanted to talk, to laugh, to hold on to the exploding fire of the night as long as she could. She didn't want to know what the day would bring her. She didn't want to know what plans Ben had for that Saturday. She would have loved to stop time. To prevent Saturday from ever arriving.

"I've got a mind to go over there and give that girl a chance to get some air. They need a station break or something."

Ben smiled. "Helen, if I were you I'd leave them alone. In fact, I don't see anything wrong with what they're doing. In fact"—he reached over and cupped her brown cheek in his hand and turned her face toward him—"I think, if we were doing what we should be doing, you wouldn't know so much about what they're doing."

Helen stared into his eyes. "And what should we be doing?"

He placed his lips on hers. They exchanged the inside air, the taste of each other. His tongue explored, lapped at her.

Helen's breath flowed hot into him. She felt herself letting go. Felt herself giving in to the feeling. At nineteen she had never given herself to anyone. She was suddenly overwhelmed by her own body.

She abruptly pulled away.

"No, Ben. Not like this. Not here."

Ben recaptured himself. For a moment he had sailed out into the deep. "I can't believe the way I feel right now. I just can't believe it." Of course he wanted to make love to her. What else was there to do at this moment? He couldn't think, there wasn't much more he could say. There wasn't much else he knew except to try to pass through her defenses.

"I know. I think I feel the same way. But . . ."

"But what?"

"I'm not like that." She looked over at Geri, who was now naked from the waist. The dark-skinned man on the couch with her was bent over, his mouth kissing and sucking her breasts.

"Is there somewhere we can go?" Maybe if they could be alone, maybe Helen would see that there was nothing else left between them.

"For what?" Helen was nervous. She knew what he wanted.

"I want to make love to you." What else could he say? Even

24

though he was comfortable with words, he didn't want to explain how bottomless he felt. How vulnerable, how small he felt in her arms. Like a little boy.

"I don't know. Why? Why do you want to make love to me?"

"Because . . ." Ben had begun the sentence without knowing what he would say. He knew what he wanted to say. He wanted to say that his body was telling him that they should make love. That if Geri and her friend could, they could too. Neither reason sounded strong enough actually to say. So he stopped and said nothing. He hoped her question would dissipate like morning fog.

"I'm a virgin." Helen pulled back six more inches to see his face in the early-morning light. She could still smell the paper plates strewn about with remnants of a spicy potato salad and fried chicken.

"So?" What difference could that make?

"Well, I just want you to know I don't know anything about sex and stuff like that."

"But Helen, the way I feel about you . . . Right now, after only knowing you for four hours . . . I know I want you. I want to touch you, to kiss you all over. Show you what love is." His words were traveling faster than his mind. That is what happened when he got confused. He wanted to know just the right thing to say. He wanted to do whatever he could to show her that this newly discovered desire was genuine and overpowering.

"I know what love is, I just haven't made it, that's all. I know what love is." Helen watched his eyes. They were still dancing. Like two black fires they glowed. His brown face, just a shade darker than her own, looked good as it pressed close.

This was like a harmonic convergence. Two people who were in exactly the same place at the same time, looking for the same thing.

"Until you make love, you *can't* know what it is. You have to feel the sweat and the energy running through you."

"I just met you. It's happening really fast, you know."

Ben felt her pulling away. "I know it's fast but that's what love is. That's the way it happens. You have to pay close attention to it when it's happening or it just goes away."

Ben looked over at Geri and her boyfriend. They were now

throwing light from the couch. They were dancing on each other's bodies. He was sitting up and she was straddling him. Ben could see her coffee-colored back glistening in sweat as she moved. The outline of her breasts was barely visible on the sides as she rhythmically rose and fell.

"That's what love is." He nodded in their direction.

"That's not love, Ben. I'm not that stupid. She really loves Jesse, the guy who left."

"Then why isn't Jesse here making love to her?"

"Because he couldn't take the pressure. He didn't want to find out who she wanted the most. He was afraid it wasn't him. So he left."

"But that's no reason to fuck the other guy."

"I know that. You know that. But Geri doesn't. She's just having fun. She could give a shit about Ralph. He was just here. That's all it is."

Ben sighed, accepted his defeat. "Damn. That's deep."

"So don't tell me about love. Sometimes what you think is love ain't it at all. I'm not stupid, you know. Sometimes it's just somebody fucking with you. Trying to see what they can get." Still, Helen was weakening. She wanted to feel him around her. He was bright, poetic, romantic. Not many of the men she had met seemed as soft as him. She had never known her father, who had been killed when she was a child, but her mother had filled her head with stories of his gentleness. So she knew there were black men with soft, careful, tender touches. But she had never met one, until now.

"But I'm not like that." Ben wanted to tell her about his future, his dreams. His flight away from the inner city. His determination to go to college. His desire to tell the stories of black people. Yes he wanted to make love to her. But he wanted her to know that he was different from the other men she'd met.

"Do you love me?"

Ben was stunned by the question. He had felt the answer in his throat all night. He had almost uttered those words earlier but stopped because he couldn't believe it himself.

"I . . . ah . . . I . . ." Helen smiled at him. "Well, maybe I do.

Maybe I'm falling in love with you right now." He knew that he was lonely. That there was something missing and that her smile and the warmth of her body filled up the empty space.

Helen looked into his dirt-brown eyes. "Maybe you are, Ben. I hope you are, because I'm falling in love with you." She paused. "But I'm not Geri."

Ben looked again at the couple on the couch. Geri was moving frenetically now and moaning loudly. Wiggling beneath her, Ralph added his voice to the sounds. They obviously didn't care that they had an audience.

Helen reached over and turned Ben's face back toward her. "I'm not Geri and I have to know that you love me before I'll be that way with you."

Ben felt a wave of emotion sweeping through him. He reached out and pulled Helen close. Into her ear, he whispered, "I love you. I know I do. If it takes a while for you to see that, I understand. I don't want you to be Geri. I want you to be Helen. That's what I want." As he finished, a scream erupted from across the room. They both looked over as Geri leaned backwards, her Afro now reduced to black flames. Her mouth upside down locked in grimace.

"One day, maybe I'll be that for you, Ben," Helen said as fatigue claimed her. She put her head on Ben's shoulder and closed her eyes.

But she could not sleep. Almost as soon as she felt his skin she pressed her lips to his neck and nibbled it. Her mind was a flurry. But it cleared as she imagined her mother seeing her cradled in a man's arms. Helen stiffened just a little. Her mother had tried her best to keep this moment from happening. When Helen was eight years old, her mother gave her the lion's share of the responsibility for the care of her sisters. Helen was already a surrogate mother.

Now, finally free of her mother's list of chores and responsibilities, she knew what she wanted: her own family. Sometimes Helen couldn't tell how much of that dream came from the feeling that her mother, a housekeeper by trade, had neglected her. But it was an understandable neglect. Her mother worked nights and days. Which left Helen in charge of the house. During Helen's childhood, her mother was preoccupied with making enough money to support the family.

Still, Helen really did love children. When she thought about a career she imagined herself as the director of her own day-care center. And she couldn't help but feel excited about the idea of being someone's wife. Of having her own family. Being with a man who cared about himself. Who had a real passion for life. Not just another hurt and confused black man, but a man on the move.

In a night of bluelight dancing and red-lipped kissing they fell into the cauldron of mutual need. Her body was so soft, provided so much strength. Helen spoke rivers of silence about family. Ben needed it.

Finally, nearly limp from exhaustion and the perpetual excitement, Helen suggested that they go upstairs to the guest bedroom where she was to sleep. Ben, his eyes heavy, tried to smile but couldn't.

Across from them, Geri and her boyfriend had fallen into a post-Valentine sleep. They drooled on each other. Ben could see a white trail in the corner of Geri's mouth as they seemed like two dead people.

He and Helen climbed the long stairway to the second floor. Once inside the dark bedroom, they found themselves standing over the bed, holding hands and looking out at the early-morning winter sun.

"Do you want me to stay?" Ben fidgeted. He wanted to sleep, to make love, to move past this point.

Helen looked into his tired eyes. For the first time in her life she contemplated going against her own rules. She had promised her mother and herself to be careful. But she also knew it was inevitable. She had to open herself to someone. She couldn't stay within the confines of her own body. All of her friends had children. Most of them were married. She couldn't keep turning everyone away. And Ben felt good to her.

Still, this wasn't the way she had envisioned it. If anyone had asked her how she would meet her dream man she would have said without hesitation that he would find her in church. They would be standing next to each other at choir practice or paired together in a sack race at the annual church picnic. Not at a party. Not high.

"Do you want to stay?" She stared out the window.

"Come on, Helen. You know I want to be with you. But I don't want to mess things up. I want to stay if you want me to."

Helen was so tired she felt her body breaking apart, as if it wouldn't wait for her to give approval for rest. She heard herself say, "Well, Ben, I don't think anything's going to happen tonight."

"Then suppose I stay. Suppose I just get into that bed and lie beside you and hold you tight for a little while." He smiled into her ear. "You know, I would love to write a poem for you. That's what I'm going to do. I have to get this down. Tomorrow, just for you." He pointed his finger at her. "I can feel you."

"How do you know what I'm feeling?"

"That's what a poet does, Helen. I just know. I want to be able to write about all the things I feel. They act like a black man doesn't have feelings. But I do. So I just know how you feel. I know that you have something that I need."

Helen smiled and turned her head away from him as she slid, fully dressed, into the bed. Ben got in and put his arm around her. "One of the best things about my parents, Helen, is that they always told me that I could do anything I wanted to. They always told me that I was going to be great one day. But you know what?" Ben paused; he started speaking again before her tired mind could respond. "One of the things they never prepared me for was being by myself. I don't like it."

Helen heard him but didn't answer. She was tired. She pulled him closer and slipped into the euphoria of developing love. Neither of them spoke another word.

Makeba's Journal

SECOND ENTRY

I don't know if I can read this. I didn't know this part. I mean, I know what
happened, but Mom never told me about how you two met. If this is the
truth I guess I don't understand. Why were you attracted to her? You knew
you wanted to be a writer. I don't blame her. You must have seemed really
cool at the time. She was a country girl. I know she was pretty, she still is.
Is that what it was? Was she so pretty to you that night that you just fell in
love with her? I don't think it was a good idea in the first place. I met my
first boyfriend at a party too. But I'm not stupid, I'm not letting no man
mess up my life. I've learned the hard way.

If it was up to Mom, I'd be just like her, a little country girl in bows
and dresses and shit like that. That's why she and my stepfather still live
out in the boondocks. They think living out there will keep me out of the
world. Not me. I can't live like that. They want me to be some little
"thing" with a dress on. But I'm determined to break out. I don't feel like I
have a choice. I'm trying my best to be my own person. It's hard though. I
always hear Mom's voice in the background. Evaluating me.

So, little by little, I'm trying to show her that I am my own woman. I
appreciate who she is. I really do. God, think about what would have happened to me if she wasn't who she was. Obviously you weren't ready for
it. You obviously had more important things to do. Don't you see, that's
the hardest part: accepting that you had something more important to do
than be my father.

Anyway, I'm going to try not to just rag on you. I could probably fill
this entire book up with stuff like that. What I'm trying to say is: I know I'm
confused. I know I don't know much about a lot of things. But I do know

that I want to be Makeba, whoever that is. And Makeba is not going to wear miniskirts and low-cut dresses and high heels. And she is not going to spend hours in the mirror trying to get right for some "catch." That is not me. I'll never dress for men again. This is one young black woman who ain't going for it anymore.

People think I'm out of it, but I don't care. That's just where I'm at. I've had it with the dating game. I don't know where that's going to take me but I'll figure it out as I go. I know one thing though, when you look at all the so-called couples around, you have to wonder. Nobody's happy. Nobody stays together. It's all bullshit.

There was a time when Mom and I did everything together. It was right after we moved back from North Carolina. She was very weak then and Nana had stayed down South. I remember coming back to Philly in October. It felt really weird. Everything seemed so dark and dirty. But Mom tried to put on a strong front. She would wake me up in the mornings and drag me all over town. We went to lunch together, to museums and movies. At least once every day for about a month she would grab me by the shoulders and say, "How are you doing, kiddo?" I never knew what to say except, "Fine." I wasn't fine. Neither was she. But what else could I say? I knew what she was asking me. And I knew why. She wanted me to have hope. She wanted me to believe that things were fine. I knew that she needed that from me.

Believe it or not, for at least a year she really thought you were coming back. That we were going to be a family again. There was this one time not long after we got back to Philly and we were staying at Aunt Geri's house, when we were having dinner and she asked me did I miss you. I said yes. And she said she missed you too and that we just had to hold on. That you were probably gonna come to your senses soon. We were eating meatballs and spaghetti and she just sat there for the longest time with a meatball on her fork, holding it up in the air.

"Aren't you going to eat?" I asked her. And then I saw the tears. They were streaming out of her eyes, dropping in her plate. "Don't worry," I said. "Daddy will be back." I told her that and I reached over and wiped her eyes. She was so sad. I remember it like it happened yesterday. "Daddy will be back."

She told me that she knew that but that she got tired of having faith in other people. That was when she told me that I was the only one she knew would never leave her. It was her and I. I guess I never felt that bad about it because I was so worried about her. She was all I had.

Where were you then? I couldn't believe that you were still alive. That you could know we were somewhere and you wouldn't come back.

Three

In the days that followed, Ben could think of nothing but Helen. He was either at Geri's, where Helen had extended her visit, or he was on the telephone talking to her. For the first time since he had left the Navy, he was not interested in his studies. He was not hustling at his job driving a cab. And he couldn't write. What he first thought was inspiration had turned into paralysis. He never wrote the poem for Helen. It was present in his head, and he spoke the words to her, but he never put it on paper. He was too preoccupied with being in love to do anything else.

All of the emotion that Ben felt about Helen was now focused on sex. Somehow sex had become the most important thing. Ben knew better. But he couldn't help it. A budding love has to grow. And to Ben, the blossom of love was sex. He had cajoled, begged and, once, even cried in an attempt to get her to open herself to him. But she always changed the subject. Helen had decided on the night she met him that she would sleep with Ben. But she would pick the time. She knew what would happen to her. She knew she would be caught in a vortex of stored-up energy and emotions that would be hard to disentangle herself from. She had been waiting for this love. She was ready to dance but she wanted to call the tune.

So instead of her body, she fed him food. Every time Ben came over, Helen's table revealed the success of her tutelage under her mother. They ate and kissed and hugged and pushed each other to the brink of restraint.

And then, finally, three weeks from the night they met, she called him. That alone was surprising because she never dialed his number. Helen's mother had taught her never to call a man. But she did.

"What are you planning to do tonight, Ben?"

Ben laughed. "What do I do every night, Helen? I come over there or we talk on the telephone all night."

"I love our conversations." There was a breathless quality in her voice.

"Me too."

"Well, Ben, when you come over here tonight, what are we gonna do?"

Ben laughed again, but this time it was a nervous laugh. He couldn't tell what she was getting at. "I don't know, Helen. Maybe what we always do. I beg you and you act like you don't know what I'm talking about."

"Maybe I haven't said much, but I know what you've been talking about. And tonight I don't want to hear it. I want you to show me."

Ben sucked in all the air around him. He teetered. The telephone was delicate in his hand. He tried not to act excited. He didn't want to scare her. "Well, fine. I'll be there at ten. Maybe nine-thirty. Soon as I get off work." He hung up the phone quickly.

And then, within hours, he became a splash of color inside her. And once there, he painted his name on all the walls, in corners, on the floors, everywhere inside her that there was a clean space, he put his name.

They professed undying. They gathered themselves and their spirits and danced a skin-to-skin, heart-to-heart dance. Smokey Robinson flowered the air with "More Love" and they gave in to each other.

Helen felt herself holding him so tight. Her fingers seemed to plunge past his skin into some region that was without flesh. Her fingers played with the air in his limbs. She dug as deep as she could. She pulled as hard as she could. She wanted to mark him.

After all, he was in a place that no man had ever visited. He had to be invited there. He had to immerse himself in her. And he had to bear the mark of his adventure. She would have it no other way.

And Ben was lost in the overwhelming cascade of hope and strength he felt in her. He tried to hold back, to be the center of power, to move her. But her energy was too strong. He could only accept the feeling of being lost in someone. Of swimming in a pool without walls. Of needing that someone desperately.

And he did. There was no floor beneath his feet. No walls. Nothing to hold on to but her. No other foundation than her sounds.

He felt her hand on the small of his back, instinctively pulling him deeper into her. He felt her long fingernails piercing his skin, plowing it like a field of rich black dirt.

He felt her thighs against him. The soft wetness that held them. He whispered pictures into her ear. And she heard him. And Smokey creened, "More love. More love."

Makeba's Journal

THIRD ENTRY

The first time I had sex I was drunk. I was young, too young to be drinking, too young to be with this guy. I barely remember the details. You probably don't want to hear them anyway. But I remember that the next day I was so sad. Mom kept asking me what was wrong. I couldn't tell her. But you know Mom, she came right out and asked me if I was still a virgin. I tried to lie to her. I knew she would freak. But she just kept on me until I told her. I realized as soon as I told her, I had *wanted* to tell her all the time.

She jumped all over me. She made me tell her who the boy was and everything. And then she called him and told him he had better never see me again. I was totally embarrassed. I mean, I knew she was right, but . . .

Anyway, I guess the hardest thing was how I felt. I was sad for a long time. Mom said it was because fifteen wasn't old enough to deal with sex. She said that if you didn't love the person sex could make you feel lonely. And that I was too young to know how to love somebody. It made sense to me but it didn't make me feel better. If you feel sadness because you're alone and sadness after you make love to someone, then where is joy? I don't understand that.

But guess what? It's to the point that I like it. I'm comfortable when I'm sad. I'm feeling sad now. I knew I would.

Four

As Mates watched Ben and Helen make love he knew there would be trouble. He pitied people who fell in love. They made love with the hope that the intensity of their feelings would forever enfold them. But he knew, and he suspected they knew, that everything changes. Still, his purpose was not to pass judgment, only to haunt the guilty one.

And it didn't matter to Mates whether the person was black and American and suffered from the ravages of slavery. It didn't matter that there was this urgent need for an entire race to seek unity and healing in the cliché of the strong family. And yet, Mates knew, the need for family did not make it any easier.

In the throes of love Ben made many promises to Helen. With his mouth, with his hands, with his entire body he pledged himself to her. He fell fully. His four lonely years in the Navy and the years since had rendered him powerless to the desire of love. He remembered, as he kissed Helen's soft brown skin, what it felt like to be out at sea, the ship rolling through the valleys of the Atlantic, with no one back home missing him.

The thing about being away, especially in the armed forces, is how quickly you realize how much you need someone waiting for you. Someone standing on the pier as your ship comes in.

Ben had returned from three Mediterranean cruises and one in the Caribbean to a pier full of strangers waving flags and blowing kisses. He had always wanted someone there waiting for him. And Helen felt like that person. She was the one who should have been there for him. She felt like home.

When he looked at her sleeping he saw his future. Ben had been energized by the political energies of the sixties. He had flirted with the fervor of the black revolution. Now, as a developing writer, he was an invisible Young Turk in the blossoming Black Arts Movement. Even though he had not published a single poem, he was reading everything he could get his hands on. And suddenly, there was so much work by African American writers available: Baraka, Madhubuti, Sanchez, Reed, Evans, Troupe, Toure, Webster and countless others. Fire and righteous thunder from the modern-day *niggerati*. Suddenly, being a writer seemed possible.

Buried in the rhetoric, the strident pronouncements of black power and black chauvinism, was the notion of family. That the real power of the African American community was in the love found between black men and women, the children they brought into the world and the community they lived in. There was a way in which the struggle for unity and healing was screwed into the cliché of the strong family.

And when Ben looked at Helen his stomach quivered from the realization that he had met someone who could give him everything he didn't have: love, companionship and the promise of significance.

We hardly ever examine the way promises are made. The way we commit ourselves. As if each promise is equal. There are times when our lives are turned by moments of confusion, when the thrill of commitment is reached in a veritable dust storm of feelings. The truth is that judgment is displaced by drugs or alcohol, by fear, by loneliness just at the moment when we must promise someone something. And these promises exist with the same weight as any other, regardless of whether they were made drunk or in the palpable need to be held.

Many men suffer through this dance with life. They promise. They leave. They try to act like they don't hurt. But they do. If you are a child of a missing father, you already know this. Then again, maybe you don't.

Makeba's Journal

Reading this almost makes me silent. So many things are flashing in my head that it's hard to keep writing. Maybe it wasn't a good idea. You have your own pain. This story is about you. About your feelings. None of us have had a chance to speak. Not me or Mom or you. I never knew this stuff. I never realized how much you must have loved her. I mean it's a goddamned love story.

I don't have one of those yet. Now that I'm older I *can* have sex if I want to. And sometimes I do. But I don't think I'm going to have a love story happen to me. People like me don't have love stories. I have no patience. I have never met a man worth believing. Nana says the same thing. She's the one who's got it in for men. She hates them. But I think you know that. I don't know what happened but you did something to her that made her really hate you. We can't even talk about you with her in the room. She just goes off.

I knew the day Mom came home and told me that she had met this guy that everything was going to change again. We had moved out to the suburbs by then but we still spent a lot of time together. She was helping me with school and everything. But suddenly she was always going out. She would take me back into Philly on Fridays and pick me up Sunday night. I was staying at Aunt Geri's all the time. And then, when Nana came back to New Jersey I spent a lot of time there too. His name is Dwight Stones.

In one year I lost you and in a way, I lost her too. I could tell the moment he came into our house that it was no longer just her and I. She waited on him hand and foot. Now I think Mom thought that it was her fault you left. Something she did or probably didn't know which drove you away. And she wasn't going to let that happen again. You have to remember she didn't have anything. We had nothing. We were getting government assistance. The telephone was always getting cut off. I know she always talked about starting a day-care center but she didn't act like she was going to do anything. So she needed him, or somebody, to help take care of me and her.

But when he came over he was the most important. And he was so different than you. It was like he just sat back and accepted all that attention from her. I guess he was thinking, if you didn't want it, he'd take it. And all I could do was watch.

At first I was never in their plans. It was like they forgot I was around sometimes. One night after he came over they left to get some pizza. I was supposed to be asleep, but I heard them leave. I was terrified. I just lay there in the dark waiting. I know I probably wondered why I was so alone. I was always thinking that. Then they came back and ate. They ate the whole pizza. I could hear them in the living room, laughing and eating. It was like Mom had suddenly just stopped being sad. And then I didn't hear anything for a long time and I got scared again. So I quietly got out of bed and walked to the stairway. I slowly went down the steps until I could see them on the couch. He was on top of her. I could see his long, narrow back full of sweat. I didn't realize what I was doing but I just kept walking toward them. I was like a spirit or something. Before I knew it I was standing right over them. I heard him breathing and saying "uh . . . uh . . . uh . . . uh." I don't know what came over me but I just starting hitting him. My hands were fists and I was pounding on his back. For a second he didn't know what was going on. But then he turned around. I'll never forget his eyes. They were shining like a cat's. It was like I woke up from a dream right then. I turned and ran back up the stairs, into my room and under the covers.

Mom came up and sat on the side of the bed. She explained all that love stuff. That "we're adult" stuff. She didn't want me to be upset. She wanted me to like Dwight. He was thinking about moving in. She was thinking about it too. She asked me to also think about it. That was when I began practicing silence. I didn't say a thing. I think I went to sleep.

Five

Ben was with Helen every moment he could break free from his studies and his job driving a yellow cab. Helen had stayed at Geri's, taking a spare bedroom in the three-bedroom house. She was in no hurry to go back to her mother's house in Woodbury, New Jersey, where she had grown up. She had found a job working at the telephone company and Geri had welcomed her like a little sister, encouraging her to explore her new-found freedom.

But Helen limited her exploration to Ben. With the whole world to traverse, she was happy, blissfully happy, working in Philadelphia and living in Geri's house, waiting for Ben to come to her.

She and Ben had quickly settled into a routine. Helen was home from work every afternoon by four-thirty and Ben would often meet her at the front door. He was fresh from the university, bursting with creative energy, talkative and fiery. They would eat and frequently make love after. Later he would leave to drive the night shift. At about one-thirty in the morning, he would return and they would lie in her bed and watch the moonshadows and the creases of golden light that were present in Geri's house.

And then one day everything changed. Helen was pregnant.

"Girl," Geri nearly screamed, "I know you ain't gone and got yourself pregnant already. You was just a virgin a month ago. I told you you had to do something 'bout that."

Helen had just returned from the doctor. She was churning with confused energy. She was pregnant. Her first sensation was intense joy and then she thought about Ben. She wasn't sure how he would take it.

"I know," Helen said meekly.

"Then how come you're pregnant? Ain't nobody ever told you nothing about birth control?"

"I know about birth control, I just didn't think I was gonna get pregnant so quick." Helen felt dumb.

"What do you think happens when a man sticks his dick in you? Huh? Babies, Helen. That's what happens, babies. And you can't tell me you didn't know that."

Helen looked away. "I know that, Geri. I know that. But I never made love with nobody else. I just never put it all together."

"Didn't Lena teach you about sex and babies?" Geri stared at the side of Helen's head, which Helen held perfectly still. "You mean your mother hasn't told you about all this?"

"You know my mother. She acts like she's afraid to talk about it. The only thing she always said to me was, 'Keep your legs closed.' That was the main thing. 'You just keep those long legs of yours closed and you won't have no men problems.'" That was why she hadn't gone back home. Helen knew that when her mother looked into her eyes, the image of Ben lying between her legs, sweating and moaning, would reflect out.

Geri stared at her, then burst into a muffled laugh. "That's probably why you got two sisters that Lena don't know what to do with. I swear, I can't believe it." She paused again. "So you two never used nothing?"

Helen shook her head.

"And what about Ben? What the hell has he been saying? Seems like to me he should know better. It ain't all your fault. The only problem is you're the one stuck with the baby, not him."

Helen was silent. Geri made her feel simple, like the country girl she was. Why hadn't she thought more about birth control? Why hadn't he?

Geri gathered her coat and scarf and headed for the door. "Anyway, I think you better tell him fast and decide exactly what y'all gonna do. This ain't no joke, girl. I knew ya'll was up there burning up the sheets but I had no idea y'all was two fools. Anyway, you can always take care of it."

"What do you mean?"

"You know what I mean. Don't look at me with those dumb eyes. You could get an abortion."

Helen's face froze. It seemed to take the air out of her body. The image of her mother loomed in front of her.

"My mother would die. She would put a curse or something on me and then she'd just die. I can't do that, Geri."

Geri shook her head, silently put her coat on and left.

Their conversation played over and over in Helen's head as she waited for Ben. She raced from euphoria to anger to panic. When she heard Ben at the front door, her heart ran ahead.

Ben was tired. There was a hint of blue under his eyes. His Tootsie Roll face was dull, its vibrancy drained by the long schedule of lovemaking, studying and driving the taxi. He collapsed next to Helen on the sky-blue couch.

"You look tired."

"Wiped out, baby. I'm totally wiped out. And I've got to get up early tomorrow to study for a sociology test."

Helen put her hand on the soft outline of his short Afro. Her fingertips played on the edges. "I guess this isn't the best time to tell you."

Ben couldn't tell whether it was a question or a statement. "Tell me what?"

"Ben, you have to promise me that you won't hate me."

"Hate you?" Ben immediately went with the feeling. Had she already met someone else? Was it ending before it actually began? He felt his breath leave and not return. His body hardened and grew a protective moss. "What's going on, Helen?"

"You know I love you very much, don't you?"

"Just tell me, Helen." Ben was suddenly very afraid. His fatigue forgotten, he wanted to get up from the couch and head back into the night air. In the short span of their time together he had discovered safety. A place so strong, so completely sheltering that he could be safe there. It was inside Helen. Not sexually inside her. Not in the juice of her life that flowed between her legs. But in her heart. In the cavity where life is pure, and cloistered.

Helen knew how to make him feel quiet. She knew how to provide the night moments all day long. That time when you know nothing is searching for you. Nothing wants you. Where there is no fear. She knew how to give that to him without saying anything and without him having to articulate the need for it. In fact, he had never known that he needed it. This quietness, this peace, was so unknown to him that he would never have thought to ask for it.

And in those moments when he was mindless, within Helen's environment, he could discern the beauty of silence. He could actually know peace, even in the swell of anxiety that accompanied the growing brutality of the Philadelphia police. He could overlook the confused looks of his younger classmates who knew somehow that they would graduate and go on to dominate his life. When he was with Helen those feelings dissipated like the image of O. J. Simpson running for a touchdown.

He looked at her, her fear crackling like sparks between them, mingling with his fear and the long awkward pause to create a volatile, combustible energy. Suddenly he realized he didn't want to face a life without her. Without that protection. He didn't want to think about Helen leaving him.

Helen stared at him. "I don't think I can tell you, Ben." She quickly averted her eyes downward.

In an uncontrolled moment of terror, Ben's body began to prepare for trauma. He felt his stomach lurch. Water collected just below the lids of his eyes. "Helen, I can't take it. Will you please tell me. Is it another man?"

Helen was swimming in her own sense of dread when she heard the question. It snapped her to attention. She put her face close to his. "Ben, I don't think I'll ever want another man, ever."

Ben breathed. He sat forward. "Then, what is this all about?"

"I'm pregnant. I'm going to have our baby."

Ben grew wings. He slid through a narrow opening in the doorway that led into the basement. He fluttered down the stairway and circled the dark, stone-walled room. There were old paint-flecked bicycles and rusted garden tools and tan cardboard boxes all around. The musk nearly choked him. But there was no opening; the cellar windows, narrow and rectangular, abutted the ceiling and were sealed with cardboard to block out the weather.

There was no way out.

And then he found himself drawn into the light. He moved closer and closer, mindless and given up to air. He closed his eyes and passed into the fullness of Helen's lips.

Helen opened her mouth to speak and Ben found himself staring into the eyes of a woman who offered him life. He pulled her close.

"I'm going to be a father?" He put joy into his voice because he knew he had to. He felt her fear and he knew that this was a big moment. He couldn't believe that he hadn't thought about it. Of course, he and Helen had already talked about the possibility of mar-riage, and she had made it clear that she wanted children. And yes, he had agreed that when he got married, he wanted children. But he hadn't *really* thought about it.

Already Ben began to recognize a pattern in himself. He wanted to ask her whether she really thought this was the right time to have a child. He wanted to talk about the responsibilities that having a child would place on both of them. He wanted to say that he wasn't sure this was the right time for him to become a father. He knew that he should have thought about this earlier. This was his fault. He knew that Helen would be very disappointed if he expressed the slightest hesitation. And he knew enough about her already to know that she wouldn't really consider having an abortion.

And he loved her. Her growing dedication to him was over-powering. No one had ever completely succumbed to his presence before. He was usually drawn to women who held their nurturing urges at arm's length. Women who were more interested in their own careers, their own dreams, not his. But Helen seemed to be saying that his aspirations, his dreams, his life could be hers. That she would be the force in his life which ensured his success, and that that role would make her happy.

So he took a deep breath and injected all the joy he could find into his speaking voice. "We're having a baby. A baby." He said it over and over into her ear. Each time with a different inflection. Each time discovering more happiness, more anticipation. Until it sounded exciting. Until he was swelled big with the energy of impending fatherhood.

Helen was now crying and laughing at the same time. She was spent, relieved. She buried her head in his chest and sobbed directly into his heart. And his heart heard. He held her tightly and looked at the ceiling. His arms were not wings and there would be no flight from here. Instead the chant "We're having a baby" continued to flow in his head. And he felt the moving chest of this warm woman in his arms and he wanted to make her happy.

He was a proud man. He could come through for her. He would show her that a black man could stand up and be responsible. For the first time in his life he thought about morality. This was what the shouting was about. How could a man create a life and then not be there? But this was exactly what was going on. There were men who could boldly tell television reporters that they liked to have children by different women. That it was a badge of masculinity.

Not Ben. He would do the right thing.

Later that morning, just as the sun came up, Ben asked Helen to marry him. She quietly said yes. She kissed him and held him tightly. A sense of relief cascaded through her body. And in the next instant a picture of her mother, Lena Brown, flashed in her head. They would have to go through Lena before there were any ceremonies or any birthings. Helen stiffened.

"Ben, you've got to meet my mother. We've got to go see her."

He felt the tension in her voice. "I never said I didn't want to meet your mother. In fact, I think it's about time."

Helen got up from the bed and walked to the window. "My mother is a little weird. She's . . . ah . . . well, she's just different, that's all."

"Is she going to want to kill me?"

"She's going to want to skin you alive." Helen laughed. "On the outside she can be pretty tough, but inside she's a sweetheart, really."

"Well, that's good to know. Because I don't want to have to fight with your mother."

Helen slowly turned around to face the bed where Ben lay, bathed in the first dusting of sunlight. "She's kind of religious," Helen said meekly.

"How religious are we talking, Helen? Southern Baptist?" Helen was silent. "Pentecostal? Voodoo? Apostolic? Santeria? Holiness? What are we talking about here?"

"She sort of mixes up a bunch of different religions. She believes in a lot of things."

Ben was uneasy. "Well, does she believe in God?"

"In a way. I guess. In Lena Brown's world God is everywhere. She used to be a righteous Christian but somewhere along the line she fell out of it."

"It doesn't matter, I'll be very nice to your mother." Ben smiled. He was not the type who had problems with the mothers of his girl-friends. They were almost always impressed with him. He knew how to present just the right image: sensitive, intelligent, serious.

"I'm not joking. Don't play around with my mother. Be straight with her. Because if she thinks you're making fun of her it could get very ugly. She's my mother and I love her to death, but I swear she's a very unusual woman. Sometimes I think she really has some kind of power or something." Helen crawled back into the bed as she talked.

Ben was suddenly very curious about Helen's mother. "You can't stop there. What kind of power are you talking about?"

"Not now, Ben—I don't want to go into it now." Helen closed her eyes. "I'll tell you later, maybe after you meet her. Just telling you what I've already told you makes me nervous. I want you to like her."

The next day Ben took off from school and work and Helen stayed home from the telephone company so they could drive to Woodbury to see her mother.

As they turned off the freeway and headed toward the street of Helen's mother's house, Ben was keenly aware of the landscape. The dense standing structures of the city had completely given way to the brown scruffiness of the Jersey country. The trees stood bare. The ground showed its scuff marks. But it was different from the shadowy gray of the inner city.

They surprised Helen's mother, who was sitting at the dining room table cutting coupons. Lena Brown was thin and short, two shades darker than Helen's coffee complexion. She sat in a chair at her dining room table in the tight two-bedroom A-frame house. The room, like the house, was thick with the clutter of pictures and bric-a-brac. Ben thought the house smelled like peanuts and uncooked fish mixed together. He was immediately uncomfortable as they walked through the small living room. He noticed the painted porcelain figurines posed all around them. Doilies of petrified snowflakes lay under them and every other standing inanimate object that crowded the room. The exact same large gold-painted Crucifixion cross, with Jesus attached, bowed and bleeding, appeared on the three walls surrounding the large table.

Lena looked up at them. She looked first at Ben. Then she quickly turned her eyes to Helen. She smiled. "I got a coupon here for Van de Kamp's. You want it? Fifteen cents off."

"No thanks, Mom." Helen pursed her lips with a smirk and bent down to meet Lena's cheek. "Hello, Mother. How are you? It's good to see you too. Oh my, what a surprise. It's so nice of you to drop by," she teased.

Lena kept her smile. "Don't be foolin' with me, girl. You know I'm glad to see you. I just looked at you standing there skinny and all and I thought you'd be needing this here coupon for some food or something."

"No, Mom, I eat fine. Geri always has a full refrigerator. Everything's fine."

"That's good, Helen. That's good. I want my little girl to be fine."

Helen looked back at Ben, who kept shifting his weight as he stood in one spot. "This is Ben, Mom. I brought him with me so you could meet him."

Instead of looking up at Ben, Lena looked back at her stack of torn-out newspaper pages with blocks of coupons on them. Ben and

Helen now stood side by side and waited for her mother to say something. But the small woman took her time. She fished through the sheets of paper. Finally, she said, "I kind of figured you wanted me to meet him. Otherwise there'd be no reason to drag him all the way down here."

Helen stared at her. "Well?" Ben instinctively grabbed Helen's arm, hoping she'd take the sting out of her voice.

"Well what?" Lena looked up at her daughter. Helen took in a breath. Ben felt his body tense. Lena stared directly into Helen's eyes when she said, "So you want to marry my baby?"

Ben heard her, saw her lips move, but because Lena was looking at Helen he missed his cue. Finally, Helen looked at him. "Ben?"

"Huh, ah yes? Yes." He grabbed Helen and pulled her close. Suddenly he realized what Lena was waiting for. "Yes, Mrs. Brown, I love her."

Lena still stared at Helen. "You want to marry him?"

Helen smiled. Her mother was stubborn and whatever process she was intent on would be exactly the way it would go. Lena could "work" on somebody until they came undone.

Lena had a habit of talking a subject into the ground. If Helen forgot, for example, to wash the dishes on a given night, or to make sure one of the other children did, Lena would wake her up early the next morning, fussing. And she'd fuss all day long and into the night. Even as Helen stood at the sink washing the second night's dishes, Lena would still be talking about how lazy and forgetful Helen was. Maybe the next day, Lena would suddenly grab Helen's hand and say, "You're a fine girl, Helen."

Helen wondered what Ben felt as they sat down side by side at the table. He stared at her with a blank face. She knew he had no idea what to expect from Lena. But even Helen, who had lived with Lena all of her nineteen years, couldn't predict the way her mother might act.

And now, looking across the table, she realized from the iron-cast features that Lena would play it to the fullest.

"You know I do, Mom. We wouldn't have driven all the way down here if I didn't want to marry him."

"Why? What makes you think you love this boy?" Lena, still ignoring Ben, looked at her daughter.

"Because, Mom, Ben is one of the nicest men I've ever met. He's smart. And I love him. I just know it. That's enough."

"You think that's enough?" Lena still showed her emotionless face.

"Yes, I do."

Lena turned to Ben. "This is my baby girl. You understand that?"

Ben stared into her stone-brown eyes. "Yes, Mrs. Brown, I understand."

Ben felt her right up in his face. Even though she was across the table he felt the heat from her body. He felt his hand being grabbed. The touch was warm and thin. He could feel the hint of strength on the surface and the frailness just below. But the grip was solid. He couldn't let go. Suddenly he couldn't see or feel Helen's presence. The room seemed filled by a silver-gray haze. With his free hand he rubbed across his eyes.

"We must pray." Ben recognized the sharp voice as Lena's. "Dear Mother, you know my body is your vessel. And this girl, who knows my insides, wants to give herself to this man."

Ben felt fingernails scratching the back of his hand. He wanted to look down and see what held him but he was frozen.

"This man. You know who this man is, don't you? You know where's he's been and what he's made of. You know everything about him. But I don't know nothing about him. Only that he wants my baby. And he has come here to get my approval. How can I approve of this man taking my daughter? What woman would give her girl to a man from nowhere? Especially when you know what's in store for her. But I know that if I try to stop her she will go on and do what she wants to anyway. Yes, I know she'll just do what she *thinks* she wants to do. So I can't stop her.

"But you can put the mark on him. You can put the fear in him that will let him know that just because he's a man don't mean he's holy. It don't mean he can treat my daughter any which way. It don't mean nothing except he's got something hanging out of his stomach.

"I want to you scare this boy out of my house. Make his hair turn white or even fall out. Make him wish like hell he'd never met Helen or come here to see me. Give him to somebody else, Lord. I don't need him. Neither does my girl.

"But if you won't do that, if he ain't gone in two shakes, running up the road toward Philly after I'm done, then I'll accept your will. I got to. You are what makes me happy. Living in your light."

The hand let go, the room cleared and Ben instantly turned his face to Helen's. He wanted to see if she'd seen or heard what he had. But Helen was staring at her mother. When Ben looked at Lena he realized that she was talking. Her voice seemed to grow in the air as if someone was controlling the volume.

"It's a struggle, Helen. You know that," Lena was saying. "Staying together nowadays is a real test."

"I know, Mom," Helen said. "But I really feel like we can do it. Don't you, Ben?"

Ben nodded. He tried to remember what he had heard. The exact words. But he couldn't. The message was clear though. Now he wanted to get up and leave. He didn't feel right. The thought of a lungful of fresh air seemed good to him.

"Helen." Ben leaned into Helen's ear. "Can we leave? I need to get out of here."

Helen continued talking as if he hadn't said anything. She turned to Ben and tried to tell him with her eyes that she wasn't ready to leave. If they got up from the table now, her mother would have every right to be angry. She wanted Ben to read her eyes and relax. Based on the range of responses her mother was capable of, she felt everything had gone rather well.

"Ben's going to college and working full-time. He's a very talented writer, you know. And I've got a new job. I just feel like we're going to make it."

Ben couldn't sit still. He slid the chair out and stood up. Lena put her eyes on him. Helen kept talking. But Lena watched Ben, who was now walking around the room. He picked up a small white porcelain unicorn. It was the newest of the figurines in the room.

"We're going to have the best family. I just know it."

Ben started walking toward the door. He couldn't listen to any more. The whole thing suddenly seemed ridiculous. He was sweating profusely. He wanted to get out. He reached for the front door.

"Ben," Helen shouted. "Mom's got a sweet potato pie. We are not leaving until I eat me a piece of this pie. And I know you want one, so get your butt back in here and find some plates in the kitchen."

Lena's eyes had followed him all the way to the door. Now she looked at him straight on. They were frozen together. No words passed. Helen was up at the breakfront slicing the pie.

"Ben, if you don't get in here and get us some plates I'm going to get mad at you and you know you don't want that."

Lena still stared at him. His body wanted to leave. But he couldn't leave without Helen, he didn't want to do that. He looked at her, immersed in the cutting of the pie. Then back to Lena, the trace of a smile gracing her lips. He felt suddenly light-headed, the tension crumbled. He exhaled a strong shallow breath. "For a minute there I thought I left my keys in the car. But now I see they're on the table. Did you say sweet potato pie? You know those are magic words. Ain't no telling what I'd do for a piece of homemade sweet potato pie." He grinned. Lena winked at him. There was a glint in the crease of her eyes.

"So, Ben, Helen. I guess you might as well tell me now about my new grandchild." The pie knife fell out of Helen's hands and hit the wide-slatted wooden floor, sweet potato pie splattered. Ben walked by Lena and into the brown kitchen as if he hadn't heard her.

But he had. As he gathered three small plates for the pie he tried to quell the disturbance that clanged inside him. How did she know that Helen was pregnant? Why hadn't Helen heard what he had? What was he in for? He thought about his classmates at school and what they would have thought about Lena. Not many Ivy League students would have to deal with a mother-in-law who had "powers."

Ben and Helen were married in May, three months after they met. Makeba was already deep in Helen's womb. It had been a whirlwind. A relationship of cascading waves. Like sugar and water, they had instantly become a confection.

Makeba's Journal

I hated this chapter. It explains so much. I feel like that hesitation that you felt is in my blood. Somehow you gave that to me. It's a part of how I am. Tentative, nervous, certain that I am wrong.

You should have spoken up. Maybe I was a mistake. Maybe you could have stopped it. You didn't have to be so proud. You could have just said, I don't want to have a child right now. Maybe she would have done something. At least she would have known how you felt. Don't you see? I can never make a direct, decisive move. I always feel like I'm making a mistake. It comes from you. It makes everything so much clearer. I know you loved me, but every child should be wished for. That's what I think. Not discovered.

Good old Nana. She knew what was going on. I believe that part. She tried to help. I bet she scared you good.

Six

Mates was nearly rolling over with laughter. Ben should have gotten the hell out of there. Lena was trying to warn him. She tried to tell him that there was something, something hidden in the airborne particles that fluttered around him, just beyond his eyesight, that was watching him. That something was Mates.

Mates was amused by the arrogance of people. They think that the worst can't happen to them. They always walk into his open jaws.

What was it people sought in marriage? What were they looking for? Mates knew that the creation of family satisfied some raw emptiness in their lives. Marriage was the way they were taught to make family. It was the cornerstone of faith. It was the frame around the picture. Still, it seemed, if they were aware of how difficult it was for two people to live together, wouldn't you expect that there would be many fewer marriages?

There could still be family without marriage. There could still be that fulfillment of the human drive to keep themselves going. They could still make babies.

Ben had been terrifically shaken by his visit to Lena's. When they were in the car he asked Helen if she had heard a voice while they were in the house. She shook her head. But Ben couldn't let it go. "Are you sure you didn't hear your mother say anything weird or anything?"

"What are you talking about? I think my mother handled it all very well."

Ben focused his eyes straight ahead. "And you didn't hear her get into that prayer thing or about God or somebody scaring me out of her house or anything like that?"

"Ben, this isn't funny."

"I'm not laughing. When we sat down at the table I heard her start this long prayer about how you were her little girl and how could she give you to me and all this shit." Ben paused. "You mean you didn't hear any of that?"

Helen didn't say anything. She wanted to say he was crazy or hallucinating, but she could tell by his voice that it would be a mistake to do so. Instead she thought about the odd things she had experienced growing up with Lena. But more than anything it was the way other people had treated them. Everyone was fearful of Lena. Helen had heard rumors of hexes and curses that Lena had put on people, but she had never heard her mother utter one unpleasant thing about anyone.

She *had* seen her mother heal a blind woman once. The woman, about sixty, dark-skinned with graying hair, had been brought to Lena by her daughter. Helen had watched as the younger woman gave Lena two hundred dollars. After she had taken the money Lena realized that Helen was standing in the kitchen doorway watching. She shooed Helen upstairs, but Helen had crept halfway down the steps to see. Lena sat in candlelight with the woman in front of her. Helen couldn't hear what Lena was saying but she did see her put her hand over the woman's eyes. The woman instantly fainted.

While she was unconscious, Lena had wrapped a bandage around her eyes. When the woman regained consciousness, Lena then whispered some instructions, gave the daughter a small bundle and ushered them out of the door.

Two weeks later the two women came back screaming with joy and praise. They swore that it was Lena, not the doctors, who had brought the woman's sight back. Lena just smiled and said how happy she was that she could help "in any small way."

"Look, I know my mother is different but she's not bad or anything. I didn't hear her say anything like that. I'm sorry. Maybe I was cutting the pie or something. I just didn't hear her."

"She scared the shit out of me. I almost lost it in there."

"Well, it's over now. We've got her blessing."

"I don't know. I'm still pretty shook up." Ben couldn't lose the feeling that something was wrong. It wasn't supposed to be that way. At the moment a person knows they are in love there shouldn't be a feeling of foreboding. And that was what Lena was. Foreboding.

The next day they visited his parents, Margaret and Benjamin Crestfield, Sr. Margaret was a social worker for the Health Department and Benjamin was the foreman for a construction company. They had long since left the tightness of the inner city and moved to the outer reaches of Mount Airy.

Sitting together on the mauve sectional couch in their sunken living room, both Benjamin and Margaret smiled approvingly at Helen. They were smitten by the way she acted as if she already knew them. They could sense her desire to make Ben happy. And they liked that.

Benjamin was the first to speak after Ben had announced the marriage. "To tell you the truth, honey, I'm pretty damned happy. I thought this boy of mine was never gonna do a damn thing with his life. Least I can tell he's got good taste."

"You ought to hush, Benny." Margaret poked her husband in the side. "Don't mind him. If you two think you can make it, we're right behind you."

After they were married, Ben threw himself into their new dream: the family. They lived in a cavernous Victorian house on the 4500 block of Sage Street in University City. By August he sat at the dining room table fanning a stack of bills to ward off the heat as he struggled with numbers on a pad of paper. There were two thoughts crowding his mind at the same time. He still had not been able to write. He was barely keeping up in school. And in his African American Poetry class he was actually falling behind. He didn't understand what the problem was. Since he had decided to become a writer he had never experienced a silence like this.

He began to think that whoever said writers had to be unhappy to create might have been right. He was happy. He enjoyed getting into bed with Helen. He enjoyed knowing she would be home when he got back from school or work. Her smile was larger now than it was when he met her. And that smile was so sweet, so joyful that it was hard to feel anything but happiness. Still, when his mind turned to writing, no stories, no pictures were there. And there was one other thing which he had slowly begun to realize. Helen didn't know how important writing was to him and didn't know how to stimulate him in that way. He counted this as a minor thing, something that would change or that he would learn to accept. He knew she loved him. And that love, expressed by her as "an unqualified love," was more powerful than anything he'd ever experienced.

But the other thought that fought for his mind's attention was their growing economic crisis. They were broke. He tried to still the uneasiness, the stress of not having enough money, but it wasn't easy. He told himself that if they could just hang on until he graduated, everything would work out fine. Luckily he had a job and his tuition was covered under the G.I. Bill, so the basics were taken care of. It was the unexpected bills that were wearing them down. His car had sucked up a lot of the money lately and Helen had taken to buying things he hadn't known she was going to buy. He wasn't angry, just nervous, worried that they would collapse before he was able to properly provide.

Still, he wanted to let her know that they were living dangerously. He looked at the list of bills. There was another mysterious payment.

"Hey Helen." He heard her upstairs cleaning the bathroom. It was Saturday morning and time for cleaning. He imagined her up there, on her knees, creating white clouds of Comet as she scattered the cleanser over everything. Then she followed it with a wet football-shaped scrub brush and a strong circular motion, spraying water about like fireworks. The only thing she'd leave behind was a thin white film of cleanser residue.

Ben heard her drop the brush into the bucket that sat beside her.

It was already hot. The late-morning August sun caressed the white enamel windowsill and threw the remaining brilliance throughout the small bathroom. Already she had cleaned the kitchen and the bedroom.

Kneeling in the bathroom, Helen watched the water settle into the yellow plastic bucket. She felt her daughter shift positions in her stomach. Yes, she loved the act of cleaning but not in the way that Ben thought. In a way, he seemed to be almost ridiculing her when he teased her about her methodical and painstaking effort. As if to take care, to make something glisten, was somehow wrong. It seemed at times that Ben could be moved by a lecture in behavioral psychology to criticize her for being anal or insecure.

But cleaning her house was one of the things in her life that she loved. She loved its transporting energy. It almost always took her back in time. She couldn't help but think of her mother, probably in her room with the door closed reading or sleeping. Her sisters in the yard playing. Gospel music on the radio. The smell of ammonia, soap and sweat. The swinging light of a high sun. Those were peaceful, tranquil times. She loved the feeling of being solid, persevering— always able to change the reality of poverty with a shine and a smile.

Since she was a little girl, she'd been preoccupied with family. Perhaps it was because hers was so porous, so incomplete. She'd never really known her father, a construction worker who died at work one day when she was three. Her mother rarely talked about him and had never brought another man home.

Helen had grown up in a house of women. And although she was always conscious, especially at school, that she didn't have a father, life at home had always been decent. It was true that her mother did very little in the house. Helen cooked, cleaned and tended to her sisters. But in a way, it was smooth. Normal. What was joy anyway? Where could it be found outside the walls of her home? They all played together, including her mother. They ate together. Danced together. And no man ever crossed their threshold except to share a meal or fix the toilet.

Yes, there was public assistance, and food stamps and times when the electric or the telephone was disconnected. There were those times. But mostly it was a life of labored joy. There was no wild-eyed euphoria but neither was there abject sadness.

Still, Helen had always felt trapped. She'd been only a fair student in school. Had no patience whatsoever with what she considered mental masturbation. What she wanted was real, not theoretical. What meant something to her *happened*. Anybody could talk about *things*. Her mother had taught her well: Talk meant nothing. It's about what you do.

And now she was married. She was who she had wanted to be. A mother-to-be. A wife. Of course, Ben wasn't the kind of man she had expected. His weaknesses were many, but she liked his sense of humor. His passion. And, God forbid, in spite of her mother's admonitions, she liked his words.

She had heard Ben call her name, but decided to finish wiping the sink. After she was done, she walked to the top of the stairs. "What do you want?"

Ben looked up at the narrow oak banister with its white, one-inch-square spokes ascending alongside the stairs. "What're you doing?"

"I'm cleaning this house, that's what I'm doing. What kind of a question is that? It wouldn't hurt if you found something for yourself to do."

"I *am* doing something. I'm down here trying to pay these bills. Can you come here a minute?"

"I told you that I was busy. I can't be running all over the place for you."

But even as she said that, Ben heard her begin her descent. He watched her move down the stairway. The yellow flowers in her dress picked up the sunlight and made her fairly glow in contrast with the white wall behind her. Her tall cinnamon body, full with the fresh flush of pregnancy, her bright overlarge smile, her swirling hair, bounced down the steps. He couldn't help but meet her smile with one of his own.

"You been cleaning the bathroom?" Ben knew what she had been doing, but couldn't stop himself.

"No, I been swimming in the pool." She winked and sat down at the table. There were beads of sweat on her temples.

"Well, just knowing that my baby is busy trying to make this house a home gets me right here." He touched his heart.

"It don't get you in the right place if you ask me." She held his eyes in her soft hands.

"What's that supposed to mean?"

"It means that when a newlywed couple moves into a new house, both the husband and the wife are supposed to work to make it livable and nice." She turned to face the living-room window, looked through it and out onto Sage Street. "You've been sitting here at this table for quite a while now."

Ben couldn't tell whether she was joking or not. "I'm trying to get these bills organized. I can't believe it got this bad this quick. We're already sinking." The plan was that he would finish his education and then she would get hers. They would do whatever they had to to make ends meet. Still, Helen had insisted that she quit her job at the telephone company. During the early days of her pregnancy, Helen was sick nearly every morning and getting to work had proven too difficult. Ben had reluctantly agreed that she should stay home. He loved her. And even though he knew better, sometimes their love felt like enough. A guarantee that everything would turn out good.

"I'm sure you'll figure out what we have to do. That's why you're the one doing the bills. Right?" Again she smiled an ambiguous smile. Being coy was one of Helen's great pleasures. It was a power. She realized how weak Ben was. She understood his insecurities. She met his arrogance with bewilderment. His seriousness with playfulness. She smiled to herself at the wonderful way love accommodates. "Anyway, why did you call me?"

"Well, I just wanted to know what this bill was for." Ben held up a blue sheet of paper.

She didn't even look at it. Instead she turned back to the window. "Which one?"

Ben couldn't help but laugh at her attempt to play him off. This was one of those little moments. One of those barely perceptible little spurts of growing love.

Ben held the bill up and waved it in front of her nose. "This one right here."

But she still wouldn't take it. She wouldn't even look at it. She just stared at him, smiling. She tried to act like she could care less about what he was saying.

"Woman, will you take this piece of paper and read it please? Then would you tell me what you spent twenty-two dollars on?" Ben mustered as much strength as he could. It was a game. They were playing with each other and in the playing was every inflection of love.

She finally took the bill out of his hands but still did not look at it. "I don't remember buying nothing from Kresge's."

"Did you look at it?"

"Well, no. Not yet."

"How did you know it was Kresge's? Will you please just take one little peek at it and tell me if you know what it's for." Ben's smile grew tired on his face.

But Helen held her ground and didn't look. "Oh yes, I think I remember this bill. Twenty-two dollars did you say? Yes. I remember it." She got up from the chair and headed for the stairs.

"Helen?"

She climbed three steps, then stopped and spoke deadpan into the dense air in front of her. "Yes dear?"

Ben could barely make out the tight roundness of her ass underneath the yellow flowers. "What the hell is it for?"

Still standing on the steps, she turned toward him and said in an oblivious, matter-of-fact way, "The wallpaper for the baby's room." She tapped her stomach to punctuate the sentence.

"We could have waited at least another three or four months before we spent money on wallpaper. I don't have time to wallpaper nothing now anyway." Twenty-two dollars was a lot of money. Ben felt a tightness in his head. They couldn't do everything. They couldn't buy it all at once.

Helen held her lightness. She smiled fully, flashing a sugared smile that was like a poisoned dart. It was her smile that thickened Ben's tongue and made him giddy.

"I suppose we could have waited," she said simply.

"Then why didn't *we*?" He tried to ignore her standing smile.

64

"It was on sale. Is this what you gonna do to me? You gonna constantly be asking me about everything I buy?" But before Ben could respond she added, "Anyway, why wait? The wallpaper was on sale this week. I swear. Why wait another two months when I'll be so pregnant I won't feel like messing with no wallpaper? We can't afford to pass up a good buy when I can find one."

Ben picked up the stack of bills and scattered them across the table. "If you looked at these bills, you'd know we couldn't afford no kind of buy. Good or otherwise. We just have to be careful, that's all. That's all I'm saying."

The smile disappeared. He tried to hide the strain sweeping across his face. Suddenly, at precisely the same time, they were both tired of playing.

"I don't think I did anything wrong." The words rolled like stones from Helen's mouth and at Ben.

She turned around and came back toward him. For a moment Ben was paralyzed. He wasn't sure what she was going to do. But the smile came back. "I'm sorry, sweetheart." She slid herself into his lap. "Are you mad at me?"

Ben could smell the acrid perfume of cleanser on her. It reminded him of many Saturday mornings spent scrubbing the stone steps in the front of his family's house in North Philadelphia. "No, baby, I'm not mad. I can't be mad at you. We just have to be careful, that's all."

"Well, when you're out of college we'll be doing just fine. We won't have to worry about a thing." Helen believed what she was saying. She expected them to be happy. She gently trailed her hand over her softly swollen belly.

"Guess what?" Her voice was now recharged, the twenty-two dollars gone into the distance.

"What?"

"I was thinking about names for the baby today."

The baby was still an abstract idea to him. But Helen felt the growth of life inside her. She journeyed through the physical kaleidoscope of changing shapes. She felt the sweep of emotion, of love, of dedication, of reverence, of revelation. Ben tried to sink into her so he could feel the same things. He tried to understand what was going on.

Men struggle with the concept of childbirth. They are challenged to love and bond in spite of it.

"I know it's gonna be a girl. I just know it. So, I was thinking about Makeba. What do you think about Makeba?"

He liked it. He knew that Miriam Makeba, the South African, was one of her favorite singers. Miriam Makeba could conjure heavy duty. Spirits flew when Makeba sang. "Makeba sounds real good to me."

Helen faced him and moved her full red lips close to his face. "I'm so glad I met you. I think we're gonna make a great team, you and me."

Ben turned into her open hearth. The wallpaper forgotten. The bills still unpaid.

He kissed her softly, reached his hand under the dress and felt her breasts, heavier now than ever before. "When I asked you to marry me, it was because you were just what I had been searching for. We belong together." He kissed her again, allowing his tongue to run into her mouth. He tickled the underside of her tongue.

"Besides, you've got a part of me in there." He poked her lightly at the navel. "Now, who else could be the father of your child? Who else could get that close to you?"

She pecked him on the cheek and got up from his lap. "You know there will never be anyone else. I love you."

Ben took a deep breath as she stood and glanced at the table where the Kresge bill stared back at him. "And don't worry about the bill, sweetheart. I think we can take care of that."

She kept moving toward the stairway without turning around. "I wasn't worried," she said into the stairwell space.

Makeba's Journal

How strange. How completely strange it is to read about me. To read how unsure you were. I don't understand what you mean about men and childbirth. All you have to do is love your child. What's the big deal? You didn't have to tell me about Mom. I could just see her acting like she was a queen or something. You were her knight. She thought you were the man. Yes, I could sure see her thinking she was in seventh heaven. She acted like that with my stepdad sometimes. Not that much though. He's okay—very different from you. I've never seen him *write* anything but checks and money orders.

I have a whole collection of Miriam Makeba's tapes. I'm hoping I can see her perform sometime. For a while I followed everything she did. She's an incredible woman. Her music is a religious experience. My favorite song is "Pata Pata Pata." I don't know why. Maybe it's because she makes me feel so happy, so strong. But you know, whenever I think of you I always end up wondering what happened. What happened? I thought you were coming back.

There were times when we didn't have anything. I mean nothing. We'd eat pork and beans three times a week. I got so sick of pork and beans that I couldn't stand to be in the same room with that sweet cinnamon smell. To this day, it makes me throw up. And whenever there was no money there would be arguments. There were times when I heard Mom and my stepdad fighting and prayed for you to come and rescue us. And when they argued I couldn't help but think that he was always mad because I was there. I was another mouth to feed. I wasn't even his daughter.

What happened? You were supposed to come back for me. You promised.

Seven

Mates knew from the beginning that Ben and Helen would have a tough time. They were trying, but there was something in the air, in the texture of the connection between them, which made him anticipate trouble. He didn't know how long it would take but he knew there would come a time when he would move into physical existence. When he would become the flesh he now began to long for.

Mates wondered how long a relationship that began in the clutch of sweat and music could last. Add the responsibility of a child and you had a problem. Then, of course, there was Lena.

Mates could now hear Ben's thoughts. He knew Ben wanted to write. But the world Ben lived in didn't make a space for that kind of desire. Ben was going in the wrong direction. His loneliness had led him to Helen and now he was fixed on living out an expected role.

But Helen was clear. Her focus was on Makeba and her family. To Mates this tension was like the smell of fresh meat.

During her pregnancy Helen sucked in everything related to new life. She grew plants and tended her flowers in the backyard. She continued her household routine as long as she could and she began to fashion the world of motherhood.

Ben stood back. He tried to be helpful. He watched Helen's stomach grow. He kissed her often and told her how beautiful she was pregnant. And she was. Helen couldn't understand why some women felt ugly when they carried their children within. How could they not understand the changes a body *had* to go through for the sake of the next life. It was a chain to God. A God's life. An internal vision realized.

Her mother had worked too hard. Had shunted Helen off in domestic service to her siblings. But she vowed, from the moment she awoke with a queasy stomach, to dedicate herself to being a real mother. A modern mother.

She felt Ben's hesitation. He stuttered sometimes when talking about the baby. About the lump in her stomach that kicked and cried loud enough for her to hear. At night, when she turned for two, trying to find the place that two could lie comfortably, she had to reach over and grab his hand and place it on her stomach.

"Feel that?" she asked.

"Is it moving?"

"Yes, she's moving, Ben. Right here." And she moved his hand again. "There. Feel her now?"

Ben felt the tremble. The rumble. The small bulge in the pit of her stomach. It was like a small ball rolling slowly. And when he did feel it, it shook him. "That's our baby. That's our baby, isn't it?"

"Yes. That's Makeba."

"I wish you wouldn't make such a big deal about it being a girl. Suppose it isn't? I don't want to have a boy who you thought should have been a girl."

Helen sighed. "First of all, I know it's a girl. I just do. Second of all, even if it is a boy, he will know the only sense of true love he will ever experience, with me."

Ben chuckled. "You think you're going to be the greatest mother that ever lived, don't you?"

Helen shifted her weight. Makeba stirred again. She was comfortable there in the womb, in the position that Helen was now in. She slipped again into anticipation. Helen smiled. "Of course. What do you think? Do you think I'm not going to be the best damn mother a child has ever known?"

"No doubt about it, Helen. No doubt. If ever there was a woman ready to love a child, you are it."

Helen looked at him in the darkness of the room. "And you? What about you? Are you ready to be the best father in the world?"

It was something that Ben had been thinking about. He was anxiety-ridden. He had promised Helen's mother, Helen, his parents, himself, everyone, that he was ready. He could take care of a family. He was ready to be a father.

Everyone expected as much from him. He absorbed the expectations and put them into himself. But in the darkness he shivered. It seemed so big. And Helen's serene confidence rattled him.

"I'm going to try, Helen. I really am."

"Do you love her?"

"Who?"

"Makeba. Do you love her?"

"I'm trying, Helen. I love you. I love what we're doing here. I love being with you and expecting a child. Of course I'll love her." Ben felt frustrated. How could he talk to her? She seemed the blessed one. The loved one. She exuded the knowledge of fullness.

"I love her now. Right now." Helen placed her own hand on Makeba's small back.

"I know you do. I can see that. But you are her. You have her right there inside you." Ben stopped. This was the stuttering conversation that Helen was growing to hate.

"What are you saying?"

"I don't know." He paused. "Sometimes I feel left out. You and the baby have so much together. I don't know how to get in there."

Helen laughed out loud. "You do so know how to get in there."

"I'm not joking. Sometimes I feel so separate."

Helen closed her eyes. "Separate? Well, I guess you are. I'm a mother. This is one of the reasons I'm here. To bring Makeba into this world. And I loved her from the first thought. From the first instant I knew she was there."

The room fell silent. Then, after a long wait, Helen finished her thought. "I feel sorry for you. You will have to learn to love what I have loved from the beginning."

"I will though. I will." Ben felt a sense of desperation. He didn't want her to think he was incapable.

"Oh, you don't have to reassure me. I know you will. We could not conceive a child that you couldn't love. So I'm not worried about that at all. Plus"—she leaned over to kiss him—"you're just about the sweetest man I ever knew and I love you very much. Any daughter of mine will love you too."

Ben slipped into a sleepy reverie with a fresh coat of security. Just before passing into the mists he said again, "I love you."

Makeba's Journal

It seems like you were really weird about her being pregnant. What's the point? Babies come from women. That doesn't mean men have to be separate. But that's the way you felt so I guess that is the point. Are you saying that's why so many black men aren't with their children? I don't think so.

And you don't have to tell me that Mom loved me. I know that. She's always been with me. She's been with me through everything. Even when I made it hard on her. And I did make it hard on her. I blamed her. Still do in a way. That's partly what this journal is all about. I'm trying to figure out what to do with all my feelings about this. But she was there and you were gone. So I blamed her. She told me it wasn't me that made you leave, so I figured it must have been her. Sometimes I just totally acted out. I'd do anything to make her angry. My secret weapon was silence. I'd go days without talking. She'd totally freak out. You know her. The one thing that drives her absolutely buggy is not talking to her. She can't stand it. I'd just sit in my room and read. Sometimes I'd write poetry. I guess that was how I kept my connection to you. I'd write stupid little poems about every little thing. Sooner or later she'd come into my room and try to get me to talk. I'd make her sweat. I knew the thing she feared even more than my silence. Losing me. If I turned against her, she would have died right there on the spot. I held her life in my hands. If she got on me too tough, I'd threaten her with silence and make her wonder if I had stopped loving her. Make her wonder if I wouldn't rather be with you. She was terrified of that. She never said it, I just knew it.

Anyway, when I turned sixteen, I took all the poems, a big stack of paper, out into the woods near our house and made a little fire and burned each one. I just didn't want anyone to see them. They made a pretty, light blue-gray smoke. It was like a ritual. Just me and the fire. But I decided then that I would never use you as a threat to her. I love her unconditionally because that's the way she loved me.

Eight

It was 3:23 on Monday morning, December 15, when Helen shook him roughly. She was ready to go to the hospital.

"Makeba's coming today," was all she said as she went down the steps.

In the waiting room Ben found a seat in the corner. In 1975 men still paced the room. There was the gratuitous path worn into the carpet. Men still followed the pattern of their fathers and found consolation in the isolation from the miracle of birth. They smoked cigarettes and read sports magazines.

Ben was in a room with five other men. None of them talked. They smoked and walked. Smoked and read. Drank coffee. Had no idea of what was going on down the hall. Didn't see the sweat, hear the grunts, smell the thick floral smell of new birth.

Ben didn't hear Helen's gospel screamshouts of anguish, pain and purpose. He didn't know that she wanted him to see her there. He didn't see Makeba when she was pulled two hours later from her temple. He wasn't there to hold Helen's hand as she prayed silently when she saw the top of her daughter's head.

Even though he didn't smoke, he bought a pack and lit a

cigarette. It fell out of his mouth when a nurse came to take him down a long hallway to see a molasses drop swaddled in a pink blanket.

He lost his breath there. He pressed himself against the glass and felt something deep within him. He waved and kissed at Makeba. She smiled at him. Now, he was a father.

Makeba's Journal

Wow. I was alive. And you were there. When I was the size of a loaf of bread, you held me in your arms. And you kissed me. And you smiled at me.

It was such a short chapter.

I'm sure you know about Kwame. Well, I think that when Mom got pregnant with him everything changed again. I was always the one who had to make adjustments. I was the one who had to figure out how to deal with the way things were. Mom tried to act like she really cared about me. I know she loved me. I mean, nobody could probably have a better mother. I knew she wouldn't abandon me. But I lost something in her when you left. She seemed so desperate. Every problem was a disaster. I was constantly worried that she was just going to have a breakdown. Maybe she did anyway. Now that I'm thinking about it, and with what I know now, I think she did have a nervous breakdown. She would just start crying for no reason. And until she met Dwight she never took that damn housecoat off. And even though we were spending a lot of time together, I remember being more sad than anything. Nothing felt right.

One time we went to a play. I don't even remember what it was but it was supposed to be funny. We sat behind this other black family and the man kept putting his arm around his wife and hugging her. It was so tender. So sweet. After a while I could feel my arm shaking. Then I realized it was Mom, she was trembling. I looked at her and saw her trying to hold back the tears. Some days I really hated you. I couldn't believe how you destroyed her like that. You were everything to her.

Anyway, it wasn't long after Mom and Dwight were seeing each other, maybe seven or eight months, that they took me out to dinner. We went to that restaurant we used to go to on Chestnut Street in University City. You know, the one with the prime ribs. I can't remember the name. But anyway, we got all dressed up. Dwight is really skinny. He's tall but almost like a stick. And he's bald too. So I remember thinking he looked like an undertaker in his black suit that night. He can be really stern too. Rigid. But that night he was smiling and laughing. And he called me Buttons. I could see why Mom liked him. He was serious about family stuff. He couldn't understand how any man could leave his children.

He told me that he loved Mom and that they wanted to get married as soon as they could. I remember staring at Mom, wondering what in the world was going on in her head. What was I supposed to say? She had made me promise to keep hoping you'd come back. I went to sleep every night for at least a year praying that you would call or something. So I was stunned. I was too young to understand what was going on. I couldn't know how lonely, how frightened Mom must have been. I could tell, sitting there, that she was really nervous about my response. There was such a pressure on me. I didn't dislike Dwight, but I didn't want another father. I didn't know what I wanted. So I shrugged my shoulders and kept eating. They talked at me all night. When I got home I grabbed Ka and went to sleep.

But what I didn't know was that Mom was already pregnant with Kwame. About two weeks after the dinner, Dwight and I went for a walk. He told me then he wanted me to call him Daddy. He said he was going to be my father and that he'd never leave me or Mom. And then, when we got back home, Mom came up to my room and told me she was pregnant. I was numb. Empty.

Nine

It amused Mates that Ben and Helen were so impressed with Makeba. They thought her life was something special. Something that would solidify their relationship. Actually it added a weight that they had to shoulder. The delicate equation of love, marriage and family would be too much for them. How did he know? He listened to the way Ben thought. Ben was already fighting himself.

Still, Mates also knew there was a light that shone on a facet of life that could only be seen by those who had created children. It was a brilliant light, pointed always to tomorrow and the journey of growth. Parents saw the subtle tightening of bone. The slow movement of hair. They were sometimes frightened by the brightness. Sometimes suffocated by it.

The decision to have a child should be cause for serious thought and consideration. But it often isn't. More likely the fact of pregnancy is present before the parents have fully contemplated their lives, as it was for Ben and Helen. People meet, they fuck and then, suddenly, they must learn to love the idea of parenthood.

Ben was scared. With Makeba's birth, he was suddenly aware of what he had helped to create. He was now responsible for another person's life. And he was committed to becoming a writer. Both were intense and uphill. One had to do with real life, the other with an imagined one.

Ben was open to obsession. It had become apparent as he delved into black literature. He read voraciously, trying to catch up on the continuum of African American literature. He read Zora Neale Hurston's *Their Eyes Were Watching God* and lost himself to the sweet smell of Florida and cane fields. He felt the thick drape of accents and the southern struggle for survival. It was Zora and then Alice Walker in her collection of short stories *In Love and Trouble* that revealed the truth: Black writers could write stories about black people for black people. This is what he wanted to do. He wanted to explore the details of black life in the same way that white writers could for white people. He loved the way D. H. Lawrence, for example, could get under the skin of sensuality and reveal the complexity of feelings while at the same time providing a critique of the life-changing Industrial Revolution.

From the abstractions of Ted Joans to the earthy truths spoken by Amiri Baraka, Ben absorbed everything. And because he was in school, his elective reading was always forced into the context of Western culture. Shakespeare and Hansberry, Frost and Hughes, Faulkner and Wright—everything ran together.

This was one obsession. The other was fatherhood.

The *idea* of being a father wasn't what frightened him. He had become used to that. He was actually excited about that. The problem was more connected to the *reality* of being a father. The expectations that he provide, teach, be present, be "in" the world for his child were etched in his mind. He wasn't sure he could do it. And the more he learned about the lives of the writers he admired, the more he wondered whether it was possible to be a good father and a writer. His life, if lived true as a writer, would be a struggle itself.

His loneliness had led him to Helen and now he was fixed, in a way, set in a place. The same magic which swooned him now defined him. And when Makeba was born, though his obsessions were a part of the air, there was a joy, like strong hands, holding him up in the rarefied atmosphere of parenthood. He and Helen would sit in the hospital room and just stare at the little girl that was them. Suddenly, for Ben, there was little thought of anything but his daughter and Helen.

Makeba's Journal

NINTH ENTRY

I'm trying to hold on to the belief that I've always had that I wasn't the reason you left us. But it's difficult the way you've written this. It was me that made you afraid. It was me that made you worry. Your two obsessions? Right from the beginning you were pitting Mom and me against writing. And I never even understood what was going on. I don't think Mom did either.

Ten

Mates lived with them. He watched them. He never slept, always observant. He shared with them the joy, though he knew it was only a flash, of their new family. He marveled at the transformations people must make for their children. When a baby is born, the concept of love is defined. No matter the circumstances of the mother and father, the birth of a child grabs everyone by the collar and shakes them. And even the confused can feel, at the witnessing of birth, the sharp clarity of love.

And then new decisions must be made. The people who created the child must decide individually how they will live out their love. People who are not fathers or mothers don't have this demand put upon them. Their lives are not awash in the bittersweet colors of parenthood.

Makeba's birth was the culmination of the euphoria that accompanied the joining of two people. In her, both Ben and Helen could see themselves, and the promised idea of love and marriage became reality.

Helen was only in the hospital for two days. During that time she had many visitors, but Lena never came. Helen had talked to her mother on the telephone, but Lena would not set foot in the hospital.

On a brisk Wednesday morning they brought tiny Makeba home with them to West Philadelphia. When they reached the front step of the house they were surprised to find Lena waiting for them on the porch.

As soon as Ben saw her, his heart stopped. Lena frightened him. At the wedding, Ben had felt her eyes tearing holes in his back as the minister conducted the ceremony.

After the vows were given, Ben remembered turning around to face Lena. He almost walked into her eyes. He wasn't threatened, just admonished. He saw her nod at Helen, who shook stardust every time she moved. Their new house was charged with happiness.

Now Lena sat, clad in a heavy gray coat, in the only chair they had on their porch. It was December and the weather had settled into its winter blanket. Beside her was a large brown paper bag.

"Mom? What in the world are you doing sitting out here in the cold?" Helen said as she gingerly began ascending the stone steps. "And why didn't you come to the hospital?"

"Helen, you know I don't go to hospitals. Don't believe in them."

"But I was there. You could have visited."

"It don't make sense to believe in something if you don't pay attention to it. I swore after your daddy passed I wouldn't ever go into another hospital as long as I lived. Now you just have to forgive me, but that's the way I feel. Anyway, that's why I came out here to meet you. I've just been sitting here waiting to see my granddaughter. I may not be the first visitor but I'm the most important." Lena slowly got up from the chair.

Ben held Makeba like a bag of groceries he was afraid would spill out. He could barely see the steps as he trailed Helen. "Hi, Mrs. Brown."

"How are you, Ben? Is that my granddaughter you got there?"

"Yes ma'am. This is Makeba."

Helen waited at the forest-green front door for Ben, who had the keys. She kissed her mother. For the first time, including the sunny May day when they were married, he saw Lena's teeth flashing. She was obviously very happy.

Helen was barely inside the house before she headed for the

couch. "I am really glad to be home. Bring my little girl over here. Sit down beside me, Grandma." Helen patted the cushion next to her. She watched Lena bring the bag over to the couch with her. "What's in the bag, Mom?"

"Nothing much. Just some things I brought with me."

"For who?" Helen was preoccupied with getting comfortable.

"Don't you worry about it. It's not for you. I didn't know anything when you were born. But now . . ."

"Now what, Mom? What are you talking about?"

"I told you, Helen, you just hand me that little girl. Let me take a good look at my grandbaby."

Lena took off her coat and eased herself into the soft brocade couch. Ben ran back outside to get Helen's bag. By the time he had brought everything inside and taken off his coat, Lena and Helen were both transfixed with Makeba.

He sat in a chair across from them and watched an animated Lena make baby sounds. He felt his heart beating rapidly. He could have dismissed it as the result of running out to the car and back, but he knew better. Helen and now Makeba were the objects of his love. That was what caused the fast-beating heart.

He marveled at Makeba's tiny brown hands, her twinkling eyes, her soft, two-toned feet which were now in the world because he loved her mother. And now, he loved *her*. He imagined a series of poems about them. Odes to mother and daughter. And then he looked at Lena. At this moment there was nothing frightening about her. She almost looked young, playing with Makeba's fingers. Perhaps there would be a grandmother poem too.

Ben sat, quiet, deep in thought, as the afternoon light dimmed the room.

Lena noticed Helen's eyes drooping. "Having a baby is hard work, ain't it?"

"All of a sudden I'm really tired."

Ben jumped up from his chair. "Maybe we should get you upstairs to bed. You could take a short nap."

"Maybe I should."

Lena smiled gently. "Sure you should, Helen. You got a lot of time to be worn out. This here girl is gonna keep you hopping from now on. Now, you go get yourself some rest. I just want to sit here and hold her for a while."

Helen looked at Ben, who shrugged his shoulders. "C'mon, sweetheart. I'll help you upstairs. Then, after your mom leaves I'll bring Makeba up."

Helen turned back to kiss her new daughter. "You're so pretty, so pretty. Mommy's just going to lie down for a little while." Then she kissed her mother and began her ascent up the steps.

With Ben by her side, they walked into the bedroom. "You know, I think your mother's going to be a pretty good grandma."

"Of course she is. I told you. She's really a sweet woman. Now remember, as soon as she leaves, you bring Makeba up, okay?" Ben nodded as Helen lay back on a stack of pillows and closed her eyes.

When Ben came back downstairs, Makeba was asleep in Lena's arms. Lena was humming a soft, unidentifiable song.

Regardless of Helen's assurances or his own attempt to quell his fear of Lena, he didn't like being in the room alone with her. He watched her sitting on the couch rocking gently. He tried to engage her in a conversation, but she responded tersely, as if she didn't want to be interrupted.

Even in his own house Ben didn't feel comfortable. He got up from his chair and headed toward the kitchen. "Would you like some herb tea, Mrs. Brown? I have some peppermint and some chamomile."

Lena didn't lift her head from Makeba, but asked, "Do you have any sassafras?"

"No," Ben called back. Ben's mother was also fond of sassafras tea. It was the tea that black folks from the South drank. His mother thought it could cure anything from a stomachache to asthma.

"Too bad." He heard Lena's voice. "Sassafras would be good right now. But that's okay. You just make whatever you like. I'll try some."

Ben smiled. Perhaps there was hope. He had felt a familiarity in her voice that penetrated the tension between them. Maybe, if he was especially nice to her, they could eventually become friends.

In the living room Lena reached down and opened the bag that sat at her feet. She retrieved from it another brown paper bag. It was smaller, an old, intensely wrinkled lunch bag. As she carefully balanced Makeba in her lap, Lena slowly pulled out three small leather pouches. Both paper bags were now back on the floor.

She opened the first pouch and the room was instantly awash in the strong scent of rose. With her thumb and forefinger she produced a pinch of deep crimson powder. "This, my child, is the rose and pomegranate's powder. A touch on your sweet baby skin will make you beautiful and let you live forever. " Lena placed a powder-caked finger on the bottom of Makeba's tan foot. A dot of redness remained after Lena removed her finger.

The whistle of the boiling water startled Ben, who had been standing at the stove staring into space. He poured the tea and headed toward the living room. But just as he passed across the threshold of the kitchen, he heard Lena's voice. He stopped still.

"And this, sugar, that I put on your eyes is the feather of an owl." Ben tried to say something. He wanted to ask what she was doing. But he couldn't move.

He heard Makeba gurgle, an unfolding shriek bouncing around in her small throat. "And last, Makeba, to protect you, the hair of a dog." Ben was stapled to the maple floors. He heard the rustling of paper as Lena continued talking to Makeba.

"There's just a bunch of stuff I'm going to teach you, girl. You are going to grow up and be the best and strongest. I promise you that. I didn't know nothing when I had your mother. But you don't have to worry."

Ben made his legs work and entered the room. He sat the tea on the coffee table and quickly moved to Makeba, sweeping her out of Lena's hands. "How's my little girl? You're tired, aren't you? Yes." And then, to Lena, he said, "I'm going to take her upstairs now."

"Ben," Lena said softly, "don't worry. I'm not going to hurt her. Or you."

Ben couldn't hold himself back. "What were you doing out here?" Makeba started to whimper.

"I was making sure that this little girl survives all the ugliness she has to face in this world. I want to make sure that she stays beautiful, and happy and safe."

"But that's our job. Helen and me. We can do that." Ben felt a sense of rootless desperation.

"It's bigger than the both of you. You have no idea how hard it is. But don't you worry, Ben. Everything is going to work out fine. I just know it."

Ben forced a weak smile and turned to carry Makeba upstairs. As he started up the stairs, Lena called strongly, "Wait, there's one more thing I have here for my granddaughter." Ben stopped and turned around. He watched as Lena pulled a small stuffed animal from her bag. It was a golden-brown lion. She held it out to Ben. "I want her to have this."

Ben reached out his hand to take it.

"Would you just do me one little favor? Would you let her touch it first?" Ben was weary of Lena. He held Makeba's tiny body out to Lena.

"This is yours, sweetheart," Lena said as she put the lion next to Makeba's skin. "See, his legs move around like this." The lion's legs were fitted to its body in such a way that each leg could rotate in position. Lena demonstrated the way the legs moved. Then she pulled the front legs up over the lion's head, so it looked like it was standing straight up with arms outstretched.

"She must never part with this. It's hers. I got it especially for her. Its name is Ka."

"Whatever you say," Ben said flatly, as he turned and walked up the wooden stairs. As he laid Makeba in her bassinet next to Helen, who was already asleep, he heard Lena gather up her paper bags and coat and leave.

Makeba's Journal

TENTH ENTRY

You know, the thing I said about children should be wished for and not discovered is still going around and around in my head. I don't think I'm going to have children. It doesn't make any sense.

Nana told me about what she did when I was a baby (the powder and stuff). I love her very much. You got her right though, she does know magic. I've seen her do it. And I think if it wasn't for her I wouldn't have made it. Lord knows Mom is not the strongest woman in the world.

When we were in North Carolina I can remember laying in bed, listening to her cry, thinking that I would never ever be in that position. Never.

And Nana just made it worse. Every day she would make sure she talked about you. She wouldn't do it in front of me, but I could hear her anyway. She ragged you out. And when she started getting on you Mom would start whimpering, but Nana wouldn't stop, she'd just keep on, all day long, until Mom was bawling like she was a little baby. It went on for weeks. We were staying in North Carolina at one of Nana's sisters.

But Nana still didn't stop. Even on the days when Mom was like stone and nothing seemed to bother her, Nana kept on. She'd say stuff like: You had gone crazy in college. And college kills black men. She said you were probably somewhere acting like you weren't even black anymore. Probably with some other woman. Probably saying the same things to some other woman that you said to Mom. Stuff like that. I mean to tell you, Nana can completely go off on you. One day she even told Mom that you were evil and that she had fallen under your spell.

Anyway, one day Nana said something about you, I don't remember exactly what it was, but it was totally wild. Something like, "Helen, that boy is the real devil walking the streets." Something completely crazy like that and Mom just burst into laughter and said, "Mom, you ought to go on with that stuff. Ain't no man on the face of the earth as bad as you make that Ben out to be. You ought to just hush up." And that was the end of it. Well, nearly the end. Nana's pretty sick right now, but she can still find something bad to say about you.

Eleven

When Lena produced Ka, Mates stopped laughing. Mates wasn't exactly afraid of the toy lion but it worried him. He wasn't sure what Lena was capable of. But the way she was going about spooking Ben made it clear that she wasn't to be taken lightly.

In the days that followed, Ben found his heart thoroughly opened by his love for Makeba. Lena's words thumped in his brain. He too wanted Makeba to be safe. He plunged himself into her child life. He wanted to do everything. He wanted to change her. To feed her. He was aware of how black men were portrayed. He wanted to be a model. His father had done it.

The days passed, just as they did for his father, and he began to learn more and more about himself. He discovered that as long as he was writing, he could be silent about his fears. He never talked to Helen about them. Indeed, as time passed they seemed the perfect family.

Slowly a sigh, a rolling sense of relief enfolded him. He was a father, a husband.

Sometimes as he came home from work, tired and hungry, he faced Helen with a heart full of love and admiration. He could almost hear the music in the background. They could have been on television. Makeba was the daughter of two people who expected success. And she grew that way, loved, even pampered, self-aware and confident.

As a baby Makeba knew Ben's hands and face just as much as Helen's. Helen tended to go to sleep early, leaving Ben up, staring into an open space of the empty page. When Makeba was young, still breaking the night, still with demands for milk, for dryness, it was Ben who materialized over her.

And most of the time he embraced the interruption. He had a hard time writing at home. He spent a lot of time in his den trying, but there was something about the house, the air. He always felt Helen over his shoulder.

At school it was a little different. He was taking a poetry class and there were a lot of in-class assignments. He liked that because it forced him to write and he got immediate feedback. His classmates and the professor loved his sensitivity, his boldness. For some reason nearly all of his poems in class were about sex. They were erotic and often graphic. The first time it happened, the class was stunned and nervous, but they liked it. And he wasn't ready to throw the political stuff at them. So he hid behind sex. Besides, his classmates were much more open to expressions of love than of anger.

At home there was no such inspiration. Most nights he gazed at his typewriter as if it was supposed to talk to him. So he welcomed Makeba's interruptions. And he didn't mind changing and feeding her. Ben's early years as a father were successive waves of revelation, frustration, fatigue and recommitment.

Every day he came home to a growing little girl who met him with youthful anticipation. He could almost hear her as he got off the bus, her soft footsteps caressing the concrete. She came gloriously, running to him, her arms outstretched with one hand clutching her Ka.

Time ran too. He watched Makeba unfurl like a morning glory in a blushing sun. They all felt the special light of a fledging family.

Every night, after dark, deep moving shadows rose up in the old house and became a part of the family. They had names. They had distinct personalities. Like the shadow on the wall that faced the bathroom door or the shadows that lurked in the living room or the upstairs hallway. And given the way her clothes were strewn or the way her toys were positioned, the shadows continuously changed shape. Makeba had a room with shadows of her own. And of course there was Ka, always near her. It was her favorite toy.

They re-created Sage Street. Turned it from a sleepy block of white college professors and post-hippies into a running discussion of African American community.

Six months after Makeba's fourth birthday another African American family, Rita and Scoby Rollins, moved across the street from them. Three months later, Hannibal, a tall, gleaming young man, moved into the upper duplex next door to the Rollinses.

As Makeba got older, Ben spent increasing amounts of time alone with her. He read to her. Told stories. Talked. He would often bundle her up and take off for long drives, leaving Helen smiling in the doorway.

Helen liked the idea that he would spend so much time with Makeba without her. She reveled in the image that Ben tried so hard to create.

When Makeba was five he began to make up stories about the shadows.

"On dark nights when you're tired and you want to sleep good, you just tell the shadows to put you to sleep. They'll take care of you." Ben's voice dropped to a whisper. "And if you wake up in the middle of the night and you've had a bad dream or something, don't worry. The shadows will take care of you. Nothing gets into this room that doesn't love you."

"Not the boogie man neither, huh Daddy?" Makeba asked in total seriousness.

"Not the boogie man or no other kind of man or woman. The only people that can come in here are people who love you."

"And what about Ka, Daddy? He wouldn't let anything bad happen to me either, would he? That's what Nana says."

"That's what she says."

Makeba just smiled. She loved her father and felt completely safe when he was around. She liked the sound of his voice and his laughing eyes. She knew nothing bad about him. She only loved him absolutely.

For a while there was so much laughter in the Crestfield house that Ben accepted his stuttered growth as a writer. Forgot that there was a world outside the world which dominated him. He was home by choice. He was a father by choice.

Within their world there was constant celebration. Every new phrase Makeba learned. Every new food. Every circus, zoo, animated film. Everything new was celebrated. He thought it would go on forever.

Makeba's Journal

This must be the fiction part. I don't know. Maybe you did used to tell me stories. Maybe it was happy. I just don't remember. And I've never heard Mom or Nana talk about anything that was good. All I've heard about are the arguments and confusion and all that. I've actually tried to think of the times when I had fun with you. Because whenever somebody asked me about you I wanted to have something to say. But I never came up with anything. I knew that you liked to write. That was all I knew for sure.

By the way, you have no idea what it's like when one of my friends asks me a question about you. Hardly anybody even knows that my stepdad isn't really my father, but I have told a couple of people. Almost as soon as I tell somebody, I regret it. Because then they want to know stuff that I don't know. Is he nice? Why don't you communicate with him? Where does he live?

Do you know how it makes me feel? Can you imagine?

Anyway, I know there must have been *some* good times because I still love you. But I don't know why. So now that I'm reading this I'm really confused. It's hard for me to remember specific details. I just don't know whether to believe you or not.

Twelve

Lena was proving to be a force in Makeba's life. She did indeed have a connection to a knowledge that neither Helen nor Ben was even aware of. She *was* strong.

Lena had found Makeba's Ka in a toy store and transformed it, using an art known only to her, into the child's twin and protector. Lena knew that the ka was a great ancient power. The ka was better than a shadow because it could actually challenge one's enemies. It was an aggressive guard, able to see what its double was unaware of.

She had learned this from a book which had picture after picture of Egyptian deities with their kas, miniature doubles of themselves, at their heels. And she knew instantly that that was what Makeba needed most. Someone to watch over her. Someone who could see what she couldn't.

Every child could use a ka. Parents have to make money and live out their own lives. Children become the victims. They are the helpless, innocent by-products of life's complexity.

And children need everything. They are brought to this festering world with nothing. They are completely at the mercy of mostly unqualified people who do not yet know much about themselves or their place in the world.

Makeba's Journal

TWELFTH ENTRY

I'm reading this and I'm thinking yeah, that's right. Children do need everything. That's something incredible. You know this and yet . . .

I don't know how to talk about being your daughter. I know we have a history. But I don't know what it is, or how to talk about it. I know we did things together. I know we ate together every day. Went to the park. Visited relatives. I know we went to Rehoboth Beach together, we saw movies and you read to me. I know that we played together a lot. I remember all of that. But those memories feel empty. It's like that's all I can do—remember them. I don't feel very much about them. Maybe I once did. But to tell you the truth, this is what I really think happened. I think that I couldn't stand to think about you. That I couldn't stand feeling the way I felt when I thought about you. Do you understand? So I understand the idea that you are my father. But in reality, I guess I have to say that Dwight is more of a real father than you are. Even though living with him was hard.

If I was already quiet, he made me stop talking completely. I was always afraid of him. He had a terrible temper. Just saying that makes me tremble. Why am I telling you this? I don't know. But I've never told anyone what I'm telling you now. This is why I like to write. Because I can communicate without speaking. And if I decide not to give this journal to you, you'll never know what I'm thinking. That's how I am. It's all inside.

Anyway I don't want to talk about Dwight. But I guess since I started I'll just say that yes, he did beat me. It was probably for talking back to him or saying something I shouldn't have. He only had to do it once or twice for me to see how crazy he really was. I can see his face, contorted in rage, ripping off his belt, coming after me. After that I just kept my mouth shut, or I said what I knew they wanted me to say. For most of my life I have been the perfect daughter. He loves me. I know he does. I love him too. But I also know he loves his son, Kwame, more than me. Ever since Kwame was born, I've known the difference between living with a man who is your father and a man who loves you like his own.

So, I just wanted to say that there is one memory I have of you that makes me smile when I think of it. It is the one memory of you that, I think, makes me think of you as my father. Remember when you took me to see your friend Harold in North Philly? I don't know how old I was, I must have been really young. But I knew my telephone number. That was one of the games we played. Remember? If I said our phone number right, you'd pick me up so that my stomach would be on your head and you'd twirl me around. I used to love that. Anyway, we were at your friend's and he had a little boy—his name was Troy I think—and we went outside to play. I don't know what you were doing. So we were running up and down the street. I remember it was very hot and there were a lot of people on the streets. Then, Troy went in the house and got some money and we went to the store.

We went to this dark little corner store on a street full of people. In the store, Troy was first and after he bought something he went outside. He had given me some money and I was buying a strip of button candy. Then when I walked out of the store, I didn't see him anywhere. I had no idea where I was. I stood there for a long time and then I just started walking, thinking I could find my way. I don't know what I was thinking actually, because I was in a completely unfamiliar place. And there were so many people walking around and all the houses and streets looked the same. After a while I just started running.

Have you ever been lost? I'll never forget that. I was running up and down those streets. Everything around me was like streamers of color. I only remember seeing colors of things passing me by. I know people were probably wondering where this little girl was going, running and crying. And it was getting darker and darker. At some point I started screaming for my mom. I remember screaming "Mommy, Mommy." That was when somebody stopped me and took me into a different store. I just kept saying I was lost. Finally somebody asked me if I knew my telephone number. They called my mother and she called you.

When I saw you come through the doorway of that store I burst into tears. So did you. You scooped me up in your arms and hugged me so hard. I'll never forget that or the look in your eyes. I knew then I was important to you. I knew it that day.

I didn't know you knew so much about Ka. I still have her. Probably always will. That's right, her. Ka is not a man. All lions are not men. She's really the one who convinced me to confront you. She's always liked you. Ka told me that you would never forget. I wasn't sure, but Ka has never lied. When I told Nana that Ka had told me not to forget you, she said that I probably didn't understand what Ka was saying. When it comes to you, Nana even disagrees with her own creations.

I took Ka's advice.

P.S. You'll probably think I'm nuts or something to still believe in Ka.

Thirteen

Children are not miracles. Just little people who give off a blinding, directionless light. It shines into the eyes and asks important questions like, "Will you show me how?" Parents gaze into the light, become enraptured and scream back, "Yes. I will show you."

But the child does not know the better question to ask and the light it throws off confuses. Instead, the newborn breath of life might ask, "*What* will you show me?" It is the "what" of life that sets the course.

And it was the "what" that Ben confronted at college. He was slowly being sucked into a world which filled his head with ideas, information and dreams. Suddenly after six years as a part-time student his professors and fellow students began to recognize his talent.

When Ben was on campus, he lost all contact with Makeba and Helen. He was known as a budding writer. He wore a fatigue jacket, jeans and combat boots as his uniform. He hung around a group of younger black students who were also fascinated with the celebration of culture. They believed that the culture of a people defined its political viability. They believed the battle was over ideas and self-identity. African Americans had to know their history, had to believe in their own beauty before white America could be forced to reckon with them.

Of course, except for the Black Writers Workshop, he was usually one of only two or three blacks in his classes. In those classes, he was considered to be a fiery, sensual, edgy writer. Ben could be depended on to say "fuck" in a poem that *wasn't* a diatribe against the system. His professors weren't always so impressed with his work. In his poetry class he was constantly encouraged to find a form, iambic pentameter for example, to channel his thoughts.

And in the short story class, his professor, Molly Berner, told him, "Mr. Crestfield, I think you have an ability to make us feel, but I can't *see* the places you're writing about. I can't *see* this house. I don't know this neighborhood. I want to *see* it."

"What difference does it make where the action takes place?" Ben knew what she was talking about. He just disagreed.

"Making love is different in Beverly Hills than it is in North Philly."

Ben opened his eyes wide and hardened his jaw. "You must be kidding. Right? You don't believe that bullshit, do you?"

Molly Berner, in her mid-forties, a published novelist who had been teaching for five years, rushed to protect herself. "Are you saying that two people who have all the money they could possibly need, who are having sex, is the same as two people with absolutely nothing who are making love in the ghetto? When they don't know how they're going to eat when they're finished screwing? It's not the same, Ben. Place is everything."

"Place ain't shit. When a man and woman come together it don't matter where they are. What I think is that white people need black writers to describe these squalid situations just to make them happy. It satisfies some weird need to minimize or even exoticize the idea of black love. Shit, of black life in general. It all happens in the goddamn ghetto. Anybody can fuck anybody in the ghetto. That's what you people think."

"I resent that, Ben. That's not what I was saying at all." She wasn't sure where this conversation was going and it worried her.

"What I'm saying is if you can describe the 'squalor,' as you put it, and then show me the beauty in it, then it's more powerful."

"That's bullshit. What about Camus and Sartre? All those existentialist white boys who could do anything they damned well pleased and everybody just accepted it. You can't name me one black existentialist. Why? I'll tell you why, because everybody wants us to tell the same damn story."

Molly didn't know much about black literature and was feeling very uncomfortable. "Okay, okay. I'm just trying to tell you what I think will make you a better writer. You have to follow your own beliefs. You have to discover what works for you."

Ben appreciated her surrender. He wasn't sure how much further he could push his argument. He wasn't even sure he was right. It was just what he felt. He knew there were black existentialists. He had even been influenced by them. And he had correctly guessed that the good professor would know less than him.

That conversation, as well as others with other professors, made it all the more surprising when one of his short stories and five poems were selected for the annual English department literary journal.

When he saw the list and the announcement of the reading in which he was predominantly featured, in the hallway outside the department office, he almost flew home on a wave of images and colors that flowed like jet streams right from his stories.

"Helen, Helen!" He was barely within the house before he was screaming her name.

She and Makeba were in the backyard. Helen was turning the brown soil in anticipation of planting her annual garden and Makeba was playing with Ka in the sandbox by the fence near the alley.

Ben felt the breeze rolling through the house and moved in that direction. It was like magic, the way he could always sense where Helen was. If he came in and she was upstairs, he would instinctively know it. If she was downstairs washing clothes, he would know it. He had internalized her.

Ben passed through the house like the breeze itself, through the kitchen and to the back door, where he stood facing the afternoon sun.

Helen was bent over, her face focused on the earth. Makeba was absorbed in a game with Ka. The toy lion looked just a bit weathered over the years but still smiled on the child. Ben stood there inhaling the image of the two of them for a moment before speaking. When he spoke, he startled both Helen and Makeba.

"Hi there, sweet stuff." And in the same breath he called to Makeba, "How's my African princess?"

Helen jerked her head up at the sound of his voice. She dropped the garden fork. "How long have you been standing there?" Makeba jumped up and ran to him with her arms open.

"Long enough to see a fine woman digging in dirt." He was dying to tell her the news. He had driven home in a fog of surging hopes. He was very excited and yet he felt like he had to control it. He couldn't appear too much so. For some reason he almost felt guilty about his good news.

Helen had steadily gained weight since Makeba's birth. Ben couldn't help but notice the roundness of her stomach which marked the place that Makeba had been.

Helen smiled and demurred. "What's wrong with you?"

"What do you mean?" Ben grinned as he released Makeba.

"Anytime you start talking like that I know something is going on. Most of the time you walk around here with a frown on your face."

"C'mon, that's not true. Anyway, there *is* something. I've got incredible news."

"What, Daddy?" Makeba looked up at him. Ben looked into her eyes. He felt the late April sun on his face. He felt Helen's presence just on the edge of his field of vision. He took it all in.

"Well, sugar, your father is going to have a whole bunch of his writing in a magazine and then, when it comes out, I'm going to stand up in front of a lot of people and read the poems and the story to them."

"Oh." Makeba's response was quick and flat. Ben let his hand rest on her head. He knew she had no idea how important it was to him.

"Your own work? That's great. That's really terrific. At least now I know you're doing something when you're up late trying to write." Helen stood up and hugged him. "That's fantastic. How? Where?" He felt her arms pull him close. He smelled the sweetness of her perfume diluted by the sun and light glaze of perspiration over her skin.

"Well, it's an English department thing. Really shocked me. I thought they thought my shit was lame. Anyway, most of this stuff I wrote at school. Like I said, they're going to publish it and then there will be a reading." Ben tried to contain his excitement. He didn't feel comfortable screaming or jumping up and down but that was how he felt.

"Wow. I'm really happy for you." He heard her words but there was something buried in the sound of them. Some reservation, a hesitation. Helen stood back; he watched the news sink into her. Slowly a smile, an understanding flicker of a smile flashed. "Am I married to a famous writer? Are you going to be a black Shakespeare or something?"

"More like Langston Hughes." He hated comparisons to white writers. He was constantly fighting his colleagues and instructors in school on the same point. They wanted him to pick a mentor, someone who *they* thought was good. But they had no idea of the influences pulsing inside him. None of his instructors knew about the Black Arts Movement, the young artists in New York and in the South who were defining a new aesthetic.

"Anyway, it's a beginning. My first publication."

"Well, I'm proud of you. This calls for a celebration, doesn't it, Kayba?" Helen grabbed Makeba's hand. "Daddy's going to be a famous man one day."

"For your poems, Daddy?"

"Maybe, sugar. We'll see." Suddenly he felt nervous. Was he going to be famous? Could he be? How could the artistic expression of an African American man penetrate the same culture that enslaved him? How? And how could it ever come to mean as much to them as it did to him? And why did he care?

"You know what?"

"What, Daddy?"

"If you grow up and think that my poems are great, then I'll be happy." That was what mattered. That she would see what his art was. That she would see what art could be.

"Who knows, Ben. Maybe she'll become a writer too." Helen kissed him on the cheek.

Ben felt her lips burn the side of his face. That kiss was an unconscious message. Helen didn't know it but her kiss was a question. "How?" How was he supposed to be a writer? They were barely making it now. How would he ever pull it off?

And yet, the kiss also gave him a sense of security. She would be there. Makeba would be there. Every empty space he had felt when he first met Helen was full. He wasn't sure if it was Helen or Makeba or what was happening with his work in school, but suddenly he wasn't lonely anymore. Maybe he would never feel lonely again.

As they walked into the house Helen asked Ben to show her the work that had been chosen. "You never let me see what you're doing." She watched Makeba run ahead, and up the steps, cradling Ka like a baby.

"That's not true, Helen. I've read you poetry. You know how I write."

"I know that. But that was a long time ago. Most of those poems you had written before I even met you. When you were in the Navy or even before. But you haven't shown me any of your new stuff. I have no idea what you've been doing in school."

"Well . . ." Ben had purposely not shown Helen his work. "I guess I just wasn't sure I was ready to let you see them."

"Why?"

"I don't know. I guess I'm a little worried you won't like them." He knew she wouldn't like them. He knew that once she found out that he was primarily writing about women, about sex, she'd freak out. Particularly since they weren't about her.

Helen turned to face him. "Now I honestly don't understand why you would say that. When have I ever said anything bad about your writing?"

"I didn't say you did. I just said—"

"I know what you said. Now why don't you just go and get some of that stuff so I can see what my baby is going to be famous for."

They were standing in the living room. The sun flowed in the front window, exposing the airborne dust around them. Ben shuffled his feet. He was trying to determine how much he would say. Finally, realizing his silence was going nowhere, he said, "Most of my work is at school. But I do have a couple of poems in my bag." He lied. All of his work was in his schoolbag. He never went anywhere without all of his manuscripts with him. That was one of his idiosyncrasies. He needed his work with him. He couldn't imagine being separated from it.

"Well, get it. I don't understand you, man. Why are you acting so strange?" She watched as Ben fished through his bag.

"Here it is." Ben pulled the two tattered sheets of paper free. He handed them to her.

Helen took the poems and sat down on the couch. She patted the cushion next to her. "Sit down. Now, let me see what you're being so mysterious about." She was about to look at the paper when she looked back at Ben as he sat down. "This is fun. I finally get a chance to see what you're writing now."

Her smile seized as she finished the first poem. She opened her mouth to speak but nothing came out.

"Helen, listen, it's no big thing. I just write what I see."

Helen was trying to gather her thoughts. She knew that the woman who was the subject of the poem couldn't have been her.

"Who is this? It's not me. That's for sure." She tried not to sound frantic, but she felt that way. "Who is this?"

"What difference does that make? She's just someone I saw on campus. A student. No big deal."

"Oh, I see. That's what goes on when you're at school? You spend your time trying to find young girls with hips like 'rock butts' to write poems about?"

"No. That's not it at all. Anyway that's 'like a butte of rock.'

Butte, not butt. But why would I try to explain it to you? I'm a poet and a writer, I should be able to write what I want to. There's nothing going on here."

"I told you once before that I'm not stupid. I know this woman isn't me and I wonder why you had to write a poem about some other woman." Helen looked at the other page. Why was he writing this stuff? She began reading aloud: " 'There is nothing dangerous between her legs/nothing warlike as a penis fully armed/only the promise of peace/the complete understanding of life/and the stream of truth.' What kind of poetry is this? You're always talking about the black man this and the black man that. What's this got to do with being a black man?"

"I don't know. I'm trying to figure that out myself. But right now this is what I'm writing. That's why I haven't been showing them to you. It's hard enough doing the work, that I have to justify it to you. And I knew that if you saw them you wouldn't understand."

Helen had heard enough. "You're damn right I don't understand. Why do you have to write about sex and other women?"

"Because there's something there I'm trying to figure out. There's so much connected to sex that we don't understand. It rules us and yet we don't understand it."

"Yeah, right." Helen dropped the papers on the couch. They fluttered briefly before coming to rest. She stood up. "I know you want to be a writer. And that's okay. If you have to write about women and all this, I'll live with that too, but I don't have to like it." She walked into the kitchen.

"I guess you don't." Ben picked the poems up and put them back into the portfolio. He was confused. He'd known all along how she would react, and yet he was unprepared. How was he supposed to do what he wanted and what Helen wanted him to do at the same time?

He followed her into the kitchen. "Come on, baby, it's not that big a deal. I'm not interested in the women I write about. Except that I have the same feelings all men have. I'm just trying to put it in context. Sometimes I just try to shock people. You know. In a way, what I'm doing has nothing to do with sex."

Helen, now standing at the sink, wheeled around. "I told you, if this is what your writing is all about, fine. I'm not going to stand in your way. Write away. Or write on, I guess I should say. I don't care."

Ben could feel the dirt flying in his face as she dug the trench between them. The next part wouldn't be any easier. "Okay. Okay. Well, will you come with me to the reading?" At this moment, he wasn't sure he wanted her to come. But he knew he was *supposed* to want the woman who loved him to accompany him to one of the most important nights of his life.

Helen turned her back to him. "Do you really want me to?"

Ben sighed. "I wouldn't ask you if I didn't."

"Then I'll go. I don't want you to think that I don't care about what you're doing, because I do. I just want you to be honest with me."

The weight that had been gathering in Ben's body lightened. "I will be honest, Helen. It should be a fun night."

The reading was two weeks later. He had decided to read the beginning two pages of his story and two poems. He practiced every night as the event approached.

On that day, Ben worked a short shift at the cab company and came home with a racing heart. Helen met him at the door.

"Makeba's sick."

His stomach turned instantly sour. "What's wrong?"

"She woke up this morning with a fever and wheezing. I finally had to take her to the doctor's. She's got some kind of flu. She's got to stay in bed. He gave me a prescription."

"Oh no. How's she doing now?" Ben was struck by how fast things changed. He always kissed Makeba before he left for school. He remembered now that she had been sweating in her sleep. When his lips touched her she had started mumbling something about Ka.

"She's sleeping now. I know you really want me to go with you tonight, but I think I should stay here with Makeba."

"But I thought Lena was going to come over."

"She is, Ben, but Jesus, Makeba could be really sick."

"I know, but you've seen a doctor. She's got medicine. Your mother's going to be with her. Everything's going to be fine." In the days leading up to the reading, Ben had gotten accustomed to the idea that Helen was going with him. Now he really wanted her to go. It wasn't that he wanted her on his arm for decoration, he wanted her to see his classmates and friends. And he wanted her to see how they reacted to his work. *They* wouldn't be embarrassed by it. He wanted her to see the world he wanted to be a part of.

He went up to Makeba's room. The shadows were thick there. Makeba was curled up with Ka, in a deep sleep and breathing heavily. He sat down on her bed. He placed his hand on her forehead. "How's my baby? You're going to be just fine, sweetheart. Daddy loves you." He kissed her lips. "Daddy loves you very much."

Helen's shadow joined the others. "I'm worried," she said in a whisper.

Ben was now up and standing beside Helen. They both stood there looking at their daughter, her little chest heaving fitfully. "I know. But I think she's going to be okay. Now, why don't you get dressed. Everything will be fine. Besides, Lena can always get in touch with us if she needs to."

"All right. If you think it's okay."

"I do."

Helen slipped into their bedroom to get ready.

An hour later Ben sat downstairs waiting for Helen. He was dressed in a black cotton cavalry shirt and black Levi's. He planned to wear a black cowboy hat he had bought while he was in the Navy. The perfect costume for a writer's coming out.

He had changed his mind three or four times. One idea was to dress in one of his dashikis and lots of African beads. At the last minute he decided against it because on this night he wanted to make a different impression. He was a renegade, a modern-day cowboy, demanding respect for his work.

Helen wore a blue pants suit. As she came down the steps, Ben couldn't help but feel a little disappointed. He had wanted her to wear something more exciting, more bizarre, something people would remember. But that wouldn't have been Helen. He swallowed and got up from the couch.

"Black? Are you wearing that?" Helen was shocked.

"What's wrong with what I'm wearing?"

"I don't think you look good in that much black. I mean, it's so dark. I think you look better in colors. Are you sure you want to wear black?"

"Yes, I know how I want to look. Now, if you've finished giving me a critique, can we get ready to go? Where's Lena?"

"Don't worry, we won't be late. Mom's on her way."

Lena arrived and assumed residence among the shadows in Makeba's room. Ben and Helen left for the university.

As they walked into the room, Ben felt the tension rise in Helen's body. This was not her territory. The room was full of chairs. The dark mahogany wood which spoke of the years of contemplation. Contemplation about words and life, about good and evil. And in this room were the bright eyes of those struggling to take their time in the same space.

Ben spotted two seats in the second row near the middle of the small wooden stage on which a chipped but newly varnished lectern sat. He tugged at Helen and began moving toward them, but was stopped by a young woman, a classmate named Monica. She was tall with straight black hair that ended abruptly at her shoulder. She wore a black-and-white checked sweater and black toreador pants. Ben sat next to her in a number of his classes. She was a rebellious preppie from Connecticut, but he thought she was blessed with an incredible wild energy that exploded in her writing. Monica slid her head through the air and kissed Ben on the cheek.

"I saw your stuff in the ragmag, Mr. B." Ben couldn't help smiling. She had never called him that before. "Spread out big as day. It's all the hush, you know. It's magnificent. It's the hit of the magazine." She stepped back and looked Ben up and down. "Urban cowboy. Heaviness. Right on." As she finished speaking she turned her head to Helen and stuck her hand out.

"Helen, this is Monica."

Helen put her hand into Monica's. She was conscious of not shaking Monica's hand, but of having hers shaken. She smiled.

Monica returned the smile and switched her attention immediately to Ben. "This is gonna make you, Ben. I swear. This is it."

Ben turned to Helen and said, "Monica's short story is in the magazine too. You'll like it, she's totally wild."

"I don't believe this. You're calling me wild? I think not. You're the one with the line, how does it go?" Monica shook her hair gently and flipped opened the *Touchstone Review*. "Ah, here it is, and I quote, 'as a penis fully armed.' No, my black brother, you're the one who's wild."

As she talked, Ben tried to keep his smile. He thought Monica was cute with her stark, angled face. She was obviously interested in being his friend. But he could also see the shock and anger rising in Helen's face. He didn't know what to do. He hoped the story would end soon. He had made a mistake in introducing Monica that way. He should have known better. Monica had no sense of control, no sense of consequence. She was so full of Monica she was oblivious to Helen. Ben couldn't tell whether it was deliberate or not. But he knew that Helen thought it was. She was starting to narrow her eyes in a way that made Ben immediately nervous. If Helen "went off" on Monica it would be nuclear.

Luckily, as she ended her monologue, Monica caught the eye of another student across the room. She waved at him and turned to face Ben. "Give 'em hell out there, my black brother. I'm really proud of you."

"You too." Ben felt a surge of relief sweep over him. While Monica was standing with them, the tension had thickened the air around them. For a moment he felt it subside. And then he looked at Helen.

Ben smiled an awkward discomforted smile. He knew Helen had had enough. He felt her pushing him quickly to their chairs. Almost running from any other interruption. He watched as other students would catch a glimpse of him, start in his direction only to flash on Helen's face and change directions. When she smiled, rooms lost their walls and were awash in light. When she frowned, she was a protective amulet, a force field.

He brought his eyes back to Helen. "Are you okay?"

"Okay? Why yes, Mr. B, my black brother, I'm doing just fine. My beautiful black brother."

"Come on. She didn't mean anything."

"Since when do you let some white bitch call you a black brother?" Helen's voice was held in the air by the thinnest of threads. It sounded on the brink of breaking away.

"I don't know. When I first met her I got into this really heated argument about race. Ever since then she's been calling me that. It's no big thing. She's okay."

"Yeah, uh-huh, I'm quite sure she's okay. Long as she can be up in your face."

"She wasn't up in my face, Helen." Ben was trying to act like they were talking about the stories and the poems in the magazine, or the impact of the hostage crisis on the election or anything important.

"Well, she damn sure wasn't in mine. For all she could care, I was your goddamned breeding whore or something." Helen was crumbling inside. The entire time that Monica hovered in front of Ben she had chewed the inside of her bottom lip. How dare she? How dare he?

Ben would have done anything to change the subject. "I've got to go up there and find out when I'm reading."

"Go. Am I asking you to sit here with me? You know, Ben, that really hurt me. You didn't even say I was your wife. What was that about?"

"It's not about anything. I just didn't think of it, that's all."

"Right. Go ahead, I know you'd rather be over there with them anyway. I think I'm going to find a telephone somewhere and check on Makeba."

"There's no need to do that. Can't you just sit here for a few minutes. It's just about to start." Ben was half out of his chair. He wanted to go but he wanted to know that Helen was okay.

"Will you just go. I'll be right back."

Ben made his way to the group of young writers standing at the front of the stage. Most of them he didn't know, but there were two others besides Monica he had talked with. One was Derek, the only other African American who was a part of the program. And Derek was whisper-quiet. He hardly spoke at all. They nodded to each other. Both recognizing the significance of the event.

"Is that your wife? She's pretty." Monica was at his side.

"Ah, yeah, thanks." Ben quickly looked to Helen's empty chair and again breathed relief. He gathered himself, put on his aspiring writer's face. "So what's the order, who's the first to get executed?"

Monica's hazel eyes gleamed. "You are, my black brother. You are the first to be sacrificed."

Ben looked at Derek. "Where does it say that the black man has to be the first up there?" Derek hunched his shoulders.

"They wanted to hit them hard, right from the beginning." Monica smiled.

They were signaled by Molly Berner to take their seats. Ben stood at the steps of the stage waiting for Berner to introduce him. He kept looking back to Helen's chair, but she hadn't returned yet.

He was introduced. He walked up to the podium and lost his physical body. From the moment he began speaking, he was transformed to a flow of words. His body disappeared under him. He read a selection from his story "Fast Feet on Cement" first. It was about an old man who sat outside a North Philadelphia candy store and his fantasy about a young woman who walked by each day. The audience laughed at the right time and were deadly silent as he finished. He knew he had them. And they erupted in applause. Helen was still not in her chair.

And then, he began to read his poems. He was just beginning the second one when he saw Helen creating a shadow in the doorway. His poetry always made people uncomfortable. He liked it that way.

> As she turned to face me
> my eyes became shutters open
> for natural light
> and she posed, her hip
> like a butte of rock
> teasing climbers into
> adventure.

When he stopped, there was a brief moment of indecision and then the audience complied and clapped again. As he turned to walk off the stage, he was once again conscious of his body. Of his legs and his feet hitting the floor. He sat down in the first chair that was empty. Ben sat there, nearly numb, unhearing of the other readers until Monica took the podium. He summoned his attention back and listened to her read. Her voice was soft and almost broke at times as she read an intense story about a nightclub on South Street.

There was an intermission after she finished. He quickly rose and started to make his way to Helen. Suddenly, he wanted to be with her in the worst way. But it was difficult. People were all around him. Telling him how good the story was. How much they appreciated his writing.

When he finally got to Helen she was standing by her chair. Her face was softer now. She was smiling. Helen had realized, for the first time, as she watched Ben read the end of the second poem, how important it was to him. She had never been to a poetry reading. She had never been on a college campus. The whole thing was intimidating to her and she wasn't sure what she was supposed to do. But she was happy for Ben. She could see how much it meant to him.

They nearly fell into each other's arms. "Congratulations, you were great."

"You only heard the last bit. I saw when you came back in."

"I'm sorry, I just had to talk to Mom. I had a funny feeling."

"It could have waited." Ben wasn't angry, but he couldn't stop himself. He wanted her to know that he had missed her and she should have been there.

"I told you, I had a funny feeling. Aren't you even going to ask about Makeba?"

"I was just about to. How is she?"

"She was coughing a lot but she finally got back to sleep. I think we should go home."

"Go home? I can't go home now. I've got to stay long enough to hear the others. And there's a party after that."

"Except for yours, this other stuff is boring. Makeba could write better than that. *I* could even write better than that. I was almost falling asleep."

"Are you kidding? There was some good work being read up there."

"I couldn't even figure out what the hell they were talking about. And that little Miss Thing over there almost drove me crazy with that stupid voice of hers."

"Come on." Ben was completely deflated. The lights flickered.

"Ben, please. I need to go. I don't want to be away from Makeba. I would think you'd feel the same way."

"I don't. I need to stay. I need this." Ben waved his hands like a magician. "I need this. This is important too."

Helen stared at him. He could see the hurt deep in her eyes. He had never turned her back this way. Never directly challenged her. He didn't want it to be a choice. This wasn't about choosing Makeba or writing. Was it? Makeba was in good hands. This was Helen's discomfort. This was her problem. If she had something else in her life besides Makeba and her family, maybe she would understand. But as he looked at her, he knew there wasn't a chance that he could get through.

"Suppose I take you home and come back? Would that be okay with you?"

"Sure. If that's what you want to do. That's fine. You can come back and be with your stuck-up writer friends." Helen was breathing heavily. She couldn't understand why he didn't see what they were supposed to do. They were supposed to go home to their sick child.

A form of panic fluttered in his body. He knew she was angry, but so was he. He hated the way he couldn't be right. There was no way that he could be right. To Helen, it *was* about making a choice, and he had made it.

They made their way to the door. He waved to Monica and the others, calling over his shoulder, "I'll be right back."

Ben could only think of the sound of his voice reading his story as he drove home. Helen was perfectly silent. She didn't want to believe that he could just drop her off like a package at the front door.

When the car stopped in front of their house, Helen was out like a rabbit jetting to freedom. She wasn't going to talk about it. Ben watched her run up the steps into the house. He knew she was crying, he heard her disintegrating even as she opened the car door. By the time she was at the front door, he could tell that the tears blurred her vision because she dropped her keys and in a fit of exploding frustration, she stomped her foot. Lena appeared at the door.

He slowly let the car roll down the street. When he reached the corner, he gunned the engine and raced back to the university. On this night, that was where happiness was.

Makeba's Journal

THIRTEENTH ENTRY

I wish I could have seen you read your writing. I wish I could have known more about what you were trying to do. It might have made a difference. I understand the struggle of black men. I know it's not easy. And I think that Mom understands too. She's hung in there with my stepdad ever since you left. She's stood by him through all kinds of bad stuff.

Mom never mentioned the reading to me. If it happened the way you say it did I guess you felt pretty bad. But look what happened. In the past six months I've been secretly clipping articles about you and this book. You finally are a writer. And it all started on that night. And I was home sick. I don't even remember hearing Mom come back in that night. There's so much I don't remember. Anyway, from the articles I have learned more about you than I ever did from Mom. I know how hard you had to work to get where you are. You probably figured if it was going to be that hard, you should just be by yourself. I read in one story that you had a nervous breakdown. That you were in an institution for a while. Was that because of us? I can't imagine being out of control.

By the way, I wasn't going to tell you this, but since you wrote about that girl Monica, I will. The one thing that Nana used to say that would make Mom go nuts is that you left her to be with a white girl. She'd go nuclear when she heard that. And Nana would say it all the time.

Fourteen

There was a tear in the fabric that connected Ben and Helen. Helen wasn't enthralled with literature and writing. She wasn't interested in the same people he was. And at times Ben's desire to be a writer overshadowed everything. At those times it was clear that he didn't care as much about family as she did. It was happening right in front of them, and yet, life seemed to just keep going.

It was Makeba who would feel the brunt of this tragedy. It was her heart full of hope that would eventually be ruptured. It was her idea of future that was in jeopardy. She was defenseless. Immersed in a love for her mother and father that defied qualification. She was a child.

Mates began to spend more time with Ben.

It was the unqualified, unquestioning quality of her love that scared Ben. "I tell you, man, that little girl is so goddamned pretty sometimes when I look at her I almost start crying." He was sitting in a downtown bar with his friend Ramsey. He had left school early and decided to play hooky from work.

He had first met the plump, plum-colored Ramsey in Naples, Italy, in the Hole in the Wall bar. It was a favorite of the black sailors that were in port. Over tequilas they had discovered they were both from Philadelphia. Ramsey, a welder, was a crew member of the U.S.S. *Forrestal,* an aircraft carrier, and Ben was stationed aboard the U.S.S. *Kenosha,* an oiler.

In their first conversation they discovered that the night before, they had unknowingly been connected by rubber hoses which pumped black oil from one ship to the other in the deep pitch of the wavering, ever shifting swell of the Mediterranean Sea. It had been just after midnight that the *Kenosha* had steamed alongside the hulking aircraft carrier to give it oil and jet fuel.

At-sea refueling, especially at night, conjured a different reality. The deep darkness of the ocean. The flickering deck and running lights of the ships. The sound of men working, screaming, singing. People who lived a life separate from those who make the choices of war. Time was suspended. The hoses of the oiler were slowly pulled across the churning alley of white water that sprinted between the two ships. Two ships that pursued completely parallel courses at precisely the same speed.

When the hoses were connected, the *Kenosha* would give its liquid cargo over to the larger ship. And all this in the middle of the night. While nearly everyone else slept. In the vacuum of the vast desert of water.

Both ships had arrived in Naples the following afternoon. And Ben had chosen a seat at the white-walled grottolike bar of the Hole in the Wall right next to Ramsey's. From that day their friendship began a blooming life. The two ships were often in the same ports and when back in the States, both ships docked in Norfolk, Virginia.

Now, nearly eight years later, there was a deep affection between them. Ramsey picked his drink up, held it up to the red lights that glowed from behind the bar. They had been drinking shots of tequila for two and half hours. Ben's head was reeling. Ramsey's eyes were like marbles, round and glazed, and his grin seemed set in brown concrete. "You're a lucky man. You've got a wife and a kid. I keep thinking that one day I'm gonna find me a woman I can settle down with." Ramsey had continued to gain weight and was bordering on being fat.

"Yeah, Rams, just be patient man. You'll find one."

"I guess I should've gone to that party with you. I always think about that night. That night you met Helen? How come I wasn't with you?" Ramsey took a sip of his drink and put it back on the table. "I still don't know how I missed that jam. We *were* out together that night, wasn't we?"

Ben smiled. He had been deflecting Ramsey's inquiries about that party for six years. "Yeah, you know good and goddamned well we were hanging out that night."

"Then why the fuck didn't I go to the party? You never said a goddamned word about it. Next thing I know, you're getting god-damned married."

"Maybe you should have come." Ben laughed.

"You're laughing, my brother, but I still don't know why you didn't tell me about it."

"I guess I just forgot. We were doing some heavy drinking, remember?"

"All I remember is you leaving me at the Thirteen saying you had to go home. You were bullshitting me, man. You wanted to go to that jam by yourself."

Ben stared down at the table and in a barely audible voice said, "That's the way it happens, man. You go to a party and bam, next thing you know, you're out looking for a crib."

"Thought you was into the family thing."

"I am, man. That's just it. You know how it is. I'm a father. I'm supposed to do the right thing. I'm the one who talks shit in my classes. You know—'Black men have to take care of their families,' and all that stuff. I mean, I'm supposed to make it so Makeba can deal in this white man's world."

"Yeah, I've heard this before, so what's the problem?"

"I'm not sure, man. I sit in my classes and write my poems and stories and I realize the kind of commitment it takes to be a writer and the way most writers have to live, nearly starving all the time, and I can't see how I'm going to make it."

Ramsey ordered another drink. The bar was nearly empty in the late afternoon. The after-work crowd hadn't started arriving yet. He turned to Ben. "Man, you better forget that poetry shit. Your ass is a motherfuckin' family man now. That poetry shit is history, man. If you want my advice you'd do better to drop it and get with something useful like accounting or computers or some shit like that."

"Ramsey, my brother, you are a good friend and if this was about a prizefight or a football game or something like that I'd be all ears, but to be honest with you, I don't need your advice about my career."

Ramsey pulled the glass away from his mouth. "You need somebody's fucking advice. Let me tell you. Somebody needs to straighten your black ass out right now."

Ben leaned back in his chair. The Budweiser light behind the bar competed with the waning sunlight to throw a faint glow against the charcoal interior. The air was slow, woven with stale beer and cigarette smoke. The carpet beneath them held memories which murmured in indistinct odors.

"I guess you're the one who's gonna straighten me out?" Ben smiled and looked into Ramsey's eyes.

"I just want to see you make your mortgage payments being a poet after your fucking G.I. Bill runs out. That's when I'll believe this shit. You're fucking up big-time. Here you are, getting money from the government to go to school. Not like me. You're in goddamned school and here you are talking about being a goddamned poet? Who the hell is hiring poets? I hear about computer programmers and advertising executives and shit like that, but I never heard nobody rushing in to hire poets. In fact, I ain't never seen no ad for poets in the paper." He paused to take another swig. "You're fucking up, Ben. That's what I say."

"Ramsey, you've known me for eight years and you know I have never listened to a goddamned thing you had to say." Ben was chuckling. "Shit, if I had, I'd have been court-martialed at least three times. I just want you to know that I have this thing . . . ah . . . I don't understand it. Sometimes I wish I could be a fucking insurance salesman or something like that. Sometimes I wish I could. But there's something going on in here." Ben tapped his chest. "Something's pushing me, man. Talking shit to me. You know?"

Ramsey looked into Ben's clouding eyes. He studied them. He

saw the fear that danced in his pupils like water drops on a thin layer of hot oil. He stared at Ben. He had a feeling that Ben wanted him to soften up, to open up, so that Ben could tell him something. He felt that whatever Ben wanted to say was big, important. And yet, he didn't really want to hear it. What Ramsey wanted to hear from Ben was that being a father and a husband and having a good job were the important things. Nothing else.

And in spite of his feelings, or perhaps because of them, he broke into a broad smile. "No, motherfucka, I *don't* know. What I know is that you better be getting yourself together so you can get yourself a job. Get your ass out of the taxicab-driving business and get behind a desk. Dumb motherfuckas like me, who can't get into college, barely even finished high school, well, we ain't got a chance. But you, you can make it, man. This is your time."

Ben looked away. "I don't think I can do it that way."

A woman came in the bar. She was followed by a man who quickly put his arm around her and guided her into a booth. Ramsey watched the couple as he said, "You're in deep shit, brother."

"I know, man. It's starting to feel that way to me too."

"Let me try to get this shit straight. Okay. Now, do you love Helen?"

"Of course. Yes. I love her. I mean, it ain't like I thought it was going to be, but yeah, I love her."

Ramsey nodded. "And you love your daughter?"

Ben feigned a menacing grimace and brought his fist into the air.

"Okay, okay, be cool, my brother. Just be cool." Ramsey smiled and relaxed his body. He seemed to grow into the chair, filling all of its empty spaces. "So, let's see here. You love your family. You're doing okay in school. Just about to graduate after all these god-damned years part-time. You're using the fucking G.I. Bill, so you've got some change in your pockets. The future looks bright and all that good shit. What the fuck are you complaining about?"

The bar was filling with the after-work crowd. Ben's blurred vision locked on a black woman in tight jeans. She wore a leather jacket that outlined a head-turning figure. Which is what happened. Heads swung in her direction as she came in the door. She didn't look like one of the refugees from the office buildings in the area. She maneuvered her way to a table directly across from Ben and Ramsey.

Ramsey hadn't seen her, but Ben had followed her all the way in. He nodded in her direction. "Now *there's* a woman."

"Boy, what has gotten into you? One minute you're crying the blues about being married and the next you're slobbering over some other woman." Ramsey's smile was still strong as he shook his head.

"I'm not interested in her, Rams, not like what you might think. I was just admiring, that's all." Ramsey looked in her direction.

He quickly turned back to Ben. "Wow, man. You wasn't lying about that." In the same instant, he was moving toward her. Ben could hear him say, "Hey momma, my name's Ramsey, what's yours?"

"Vicki," she said flatly, as she found a cigarette. Her skin was like ermine. Her hair fell alongside her face, creating flattering shadows in the dim light of the bar.

"Well, hey Vicki, why don't you join us over here? Let me buy you a drink."

Ben tried not to act interested. But he was. His heart was moving a little faster. He wondered if she'd respond.

"No, thank you, I'm waiting for someone."

Ramsey accepted his rebuff and faced Ben again. "I tried. Woman like that ain't interested in me no way." Ben smiled back. They ordered another round and another after that. Ramsey had forgotten their previous line of discussion but Ben hadn't. In between the lines of his spinning head, he thought about Helen. Where were they going?

He thought about telling Ramsey about Monica. It wasn't just Helen's imagination. Monica had made it quite clear she was interested in him. But Ben had decided then not to open up to her. He was curious, but he didn't want to risk his relationship with Helen. Besides, this was Philadelphia with its East Coast tightness and he wasn't ready for an interracial relationship in a city where a hysterical mayor, Frank Rizzo, had the city in the grip of a palpable racism. And finally, he knew that it would really hurt Helen. Not just the infidelity, but the race thing. She would never be able to get over that.

He had seen the growing number of interracial couples on the streets of downtown Philadelphia. And on campus, there were a number of interracial liaisons happening under the protection of the safe university environment. He had also heard the not-so-quiet rumblings from black women who took it as a personal affront. Helen was one them. She would set fire to his pants while he was in them if she ever caught him with a white woman.

In the throes of this contemplation, Ben missed it when the man Vicki was waiting for arrived. At some point Ben looked over at her and saw she was talking to someone. But she caught Ben looking and winked her eye at him. She painted a faint smile in the smoky air. Ramsey was now talking about the Philadelphia 76ers and Dr. J. Ben could barely make out what he was saying. He turned his head away from Vicki just long enough not to appear to be staring at her.

Ramsey kept talking and Ben drank and nodded his head and played eye games with Vicki. She was sitting so that he could see her without having to cross eyes with the man she was with. Music was now all around them. He had slipped into a cocoon of music, smoke, noise, basketball talk and Vicki. Somewhere in the folds of his reverie he heard Ramsey say he was going to the bathroom. He heard the chair slide back and Ramsey's presence dissipate. But he was fixed in his dream.

Now, maybe he *was* staring at her. Even when she wasn't looking at him. At first her open eyes had drawn him in. He had traced the delicate contour of her cheeks, the fullness of her lips. He watched her as her pink tongue formed a lisp at the back of her teeth when she talked. But it was also like a hypnosis. He was lulled through her and into a different place. Suddenly he wasn't looking at Vicki anymore but at a picture of himself standing in front of a new house. There was his station wagon in the driveway. There was Helen in the window. Makeba was tooling toward him on a bicycle augmented with training wheels. She was moving at full speed. He realized she wasn't going to stop. The bicycle began to get larger and larger, its wheels growing into tank treads. Her legs became huge pistons which pushed the vehicle at increasing speed. She was bearing down right on him. In an instant he felt panic deep in his stomach. He was just about to scream when everything became blue. He blinked his eyes.

Ramsey was still gone. But now, standing in front of him, was the man from Vicki's table. He was even larger than Ramsey. Except he wasn't fat. He was a hulking mountain of weathered dark skin. Ben's eyes reached up in confusion.

"What the fuck were you looking at?"

"What do you mean?" Ben couldn't think of anything else to say.

"Just what I said. I'm tired of you staring at my woman. I don't play that shit."

It was then that Ben realized that the man was angry. That he had committed a cardinal sin. It was dangerous to let your eyes linger too long on a woman who was with another man, even accidentally. If the stare held there too long, war was certain. Ben's stomach jumped again.

"Is there some reason why you got to be checking her out so tough?"

Ben's throat was suddenly dry. "Naw, man. I was just day-dreaming, that's all. I didn't mean no harm."

The man bent down and set his face an inch away from Ben's. "I'm gonna tell you something. I don't like you. I don't like nobody staring at me or her like that. You understand?"

"Yeah." Ben's voice was a cloud. "I understand."

" 'Cause I'll kick your motherfuckin' ass. Clean this whole god-damn bar with your skinny behind. You hear me?"

Ben was trying to swallow but he couldn't. He was frozen. The man seemed already out of control. All kinds of warning bells were going off in Ben's head but he didn't know what to do. Vicki's voice rose from behind the man's body. "He didn't mean no harm, Donnie. It's cool."

But the man grabbed Ben's right hand and held it tightly. The touch of skin was startling at first. The connection between them. And then he felt the pain. The man closed his fist tighter and tighter, as if Ben's hand was made of clay and would give.

"You need this?"

"I need my hand, man. I need my hand," Ben said, tears forming in his eyes.

"What you need it for? You gonna hit me with it?" The man's breath was in Ben's nostrils. His sweat was there too.

"No, I don't want to hit you. I'm sorry, man. I didn't mean no harm. I was just thinking. Just daydreaming."

But he wouldn't loosen his grip. It had stopped getting tighter but there was no blood moving in Ben's fingers. His hand felt like a dishcloth that was being wrung dry. Time seemed to stop. His mind flashed on an unfinished poem sitting in his typewriter in his den. It was a poem about a woman and her daughter sitting on a stoop in front of a house on Diamond Street in Philadelphia. He was going to call it "Safe." But could he write with one hand? That was what he was thinking when Ramsey came back.

Ramsey was drunk; his voice instantly found the right edge for a barroom confrontation. "What's the problem, brother?"

"I ain't your fucking brother. Dig it?" And then to Ben: "I think you should apologize to me and my lady."

"Sure man, I told you I was sorry. I didn't mean to bother you."

"Let his hand go." Ramsey was surging now, Ben could sense he was about to get into it.

"It's okay, Rams. Just a misunderstanding, right? I mean, I didn't mean no harm."

Ben felt the pressure release from his hand and a swift wave of pain shot through it. Ramsey stood staring as the man turned back to his girlfriend. But now she was up and walking toward the door. He grabbed his coat and followed her.

Ramsey eye's followed them. "That motherfucka is crazy. What the fuck did you do?"

"I didn't do a goddamned thing. I was just thinking, man. He thought I was making eyes at his girl. I mean, I was for a minute, but shit, man, he fucking crushed my goddamned hand." Ben felt like crying.

Ramsey collapsed into his chair. Ben got up from his seat; his right arm felt as if it stopped at his wrist and all the blood was dripping onto the floor. He had no feeling in his hand at all.

"Rams?"

"Yeah?"

"I think he did smash my goddamned hand, man. I think he really did. I can't feel shit. I think I'm going to have to get to a hospital. I got to have my hand. I can't write without it." Ben was afraid of the words that came out of his mouth. He shuddered at the idea of utter silence.

"Write? Is that what you're worried about? Let's get your ass to a hospital. You should have kicked him in the nuts or let me smash his fucking head in. Motherfuckas walking around thinking they can do whatever they fucking want to. And you're talking about writing. Shit. Let's go, Ben. We better take care of that hand of yours. I'm telling you, brother, like I was saying, you're gonna have to get your shit together."

Makeba's Journal

FOURTEENTH ENTRY

My love scared you? My love scared you? Maybe I should put this book down. Maybe I don't need to read this. I definitely don't appreciate knowing that because I loved you as my father, you would take that love as a threat. As something to be feared.

The story about Ramsey and that man is interesting I guess, but even now, just a minute after I finished reading this chapter, the only thing I can remember is that it was my love that made you afraid. I didn't choose you. I didn't choose this life. You're damned right I felt the "brunt," whatever the hell you mean by that. If you mean did I have to figure out why you left? If you mean that I had to get used to some other man who wanted, insisted that I call him Daddy? If you mean that I had to try to act like you never existed? If that's what brunt means, then hell yes, I felt the god-damned brunt.

Fifteen

Mates could feel himself becoming stronger, his senses more acute. He looked at Ben and his poor little hand. What irony. Mates wondered how in the world Ben would be able to write those wonderful stories and poems he expected to write.

Tragedy comes to people in more convoluted ways than one might think. Ben's hand could have been crushed and he could have lost the ability to write forever and that would have been that. Perhaps such a disability would have ended the anguish. But it doesn't happen that way. His hand suffered only a bad bruise and in time he was back at the typewriter. If only he could write a new life. If only he could write himself a way to live up to the image he promised.

It was June 1982. Ben had finally graduated from the University of Pennsylvania with a degree in English with a creative writing concentration. That spring he had applied to the Iowa Writers Workshop. He'd sent them a short story as a writing sample and immediately started praying every night before he went to bed. "God, please, please let them accept me." That was his prayer. "Please."

But Ben was sure that God would see through the lie. Writing had become his religion. He felt called, as a minister would be called. But called to what? To continue the effort of African griots and scribes to capture the full stroke of black humanity? To tell lies in the search for truth? To talk shit on paper with the bluster of Superfly on the hustle? It was all that. Ben was developing in a new breed of African American writers. Having felt the energy of the revolutionaries of the generation just before him, he was driven to define the contemporary black man. And it wasn't all fight and fire. The activist writers of the sixties and seventies had burned out. They had screamed and scratched and fought until there was nothing left. Only a handful of black writers survived the revolution. From this Ben knew he had to control his rage so that it would not destroy him.

Still, as he approached the end of his undergraduate life, he was worried about money. How would he make enough money? In a fit of anxiety, he had taken to scouring the want ads, and actually sending his résumé out.

He told himself that he would leave it up to fate. If he was accepted into Iowa and was not offered a job, it would be a sign. If he got a job but couldn't get into school, that too would provide direction. He made it as hard as he could. He applied to only one school and was very selective about where he sent his résumés.

He actually didn't expect to be accepted into graduate school. There was something about the way he wrote that began to turn his classmates and his professors against him. He'd finally lost his appetite for the shock and the erotic. Now he was trying to deconstruct the lives of African American people to reveal the interior. Not the perceived stereotype of drugs and violence and welfare, but the inner life. He wanted to go beyond the superficial effects of slavery. He wanted to go deeper. To explore the detail of complexity. Now, suddenly he was obsessed with the spirit. The essence. The humanity.

But he'd noticed a distinct change in the way his classmates responded to his latest work. When he dropped the clever sexual references and began talking about the strength of his father, the quiet exuberance of his mother, the beauty of Makeba, they weren't interested. When he started to write about the way black people lived with such dignity in an unbroken struggle against the system, the excitement about his work disappeared. Even Monica had said some-

thing about his need to "find that edge that was in your other work."
He couldn't get Baraka's words out of his mind. If you really told
white people what you were thinking they'd have to kill you.

So when he put the application to Iowa in the mail, he was sure
he would not be selected. And when a personnel manager at Benson
Glendale, a young public relations firm, called and asked him to
come in for an interview, he did.

He actually went out and bought a suit at Krass Brothers down
on South Street. He tied a tie around his neck and walked into the
company one day. The next day he was offered a job as copywriter.

And on this same day, when he opened his mail he was stunned
with the news that he had been accepted at Iowa. He had hoped the
choice would be made for him but suddenly it was harder than
before. He had to choose.

Helen tried to be supportive. After the episode at the reading,
she had shied away from talking about writing at all. And then, when
he talked about considering going to work or back to school, she had
tried not to reveal her desire that he pursue a career in business. She
was convinced that he could never make a decent living as a writer.

And yet, when he told her about the two offers she again tried to
make it clear that he was the one who had to make the decision.

"We can make it," she said. "I know how badly you want to
write. I don't want you to feel like me or Makeba are going to keep
you from doing that."

"But how will we make money? I would do it if I could figure out
a way, but I can't," Ben said softly. It was clanging in his head. His
own expectations of himself. It was his job to provide for them.

It wasn't Helen screaming at him all the time to get a better job,
even though he knew that's what she wanted. It wasn't that she didn't
contribute money to the household budget or that she wasn't even
working. It wasn't anything Helen was or wasn't doing. It was him.
Something inside *Ben* made him want to take full responsibility for
his family. Even though their marriage was already slipping, Ben
clung to the image of himself as a stereotype buster. Someone
everyone could point to as an exception to the rule of black men.

Helen stared at him. She was thinking too. She remembered

Geri's warning about Ben being a writer at the Valentine's Day party where they met. Then, it had been a joke. But now it wasn't amusing. Ben was much less concerned with the details of their lives than she thought he should be. Doing the things he should have been doing around the house, keeping the family tight and strong—she felt as if he left all of that up to her. He worked hard, that was true, but he also came home and closed himself up in his den. She knew he had an enormous sense of responsibility for her and Makeba, but she wanted more from him than money.

And yet she realized how serious writing had become to him. And now, faced with this choice, she wasn't sure what to say. He was right. There was no way they could survive if he didn't get a full-time job. Without the G.I. Bill, the cab-driving job wasn't close to bringing in enough money.

Helen wanted to be home with Makeba. What she saw on the evening news only strengthened her conviction that a mother, a father, someone, had to be home to raise a child. A parent had to know where their child was, and what they were doing. The way she saw it, anytime a young person was killed, or in a gang, or taking drugs, it was the parent who was at fault. In her way of thinking, there was no choice except for one of them to be home with Makeba. That was why, after Makeba was older, she wanted to start her own day-care center. She knew what was needed. It was love.

Ben knew how to read her silence. He knew that she didn't want to say out loud what both of them were thinking: that he had to take the job.

"It's okay, Helen. I think I'm going to take that job at Benson Glendale anyway. I was talking to one of my instructors and she thought that I wouldn't learn that much more about writing anyway. Her advice was to 'live.' She said, 'Live and then write.' So that's what I'm going to do. I'm not exactly the next Richard Wright or James Baldwin. They're not ready for my shit anyway."

Helen remained silent. There was nothing she could say. She agreed with him on all counts. She didn't want to acknowledge the pain that she heard on the inside of his voice.

Makeba's Journal

FIFTEENTH ENTRY

I can't help but be suspicious about all of this. I don't get enough of what Mom was thinking. You thought you knew her so well, but I don't think you did. Yes, she is really traditional but she is also very smart. She reads a lot. And she's very sensitive. If she wasn't so wrapped up in the church there's no telling what she would be. And even at that she's accomplished a lot. I don't feel like you know her.

Besides I don't know why you never did what you wanted to do. If you just wanted to sleep with her, why did you marry her? If you didn't want me, then why weren't you more careful? If you didn't want to take the job, why did you?

In spite of myself, I was very proud when I read those articles about you, but now, I don't know. The problem is that I don't understand what this is I'm reading. I remember when you got the job, but I thought it was a happy time. You and Mom had champagne and we had this great dinner. Do you remember that? I do. I even remember how you gave this toast to us, me and Mom, and said how happy and excited you were to finally get a chance to make a lot of money. I remember that. How come you didn't write about that?

Sixteen

He took the job. And with that decision Ben had chosen a direction. He wormed himself into a young company where the only thing as dark as him were the desktops and the suits his colleagues wore. He was the only one who had known the blue lights of basement parties. The only one who had run from pursuing street gangs. Out of twenty he was the only one.

From the beginning everyone at Benson Glendale smiled a lot. Ben did too. It was a new world. He worked in a department with two other copywriters. Benson Glendale, though a young company, wasn't the typical laid-back advertising/public relations firm. In fact it was quite conservative. Ben was expected to wear a tie, to be in the office all day and to be involved in the life of the company. He was expected to become a part of the Benson Glendale family.

Ben's history was work. His father had always worked hard, as had his mother. His experience in the Navy had solidified this legacy and now he applied himself at Benson Glendale.

Almost immediately he began to feel the way he had felt in the Navy. Used, manipulated. His superiors were always surprised that he was articulate, that he was well-read, that he was smart.

In the Navy, *he* was the one the captain would usually ask to compose official letters and messages. He was the one the captain asked for private advice. But when promotions and special privileges were being handed out, Ben never got any. At Benson Glendale it was working out the same way. People were surprised at his ability, impressed even, but they expected him to completely assimilate himself. To prove he was one of them.

In the early days at Benson Glendale, Ben tried to do that. He worked the long hours. Volunteered. Socialized. And when he came home he tried to write. But he was often weary by the time he made it to his den.

At night his hand still ached from his altercation in the bar. Even though no bones had been broken, pain would unexpectedly erupt. He still found it hard sometimes to make a sudden movement. To hit the *o* or the *i* keys on the typewriter. It made the fight to write more real, more immediate.

Still, every so often he became totally deflated. Empty of all energy. Then he would collapse on the living room couch and open himself up to the mindlessness of television.

This was such a time. He was flopped on the couch, waiting for an early-season Phillies game to come on television. Just the night before, he had been up late trying finish a short story. On weekends and holidays, he tried to throw himself into his writing. After which he always felt sluggish, almost sleepwalking on the fringe of the family life. But he was committed to not letting his dream of being a writer slip completely away.

Helen was sitting next to him, reading *Tar Baby,* a book by Toni Morrison. After a while Helen put the book down.

"I don't know why Mom has to get Makeba so much. It's like she's trying to be her mother or something."

From the time Makeba was six months old, Lena had insisted on spending time alone with her. Every other Saturday she would drive up from New Jersey to pick up her granddaughter. Most of the time Makeba's outings with Lena were welcomed by Helen and Ben. But there were some Saturdays when Helen didn't want to let Makeba go.

"Oh really, I didn't know you cared. I've been saying that since

Makeba was born. She's always taking that child somewhere." Ben was surprised by Helen's statement. She had never before questioned the amount of time Lena spent with Makeba.

"I really don't mind. A girl needs to know her grandmother. They should spend time together. It's just that on some of these Saturdays I'd like to spend some quiet time with my daughter. The week is so hectic I hardly have enough time with her."

"You're not working. You could do things during the week if that's how you feel." Ben couldn't help wanting Helen to go back to work. He didn't buy her argument that Makeba needed her at home full-time. Besides, if Helen went back to work, maybe he could eventually plan to go back to school.

"I know I'm not working. Don't throw that up in my face. You know as well as I do that even if I was working, day care and transportation would eat up all the extra money I would make. It's cheaper for me to stay home and take care of Makeba."

Ben decided to let the conversation, one which they had periodically, fade. "I wouldn't worry too much about your mother. I guess all grandmothers are like that. That's one of the benefits. They get to spoil their grandchildren." The truth was that Ben had never figured out how to handle Lena or even how to talk about her to Helen. If he tried to voice his apprehension, Helen immediately came to her defense. But when Helen complained, he knew he had to be careful. If he agreed too strongly, she would turn the tables on him.

Helen had succeeded in convincing Ben that Lena wasn't capable of doing anything mean. So now, as he thought about Lena's influence on Makeba, he tried to be more accepting. It was ironic that it was Helen who was suddenly asking questions about it.

"I know. It's just that she never spent that much time with me. I can't remember a time when just she and I went out together. Or even just sat around the house alone. She hardly ever talked to me. Except to tell me to clean something, or to criticize something I did."

Ben got up from the couch and walked to the television. The game was coming on. He could feel Helen wanting to talk. He decided not to turn it on. Instead he faced her.

"Do you want to tell her to maybe only make it once a month?" As he listened to Helen talk about her mother, he realized that there was something fundamental missing in her relationship with Lena.

"No. I don't think so."

Against his instinct, Ben asked, "Do you think maybe you're a little jealous?" It was the best way for him to say what he was thinking.

"Jealous? Of what, Ben?"

"Of how much attention your mother gives to Makeba?" He watched her facial muscles knot.

"Do I have to be jealous just to want to spend more time with my child? Do I sound jealous to you?"

Helen's voice had gone cold. When Ben heard it, he realized he was in deep weeds. "I didn't say you sounded jealous. But I never thought I'd hear you complain about how much time Lena spends with Makeba."

"I wasn't complaining. Why do you have to twist everything up? You stand there, detached from everybody and everything around here, and make judgments about me."

"Helen, what are you talking about?"

Helen tried to rein herself in. She tried to get a grip on the life that moved around her like a rope. She didn't want to be angry at Ben, or her mother. But something was happening. She could feel Ben's anxiousness. She knew he didn't really want to work at Benson Glendale. She knew he really wanted to write. She couldn't suppress a feeling, deep inside her, that her life was unraveling.

And her life depended on stability, the continuity of their family. She just wanted to be a woman who read books, took care of her daughter and loved her husband. But everything seemed to be getting more and more complicated.

"Oh, so now you don't know what I'm talking about? You have the nerve to stand there and tell me I'm jealous of my own mother. What do you know?"

Ben retreated further. "Forget it. I'm sorry I brought it up."

"So am I."

He turned the television on and tried to lose himself in the baseball game. Helen went back to her book.

The next morning as Ben still slept, Lena rang the doorbell and walked into the house. Makeba was waiting for her on the couch alongside Helen. It was a gray Saturday morning, a cover of rain clouds hovered.

Helen kissed her mother. "How was your drive?"

"I hate coming into the city, Helen. This place is filthy. I don't know how or why anybody in their right mind would want to live in this mess. It's the middle of the morning and there's gangs of people all over the place, like there ain't nothing better to do than hang out on a corner."

"It's Saturday, Mom. What do you think people should be doing?"

Lena untied the soft baby-blue scarf from around her hair. "They should be finding something to do. It ain't like there's nothing to do in this godforsaken city."

A seven-year-old Makeba hugged Lena's waist. "But Nana, you're supposed to play on Saturday. No school or nothing."

"I'm not talking about you, sugar, I'm talking about those good-for-nothing lazy bums standing around all over the place. Saturdays don't mean nothing to them. You can find them doing the same thing on Mondays that they doing now."

Helen had gone back to the couch. She knew her mother well enough to know that if she didn't respond Lena would eventually change the subject.

"Where are we going this week, Nana?" Makeba wasn't interested in the discussion about people standing around on the streets. She was tall for her age. Her freshly straightened dark brown hair rested just below her ears. She was nearing the end of first grade and seemed to everyone, especially Helen and Ben, older than she was. She had personality.

"I was thinking about a nice June picnic. I know just the place."

"Where's that, Mom?" Helen let out a slow sigh. She had never been on a picnic alone with her mother. There was the annual church picnic and the family reunion in Clinton, North Carolina, but she had never sat with her mother in the grass and looked up at the sky.

"It's a small, beautiful little park in North Philly, Rock Garden."

"Are there lots of rocks there?" Makeba asked.

"Well, in a way. It's like a little mountain in the middle of the city. There are caves and little streams running through it. And they've put in paths so we can walk around up there."

"Really?" Makeba's excitement rushed forward.

"Yes, dear. I just hope those North Philly hooligans haven't ruined it since I was there last."

"So how long was that, Mom?" Helen fiddled with Makeba's hair.

"Hasn't been that long. About a year." Lena opened her eyes to her daughter. She wondered about Helen's tone of voice. She slowly walked to the couch and sat down beside her.

"So, do you go there often?"

"Every year since your father died." Lena leaned back into the soft chair. "You mean you don't know about Rock Garden?"

"No, Mom, I don't know anything about Rock Garden. Why would I know about Rock Garden? Have you ever taken me there?" Helen couldn't control herself. Her anger close to the surface.

Lena felt the chill. She turned to face her daughter. Makeba stepped back from the two of them and stared first at Lena, then her mother and then to Lena again.

"Is there something wrong, Helen?"

"No, Mother. Nothing's wrong. Everything's fine." Helen looked into Makeba's eyes. She could tell that Makeba was uncomfortable.

Makeba was trying to figure out what was going on. She had never heard her mother unveil her sharp-edged voice to her grandmother before.

Lena spoke softly, almost into Helen's ear. Makeba even took a step forward but still couldn't hear.

"You are a woman now. I'm sorry if I wasn't a good mother to you. Maybe I didn't tell you everything you needed to know. But I didn't know myself. I was doing the best I could do. There were so many things I was learning when you was just a little girl."

Makeba tried to see into her mother's eyes. Maybe there she would be able to find the words that she knew were coming out of Lena's mouth. But Helen's head was slowly dropping, a little at a time, and already her eyes were hidden from Makeba.

Lena continued. "But I'm getting old now, and I *should* know more than I did then. Every day I put something together that I didn't realize before. That's what I'm doing these days. I'm reading and studying and putting things together. Trying to make sense out of everything. Especially you. I've been trying to figure out what I could have done better."

Still moving very slowly, Helen lifted her head. "Do you know?"

"I think I do. I taught you how to tie your shoes. I taught you how to wash dishes, how to talk. All that kind of stuff. But I didn't teach you how to feel. How to see through all the mess in front of you so you could find your way. That's what was missing in my life. Probably missing in yours. Unless you learned it somewhere else. I know you couldn't have learned it from me, because I didn't know it myself. But now I know. I can teach it to Makeba. I can show her how to protect herself. To transform the energy of all of us into something strong. Something fierce. Something that will define her and help her turn back all them forces out there that will try to stop her."

Helen closed her eyes and let her head drop back on the couch. Lena fell silent and looked up at Makeba, who was still standing there looking very nervous.

"Come here, Kayba. Come to Nana. Don't you worry about nothing, child." Lena opened her arms and enfolded Makeba in her thin black grasp.

"Mom?" Helen sat up. She had thought about what her mother had said. Inside, her stomach was quivering. "What about me? What's going to happen to me?"

Lena slowly rose out of the chair and brought Makeba with her. "Kayba, get yourself a sweater. It's liable to be chilly later on. Get the red one. And bring Ka too." Makeba, thankful to be dismissed, raced up the stairs.

"I been thinking about that, Helen. I been thinking a lot about that. And I just don't know."

"So you're just gonna pass me by." Helen felt tears on the inside holding themselves there.

"No, girl. What's wrong with you? I ain't planning on passing nobody by. But I'm gonna work with that daughter of yours first. So I know she's taken care of. But I'm still your mother and I ain't gonna let nothing happen to you. I love you." Lena reached over and put her arms around her daughter. Helen made herself small and crawled back into the belly of her mother. She lay there for a second before slowly pulling away.

She took in a deep breath. She felt better. Her mother was probably stronger than she was. Her mother could at least see the future in Makeba. Helen was still stuck on Helen.

Makeba's Journal

Nana took me everywhere. Every week it was something else. We'd go to the Franklin Institute or to the zoo. And she taught me all kinds of things. The most important thing she taught me was how to let all parts of life exist at the same time. That was how Ka came to me.

I know you don't believe it, but one day, after Nana had taken me to this restaurant for lunch and we were driving back home, she asked me to give Ka to her. I thought, for a minute, that she was going to throw her out of the car or something. But she just propped her up between us as we drove through the city.

About a block before we got home, she pulled the car over and turned to me and told me to close my eyes. And then she started talking to Ka. Just like she was a real baby lion. No, like she was me. A girl like me, but older. It was like a prayer. She asked Ka to love me like she did. To soothe me whenever I hurt myself. And then, after this long list of things she wanted Ka to do, Nana asked her: "Will you stay with her, be her living shadow and show her what you have learned?"

And then, believe it or not, I heard Ka's voice, only it sounded like me. And Ka said, "Don't worry. This child will live to discover the truth."

I swear to God. I heard her. With my eyes shut tight I heard Ka's voice. Later, I asked Nana what Ka meant about discovering truth. She said that Ka would let me know when it was time to know. Ka has led me back to you.

Seventeen

Mates was very comfortable in the shadows. He liked the feeling of freedom, of being disconnected from a body, of being present and yet unseen. People often knew he was there, but were unable to explain it. People needed substance. They were helpless to explain those things which couldn't be touched.

Of course, Mates knew there was this widespread belief in God which he understood. The problem was that people thought that their God was supreme. That no other God existed. In his world there was a different god for everything. He was one of them and an emissary for them.

Mates could see now that Ben was the chosen one. So many promises. So many hopes. It was clear that it wouldn't be Helen. She was committed in a way that was unshakable. He knew that Helen would never feel guilt. If their life together fell apart, it would be Ben who would shoulder the weight of guilt.

And if Ben had known better he would have feared Lena more than he did. She held the voice. She was in touch with the other world.

Lena's tutelage of Makeba worried Helen. As a young girl, Helen had been brought into the church by her mother, who was then a devoted Apostolic Baptist. But as the years passed, Lena had become increasingly disaffected with church.

"They don't do enough for me, child," she would say every Sunday after services. "Just a lot of screaming and hollering and shouting and babbling and nothing happening. People don't get stronger, they don't get richer. Ain't nothing changed."

But for Helen the church took on greater significance. At about the time her mother was leaving the church, she joined. And now, every Sunday was her day to spend there among her friends. Ben never went and did his best to keep Makeba home with him. But every Sunday, Helen would try to talk Makeba into going. Sometimes she was successful.

On those Sundays, Makeba would sit uncomfortably next to her mother in the third pew of the small storefront church. Helen could tell that Makeba didn't enjoy it. She wouldn't learn the hymns. She was nervous when people started shouting. Makeba didn't like church.

It made Helen more aware of how dissatisfied she was with the influence both her mother and Ben had on Makeba.

"I'm telling you, Ben. I think this stuff my mother is filling Makeba's head with is not good for her. She shouldn't talk about ghosts and visions and all that stuff in front of my child like that."

Even though Lena still scared the bejesus out of him, Ben wasn't worried about Makeba. He could see how much Lena loved the child. He knew she wouldn't do anything to hurt her.

"I don't think it's such a big deal."

"I wouldn't expect you to. What do you ever think is a big deal? Makeba is too young to believe in all this crazy stuff. I'm going to talk to Mom about it. I can't just let her ruin my child's life."

Ben decided not to respond. The same unresolved issues were always present. Helen seemed to worry about everything. What he wanted was a simpler life, an existence that would lead him back to his writing full-time. He wasn't worried about Lena and Makeba because it wasn't worth the effort. There was no way they were going to stop Lena from saying things to Makeba. Besides, he was convinced there was nothing damaging happening. So instead of plunging deeper into the budding argument, he walked over to her and kissed her on the cheek.

"Oh." Helen was not mollified. "Are you patronizing me? A peck on the jaw. Just be quiet, Helen. Don't make a fuss, Helen. I know what you're doing."

"Come on. I kissed you because I just wanted you to know that I love you." Helen always caught him when he tried to steal her anger. And yet, even though she suspected what he was doing, it worked. A simple kiss and the statement of love touched her. He saw her expression change.

She looked into his eyes and remembered the soft sounds of Smokey Robinson. The blue lights. The love that brought them Makeba. "I'm sorry. I love you too. It's just that my mother is getting to me."

Ben kissed her again, saying, "I know. But you have to relax about it. I just don't think she means any harm." He kept moving into the kitchen. There he found a black cast-iron frying pan and placed it on the stove, poured a ribbon of oil into it and turned the burner on.

Helen walked toward the kitchen, still talking to him. "And I never thought I'd hear you defend her."

"Me either." From the freezer he retrieved a rock-hard patty of ground beef.

"Well, I've got to talk to her. Anyway, I'm on my way over to Geri's. Makeba's upstairs playing some kind of godforsaken game Mom taught her. Keep an eye out."

Ben walked behind Helen as she left the house. He couldn't help but admit to himself that he liked it when she left. He loved Helen and Makeba *and* being at home. But sometimes all together it was too much.

There was a serenity in the house that was only present when she was gone. In the beginning, he had discovered peace when he and Helen were together. Increasingly that was lost. Now he found his quiet fullness more when he was alone, or with Makeba.

It was ironic because he loved the house they rented. It was big enough to give him much of what he needed: privacy, a place to do his work. In fact, Sage Street had become home. The small group of African American families on the otherwise all-white block made it feel familiar. Like the streets they had all known as children.

Hannibal, who lived across the street, was a young banker. Next door to him Rita and Scoby Rollins lived in a lower level of a duplex. Rita had just started teaching elementary school and Scoby was trying to make a go of it in his own pest extermination business. They were all struggling with the idea of success. They were all unfolding believers.

At night they ignored the porches and sat on the steps, as they had when they were young in their respective neighborhoods, and talked about the changing world. They talked about the continued threads of racism that wound their way into every aspect of their lives. They talked about their parents and how they had grown up.

They had high hopes for their children. They sketched their love for them and their future on the asphalt river that flowed at their feet.

But Ben was growing more and more cynical about the outside world. The world of junk bonds, corruption and scandal. He knew it was against *them*. Not far from where they lived, the radical "back to nature" group, MOVE, had taken root. Every day on his way home from work, Ben would pass the MOVE compound, a large house in Powelton Village with a tall wooden fence that nearly closed it off from view. But sometimes, when the gate was open, Ben could see the naked children and animals playing in the yard.

People claimed they were unclean, unhealthy, dangerous. But Ben was fascinated with MOVE. John Africa and his clan, all of whom took the surname of Africa, defied everybody and everything. They ignored health laws, they gathered weapons, they wore dreadlocks. They frightened white people. And later, many African Americans would sigh with uneasy relief when, in a hail of gunfire and even explosives that reminded Ben of televised accounts of Vietnam, the group was horrifically dismantled by the city.

The brothers and sisters of MOVE stood in stark contrast to his effort to live the life that was expected of him. He had given up the idea of being a professional artist. He had started wearing suits and sitting behind a desk. He silently cheered when MOVE stared down the police. When they spit at the rules and proclaimed the law as null and void.

And, along with the growing tension that surrounded MOVE, there was the brutality of the police. They were completely out of control. Even his white co-workers were aware of it. In fact the police had crossed the line and were brutalizing white people. No one felt safe. Indeed, feeling safe had become a concept, a dream. There was, in effect, no true safety. Not from the villains on the street or the villains behind the badges.

Slowly, Ben began to feel like he *couldn't* be happy. The happiness that filled him up when he read his poems to the small campus audience was all but gone. There was so much wrong around him that he couldn't allow himself the luxury of happiness.

He began to think that there was something wrong with the *idea* of happiness itself. That the mere presence of happiness in a person's life could block out the truth of suffering. That it could actually obscure the truth of racism and oppression.

He was beginning to think that he would never actually be what he was supposed to be. Not the writer, the father, or even the righteous black man. And yet, he began each day as a continuation of the quest for success.

In the quiet moments at home with Makeba he allowed himself to get as close to happiness as he ever did. He relinquished himself to her and accepted whatever joy she gave him in return.

He watched Helen close the door behind her. And then instantly, mindlessly he left the kitchen and bounded up the stairs and into Makeba's room. The walls were covered in a deep ocean-blue wallpaper with pictures and stickers tacked all over it. There was a yellow plastic pony in one corner and a pile of clothes in another. Dolls and miniature cooking implements were scattered through the room. On the bed Makeba sat, cross-legged, like a spiritual figure facing the wall. Ben heard her mumbling.

"Hey little girl. Who are you talking to?"

Makeba jumped. She had been completely absorbed in her conversation. "Just Ka, Daddy. I was just playing with Ka."

"Well, do you want to do something this afternoon? How about a story or something?"

"Do you want me to tell you a story?" Makeba was smiling at him. When she smiled like that all the lights in the house would dim, so that she was the only thing visible to him.

"Well, actually I was thinking I might read to you. What do you say?"

"Okay."

Ben began reading a book of African and African American folk tales. She sat with her bony brown knees curled up to her lips. Her hands embossed on her sugar face, which now rippled in intensity. Her hair, straightened, was pulled back and in two ponytails. She was in a red plaid sleeveless dress. He felt her radiating. She was someone he loved. It was proof that there was *something* worth being happy about even if he had to struggle to accept it. Makeba was happiness. He loved her.

After listening to him read for a few minutes, Makeba interrupted.

"Daddy, who wrote that book?"

Ben stopped reading and showed her the cover. "Julius Lester. He's a writer. Just like me."

"Did he see Br'er Rabbit?" Makeba's eyes were like torches in the dim light.

"No, baby, he didn't actually see Br'er Rabbit. He's just writing stories he's heard from other people."

"Who saw the rabbit?"

Ben felt the joy he always felt when she embarked on a journey of discovery. "These stories, all of them, are stories that people have told to their children for hundreds of years. It's been so long since they were first told that nobody even knows if they were true. But they might be. Anyway they're fun, aren't they?"

Makeba stared at him, her little brown face turned up. "Yeah, but is it true or is it made up?"

As Ben thought about the question, a thick acrid aroma seemed to assault his nostrils. "What's that smell?" he asked her.

"I don't know."

Ben sniffed the air. Like a finger snap he realized what was wrong. He had left the burner on. The inside of his mind turned red and yellow. He could see the flames, feel the heat.

He grabbed Makeba under his left arm like a rifle. She was completely silent, almost not breathing. He ran with her to the telephone in his room and dialed 911.

"There's a fire. We've got a fire. I've got to get my daughter out. My house is on fire." He gave the dispassionate dispatcher his name and address, hung up the telephone and ran to the top of the stairway.

"Daddy! Daddy! Ka. Ka. We didn't get Ka."

"Makeba, we've got to get out of here. Ka will be okay." Ben had reached the top step.

Now Makeba burst into tears and fought to free herself. "No, Daddy, no. I have to get Ka." He struggled to hold her.

The air swirled with thin ribbons of smoke. "Okay, okay." He gave in and quickly turned back down the hall to her room. Ka was sitting on the bed where she had left it. Ben grabbed the lion by one of its outstretched arms. Makeba snatched it from him and held it close.

They then quickly descended the stairs and headed for the front door. As he reached the doorway, Ben looked back toward the kitchen. He saw new shadows swimming on the wall, like black lights at a disco. He couldn't see the stove, only the side wall of the kitchen with the new shadows.

"There's a fire back there," he said as he opened the door and stepped onto the porch. He heard sirens in the distance. He saw a few of his neighbors coming to the windows of their safe, non-burning homes.

He looked down at Makeba, and realized how lucky he had been. They were safe. He had been there to save her. To hell with the kitchen, or the house for that matter. His daughter was safe. It was then he thought about his manuscripts lying there in his den, innocent and vulnerable.

The fire engines were on the street now and heavy-walking men pushed their way into his house. As they entered, smoke buffeted at the door.

Ben stood trembling now as the weight of the situation set in. He waited, expecting to hear the shatter of glass breaking and the loud chopping and crashing that usually accompanied urban firefighting.

If you were unlucky enough to have the misfortune of a fire in your house, only prayer could keep the firefighters from destroying what the fire didn't.

But those sounds did not issue forth. Only darker clouds of pungent smoke.

"Daddy, is our house going to burn down?" Makeba looked up with onyx eyes.

"I don't know, baby. I hope not."

"Do you think my room is on fire?"

Ben didn't want to think about the details of a disaster. "The important thing, sweetheart, is that you are safe. We made it out. And your mom's safe. That's the important thing."

Makeba didn't say anything more. She was suddenly fascinated by the blinking, spinning lights that flew whirligig up and down the block. She kept turning around and around, trying to follow the pattern of the fire truck's lights.

Hannibal walked over from across the street. "What's going on, man?"

"My house is on fire. In the kitchen. Shit. I think I left something on the stove." Ben was grateful for an adult companion.

"Don't worry, man. These dudes will take care of it."

"Yeah, I know. That's partly what I'm worried about. But damn. Helen's going to kill me."

At that moment a stout man swimming in his firefighter's coat walked out of the house and up to Ben. "This your house?"

"Yes."

"You the one who called the alarm in?"

"Yes, but how bad is it. Is it bad?" Ben's heart pounded.

"You Mr. Crestfield?"

"Yes. Goddamnit, I said yes. Now what's going on in there?"

"Well, Mr. Crestfield. All we had here was a little grease fire. Just a little frying pan with oil in it that got too hot. That's all. No big damage. Do you have a fire extinguisher?"

"Uh, no." Ben was starting to feel a little embarrassed. There were people standing around him and his daughter was below him and the tone of the big fireman seemed just a bit parental.

"Well, Mr. Crestfield. All you had to do was turn the fire out, put a lid on the pan and open some windows. Or you might have used some baking soda."

"I see. Well, I'm sorry. I didn't know. You see, I was upstairs and I smelled the smoke, and I . . ."

"You called us. I understand. No harm done. In a way, you were lucky. It could've turned nasty if nobody had called us and you weren't home or something. No harm done."

The rest of the firefighters filed out of the house. After the trucks left and the neighbors went back to their houses, Ben and Makeba sat on the steps to wait for Helen. Hannibal had stayed on as well. The kitchen was a mess, the stove a disaster. Ben had decided he would clean it up later. He just wanted to breathe the chilly night air for a while.

The quiet Sage Street night had been stained by the smell of burning oil mixed with that of the firefighters. The people who fight fires smell like all the fires they've fought. Their coats and boots and gloves hold the history of destruction and death. They left that smell on Sage Street.

But Sage Street also had found a new kind of quiet. The kind that came after a sudden burst of clatter. The kind of quiet that was restorative. That was still influenced by the noise just ended.

Ben sat there on his stoop holding a sleeping Makeba in his arms as if she was the most precious thing he had ever known. Hannibal now sat silently beside him. Ben told Hannibal how afraid he had been for Makeba. How panicked he was when he smelled the fire.

Among his friends on Sage Street, Hannibal was the most focused, clear about the direction of his life. He was a pure striver. He was intelligent and strong-willed. A confirmed bachelor. He held himself in the playboy image. He drove a canary-yellow Pontiac Firebird. He dressed like a picture. The women whom he coveted as prize often took the challenge in hope that they could change him. No one ever really did.

And yet, Hannibal watched with learning eyes as Scoby and Ben worked the arid, dusty landscape of fatherhood. He would walk across the street to talk to Helen or to play around with Makeba.

"It's understandable. I mean, this is your family. This sweet little bag of sugar is your daughter. You're supposed to be afraid for her."

"I know. But you don't know how hard it is. You zip around in your 'bird and hang out with all those fine women I see falling out of your crib and yet I always get the impression that you think *I'm* doing something special."

"You are. Sometimes hanging out like I do gets very dumb. Sometimes I wish I had what you have."

"Naw, man, I don't know about that. I'm struggling. Really struggling with it."

"What you need to do, Ben"—Hannibal stretched his long legs over the steps— "is stop worrying so much and learn how to make the best of the situation."

"The best of a bad situation," Ben said into the silky summer-night air.

"It's only as bad as you make it, brother. I mean really, if you get about the business of making some money and move beyond this self-pity bullshit, you might make it." Hannibal had moved to Philadelphia from Washington to attend the University of Pennsylvania. He had attended white private schools all his life.

Ben looked at him. Hannibal was *the* tall, dark and handsome equivalent in black. He liked Hannibal for a lot of reasons, but one of them was that he was unequivocal. He believed. "It isn't that simple, man. Do you really think that if you put all your energy into doing your job at the bank you're going to end up being president of the Girard National Bank?"

"If I wanted to. If I wanted to I could run that motherfucka without any sweat. This money shit is a piece of cake. They try to mystify the whole thing so folks like us won't think we can understand it. But shit, man, making money isn't that hard. You watch me."

Ben smiled. Hannibal believed. "So you're going to make big money, huh?"

"Watch me. You just watch me. But let me tell you. . ." Hannibal's soft voice raised a notch. "I'm not going to be no goddamn bank president. Because I do know I'd have to wait forever to get there. I mean, I know I can get there, but. . ."

Laughter left Ben's mouth. "But what?"

"I don't *want* to be bank president. I'm going to do my own thing. We got to get to the entrepreneurial thing. For a man to make things happen for him nowadays, you have to control your own destiny. You have to have your own thing."

"So what's your thing, Hann?"

Hannibal stood up, came down the steps and stood on the sidewalk facing Ben. "Don't know yet, Ben. I haven't figured that out yet. But I will. I'm not ready anyway. You see, even though I said it wasn't hard, there is a lot of shit you have to know." Hannibal stared into Ben's eyes. This was when Ben liked Hannibal the most. Not when he was talking about manipulating his many women friends, or when he hid his closest, warmest emotions. But when he was engaged.

Hannibal continued. "You want to know something? Something I discovered in college?"

"You're not going to tell me any more of those hot coed stories, are you? Because I don't want to hear none of that shit tonight. Helen's not even at home," Ben joked.

"I found out that the whole study of money is the study of white men. If you know it, you know them. If you master the knowledge of money, you master the white man and therefore you become the master of your own life."

Hannibal stood up, satisfied that he had articulated his philosophy. Ben had listened carefully. Something about the preoccupation with money as the primary vehicle to self-determination seemed wrong. But he was fascinated by what Hannibal had said.

"I don't know, man. . . but the more I work—the more I fall into this stream of people who are trying to prove how capable they are at everything, including making money—the more I think about punching out."

"You can't punch out, brother." Hannibal laughed and pointed to the house where Makeba and Helen slept. "You ain't about to go nowhere."

Ben gave up the seedling of thought. Of course he wasn't going to punch out. He had a life of lives to be there for.

"All I'm saying is that I can't help wondering what I'm doing with my life. I'm not writing very much right now. All I do is go to work. I mean, maybe I should be doing something else."

"Like what?" Hannibal yawned. He was ready to go back home.

"I don't know. Just like you. But when I know, you'll be the second person to know." Ben smiled.

"Yeah, well, I got to get up early tomorrow."

"Me too."

And now, in the barrel of the night, as he waited for Helen with a sleeping child in his arms, he wondered again about his life.

Makeba's Journal

It's eerie to read about me from your point of view. I have to keep trying to remember that you are my father and that the child in the book is me. But it's very hard to trust you. The things you say are basically true. I remember the fire. I know I was very scared. And I remember making you go back to get Ka. But there are little things which don't seem right. The problem is you have to lie to write, don't you? I mean, like the way I remember it, there were no firemen. You put the fire out yourself. The kitchen was a wreck but there weren't fire trucks and all that. And I thought you were in your den writing when the fire started. I don't remember you being in my room.

And then, on top of everything, whenever you mention me or Mom it's always bad. Like we were just dead weight on your career. Is that all I was?

The confusing part is that I wanted to read this book because I wanted to know what you thought. But the more I know, the more I'm not sure I should know it. I also want to know whether or not I can trust you. You left me. You walked away. How can I ever trust you after that? I thought maybe as I learned more about your story I would feel something. Maybe it would let me believe in you again. That's what I want. There are things you should know about me, but I can't tell you until I feel it's right. Too much time has passed and the only clear feeling I have about you is that no matter how much you protest, you couldn't have loved me very much.

Eighteen

An alarm went off within the darkness. The air was thick. The fire was a wake-up call. Mates could feel a gathering of strength surging around him. Ben was walking a thin line and would not be able to keep his balance forever. He was looking for an escape but he wasn't a butterfly. He had no power. He was just a man. Poor man. Poor poor man.

Ben was in a relationship with destiny. His race, his sense of history, his education, were meaningless. Ben wasn't doing what he wanted to do. Mates could see it easily. But Ben was already in too deep—a wife, a child.

From where Mates was, ensconced in the shadows, this was shaping up to be very amusing. He'd seen it before. There were men strewn all over this world who had decided that the only way to reach their dreams was to run from their history.

As hope and promise dissipate, a sound is made. Like an envelope being opened, except the ripping goes on until your ears become accustomed to it. And when that happens it is likely that you will lose something. Promises made and held hopes are adhesives and need at least two things to be attached to. They stand between us.

Helen heard the sound. She knew something was very wrong.

She had taken to spending more and more time with Geri. This happened mostly during the weekdays. Geri was hardly ever available during the weekends. Her life was consumed in men and parties. Helen would sit and listen to the details.

She couldn't help but admire Geri. There was something about her friend's complete lack of interest in having a family that both upset and intrigued her. Geri, on the other hand, was oblivious to the issues that preoccupied Helen.

And yet Helen would look for opportunities to say how unhappy she was becoming. How she was growing more and more afraid that she and Ben were coming apart.

Finally Geri got the point and asked, "Okay Helen. What's the real problem here? Do you think he's seeing somebody? What's going on in the boudoir? Does he still make your hair go back?"

Helen was surprised at the directness of the question. She swallowed. "I . . . We . . . Well, everything's not going super in that department right now." She looked down at the pink faux-marble kitchen tabletop in front of her. And then quickly added, "But I don't think he's involved with anybody else. I don't think so. But he doesn't come straight home from work the way he used to. And he's started spending so much time in his den."

"Well, what's he do in his den?"

"I don't know exactly." Helen picked up her glass of orange juice. Geri was eating a chocolate chip cookie. The brown crumbs were collecting in a pile in front of her. "He won't let me in there anymore. And he won't show me what he's working on. He's just become very quiet. It's not like he talked all the time. But now it's like he hardly says anything to me. He spends most of his time with Makeba or in his room. He's up all night in there."

Geri turned her head to the silent television on the counter, where the soft brown face of Oprah Winfrey stared back. "So where does he go after work?"

"He says he's with Ramsey. I don't think he's lying to me. I just think he doesn't want to be home."

"No, Helen. I don't think he's lying either but you've got to admit that he ain't up on it either. I mean, he's acting kind of weird.

You ain't done nothing but be a do-right woman and here he is throwing shit in your face."

"Maybe it's not that bad. It's pretty hard on him really. He wants to be writing. I'm thinking that I should probably go back to work."

Geri looked at Helen as if she realized for the first time that Helen wasn't working. "Yes indeed, girlfriend. If I was you I'd get myself some employment. You just never know. It don't smell like roses over there on Sage Street. Y'all been together a long time, and the way I see it, nothing don't go on forever."

Helen tried not to look into Geri's eyes. "Why not? I don't understand. I mean, we're just getting started. Makeba's only nine. I was thinking about having another child. I want a family."

"But Helen." Geri hunched her slim shoulders forward, her almond eyes sparkling, her now trimmed Afro glistening. "Look around you. Who the hell is staying together? Nobody. I don't know one damn couple in the entire city of Philadelphia that's been together more than ten years. None. Maybe you do, but I don't. All I see are people breaking up like teacups falling out the cupboard. And everybody is always asking me when I'm getting married. Shit. I wish I would get married. Let some asshole sonofabitch treat me like I ain't nobody. Na-uh, baby. I'm staying single. I'm keeping myself in good shape and I'm taking names and kicking ass. If they want to spend time with me they gonna have to sing a pretty tune."

Helen couldn't help smiling. Geri could talk shit like a corner girl. Which made sense because Geri had indeed been a South Philly corner girl. And now, she was working at the phone company by day and playing the streets by night. And she still had a gang of women friends who nearly worshiped her.

Geri continued. "But if I was you, I wouldn't be thinking about having no more kids. That would be just about the dumbest goddamned thing you ever done."

"I'm not so sure. I remember the way he was when Makeba was born. He wanted to be there all the time. You know how close he is to that girl. If we had another baby, it might make a difference."

Geri played in the cookie crumbs. "Tell me you ain't that dumb? Please, chile, please tell me that you are just bullshitting me."

"I'm serious. You never know."

"I know one thing. Having another baby when you and your man ain't down together is like building a house without a foundation. The goddamn thing is going to fall in one day."

"But it might fall anyway." Helen felt very sad. She hated giving voice to her fears. "It's not Ben. I can live without him."

"Well, thank you, Jesus. You ain't totally ignorant."

"It's the whole idea of our family that I don't want to lose. We can do it. Makeba and Ben are my family."

"Not if he doesn't love you. Not if he doesn't want to be there."

Helen was tired of the discussion. She was ready to head back home. "He doesn't know what he wants. His head is so full of all that white folks' stuff he learned in college and his writing that he don't know whether he's coming or going. So I'm not worried about what he wants. We have a daughter and she deserves a father and a mother and that's the way it's supposed to be."

Geri just stared at her. Soon Helen got up from the table and left for home.

When she got back to Sage Street Makeba was already asleep. Ben was upstairs in his den. Helen thought about knocking on his door but decided instead to go to bed. After having spent the evening laughing with Geri the silence of the house was welcome anyway.

Makeba's Journal

EIGHTEENTH ENTRY

I feel sorry for Mom. She had no idea how bad everything was. You could always count on her to keep going when things got rough. I respect her a lot. But I wish she had been different. Maybe things would have been better between the two of you.

Now I understand what you meant in that *Ebony* magazine article when you said that "most writers will declaim themselves in their work. There is no reason to deny my own story through the creation of fictional characters. My life is fiction." I wrote it down because I didn't understand it. I am not fiction and I am a part of your life. But now I see what you mean. You've made all of us a part of a fiction. And yet, it is our lives. We exist.

Maybe there is hope.

Nineteen

Mates could feel his muscles twitching. That was living. With twitching muscles and a nose that never quit smelling. It was coming soon. He ached for the solidification, the transformation into his fated existence. Mates was a natural predator, he needed only prey.

Ben feared Mates even then. Even when he had no idea that Mates was real, Ben was possessed with the need to exonerate himself for his own selfishness. Ben knew that there would eventually come a time when something would force him to confront himself. But he didn't know it would be Mates, the dog. If he had, things might have been different.

One of the driving energies pushing him into new terrain was that he was unhappy at Benson Glendale. He couldn't believe how superficial the world of business was. How intensely people felt about the finite elements of making money. In the Navy he had grown accustomed to incompetence and pettiness. And now, in the private sector he was confronted with a hypercharged, almost frenetic energy to make money. In this world, even the smallest, most minute of functions was considered, discussed and planned. It drove him crazy.

He was supposed to be there on time. Smile. Be neatly dressed—indeed, to reflect his belief in the system simply by the way he dressed. He was expected to make small talk with people he didn't like and who didn't like him. No one ever asked him about his writing, even though everyone knew that's what he did when he wasn't at work. No one cared about that.

"Why were you late this morning?"

"Why didn't you come to the office party?"

"Why do you always look so angry?"

"What's wrong, Ben, aren't you happy here?"

"Hell no, I'm not happy here. How can I be happy here? You people have no idea what I'm up against here. I'm already mimicking you stupid assholes, trying to act like I believe that you will actually give me something if I do right. I'm already selling the fuck out."

This is what passed through his head every day. He'd sit at his desk and try to write "zippy" copy. That was the phrase around the office. "Peppy," "pithy," "electric." And he wasn't bad at it. But it leached something from his reservoir of creativity to have a job in which he was paid to lie. It hit home when he was asked to write ad copy for a fashionable Society Hill furrier.

"We're giving you this account because you've had so much success writing for the downtown crowd, Ben." That was what John Glendale had said as Ben sat facing him in the vice president's loft office. Ben knew that was a lie. He had had terrific success with their largest client, the department store Strawbridge and Clothier. He thought his real talent was in his ability to reach working-class consumers who were seeking a bargain. But of course, he could only assist on such an account. They would never give such a plum to him.

He knew that the reason he got the furrier was because three of the writers had refused to write copy for them. Ben studied the man who sat behind the desk, trying to decide what he wanted to say. John was only five years older than Ben and was a phenom in the business. He'd started out with a small company and wild ideas and built a very successful advertising and public relations firm.

John faced him with his rounded shoulders, thinning blond hair and horn-rimmed glasses. When he smiled his fading San Juan tan seemed to crack open. His conservative blue pinstripe Brooks Brothers moved with him.

"I'm not sure I want to work for them."

"What do you mean?" There was a tone in John's voice which told Ben there wasn't much room to operate.

"It's just that I don't think we should have a company like that as clients. Nobody wants to work for them."

"Ben, this is a great opportunity for you to show what you've got in terms of account management. You don't want to be a writer all your life, do you? I mean, the money's in the management and the sales. I think maybe you could make it here. But you've got to step up to the plate."

Ben played the last sentence over in his head. "Step up to the plate." What the hell did that mean?

"Well, I'd love to try account management," Ben lied. "I just don't want to be the manager for an animal killer." Ben knew this would anger John. He also knew he hadn't ever thought about animal rights before in his life. He knew almost nothing about it. But he did know that there were three white copywriters who refused to do the work and he didn't want to be seen as different from them. He didn't want to be the Negro who'd do anything to ingratiate himself with his white employer.

"An animal killer, huh?" John stood up abruptly. "Let me tell you something, Mr. Crestfield. I don't appreciate your tone of voice or your choice of words. And you get this straight. You work for me. If I tell you to write for the fuckin' Martians you do it. You got that?"

Ben couldn't believe this white man was getting in his face like that. Granted he was a long way from North Philly, but it was still in him. Deep inside him the instincts began to form into action. He stood up.

"Listen man. I won't let you talk to me like that. *You* got that?" Ben threw John's words back at him. "I'll kick your motherfuckin' ass if you raise your voice to me again." Ben couldn't believe he was saying what he was saying. But something was going on inside him and he couldn't control it.

"Get out of my office. I should have known better. This affirmative action bullshit is just that. You're lucky Benson likes you or you'd be history. But I'm warning you, Ben. This is the beginning of the end. He won't be able to protect you forever."

Ben turned and walked out of the office. He'd learned at least two things. One was that Seth Benson liked him and the other was he didn't give two shits.

Makeba's Journal

I'm tired. I'm not used to sitting so long. And I'm uncomfortable. What was I to you? Sometimes I feel like you never saw me as a person.

I hate feeling uncomfortable. When your skin feels creepy and your stomach quivers. I hate that. Okay, you have to know something. I wasn't sure I was going to tell you but suddenly I feel like it's a part of the reason I'm writing this at all. About five months ago I was at this coffee shop downtown. I like to come into the city every now and then. Sometimes I meet friends, other times I just go to a movie. Well, I stopped in this place where I always get a sweet roll or a croissant and a cup of coffee.

Well, this guy comes in and sits at my table. I didn't mind that too much. Actually he seemed pretty interesting. He had the prettiest wavy black hair I have ever seen on a black man. He said his name was Ricky. So anyway, we started talking and he told me he was in college at Drexel studying to be an electrical engineer. I told him about me. At the time I was thinking about taking a course in computer repair.

I met him a few more times over the next week. Then he asked to take me to the movies. I said yes. I really liked him. Ka warned me. But Ka has never liked any boy I liked. She and Mom never approved of anybody who was interested in me. I always left Ka home when I went out with Ricky. That was stupid.

Well, after the movie he drives me to Fairmount Park and cuts the car off. We kissed. I knew what he wanted but I wasn't sure about him. He acted kind of strange sometimes. Like one time we were buying some ice cream and the guy who was serving us was real nasty. He didn't look up at Ricky or me or nothing. So when Ricky gets the ice cream and the man sticks his hand out for the money, Ricky turns the ice cream upside down in his open hand. Both cones. And Ricky says, "This is for your funky vanilla self and the ice cream too." And we walked out. So I knew he could be weird. I understand that. Almost every black man I know is like that. Like a balloon, full of anger just waiting for a pin. If I couldn't love a man who was angry then I could never love a black man.

Anyway, so Ricky starts trying to feel my breasts. I pushed his hands away and he shoved me up against the car door. At the same time his hands were already under my dress. I couldn't believe it. He wasn't saying anything. Not "I love you" or "I need you" or anything. I just remember his heavy breath and the feeling that his hands were penetrating my skin.

He got his black ugly fingers all the way up my dress, pushed under my panties and into me. I was screaming. I screamed so loud. And I started kicking him. I had on heels so it didn't take long before he backed off of me and slid back under the steering wheel. He started crying and apologized. He said that sometimes he couldn't control himself. And then he started talking about all his problems. *His* problems. He reminded me of Mike Tyson and that Kennedy guy. He had practically raped me. And he had the nerve to sit there, while I'm stinging from his brutality, and talk about his problems. But I was scared. I didn't have anything that I could use to defend myself. Ka was not with me. I was in his car. In the park. In the dark. I was at his mercy.

It was at that moment that I thought about you. That was when I realized I had to talk to you. That no matter how mad I was at you, how disappointed that you left us, I had to talk to you. I promised myself that if I lived through that moment I would come to you. That was before I even knew this book existed. I also made one other promise. That if Ricky didn't kill me that night, right then, in that car, I would kill him. I have been possessed by this thought ever since. I will never be defenseless again.

Twenty

At night, in his room, Ben traveled further and further into the made-up world of his stories. His hands danced in some spiritual harmony with his mind as they struck the keys of his electric typewriter. They seemed to take on a life of their own. He often stared at them. Particularly the backs of them. Sometimes, while he typed, it was the back of his hands that he focused on. He loved the way they moved. The way his skin, like an incredibly detailed brown map, stretched to accommodate their every movement. The pronounced crisscrossing of veins. He often reminded himself how close he had come to losing the fluid grace of his right hand. In one instant, his hand could have been crushed by a rageful stranger in a dark bar. Even now, after he was finished writing, his hand ached. It was a deep, stabbing pain which could not be reached. A pain that seemed buried in the bone.

And yet he was suddenly possessed by his work. Consumed in his need to translate what had become an increasing turmoil into art. Ben's current subject was Makeba. He was trying to write a series of poems to her. Makeba's face was now ever present wavering in front of him like a hologram. Her eyes following his every action.

He couldn't tell her, or Helen for that matter, that he was writing so much about Makeba. They would want to know why. And he wasn't sure about that. They would want to know why the poems and short stories all ended with Makeba in deep sadness. He couldn't help feeling that there was some great tragedy lurking in her life.

Ben didn't want to hear the questions because he didn't know the answers to them. He only knew that he was trying to transform his purest feelings about Makeba, his unexpressed love, his hope for her future, into a poetic language. He wanted to write something that would be like a blanket for her. And he wanted to discover what being a father meant.

Ben was beginning to realize that his presence in her life was tenuous. More and more he could see himself living somewhere else, surrounded by paper. Living a life on the outside of the walls that were presently around him.

But he was not in control of the images that grew on the paper in front of him. He would struggle home from work, eat dinner, play with Makeba and make his way up to his second-floor den. Once there, he would sit in an old, chipped wooden secretary's chair under candlelight and stare at the typewriter until the night opened up. The flicker of the flame from the candle would create hypnotic shapes that shimmied across the walls. Eventually he would begin to mark the paper with little black marks. Clack clack clack clack. His hands would begin a journey of love and adventure.

But increasingly the words were more desperate. There was a growing cynicism about Makeba's future. Or rather it was a cynicism about Ben's future with Makeba.

On an impulse, he jumped up from his desk and walked into Makeba's room. She was carefully folded into her bed, lightly snoring. He looked at her face. Her innocence was so powerful. He moved close to her bed and found himself whispering, blowing flowers of pain into her ear.

"What am I supposed to do, Makeba? How can I do this? I want you to be strong. To feel safe.

"But I didn't exactly plan to be a father. It just happened. Suddenly you were coming and I wanted everything to be okay. I wanted your mother to feel safe. I needed her. And then, I started needing you.

"People say that I've got a special responsibility for you. I made you. If it wasn't for me, you wouldn't be here. And God, how incredible that is. You exist because I do. Okay, maybe I do. I want to take that responsibility on too. Makeba, you probably won't believe it, but I really want to do the right thing. People will say the right thing is obvious. That I belong here, with you and your mother. People will say there is no excuse, no reason strong enough to justify walking away from your family.

"Makeba, please forgive me. I want to be more than a faceless spot in the black crowd. At this moment, I can't think of one black man who has been the father of a family and created great art. That scares me.

"It's really hard to say that I love you and that I love your mother and yet I'm afraid that I'm going to die. That if I don't find a way out of here I'm not going to make it. We need so much. We need black men to be fathers. We need black men to be artists. We need them to make a statement, a final, summary statement to the world that what we see and feel might hold the key to our existence. Might save everybody. I believe that. And yet I don't think I can do it all: be a husband, a father and me.

"So listen, sweetheart, this is what I want to know. Do you understand? Can you forgive me? I mean, if you knew that I was fighting for identity, a chance to concentrate on my gift, would you understand? Would you insist I be with you even if it meant I would never write again? If you were certain that no matter how much I loved you, if I stayed here I would be unhappy, would you still want me to stay?"

Ben stood silent for a long time, staring at the image of his daughter frozen in front of him. Her body pulling in air, holding it, letting it go.

"Makeba, listen. If I ever leave, I won't be leaving you. This thing I'm fighting is not against you. No matter what, we will never disconnect. I will always be your father. We won't be separated so easily.

But I may not be able to live this out the way we first thought. Things may have to change."

Ben heard something just behind him; he whirled around, to face Helen. "What are you doing? I woke up and thought I heard someone talking in here. What were you saying?" Helen's voice merged a hushed whisper with anger and suspicion. She wore a summer-weight blue nightgown. Her hair was wrapped in a silk scarf. She looked at a sleeping Makeba to emphasize the questions she was asking.

"Nothing. I was just checking on Makeba. Sometimes I just like to watch her sleep," he lied.

"Really? I didn't know that." Helen was suspicious. She had clearly heard him whispering. "Did I hear you say something about leaving? That's not what I heard, was it?" She was getting very tired of his lethargic, tortured posture. "Stand up, damn it. Just stand up." She wanted to scream at him.

"I guess I was thinking out loud. I'm sorry if I disturbed you." Ben walked past her and into their bedroom. He bounced himself onto the bed with a heavy sigh. He knew there would be no peace until they talked.

"I don't get it. What's the matter? What's wrong with you?" Helen was still in the hallway when she began talking. And she was speaking clearly now. Not in a whisper. Her voice rose as she passed through the bedroom threshold.

"I don't know." Ben lay back. "But this is really hard."

"What is? Being a father? Being a husband?" Helen paused. She was holding herself together as well as she could. But there was a limit. She was ready to let it out. "I'm tired of you complaining all the damn time. All you have to do is act like a man. Is your life so awful? Are we so awful?"

Ben turned away from her. This would be the perfect time to say what he needed to say. This was it. He exhaled. "My life . . . Helen . . . my life is pretty awful."

Helen looked through him. She was very sleepy all of a sudden. And yet, she summoned more energy. Ben was confused and falling apart and he needed her to help him find his way. She didn't want to hear any more about his life. She didn't want to know how hard he thought it was. She just wanted him to live up to his promise. They had to make it.

She sat down on the bed and gently but firmly turned Ben's head back toward her. "Listen, we can work this out. I know we can. We have the beginning of a great family and I don't want to lose it. I'm not letting this whole thing just fall apart because it's difficult."

Ben put his arms around her. Her body was still warm from sleep. "Why is it that what I want to be seems so far away from here?"

"It's because, Ben, you don't know how close you are to where you really belong. But I'll help you. Together, we'll make it. I know we will."

And with that, she curled up beside him. They held each other and slipped into dream.

The next morning, a Saturday, Helen and Makeba were up and out of the house early. Ben was still lying under the covers. It was midday and the sun fractured the settling dust in the room. He slowly opened his eyes. He knew that Helen and Makeba were at Geri's. That afternoon he was supposed to get together with Ramsey and Hannibal for drinks.

But something wasn't right. As he lay in bed he thought he heard footsteps downstairs. There was someone else in the house. He knew it. There were little movements that disturbed the general stillness. Ben knew he wasn't the only living thing there.

He rolled out of bed and pulled on his sweatpants. Then, shirtless, he walked through the hallway and stood at the top of the stairs. He listened. He was certain there was someone downstairs.

"Hello. Helen? Makeba?" he called as he started slowly down the steps. He grew increasingly uneasy. Now the sound was in the kitchen. "Helen? Are you in there?" he almost screamed.

"You don't have to holler. I was coming out here." Lena, dressed in a peanut-green polyester pants suit, her thin body rattling inside it, came out of the kitchen. "I was just trying to find some tea or something."

"Lena, what . . . ah . . . How are you? Is everything okay?" To his recollection, Lena had never been in the house when Helen wasn't there. "What are you doing here?"

"Well, I just thought it was about time we had a talk."

"You and me?" Ben stood there staring at her.

"Yes. Now you go put on a shirt and come on down here and sit down. I'll make you some coffee. There's some things I want to say."

"Lena, what is this all about?" Even as he asked her the question he was beginning to head back upstairs for his shirt.

"It's about your family. It's about all of us."

Ben took his time as he walked back up the steps and found a shirt to put on. He went into the bathroom, where he carefully washed his face and put his shirt on. Did she know things weren't working out? He headed back downstairs.

Lena was already sitting on the couch in the living room, sipping her tea. On the coffee table was a cup of coffee for him. He bent over and picked up the coffee. "Thanks. This is very good."

"You're welcome. Now, sit down." He did. Suddenly he felt sheepish, like a little boy. "I talked to Helen early this morning. She was pretty upset."

Ben took a deep breath. She knew. "What did she say?"

"She's worried. And that makes me worry. I don't want my daughter to be worried like she is. You know what I mean?"

Ben nodded. He was listening but he was also trying to formulate some kind of response.

"I mean, it just seems that you two have got to get it together. Life's hard. I know that. But I don't know what you must be thinking. You got a beautiful daughter. Helen's wonderful. What's the matter with you, boy?"

"Why do you think something's the matter with me?"

"Well, my daughter is all worked up thinking you're gonna leave her. Now, that's what she told me. You sayin' that ain't true? 'Cause if it is true, then I'd say something was mighty wrong with you."

"I didn't say I was leaving. The only thing I've said is that things don't seem to be working out. That's all." It was hard enough trying to talk to Helen. With Lena it was impossible.

"Well, what do you mean by that? What's not working out?"

Ben just sat there looking into the midmorning. He couldn't say anything.

What Lena saw was a man whose face had hardened into wood. She could perceive his sense of paralysis. She knew he couldn't tell her what he felt. But she could tell him. She leaned forward and pointed herself at him.

"I wasn't in favor of this thing from the beginning. And I told you then I wasn't gonna have no messing around with my daughter. You made a promise and you had better keep it. This ain't nothing to play with. If you're aiming to hurt my daughter or my granddaughter, you had better think twice. Because I'm just not gonna let you walk away from here like that."

Ben pooled his energy and forced himself to speak. "I know you mean well. But don't you think Helen and I should deal with this?"

"No," Lena snapped. "No I don't. If I don't get involved in this ain't no telling what will happen. Just because you think you're so smart and can write all this godforsaken junk you write. You think you brought the world into being when you stepped on the earth. And you think you can decide what is right and wrong. But you can't. This is my business too. My daughter is my business. Now, I'm trying to talk to you nicely about this. But I don't think you have put yourself into this family strong enough. They need more from you. You're going to have to find a way to do that for them. You just are. I know you don't want to hurt them.

"But I want you to know this: I'm not kidding. If you do hurt them, I swear to you, you will have to search the earth to find a way to forget it."

Ben now held his head up. He was on fire with anger. She had no right to intrude into his life this way. He wanted to attack her. He wanted to ask why Helen was so afraid of a future without him? Why hadn't Lena raised her daughter to know her own strength, disconnected from a man? Why did he feel as if Helen had been waiting for him? Waiting to become a wife and mother instead of creating something special for herself, like his writing was for him. But instead, he smothered his thoughts.

"Are you finished? I appreciate your concern," Ben said through clenched teeth. "But I want you to know that this is between Helen and me. It's got nothing to do with you. You have no idea who I am or what I think and I'm not going to waste my time trying to explain anything to you. Now, I've got to go. Are you going to stay here and wait for Helen to come back or are you leaving? By the way, how did you get in?"

"Helen left the door unlocked for me. I just wanted you to know how I felt. And I did that. Now I'm ready to go. So, you tell Helen I asked about her and kiss Makeba for me."

Ben watched Lena gather her things and leave. He leaned back in the chair as she closed the door.

Makeba's Journal

TWENTIETH ENTRY

I know what happens from here on. I know how this turns out. I don't really need to read any more. You got mad one night and left. I remember that much. The argument. The shouting. I remember that. I wonder how you'll write that.

How was I supposed to answer you? What father would ask his daughter to make a choice?

Ricky's face just flashed in my mind. I haven't talked to him since that night. I bought a gun. It's laying on my bed right now. I was really going to kill him. I still might. I promised myself I would.

Twenty-one

Love is a slow walk to madness. To being haunted. And when it wears thin, love knows only desperation. Some of it swims into Mates's body like blood as a clutching, grabbing kind of energy that seeks to prove its own existence. It breathes life into his limbs.

The rest of it escapes and maintains residence in all the spaces where it was expressed. It remains deep in the crevices of the wood or in the small cracks of the mortar, forever. You can go back to a spot where you held hands with a former lover and feel the same intensity, the same emotion. It may make you sick or make you swoon. You may want to flee. But you know it is there just the same.

Things between Ben and Helen had slowed to a crawl. Ben turned further inside, into his writing, into the seclusion of his den. He and Helen now spent little time together.

Every day, Helen became more and more anxious. She had taken to a daily harangue to draw Ben out. She complained about the things he did. What he talked about. Some days her sole objective was to instigate some confrontation between them. She could tell she was losing him. That they were disintegrating. And his inability to talk about it infuriated her.

Sometimes she was sure that he was losing his mind.

At night, after Makeba had gone to bed, after the kitchen was cleaned, after the nightly news, she'd watch him sit in his bent-wood rocker in the living room, ignoring the television, staring into space. Sometimes he would sit there for hours. And then suddenly he'd jump up and run upstairs to his room.

But as Helen watched him sit there, night after night, she wondered if he would ever wake up and see her waiting for him to return as her lover. She hoped he would eventually snap himself into sync with her.

Ben knew what she was doing. He watched stoically as Helen tried to pry open a part of him that had closed. Every time he told Helen he loved her, he felt stupid. He felt incompetent to put his exact feelings into words. He wanted Helen to see that even though he loved her, it wasn't enough.

He was there with her. But it wasn't an honest life. He began feeling guilty and he didn't want Helen to think it was her fault. He didn't want her to believe that their love had already died. He didn't want her to think that he was backing out on any of the promises he had made.

But he was. He felt himself slipping deeper and deeper into a place where she could not reach him. He hoped she would not see how, like evaporating water, he was leaving her all along.

But Helen knew. She felt it, saw it. She couldn't believe it but there it was. When he was home he was usually with Makeba. He rarely came barreling up the steps just for her. He had stopped pulling her out of sleep to crawl into her body.

And yet, while she knew this, she was not willing to accept it, to let it undermine her hopes for the future. If it took her will to hold things together, then her will was strong enough. She expected Ben to emerge from the abyss any day. Every day. She waited.

And so she kept thinking up things for them to do. Trips to the zoo, bowling, miniature golf, romantic dinners out. But one day as she waited for Ben to come home from work, she got an idea.

She was flipping through the classifieds when she came upon the Houses for Sale section. Suddenly she knew what it would take to get

Ben to understand where his priorities should be. They had been renting the house they were living in and if she could get Ben excited about buying a house maybe it would reenergize his interest.

Besides, she reasoned, they needed a house. They needed a place that was theirs. That had a lawn and a garage. A house on a tree-lined street with other black families. Out of the city. The picture was incomplete the way it was. How could she expect Ben to focus on his family life if they had no long-term financial commitments? No long-term commitment to be in a place together? They had to make a change. It was the logical next step.

Later that evening, after Ben came home and they had dinner, she went to their bedroom and changed into her favorite nightgown, a sheer pink peignoir. It fastened up high, near her neck, and draped her tall body. Its flowing chiffon, in two layers, reached the floor. She lit three candles on her dresser, reclined on the bed and called Ben.

When he walked into the bedroom, she looked into his eyes and saw the strain of the mere act of walking up the steps.

"Come here and sit down," she said.

"Helen, please. I don't feel like it tonight." Ben didn't even want to play the game. He was tired of forcing his physical self into action. "I'm tired and I just don't want to make love right now."

"You could at least sit down with me."

Ben looked at her lying there. He hated that nightgown. He knew she thought it was sexy, but he thought it was old-fashioned, conservative. If she wanted to excite him, that wasn't the thing to wear. Still, he forced a smile. "I know you didn't put that on just to get me to sit with you."

"Ben?" Ben recognized the inflection of her voice. This was the voice of incredible hope. This was the voice of excitement.

Helen shifted her body so that she nearly faced him. "Well, I've been thinking that maybe we should move."

"Move? Why?" Ben had never thought about leaving Sage Street with Helen. He *had* begun to contemplate leaving. But not with her. Why would they move anyway?

"Because I think Makeba should grow up in a different environment. You know what I mean? I mean, what if we decide to have another child? Of course Sage is fine but, you know, every year when the school year changes there's all these new people moving in. It's not the kind of place you want to have your children spend their whole lives."

Ben's heart paused. "Children? What do you mean *children?*"

"You never know." Helen broke a sweet, obviously teasing smile. "We might have another child."

"Another child? No, Helen. Not another child. I don't want another child and we can't afford to buy a house." They had battled the bills since the first week of their marriage.

"I didn't say we should have a baby now, but maybe . . ." Helen almost whispered.

"No. I'm not talking about another baby. Don't start that."

Helen sat up, reached her hand over and grabbed his face, turning it to her. "I think we can afford a house. We have to. It's something everybody else does."

"But we're barely making it now." When she called him upstairs, Ben had been thinking about going to his room. He had come into the bedroom on his way there. This was an ambush. He wasn't prepared for it.

"Don't think about the negative part. Just listen to me. Suppose we had a smaller, newer house on a beautiful street in Chestnut Hill or somewhere like that. And Makeba had friends. And we had families, just like us, all around. We could have a front lawn. And a garage. A big brick barbecue pit, you know." She paused, breaking into a big smile. "And you could put up a basketball hoop." She nudged Ben's side with her elbow.

He fought a smile. She was so strong and able to penetrate his first line of defense. She knew him well. He had always wanted a basketball hoop. But in North Philadelphia no one had garages. You put the hoop on a tree or a telephone pole.

"I mean, just think about it. It could be just the thing we need. Just the thing that . . ."

"That what?"

"That might make us all very happy. Happy as a bunch of little piggies in mud." She tried to keep from laughing at her inability to use the right word in the old saying.

"Pigs in shit, Helen. It's pigs in shit."

"Who cares? We can be happy. We've been happy." Helen knew how to fight the negative energy that rose from his body like puffs of smoke.

Ben wanted to change the subject. He didn't know how to respond. He knew he didn't want to dig the hole deeper. He knew that. Still, unprepared to tell her the complete truth, he said, "Okay. If you want to look into it, go ahead. I just know one thing."

"What's that?" Helen slid back down on the bed, satisfied that they were on the verge of a new beginning.

"I want you to be happy." Ben looked into her eyes and tried to make her believe him. And it was true. He really did.

Helen reached up and pulled him down on her. She kissed his lips. "Then we got this thing under control, baby. Trust me. We'll make it."

Ben returned her kiss and at the same time began pushing himself up. "I've got work to do, Helen." As he walked down the hall toward his studio, Ben hoped that their lives would soon find new light.

Makeba's Journal

TWENTY-FIRST ENTRY

Have you ever held a gun? I bet you haven't. They're heavier than you think they'd be. I've never fired it. I just hold it a lot. But do you know what? The longer you have a gun that you haven't fired, the harder it is to not pull the trigger. Actually I can't wait to shoot it. Every day I imagine Ricky standing over me thinking he can do whatever he wants and then I pull out the gun and he knows it's all over. I can see his soft brown eyes wide open, gleaming, frightened out of his stupid mind. His body trembling. Maybe he'd be begging me to let him go. I know just what he'd say too, he'd say something lame like, "I didn't mean it. I'm sorry. I didn't mean to hurt you." And then I'd smile at him and pull the trigger. Fuck him. He doesn't deserve a break. I don't care whether he deserves it or not. He wouldn't get one from me.

Does it surprise you that I have a gun? Your little girl a gun-toting hoodlum. Well, it's treacherous out there. It's not even safe out in the suburbs where we live, much less in the city. But I didn't buy it because I'm afraid of the knuckleheads in the streets. I can pretty much handle them. Nobody messes with me too much. It's just that after Ricky tried to pull a number on me I had to have a way to take care of myself. I don't want to go out that way. At the hand of somebody I actually know. I'm not having it.

Okay, I'm finished venting about Ricky. But I wanted you to know. To be honest I don't really want the gun. It has a sort of personality to it. Sometimes I find myself standing in my bedroom touching it, stroking it like it was Ka or a pet or something. And you know how Bilbo Baggins in *The Hobbit* finds the ring that Gollum lost? Well, remember how hard it was for Bilbo to let the ring go even though the longer he kept it, the more dangerous it was to him? How its power of invisibility was actually driving him crazy? Well, that's how this gun is. It's getting to the point that I should either shoot it or give it away.

Mom should have realized it was hopeless.

Twenty-two

Two weeks later they sat on the porch waiting for the realtor to pick them up. Ben couldn't sit still. "There are so many things I could be doing. Why are we doing this?"

Helen was resolute. She hoped that Ben would get excited about buying a house—about starting over. "You know why we're doing this." She was relieved when she saw the white LeBaron pull up to the curb.

The agent, Sam Moser, was a white man who specialized in selling houses to upward blacks. He knew just the right neighborhoods where his clients would find what they were looking for and be welcomed at the same time.

Ben and Helen climbed in the car. Ben sat in the back seat as Helen, with paper and pen in hand, sat next to Sam. She had already spent an hour in Sam's office the week before, discussing price range and general areas of interest.

"To tell you the truth, folks, I don't think this is going to take a long time. I've got a couple of beauties that I have a feeling you're going to like."

Helen, riding the moment, gushed, "I hope so. We don't want to waste a whole lot of time looking at houses we don't want. We want to find the right place as soon as we can."

Ben felt like he was being chauffeured by two people who didn't care where they were going. He heard them talk about the weather and the crime rate. He heard them talk about schools and block clubs. But he was hopelessly disconnected from them. He was missing a day of work for which he'd have to atone. He was already missing the house on Sage Street. Even if he didn't own it.

Finally they stopped in front of a house that looked a lot like his parents' house. It looked a lot like all the rest of the houses on the block. And the houses in the neighborhood. He heard words flying by him. Two-car garage. Lawn. Quarry kitchen. Finished rec room.

He heard the words fall like water balloons splattering all around him. Helen was now not touching the ground. She glided through the house. The kitchen brought yelps. The master bedroom a sigh. The living room, with a dramatic fireplace, a scary silence. She looked in every closet. Opened every cabinet.

But Ben took only two steps through the door. He stood like a tree in the clay-toned foyer. He listened as the agent led her from feature to feature. Sam talked incessantly. The price was right. The terms were right. He thought they could qualify. After all Ben had the G.I. Bill, right?

Ben felt his roots digging into the shag carpeting, searching for some sort of nourishment. But there was none and the foundation on which he stood could never support his weight. If trees could scream he would have screamed. He would have opened a knothole in his trunk and let out the loudest, fiercest scream he could muster. "No! Helen, stop this madness right now!"

"Is this perfect or what?" Sam said simply and triumphantly as they reached the front door again. "Everything you want. Ready to move in. What's more to ask for?"

Sam was looking at him. Helen was looking at him. He saw the questions in her eyes. Ben's body began to unravel. Suddenly he realized that this was a life or death situation. He had seen the sheaf of commitments he would have to make brimming forth from the portfolio that Sam carried. He felt tight, stuffed, full. The house was now very small. He was swelled with panic. He could have said it then. He should have. He wanted to but he couldn't. He forced another smile.

"What do you think, Ben?" Helen looked at him, this time incapable of reading his thoughts.

"I like it." It didn't matter what he thought about the house. He wasn't buying a house. From what he could see the house was fine. It was like all the other houses. He just didn't care. "I think we should talk about it some more at home."

His words breezed by Helen. "Yes, Mr. Moser. We love this house. This is perfect. Suppose we look at the others you have too though, just to be sure?"

"Of course." Sam led them back to the car. "By the end of this afternoon, your head's gonna be swimming in beautiful homes." Then Sam turned around and spoke over his shoulder to Ben. He knew that if there was a barrier to making this deal it would be Ben. Real estate agents have a way of sensing where the resistance will come from. "And don't worry, Mr. Crestfield, everybody feels the same way the first time. I can tell you're a bit nervous. Everybody is. It's a big decision."

Helen stared ahead, beaming.

Ben rode the afternoon out in the back seat. Followed Helen through houses he didn't like. Smiled approvingly when he was supposed to and breathed joy when it was over.

He was silent during the ride back. He had told her he was wasted, burnt out from the house search. He just wanted to go home and lie down.

Ben found a way to avoid the subject for the next two days. He managed to be out of the house during dinnertime each night, claiming work held him. But Helen was growing more and more anxious.

On the third night, as he used his briefcase to push the door open, she met him there already deep into the discussion. She was beside herself with frustration. There were applications to file. Money to get together. In her hands was a yellow notepad, and two pencils. The first sheet of the pad was full of numbers and lists. As she talked she tapped the pencils on the paper like it was a drum.

"Ben, what the hell is going on? Why haven't you at least talked to me about the house? Huh? You haven't said one single word. Nothing. Not 'I liked them' or 'I didn't.' Not 'We have to keep looking,' or anything," she said as he passed her in the door.

Ben knew he had to face her. Had to deal with everything. Not just the house. But he was afraid. It could also be the end of everything.

He slowly put his briefcase and newspaper down. "Why do we have to buy a house now?"

"Because it's time. We should give Makeba a better environment to grow up in."

"There's nothing wrong with where we live. This is just fine for me. I don't see why we've got to go deeper in debt right now. I just don't think we can do it."

Helen drew a deep breath. She wanted to penetrate him. Go beyond the surface and insert herself into him. To make his mind work for her. "What are we waiting for? For you to get a promotion? Publish your poems? What? Listen, if it's your job, I know that you hate your job. But you can change jobs. You've been there almost three years. If you hate it so much why not just get a new job? And let's face it, your writing isn't going to get us anywhere. You've said yourself that it's almost impossible for a black man to publish a book. I just want to know what are we waiting for?"

Ben stared at her. What did she know about his work? She never tried to understand what he was about. She didn't understand that whatever it was that was pushing him to write had to do with something greater than his connection to her. He wanted what Langston wanted. What Hurston wanted. What Baldwin wanted. He wanted to be free enough to tell the truth.

He couldn't imagine taking such a journey while in the grip of the pressures of mortgage payments and the middle-class life Helen wanted to lead. Ben was afraid that her dream realized would be his deferred. And he knew, and flinched whenever he thought it, that Helen's dream was Makeba's future. And here he became speechless. Speechless but not thoughtless. Ben realized that he could not let Makeba suffer. That couldn't be the cost of following his heart. He was becoming more and more clear that he didn't want the life that Helen wanted. His challenge was to separate Makeba from the gravity of Helen's control. It was Helen he was falling out of love with, not Makeba.

He knew he couldn't buy a house.

"I know you're not going to like this, but I can't do it. I just can't. In a way, I want to. I mean, I want you to be happy, but I don't think I can make myself do it."

Helen planted her feet firmly to stem the rush of energy flowing over and through her. She wanted to uncoil all of her anger and fling it at him. "You can't do what?" She flung the pencils and pad across the living room. Ben shuffled his feet. "You can't do what, Ben?" This time her voice was bottom-heavy with feeling.

"We can't buy a house. It's not the right time."

Helen lost her sight. The room shaded into early pre-evening shadows. Not the familiar ones but some others she had never seen before. These shadows formed the shapes of animals.

She screamed, "There is no right time for you. You're being ridiculous. This is our chance at a new start. Isn't that what you want? Don't you want us to make it? This is it."

As the shadows gathered in the corners of the room he saw Helen's face change. Suddenly he could tell that she had finally realized that they had already peaked. That they were somewhere on the downslide. He just stood there and prepared for the storm he knew was coming.

"And I guess you don't care. You don't give a shit. Not you. Not selfish Ben. What the hell do you care if Makeba only has half a father? What do you care if we just go through the goddamn motions? Always talking some shit about African American men and how great you are. You ain't shit, Ben. You understand that? You ain't shit. Can't be a goddamned husband. Can't be a father. What can you be? Huh? What can you be?"

Helen's eyes were red. Ben was still. The air skipped with yelps. The passing wind. The shadows completing their transformation. His life was being judged. Everything had come to this.

Helen wanted to hit him. To nail her disappointment to his face.

But instead she abruptly began walking toward the stairway. She walked through Ben, reducing him to painted air, and ascended the steps.

Ben was left to a pack of shadows, their eyes holding Helen's anger.

Makeba's Journal

When you went to look at houses I remember talking to Grandma Crest-field about the kind of house I wanted. I even drew her a picture. I imagined that when you and Mom came back, I'd get in the car and we'd drive to our new house and live happily ever after. All of the things that scared you were the things I dreamed of. A lawn. A garage. All that stuff. It wasn't just Mom.

And I remember when the two of you came back, you were so quiet. I knew something was wrong. I just thought you were disappointed that you didn't see a house you liked.

I didn't know that that was almost the end. I didn't know. It's too bad that when you're young you don't even know things are just about over. I guess I shouldn't feel too bad. Mom didn't know either. I know she was pissed, but I think that she never believed for one minute, up to the absolute end, that you and her would ever not be married. She believes in love in the purest sense. No matter what was actually going on between the two of you, I *know* that she always romanticized your relationship. And she thought it would go on forever. So did I. What was I supposed to do? How could I have known you were so unhappy? What a mess it turned out to be.

Twenty-three

Finally Helen's growing anger had bloomed and Mates became immediately stronger. It would be only a matter of time before he breathed Ben's air.

Mates's blood, transformed from anger (which itself was transformed from love), now flowed. Even as a shadow, he had a heartbeat. And he could hear the crying. It cascaded inside Helen's body.

In the end there is always a scream of anguish, of abject pain, of being lost, cut loose, set adrift in a mysterious sea. Suddenly you can't remember the beginning. The time when everything was new and magical. You don't know why you are where you are. How could you have given yourself, your heart and soul to such a magnificent emptiness? And yet, when all the things connected to love have gone, the emptiness is immediately filled with mournful silence.

Helen's grip on her own future began to slip. Ben was resolute in his refusal to sign his name to a mortgage. She cried and pleaded, but it was clear that he wouldn't change his mind. Slowly, over time, the house receded to dream.

And by 1985, ten years after they were married, life had spoiled. The unraveling had ended in a pile of thread. Everything hoped for was now unmoored and ambient.

The end came one dark, cold March night. A night before the brisk winds brought spring. Makeba was upstairs, trying to be invisible and formless, like a breath of air in a warm house.

Her childhood world had deteriorated into a cavern of dread. What Makeba now heard pass between her mother and father was not love. Indeed, it was the raw nerve of disconnection.

She listened.

Makeba looked down the dimly lit stairway. The white-yellow light from the outside brought life to the shadows. There was nothing present to soften the harsh, unthinking words that came from below, except her Ka, who still smiled at her. Nothing protected her.

And when the voices below rose like smoke, up the stairs and into her room, she began an involuntary tremble. She clutched Ka tightly. His soft golden body gave in to her hug. Ka had remained remarkably well kept during the years. Makeba had kept him scrupulously clean. If he fell in the mud or had cereal spilled on him, Makeba would stop whatever she was doing and wipe her beloved Ka clean.

She confided everything in Ka. Ka *was* good for her. He was the perfect balance. When Makeba was sad, he could make her smile. When she was giddy, he would sit quietly until she calmed down. Now she held on to him. The muscles in her face knotted. Her nine-year-old mind flexed as she tried to measure the severity of the storm below her.

From the bedroom, Makeba could only hear the aura of the anguished exchanges through the filter of the shadows, the night light and the tall stairwell. The words were indistinct but the sentiment made her anxious. She was loath to move. Actually she wanted to be somewhere completely different. She wished she could just leave by the window. And she would have if she had money or clothes or somewhere else to go. But this was her home. Makeba heard the resonance of her father's voice ripple through the air.

Downstairs, Ben and Helen Crestfield were engaged in a battle of futures; theirs and Makeba's teetered on the rim. Weeks of border skirmishes had finally yielded full-fledged war. Ben had finally struck the match to the keg.

"Helen, I don't see how we can go on with this." His future had suddenly become very dark.

He wanted to say something different. He wanted to say he loved her. That he thought she was a wonderful woman, a terrific mother. That he had always wanted them to be television's Dr. Heathcliff Huxtable and his lawyer wife, Clair. He and Helen had always had at least as much passion as they did.

Ben wanted her to know that he didn't want to hurt her. He needed space. Everything smoldered like burning trash and the smoke hung over his head in a thick cloud. He just needed to be out of the relationship.

He couldn't believe how hard it was to say. He knew she would not understand. Helen had so much invested. For a second as he watched her standing in the kitchen doorway, he prayed she'd make it easy. He wanted her to smile calmly at him and say, "Yes, Ben. I understand how things can change. I understand that sometimes a person can fall in love with someone and love them deeply for a certain period of time and then after a while, when it wanes, feel lonely and unsatisfied. I understand. I'll make sure you get all the time with Makeba you need. I know you'll be a good father to her." He wanted her to say that. If he could write the words that formed on the inside of her brain that's what he would have written. But that's not the way it went down.

"You can't go on with this?" Helen repeated. "What does that mean?" She had emerged from the kitchen, her caramel skin sparkling with beads of sweat. She had a queasy feeling in her body. She stood there silent. She wanted Ben to drop it. Simply to stop talking. She hoped he wouldn't take the subject any further. She didn't know what happiness was either. But Helen did know that she felt full and wonderful when she gazed into Makeba's eyes or when they were all gathered together in their darkened living room, in front of the television on a Sunday night.

"I'm not happy. Are you happy?" Ben asked in his softest voice. As if its gentleness would let it pass.

"Am I happy? That's kind of stupid, isn't it? I thought you didn't want to be happy." Helen felt steam rising inside her. She deflected the question by asking one of her own. She felt little sympathy for him. Life was hard. But in the hardness a person could still find happiness. They had their family. They had their health.

Ben knew she'd turn the question back at him. He didn't have a good answer. He had changed. Once, being happy hadn't been important. But now . . .

"I've changed. We can't go on living together like this."

"Like what?" She challenged him. "I thought you loved me." Helen slid into a chair at the table, where drying spaghetti sauce stared back at her. She tried not to get up to find a dishcloth to wipe up the spill. Instead she began picking at it with her candy-red fingernails. Sometimes when she looked at Ben she would feel liquid from the intense emotions that coursed through her. And sometimes, like now, those same emotions made her want to strike out at him.

"I do love you. But life is flashing by us. Like a slide show we can only watch. It's not about us. We aren't living. We're being parents, Helen. We're working and we're taking care of Makeba." He looked her in the eye.

"If you wanted to, you could do more. We could go to a marriage counselor or we could talk to my minister. We could do a lot of things. You could spend more time with us. You used to. Remember how we used to drive out to the country? We don't do things like that anymore."

Ben hadn't broken his stare. She was right. There was no way he could blame his boredom, his lack of enthusiasm, on anyone but himself. But that didn't stop him from trying.

"It just always seems like too much work."

"Too much work? What the hell does that mean?" She hated to hear him complain. That's all he did. Her anger was forged into a point.

"I'm an artist. I don't want to think about bills and buying houses. I don't want stocks and mutual funds. Sometimes I don't even want to be Makeba's father. She deserves better than me."

"Yeah, so?" Now, armed and willing to fight, she connected her eyes to his. Ben could see the pain etched into her forehead. He could see the beginning of a tear form. He knew he had turned a corner. He had never expressed any regret regarding Makeba. And then, what he had said wasn't true. He knew it wasn't Makeba. It was Helen. Their relationship was paste now and he wanted more, or less. But between them now was Makeba and the connection seemed unbreakable.

"It's too hard." There were no words in him, only rocks in the bottom of his stomach, rolling around. There was nothing he could say that would help.

"Too hard! I do all the damn work. All you do is complain about how hard everything is." She was tired. Weeks of trying to anticipate Ben's moods, trying to understand why he wasn't as excited about everything as he once was.

"That's part of the problem." He picked up the classified section of the newspaper that sat on the table in front of him. He didn't look at it, dropped it back on the table. There was no painless way to do it. He knew Helen would not let go easily.

"You bastard. How dare you? Ten years. Ten years of this shit and you want to just leave? I've worked like a slave around here and you have the gall to tell me it's *too hard*." Her scream broke off into a chuckle. He watched her compose herself. "You have a responsibility to your family." He knew that was coming. That was it. It was the formula for the survival of a people.

"This is your family. You have to make it work."

"I'm sorry."

"Sorry?" Helen was enraged. There was no turning back.

"Sorry?" she repeated. "It really doesn't matter to you, does it? Ten goddamned years. You're a selfish, egotistical ass who's tired of playing and wants to take his toys and go home. Well, this ain't no game. You can't be a part-time husband or father. This is some lame shit, Ben. What is wrong with you? You don't understand a goddamn thing about being a man, do you?"

She paused to catch her breath, then she changed her tone. "I'm not just worried about me, you know. What about Makeba?"

"This is not about Makeba. It's you. I just don't love you the way I used to."

Helen's eyes widened. She jumped up from the table. For an instant he wondered what she was going to do. She started toward the kitchen but stopped, turned around to face him. She leaned forward on the table opposite where he sat; Tina Turner whispered in her ear, "What the hell does love have to do with it? We need you, Ben," she said quietly, her emotions transformed to water.

Helen turned her back on him, trying to gird herself. She grappled with the fleeing energy inside her trembling body. She loved him. Loved her daughter. She wanted everything to work out. She softened her voice even more. Reached inside herself to find the thin thread of their life together. Perhaps she could give more. Do more. Still with her back to him she said, "Is it me? I mean, is there something I can do . . ."

Ben felt her in his head. "Helen, please try to understand. I don't want to hurt you."

Again she wheeled around to him. "You don't want to hurt me? What do you think you've been doing for the last five years? This whole marriage has been a string of hurts. You're never home and when you are, you're upstairs in that stupid room writing stuff nobody wants to read."

"It's depressing being here." Ben realized immediately, and really for the first time, how difficult it would be to separate the life of his child from hers. He didn't mean that Makeba depressed him. It was Helen. But in a way, Helen *was* Makeba. At that moment, he couldn't tell where Helen ended and Makeba began.

Helen didn't hesitate, didn't flinch this time. "Then leave. I don't care anymore. If you want to go, you can get your things and get the hell out of here. You can just get the fuck out of my life. I'm not going to spend the rest of my life trying to convince you that you belong here with me and Makeba." The terror in her voice scared him.

"Listen babe." She turned away from him at the word. She wasn't his "babe" any more. That was for sure. And she didn't want him to confuse the issue. But Ben couldn't help it. He still cared about her. They still had a history. She was the mother of his daughter. "I've stayed here, tried my best, *for* the family."

"Well, don't do us any favors, okay? Just get the hell out of here."

"Helen, please, don't make this—" Ben never got a chance to

finish his sentence. There was a stack of dishes on the breakfront in the dining room. Helen had slowly walked over to them and in a flurry of motions flung them to the floor. The pieces of blue-trimmed white china crashed into themselves and threw a chilled air throughout the house.

Along with the crescendo of breaking dishes, there was a smothered yelp from Makeba's bedroom upstairs. Ben heard her jump up and run into the bathroom.

He had almost forgotten about her. But she was there, upstairs, listening.

Makeba sat on the toilet and faced the closed bathroom door. She still held fast to Ka. "They're cursing," she said to the lion. There was a long pause as the sound of two people arguing rolled up the steps.

Like a tornado, anger swirled everywhere throughout the house. Every now and then a car would pass in the street and break the arrangement of the other shadows but they would quickly resume their places and their smiles.

With a sigh, she said again to Ka, "I don't believe it. I'm afraid." The smiling shadows held their pose. Even among smiles there was sadness. Makeba had lived through many fights between Helen and Ben but there was no preparation for this moment. Everyone in the solid, middle-class stone house was unhappy at this moment.

Makeba thought about going downstairs for a glass of milk. Maybe it would change the atmosphere. Sometimes her presence was enough to soften the air between them. She tried to move but found herself stuck to the toilet. And instead of really caring about what was going on, she abruptly turned to face the wall behind her. She found her free hand at the wall picking at the blue wallpaper. There was greater distance now between her and the spoken words that originated below.

Makeba repeated everything she heard to Ka. And as she did she pulled small sections of the wallpaper away from the bathroom wall. "She's gonna make him leave if he don't start changing. She's saying she's gonna make him go. And he don't care, he will go if he has to but he don't love her anymore and he's tired of trying to act like he does just because they got me." At the last word Makeba's mouth froze like a jammed sewing machine. What was going on?

"He's really mad now. He's calling her names again. Saying she don't know how to love him. And . . . and . . . and she's saying how can she love somebody like him?"

Makeba closed her eyes. It almost sounded funny. She felt a smile creep across her face. But before the smile became a laugh the humor was gone entirely. It evaporated into the deepening darkness.

Soon she heard a clear, scream from her mother's body. "Get the hell out of here. I don't need this. Get out."

She could tell that her mother meant business. Her scream lacked terror. It was solid and backed by a leaded emotion.

Helen had finally let go. All of the energy she had used to hold on to Ben for the last two years had now reversed itself. She wanted to erase his existence. To purge his image. To relieve herself. "No. You want it this way? You want your freedom? Leave. Why wait? Why keep trying? Why not just get the hell out right now?" Her pretty face was tortured. Ben couldn't keep from crying. They both cried.

Eventually he got up from the table and walked to the hallway closet to get his jacket. He left Helen crying. The early spring chill was like a spirit swimming through the house. As he got to the closet he looked upstairs. He turned and began the climb. He had been thinking about this for a while. Yes, he would leave, but he would be back for Makeba. He would do whatever he had to to convince Helen to let him have her. He would not let his separation from Helen mean separation from his daughter.

And he didn't want to have to visit on weekends and play that game. He wanted her with him. Maybe they could work something out. He had gone to school. Maybe Helen would want to do that while he raised Makeba. Something. There had to be some way he could stay with his daughter.

The maple steps creaked under his weight. Ben moved slowly up. At the landing he turned toward Makeba's room.

"Kayba? Are you asleep?"

Makeba sat in the bathroom, Ka's face buried in the space between her cheek and shoulder. She was fighting her own tears. She knew what was happening. She had friends who had described the ending of marriage to her. When it started rolling up the stairs, she recognized it immediately.

In this, Ka was no protection for her.

"Kayba?" Ben peeked into her bedroom. He flung the bedclothes off, thinking Makeba was hiding.

Makeba heard him. She tried to say something but the sound never made it past her throat.

Ben was now in the hallway in front of the bathroom. He saw the light glowing from inside. He knocked softly.

"Yes?" Makeba's voice was weak.

"It's Daddy, sweetheart. Can I come in?"

"Yes." Makeba saw her father fill up the darkened doorway. She saw his contorted face, smudged with the mud that tears make.

"You know I love you, don't you?"

"Yes."

"Do you know what's happening? I mean, what's going on between your mom and me?" Ben couldn't stand still. He bounced inside the door frame from side to side.

"I think so," Makeba said flatly. Ka was now on her lap, the lion's expression unchanged since the day it arrived. The only thing Ka could do was absorb some of her pain. But there was so much of it in that small blue room. "You're leaving us."

"I have to, baby. I have to. I can't stay here anymore."

"Why?"

Ben exhaled, nearly losing all of his remaining strength. "You've seen how we are. All we do is argue. I just don't want to live with her anymore."

"But what about me?"

Once again, he was crying. What a question. He knew it had to come. The question that never dissipates, never goes away. The question that is never completely answered. The question that perhaps cannot be answered. But at least he was prepared to try. He bent down and put his arm around her.

"How would you like to come live with me?"

"You mean without Mom?"

"Yes, just you and me. We could make it."

Makeba fidgeted. She stared first at her father and then at Ka. "Where would we live?"

"I don't know right now, Kayba, but we could find a nice place somewhere."

"But how come Mom can't be with us?"

"Because we're not happy together anymore."

"But I don't want to leave her."

"I know. I know you don't, baby." Ben hugged her and stood up again. "Listen Kayba, I want you to think about it, okay? I'll come to see you on Saturday, maybe we'll go to the skating rink or something. And you can tell me what you think about it then. All right?"

Makeba nodded her head.

"I love you. I want you to believe that. I love you now and I always will, no matter what happens. You remember that. Okay?"

Makeba nodded again.

"I'm leaving now. I've got to go. But I'll see you on Saturday. And sweetheart, don't worry. Okay? Everything's going to turn out fine."

He turned to leave, paused at the door to look back at her sitting there, holding back tears and stroking Ka's back. He walked into his den, where he closed the cover on his Smith-Corona and gathered his poems and the first pages of a novel he had started.

Helen had turned off every light downstairs, so Ben came down the steps in complete darkness. Everyone and everything was being left behind.

Makeba's Journal

No. I don't believe you. You had no intention of coming back. You left. You ran out of the door. You never meant to come back. This is a lie. Mom would have told me. I would have known. Okay, so it sounds good. I remember the argument. I remember you coming upstairs. And I remember when you asked me if I'd come live with you. I thought about it all weekend. I thought and I thought. How could I leave Mom? I didn't think I could do it at first. But I couldn't stop thinking about it. She was a basket case. All she did was cry. I was in my room almost the entire week. I know I didn't go to school. We were both really scared.

After you left she came into my room and told me that you were leaving but that she didn't think you'd be gone too long. She tried to make it sound like you were going to the barbershop or on a vacation or something. I think she really thought you just needed some time out. But I can see now that you were dying to get away from her. It just wasn't the right mix. You weren't right for each other.

Anyway I talked to Ka about it and I dreamed about it and finally I realized that I didn't want to be away from you. That's right. In my sleep I decided that I would ask Mom if I could go with you. I woke up the next day even more afraid. You were gone, she was crying, Nana was just sitting on the couch, sucking her teeth and shaking her head. I didn't know how I was going to tell them. I wasn't sure I could at all.

At dinner that night I tried to say something about you. Nana almost screamed at me. She said it was best not to mention your name in the house for a while. I think I said something like, "Do you really think he'll be gone for a long time?" And then, even after Nana tried to shut me up, I finally said what I really wanted to say.

"Well, if Daddy's not going to be gone that long, then maybe I can stay with him sometimes."

Nana put her hand up as if to tell me to shut up, but Mom said, "You mean visit your father? Of course, sweetheart."

I remember that I was instantly excited. There was a moment there when I understood what was going on. And then I went too far: "And do you think I could live with him for a while? I mean—" Mom's eyes lit up and I knew I had said something wrong.

"Did he say something to you about that?"

I didn't know what to say so I told her that you had asked me if I would want to. She looked at me and then at Nana and got up from the table.

But you never came. And you never called. And like magic we were suddenly in North Carolina. I had chosen you and you never even came back to get me. What am I supposed to do with that?

Ka has always said that this story wasn't over. I didn't know what she meant, but I guess I'm beginning to.

How much of this is true? I can't keep it all straight anymore. I just know that I've always thought you walked out and never came back.

Twenty-four

Mates could feel the tightness of his body coming together. The shadows around him had congealed into a solid blackness. At the same time he felt a strong force pulling him away from the darkness. He was being separated and moved toward Ben. He floated like a kite just behind Ben. Inside Mates's stomach was an urge to lunge at Ben. But the terror was still not real. There remained only the call to bring him forth.

Ben checked into a hotel near the university campus. He was struck by the silence that immediately invaded his life. There was no wondering Helen to evade, no needing Makeba to tend to. Exile gripped his heart.

Ben sat in silence, staring at the thin white walls of the small room. From the first moment he began to miss Makeba. Miss her intensely. He cried for her. He wondered how he could face the pain of missing his daughter.

He didn't turn his television on. He didn't read. He didn't try to write. His eyes couldn't focus on small images. He could only see the wavering reality as it trembled under the veil of his tears.

On the second night Ben began to hear Makeba's voice. Her voice invaded his silence. When he ate, took a shower or sat in the gray armchair, Ben was likely to hear her soft voice. He couldn't tell what she was saying. But he sensed she was talking about him.

Ben was stuck there in that room, listening to her voice, imagining her thin body, feeling her hurt. He wallowed in it. He didn't call anyone, not even Ramsey. He wanted to face this life alone. But he knew it was to be a journey. And that it was just beginning.

At night, Makeba's eyes sparkled like tiny torches. Disappointment flickered. Her eyes were nighthawks in the bluedark sky, free-flying and sorrowful.

Ben couldn't conceive of living his life without her. Visiting her on weekends. Buying toys that he wouldn't get a chance to see her play with. Maybe he had moved too hastily. How could he write? How could he survive being disconnected from Makeba? Helen was his problem. Their relationship was over. Right or wrong he saw her as the symbol of the barriers he had to overcome to be a writer. But Makeba? Makeba was an innocent. Even more, he needed Makeba. She was his blood. His inspiration.

How could a man leave his child? How could he make a decision that would take him away from her? Break the bond that is special and unique between a father and daughter?

Could the cost for identity, for freedom be so high that he would have to let go of the one person in his life who belonged? He had already chosen a path. He was living in a hotel away from his wife and his daughter. He had broken the connection between him and Helen.

And yet, in his new freedom, he felt immediately paralyzed. With one breath, he looked forward to visiting Makeba. With the next he dreaded facing Helen. All of the feeling that had been love was now something else, something which made him want to run, to escape its lingering power. Ben knew it was shame. He was profoundly saddened by the shame that swam through his body. He had destroyed all of Helen's dreams in an attempt to keep his alive.

But he could save Makeba. He could go back and get her. He could show her that he wasn't deserting her. Maybe she would want to live with him. When he went back on Saturday to get his things, he would ask.

And then Saturday became the only day of the week. Ben

planned his speech to Makeba. He wanted to relieve any fears she had that he was leaving *her*. She could choose to live with him.

Friday night he dreamed he was on trial. The judge was a black woman, not Helen, but someone who could have known Helen. Someone who had felt the crush of a family being torn apart. Perhaps she was the daughter of a divorce. Perhaps . . . Ben sat in the witness box terrified.

His defense was presented by Ramsey:

"This man is a good man. This man has climbed out of the shadow of slavery and formed himself into something strong, full of potential. He is an educated man. Not a 'trained' man, mind you. Not like those which society 'trains' to do its dirty work. He is not an accountant, a lawyer, a teacher or a bus driver. He is an artist. A thinking man. A dreaming man. And you would want him to reduce himself. To limit his potential simply to follow through on a commitment to his wife."

The judge stared down at Ben, all but ignoring what Ramsey was saying. "You know of course, Mr. Crestfield, that you are guilty. There is no defense in a situation like this. You had your obligations and responsibilities clearly outlined for you. Indeed, you created them yourself, in a partnership. Besides, you are not separate from your people. You are only an 'educated' man because your parents stayed together to give you a proper life. How could you want any less for your child? You are guilty. There is no defense."

Ben woke up before he found out his punishment. He had made his decision. His only chance at redemption would be to persuade both Helen and Makeba that he could provide a decent home for his child. That he didn't need Helen to do that.

In the morning, when he approached his house on Sage Street, it was like he had never been there before. The sun blasted the street in light. And it was quiet. Eerily quiet. After five days in a hotel room, he was disheveled, tired. His body ached. Parts of him felt like they might simply fall off.

For a second he thought about stopping off to see Hannibal before he faced Helen, but he didn't see Hannibal's yellow Firebird. For some people Friday night could extend into the next week.

He walked up the steps, passed through the porch. There was an empty, crumpled brown paper shopping bag sitting by the door. In the window of the door was an envelope with his name on it.

Ben reached for the envelope and as he grabbed it the door swung slowly open. He began to tremble as he snatched the letter open. But he kept moving into the house.

There were no lights on inside. The house was empty. He strained his ears. No. There wasn't even the hum of electricity. There was no energy, electric or human, flowing within the house at all. It was perfectly still. Instinctively he ran up the steps to Makeba's bedroom. It was empty there too. To the closet. Empty. Hangers lined up like functionless sculpture. Barren.

There were no sheets on Makeba's bed. No clothes in the dresser. No toys, no dolls, no books, no jacks. Makeba and her Ka were gone. Her paintings from school were the only things left. Foremost among these was a picture she had drawn of the house when she was in the third grade. It was a simple, crooked drawing of an A-frame house. In it Makeba had placed Helen, Ka and Ben. In jagged writing underneath: "I love my house."

Ben stumbled into the bathroom and sat down on the toilet as his body dispersed into the air. It was then he unfolded the letter. His stomach dropped into the still toilet-bowl water. His head began unraveling like a ball of string. The tears started, one at a time, until unchecked, he was breathing them out like air. He read the letter.

Dear Ben,

I know this letter will come as a shock to you. I know that it will hurt you. But you did this to yourself. I didn't begin the last ten years knowing that at this point I would be doing what I'm doing. I have no choice. You've made your mind up about what you're going to do, and now, I've made up mine. Your decision hurt me deeply.

I love you, Ben. I truly do. I wish things were different between us.

But like I said, you created this whole mess. My mother taught me wrong. She always told me to find a man that is closest to the ideal and then stick by him no matter what. She never taught me how to let go.

Anyway, I'm not about to let you talk me into giving Makeba up. After you left she asked me about living with you. Do you think I'm crazy? You have no idea who I am if you think I'm going to let you take Makeba away from me. I can hear you now, telling me how it will be for my benefit. All the things I could do if I was free to do what I wanted.

You can forget that. I'm sitting in your den writing this letter. At your desk. In your house. I know you'll hate me for this. I've already accepted that. They say love is really very close to hate. Well, I'm prepared for your hate now, just as I once was open to your love.

I am Makeba's mother. I brought her here. And I'm not leaving her.

Actually I'm feeling very calm and peaceful. I know what has to be done. It's taken me a little while. I guess I knew it was over long ago. I should have done something. But I didn't. Neither did you.

So, by the time you read this letter I will be gone. Makeba will be gone. I'm sorry. I don't want to deprive you of your relationship with her forever, I'm not cruel. But for a while, I think it will be best if you don't know where we are. I'll get in touch with you later.

I'm doing this for me and Makeba. Be happy if you can. And don't hurt too much.

Helen

Ben's head was swimming. He had made a huge mistake. If he had had any idea that Helen would leave, he would've stayed there. He didn't really want to leave the house. Just her.

He sat there for a long time. Most of the afternoon. He had stopped crying. Stopped reading the letter. Stopped thinking. He was like stone. Like the house, empty. Finally Ben regained consciousness and left the bathroom. He was in no mood to move his things. He wasn't sure what he was supposed to do. Helen had become the enemy. And now she was gone. With no one to fight, he was purposeless.

He dragged his body down the steps, into a shadow-drenched living room. Without thinking he walked toward the front door. But he was struck stiff by a movement in the vestibule. Someone was standing there.

His heart fluttered but he found no escape. His body was stuck. He tried to speak. He moved his mouth. His brain was screaming. Inside him was a swirl of noise. It wanted release. His head was spinning under the stress. Had Helen come back? Was it Makeba standing there? If he had known terror before, then this was worse. More powerful.

He tried to grab the words that were flying around him. "Helen?" came weakly from him. "Helen?"

"It's not Helen. Helen is gone." Lena stepped into the house. "I wanted to see you. I was here earlier but I guess you hadn't got here yet."

"Where's Helen?"

"She's gone, Ben. You drove her away."

"I didn't drive her away. I left. I've only been gone five days. This is ridiculous."

"You've been driving her away from you since you met her. What did you think? That you would be the one to decide everything? When you got married. When you broke up. Who was going to have Makeba. That's what you thought, isn't it, Ben? That it was all up to you?"

"Lena, ever since I met you, you've been all in our business. You've been more destructive than I could have ever been. Now, tell me, where's my baby?"

Lena's thin body railed back in laughter. "Me? You're blaming me? You're incredible. You blame my daughter. You blame your daughter. Now you want to blame me. You're less of a man than I thought. You're nothing." Lena paused, shutting her laughter down like a powerful engine. Then she was ice. "If I could have I would have made Helen leave you years ago. You always talked a good game but you never did a damn thing. Typical good-for-nothing nigger of a man is what you are. College-educated. Ha. You're nothing. And now you have nothing."

Ben's skin felt suddenly warm, like he was oozing blood. A wet sticky warmth. This was a war. And he was losing it. Perhaps it was already lost. Lena stood in front of him, shielded by the shadows, and continued the pummeling.

"I can't cry anymore. And I don't know what to do with my anger. Please. Can't you tell me where they are?" Ben's voice bounced around the empty room.

"Why? Why should I tell you anything? You're just going to make their lives miserable."

"You're talking about my wife and my daughter. What is wrong with you? I just want to know where they are." He took two steps in her direction and stooped over so that his face was close to hers.

But Lena didn't flinch. "Ben, the only reason I'm here is to tell you to leave them alone. You hurt my daughter. I warned you. I told you to take care, but I guess you didn't take me seriously."

Ben felt himself slipping away. He couldn't intimidate her. He wheeled away from her, his control crumbling. "What the hell do you know? You're some crazy-ass old woman who thinks she can scare people by walking around in the dark and carrying weird shit around in bags." He turned back to her. "You're as responsible as I am. If you knew how to be a mother instead of a fucking witch or some shit, things might be different. Maybe Helen wouldn't be so afraid of her own life and she wouldn't focus so much on me if you had raised her better."

Ben reached out and grabbed Lena by her wrists. He brought them up into his face. "Where are they?" he screamed at her.

Again Lena smiled. "They will always be behind you. At your heels. In your shadow. Forever, Ben. You will know them when you can't sleep. When you are tired and unable to rest. You have created ghosts. Your dreams have created your own haint. And if I have anything to say about it, you will never be free."

Ben threw Lena hard to the floor. She made no sound. Her eyes shot fire up at him. He stood over her with his hand raised. He wanted to beat her into the floor. Banish her from his life. Instead he turned and walked out the door.

And Mates took his first real breath. He was there, waiting just behind Lena. When she hit the floor, there was an explosion inside him, which, instead of breaking him apart, pulled him together. The truth was that Mates had been waiting there for ten years, following them around, watching. And now, he *was* them: Lena, Helen, Makeba and Ka. Everything they held inside, their hope and their frustration, was his blood. Their anger, his heartbeat.

Mates stepped over Lena as he followed Ben out the door.

Outside, Ben was frantic. His skin crawled, his stomach hurt. Sage Street seemed alien. Hannibal was on the porch across the street. He called to Ben but Ben ignored him. He thought the car coming down the street was being driven by Ramsey and that Geri was a passenger. He started trotting. Going he didn't know where—just going.

Ben ran out of Sage, out of concrete. He ran across asphalt, over grass. He ran through alleys, across front yards. And Mates was right behind him. At first, like so many times before, Ben didn't know Mates was there, ten paces on his trail. But when Ben turned to look behind him, for the first time he could see Mates, panting, galloping behind like a hound. His thick coat glistening in the afternoon sun. Mates saw the recognition in Ben's eyes. Ben knew then that Mates was pursuing him.

A low growl groaned from the black dog. Ben heard it as a voice. Mates knew by the look in Ben's face that he could hear him. That Ben would twist the sounds that flowed from his new body into words. "Ben, it has finally happened, you have disappointed everyone. Only Ka has the faintest faith in you and that's only because Ka will hope to the end for Makeba's sake. Not me, Ben. I already know the truth. You are mine."

Ben was stricken. He turned a lighter shade of brown. There was a dog, a huge, bounding, frightening black dog, just strides behind him. And it had spoken to him.

As his breath shortened until there was barely space in his chest for any air at all, he tried to reassert some semblance of internal control. He was running to madness. He felt it. Everything he had tried to fashion for himself was shredded. He had nothing, no one—except Mates. And what was Mates? What was happening to him?

Then Ben did a curious thing. He slowed down. Mates could have pounced on him then, but he didn't. Ben came to a full stop and turned around to face the dog.

Mates pulled up quickly. He bared his teeth and let his fiercest growl rise out of his chest. Mates stood up on his hind legs and swung at Ben with his right front paw. Ben jumped back, just out of reach.

"Mates wants you now."

"What's going on? What the hell is happening?"

"You watched each piece fall into place. You know all there is to know."

"My daughter?"

"She is Mates."

"My wife?"

"She is Mates too. And Lena. And everyone who cares about them." Mates lunged again.

Ben turned away and began running. He was unhinged. This was the way Mates wanted him. Running through the city terrorized. Afraid to stop. Afraid to do anything but try to elude the demon just behind him.

And do you know what? He would never be able to do that.

Makeba's Journal

TWENTY-FOURTH ENTRY

I remember being awakened early that Thursday morning by Mom and Nana. We got dressed and packed everything up and went to the airport. My mind was swimming. I didn't know what was going on. I kept asking Mom if you were coming. And she just told me to not ask her any more questions. She said that everything would turn out fine.

We flew that day to Clinton, North Carolina, where we stayed for about six months. I kept asking Mom if you were coming or if you were going to call or what. She would say that when you were ready you would call. That you knew where we were. I know that Mom wrote you a letter. She told me that. And she said that she had also told Nana to tell you where we were. And I heard Nana tell Mom that she had given all of the information to you.

So I waited. Every day when I came home from school, I'd ask if you'd called or written. Nothing.

And now you're trying to say that Mom and Nana never told you where we were? I can't believe it. It doesn't make any sense. Why would they do that? They knew I loved you. They had to know how much it would hurt me. They had to.

And you. All of these years. Through all this time . . . if you had wanted, you could have found me. Even if they never told you anything, it's been a long time. You could have done something.

Ka always said that you had not lost your love for me. She told me not to forget you. And I haven't. And recently, Ka has encouraged me. She told me to find you. I guess to learn what I've learned about you. I just wish you could have made contact with me. I've needed you.

The thing is, regardless of how long it's been, I can't get you out of my mind. I still remember you and I guess I still love you. Maybe this whole story is just a lie. Maybe it didn't happen like this at all. It really doesn't matter. I feel like I've gotten to know you again. I hope that we can find a way to talk.

I've also decided to get rid of this gun. I can't actually use it. I think if it gets to the point you have to use a gun, you've already lost control. And like I've been telling you, that won't happen again.

Yours, Makeba

Twenty-five

Ben ran all afternoon. He ran through West Philadelphia like it was scenery scrolling by. He ran through the streets of University City seeing only the speckled pastiche of cement sliding under his feet. He couldn't think. Couldn't see. Only run. He felt Mates behind him. He heard Mates occasionally screaming at him. Growling. Sometimes he could even feel the dog's sweet hot breath encircle his head, then fade away. He ran until he passed into darkness.

Suddenly the moonlight was in the trees. It illuminated the leaves, which were full of speech as the torrent of movement passed below them. Ben Crestfield was running and splashing and reaching for something which would save him. He was frantically trying to outrun Mates. But the dog was not impatient. It pursued Ben in a measured pace. It seemed content to follow, staying just a step or two behind him.

Inside Ben's head was a swirl of colors and lights. Exhausted, he realized he had run into the park, except that now it seemed thick and dense. There was only the narrow path on which his feet barely touched as he pressed forward. The trees were wide and dark and leaned together, creating a shroud. He felt the skinny limbs reaching out to scratch him. And then there was a sudden break. There, the narrow path opened into a wide patch of green grass, shimmering like water. It wooed him there. It silently promised safety. And, since safety was something he desperately needed, Ben put everything into his pumping legs.

The air was still very thick among the trees. Whispers died there. Only the laughter of the leaves and Mates's heavy howling breath followed him. Mates was his approaching dread.

But Mates was having fun. For the first time in ten years he was alive. His prey was right in front of him. He could feel Ben's heart thumping. Every beat.

Mates imagined that Ben was probably praying that his heart was strong enough to withstand this terror. Mates wanted to be close enough to Ben so that the man could smell him, feel the strength of his power moving near him.

Mates was in ecstasy. He knew that it was Ben's fear which made him run as if he were made of wind. Mates barked at him. He wanted Ben to see his tongue, long and red, dripping with the taste of the first taste of him. Every now and then Mates lunged even closer and snapped at his churning legs. He toyed with Ben.

Mates was at his best in the chase. He loved the pure freedom of running, the streams of color that passed through the corner of his eyes, the internal combustion which pushed him forward.

But Ben was fast. Strong enough to keep his pace. He broke into the clearing. Mates abruptly stopped and stood still in the dark behind an elm tree, staring at Ben.

Ben had finally stopped running. He had slipped to his knees and was now crawling on the wet grass. Slowly he pulled himself up on a fallen tree.

All was silent. No crickets. No owls. No skittering mice.

Ben tried to bring his eyes into focus. He craned his neck in each direction, straining to see if what he thought he had seen was indeed real. Was there really a dog—a dog who talked—chasing him?

Slowly Ben recaptured some of his composure, caught his breath. He sat still, his breathing becoming lighter. He tried to become invisible. He tried to disappear into the scaling bark of the tree trunk that he was sitting on.

But the more his body returned to its natural state, the more his mind asserted itself. Where was Makeba? Where was she? Why had he let himself stray this far from what he lived for? How long would this thing chase him? How long did he have to run? And then his heart froze again. He saw Mates's eyes peering from behind a tree. It *was* real. What he thought he had seen, he had seen. And at that moment he was willing to give up. He had claimed to be a father. He had created a child. He was incapable of being what she needed him to be. Clearly he was not able to do it. He was, in fact, caught in a waking dream. Pursued by something he didn't understand and crumbling inside like sandstone to a rough touch. He was falling apart. It was the last thing he was supposed to do. He was a black shout in a white whisper world. He was supposed to stand up and scream back. He was the bad motherfucker. What terror could frighten him? Ben stared at the silhouette of the animal and suddenly couldn't control his voice.

"Come on, then. If you want me, come and get me. I'm tired of running. I can't get away anyway. Come out into the open and let me see you."

"I want to. I want to put myself in front of you. Force you to flee again into the forest where I can dominate you . . ." Mates's speech broke into a howling. It was a mix of feelings. He wanted to continue his patient wait for Ben to get up and continue running, and yet there he was, just sitting there taunting. Asking for him.

"Ben, you know what I am. You know why I am chasing you. It is a common story really. I have pursued many before you and there will be others.

"The disappointment and pain you have caused is not a fleeting memory. I am here to remind you that there is a place for those who destroy the dreams of children.

"I want you to contemplate being torn apart by me. Being ripped apart, your fingers snatched from your hands, one by one, as appetizer. The blood a sauce, the bones toothpicks. We are meat, all of us.

We all have our predators, the things that would eat us as we do others."

The darkness of the woods around the clearing made the voice seem to come from everywhere. "What do you want? What are you?" Ben tried to sound strong. He waited for Mates to respond. "You heard me. I asked you a question."

Mates considered what to say back to him. But he didn't want to give Ben any comfort. His silence was as strong as his teeth. Mates sat back on his haunches.

Ben stood up and began walking toward Mates.

"That's right. That's right. You come to me."

"I can't run anymore. I'm tired. I've dodged and ducked and lied and slithered long enough. I'm tired."

"Yes, I know." Mates's whole body quivered. Now *he* was drooling. His jaws muscles spasmed. "I want you, Ben."

"What was I supposed to do? What was I supposed to do?" He was crying, he was already beginning to fold up. His knees were buckling. He was moving forward toward Mates, but only barely so.

"There is nothing to do now but give yourself to me. There is no other way out." Ben was just to the edge of the clearing. The shadows of the trees were caressing his face. "Just a little more. Just a little more."

Ben collapsed. He was throwing up and crying and gasping for air. Makeba's face hovered over him, Ka floated next to her. There were tears in the lion's eyes. Lena was laughing. Helen stood back in the darkness, trembling.

Mates took a step forward and bared his teeth, his red gums like neon. Now he was standing over Ben. All Mates wanted now was for Ben to open his eyes. To watch his long white teeth plunge into his chest. Mates couldn't wait any longer. He lowered himself, swiveled back on his haunches in recoil. Mates then let out a scream that was made of all the pain of all the innocent people throughout time.

The scream was a red light in Ben's head. He turned toward Mates and saw the dog two feet away, eyes like candy apples, glistening in the night light. Ben looked into the animal's mouth, was drawn inside as if it were a tunnel with the faint sound of trickling water deep inside it.

Mates threw all of his weight into his leap at Ben. He was in the air like a bird and would land in the middle of Ben's back.

Ben twisted around quickly, raised his hands in a futile attempt to ward Mates off. At the same time, Ben found himself screaming too. "No. No. No. I'm sorry. I didn't know what else to do."

Ben was startled into frenzy when Mates landed on him. There was no pain, no tearing of flesh. Nothing. Mates simply vanished into his skin. And then he felt it. Like spontaneous combustion, his stomach began to quiver uncontrollably, a pounding began in his head, his mouth went dry. He opened his eyes and saw only red; a deep crimson on the edges and nearly pink at the center. And he felt it moving around inside him. Suddenly there was only red running through him.

Epilogue
Part One
1994

For days, Ben wandered the streets of West Philadelphia. He felt like his stomach was slowly being chewed up. He could hear a fierce growling inside of him. There was a buzzing sound in his head. He couldn't stop crying. He no longer had a job. He had no money. He slept in alleys, ate garbage. He was dirty, vagrant. He was on the streets like that for two weeks before Ramsey found him.

"Ben, is that you?" Ramsey had been searching West Philadelphia for Ben. He had been calling every possible place Ben might be. Finally he began driving through the streets of University City, and going in and out of bars. He'd been at it for about six days when he got a notion to head downtown. He instinctively parked his car in the lot behind the Thirteen Bar and as he walked through the alley adjacent to the bar he saw Ben, huddled in a doorway, talking to himself. But it was clear as he approached that Ben was completely disoriented. And when Ramsey grabbed him and hoisted him up, Ben was lifeless, a smelly muttering sack of a man. The only thing Ramsey could think to do was take Ben to the hospital.

As he stood Ben up, Ben opened his eyes and stared at him without a glimmer of recognition. "How can we be fathers in a world that won't let us be men?" He stared at Ramsey like a child. As if Ramsey was his father. At that moment Ramsey felt sad because he was holding something less than a man. He looked into Ben's soft brown eyes, dirt and scratches making a mask of his face, and he thought that maybe Ben should have actually asked his own father that question. Fathers should teach their sons what it means to be men.

"You got to get yourself together, brother. This ain't cool."

"Do we have to choose? Is that it?" It was the last lucid thing Ramsey heard Ben say. He had lapsed into a deep growl that scared Ramsey.

Two days later Ben awoke in a fresh-smelling white bed in the psychiatric ward of Pennsylvania General Hospital. He was on his back and strapped to the bed. He had suddenly erupted from his catatonic stupor into a violent flurry of activity. He had hit two nurses before being subdued.

That was the nadir. But time and a lot of therapy had allowed him to slowly regain his stability, his ability to manage his life. As he recovered he tried a halfhearted search for Helen and Makeba. But Lena's house had been sold and all the telephone numbers he had were disconnected. And almost with a sigh of relief he packed his things and left Philadelphia.

He told himself it was for the best. That his tortured mind was not functional in the small, articulated world of family. He taught himself numbness about his daughter. At least he tried to numb his heart. He knew it was Mates. He knew that Mates had damaged him. The guilt that Mates had buried like bones throughout his body occasionally erupted in a fit of questions.

"Will you face your guilt? Will you fight me?"

"Will you run, be my plaything?"

Ben's first instinct had been to run. Believing that his ability to carry Mates around with him was easier than trying to change history.

He had gradually started writing again. But the only story he had to tell was his own. And after he tried writing everything but the truth, he finally gave in. But Mates was there again. Taunting him.

"Tell it. Tell it. I dare you. You can't survive it. I'll have you all to myself then."

But Ben wrote anyway and found himself embarked on the

hardest task of his life: the telling. And the telling was a painful, healing thing. The telling rendered Mates docile, less destructive.

In a way he had written the story for just this moment.

This moment. This glorious, incredible moment when his daughter, Makeba Crestfield, sat across from him, looking like a lost soul. The overalls, the combat boots, the slumping boyish demeanor, revealed a young woman who was completely out of Ben's range of understanding. Where was his cute little Kayba? Where was his baby? That woman whose face was now just two feet away from his was a reflection distorted by time and distance. He knew he would have to start over.

"I know you think your mother is the hero in this drama. I understand why someone could think that. But I've fought the monster too. I've survived the guilt. I still love you. It may not seem like such a big thing to you. But I still cling to the idea that we can be close. That family with you is possible.

"After everything I still have hope. I know we will be for each other in the end. I know life is strange. That people go their ways, seem totally unconcerned, but that's only how it looks."

At first, Makeba wasn't going to say anything, but something inside put words in her mouth. "But Dwight and Mom both have drilled into my head, it's what you *do* that counts. They were the ones who *did* things for me. Because I was a child and because they loved me. You can't ask me to condemn them."

"I'm not asking for that. I'm asking that you just understand that what seems simple isn't simple. Some people choose to see the complexity in life. I'm like that. There isn't anything simple about life. I know that responsibility and obligation are important. I know that I ran from that. But I would have been a tragedy if I had stayed with your mother."

"So you'd rather I be the tragedy? That's it, isn't it? You sacrificed *me* for you."

"Makeba, I think I would have sacrificed both of us if I had stayed."

"Tough life, eh?" It was out of her before she could stop it. "Well, actually I shouldn't have said 'sacrificed.' My life hasn't really been that bad. If you hadn't written this book, if I hadn't thought about finding you, I would probably have left town about now. I'm not a disaster." She jumped from the bed, walked into the bathroom, where she found tissues. She hadn't known what she would feel when she actually saw him. Heard his voice. But now she was very sad. There had to be a way out. She looked, for just a second, at her tired face in the mirror before rejoining him. "It's just this father stuff. If it wasn't for you I could just go on like children do and have a life."

And then, without realizing it, he was crying again. But this time the tears flowed in streams of complexity. He was happy and sorry. Yes, he had put her behind him. He had had to. How could a man suffer through the loss of a child every day? He wasn't that strong. Yes, he had, at some point, decided he wouldn't call. After he recovered his health, he was afraid even to talk to Helen.

He was embarrassed that his relationship with Helen had destroyed his ability to have a relationship with his daughter. That was what was wrong. The way men relate to children. The way men are taught to make their connection to children through women. That was what had separated them. When the love dies between mother and father, it is the father who catapults away. Anything else was a fight upstream. What else had history demanded?

Throughout the time he had been separated from Makeba, Ben had felt the sting of anonymous criticism from social workers, lawyers, the government and an assortment of other angry voices who all saw him as a criminal. But his own conscience was stronger and more merciless than all of them. He had been a father without a child. And he was ashamed.

Makeba had no tears for him. She felt his anguish. She knew her appearance would unsettle him, but she wasn't sorry. This was the best thing she'd ever done. Even sitting there as she was now, back on the bed, watching him try to keep from completely collapsing, she felt lighter than she could remember. She fondled Ka's remaining strands of fur. Ben pulled his chair close to the bed.

When they'd reached the hotel, Ben had ordered food. She had eaten the hamburger and fries and apple pie à la mode while he read her journal. Occasionally he would hold his head up and look at her. More than once he said, "I love you. I've missed you so much." At those times she'd avert her eyes. Inside she smiled. This was what she needed. What she had wanted for so long. But she wasn't ready to do anything but sit there.

Makeba's nervousness was gone. She had traveled the distance. Had done the thing she set out to do. She felt strong. Able for the first time to think clearly. Her emotions, buried in the journal, in her life, had receded. She felt calm for the first time since he had gone.

After Ben was finished reading, he leaned forward and hugged his daughter. She was stiff in his arms. But he didn't care. She was in his arms.

"What can I say? What can I say to you?"

Makeba looked at her father. She was still getting used to being with him. "I don't know. Maybe nothing right now. We have to start over. But I can't do that right now. I just wanted to see you." She reached into her bag and took out a sheet of paper she had written her telephone number on. "Here is my phone number." She handed him the piece of paper.

Ben was dumbfounded. He wanted Makeba to drop all of her coldness, her aloofness. He wanted her to open her arms wide and accept him back into her life. But he watched as she got up from the bed and put on her coat. He watched her moving deliberately, gracefully. She came back to him and hugged him lightly.

When she reached the door, she turned around and again reached into her black bag. This time she pulled out a stack of pictures held together by a rubber band. "Every year I took a picture of myself for you. So you could see how I grew up. I didn't know if I'd ever give them to you, but I guess now is as good a time as any."

Ben saw the flash of brown on the Polaroid squares. In her hand was missing history, formed images of his imagination over the years. Makeba fondled the pictures, fully aware of the moment. And then she gently tossed them on the bed. "Maybe we can have breakfast tomorrow morning. I'll call you."

Ben watched the flight of the pictures, picking out her little face as it hit the pink bedspread. She was with him now and she would always be there.

He thought she'd simply walk out. But instead of opening the door to leave, she smiled at him and said, "I hear it's pretty cold up there in Minnesota."

"Yeah, it is. Sometimes I wonder why I'm there."

"Why *are* you there?"

"Where else is there to be?"

"I'm headed for California, I think."

"Really? Where in California?"

"San Francisco."

Ben looked at his daughter. She was beautiful. Full of tomorrows. "I've thought about living out there, but . . . I don't know, earthquakes . . ."

"You could live anywhere, couldn't you? I mean it's not like you have a job or something."

Ben chuckled. It was the first time in a long time he'd done that. A laugh caused by the smart mouth of his own daughter. "That's true."

"You could follow me for a change." Makeba didn't know what the hell she was doing. This was delicate china. Rice paper.

"You mean move out to California and live with you?"

The "with you" part brought Makeba back to reality. "I didn't say nothing about living with nobody. I just said you could live out there if you wanted."

"But you would be there too, right?"

"That's where I'm going."

"But you wouldn't want us to live together?"

"Listen, ah . . . I don't know what to call you, but I'm not looking for a father in the way you might want. I just want to feel you. Feel you, you know, like take a deep breath and not have any doubts about anything . . . you know. Like Terry McMillan talks about in *Waiting to Exhale,* I just want to breathe. So if you wanted to live in the same town with me, that might be cool. We could have dinners and get to know each other. Anyway, we can cross that bridge when we get there. Besides, I'm not making any promises about anything. *If* I call you tomorrow and *if* you're still here, we'll go from there."

"I'll wait right here until you call, sweetheart." The door closed and so did Ben's mouth. But not before Mates, once again a shadow, escaped and took position for his new vigil.

Part Two
1995

Ben was on his hands and knees applying a coat of wax on his kitchen floor when the telephone rang. He had his portable clipped to his belt. He unhooked it and pressed the talk button. It was Ramsey, calling from Philadelphia.

"I just called to wish you luck. I know this is going to be hard for you but I think it's right. I mean, it had to happen." Ben could hear in his friend's voice an appreciation for the way events were unfolding. He thought it was actually quite ironic that in the year since Ben had left Philly, Ramsey had met, married and was expecting his first child.

"I'm ready, though. I'm cleaning my apartment from top to bottom. When she gets here I don't want anything to be off, you know?"

"Yeah, I know. Delores told me to tell you to hang in there. She thinks this will be good for you."

Ben had never met Ramsey's new wife, but he knew that the news of Makeba's reentrance into his life had filtered way beyond Ramsey's household. It seemed to be quite the topic of conversation.

"You tell Delores that I don't have a choice. I have to hang in there, if you know what I mean."

"Yeah, well, I just think that you needed this. You can't walk around in this world being a father of a child you don't know. That ain't right. I been telling you this for ten years or more. I'm just glad Makeba made the first move."

And it was true. She had made the first move. How hard was it for a child to do that? If the father wasn't capable of making that contact, then what could be expected from the child?

"Yeah, so am I." Ben thought about all the years between him and Makeba. It was clear that she was still searching for a way to explain his absence. It was the main reason *she* had insisted on only talking on the telephone, even though Ben had tried tirelessly to get her to visit him or allow him to come to Philadelphia to see her. But it took nearly eleven months for her to *want* to come to him. And almost a year of daily telephone conversations before Makeba could actually trust that he was really going to be there for her.

She understood the confusion. The way in which he and Helen split. She understood that Lena, probably with Helen's implicit consent, had sabotaged any chance of Ben gaining custody of her. They had helped to push Ben into oblivion. But why oblivion? Why not just a short absence and then a reconnection? Why had it taken ten years? And then why was she the one who had to make that contact? In a way, she was asking the question: "If I am your daughter and you love me, why am I chasing you down?"

Whenever it came up in their conversations on the telephone, he would answer by saying how ashamed he was. He tried to tell her how the breakup of his marriage to her mother had happened at a time when he just wanted to get away. And the way things had exploded had made it easy. He did get away. And the longer he was away, and the greater the distance between them, the harder it had been to do anything about it. He tried to tell her how difficult it had been to *think* about calling, much less visiting. But even as he tried to say it, he realized how silly it sounded. *No one would understand this—especially Makeba.*

"Now you're going to see what you should have been experiencing all along. You better dust off your checkbook while you're cleaning your house."

Ben flinched; he was now sitting at his dining room table. He couldn't help but resent the attitude—even from a friend—that he *should* suffer because of his absence. Besides, he thought, no one could ever know how miserable he had been. "Well, I'm not thinking about money right now. That's the problem. Everybody always connects being a parent to money. I just want to get to know my daughter again. I feel like there's a lot I can teach her. Maybe she can teach me some things too."

"Yeah, right. Not about money." Ramsey chuckled. "You have to purchase the right to teach your children, brother."

"Well anyway, I'm down for whatever." Ben was trying his best to conclude this discussion.

Ramsey got the hint. "So, what time is she coming?"

"Her plane gets in at five. I'm kind of sweating bullets." Ben caught a whiff of his hands still smelling of wax. "I've been cleaning for days, it seems like. I didn't realize how filthy I really am. Listen, I'd better go. I still have a few things to do before I pick her up at the airport."

It had been over a year since Ben had last seen Makeba. He thought back to the moment she had walked out of his hotel room. He had spent the night trying not to feel too sorry for himself. The television had been on, but he only remembered lying in his bed, looking at the pictures of his daughter and crying.

It was all such a surprise. He had come to Philadelphia that day to promote his new book. He had been happy, almost delirious about the reception it had gotten. Ben had to admit to himself that he had tried to slip quietly into town, do the book signing and head back to Minneapolis. But Makeba had walked herself back into his life. Reasserted herself, like children often do. Ben had thought that night that there was no way a father could, indefinitely, forever, deny what was true. And that's what he had been doing. Denying. For nearly ten years he had buried himself, dug deep into the ground and tried to disappear. He was in Minnesota for Christ's sake.

And now so was Makeba. Ben walked up to the gate. He was about three minutes late. He saw her as soon as he passed the check-in counter. She looked up and smiled at him.

She transformed to mist. A slate-infused mist with a strong, heat-generating smile. Ben moved toward her. He opened his arms and drew in his breath, inhaling her. And she settled, nestled really, in the heart of his grasp. And this time, all the hesitancy, the stuttering, halting energy, was gone. They melted into each other. Not lovers. Father and daughter. Spirit to spirit. Suddenly the world became narrow. The lights dimmed. Everyone left, rushed out to their appointed flights, back to their cars. Somewhere. Everywhere.

And there were no public announcements. Nothing was there except them and they spoke nothing audible to each other. No admonitions. No pleas. No shame. And Ben rolled himself backwards, regressing beyond all of his sophisticated escapism and into the space where he understood completely the nature of parenthood. The solid-gold quality of stewardship. Suddenly he understood how people could sacrifice *their own lives* for those of their children. Indeed, maybe it wasn't even a sacrifice. Maybe it was a privilege. To feel like this. To feel expanded, multiplied, exponential.

"If you hadn't come soon, I was going to catch the next flight out of here," Makeba lightly whispered. Her face rested in the curve of his shoulder so he heard only the suppressed giggle.

"Do you think I'll ever be on time for anything? Believe me, I was racing to get here as fast as I could."

"Don't worry about it. I was just kidding." Makeba now stepped back, allowing Ben to see her. Her hair had been straightened and curled. It turned up and under her chin from the sides.

"Well, anyway you're here. At least I don't have to talk to you on the telephone for a while." Ben grabbed her bag and pointed her toward the baggage claim area. Now there were people around them again. Moving walkways with people gliding by. But Ben and his daughter walked on solid ground. Their movement was much slower, more deliberate than everyone else's.

"Oh, so you don't like talking to me on the phone, huh?" Ben sometimes forgot how sarcastic and wry Makeba could be. Over the past year they had talked on the telephone nearly every day, sometimes more than once.

"You know I love talking to you. But my phone bill . . ."

Makeba burst into laughter. "Your phone bill must be as high as your car payment or your rent."

"That's what I'm saying. It's definitely cheaper to have you here."

"Now there's a welcome I didn't expect."

"You know what I'm talking about." Ben smiled. And she smiled.

"This way I know what I'm worth to you." Makeba flipped her head back to show even more teeth. "So let's see now, how much am I really worth? The phone bill has to be at least two hundred a month and that's for twelve months. Hmmmm. And the plane ticket cost three hundred and fifty. Yeah, now we're talking. And that's not including any gifts I might happen to get while I'm here."

Ben laughed out loud. It wasn't a nervous laugh. He was bounding. They were moving through the airport. It wasn't that he had money. Actually, he didn't. Having one book that did moderately well barely took care of the basics. The difference was, Makeba was now in that category. Her emotional needs—because that's all he could really attend to now—were of central importance to him now.

"The phone bill is more like three-fifty a month if you want to know the God's honest truth."

"Good."

He laughed again. "Is it that you *like* spending my money?"

"Your money? I thought you were supposed to be my father."

"Not supposed to be, Makeba. I *am* your father. The guy that married your mother is *supposed* to be your father. But, for good or for bad, I really am."

Makeba fell instantly silent. Ben knew he had brushed past the safe zone. But in the year they had been talking, he had had to stifle his resentment, his shame at having his place filled by someone else. She had had a rough life, and yet, there was a man in her house who performed the function of father. And she loved him. Sometimes she would call Ben when she was upset with her stepfather and Ben would feel stronger, keener as he silently listened to her complain. But if he ever contributed, was outraged or joined her anger, she would immediately turn on him. It presented a dilemma for him. On some level he had great respect for this man. On the other, as he became privy to the way he had raised Makeba, he was saddened. Angered. How dare someone undermine the self-esteem of another person! Of someone you claim to love *like* a daughter.

They were now at his car, a red '89 Jetta. "You know, one of the things I've been thinking about is what makes a father. I mean, you say you're my father. I know you are on some level. I mean I do remember you. I remember a lot about the things that we did. But like I said in my journal, it's all unclear. But anyway, the thing that bugs me is, how important is biology? I mean . . . you know . . . I don't really know you. I call somebody else 'Dad.' "

There it was. Ben felt his gut drop. He became the windshield. The steering wheel. The tires. The axle. He was rolling down I-35W toward his house. He was everything in motion except himself.

She continued. "Don't get me wrong. Even though I don't know why, I know that I love you. There *is* something genuine in you that is me. I know we're a lot alike. You're always disorganized and confused. You have a hard time making decisions. You're a dreamer. We are a lot alike. I know that you are my father. But my dad . . . ah . . . my daddy has been there for me. He's taken pretty good care of me. I know he's a pain, but he's been there."

"I know." What else could he say? She wasn't trying to be mean. She was just saying what was true. And then they were downtown. And then into his garage. Now he was taking her bags out of the trunk. And he couldn't stop thinking, wondering. Where were they going? There was nothing new in what she was saying. She said the same things periodically on the telephone. But she was with him now. And he realized that the scar she carried was just that: a scar. It would not go away with a telephone call—not even a hundred telephone calls. It was a scar. The mark of Mates perhaps. No. No. He couldn't call Mates into this again. He was a shadow now and even when he was real, he was only guilt. And guilt could be erased through action. And he was acting. And maybe even scars over time could be healed. Yes. Yes. That's right. Some scars do go away. There is that possibility. Sometimes when you hurt yourself and you look at the results, you say, "That's a nasty scar," and you think it's going to be like that forever. But then, ten years later, you're lying in bed with someone and they touch you on that spot and you look and you realize only you can see it. Only you know it was once a nasty scar. But. But. You really never forget it. Even though no one else can see it. You still know it was there.

And then just as he was bending down to grab her suitcase, a Samsonite number with fabric on the sides like a carpetbag, she touched him on the arm. He turned around. The top of her head came just to the level of his eyes, so he had to look down. She extended her hand. He took it. "I forgive you. I want you to know that. I don't know why. People tell me I'm stupid. But I forgive you."

And even though he knew her well enough—or rather he knew himself well enough—to know that if she was like him, that statement was an intention, a desire. She *wanted* to forgive him. She had never said that before. She had to say it before it could become a possibility. And even though he understood that, he accepted her intention, her desire, as absolute joy. As redemption.

And then they were outside. In the park. Walking. Hand in hand. And the weather was nonexistent. And there were no people, only things to do. Only places to see. Restaurants to eat in. And there were birds there. And they sang. And the waning sun waited while they walked, thrilled to be late for the setting. And the moon looked on, anxiously awaiting its turn to christen.

And eventually the moon did present itself. Nearly full. Contented. And they talked about books she'd read and Geri and Lena and Helen and Hannibal, whom Makeba barely remembered, and Ramsey, whom she remembered well.

It was now nearly midnight of the first day Ben had breathed clearly in years. He remembered Makeba mentioned that thing about wanting to breathe freely. Without hesitation. Without the threat of Mates. Without shame. Just breathe like anyone would who was in the process of making amends. His mind was so clear now that he felt disconnected from everything else in his life. This night, as they sat on his couch in his apartment, it was as if it was a first date in the

1800s where you would linger as long as possible in the parlor. Hoping.

And in a way he *was* hoping. Hoping that this was truly a beginning. That they would bond in the most perfect of ways. That he might tell her a bedtime story and she might slowly slip into the folds of sleep and he might kiss her gently on the cheek, stand back and admire his Makeba as he had once done.

That was the thing. Sitting next to her now or across from her at the restaurant, he was struck by the complexity of his own memory. He looked at her. He saw the frayed jeans. The thick shoes. The fatigue-green T-shirt. Her softly blemished face. The glow of a young woman. A smart, alert young woman. He saw all these things with his eyes but in his mind she was still nine or ten. Still a gangly, precious little child. Or she was two and he was teasing her. Holding out a ball, offering it to her. Waiting until she reached for it, only to pull it away. Only to entice her into the same game again. Suddenly he was remembering things he had not been able to remember before. No matter how hard he had tried to tell the story about their separation, there was always so much information that was lost. Gone. He couldn't remember it. He couldn't make it up. He had to be here at this moment thinking it.

Oh, how wonderful it was to return home. That was what he thought. "I'm really glad you did what you did. You know that, don't you?"

"Yes. I know." Makeba was tired. She had been completely enswirled in the vague familiarity of the smell of the man who sat next to her. The man who truly was her father. And her journey to Minnesota had been harder than riding the train into the city that fateful day. She had hated explaining to her mother and stepfather that she had to do this. They reminded her over and over that Ben hadn't really lifted a finger to find her. That she was the one who was making all the effort. And this was true. But it was her life that she was trying to save. "Somebody had to get you straight." She yawned. "I think I'm going to bed."

"Do you like your room?"

"Yes. What are we doing tomorrow?" She slowly got up.

"Mall of America sound good to you?"

"Sounds fine. Well . . . ah . . ." She still didn't know what to call him. There wasn't enough room in her head to call two people Daddy. Maybe in time. But now, there was no appropriately affectionate name. And she was beginning to feel affection. The hours on the telephone. His willingness to listen to her ramble. To push her to *do* something with her life. There were moments when he *felt* like the real daddy. But it would be too much to give right now. "I'm heading to bed. Good night." She reached down to an expectant father and kissed him on the cheek.

And then it was them eating a breakfast of pancakes which he made for her, using a recipe he had learned by watching her mother. And then they were driving. Strolling through the ridiculously large megamall. They watched the kids in Snoopy World. Shopped. Went to see a movie. And all the time, Ben knew he was doing an abnormal thing. He was trying to remove the scar. To be unblemished again. He wanted it off of him. Off of her. He was scrubbing as hard as he could. And it was easy. She was making it easy.

She was making it easy because she needed it more than he did. And suddenly Ben understood that they really were bound together. Children who are separated from their fathers and their fathers who are missing, both need the same thing. Each of them must come to see that they need each other to live a whole life. A life without doubt and shame. That what had passed for living before their reconnection was just not acceptable. It had nothing to do with money. It had to do with salvation.

When they returned from the mall, Ben was tired and retired to his bedroom to take a nap. But instead of sleeping, he lay there, fully dressed, thinking about how lucky he was. He had recovered something very valuable that had been lost. He wanted to sleep but he couldn't shut off his dancing mind. His daughter was in the next room reading. Her presence in his home had changed it instantly. He got up from the bed, opened his bedroom door and saw Makeba sitting at the dining room table. But she wasn't reading. She was writing.

Ben wanted to interrupt her. To say something more. To let her know again, how happy he was. But instead, he stepped back into the bedroom, closed the door and eased himself back onto the bed.

His mouth still moving. His mind still keen. His heart still full. He had covered the distance. Had been lost in it. They would be okay. Whether she stayed in Minneapolis or moved to San Francisco. Whether he moved to be with her or not. They could survive anything now because they had survived. He knew it as surely as he knew that Mates would always be a shadow in his life. He had faced everything. He was alive. He was a father.

And don't miss

by ALEXS D. PATE

A provocative and often hilarious tale of race and class,
murder and mayhem, in contemporary America.

A Bard hardcover available October 1999

STEPHANIE LAURENS, asidua de las listas de libros más vendidos del *New York Times*, comenzó a escribir para evadirse del árido mundo de la ciencia en que se desarrollaba su profesión. Su afición no tardó en convertirse en una brillante carrera como escritora. Sus novelas, ambientadas en el periodo de la Regencia en Inglaterra, han cautivado a miles de lectoras en todo el mundo, convirtiéndola en una de las autoras de novela romántica más queridas y populares. Vive en Melbourne, Australia, con su marido y sus dos hijos.

Títulos de Stephanie Laurens publicados en Zeta Bolsillo:

La promesa en un beso
El juramento de un libertino
Tu nombre es Escándalo
La propuesta de un canalla
Un amor secreto
Todo sobre el amor
Todo sobre la pasión
Una noche salvaje
Sombras al amanecer
La verdad sobre el amor
Pura sangre
El amante perfecto
La novia perfecta

ZETA

Título original: *The Perfect Lover*
Traducción: Ana Isabel Domínguez Palomo y María del Mar Rodríguez Barrena
1.ª edición: marzo 2011

© 2003 by Savdek Management Propietory Ltd.
© Ediciones B, S. A., 2011
   para el sello Zeta Bolsillo
   Consell de Cent, 425-427 - 08009 Barcelona (España)
   www.edicionesb.com

Printed in Spain
ISBN: 978-84-9872-484-4
Depósito legal: B. 2.054-2011

Impreso por LIBERDÚPLEX, S.L.U.
Ctra. BV 2249 Km 7,4 Polígono Torrentfondo
08791 - Sant Llorenç d'Hortons (Barcelona)

El amante perfecto

STEPHANIE LAURENS

ZETA

El árbol genealógico de la Quinta de los Cynster

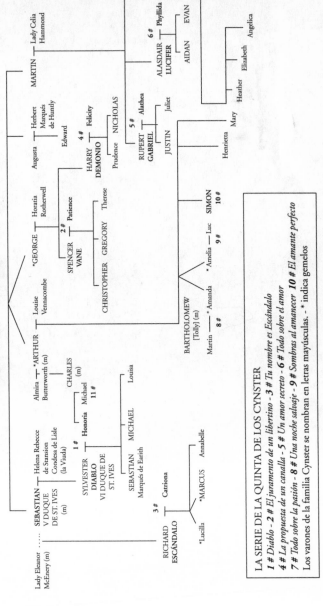

LA SERIE DE LA QUINTA DE LOS CYNSTER

1 # *Diablo* - *2 #* *El juramento de un libertino* - *3 #* *Tu nombre es Escándalo*
4 # *La propuesta de un canalla* - *5 #* *Un amor secreto* - *6 #* *Todo sobre el amor*
7 # *Todo sobre la pasión* - *8 #* *Una noche salvaje* - *9 #* *Sombras al amanecer* *10 #* *El amante perfecto*
Los varones de la familia Cynster se nombran en letras mayúsculas. - * indica gemelos

Este libro está dedicado a mis lectoras,
a las nuevas y a las de siempre,
que han seguido a los Cynster
desde su primera aparición.
Vosotras sí que sois el viento bajo mis alas.

Personajes

Simon Cynster	amigo de James Glossup
Portia Ashford	acompañante de lady Osbaldestone
Charlie Hastings	amigo de James Glossup
Lady Osbaldestone (Therese)	prima lejana de lord Netherfield
Vizconde Netherfield (Granville)	padre de Harold, lord Glossup
Harold, lord Glossup	actual dueño de Glossup Hall
Catherine, lady Glossup	esposa de Harold
Henry Glossup	primogénito de Harold y Catherine
Kitty Glossup, de soltera Archer	esposa de Henry Glossup
James Glossup	segundo hijo de Harold y Catherine
Oswald Glossup	tercer hijo de Harold y Catherine
Moreton Archer	padre de Kitty
Alfreda Archer	madre de Kitty
Swanston Archer	hermano pequeño de Kitty
Winifred Archer	hermana mayor de Kitty
Desmond Winfield	en pleno cortejo de Winifred Archer
George Buckstead	amigo íntimo de Harold Glossup

Helen Buckstead	esposa de George
Lucy Buckstead	hija del matrimonio
Lady Cynthia Calvin	viuda amiga de los Glossup
Ambrose Calvin	su hijo
Drusilla Calvin	su hija
Lady Hammond	aristócrata de renombre, emparentada con los Glossup
Annabelle Hammond	su hija mayor
Cecily Hammond	su hija menor
Arturo	el apuesto líder de un grupo de gitanos acampados en las cercanías de Glossup Hall
Dennis	gitano contratado como jardinero temporero durante los meses de verano
Blenkinsop	el mayordomo
Basil Stokes	inspector de policía enviado por Bow Street para investigar

1

Finales de julio de 1835
Ashmore, Dorset. En las cercanías de Glossup
Hall.

—¡La madre que la trajo! —exclamó Simon Cynster mientras refrenaba a sus caballos y contemplaba con los ojos entrecerrados la loma que se alzaba a espaldas de Ashmore. Había dejado el pueblo atrás hacía sólo un instante y enfilaba el frondoso camino que llevaba a Glossup Hall, a un poco más de un kilómetro de distancia.

Nada más pasar las casas, el terreno comenzaba a ascender de forma abrupta. Una mujer paseaba por el serpenteante sendero que bordeaba la loma. Desde la cima, alcanzaba a verse el Solent; y en los días despejados incluso se atisbaba la isla de Wight.

No era de extrañar ver a alguien allí arriba.

—Y tampoco es de extrañar que nadie la acompañe... —Con creciente irritación, observó cómo la delgada, ágil y elegante figura de cabello oscuro ascendía por el sendero. Una figura de largas piernas que atraería sin remisión los ojos de cualquier hombre de sangre caliente. La había reconocido al instante: Portia Ashford, la cuñada de su hermana Amelia.

Portia debía de ser una de las invitadas a la fiesta campestre de Glossup Hall; era la única propiedad importante de las cercanías desde la que podía haber llegado paseando.

De repente lo invadió la impotencia.

—¡Maldición!

Había cedido a las súplicas de su amigo James Glossup, al que conocía de toda la vida, y pensaba detenerse en la propiedad de su familia de camino a Somerset para ayudarlo a soportar el agobio de la fiesta que celebraban sus padres. Pero si Portia estaba presente, bastante agobio tendría él...

Portia llegó a la cima de la loma y se detuvo mientras alzaba uno de sus delgados brazos para apartarse la melena azabache de la espalda; acto seguido, alzó el rostro hacia el viento y contempló el paisaje antes de bajar la mano y seguir caminando hacia el mirador, de manera que acabó desapareciendo de su vista.

«No es asunto mío.»

Las palabras resonaron en su cabeza. Bien sabía Dios que ella misma se lo había dicho con bastante asiduidad, de varias formas y casi siempre con palabras mucho más tajantes... No era su hermana ni su prima; a decir verdad, no había ningún vínculo consanguíneo entre ellos.

Apretó la mandíbula, les echó un vistazo a los caballos, tensó las riendas que había aflojado...

Y soltó un juramento para sus adentros.

—¡Wilks, despiértate, hombre! —Le arrojó las riendas al lacayo, que hasta ese momento había estado echando una cabezadita a su espalda. Echó el freno y bajó del carruaje—. Sujétalas, volveré enseguida.

Se metió las manos en los bolsillos del gabán y enfiló el estrecho sendero que llevaba a la cima, donde se unía al que Portia debía de haber seguido desde Glossup Hall.

Lo único que iba a conseguir era meterse en problemas; como poco, entablarían una discusión mordaz. Claro que la idea de dejarla sola, desprotegida ante cualquier hombre que pudiera pasar por allí, era impensable. Al menos para él. Si hubiera seguido hacia Glossup Hall en el carruaje, no se habría quedado tranquilo hasta verla aparecer sana y salva en la mansión.

Y dada la inclinación que Portia mostraba por los largos paseos, habría tardado horas en regresar.

No le daría las gracias por su preocupación. Si sobrevivía sin que su ego acabara maltrecho y apaleado, podría darse por satisfecho. Portia tenía una lengua muy afilada; no había modo de escapar ileso. Sabía perfectamente cuál sería su reacción cuando lo viera aparecer; la misma que había demostrado a lo largo de la última década, desde el preciso momento en el que se dio cuenta de que era una mujer muy deseable que no tenía ni idea de la tentación que representaba y que, por tanto, necesitaba protección constante a causa de las situaciones en las que ella misma se metía de forma despreocupada.

Mientras estuviera fuera de su vista, lejos de su órbita, no era responsabilidad suya. Sin embargo, si ése no era el caso y se encontraban en algún lugar estando desprotegida, se sentía obligado a mantenerla a salvo. A esas alturas ya debería saber que era inútil luchar contra ese impulso.

De todas las mujeres que conocía, ella era indiscutiblemente la más difícil; y no por su falta de inteligencia, porque en ese aspecto también superaba a las demás. No obstante, allí estaba él... siguiendo su estela pese al recibimiento que le esperaba; eso decía mucho de su propia inteligencia...

¡Mujeres! Había pasado todo el trayecto reflexionando sobre el tema. Su tía abuela Clara había muerto hacía poco tiempo y le había dejado su casa de Somerset. La herencia había supuesto un punto de inflexión y lo había obligado a replantearse su vida y a redirigir sus pasos. Había llegado a la conclusión de que su estado tenía un origen mucho más profundo. Había comprendido por fin aquello que otorgaba sentido a las vidas de sus primos y sus cuñados.

Y era algo de lo que él carecía.

Una familia. Su propia familia, sus propios hijos. Su propia esposa. Jamás le habían parecido importantes. En esos momentos se alzaban ante él como algo vital, como algo imprescindible si quería una vida plena.

Como vástago de una familia prestigiosa y acaudalada, había llevado una existencia cómoda hasta ese momento; no obstante, ¿qué valor tenía la comodidad frente a la vacuidad que había descubierto en su vida? La incertidumbre no radicaba en su habilidad para lograr lo que se propusiera (al menos no creía que pudiera tener problemas al respecto en ningún sentido), sino en el objetivo en sí, en la necesidad, en la razón de ser. Eso era lo que le faltaba.

Le faltaban las necesidades que hacían satisfactoria la vida de un hombre como él.

La herencia de la tía abuela Clara había sido el último empujoncito. ¿Qué iba a hacer con una idílica casa solariega en el campo sino habitarla? Necesitaba buscar una esposa y ponerse manos a la obra para formar la familia que daría sentido a su vida.

Claro que no había aceptado la idea con docilidad. Durante los últimos diez años había llevado una vida ordenada y tranquila, en la cual las mujeres sólo tenían cabida en dos ámbitos muy distintos, ambos bajo su control. A sus espaldas llevaba incontables relaciones sentimentales discretas, ya que era todo un experto a la hora de manejar (seducir, disfrutar y por último descartar) a las damas casadas con las que solía enredarse. Aparte de ellas, las únicas mujeres con las que se relacionaba eran las de su familia. No iba a negar que en el ámbito familiar eran ellas las que gobernaban, pero puesto que ésa había sido la norma desde siempre, nunca se había sentido limitado ni había considerado la situación como un reto que superar. Era un mal necesario y punto.

Su participación en las inversiones de la familia y en las distracciones de los eventos de la alta sociedad, junto con sus conquistas sexuales y su asistencia a las reuniones familiares que se sucedían a lo largo del año, habían hecho que su vida estuviera agradablemente ocupada. Jamás había sentido la necesidad de asistir a los bailes y saraos que preferían las jóvenes en edad casadera.

Lo que lo dejaba en una situación insostenible, ya que

deseaba una esposa pero no podía recurrir a los métodos habituales por temor a alertar a toda la alta sociedad. Si era tan imbécil como para comenzar a acudir a esos eventos, las amantísimas madres se percatarían de inmediato de que estaba buscando esposa... y comenzaría el asedio.

Era el último Cynster soltero de su generación.

Se detuvo al llegar a la cima de la loma. El terreno descendía de forma abrupta a un lado y el sendero continuaba unos cincuenta metros más hacia la izquierda, en dirección a un mirador excavado en la pared de piedra.

Las vistas eran magníficas. Allá a lo lejos, el sol arrancaba destellos al mar y entre la calina veraniega se vislumbraba la silueta de la isla de Wight.

No era la primera vez que contemplaba el paisaje desde allí. Echó a andar hacia el mirador y hacia la mujer que lo ocupaba. Estaba de pie junto a la barandilla, mirando el mar. Por su postura e inmovilidad, supo que no se había percatado de su presencia.

Apretó los labios y siguió caminando. No tendría por qué darle explicación alguna. Llevaba diez años tratándola con el mismo afán protector que dispensaba a todas las féminas de su familia. No le cabía duda de que era la relación que los unía (Portia era hermana de su cuñado Luc) lo que dictaba sus sentimientos hacia ella a pesar de que no hubiera vínculos consanguíneos entre ellos.

En su mente, Portia Ashford era de la familia y había que protegerla. Eso, al menos, era indiscutible.

¿Qué tortuosa lógica había llevado a los dioses a decretar que una mujer necesitara de un hombre para concebir?

Portia contuvo un resoplido asqueado. Ése era el quid de la cuestión a la que se enfrentaba. Por desgracia, no tenía sentido rebelarse; los dioses lo habían dispuesto así y no había nada que pudiera hacer al respecto.

Salvo encontrar el modo de sortear el problema.

La idea aumentó su irritación, que en su mayor parte

estaba dirigida a sí misma. Nunca había deseado un marido, jamás había creído que el camino habitual que dictaba la sociedad, ese que ensalzaba las virtudes del matrimonio a pesar de sus restricciones, fuera para ella. Jamás había pensado en su futuro en esos términos.

Pero no había otra opción.

Enderezó la espalda y se enfrentó a los hechos sin más. Si quería tener hijos propios, tendría que buscar un marido.

El viento arreció, acariciándole las mejillas con su frescor y enredándole la abundante melena ondulada. La certeza de que los niños (sus propios hijos, su propia familia) eran lo que de verdad ansiaba, el verdadero reto que debía conquistar y vencer, para el que había sido educada al igual que lo había sido su madre, se había alzado ante ella con la misma delicadeza que la brisa. Durante los últimos cinco años había trabajado con sus hermanas, Penélope y Anne, en un orfanato de Londres. Se había embarcado en el proyecto con su habitual entusiasmo, convencida de que sus ideales eran correctos y satisfactorios, pero había acabado por descubrir que su propio destino yacía en una dirección hacia la que nunca se le había ocurrido mirar.

Por eso necesitaba un marido.

Dado su apellido, su estatus familiar y social, y su dote, sortear semejante impedimento sería fácil, aun cuando ya tuviera veinticuatro años. Claro que no era tan tonta como para creer que le valdría cualquier hombre. Teniendo en cuenta su carácter, su temperamento y su enérgica independencia, era imperativo que eligiera con sumo cuidado.

Arrugó la nariz sin apartar la mirada del horizonte. Jamás había imaginado que llegaría ese momento, que acabaría por desear un marido. Puesto que su hermano no tenía prisa alguna por que se casaran, tanto ella como sus hermanas habían disfrutado de la posibilidad de elegir sus propios caminos. El suyo la había excluido de los salones de baile, de Almack's y de ese tipo de acontecimientos sociales donde las jóvenes de la alta sociedad buscaban esposo.

Aprender a buscar un marido siempre le había parecido una tarea insignificante; una empresa muy inferior a los sustanciosos retos que su intelecto le demandaba...

Los recuerdos de esa pasada arrogancia, del desdén con el que había despreciado un sinfín de oportunidades para aprender el modo de seleccionar un marido y de engatusarlo, no hicieron más que avivar su irritación. Era exasperante descubrir que su intelecto, cuya superioridad nadie cuestionaba, no hubiera previsto la situación en la que se encontraba.

La puñetera verdad era que podía recitar a Homero y a Virgilio al pie de la letra, pero no tenía ni la menor idea de cómo conseguir un marido.

Mucho menos de cómo conseguir al adecuado.

Enfocó la vista para contemplar el distante mar, los reflejos del sol sobre las olas, unas olas que cambiaban constantemente de dirección al compás del viento. Igual que lo había hecho ella durante el último mes. Algo tan poco habitual, tan opuesto a su carácter (siempre había sido decidida y jamás se había mostrado tímida o débil) que le ponía los nervios de punta. Su forma de ser quería... No, le exigía que tomara una decisión, que fijara un objetivo sólido, que trazara un plan de acción. Las emociones, una parte de sí misma a la que apenas prestaba atención, le dictaban que no se mostrara tan segura. Que no se lanzara de cabeza a ese nuevo proyecto con el ímpetu habitual.

Había revisado sus opciones *ad infinitum;* no le quedaba nada más por analizar. Había acudido al mirador con la intención de aprovechar las escasas horas que le quedaban antes de la llegada de los restantes invitados y del comienzo de la fiesta campestre en sí para formular un plan.

Apretó los labios y entrecerró los ojos aún mirando hacia el horizonte, consciente de la reticencia que pugnaba por hacerse oír, que la instaba a retroceder. Era una sensación enervante, pero tan instintiva y poderosa que se vio obligada a luchar contra ella para continuar... No iba a marcharse sin haberse hecho una firme promesa.

Se aferró a la barandilla, alzó la barbilla y declaró con una voz firme:

—Utilizaré las oportunidades que la fiesta me brinde para aprender todo lo posible y elegir de una vez y para siempre. —Descontenta con semejante promesa porque la consideraba demasiado tibia, añadió con más decisión—: Juro que tomaré en consideración a todo invitado cuya edad y posición social sean las adecuadas.

Ahí estaba. ¡Por fin! Había dado voz al siguiente paso de su plan. Lo había convertido en un voto solemne. Como siempre que tomaba una decisión, sintió que la invadía la euforia...

—Vaya, vaya, se te ve muy animada, si me permites decírtelo. Aunque ¿para qué necesitas tener en cuenta la edad y la posición social?

Se giró con un jadeo de sorpresa. Por un instante se le nubló la mente. No a causa del miedo. A pesar de las sombras que rodeaban al recién llegado y de la brillante luz del sol que tenía a su espalda, había reconocido su voz y sabía muy bien a quién pertenecían esos anchos hombros que bloqueaban el arco de entrada.

Pero, ¿qué diantres estaba haciendo Simon allí?

Sus ojos azules la miraron con más intensidad. Una intensidad que era demasiado directa como para tacharla de educada.

—¿Se puede saber qué es lo que tienes que considerar? Por regla general, sólo tardas dos segundos en tomar una decisión.

La calma, la seguridad en sí misma..., la temeridad..., regresaron al punto. Entrecerró los ojos.

—Eso no es de tu incumbencia.

Simon se movió con deliberada lentitud y en tres zancadas se puso junto a la barandilla. Portia enarboló sus defensas. Sintió que la tensión se apoderaba de los músculos de su espalda al tiempo que algo le oprimía el pecho, como si reaccionara a su presencia. Lo conocía muy bien y, sin embargo, allí a solas, rodeados por el silencio del campo y del cielo, le pareció más corpulento, más poderoso.

Más peligroso en un sentido que no atinaba a comprender.

Se detuvo a dos pasos de ella y señaló el paisaje con la mano.

—Parecías estar declarando tus intenciones al mundo.

Clavó la vista en ella. A sus ojos asomaba una nota burlona por haberla pillado en mitad de su voto, junto con una expresión alerta y cierto grado de desaprobación.

No obstante, sus facciones siguieron impasibles.

—Supongo que sería demasiado esperar que tuvieras a un lacayo o a un mozo de cuadras esperando por aquí cerca, ¿verdad?

No estaba dispuesta a discutir semejante tema, y mucho menos con él. Inclinó la cabeza con rigidez a modo de saludo antes de girarla para seguir contemplando el paisaje.

—Buenas tardes. Las vistas son magníficas. —Hizo una breve pausa—. No sabía que fueras un admirador de la naturaleza.

Sintió que contemplaba su perfil antes de desviar la vista hacia el paisaje.

—Por supuesto. —Se metió las manos en los bolsillos y pareció relajarse—. Hay ciertas creaciones de la naturaleza que venero con adicción.

No le costó mucho adivinar a lo que se refería. En el pasado, le habría replicado con un comentario mordaz... En ese momento, lo único que pasaba por su mente eran las palabras de su voto.

—Has venido a la fiesta de los Glossup.

No era una pregunta, y él contestó con un elegante encogimiento de hombros.

—¿Para qué si no?

Se giró hacia ella en el mismo instante que soltaba la barandilla. Sus miradas se encontraron; había escuchado su voto y era imposible que olvidara...

De repente, estuvo segura de que debía poner más distancia entre ellos.

—He venido en busca de un poco de soledad —le informó sucintamente—. Ahora que estás aquí, me marcho.

Se giró hacia la salida, pero él le bloqueaba el paso. Con el pulso acelerado, lo miró a la cara.

A tiempo de ver cómo sus facciones se endurecían y de percibir cómo se mordía la lengua para no replicar. Cuando la miró a los ojos, sintió su contención de un modo casi palpable. Con una serenidad tan deliberada que resultaba amenazadora de por sí, se hizo a un lado y le indicó con un gesto que lo precediera.

—Como desees.

Todos sus sentidos siguieron pendientes de él mientras pasaba a su lado. Sintió un hormigueo en la piel, como si su proximidad fuera un peligro potencial y muy real. Una vez que lo dejó atrás, pasó bajo el arco de entrada con la cabeza bien alta y enfiló el sendero con una fingida calma.

Simon tensó la mandíbula y reprimió el impulso de detenerla, de extender el brazo y obligarla a darse la vuelta... aunque no estaba seguro de para qué. Eso, se recordó, era lo que había estado buscando: que regresara con paso arrogante a Glossup Hall.

Inspiró hondo, retuvo el aire y se dispuso a salir de nuevo a la luz del sol para seguirla camino abajo.

Cuanto antes regresara a la civilización y a la seguridad que ésta representaba, antes acabaría su viaje. Había hecho el trayecto desde Londres sin detenerse y estaba sediento. Una jarra de cerveza no le iría nada mal.

Dado que sus pasos eran mucho más largos, podría adelantarla en un momento. En cambio, prefirió seguirla sin prisas, disfrutando así del paisaje... La moda del momento, que dictaba que las cinturas de los vestidos coincidieran con la cintura natural de la mujer, le sentaba de maravilla ya que resaltaba su esbelta silueta, sus delicadas curvas y sus larguísimas piernas. El azul violáceo del ligero vestido de paseo que llevaba acentuaba el impactante contraste entre su cabello negro, sus ojos azul cobalto y esa piel tan pálida que casi parecía translúcida. Era más alta que la media femenina. Su frente le llegaría a la barbilla... si alguna vez se acercaran tanto.

La idea de que algo así sucediera lo hizo contener una carcajada.

Una vez que llegaron a la cima de la loma, Portia la traspuso, y sólo entonces descubrió que la estaba siguiendo. Le lanzó una mirada letal por encima del hombro antes de pararse y darse media vuelta para enfrentarlo.

Cuando Simon se detuvo frente a ella, le observó con los ojos entrecerrados y echando chispas.

—No vas a seguirme de vuelta a la mansión.

Ni siquiera tuvo que preguntarle lo que estaba haciendo. Ambos lo sabían. La última vez que se vieron fue en Navidad, siete meses antes, pero apenas hablaron ya que estaban rodeados por la horda de sus familiares. En aquel entonces no había tenido la oportunidad de sacarla de quicio, ocupación que ejercía desde que ella cumpliera los catorce años, y a la que se entregaba en cuerpo y alma cada vez que se encontraban.

Clavó la mirada en ella. Algo relampagueó en las profundidades de ese azul engañosamente delicado... ¿Genio? ¿Determinación? Acto seguido, apretó los labios y pasó a su lado con la agilidad y la elegancia que lo caracterizaban, muy inquietantes en un hombre tan corpulento. Echó a andar sendero abajo.

Se dio media vuelta para observarlo. Él no se alejó demasiado, sino que se detuvo justo al pasar la bifurcación desde la que partía el camino que llevaba al pueblo.

En ese momento, se giró para enfrentar su mirada.

—Tienes razón. No voy a hacerlo. —Señaló el camino con la mano.

Ella miró en esa dirección. Había un tílburi..., el de Simon, allí abajo.

—Su carruaje la espera, señora.

Alzó la vista para mirarlo a los ojos. Con cara de pocos amigos. Estaba bloqueando el sendero hacia Glossup Hall de forma deliberada.

—Tenía la intención de regresar dando un paseo.

Sus ojos azules siguieron clavados en ella.

—Cambia de opinión.

El tono de su voz, cargado de una arrogancia muy masculina y un desafío que resultaba desconocido en él, le provocó un escalofrío. Su postura no era abiertamente hostil, pero sabía que podría detenerla, que lo haría si intentaba sortearlo.

Su temperamento, una obstinación salvaje que afloraba ante cualquier táctica intimidatoria y más aún si procedía de él, estalló; aunque en esa ocasión llegó acompañado de una serie de emociones poderosas de lo más desconcertantes. Se quedó inmóvil, enzarzada en la silenciosa batalla que se libraba entre ellos; enzarzada en la conocida lucha por la supremacía, pero...

Había algo distinto.

En él.

Y en ella.

¿Sería por la edad? ¿Cuánto tiempo había pasado desde la última vez que libraron una batalla de voluntades semejante? ¿Tres años? ¿Más? De todas formas, la liza había cambiado. La lucha ya no era la misma. Algo fundamental había cambiado. Presentía en él una actitud depredadora mucho más flagrante, más agresiva; una fortaleza acerada bajo su elegancia, como si su máscara se estuviera resquebrajando con los años.

Siempre había sabido lo que Simon era en realidad.

El voto que había hecho poco antes resonó en su cabeza. Intentó con todas sus fuerzas no dejarse distraer; aun así, escuchó esa vocecilla que la llamaba..., reconoció el desafío implícito.

No pudo resistirse.

Alzó la cabeza y echó a andar con la misma determinación que él había demostrado.

La expresión alerta que había asomado a los ojos de Simon se hizo más evidente, hasta que en un momento dado se concentró por completo en ella. Sintió otro escalofrío en la espalda. Se detuvo delante de él y enfrentó su mirada.

¿Qué verían esos ojos azules? A esa distancia, mientras intentaba descubrir qué ocultaba tras sus defensas, descubrió que le era imposible hacerlo. Algo extraño, porque jamás habían hecho esfuerzo alguno por ocultar su mutuo desinterés. ¿Qué estaba ocultando Simon? ¿Cuál era la fuente de esa velada amenaza que irradiaba?

Para su sorpresa, quiso saberlo.

Respiró hondo de forma deliberada y replicó con voz serena:

—Muy bien.

La sorpresa se reflejó en los ojos de Simon, aunque no tardó en ser reemplazada por un brillo suspicaz. Ella dio media vuelta y, ocultando una sonrisa, bajó la vista al suelo mientras enfilaba el camino que descendía hasta el pueblo. Para que él no creyera ni por un instante que había vencido, añadió con frialdad:

—Resulta que me hace daño un zapato.

Sólo había dado un paso más cuando lo sintió acercarse, mucho más rápido de lo normal.

Sus sentidos se pusieron en alerta. Aminoró el paso, insegura..., y él ni siquiera se detuvo. Se agachó y la cogió en brazos.

—¿¡Qué...!? —Simon siguió caminando al tiempo que la sujetaba con más firmeza. La llevaba como si no pesara más que una pluma. La sorpresa la había dejado sin respiración y le había nublado el sentido común. Le costó un enorme esfuerzo tomar aire—. ¿Qué crees que estás haciendo? —La perplejidad que sentía tiñó cada una de sus palabras.

Simon jamás había mostrado el menor indicio de reaccionar físicamente a sus pullas.

Se sentía... ¿Cómo? ¿Aturdida? ¿O...?

Hizo caso omiso de la confusión y enfrentó su mirada cuando él la miró de reojo.

—Te hace daño el zapato; no podemos permitir que tu delicado piececito sufra innecesariamente.

Su voz fue suave y su semblante, inocente; hasta la expresión que asomaba a sus ojos podría tacharse de sincera.

Portia parpadeó. Ambos miraron al frente. Consideró la posibilidad de protestar... y la descartó al instante. Él era capaz de prolongar la discusión hasta que llegaran al tílburi.

En cuanto a la posibilidad de forcejear para zafarse de su abrazo, era muy consciente (más de lo que debería) de que físicamente era mucho más débil que él. Los brazos que la sujetaban eran tan duros como el acero; no perdió el paso en ningún momento y siguió caminando con seguridad, dejando bien clara su fuerza. La mano que la aferraba por el muslo, justo por encima de la rodilla (decentemente cubierta por las faldas de su vestido), se cerraba en torno a ella como si fuera una garra. Estaba atrapada por la amplitud de su pecho y por la fuerza que irradiaban sus músculos. Jamás había considerado su fuerza masculina como algo que necesitara sopesar ni sobre lo que debiera reflexionar siquiera; pero si Simon estaba dispuesto a introducir el contacto físico en su ecuación, no le quedaría más remedido que reconsiderar el tema.

Y no sólo los aspectos básicos de esa demostración de fuerza.

Estar tan cerca de él, atrapada entre sus brazos, le provocaba... una especie de mareo, entre otras cosas.

Simon aminoró el paso y ella volvió a prestar atención a sus alrededores.

Con una floritura, la dejó en el asiento del tílburi.

Sobresaltada, se aferró al borde del vehículo y la fuerza de la costumbre le hizo retirar las faldas para que él pudiera sentarse a su lado; en ese instante, se percató de la mirada igualmente perpleja de Wilks, el lacayo.

—Esto... Buenas tarde, señorita Portia —la saludó el hombre al tiempo que inclinaba la cabeza y le tendía las riendas a su señor.

Sin duda, había presenciado el espectáculo completo y estaría esperando que ella estallara o al menos que hiciera algún comentario cortante.

Y no era el único.

Sonrió con serenidad antes de devolverle el saludo.

—Buenas tardes, Wilks.

El lacayo parpadeó, asintió con recelo y se apresuró a ocupar su lugar.

Simon la miró de soslayo mientras tomaba asiento a su lado. Como si esperara un mordisco... o al menos un gruñido.

No se tragaría una sonrisa dulce, de modo que miró al frente, compuesta y tranquila, como si hubiera sido idea suya acompañarlo en el tílburi. La mirada recelosa de Simon bien valió todo el esfuerzo que le estaba costando esa alegre muestra de sumisión.

El vehículo se sacudió antes de ponerse en marcha. En cuanto la pareja de bayos se adaptó al ritmo que Simon impuso, le preguntó:

—¿Cómo están tus padres?

Hubo un silencio antes de que él le contestara.

Asintió con la cabeza y se lanzó a hacerle un resumen de la salud, el paradero y los últimos intereses de todos los miembros de su familia, a la que él conocía al completo. Como si se lo hubiera preguntado, prosiguió:

—He venido con lady O. —Durante años, ése había sido el diminutivo que habían utilizado para referirse a lady Osbaldestone, una pariente lejana de los Cynster y amiga íntima de su familia. Una arpía entrada en años que tenía aterrorizada a la mitad de la alta sociedad—. Ha pasado unas cuantas semanas en Calverton Chase y después tenía planeado pasar una temporada aquí. ¿Sabías que es una vieja amiga de lord Netherfield? —El vizconde Netherfield era el padre de lord Glossup y en esos momentos estaba de visita en Glossup Hall.

Simon había fruncido el ceño.

—No.

Portia esbozó una sonrisa sincera; le tenía mucho cariño a lady O; pero Simon, al igual que la mayoría de los caballeros de su calaña, encontraba la perspicacia de la dama un tanto aterradora.

—Luc insistió en que no debía cruzar medio condado sola, así que me ofrecí a acompañarla. Hasta ahora sólo han llegado... —Prosiguió con la cháchara, poniéndolo al día de aquellos que ya se alojaban en la mansión y de los que estaban por llegar, tal y como haría cualquier dama bien educada.

El recelo con el que la miraba se agudizó a pasos agigantados.

En ese instante, las puertas de acceso a Glossup Hall les dieron la bienvenida. Simon hizo girar a los bayos y los azuzó para que enfilaran el camino.

La enorme mansión había sido construida en el periodo isabelino. La típica fachada de ladrillo rojo estaba orientada al sur y el edificio constaba de tres plantas. Las alas añadidas al este y al oeste estaban dispuestas en perpendicular a la fachada y se extendían hacia atrás. El ala central, en paralelo a las anteriores, le confería a la mansión la forma de una E y albergaba el salón de baile y el invernadero. A medida que se acercaban, distinguieron los reflejos del sol sobre las hileras de ventanas emplomadas y sobre las altas chimeneas con sus recargados remates.

Simon ya estaba completamente desconcertado cuando refrenó a los bayos al llegar al patio principal frente a la fachada. Y eso era algo extraño en él. Dentro de los límites de la alta sociedad, no había nada que lograra descolocarlo.

Salvo Portia.

Si hubiera protestado y hubiera esgrimido esa lengua tan afilada como era habitual en ella, todo habría sido normal. No habría disfrutado del encuentro, pero tampoco habría sentido esa repentina desorientación.

Aunque se devanara los sesos, no recordaba ni una ocasión en la que se hubiera comportado con esa... delicadeza tan femenina. Ésa fue la única definición que se le ocurrió para describir su actitud. Por lo general, Portia hacía gala de una armadura llena de púas. Sin embargo, ese día parecía haber dejado escudos y púas a un lado.

El resultado era...

Detuvo los caballos, echó el freno y le arrojó las riendas a Wilks antes de apearse.

Ella aguardaba a que rodeara el tílburi y la ayudara a bajar. La miró un instante, esperando que saltara sin ayuda ninguna con sus acostumbrados modales que proclamaban su independencia y autosuficiencia. En cambio, cuando le ofreció la mano, la aceptó y dejó que la ayudara a descender con una elegancia sorprendente.

Cuando la soltó, ella alzó la vista y sonrió.

—Gracias. —Su sonrisa se ensanchó y siguió mirándolo a los ojos—. Tenías razón. Mi pie está mucho mejor de lo que lo habría estado de haber regresado caminando.

Con una expresión de inefable dulzura, inclinó la cabeza y dio media vuelta. El azul cobalto de sus ojos era tan oscuro que no supo si el brillo que había visto en sus profundidades era real o sólo un mero efecto de la luz.

Se quedó de pie en el patio principal, observándola, mientras los mozos de cuadra y los lacayos iban de un lado a otro, ocupados con sus menesteres. Sin mirar atrás ni una sola vez, Portia desapareció entre las sombras que reinaban al otro lado de la puerta de entrada.

El crujido de la gravilla bajo las ruedas del tílburi y los cascos de sus caballos, que los mozos llevaban a los establos, lo sacó del ensimismamiento. Con apariencia impasible, aunque en su fuero interno estaba que trinaba, echó a andar hacia la puerta de Glossup Hall. Y la siguió al interior.

—¡Simon! ¡Excelente! —James Glossup cerró la puerta de la biblioteca y se acercó a él con una enorme sonrisa.

Una vez que hubo dejado el gabán en las manos del mayordomo, Simon se giró para saludar a su amigo.

El alivio inundó la mirada de James mientras le estrechaba la mano.

—Has llegado justo a tiempo para cerrar filas con Charlie y conmigo. —Hizo un gesto con la cabeza en dirección al salón. A través de las puertas cerradas les llegaba el inconfundible murmullo de las conversaciones de los invitados, enzarzados en la típica charla social—. Charlie ha ido de avanzadilla.

Blenkinsop, el mayordomo, se detuvo junto a James.

—Haré que lleven el equipaje del señor Cynster a su habitación habitual, señor.

James asintió con la cabeza.

—Gracias, Blenkinsop. Nos reuniremos con los invitados. No es necesario que nos anuncies.

El mayordomo, un antiguo sargento mayor, alto y un tanto orondo si bien jamás abandonaba la rigidez de su porte, hizo una reverencia antes de alejarse. James lo miró y le hizo un gesto hacia el salón.

—Vamos... ¡Al ataque!

Entraron juntos y se detuvieron a la par para cerrar las dos hojas de la puerta. Simon enfrentó la mirada de James Glossup cuando escuchó el chasquido del pestillo. Desde el otro lado de la estancia, Portia sospechaba que ambos eran conscientes de la imagen que transmitían al entrar hombro con hombro.

Dos lobos de la alta sociedad. Nadie que tuviera ojos en la cara los confundiría con otra cosa; y el efecto era abrumador cuando estaban juntos. Altos, atléticos, musculosos, de hombros anchos y largas extremidades, pero sin resultar excesivamente corpulentos. Mientras que el cabello castaño de James se rizaba ligeramente, el de Simon, que una vez fue rubio pero que se había oscurecido con la edad, caía en sedosas ondas entre las que se adivinaba algún que otro mechón dorado. Simon tenía los ojos azules y la piel algo más clara. James tenía unos ojos castaños de mirada intensa a los que sabía sacar todo su partido.

Ambos iban ataviados a la última moda; el corte impecable de sus chaquetas, ajustadas como un par de guantes, llevaba el sello de uno de los sastres más cotizados entre la alta sociedad. Sus corbatas eran de un blanco impoluto y estaban anudadas con precisión; los chalecos por sí solos eran un estudio de elegancia.

Destilaban la típica exquisitez propia de la nobleza. En el fondo eran hermanos..., un par de aristócratas libertinos; tal y como dejaron bien claro mientras James hacía las presentaciones.

Charlie Hastings no tardó en acercarse a ellos; y el trío quedó así completo. Era el más bajo de los tres; guapo y de cabello rubio, y no cabía la menor duda de que era de la misma calaña que sus amigos.

Portia observó al resto de los invitados, que se habían diseminado por los sofás y las sillas en pequeños grupos para tomar el té. Sólo faltaban por llegar lady Hammond y sus dos hijas, a las que se esperaba para última hora de la tarde.

James acompañó a Simon hacia el anfitrión, que no era otro que su padre, Harold, lord Glossup. Era un caballero de mediana edad y complexión fuerte, que había dado a sus invitados una calurosa bienvenida. A su lado estaba George Buckstead, un antiguo amigo, que tenía el porte recio de la nobleza rural y el mismo carácter afable de lord Glossup. El tercer miembro del grupo era Ambrose Calvin, un caballero de estampa un tanto diferente. Ambrose tenía unos treinta y cinco años y, al parecer, estaba decidido a abrirse paso en la política; de ahí, supuso Portia, su presencia en la fiesta. No tenía muy claro qué esperaba sacar Ambrose de su estancia en Glossup Hall, pero conocía muy bien a ese tipo de hombre; desde luego, tenía algo en mente.

Charlie, que ya había sido presentado anteriormente, se había quedado rezagado. Cuando James y Simon se dieron la vuelta para regresar con su amigo, descubrieron que la señorita Lucy Buckstead ya lo había acorralado. Lucy, una muchacha vivaz, alegre, bonita y de cabello oscuro, que acababa de cumplir los veinte, estuvo encantada de ofrecerle la mano a Simon, aunque sus ojos no tardaron en volar hacia el rostro de James. Con una elegante disculpa, éste alejó a Simon de la joven para proseguir con las presentaciones. Charlie se aprestó a distraer a la muchacha.

Portia se percató de la mirada que intercambiaron Simon y James antes de llegar junto al siguiente grupo. Estaba formado por la anfitriona de la fiesta y madre de James, Catherine, lady Glossup, una dama de cabello rubio y desvaídos ojos azules que aún conservaba cierto grado de retraimiento, un débil vestigio de una superioridad de la que carecía por completo. No era una mujer desagradable ni mucho menos, pero sí daba la impresión de estar un tanto desilusionada. A su lado se sentaba la señora Buckstead, Helen, una dama oronda cuya serena alegría dejaba bien claro que estaba encantada de la vida.

Ambas damas sonrieron con elegancia cuando Simon les hizo una reverencia; intercambió con ellas los saludos de rigor antes de estrechar la mano del caballero que las acompañaba. El señor Moreton Archer era un rico banquero muy influyente que se había tenido que labrar su propio camino en el mundo al ser el segundo hijo de un segundo hijo, y con un éxito más que considerable. La confianza que ese hecho le había deparado lo envolvía como una pátina y quedaba patente en su costosa ropa y en su impecable apariencia.

El señor Archer, que pertenecía a la generación de los anfitriones, era el padre de otra Catherine, a la que todos conocían como Kitty y que se había casado con Henry, el primogénito de lord Glossup. Estaba claro que, para el señor Archer, el matrimonio de su hija había sido la llave que le abriera las puertas del círculo social al que siempre quiso pertenecer.

Cuando le presentaron a Simon, el caballero compuso una expresión de intenso interés. Le habría gustado mantener una larga conversación con él, pero James lo apartó con diplomacia y continuó con el recorrido por los grupos.

El siguiente incluía a Kitty Glossup, que en algunos aspectos era la segunda anfitriona. Rubia, bajita y un tanto entrada en carnes, Kitty tenía una piel de alabastro, y unos chispeantes ojos azules; sus pequeñas manos estaban en constante movimiento y sus labios, a los que solía aplicar un poco de carmín, no paraban de hacer pucheros, de sonreír o de moverse mientras hablaba. Ser el centro de atención era su paraíso particular. Era una joven presuntuosa y frívola... De hecho, Portia llegó a la conclusión de que no tenían nada en común; aunque, en general, Kitty no se diferenciaba de muchas otras jóvenes de la alta sociedad.

Hasta ese momento, Kitty había estado charlando con lady Calvin y con el señor Desmond Winfield. Cynthia, lady Calvin, era una viuda muy bien relacionada que guiaba a sus dos hijos, Ambrose y Drusilla, con mucho tiento. Era la hija de un conde y frecuentaba los mismos círculos sociales que los Cynster y los Ashford. Le dedicó a Simon una espléndida sonrisa y le ofreció la mano.

El señor Winfield había llegado un par de horas antes; de modo que Portia aún no sabía mucho sobre él. Su apariencia externa dejaba claro que era un caballero solvente, sobrio y juicioso. Suponía que lo habían invitado los Archer y se preguntó si sería el pretendiente de la primogénita de la pareja, Winifred, que seguía soltera.

Winifred se encontraba en el siguiente grupo hacia el que James condujo a Simon. También estaba Henry Glossup, el hermano mayor de James, Alfreda Archer (la madre de Kitty y Winifred, y por tanto, suegra de Henry) y Drusilla Calvin.

Puesto que Simon era amigo de James desde hacía muchos años, había estado en Glossup Hall en numerosas ocasiones y conocía bien a Henry. Se dieron un apretón de manos como correspondía a las viejas amistades. Henry era una versión más callada de James, con unos cuantos años más y de complexión más recia. Un hombre afable sobre cuyos hombros recaía la responsabilidad del manejo de la propiedad.

Alfreda Archer lo saludó con efusividad. A pesar de que contemplaba la escena desde el otro extremo de la estancia, Portia se percató de que Simon enarbolaba sus defensas. La señora Archer llevaba la impronta de una madre casamentera; una madre que no dudaría en utilizar el matrimonio para ascender en el escalafón social. En cambio, Winifred se comportó con placidez y lo saludó con una elegante sonrisa como dictaban los buenos modales, nada más.

Drusilla apenas logró imitarla. La muchacha era de su misma edad, pero ahí acababan las similitudes entre ellas. Era tímida y apocada; además, se comportaba con una austeridad excesiva para su edad. Parecía verse a sí misma como la dama de compañía de su madre, en lugar de como su hija. Por tanto, no tenía el mínimo interés en James ni Simon... y lo dejó bien claro.

El resto de los presentes, aparte de lady Osbaldestone y de lord Netherfield con los que estaba sentada, eran Oswald Glossup, el hermano pequeño de James, y Swanston Archer, el hermano pequeño de Kitty. Ambos eran de la misma edad y similar actitud. Ataviados con un par de ridículos chalecos de rayas muy ajustados y fracs con faldones más largos de la cuenta, se comportaban como los gallos del corral y se pavoneaban de un lado a otro, manteniendo las distancias con los demás.

Simon los saludó con un gesto rígido de la cabeza y una mirada que rezumaba su desaprobación.

Y, acto seguido, se acercaron al sofá donde ellos estaban sentados, un poco apartados de los demás a fin de poder observar a su antojo y hacer comentarios sin tapujos.

Portia se puso en pie cuando se acercaron. No porque así lo dictaran las buenas maneras, sino porque aborrecía sentirse observada desde arriba, sobre todo si se trataba de dos hombres a la vez.

Lady Osbaldestone correspondió al saludo de Simon con un alegre golpe de su bastón sobre el suelo y no tardó en ponerlo en su lugar al preguntarle:

—Vamos a ver, ¿cómo está tu madre?

Curtido por una dilatada experiencia y, por tanto, consciente de que no había escapatoria posible, él le contestó con una serenidad encomiable. Lady Osbaldestone exigió un resumen acerca del estado de sus hermanas pequeñas y de su padre; mientras él satisfacía la insaciable curiosidad de la anciana, Portia intercambió una sonrisa con James y entabló una conversación con él y con su abuelo, lord Netherfield, acerca de las rutas de paseo más pintorescas de la zona.

Lady Osbaldestone acabó por fin de interrogar a Simon y éste se giró hacia lord Netherfield para saludarlo con una sonrisa y un par de comentarios que denotaban que ya se conocían previamente. Una vez cumplimentadas las presentaciones y los saludos, Simon, que estaba de pie a su lado, miró a lady Osbaldestone... y se quedó petrificado.

Portia lo notó y miró a la anciana... y también cayó bajo el mismo hechizo. La mirada de basilisco de la dama, que había aterrorizado a la alta sociedad durante más de cincuenta años, estaba clavada en ellos.

En los dos.

Aguardaron hipnotizados, sin saber qué hacer, preguntándose cuál podría ser la infracción cometida...

Las cejas de lady Osbaldestone se alzaron en un gesto aterrador.

—Vosotros dos os conocéis, ¿no es cierto?

Portia sintió que el rubor se extendía por sus mejillas. Por el rabillo del ojo, vio que Simon no había reaccionado mucho mejor. A pesar de ser muy conscientes de la presencia del otro, ninguno de los dos había recordado que debían saludarse como dictaban las buenas costumbres. Abrió la boca para contestar, pero él se adelantó.

—Me encontré con la señorita Ashford hace un rato.

De no haber estado delante de todo el mundo, le habría asestado una patada. ¡Esa fría arrogancia había logrado que sonara como si hubiera sido un encuentro clandestino! Con voz airada, procedió a explicarse:

—El señor Cynster fue tan amable de traerme en su tílburi desde el pueblo. Fui paseando hasta el mirador.

—¿De veras? —La siniestra mirada de lady Osbaldestone los mantuvo atrapados un instante antes de que asintiera y golpeara el suelo con su bastón—. ¡Entiendo!

Antes de que pudiera interpretar lo que la dama había querido decir, ésta continuó:

—Muy bien. —Señaló la taza vacía que había dejado en la mesita auxiliar—. Puedes traerme otra taza de té, Simon.

Con una diligencia comprensible dadas las circunstancias, el aludido esbozó una sonrisa encantadora, cogió el platillo y la taza y se alejó hacia la bandeja del té, situada en un carrito junto a lady Glossup. James fue requerido por su abuelo para que hiciera lo mismo. Ella aprovechó el momento y se disculpó para atravesar el salón y reunirse con Winifred Archer y Drusilla Calvin; las invitadas a las que suponía que Simon no querría ni acercarse...

Tal vez hubiera hecho el voto de considerar a todos los caballeros elegibles, pero eso no significaba que tuviera que estar al lado de dichos caballeros en cuestión.

Sobre todo si se trataba de Simon.

Sobre todo si lady Osbaldestone estaba mirando.

Simon le llevó la taza de té llena hasta el borde a lady Osbaldestone y se excusó con una florida disculpa. La vieja arpía le dio la venia con un resoplido y un gesto de la mano. Tras coger una taza de té para sí mismo, se unió a Charlie y a Lucy Buckstead, que estaban junto a las ventanas.

Charlie lo recibió con una sonrisa, aunque no detuvo su taimado parloteo ni un solo instante. Estaba decidido a conquistar a la frívola señorita Buckstead. En realidad, no albergaba ninguna intención seria hacia ella; simplemente le encantaba flirtear. Con su rubio cabello rizado, sus oscuros ojos castaños y su lento modo de hablar, tan de moda en esos días, estaba muy solicitado entre las aristócratas de buen gusto y mejor discernimiento.

Dichas damas discernían, por regla general con ejemplar rapidez, que Charlie ladraba mucho, pero mordía poco. Al menos en la mayoría de los casos. Por supuesto que se daba el gusto cuando le apetecía, sólo que no solía apetecerle muy a menudo.

Hasta la señorita Buckstead, inocente como era, parecía estar bastante cómoda a su lado, riendo y sorteando los comentarios de su amigo, que bordeaban la indecencia sin llegar a ser escandalosos.

Simon sonrió y le dio un sorbo al té. Tanto él como

Charlie sabían que estaban a salvo al lado de la señorita Buckstead. Era a James a quien le había echado el ojo.

Fingió estar pendiente de la conversación mientras observaba a la concurrencia. Para los Glossup, el propósito de la fiesta no era otro que el de estrechar lazos; con los Archer, la familia de Kitty; con los Buckstead, antiguos amigos; y con los Calvin y los Hammond, cuyas relaciones con la alta sociedad podrían serles útiles. Un ramillete de invitados normal y corriente, pero dada la presencia de Lucy Buckstead, era comprensible que James hubiera querido asegurarse la presencia de unos cuantos caballeros más.

No estaba resentido con James por hacerle perder unos días. En realidad, para eso estaban los amigos. De todos modos, se preguntaba cómo lograría matar el tiempo hasta que pudiera despedirse de James y proseguir el viaje a Somerset.

Su mirada se posó sobre el trío de damas reunidas junto al otro ventanal. Winifred Archer, Drusilla Calvin y Portia. Las dos últimas eran de la misma edad, de unos veinticuatro años, algo más jóvenes que Kitty, cuya estridente risa se alzaba por encima del murmullo de las conversaciones que el resto de los invitados mantenía en un tono más moderado.

Portia le echó un rápido vistazo a Kitty antes de volver a prestar atención a la conversación que mantenían Winifred y Drusilla.

Winifred estaba de espaldas a su hermana y no dio indicio alguno de haber escuchado la aguda carcajada. Era mayor que Portia; tal vez se aproximara a su edad, veintinueve años.

Observó el grupo que presidía Kitty y vio que Desmond Winfield echaba un vistazo en dirección a Portia. ¿O hacia Winifred? El hombre se crispó, como si deseara acercarse a ellas.

Kitty le colocó una mano en el brazo y le preguntó algo; el caballero se giró hacia ella y le contestó con voz queda.

A su lado, Charlie se echó a reír. Lucy soltó una risilla. Puesto que no tenía la menor idea de lo que habían dicho, Simon les sonrió, alzó la taza y bebió un sorbo de té.

Su mirada regresó a Portia.

Estaba bañada por un rayo de sol, que arrancaba destellos azulados a su cabello.

De forma inesperada, evocó la fragancia que desprendía su abundante cabello. Ese dulzón aroma que había resultado toda una provocación para sus sentidos mientras descendía el camino con ella en brazos. El mismo aroma que en ese momento espoleó su memoria, de modo que los restantes recuerdos acudieron en tropel: el peso de su cuerpo entre sus brazos, la tensión que se apoderó de ella, esas curvas tan femeninas... Las sensaciones que experimentara en aquel momento volvieron a apoderarse de él y lo excitaron.

Había sido muy consciente de ella como mujer. Algo que jamás se le había pasado por la cabeza. El hecho lo había dejado atónito, no tanto por el descubrimiento en sí como por el deseo que lo invadió de llevarla a algún otro lugar... A un lugar muchísimo más privado.

Y no la había confundido con otra ni mucho menos. Había sabido muy bien a quién llevaba en brazos. No había olvidado su lengua afilada ni su terrible temperamento. Sin embargo, había sentido deseos de...

Extrañado consigo mismo, miró hacia Lucy Buckstead. Si quería una esposa, ella era el modelo perfecto a tener en cuenta: dócil, de maneras agradables..., manejable. Clavó la vista en ella... pero su mente se empeñó en tomar otra dirección.

Dejó la taza y esbozó una sonrisa.

—Si me disculpáis, me gustaría asearme un poco y librarme del polvo del camino.

Tras despedirse de la pareja con una breve reverencia, le devolvió la taza a lady Glossup, le dio una excusa elocuente para retirarse y escapó.

Mientras subía las escaleras, su mente se vio invadida de nuevo por Portia, por su inesperado interludio en el sendero y por la más que inesperada actitud de Portia en respuesta. Glossup Hall lo había provisto de un paisaje que no había anticipado; tenía todo el tiempo del mundo... No había razón para no explorarlo.

Aparte de todo lo demás, el desafío de descubrir qué quería aprender de la vida una dama de refinada educación se le antojaba prácticamente irresistible.

2

—Jamás te habría tomado por un cobarde.

Las palabras, pronunciadas por una voz femenina y con una cadencia decididamente provocativa, hicieron que Portia se detuviera en seco en el descansillo de las escaleras del ala oeste. Había estado practicando al piano en la sala de música situada en esa misma ala, pero en esos momentos se dirigía al salón, donde el resto de los invitados se reuniría antes de pasar al comedor para cenar.

Había elegido las escaleras del ala oeste, unas escaleras que las invitadas a la fiesta no solían utilizar, ya que sus habitaciones se encontraban en el ala este.

—Aunque tal vez todo sea una estratagema.

Las palabras quedaron suspendidas en el aire como una caricia. Era Kitty quien hablaba.

—¡No es ninguna estratagema! —exclamó su cuñado entre dientes—. No estoy jugando a nada... ¡y jamás se me ocurriría hacerlo contigo!

Se encontraban fuera de su ángulo de visión, al final de las escaleras, pero eso no impidió que se percatara de la evidente repulsión que sentía James Glossup. Y de la sutil desesperación de su voz.

Kitty soltó una carcajada. Su incredulidad (o más bien la incredulidad de que un hombre no la deseara, sobre todo uno como James) reverberó en las escaleras.

Sin pensárselo dos veces, Portia continuó escaleras abajo con paso tranquilo y seguro.

La pareja la oyó y se volvió hacia ella. Ambos rostros reflejaron una incómoda sorpresa, aunque sólo el del hombre traslució una emoción cercana a la vergüenza. La expresión de Kitty era de absoluta irritación.

En ese momento, James Glossup la reconoció y el alivio le suavizó el semblante.

—Buenas tardes, señorita Ashford. ¿Se ha perdido?

No era así, pero Kitty lo tenía arrinconado contra la pared.

—Sí. —Se encogió de hombros para darle un toque de impotencia a su expresión—. Creí que iba por buen camino, pero... —Hizo un gesto con la mano.

Él se apresuró a apartarse de Kitty.

—Permítame... Me dirigía al salón. ¿Es allí adonde iba?

Le cogió la mano y se la puso sobre el brazo. Cuando lo miró a los ojos, vio la súplica que escondían.

—Si es tan amable... Le agradecería muchísimo su ayuda. —Esbozó una sonrisa afable antes de volverse hacia Kitty.

La dama no correspondió el gesto; se limitó a asentir con cierta sequedad.

Portia enarcó las cejas.

—¿No nos acompaña, señora Glossup?

James se tensó a su lado.

La aludida los despachó con un gesto de la mano.

—Iré enseguida. Vayan adelantándose. —Y tras esas palabras, dio media vuelta y subió las escaleras.

James se relajó y ella dejó que la condujera hacia el ala central. Lo miró al rostro y se percató de que tenía el ceño fruncido y de que estaba un poco pálido.

—¿Se encuentra bien, señor Glossup?

Él la miró y esbozó una sonrisa... de lo más encantadora.

—Llámeme James, por favor. —Y con un gesto de cabeza, añadió—: Gracias.

Se vio incapaz de contener la pregunta más obvia:

—¿Suele ser tan... molesta?

James titubeó un momento antes de contestar.

—Parece que va empeorando cada vez más.

Era evidente que el tema lo incomodaba. Portia clavó la vista al frente.

—En ese caso, tendrá que acercarse a otras damas hasta que se le pase.

La mirada del hombre la atravesó, pero no la conocía lo bastante como para saber si el comentario había sido irónico. Se dejó guiar por los pasillos de la mansión mientras se esforzaba por contener una sonrisa ante la extraña idea de que un libertino como James Glossup hubiera recurrido a ella para... Bueno, para proteger su propia virtud.

Sus miradas se encontraron al llegar al vestíbulo principal y supo que él albergaba la sospecha de que se estaba riendo, pero no estaba seguro del todo. Dado que estaban a punto de entrar en el salón, Portia miró hacia delante. Simon habría sabido la verdad.

Mientras entraban en el comedor, lo vio junto a la chimenea, charlando con Charlie y con dos alegres jovencitas, las hijas de lady Hammond, Annabelle y Cecily. Lady Hammond, una dama afable y jovial, estaba sentada en un diván con lady Osbaldestone.

Sus miradas se encontraron. James se despidió y se marchó para charlar con su padre. Ella se detuvo para saludar a lady Hammond, una amiga de su madre, antes de reunirse con el grupo de Simon.

Las muchachas supusieron una bocanada de aire fresco. Aunque eran muy inocentes, estaban como pez en el agua en ese ambiente, decididas a ser el alma (o las almas) de la fiesta. Las conocía desde hacía años, y la recibieron con su típica jovialidad.

—¡Maravilloso! ¡No sabía que estarías aquí!

—Ay, será estupendo... ¡Estoy convencida de que nos lo pasaremos en grande!

Con esas miradas resplandecientes y sus deslumbrantes sonrisas, era imposible no corresponder a su alegría. Tras intercambiar las cortesías habituales acerca de la familia y los conocidos, la conversación se centró en las actividades que tendrían lugar durante los días venideros, así como en los entretenimientos que ofrecían la propiedad y los alrededores.

—Los jardines son increíbles y tienen un sinfín de senderos. Lo leí en una guía de viajes —confesó Annabelle.

—¡Ah! Y también hay un lago... La guía decía que no era artificial, sino que se nutría de un manantial natural, y también que era muy profundo. —Cecily arrugó la nariz—. Demasiado profundo para hacer pie. ¡Quién lo iba a decir!

—Bueno —intervino Charlie—, no creo que quiera arriesgarse a caerse. Está helado... Y lo digo por experiencia.

—¡Válgame Dios! —Annabelle se giró hacia Charlie—. ¿Lo ha hecho? Me refiero a caerse al lago.

Portia captó la mirada de soslayo que Charlie le dirigió a Simon y la mueca burlona que apareció en los labios de éste; a tenor de dicha mueca, estaba claro que alguien había lanzado a Charlie al lago.

Un movimiento al otro lado del salón le llamó la atención. Kitty había entrado y estaba observando a los presentes. Henry se separó de un grupo y se acercó a ella. Le habló en voz baja con la cabeza inclinada, a todas luces para que nadie se enterase.

Kitty se tensó y alzó la cabeza. Fulminó a su marido con una mirada de ultrajado desdén antes de responderle con una breve réplica, darle la espalda y, con un mohín beligerante, alejarse a grandes pasos para charlar con el señor Calvin y su hermana.

Henry observó la marcha de su esposa. Su rostro estaba crispado, aunque logró controlar sus emociones. Sin embargo, daba la impresión de que el rechazo le había resultado doloroso.

Era evidente que las cosas no marchaban bien entre ellos.

Se concentró de nuevo en la conversación que se sucedía a su alrededor. Annabelle se giró hacia ella con una expresión ansiosa en los ojos.

—¿Lo has visitado ya?

A todas luces se había perdido algo. Miró a Simon.

Él le devolvió la mirada. Las cejas castañas se arquearon, pero accedió a echarle una mano.

—Es la primera vez que Portia visita Glossup Hall. Al igual que ustedes, todavía no ha visto nada. En cuanto al templete... Debo admitir que prefiero el mirador que hay junto al lago. Tal vez esté en un lugar demasiado recóndito para algunos, pero la tranquilidad del agua es relajante.

—Pues tenemos que ir por allí. —Cecily no dejaba de hacer planes—. Y tengo entendido que también hay un mirador por algún sitio...

—Ya he estado allí. —Portia se negó a mirar a Simon a los ojos y se concentró en aplacar la insaciable sed de información de las Hammond.

El tema los mantuvo entretenidos hasta que se anunció la cena. Una vez sentada a la larga mesa, muy consciente de su voto, se concentró en reconocer el terreno.

«Juro que tomaré en consideración a todo invitado cuya edad y posición social sean las adecuadas.»

Pero ¿a quiénes tenía que considerar? Todos los caballeros sentados a esa mesa eran, al menos en teoría, adecuados según su posición ya que de otro modo no estarían presentes. Algunos estaban casados, lo que los eliminaba sin problemas; de los restantes, a algunos los conocía mejor que a otros.

Mientras cenaban y charlaban, y ella le prestaba atención primero a una conversación y luego a otra, dejó vagar la vista por los presentes, tomando nota de todos los caballeros, de todas las posibilidades.

Su mirada se detuvo en Simon, que estaba sentado al otro lado de la mesa, dos sitios más allá. Se afanaba por conversar con Drusilla, quien parecía especialmente reservada y adusta, aunque también incómoda. Eso la desconcertó; dejando a un lado sus frecuentes discusiones, sabía que los modales de Simon eran exquisitos en extremo y que jamás haría nada indebido en un evento social. Era Drusilla quien tenía problemas para relacionarse.

Hubo un intervalo en la conversación que mantenían los invitados más próximos a ella; con la vista clavada en Simon, se fijó en los reflejos dorados de su cabello, en el modo en que sus largos y elegantes dedos se curvaban alrededor del tallo de su copa y en el rictus resignado de sus labios cuando se reclinó en su asiento al dejar a Drusilla en paz.

Llevaba observándolo demasiado tiempo y él se percató de ello.

Justo cuando miraba hacia ella, Portia bajó los ojos al plato y con mucha calma se llevó un poco de comida a los labios antes de girarse hacia el señor Buckstead, que estaba sentado a su lado.

No volvió a respirar tranquila hasta que sintió que los ojos de Simon se apartaban de ella.

No se dio cuenta de lo extraña que era su reacción hasta ese preciso instante.

«... a todo invitado cuya edad y posición social sean las adecuadas.»

Cuando llegó el momento de retirarse al salón para que los caballeros se tomaran el oporto, ya había anotado tres nombres en su lista mental. Era evidente que la fiesta campestre iba a ser todo un reto, un campo de pruebas en el que desarrollar sus habilidades para encontrar marido; ninguno de los caballeros presentes pertenecía al tipo al que le confiaría su mano, pero como especímenes con los que practicar le irían de perillas.

James Glossup y Charlie Hastings eran precisamente el tipo de caballeros a quienes debía aprender a analizar.

En cuanto a Simon... A pesar de que lo conocía desde siempre, a pesar de que llevaban irritándose el uno al otro desde hacía diez años y a pesar de que jamás lo habría incluido en su lista de no haber formulado su voto tal cual lo había formulado antes de saber que él estaría presente, poseía cualidades valiosas como posible marido que no iba a descartar.

Unas cualidades que ella tenía que aprender a examinar y evaluar.

A decir verdad, pensaba mientras entraba en el salón detrás de lady O, siendo un Cynster, las cualidades que pudiera tener Simon en lo tocante al matrimonio le servirían como rasero para medir a todos los demás caballeros.

Era una idea de lo más perturbadora.

Por suerte, los caballeros no se reunirían con ellas hasta pasado un tiempo y podría desentenderse de la idea con la charla de las Hammond y de Lucy Buckstead.

Más tarde, cuando los caballeros se reunieron con ellas y las conversaciones cambiaron a temas más generales, se encontró en un grupo con Winifred Archer y Desmond Winfield. Ambos eran muy agradables, un poco tímidos pero en absoluto inseguros; le bastó muy poco tiempo para llegar a la conclusión de que había una relación entre ellos... o al menos que estaban intentándolo. La actitud de Winifred era incierta, pero la de Desmond estaba clara a pesar de sus exquisitos modales; sólo tenía ojos para ella.

El lápiz imaginario que tenía en la cabeza estaba a punto de tachar el nombre de Desmond cuando se detuvo. Tal vez y dada su relativa inexperiencia en la materia, debiera esperar un poco para hacerlo; seguiría en su lista no como marido potencial, sino como ejemplo de las cualidades que las damas como Winifred, que si bien algo tímida parecía muy sensata, buscaban en un hombre.

Aprender de los éxitos (y de los fracasos) de los demás era una postura inteligente.

Esa idea la hizo mirar a su alrededor. Kitty, ataviada con su reluciente vestido de seda aguamarina, deslumbraba con su efervescente encanto mientras revoloteaba de grupo en grupo. No había ni rastro del mohín y parecía estar en su salsa.

Henry estaba hablando con su hermano y con Simon; ya no parecía preocupado ni distraído por el comportamiento de su esposa.

¿Habría malinterpretado lo que había visto?

Alguien se acercó a ella. Se giró y vio que Ambrose Calvin le hacía una reverencia a la que ella correspondió.

—Señorita Ashford... Es un placer conocerla. La he visto en varias ocasiones en Londres, pero nunca he tenido la oportunidad de que nos presentaran.

—¿De veras? Supongo que eso significa que pasa mucho tiempo en la capital, ¿estoy en lo cierto?

El señor Calvin tenía unos ojos castaños muy oscuros y el cabello de un castaño mucho más claro; de facciones corrientes, tenía cierto aire de aristócrata que quedaba un tanto suavizado por su cordialidad y sus impecables modales hasta parecer agradable. Inclinó la cabeza ante su pregunta.

—Prácticamente todo el tiempo —respondió casi de inmediato antes de añadir—: Tengo la esperanza de entrar en el Parlamento en la próxima legislatura. Por supuesto, paso gran parte de mi tiempo ocupado con el desarrollo de los acontecimientos... Y para tener información de primera mano, hay que estar en Londres.

—Sí, por supuesto. —Estuvo en un tris de decirle que lo entendía a la perfección ya que conocía a Michael Anstruther-Wetherby, el representante de lord Godleigh por West Hampshire, pero la frialdad que vislumbró en los ojos oscuros de su interlocutor hizo que se mordiera la lengua—. Siempre he creído que en estos tiempos tan revueltos servir a la comunidad en el Parlamento debe de ser muy gratificante.

—Así es. —Su tono de voz no indicaba que estuviera motivado por un afán reformista—. Tengo la firme creencia de que necesitamos a los hombres adecuados en los puestos adecuados. Necesitamos a hombres interesados de verdad en gobernar, en guiar al país por los caminos apropiados.

Eso era demasiado pomposo para su gusto, de manera que decidió cambiar el curso de la conversación.

—¿Ya ha decidido a quién representará?

—Aún no. —Su mirada se desvió hacia un grupo al otro

lado de la estancia, un grupo en el que se encontraban lord Glossup, el señor Buckstead y el señor Archer. Tras una breve pausa, volvió a concentrarse en ella con una sonrisa un tanto arrogante—. Tal vez no sea consciente, pero tales asuntos se suelen tratar (por el bien de todos) dentro del partido. Espero noticias de mi nombramiento en breve.

—Entiendo... —Correspondió con una sonrisa muy dulce; una sonrisa que Simon habría interpretado al punto por su falta de sinceridad—. Entonces sólo resta esperar que las noticias que reciba sean las que merece.

El señor Calvin interpretó el comentario como ella quería que lo interpretara, de modo que también se sintió bastante arrogante mientras se reunían con varios invitados y se sumaban a su conversación.

Poco después, lady Glossup alzó la voz y pidió una voluntaria que se ofreciera a entretener a los presentes con el piano.

Antes de que nadie pudiera reaccionar, Kitty dio un paso al frente con una sonrisa deslumbrante.

—¡Bailar! ¡Eso es lo que necesitamos!

Lady Glossup parpadeó y la señora Archer, que estaba a su lado, se quedó perpleja.

—Bien... —continuó Kitty desde el centro de la estancia mientras giraba a su alrededor dando palmadas—, ¿quién tocará para nosotros?

Portia había respondido a esa pregunta tantas veces a lo largo de su vida que ya era algo instintivo.

—Me encantará tocar si eso complace a los demás.

Kitty la miró con una expresión a caballo entre la sorpresa y el recelo, pero aceptó casi al instante.

—¡Excelente! —Se giró y le hizo señas a los caballeros—. James, Simon..., ¿me hacéis el favor de colocar el piano? Charlie, Desmond..., apartad esas sillas de allí hacia la pared.

Mientras se sentaba al piano, miró de nuevo a Kitty. Parecía que sólo la motivaba el inocente placer del baile. Rebosante de esa ingenua emoción, era muy atractiva. No había ni rastro de la sirena que había acorralado a James en las escaleras; ni rastro de la sensual y malhumorada mujer que había entrado en el salón antes de la cena.

Pasó las manos por las teclas para comprobar el sonido. ¡Gracias a Dios que el piano estaba afinado! Levantó la vista al mismo tiempo que un montón de partituras caían sobre la superficie de madera lacada del piano.

Alzó la vista un poco más y se topó con los penetrantes ojos azules de Simon, que enarcó una ceja.

—Ya veo que vuelves a esconderte detrás de tus habilidades, como de costumbre.

Parpadeó, sorprendida. Con una expresión enigmática en el rostro, Simon se dio la vuelta y se reunió con los invitados que ya estaban buscando pareja.

Se desentendió del extraño comentario y colocó las manos sobre las teclas para dejar que sus dedos tocaran los primeros acordes de un vals.

Sabía tocar muchos. Siempre se le había dado muy bien la música; de hecho, era como si fluyera de sus dedos sin más, razón por la que se ofrecía tan a menudo a tocar. No necesitaba pensar para saber lo que estaba haciendo; disfrutaba tocando, se sentía cómoda sentada al piano y podía dejarse llevar por la música o estudiar a los presentes según le apeteciera.

Esa noche decidió hacer lo segundo.

Y lo que vio la dejó fascinada.

Como era habitual, el piano estaba en uno de los extremos de la enorme estancia, lejos de la chimenea, de las sillas y de los sofás donde se sentaban las personas de más edad. Los bailarines estaban en el espacio intermedio; dado que muy pocos creían que el intérprete alzaría la vista del instrumento, aquellas parejas que querían aprovechar el baile para intercambiar mensajes solían alejarse de los astutos ojos de sus mayores. De manera que se colocaban directamente frente a ella.

Portia, por su parte, estaba encantada de tocar un vals tras otro, intercalando alguna que otra contradanza y dándoles a los bailarines el tiempo justo para recuperar el aliento y cambiar de pareja.

Lo primero que notó fue que si bien Kitty disfrutaba bailando, parecía tener un motivo ulterior. Cuál era ese motivo no estaba muy claro, ya que parecía haberle echado el ojo a más de un caballero. Flirteaba, no cabía duda de que eso era lo que hacía, con James, su cuñado, para irritación de éste. Con el señor Calvin se mostraba un poco más discreta, aunque sus ojos conservaban el brillo incitante y sus labios se curvaban en una sonrisa provocativa. Y por más que estuvo observando con detenimiento, no encontró motivo alguno para responsabilizar al caballero, ya que no le dio pie en ningún momento.

Con Desmond se mostró tímida. Seguía flirteando, pero con mucha más sutileza, como si adaptara su ataque a la personalidad de su víctima. Desmond parecía titubear, vacilar; no la animó, pero tampoco la rechazó de plano. Sin embargo, cuando les tocó el turno a Simon y a Charlie, ambos parecieron replegarse tras los impenetrables muros de la más fría desaprobación. Kitty los desafió pero su puesta en escena carecía de fundamento, como si sólo estuviera aparentando de cara a la galería.

No sabía para qué se molestaba en flirtear con ellos. ¿Estaría pasando algo por alto?

Sin embargo, cuando Kitty bailó con su marido, su actitud se tornó pasiva. No se esforzó en lo más mínimo por llamar su atención; de hecho, casi no pronunció palabra alguna. Henry hizo cuanto estuvo en su mano, pero no consiguió ocultar del todo su decepción, ni una especie de resignada desaprobación.

En cuanto al resto, no le costó trabajo descubrir que Lucy Buckstead quería echarle el guante a James. Sonreía y reía con todos los caballeros, pero a James lo escuchaba embobada mientras lo miraba con los ojos como platos y los labios entreabiertos.

James tendría que andarse con cuidado, y no sólo en cuanto a Kitty, algo de lo que, según sospechaba, era muy consciente. Su actitud siguió siendo educada, pero distante.

Las Hammond no estaban interesadas en entablar una

relación; estaban allí con la sencilla ambición de divertirse y con la esperanza de que los demás también lo hicieran. Su fresca exuberancia era un bálsamo para todos. Drusilla, en cambio, se habría quedado sentada todo el tiempo junto a su madre si ésta se lo hubiera permitido. La joven soportó la tortura con el mismo entusiasmo que mostraría una aristócrata francesa de camino a la guillotina.

En cuanto a Desmond y a Winifred, no cabía duda de que el amor flotaba en el aire. Era de lo más instructivo observar su interacción: Desmond se insinuaba sin mostrarse exigente, el equilibrio perfecto entre la timidez y la arrogancia; Winifred respondía en voz baja, con los párpados entornados y la vista clavada en el suelo, aunque no tardaba en alzar la mirada hacia su rostro, hacia sus ojos.

Portia bajó la cabeza para ocultar una sonrisa cuando llegó al final de la pieza. Aún resonaba en el aire el último acorde cuando decidió que a los bailarines les vendría bien un respiro mientras buscaba otra partitura.

Se puso en pie para hojearlas mejor. Había repasado casi la mitad del montón cuando escuchó el frufrú de unas faldas que se acercaban.

—Señorita Ashford, ha tocado usted maravillosamente, pero es muy descortés por nuestra parte que al hacerlo se pierda toda la diversión.

Se giró justo cuando Winifred llegaba del brazo de Simon.

—No, no... Yo... —Se detuvo sin saber muy bien qué decir.

Winifred sonrió.

—Le estaría eternamente agradecida si me permitiera ocupar su lugar. Me gustaría descansar un poco y... Bueno, ésta es la mejor manera.

Cuando la miró a los ojos, se dio cuenta de que le estaba diciendo la verdad. Si Winifred se limitaba a sentarse en un rincón, alguien empezaría a preguntarse el motivo. Sonrió.

—Como desee.

Se apartó del piano y Winifred ocupó su lugar. Juntas repasaron las partituras hasta que Winifred escogió una y se sentó. Portia se dio la vuelta... y se encontró con Simon, quien, con una paciencia muy inusual, la había esperado.

La miró a los ojos antes de ofrecerle el brazo.

—¿Lista?

Por absurdo que pareciera, jamás había bailado con él. Ni una sola vez. Hasta ese momento, jamás se le había ocurrido que pudiera pasar diez minutos dando vueltas por la estancia bajo su dirección sin acabar en una guerra abierta.

La mirada de Simon no flaqueó. El desafío era evidente.

Al recordar su voto, al escucharlo de nuevo en su cabeza, levantó la barbilla y sonrió. De forma encantadora. Que lo interpretara como quisiera.

—Gracias.

El recelo ensombreció sus ojos, pero acabó por inclinar la cabeza y colocarse su mano en el brazo antes de conducirla hacia el lugar donde aguardaban las restantes parejas mientras Winifred empezaba a tocar un vals.

Su serenidad se vio sacudida en un primer momento cuando Simon la rodeó con los brazos, cuando sintió su fuerza y recordó, con demasiada claridad, cómo se había sentido entre sus brazos. Volvió a sentir un nudo en el pecho y se quedó sin respiración un instante; la sensación de esa mano masculina, grande y fuerte, en la espalda la distraía... y luchó con todas sus fuerzas para ocultarlo.

La música los atrapó en su hechizo y comenzaron a girar. Con las miradas entrelazadas, se deslizaron por la estancia.

Apenas si podía respirar. Había bailado el vals en incontables ocasiones, incluso con caballeros de la calaña de Simon; pero la sensación física jamás había sido tan intensa ni había llegado al punto de amenazar con robarle la razón. Claro que jamás había estado tan cerca de él; los movimientos de sus cuerpos, la percepción de esa fuerza tan masculina, su propia debilidad y el poder que subyacía bajo todo eso la atravesaron con tal fuerza que la dejaron desorientada. Parpadeó un par de veces en un intento por concentrarse... en cualquier cosa que no fuera la facilidad con la que se desplazaban, la sensación de que se estaba dejando llevar, ni la emoción que la embargaba.

Pero ¿por qué estaba emocionada?

Contuvo a duras penas el impulso de menear la cabeza en lo que habría sido un vano intento de librarse de esas ideas alocadas. Inspiró hondo y miró a su alrededor.

Y vio a Kitty bailando con el señor Calvin. Su actuación, con sutiles variaciones, seguía en vigor.

—¿Qué está tramando Kitty? ¿Lo sabes?

Era lo primero que se le había pasado por la cabeza, aunque nunca había sido demasiado tímida, mucho menos con Simon. Éste la había estado observando con detenimiento; de manera que se había cuidado mucho de no mirarlo a los ojos. En ese momento, en cambio, levantó la vista y comprobó, aliviada, que su semblante retomaba su acostumbrada exasperación.

Más tranquila, enarcó las cejas.

Simon apretó los labios.

—No tienes por qué saberlo.

—Es posible, pero quiero hacerlo... Tengo mis motivos.

La expresión de Simon se tornó ceñuda. No alcanzaba a imaginar qué «motivos» serían ésos.

—Si no me lo dices, se lo preguntaré a Charlie. O a James —lo amenazó, con una sonrisa.

Fue la última frase, ese «O a James», lo que lo convenció. Dejó escapar un suspiro entre dientes, levantó la vista y cambió el rumbo hacia el otro extremo de la estancia antes de contestar en voz baja:

—Kitty tiene la costumbre de flirtear con todo hombre bien parecido que conoce. —Pasado un momento, añadió—: Hasta dónde llega ese flirteo...

Fue a encogerse de hombros, pero se lo pensó mejor. Apretó los dientes. Al ver que no proseguía y que se negaba a mirarla a los ojos, no le quedó más remedio que acabar la frase, acicateada por el hecho de que no hubiese sido capaz de mentirle al respecto como dictaban las buenas costumbres.

—Sabes perfectamente hasta dónde llega porque te ha hecho proposiciones indecentes, y también a Charlie. Y sigue insistiendo con James.

El comentario logró que la mirara y su rostro reflejó una emoción mucho más compleja que la irritación.

—¿Cómo diablos te has enterado?

Sonrió... y por una vez no fue para molestarlo, sino todo lo contrario.

—Cada vez que estáis cerca de ella a solas, tanto Charlie como tú irradiáis una increíble desaprobación..., como durante el vals. En cuanto a James, lo sé porque me he topado con ellos *in extremis* esta noche. —Su sonrisa se ensanchó—. Podría decirse que lo rescaté. Por eso llegamos juntos al salón.

Percibió cómo Simon se relajaba un tanto y aprovechó la ventaja con la que contaba. Porque ansiaba enterarse.

—Tanto tú como Charlie habéis conseguido convencerla de que no... —comenzó, pero se detuvo con un gesto de la mano libre— estáis interesados. ¿Por qué James no hace lo mismo?

La miró de soslayo antes de replicar:

—Porque intenta con todas sus fuerzas no hacerle daño a su hermano... Al menos, no más del necesario. Kitty lo sabe, y se aprovecha de ello. Ni Charlie ni yo tendríamos el más mínimo reparo en tratarla como se merece si llega a traspasar ciertos límites.

—Pero es lo bastante astuta como para no traspasarlos, ¿verdad?

Simon asintió con la cabeza.

—¿Qué hay de Henry?

—Cuando se casaron estaba muy encariñado con ella. No sé qué siente por ella en estos momentos. Y, antes de que lo preguntes, no tengo la menor idea de por qué es como es... Nadie la tiene.

La mirada de Portia voló hacia Kitty que, al otro lado

del salón, sonreía de forma seductora al señor Calvin, quien hacía todo cuanto estaba en su mano por fingir que no se había dado cuenta.

Poco después, sintió la mirada de Simon sobre ella.

—¿Alguna sugerencia al respecto?

Lo miró a la cara y negó con la cabeza.

—No, pero... no creo que sea una compulsión irracional... Ya me entiendes; sabe lo que está haciendo, es todo muy deliberado. Tiene algún motivo en mente, algún objetivo.

Simon no dijo nada. Los últimos acordes del vals flotaron en el aire. Se detuvieron y charlaron con Annabelle y Desmond antes de cambiar de pareja para la siguiente pieza.

Se mantuvo fiel a su voto y charló amistosamente con Desmond. Se despidió con la idea de que debía felicitar a Winifred por su buena suerte; Desmond parecía un hombre muy agradable, si bien resultaba algo serio. Bailó con Charlie, con James y con el señor Calvin, e hizo gala de toda su astucia con ellos. Y se sintió muy segura al hacerlo, porque era incapaz de flirtear y sabía que ninguno de los tres caballeros vería nada extraño en sus sutiles preguntas, sólo un interés general.

Después bailó con Henry y se sintió fatal. A pesar de que su pareja hacía todo lo posible por entretenerla, era incapaz de olvidarse del hecho de que él era muy consciente del comportamiento de su esposa.

Era una situación muy complicada, ya que Kitty era muy astuta, muy hábil. No hacía nada que resultara escandaloso, pero sus constantes flirteos hacían que todos tuvieran la misma pregunta en mente:

¿Por qué lo hacía?

No se le ocurría nada, ya que Henry se parecía mucho a Desmond. Era un hombre callado, amable y decente. Durante los diez minutos que había conversado con él, comprendió el deseo de su hermano de protegerlo a toda costa, sin importar las circunstancias, así como el apoyo que recibía de Simon y de Charlie al respecto.

Estaba de acuerdo con su proceder por completo.

Cuando decidieron que era hora de poner fin al baile, siguió haciendo conjeturas acerca del número de invitados que se habría percatado del comportamiento de Kitty y lo interpretaban como lo hacían Simon, Charlie, James y ella misma. Por no hablar de Henry.

Ambrose Calvin y Desmond desde luego que se habían dado cuenta; pero ¿y las damas? Eso era más difícil de averiguar.

Cuando sirvieron el té, los presentes se reunieron en torno a la bandeja, encantados de poder descansar y recuperar el aliento. La conversación era relajada y nadie sentía la necesidad de rellenar los silencios.

Portia bebió en silencio mientras observaba. La idea de Kitty había sido todo un acierto, ya que el baile había desterrado las formalidades y los había acercado con mucha más facilidad de lo que solía ocurrir en otras fiestas campestres. En esos momentos, en lugar de las habituales tensiones entre los invitados, se presentía cierta afinidad, como si hubieran acudido a la fiesta para compartir su tiempo con los demás; una afinidad que sin duda haría que los días venideros fueran mucho más placenteros.

Estaba soltando la taza de té cuando Kitty volvió a acaparar todas las miradas. Se puso en pie, acompañada del frufrú de sus faldas, y llamó la atención de la concurrencia con una sonrisa deslumbrante y los brazos abiertos.

—Creo que deberíamos dar un paseo por los jardines antes de retirarnos. Hace una noche maravillosa y muchas de las plantas están floreciendo. Después de tanto ejercicio, necesitamos un momento para tranquilizarnos en un espacio relajante antes de retirarnos a nuestras habitaciones.

Y, una vez más, estaba en lo cierto. Los invitados de más edad, que no habían bailado, no se mostraron de acuerdo, pero aquellos que sí lo habían hecho le dieron la razón. Siguieron a Kitty por las puertas francesas que daban a la terraza; desde allí, se adentraron en los jardines por parejas o en grupos de tres.

Portia no se sorprendió en absoluto cuando Simon apareció a su lado en la terraza; siempre que coincidían en las fiestas y en situaciones como ésa, no solía apartarse mucho de ella... Su actitud no variaba nunca. Asumir el papel de protector renuente era una costumbre que llevaba años practicando.

Sin embargo, en esa ocasión rompió con la tradición al ofrecerle el brazo.

Ella titubeó.

Simon vio cómo le miraba el brazo con los ojos desorbitados como si nunca hubiera visto uno en la vida. Esperó a que levantara la cabeza y lo mirara a la cara para enarcar las cejas en un deliberado y arrogante desafío.

Ella levantó la barbilla y le colocó la mano sobre el brazo con serena arrogancia. Tuvo que reprimir la sonrisa que le provocó tan insignificante triunfo y la condujo por los estrechos escalones que daban al jardín.

Kitty iba en cabeza con Ambrose Calvin y con Desmond, charlando animadamente con Lucy Buckstead de modo que la muchacha se vio obligada a acompañar al trío en lugar de quedarse rezagada para hablar con James como seguramente había sido su intención. Charlie y James acompañaban a las Hammond y a Winifred; Drusilla había declinado la oferta de unirse a ellos con el pretexto de que odiaba el aire nocturno, y Henry estaba sumido en una acalorada conversación con el señor Buckstead.

Se internaron en los jardines.

—¿Tienes alguna preferencia en particular? ¿Quieres ver algo en concreto? —Abarcó los alrededores con un gesto del brazo.

—¿A la pálida luz de la luna? —preguntó ella a su vez mientras seguía con la mirada el grupito de Kitty cuando éste se alejó de la casa en dirección a la oscuridad de los enormes rododendros que flanqueaban el prado—. ¿Qué hay por ahí?

—El templete —contestó, sin quitarle la vista de encima.

La respuesta hizo que enarcara las cejas con altanería.

—¿Dónde queda el lago?

Simon señaló hacia el lugar donde el prado descendía en una suave pendiente, hasta reducirse a un amplio sendero verde que serpenteaba entre los parterres de flores.

—No está cerca, pero tampoco demasiado lejos como para dar un paseo hasta la orilla.

Se encaminaron en esa dirección. El resto los siguió. Las exclamaciones de las Hammond acerca de los extensos jardines, de los enormes setos y árboles, de la cantidad de senderos y de los magníficos parterres flotaron a coro en el aire nocturno. Y, desde luego, los jardines presentaban una estampa exuberante. La mezcla de aromas de las numerosas flores flotaba en la cálida oscuridad.

Prosiguieron su paseo, ni demasiado rápido ni demasiado despacio y sin rumbo fijo; disfrutar del momento parecía el único objetivo... Disfrutar del tranquilo, silencioso y, si bien inesperado, cordial momento.

El grupo que los seguía caminaba bastante más despacio, de modo que sus voces quedaron reducidas a un murmullo.

—¿Qué estás tramando? —le preguntó mientras la miraba de reojo.

La pregunta hizo que ella se tensara un instante.

—¿Tramando?

—Te escuché en el mirador, ¿recuerdas? Dijiste algo acerca de aprender más, de tomar una decisión y de considerar a todos los que sean adecuados.

Ella lo miró con el rostro oculto por la sombra de las ramas de los árboles bajo los que paseaban.

De modo que insistió:

—¿Adecuados para qué?

Portia parpadeó un par de veces mientras lo miraba a los ojos, tras lo cual clavó la vista al frente.

—Sólo... Es sólo una cuestión que me interesa. Algo sobre lo que he estado meditando últimamente.

—¿Y de qué se trata?

Pasado un momento, respondió:

—No tienes por qué saberlo.

—Eso viene a significar que no quieres decírmelo.

Portia inclinó la cabeza.

Estuvo tentado de insistir, pero se recordó que ella estaría allí los próximos días; tendría todo el tiempo del mundo para descubrir qué estaba tramando si no la perdía de vista ni un instante. Ya se había percatado de su interés por los caballeros durante la cena; además, cuando bailó con James y Charlie, y también con Desmond, se había mostrado más animada de lo normal y les había hecho numerosas preguntas. Estaba seguro de que no tenían nada que ver con Kitty; a él sí podía hacerle ciertas preguntas porque eran prácticamente familia... No sentían la necesidad de fingir que acataban las apariencias sociales cuando estaban a solas.

—Muy bien.

Esa pronta capitulación le valió una mirada recelosa, pero a ella no le convenía proseguir con el tema. De modo que esbozó una sonrisa y escuchó su suave resoplido mientras ella volvía a fijar la vista al frente. Prosiguieron su paseo en silencio, sin necesidad de poner en palabras lo que era evidente: no dejaría de vigilarla hasta averiguar su secreto, y ella ya sabía a lo que se enfrentaba.

Mientras atravesaban la última extensión de hierba antes de llegar al lago, repasó el comportamiento de Portia hasta ese momento. De haberse tratado de otra mujer, sospecharía que buscaba marido; sin embargo, ella jamás había tenido esa inclinación. Jamás había tenido en mucha estima a los hombres, así que no se le ocurría ningún motivo que la hubiera llevado a cambiar de opinión.

Era mucho más probable que estuviera persiguiendo algún tipo de conocimiento. Tal vez la manera de atisbar o conocer de primera mano alguna actividad normalmente vetada a las mujeres. Eso sí que tenía sentido... Era lo normal en ella.

Llegaron al borde donde el sendero comenzaba a descender hacia el lago. Se detuvieron y Portia pareció quedarse prendada de la imagen que se extendía frente ella: el extenso lago de aguas oscuras y mansas, como un agujero negro en mitad de la hondonada, limitada al frente por una colina boscosa; a la derecha se alzaba un pinar sobre una suave elevación y, apenas visible a la mortecina luz, en la orilla izquierda se encontraba un mirador cuya blancura destacaba entre las sombras de los rododendros.

El paisaje la dejó sin palabras, absorta por completo en la imagen que tenía delante.

Simon aprovechó la oportunidad para estudiarla. La certeza de que buscaba un caballero para que la iniciara en ciertos placeres ilícitos tomó forma hasta asentarse de pleno. De una manera totalmente inesperada.

—¡Ay, Dios mío! —Annabelle llegó junto a ellos con los demás invitados a la zaga.

—¡Qué maravilla! ¡Caray! ¡Qué gótico! —exclamó Cecily con las manos enlazadas mientras brincaba por la emoción.

—¿De verdad es muy profundo? —le preguntó Winifred a James.

—Jamás hemos tocado el fondo.

La respuesta provocó sendas expresiones horrorizadas en las hermanas Hammond.

—¿Continuamos? —preguntó Charlie, mirando a Portia y luego a él.

Había un estrecho camino que rodeaba el lago, muy pegado a la orilla.

—Vaya... —dijo Annabelle, mirando a su hermana—. No creo que debamos. Mamá dijo que deberíamos descansar bien esta noche para recuperarnos de los rigores del viaje.

Winifred también puso objeciones. James se ofreció con galantería a acompañar a las tres jóvenes de vuelta a la casa. Tras despedirse, se alejaron. Flanqueada por Charlie y Simon, Portia se encaminó hacia el lago.

Charlaron mientras paseaban, todo de manera muy relajada. Los tres frecuentaban las mismas amistades, así que fue de lo más natural que la conversación girara acerca de los acontecimientos que habían tenido lugar durante la temporada; los escándalos, los enlaces, los cotilleos más intrigantes... Lo más sorprendente de todo fue que Simon no se mantuvo callado como era habitual en él, sino que contribuyó a que la conversación siguiera por los derroteros apropiados. En cuanto a Charlie, bueno, siempre había sido un parlanchín; fue muy sencillo incitarlo para que los entretuviera con divertidas historias sobre apuestas que no habían acabado bien y con las hazañas de los caballeretes más alocados.

Se detuvieron junto al mirador para admirar la sólida estructura de madera, algo más grande de lo habitual dada la distancia que la separaba de la casa, antes de continuar bordeando el lago.

Cuando dieron la vuelta para regresar a la casa, se sentía de lo más ufana. Había sobrevivido con bastante éxito a toda una velada y a un paseo nocturno con dos de los lobos más afamados de la alta sociedad londinense. Conversar con dos caballeros, hacer que confiaran en ella, no había sido tan difícil como había supuesto en un principio.

Estaban a medio camino de la suave pendiente que ascendía hasta la mansión cuando Henry se acercó a ellos.

—¿Ha pasado Kitty por aquí? —les preguntó cuando llegó a su altura.

Negaron con la cabeza y se detuvieron para mirar hacia el lago. El camino era visible desde su posición. Y el vestido aguamarina de Kitty habría resaltado en la oscuridad.

—La vimos cuando salimos de la casa —dijo Portia—. Se marchó hacia el templete con otros invitados.

—No la hemos visto desde entonces, ni a su grupo tampoco —añadió Simon.

—Vengo del templete —les aclaró Henry.

Escucharon los pasos de alguien que se acercaba y cuando se giraron en la dirección resultó ser James.

—¿Has visto a Kitty? —le preguntó Henry a su hermano—. Su madre quiere hablar con ella.

James negó con la cabeza.

—Vengo de la casa y no he visto a nadie por el camino.

Henry suspiró.

—Será mejor que siga buscando. —Tras despedirse de ella con una reverencia e inclinar la cabeza hacia los hombres, echó a andar hacia el pinar.

Los cuatro lo observaron hasta que las sombras lo engulleron.

—Tal vez habría sido mejor que la señora Archer hubiera hablado con ella antes —comentó James—. Ahora mismo... quizá sea mejor que Henry no la encuentre.

Comprendieron a la perfección lo que quería decir. El silencio cayó sobre ellos.

James recordó con quién estaba y la miró.

—Lo siento, querida. Me temo que no estoy de muy buen humor esta noche... No soy buena compañía. Si me perdona, volveré a la casa.

Hizo una reverencia bastante tensa que ella correspondió con un gesto de la cabeza. Tras despedirse de Simon y Charlie, James dio media vuelta y regresó a la mansión a través del prado.

Ellos lo siguieron mucho más despacio. Y en silencio, ya que poco podían decir y desde luego parecía más sensato no expresar en voz alta sus pensamientos.

Habían llegado a una bifurcación desde la que partía el sendero que llevaba al templete y el que rodeaba el pinar, cuando escucharon unas pisadas.

Como si fueran uno, los tres se detuvieron y miraron hacia el sendero en sombras que conducía al templete.

Una figura emergió de un camino secundario procedente de la mansión. Un hombre. Enfiló el sendero en el que ellos estaban y salió a la luz de la luna, momento en el que levantó la cabeza y... los vio. Sin titubear, cambió de dirección y tomó otro de los innumerables caminos que atravesaban el jardín de los setos.

Su sombra se desvaneció. Escucharon el susurro de las hojas a su paso, pero luego, nada.

Un instante después los tres inspiraron hondo y reanudaron el camino hacia la casa. Ni hablaron ni se miraron a los ojos.

Aun así, sabían perfectamente lo que los demás estaban pensando.

El hombre no era un invitado, ni un criado, ni siquiera un mozo de cuadra.

Era un gitano, alto, delgado y atractivo.

Con la melena negra revuelta, la chaqueta desabrochada y los faldones de la camisa por fuera del pantalón.

Resultaba difícil imaginar una razón inofensiva que explicara la presencia de un hombre así en la mansión y mucho menos que explicara su marcha con semejante desaliño y a esas horas.

Al llegar al prado principal se encontraron con Desmond, Ambrose y Lucy que, como ellos, regresaban a la casa.

No había ni rastro de Kitty.

3

—¡Y bien, señorita...! —exclamó lady Osbaldestone mientras se dejaba caer en un sillón emplazado junto a la chimenea de su habitación y clavaba una mirada elocuente en ella—. Ahora puedes contarme qué es lo que estás tramando.

—¿Tramando? —repitió Portia con los ojos clavados en ella.

Había ido a la habitación de la anciana para ayudarla a arreglarse antes de bajar a desayunar. De pie en mitad de la estancia y bañada por la luz que entraba por las ventanas, se descubrió atrapada por su penetrante mirada. Abrió la boca para decirle que no estaba tramando nada, pero la cerró.

Lady O resopló.

—Ya veo. Nos ahorraremos mucho tiempo si no te andas por las ramas y lo sueltas de una vez. Por regla general, te comportas con tal altanería que ni siquiera te fijas en los caballeros que te rodean; ayer, sin embargo, no sólo los estudiaste detenidamente, sino que además te dignaste charlar con ellos. —Cerró las manos en torno a la empuñadura de su bastón y se inclinó hacia delante—. ¿Por qué?

Una expresión especulativa brillaba en sus perspicaces ojos negros. Era mayor y muy lista, y se sabía al dedillo todo lo que había que saber acerca de la alta sociedad, de las relaciones que había dentro de ella y de las familias que la componían. Debía de haber asistido a cientos, si no miles, de enlaces, sin contar en los que había mediado. Era la madrina perfecta para su plan. Si elegía ayudarla, claro estaba.

Aunque primero tendría que atreverse a pedírselo...

Unió las manos al frente, inspiró hondo y eligió sus palabras con sumo cuidado.

—He decidido que ya es hora de que busque un marido.

Lady O parpadeó.

—¿Y estás considerando a los caballeros presentes?

—¡No! Bueno..., sí. —Hizo un mohín—. No tengo ninguna experiencia en estos asuntos..., como ya sabe.

La dama volvió a resoplar.

—Sé que has malgastado los últimos siete años, al menos en ese sentido.

—Se me ocurrió que —prosiguió Portia como si no la hubiera escuchado—, ya que estoy aquí y he decidido casarme, podría aprovechar la oportunidad para descubrir cuáles son los criterios de selección. Para reunir la información y la experiencia que me servirán a la hora de elegir con sensatez. En resumidas cuentas, para evaluar los atributos que debería considerar. Aquello que valoro más en un caballero. —Frunció el ceño y prestó atención al semblante de lady O—. Supongo que cada dama exigirá algo diferente, ¿no?

La anciana sacudió la mano.

—*Comme-ci, comme-ça.* Yo diría que hay ciertos atributos fundamentales y otros superficiales. Los fundamentales, los más buscados por las mujeres, no difieren tanto de una a otra.

—¡Caray! —Portia alzó la cabeza—. Eso es lo que esperaba aclarar mientras estuviera aquí.

Lady O prolongó el estudio de su rostro unos instantes; después, se recostó en el sillón.

—Te observé anoche mientras estudiabas a los caballeros. ¿A quiénes has decidido tener en cuenta?

El momento de la verdad. Iba a necesitar ayuda. Al menos iba a necesitar a una dama con la que discutir sus avances, una dama en la que pudiera confiar.

—He pensado en Simon, James y Charlie. Son los candidatos más obvios. Y, aunque sospecho que Desmond tiene sus miras puestas en Winifred, he llegado a la conclusión de que también lo tendré en cuenta, aunque sólo sea para establecer el modelo de hombre adecuado.

—¿Lo has notado? ¿Cómo interpretas tú la reacción de la muchacha?

—Está indecisa. Se me ocurrió que podría aprender algo si la observo mientras se decide.

—Sin embargo, ya tiene treinta años y sigue soltera. —Lady O enarcó las cejas—. Me pregunto por qué...

—Tal vez no haya querido casarse... —Se percató de la mirada de la anciana y dio un respingo—. Por lo que he visto, parece muy sensata.

—Cierto, de ahí que me lo pregunte. ¿Y Ambrose? También está soltero, pero no lo has mencionado.

Se encogió de hombros.

—Tal vez sería lo adecuado, pero... —Arrugó la nariz y buscó las palabras que describieran la impresión que se había formado sobre él—. Es ambicioso y está decidido a labrarse una carrera en el Parlamento.

—Eso no debería pesar en su contra; acuérdate de Michael Anstruther-Wetherby.

—No me refiero a eso en particular. —Frunció el ceño—. Es más bien el cariz de su ambición, creo. A Michael lo mueve la ambición de servir a los demás, de establecer un buen gobierno. De organizar porque se le da bien hacerlo, como a su hermana.

Lady O asintió con la cabeza.

—Muy perspicaz. Debo entender que las motivaciones de Ambrose no son tan nobles, ¿no? Todavía no he tenido la oportunidad de hablar mucho con él.

—Creo que ansía la posición por sí misma. Ya sea por el poder o por cualquier otra ventaja que le otorgue. No he percibido ninguna otra motivación más profunda. —Miró a la anciana—. Pero tal vez lo esté prejuzgando. La verdad es que no he indagado mucho.

—En fin, dispondrás de mucho tiempo mientras estemos aquí. Y sí, estoy de acuerdo en que ésta es una forma adecuada para pulir tus habilidades. —Hizo ademán de ponerse en pie y ella se acercó para ayudarla—. No sé si te has dado cuenta —prosiguió mientras se incorporaba—, pero con Simon, James y Charlie a «tener en cuenta» vas a estar muy ocupada. Es posible que no tengas tiempo para ampliar tus horizontes.

Creyó ver el asomo de una sonrisa engreída en los labios de la anciana cuando ésta se giró hacia la puerta, aunque no supo cómo interpretarlo.

—Me informarás todas las noches de tus progresos, o todas las mañanas si lo prefieres. Mientras estemos aquí, estás bajo mi responsabilidad, por más que tu hermano y tú penséis que es al contrario. —La miró de reojo conforme atravesaban la habitación—. A mi edad y con los tiempos que corren, será interesante ver cuáles son los atributos masculinos que consideras más deseables.

Portia inclinó la cabeza respetuosamente, aunque ninguna se tragó el gesto. Le contaría a lady O lo que sucediera porque necesitaba ayuda y alguien que la guiara, no porque considerara que estaba bajo su responsabilidad.

Una vez que llegaron a la puerta, aferró el pomo para abrirla, pero la anciana se lo impidió inmovilizándola con el bastón. Portia la miró y se encontró con sus penetrantes ojos.

—Un detalle que no me has explicado... ¿Por qué, después de siete largos años en los círculos de la alta sociedad, has decidido de repente que deberías casarte?

No creyó oportuno mostrarse reservada. Su razón era de lo más normal.

—Por los niños. Mientras los ayudaba en el orfanato, comprendí que me gustaba poder trabajar con ellos, que me gustaba muchísimo. Cuidarlos, verlos crecer, guiarlos. —Sintió que esa necesidad crecía en su interior sólo con pensarlo—. Pero quiero cuidar a mis propios hijos. La estancia en Calverton Chase avivó ese deseo al ver a Amelia y a Luc con su prole, por no mencionar a Amanda y Martin, que suelen visitarlos muy a menudo. Es una casa de locos, pero... —Sus labios esbozaron una sonrisa melancólica mientras sostenía la mirada de lady O—. Lo deseo.

La anciana estudió su rostro con atención antes de asentir con la cabeza.

—Niños. Como impulso inicial están muy bien... El empujoncito que por fin ha logrado que te dignes observar lo que tienes a tu alrededor y sopeses la idea del matrimonio. Comprensible, natural y decente. ¡Sin embargo...! —La atravesó con una mirada siniestra—. Sin embargo, no es una razón adecuada para casarse.

Portia parpadeó.

—¿Ah, no?

Lady O retiró el bastón e hizo un gesto para que abriera la puerta.

—Pero...

—No te preocupes —la tranquilizó la anciana mientras echaba a andar por el pasillo—. Tú sigue con ese plan tuyo y considera a los caballeros elegibles. La razón adecuada (recuerda bien lo que te digo) acabará por aparecer. —Avivó el paso y Portia tuvo que apresurarse para alcanzarla—. ¡Vamos! —exclamó al tiempo que señalaba hacia las escaleras—. ¡Esta conversación sobre el matrimonio me ha abierto el apetito!

El apetito de manipular, claro estaba; aunque, a decir verdad, siempre tenía esa clase de apetito. Y la dama era toda una experta en ese arte. Lo hizo con tal sutileza mientras pedía las tostadas y la mermelada que Portia estaba convencida de que ni Simon, ni James, ni Charlie se dieron cuenta de que la idea de salir a cabalgar no había partido de ninguno de ellos.

Claro que, a la postre, la invitación a que se les uniera sí partió de ellos. Una invitación que aceptó encantada. Lucy también lo hizo. Y, para sorpresa de los presentes,

Drusilla se sumó al grupo. Winifred confesó que montar a caballo no era uno de sus pasatiempos preferidos y que prefería dar un paseo. Desmond se ofreció a acompañarla de inmediato.

Ambrose estaba enzarzado en una discusión con el señor Buckstead y se limitó a negar con la cabeza. Las Hammond ya habían engatusado a Oswald y Swanston con sus alegres miradas para que las acompañaran a pasear alrededor del lago. Kitty no estaba presente, como tampoco lo estaban las restantes damas. Todas habían elegido desayunar en sus respectivas habitaciones.

Quince minutos después de haber abandonado la mesa del desayuno, el grupo de jinetes ya se había reunido en el vestíbulo principal y estaba dispuesto a seguir a James hasta los establos.

Elegir las monturas llevó su tiempo. Ataviada con su traje de montar de color azul oscuro, Portia acompañó a James a lo largo del pasillo central que dividía las cuadras mientras ojeaba las monturas y le preguntaba acerca de los animales que le parecían más elegantes. ¿Sería uno de los atributos importantes para ella que un hombre fuera un jinete competente y conociera bien a sus caballos?

La mayoría cumplía el requisito, pero no necesariamente a su gusto.

—¿Conduce su faetón cuando está en Londres?

James la miró de soslayo.

—Sí, tengo una pareja de tordos ideales para pasear.

—Señor... —lo llamó el encargado de los establos desde la puerta—, los caballos estaban listos.

James le hizo un gesto y ella recorrió el pasillo de vuelta a la salida. Sintió su mirada clavada en ella, no con intensidad pero sí con evidente curiosidad.

—Los tordos están en la otra ala del establo... Si le apetece, un día de éstos podría enseñárselos.

—Si tenemos tiempo, me encantaría.

Él se encogió de hombros.

—Ya buscaremos un rato.

Ella sonrió justo cuando salían al patio, donde estaba

el resto del grupo. Charlie y el encargado de los establos estaban ayudando a Lucy y a Drusilla a tomar asiento en sus monturas. Portia se acercó al mozo de cuadras que tenía las riendas de la yegua castaña que había elegido... con la ayuda de James y Simon. Al llegar junto al animal, se dio la vuelta. Y esperó.

James se había detenido para dar unas palmaditas a su caballo antes de observar a las damas a las que estaban ayudando.

Portia lo miró fijamente, esperando que se percatara de ello y que se acercara para ayudarla a montar.

—A ver... Permíteme.

Se dio la vuelta al escuchar a Simon a su espalda.

Él frunció el ceño mientras le rodeaba la cintura con las manos.

—No tenemos todo el día para que lo pierdas mirando embobada a los demás.

La alzó con una facilidad pasmosa. Y ella volvió a quedarse sin respiración. Una vez que estuvo afianzada en la silla, la soltó, le apartó las faldas y sostuvo el estribo inferior. En cuanto hubo recuperado el sentido común, colocó los pies en su sitio y se acomodó las faldas.

—Gracias —le dijo, aunque ya se alejaba.

Lo observó mientras cogía las riendas de su caballo de las manos de un mozo de cuadra y se subía a lomos del animal con agilidad. ¿A qué venía esa cara? No era tanto su ceño fruncido como la expresión adusta que había asomado a sus ojos azules. Se obligó a no pensar en ello y tomó las riendas de las manos del mozo que las sujetaba antes de azuzar a la yegua para que se pusiera en marcha.

James vio que estaba lista y se subió a lomos de su castrado. La alcanzó justo cuando pasaban bajo el arco del patio. Simon guiaba a Lucy y a Drusilla, estudiando con atención sus posturas para evaluar su pericia a lomos de un caballo. Charlie no tardó en montar y seguirlos.

James y ella lideraban el grupo. Primero fueron a un paso tranquilo y luego al trote. Puesto que había nacido y se había criado en el campo, estaba acostumbrada a montar a caballo y había formado parte de las partidas de caza desde que era una niña. Si bien los años habían calmado gran parte de su temeridad, le encantaba cabalgar. La yegua, no muy grande, era briosa y juguetona. La dejó disfrutar, aunque no dudó en refrenarla cuando amenazó con abandonar el camino.

James quiso ofrecerle una yegua torda muy dócil, y ella ya había abierto la boca para protestar (algo que habría hecho sin reparo alguno) cuando Simon intervino y sugirió la castaña en su lugar. James había aceptado la opinión de Simon acerca de su capacidad como amazona con una ceja alzada, pero sin hacer el menor comentario. No le había quedado más remedio que morderse la lengua y darles las gracias a ambos con una sonrisa.

En esos momentos, James la observaba, analizándola y evaluando su estilo. Simon, según comprobó, no lo hacía. Le bastó un rápido vistazo por encima del hombro para verlo, aún con esa expresión tan seria, mirando a Lucy y Drusilla. Charlie, cuya montura avanzaba alegremente junto a la de Drusilla, charlaba con su acostumbrada afabilidad. La muchacha, como siempre, guardaba silencio, pero parecía prestarle atención o, al menos, parecía hacer un esfuerzo por prestarle atención... Se preguntó si los habría acompañado debido a la insistencia de su madre.

Lucy no paraba de echar miraditas al frente. A James y a ella. Giró la cabeza y comprendió que, en aras de la amabilidad, debería cederle su posición en breve. Esbozó una sonrisa y le dijo a James:

—Me encanta cabalgar. ¿Esta zona es buena para practicar caza?

Respondió sin indecisión alguna a todas sus preguntas mientras avanzaban por los frondosos caminos. Con mucho tiento, fue desviando la conversación hacia el tema que le interesaba: su vida, sus actividades preferidas y las que aborrecía, sus aspiraciones... Todo con mucha sutileza, por supuesto.

A pesar de todos sus esfuerzos, o tal vez a causa de

ellos, para cuando llegaron a la linde de Cranborne Chase, el antiguo coto de caza de la realeza, los ojos castaños de James la contemplaban con una expresión perpleja, curiosa y, desde luego, recelosa.

Esbozó una sonrisa alegre mientras refrenaban sus monturas y aguardaban a que los otros los alcanzaran antes de internarse por los caminos que recorrían los altos robledales. Aprovechó el momento para cederle su sitio a Lucy y dejó que su yegua trotara al lado del caballo tordo de Charlie.

Éste pareció encantado. Se giró hacia ella y dejó a Drusilla en manos de Simon.

—¡Caray! ¿Se ha enterado del escándalo que ha protagonizado lord Fortinbras en Ascot?

Y procedió a contárselo con pelos y señales. Para su sorpresa, descubrió que, pese a su naturaleza abierta y charlatana, le estaba costando mucho que Charlie hablara de sí mismo. En un principio, creyó que se debía a su carácter extrovertido, pero cuando se percató de que esquivaba todas y cada una de sus preguntas, y tras recibir una mirada penetrante y en absoluto inocente, comprendió que su cháchara era una especie de escudo protector; una defensa que había elaborado de modo instintivo contra las mujeres que querían conocerlo.

James era un hombre más seguro de sí mismo; de ahí que no adoptara una actitud tan defensiva. En cuanto a Charlie... Acabó por sonreírle con sinceridad y abandonar las pesquisas. Sólo era un juego; un modo de practicar. Sería injusto ponerlo a la defensiva y estropearle la fiesta campestre por el simple motivo de perfeccionar sus habilidades.

Echó un vistazo a su alrededor.

—Hasta ahora hemos sido muy prudentes... ¿Se atrevería a galopar un poco?

Charlie abrió los ojos de par en par.

—Si le apetece... no veo por qué no. —Miró al frente y soltó un grito de alegría. Cuando James miró por encima del hombro, le hizo un gesto indicándole que iban a galopar. James aminoró el paso y se apartó, llevando a Lucy con él, a un lado del camino.

Portia azuzó a su yegua. Pasó junto a James y Lucy al galope. El camino era ancho, lo bastante como para que pudieran avanzar dos caballos uno al lado del otro; pero cuando llegaron a la primera curva, ya le sacaba una buena ventaja a Charlie. Frente a ella se abría un amplio prado cubierto de hierba. Le dio rienda suelta a la yegua y el sonido de los cascos que escuchaba a su espalda quedó ahogado bajo la implacable cadencia del galope de su montura. El rítmico sonido resonaba en su interior, al compás de los latidos de su corazón, que hacía correr la euforia del momento por sus venas.

El límite del prado se acercaba. Miró por encima del hombro. Charlie la seguía a unos metros de distancia, lo bastante lejos como para no alcanzarla. Tras él seguían los otros cuatro miembros del grupo, a un trote vivo pero no a galope tendido.

Devolvió la vista al frente con una sonrisa y prosiguió por el camino, que al llegar al extremo del prado volvía a estrecharse. Veinte metros más allá se abría de nuevo al salir a otro claro. Con el corazón henchido por la alegría, dio rienda suelta a la yegua, pero la refrenó al llegar al centro.

El ruido de los cascos de los caballos que la seguían se escuchaba cada vez más distante. Por mucho que disfrutara de la velocidad, no era tan estúpida como para lanzarse al galope por unos caminos desconocidos. De todas formas, ya había disfrutado del momento y con eso le bastaba. A medida que se acercaba a los árboles y el camino volvía a estrecharse, instó a la yegua a aminorar el paso hasta ir a un suave trote.

Se detuvo al llegar a la linde y esperó.

Charlie fue el primero en alcanzarla.

—¡Menuda forma de cabalgar!

Portia enfrentó su mirada, lista para defenderse, pero se dio cuenta de que no estaba escandalizado. La expresión de sus ojos era bien distinta, como si el hecho de que supiera cabalgar le hubiera hecho pensar algo que antes ni siquiera se le había pasado por la cabeza.

Antes de que tuviera la oportunidad de reflexionar al respecto, llegaron James y Lucy. La muchacha reía y charlaba con los ojos chispeantes. James intercambió una mirada con Charlie quien, con su habitual encanto y su afable sonrisa, ocupó el puesto de su amigo al lado de Lucy.

Simon y Drusilla llegaron poco después. El grupo se demoró un instante para recuperar el aliento y dejar que sus monturas descansaran. James le dijo algo a Drusilla y ambos encabezaron el camino de regreso a Glossup Hall.

Lucy se apresuró a seguirlos, pero la sutil insistencia de Charlie la obligó a prestarle toda su atención. Mediante la simple estrategia de refrenar su caballo, mantuvo a la muchacha bien alejada de James.

Portia contuvo una sonrisa mientras los seguía. Apenas fue consciente de la presencia de Simon a su lado. O, más bien, no lo dejó traslucir. Sus sentidos, en cambio, estaban muy pendientes de su proximidad y de la fuerza contenida con la que se sentaba a lomos de su caballo. Esperaba sentir al menos una pizca de la orgullosa reticencia que la invadía cada vez que lo tenía cerca y que precedía a la irritación... Pero lo que sintió fue un hormigueo en la piel y una opresión en el pecho; dos sensaciones totalmente desconocidas.

—Ya veo que en el fondo sigues siendo una polvorilla.

Había una acritud en su voz que no había escuchado antes.

Giró la cabeza, enfrentó su mirada y la sopesó un instante. Apartó la vista con una sonrisa.

—No pareces desaprobarlo.

Simon refunfuñó algo. ¿Qué podía decir? Tenía razón. Debería desaprobarlo, pero parte de sí mismo respondía (y de inmediato, además) al desafío de una mujer que podía cabalgar como el viento. Y la certeza de que montaba tan bien como él le permitía disfrutar del momento sin que éste quedara empañado por la preocupación.

La causa de su irritación no tenía nada que ver con que hubiera cabalgado a galope tendido, sino con el hecho de no haber sido él quien la acompañara.

Sus monturas avanzaban tranquilamente. Le echó un vistazo a su rostro por el rabillo del ojo; estaba sonriendo mientras pensaba en algo de lo que él no tenía ni la menor idea. Esperó a que le preguntara algo, a que hablara con él tal y como lo había hecho con James y Charlie.

El único sonido que escuchaba era el de los cascos de los caballos.

Portia siguió en silencio. Distante. En otro lugar.

A la postre, aceptó que no tenía la menor intención de incluirlo a él en su empresa, fuera cual fuese. Las sospechas que albergaba se intensificaron. La reticencia con la que lo trataba era confirmación más que suficiente. Si estaba dispuesta a llevar a cabo alguna experiencia ilícita, él era el último a quien acudiría.

La certeza, o más bien la oleada de emociones que ésta suscitó, hizo que contuviera la respiración. Los remordimientos lo asaltaron con fuerza. Tuvo la impresión de que había perdido algo... algo que le era muy querido y de lo que ni siquiera se había dado cuenta hasta que ya era tarde.

Se reprendió para sus adentros e inspiró hondo al tiempo que volvía a contemplar su rostro.

Quería preguntarle, exigirle que se explicara, pero no sabía cómo formular la pregunta.

Y, de todas formas, tampoco sabía si ella iba a responderle.

Tras cambiar el traje de montar por un vestido de sarga verde y blanco y volver a peinarse, Portia bajó la escalinata mientras el sonido del gong que anunciaba el almuerzo reverberaba por la mansión.

Blenkinsop cruzaba en esos momentos el vestíbulo principal. Se detuvo para hacerle una reverencia.

—El almuerzo está servido en la terraza, señorita.

—Gracias.

Se encaminó al salón. El paseo a caballo había ido muy bien; había superado con soltura el desafío de «mantener una charla con caballeros». Estaba aprendiendo y ganando confianza, justo su intención.

Claro que la mañana había estado libre de la distracción que suponían Kitty y sus payasadas. Lo primero que escuchó en cuanto atravesó las puertas francesas y puso un pie en las baldosas de la terraza fue la voz de Kitty en su versión ronca y seductora.

—Siempre te he tenido un gran aprecio...

No era James, sino Desmond a quien había acorralado contra la balaustrada. ¡Esa mujer era incorregible! La pareja estaba a su izquierda; de modo que se dirigió a la derecha y fingió no haberlos visto. Siguió caminando hasta el lugar donde se había dispuesto una mesa muy larga en la que ya estaban colocadas las bandejas, las copas y los platos. El resto de los invitados se había reunido alrededor, aunque algunos ya se habían sentado a las mesas de hierro forjado diseminadas por la terraza y otros habían bajado al prado, ya que había más mesas a la sombra de los árboles.

Le sonrió a lady Hammond, que estaba sentada junto a lady Osbaldestone.

La anciana señaló el salmón frío de su plato.

—¡Delicioso! Tienes que probarlo.

—Lo haré.

Dio media vuelta y se acercó al bufé para coger un plato. El salmón estaba servido en una enorme bandeja situada al fondo de la mesa. Tendría que estirar mucho el brazo...

—¿Quieres salmón?

Alzó la vista y sonrió a Simon, que acababa de aparecer a su lado. Había adivinado que era él justo antes de que hablara. Aunque no sabía muy bien cómo.

—Gracias.

Para él era fácil alcanzar la bandeja. Le ofreció el plato y él le sirvió un grueso filete del suculento pescado antes de servirse dos en su plato. La siguió a lo largo de la mesa mientras ella elegía de entre los manjares dispuestos, haciendo lo propio.

Cuando titubeó al llegar al extremo en busca de un lugar para sentarse, Simon volvió a detenerse y le indicó el prado con un gesto de la mano.

—Podríamos sentarnos con Winifred.

La hermana de Kitty estaba sentada sola en una mesa para cuatro. Portia asintió.

—Sí. Vamos.

Mientras atravesaban el prado fue muy consciente de la presencia de Simon a su lado. Como si estuviera protegiéndola, aunque de qué debía protegerla era un completo misterio para ella. Winifred alzó la vista cuando se acercaron y les ofreció una sonrisa. Simon retiró la silla que enfrentaba la de la dama y le hizo un gesto para que tomara asiento. Una vez que estuvo sentada, él hizo lo mismo.

Desmond tardó unos minutos en reunirse con ellos y así la mesa quedó completa. Winifred, que acababa de sonreírle, miró su plato y frunció el ceño.

—¿No tienes hambre?

El caballero echó un vistazo al plato, en el cual sólo había un filete de salmón y dos hojas de lechuga. Titubeó un instante antes de contestar:

—Es el primer plato. Cuando acabe esto, iré a por más.

Portia se mordió el labio y bajó la vista. Por el rabillo del ojo vio que Kitty estaba en la terraza, en el extremo del bufé y con la vista clavada en ellos. Miró a Simon y éste sostuvo su mirada. Aunque su expresión permaneció impasible, ella supo que también se había percatado del detalle.

Estaba claro que James no era el único caballero que huía de las atenciones de Kitty.

La señora Archer agitó la mano y llamó a Kitty para que se acercara... a la mesa que ocupaban ella, su marido y Henry. La reticencia de Kitty fue evidente, pero poco podía hacer para no sentarse con ellos. Para alivio de todos, obedeció con cierto asomo de elegancia.

Los invitados se relajaron al punto y comenzaron a

charlar. La única que no mostró alivio alguno fue Winifred; a decir verdad, ni siquiera daba muestras de ser consciente del comportamiento de su hermana.

Sin embargo, conforme comían y charlaban, Portia se dedicó a estudiar a la mujer con disimulo y descubrió que le resultaba difícil creer que ignorara por completo los tejemanejes de Kitty. Winifred hablaba con voz suave; era de naturaleza callada, aunque en absoluto tímida o insegura. Exponía su opinión con serenidad y siempre se mostraba comedida, pero nunca sumisa. El respeto que sentía por la hermana mayor de Kitty se acrecentó.

El almuerzo finalizó con los sorbetes y los helados. Todos se pusieron en pie y comenzaron a pasear a la sombra de los enormes árboles.

—¡Esta noche es el baile! ¡Estoy deseando que llegue la hora! —exclamó Cecily Hammond, prácticamente dando brincos de la emoción.

—Es verdad. Creo que en todas las fiestas campestres debería celebrarse uno. Después de todo, es la oportunidad perfecta. —Annabelle Hammond se giró hacia Kitty cuando ésta se acercó al grupo—. Lady Glossup me ha dicho que el baile ha sido idea suya, señora Glossup, y que usted se ha encargado de casi todos los preparativos. Creo que deberíamos darle las gracias por su previsión y por todas las molestias que se ha tomado por nosotros.

El halago, tal vez un tanto inocente pero a todas luces sincero, le arrancó a Kitty una sonrisa.

—Me alegro mucho de que piensen que puede ser divertido; creo de veras que será una noche maravillosa. Adoro bailar y sé que la mayoría de los presentes también lo hace.

Kitty echó un vistazo a su alrededor. Se alzó un murmullo de aprobación. Por primera vez, Portia creyó vislumbrar cierta ansiedad, algo parecido a la inocencia, en Kitty; un deseo sincero de verse inmersa en el brillo y la elegancia del baile; la certeza de que en él encontraría... algo.

—¿Quiénes asistirán? —preguntó Lucy Buckstead.

—Todas las familias de los alrededores. Ya ha pasado cosa de un año desde que se celebró el último gran baile en los contornos, así que la asistencia será masiva. —Kitty hizo una pausa antes de añadir—: Además, están los oficiales del acuartelamiento de Blandford Forum. Estoy segura de que asistirán.

—¡Oficiales! —Cecily la miraba con los ojos desorbitados—. ¿Habrá muchos?

Kitty nombró a aquellos a los que esperaba. Aunque las damas se mostraron muy interesadas por las noticias de que los uniformes militares adornarían esa noche el salón de baile, los caballeros no parecieron muy entusiasmados al respecto.

—Oficiales sin escrúpulos y mal pagados, ya lo verás —le dijo Charlie a Simon en un murmullo.

Portia se mordió la lengua para no replicarle que dichos invitados los mantendrían alerta. No tenía sentido comentar algo que incentivara el afán protector tan típico de Simon. No le cabía duda de que se manifestaría por sí solo esa noche sin más estímulos. Tendría que estar muy pendiente e incluso tratar de evitarlo. Nada más lejos de sus deseos que tener una carabina...

Un baile rural importante prometía ser el acontecimiento perfecto para, por decirlo sin tapujos, pulir sus habilidades como cazamaridos. La mayoría de los caballeros que iba a conocer esa noche desaparecería de su vida al finalizar el baile; por tanto, eran perfectos para practicar.

Todas las jóvenes solteras se morían por asistir a los bailes; suponía que ella debía desarrollar esa costumbre. De momento, mientras paseaba y conversaba con los invitados a la sombra de los árboles, se dedicó a escuchar y tomar notas mentalmente acerca del comportamiento de las restantes damas. Del sereno entusiasmo de Winifred. De la resignación de Drusilla. De la chispeante emoción de las Hammond. Y de la romántica esperanza de Lucy.

Así como de la sincera expectación de la que Kitty hacía gala, convencida de que iba a ser una noche maravillosa. Puesto que llevaba casada varios años y habría asistido a un buen número de bailes, el fervor con el que esperaba la noche resultaba sorprendente y la hacía parecer más joven, incluso inocente.

Extraño, si se tenía en cuenta su comportamiento.

Tras apartar su mente de la confusa personalidad de Kitty, Portia tomó nota de todo lo que dejaron caer las restantes damas acerca de los preparativos para el baile y sus vestidos, decidida a aprovechar la ocasión al máximo.

Se movió de grupo en grupo, muy pendiente de todo lo que se decía. Le llevó un tiempo percatarse de que Simon o bien la seguía muy de cerca o bien la observaba desde lejos.

En ese momento se encontraba con Charlie y James, a cierta distancia del grupo en el que ella estaba. Alzó la cabeza y lo miró a los ojos, esperando arrancarle una mirada de hastiada irritación. Ésa era la expresión que solía aparecer en sus ojos cuando la vigilaba, llevado por ese afán protector compulsivo.

En cambio, cuando sus miradas se encontraron, no detectó indicio alguno de irritación. De otro sentimiento, sí. Algo mucho más intenso, más poderoso. Algo que se reflejaba en su semblante; en los austeros ángulos de sus pómulos y su frente; en su mentón, cuadrado y decidido.

Sus miradas se encontraron apenas un instante, pero fue más que suficiente para que leyera su expresión y la entendiera. Para que reaccionara.

Inspiró hondo y se giró hacia Winifred, asintiendo con la cabeza como si hubiera escuchado lo que ésta acababa de decir. Lo único que tenía claro en ese instante era que fuera cual fuese el impulso que lo llevaba a vigilarla, no tenía nada que ver con su afán protector.

Las damas más jóvenes no eran las únicas entusiasmadas con la perspectiva del baile. Lady Hammond, lady Osbaldestone e incluso lady Calvin estaban dispuestas a divertirse. Era verano y escaseaban los eventos sociales en los que ejercitar sus habilidades.

Portia no comprendió de inmediato la fuente de su interés; sin embargo, cuando a media tarde lady Osbaldestone exigió su ayuda para subir a sus aposentos con el fin de echar una siesta, pasando primero por su habitación, lo comprendió todo.

—¡No te quedes ahí pasmada, niña! —exclamó lady O al mismo tiempo que golpeaba el suelo del pasillo con su bastón—. Enséñame el vestido que piensas ponerte esta noche.

Resignada y preguntándose si serviría de algo, Portia la acompañó a la habitación que le habían asignado, situada en el ala este. Era una estancia bastante grande, con un armario enorme en el que la doncella había colocado todos sus vestidos. Tras ayudar a lady O a tomar asiento en el sillón de la chimenea, se acercó al armario y abrió las puertas de par en par.

Y titubeó. A decir verdad, aún no había pensado en el vestido que se pondría. Nunca se había preocupado por esas cosas. Gracias a Luc y a la excelente economía familiar, tenía vestidos de sobra, todos ellos preciosos; no obstante, hasta ese momento les había prestado la misma atención que a su aspecto físico: ninguna.

Lady O resopló.

—Tal y como pensaba. No tienes ni la menor idea. En fin, vamos a ver lo que has traído.

Portia obedeció a la dama y fue sacando uno a uno los vestidos que había llevado consigo. Cayó en la cuenta de que le encantaba uno de ellos, el de seda verde oscuro, y así lo dijo.

Lady O meneó la cabeza.

—Todavía no. Deja el dramatismo para más adelante, cuando lo tengas comiendo de tu mano. Sólo entonces surtirá efecto. Esta noche necesitas parecer... —Agitó la mano—. Menos decidida, menos segura. ¡Piensa en términos de estrategia, niña!

Portia nunca había considerado los colores de los vestidos en esos términos; observó desde esa nueva perspectiva los vestidos que había echado sobre la cama...

—¿Qué tal éste? —Alzó uno de seda en un delicado tono gris perla. Un color inusual para una dama soltera, pero que le sentaba de maravilla dados su cabello oscuro, su ojos color azul cobalto y su altura.

—Humm —Lady O le hizo un gesto—. Álzalo un poco más.

La obedeció al tiempo que alisaba el corpiño sobre su pecho y lo ajustaba para que la dama observara el sugerente diseño. El corpiño estaba hecho con dos capas de tejido, una inferior de seda ajustada y una superior de gasa del mismo tono, mucho más suelta y que disimulaba el atrevidísimo escote.

Los labios de lady O esbozaron una lenta sonrisa.

—Perfecto. Ni inocente en exceso ni del todo descarado. ¿Tienes zapatos a juego?

Los tenía, junto con un chal de tejido liviano en color gris oscuro y adornado con cuentas, y un ridículo. La anciana asintió con la cabeza en señal de aprobación.

—Y creo que me pondré las perlas.

—Enséñamelas.

Sacó la larga sarta de perlas del joyero y se la colocó alrededor del cuello. Le llegaba casi a la cintura.

—Tengo los pendientes a juego.

Lady O señaló el collar.

—Así no; date una vuelta en torno al cuello y deja que el resto caiga.

Portia enarcó las cejas, pero la obedeció.

—Ahora, coge otra vez el vestido.

Lo hizo y se lo pegó nuevamente al cuerpo. Cuando se dio la vuelta para mirarse en el espejo de pie que había en un rincón, captó el inesperado efecto.

—¡Vaya! Ahora lo entiendo...

—Me alegro. —Lady O parecía satisfecha—. ¡Estrategia! ¡Vamos! —Se levantó del sillón, logrando que soltara el vestido a toda prisa sobre la cama para ir a ayudarla. Una vez que estuvo de pie, la anciana se dirigió a la puerta—. Ya puedes ayudarme a prepararme para la siesta. Después, volverás aquí, te meterás en la cama y descansarás.

—No estoy cansada. —En la vida había echado una siesta antes de un baile.

La astuta mirada que le lanzó lady O mientras salía al pasillo le indicó que ella había llegado a esa misma conclusión.

—De todas formas, vas a complacerme regresando a tu habitación y metiéndote en la cama hasta la hora de arreglarte para la cena y el baile. —Cuando abrió la boca para replicar, la anciana levantó una mano para silenciarla—. Aparte del hecho de que ninguna dama desea asistir a un baile si no tiene un aspecto radiante y descansado, ¿qué tienes en mente hacer si me permites saberlo?

La pregunta fue lo bastante cortante como para que la hiciera recapacitar. Sopesó la respuesta mientras caminaban por el pasillo y al final confesó:

—Un paseo por el jardín y, después, quizás echarle un vistazo a la biblioteca.

—Y, a tenor de los invitados a esta fiesta, ¿crees que serás capaz de hacerlo a solas?

Portia frunció la nariz.

—Probablemente no. Seguro que alguien me ve y me acompaña...

—Alguien no... Algún caballero, para ser más precisas. Puedes estar segura de que las demás damas tienen dos dedos de frente y van a pasar la tarde descansando. —Se detuvo al llegar a la puerta de su habitación y la abrió. Portia la siguió y cerró la puerta al entrar—. Alguno de los caballeros, o seguramente más de uno, te acompañará. —Soltó el bastón, se subió a la cama y la atravesó con una mirada perspicaz—. ¡Piensa! ¿Eso es inteligente?

Tal parecía que le estuvieran dando una lección magistral acerca de un arte desconocido para ella hasta el momento. Tuvo que improvisar la respuesta.

—No, ¿verdad?

—¡Por supuesto que no! —exclamó la anciana mientras se recostaba sobre los almohadones y se ponía cómoda. La miró con los ojos entrecerrados—. Has pasado toda la mañana y media tarde con ellos. Darles una dieta abundante de tu compañía no va a despertar su apetito. Éste es el momento, las horas que faltan hasta el baile, de privarlos de su sustento. Después, durante la cena y el baile, estarán más predispuestos a acudir a tu lado.

Se le escapó una carcajada sin poder evitarlo. Se inclinó hacia delante y le dio a lady O un beso en la mejilla.

—¡Es una estratega fabulosa!

—¡Paparruchas! —La dama cerró los ojos y relajó la expresión—. Soy un general con mucha experiencia y he luchado, y ganado, más batallas de las que puedas contar.

Portia se alejó con una sonrisa en los labios. Acababa de llegar a la puerta cuando, sin abrir los ojos, lady O le ordenó:

—Vete y descansa.

Su sonrisa se ensanchó.

—¡Señor, sí, señor!

Abrió la puerta, salió al pasillo y, por una vez en su vida, hizo lo que le habían ordenado.

4

—No te olvides: ¡piensa en términos de estrategia!

Con semejantes palabras, lady O entró sin más en el salón y dejó que Portia la siguiera con más tranquilidad. Levantó la cabeza y entró... y se dio cuenta de que todas las miradas se posaron en ella de inmediato.

Lo más interesante fue que las damas regresaron a sus conversaciones un instante después, mientras que los caballeros siguieron atentos a ella algo más de tiempo; algunos incluso necesitaron algún comentario para regresar a la realidad.

Sabía que era absurdo fingir que no se había percatado de ello. Con un despliegue de serenidad, hizo una reverencia a lady Glossup, que le correspondió con un gesto de cabeza y una sonrisa deslumbrante, y después continuó caminando hasta llegar junto a Winifred, que estaba hablando con Desmond y James.

La admiración que pudo leer en los ojos de ambos hombres cuando la saludaron fue palpable. La aceptó con despreocupación y como si estuviera acostumbrada a semejante trato antes de unirse a la conversación.

Sin embargo, estaba aturdida. ¿Había cambiado? ¿Había cambiado algo en ella por el mero hecho de haberse decidido a buscar marido? ¿Se le notaba de alguna forma? ¿O tal vez no se había dado cuenta de que ésa era la reacción que provocaba en los demás porque hasta el momento jamás se había preocupado de ello y no le había prestado la menor atención a los caballeros?

Mientras paseaba y saludaba a la concurrencia, decidió que se debía a eso último. Una idea bastante sombría. Lady O había estado en lo cierto: su arrogancia debía de haber sido increíble. Aunque darse cuenta de ese hecho también incrementó su confianza. Por primera vez comenzaba a entender que tenía algo, un arma o una especie de poder, que podía utilizar para atrapar a un marido.

Lo único que tenía que hacer era aprender a elegir al caballero adecuado y aprender a utilizar dicha arma.

Simon estaba hablando con las hermanas Hammond y con Charlie; pasó junto al grupo y lo saludó con un indiferente gesto de cabeza. La había estado observado con atención desde que entró en la estancia. Su expresión era tensa, pétrea. No tenía ni idea de lo que estaba pensando.

Lo que menos le convenía era atizar su instinto protector; de manera que decidió unirse a Ambrose y a lady Calvin.

Simon contempló cómo Portia sonreía y encandilaba a Ambrose. Su rostro se tensó por el esfuerzo de reprimir una mueca feroz. No estaba por la labor de meditar por qué sentía lo que sentía..., ni tampoco qué eran esas emociones que se agitaban en su interior. Jamás en su vida se había sentido de esa manera. Tan... decidido. Tan aguijoneado.

El hecho de que no supiera por qué, de que no comprendiera el motivo, sólo le aumentaba la desazón. Algo había cambiado, pero era incapaz de apartar esa malsana obsesión de su mente el tiempo suficiente como para identificarlo.

Esa tarde había estado esperando a que Portia bajara tras acompañar a lady O a su dormitorio. Había querido hablar con ella, engatusarla para que le confesara lo que quería aprender.

No había hecho acto de presencia... O, mejor dicho, no había podido dar con ella; algo que le hacía preguntarse dónde había estado y con quién.

Podía verla por el rabillo del ojo; su esbelta figura cubierta por el vestido gris perla y el cabello oscuro recogido en la coronilla, mucho más alto de lo que jamás se lo había recogido. El peinado le dejaba al aire la nuca y atraía su atención hacia la elegante curva de su cuello y los delicados hombros. En cuanto al collar de perlas... una vuelta se le ajustaba al cuello mientras que la otra colgaba por debajo del diáfano escote de su corpiño y desaparecía por el misterioso valle situado entre sus senos. Llevándose con ella su imaginación. Sus sentidos seguían hechizados aun cuando apartó la vista; las palmas de las manos le ardían por el deseo de tocarla.

Portia seguía moviéndose con su elegancia innata, sin artificios; su modo de conversar tampoco había cambiado. Sin embargo, algo en su interior le decía sin lugar a dudas que su objetivo sí había cambiado.

Por qué le afectaba algo así le resultaba un misterio... Sólo sabía que así era.

Un movimiento en la puerta hizo que desviara la vista. Kitty acababa de llegar. Estaba deslumbrante con un vestido de satén blanco adornado con encaje plateado. Su cabello rubio claro estaba recogido en un complicado moño; los diamantes relucían en su escote y en sus orejas. Allí sola, era una visión magnífica, en especial porque resplandecía de felicidad; una felicidad que se reflejaba en su rostro, en sus ojos, y que hacía brillar su piel.

Se dirigió hacia los invitados de más edad como dictaban los buenos modales antes de aceptar el brazo de Henry y comenzar su paseo por el salón para saludar a cada grupo y recibir sus halagos.

Miró de nuevo a Portia. Cuando Kitty se detuvo junto a ella, sus sospechas se confirmaron. Al lado de la belleza de Portia, mucho más sutil y fascinante, Kitty parecía ostentosa. La pareja no se detuvo demasiado, sino que continuó de grupo en grupo hasta llegar junto a él.

Apenas tuvieron tiempo de intercambiar unas pocas palabras antes de que el mayordomo entrara para anunciar que la cena estaba servida.

A él le tocó acompañar a Lucy mientras deseaba con

todas sus fuerzas que... Pero no, la distribución de los invitados ya estaba dispuesta y mucho se temía que Kitty había sido la encargada. Los anfitriones, lord y lady Glossup, se sentaban a ambos extremos de la mesa; Kitty estaba sentada en el centro de uno de los laterales con Henry frente a ella, tal y como dictaba la etiqueta. Desmond estaba a su izquierda y Ambrose a su derecha. Portia estaba cerca de uno de los extremos, entre Charlie y James; mientras que él estaba al otro lado de la mesa, flanqueado por Lucy y la extremadamente callada Drusilla.

En otras circunstancias, no habría tenido motivo alguno para quejarse... Lucy era alegre y vivaz, aunque no dejaba de echarle miraditas a James, y Drusilla se contentaba con algún que otro comentario educado. Sin embargo, tal y como estaban las cosas, se vio obligado a observar cómo Portia se convertía en el centro de atención de Charlie y James durante la cena.

Por regla general, ni se le habría ocurrido mirarla, no en semejante entorno; hasta el momento, la actitud de Portia hacia los caballeros que la rodeaban había sido de altanero desdén. Ni Charlie ni James habrían tenido la menor oportunidad de hacer algún tipo de avance con ella; la idea de que respondiera a sus manidos halagos ni siquiera se le habría pasado por la cabeza.

La observó disimuladamente durante toda la cena; en un momento dado, se percató de que lady Osbaldestone lo miraba y puso mucho más cuidado en su empeño. Sin embargo, sus ojos tenían voluntad propia. No alcanzaba a oír lo que hablaban, pero su modo de sonreírles y las miradas interesadas que dedicaba a sus dos amigos hacían que no pudiera apartar la vista de ella.

¿Qué diablos estaba tramando?

¿Qué quería aprender?

Y lo que era más importante, ¿sabría lo que estaban pensando Charlie y James en esos momentos?

Porque él sí lo sabía. Y le molestaba mucho más de lo que estaba dispuesto a admitir, mucho más de lo que quería considerar siquiera.

Lady O volvió a mirarlo. De manera que entornó los párpados y se giró hacia Lucy.

—¿Sabe qué hay planeado para mañana?

Aguardó el momento adecuado; por suerte, Lucy estaba tan ansiosa como él por trasladarse al salón de baile. En cuanto lady Glossup se puso en pie y los instó a ir hacia allí, le ofreció el brazo y dejó que Drusilla los siguiera, acompañada del señor Archer.

Portia, del brazo de Charlie, iba por delante de ellos ya que su lugar en la mesa estaba más cerca de la puerta. En el vestíbulo principal tuvieron que rodear a los vecinos que habían sido invitados y que ya habían comenzado a llegar. Los invitados que se quedaban en la casa fueron directamente al salón de baile. A juzgar por el gentío que se arremolinaba en el vestíbulo, era evidente que el baile sería todo un éxito. Llevó a Lucy sin dilación al salón de baile con la intención de alcanzar a Portia antes de que la muchedumbre la engullera.

Al entrar en el salón, vieron a James justo por delante, observando a los presentes y escudriñando las caras.

Supo sin lugar a dudas que estaba buscando a Portia. Aunque Lucy seguía tomada de su brazo, se detuvo.

Kitty se lanzó hacia James y se colocó a su lado antes de que éste se diera cuenta siquiera. Le puso una mano en el brazo y se acercó a él... más de la cuenta. James retrocedió, pero ella siguió avanzando. Se vio obligado a permitirle que se apoyara en él. Su sonrisa era la seducción personificada mientras hablaba en voz baja.

Era una mujer bajita. Para escucharla, James tenía que inclinar la cabeza, de modo que la imagen que proyectaban sugería una relación un poco más estrecha que los simples lazos familiares.

Sintió que Lucy se tensaba a su lado.

James se enderezó y levantó la cabeza; por su rostro pasó una expresión de puro pánico. En ese momento lo vio y abrió los ojos de par en par.

Ningún amigo que se preciara haría caso omiso de semejante súplica.

Le dio unas palmaditas a Lucy en la mano.

—Vamos... Hablemos con James.

Por el rabillo del ojo, vio que Lucy levantaba la barbilla. Con determinación, la muchacha lo siguió.

Kitty los vio acercarse y retrocedió un paso, de modo que su cuerpo ya no tocara el de James.

—¡Mi querida Kitty! —dijo Lucy antes de detenerse siquiera; a esas alturas, todos utilizaban sus respectivos nombres de pila—. Debe de estar encantada con semejante gentío. ¿Esperaba a tanta gente?

La susodicha tardó un instante en adaptar su mente a las nuevas circunstancias, pero luego sonrió.

—Por supuesto, es de lo más satisfactorio.

—Me sorprende que no esté con su suegra para recibir a los invitados.

Simon se mordió el labio y en su fuero interno aplaudió las agallas de Lucy; tenía una expresión inocente en los ojos, pero se las había apañado para colocar a la otra dama en una situación incómoda.

La sonrisa de Kitty se tornó algo forzada.

—Lady Glossup no necesita mi ayuda. Además... —dijo al tiempo que desviaba la vista hacia James—, éste es el mejor momento para asegurarse el modo de disfrutar plenamente de la noche.

—Creo que eso es justo lo que pensaba cierto caballero —mintió Simon sin el menor reparo—. Estaba preguntando por tu paradero hace un momento... Un hombre de pelo oscuro. Creo que del pueblo.

—¿De verdad? —Eso distrajo a Kitty al punto—. ¿Sabes quién es?

—No recuerdo el nombre. —Recorrió con la mirada el salón de baile, que comenzaba a llenarse con los invitados—. Vaya, ahora no lo veo. Sería mejor que fueras hacia allí, tal vez lo encuentres...

Kitty se mostró indecisa un instante antes de sonreír (de forma muy elocuente) a James.

—Me reservarás ese vals del que hemos hablado, ¿verdad?

El rostro de James adoptó una expresión pétrea.

—Si da la casualidad de que estoy cerca en ese momento y no estoy comprometido... —Se encogió de hombros—. Tenemos que entretener a muchos invitados.

Su cuñada lo miró echando chispas por los ojos y apretó los labios para reprimir una réplica mordaz. Dado que tenía de testigos a Lucy y a Simon, se vio obligada a aceptar sus palabras con una inclinación de cabeza. Miró a Simon.

—¿Has dicho con pelo oscuro?

Él asintió con la cabeza.

—De estatura media, buena constitución. Manos cuidadas. Excelente sastre.

Era la descripción que un caballero haría de otro. Kitty se tragó la historia con anzuelo y todo... Y tras un breve gesto de cabeza, se alejó de ellos.

James lo miró a los ojos con una evidente expresión de alivio.

Entre ellos, Lucy dijo con vivacidad:

—No me había imaginado que tuvieran tantos vecinos. —Miró a James—. ¿Sería tan amable de pasear conmigo y presentármelos?

James titubeó un instante, pero luego sonrió y le tendió el brazo.

—Si ése es su deseo, será todo un honor para mí.

No le sorprendió en absoluto la mirada que le dirigió James por encima de la cabeza de la muchacha. Otra súplica, aunque en esa ocasión para que no lo dejara a solas con Lucy. Se tragó su impaciencia, ya que después de todo Portia no cometería ninguna locura, y consintió en pasear y charlar con ellos. Comprendía a la perfección la reticencia de James a dejar que Lucy se hiciera una idea equivocada acerca de una posible relación más personal entre ellos.

—Gracias. —James le dio unas palmaditas en el hombro cuando dio comienzo el baile y ambos observaron cómo Lucy bailaba la primera pieza con un joven que se había apresurado a solicitarla como pareja—. Ahora comprendes por qué insistí tanto en que vinieras.

—Yo no me preocuparía mucho por Lucy —refunfuñó él—. Tal vez sea algo entusiasta, pero se atiene a los límites marcados. Kitty, en cambio... —Miró a su amigo—. ¿Vas a quedarte una vez que se marchen los invitados?

—¡Por el amor de Dios, no! —James se estremeció—. Pienso marcharme con vosotros... Creo que le haré una visita al bueno de Cromer. Northumberland está lo bastante lejos como para disuadir incluso a Kitty.

Simon sonrió cuando se separaron. Mientras paseaba entre los invitados junto a James y a Lucy, había estado escudriñando a los presentes para localizar a Portia. En esos momentos se encontraba en el otro extremo del salón, junto a las puertas francesas que daban a la terraza y a la cálida noche. Charlie estaba con ella, al igual que un oficial vestido de uniforme; ambos estaban encandilados con ella hasta el punto de hacer caso omiso de todo lo que les rodeaba, incluida la atracción de la pista de baile.

Algo comprensible ya que Portia estaba radiante. Sus ojos azul cobalto resplandecían y sus manos gesticulaban con elegancia mientras esbozaba una deslumbrante sonrisa. Incluso a esa distancia, sintió la atracción. Cada vez que uno de ellos le hablaba ponía toda su atención en sus palabras; semejante devoción era una garantía para mantener a su lado, e hipnotizar, a cualquier hombre de sangre caliente.

En cualquier otra mujer, habría tachado semejante comportamiento como flirteo con toda la razón del mundo, pero Portia era, si nada lo convencía de lo contrario, incapaz de poner en práctica ese arte. Rodeó la estancia y esperó el mejor momento para acercarse. Tenía los ojos clavados en el trío, estudiando sus rostros, y estaba convencido de que ni Charlie ni la última conquista de Portia, fuera quien fuese el militar, interpretaban su comportamiento como la típica invitación.

Era algo distinto. Y eso, junto con el misterio de lo que andaba tramando, le confería más encanto y hacía que su atracción fuera irresistible.

Estaba apenas a unos metros de ella cuando de golpe

una mano se cerró con sorprendente fuerza alrededor de su brazo.

—¡Aquí estás! —Lady Osbaldestone lo miró con una sonrisa malévola—. Ni tus hermanas ni tus primas están presentes, así que no tienes obligaciones. Ven conmigo... Quiero presentarte a alguien.

—Pero... —Se resistió a sus tirones, ya que la anciana quería alejarlo de Portia. El maldito baile llevaba ya una hora y eso era lo más cerca que había estado de ella.

La anciana alzó la vista hasta su rostro y después siguió la dirección de su mirada hacia... Portia.

—¿Portia? ¡Bah! —Chasqueó los dedos—. No hay necesidad de que te preocupes por ella... De todos modos, ni siquiera te cae bien.

Abrió la boca para negar sus palabras, al menos la primera parte de lo que había dicho.

Lady O meneó la cabeza.

—No es de tu incumbencia si tu amigo Charlie le hace beber demasiadas copas de champán.

—¿¡Qué!? —Intentó girarse.

Lady O se lo impidió con un formidable tirón.

—¿Qué más da si acaba un poco achispada? Ya es mayorcita para saber lo que se hace y lo bastante decidida como para hacer valer su opinión. Ya va siendo hora de que abra un poco los ojos... Después de todo, esa tontuela tiene ya veinticuatro años. —Resopló y tiró de él—. Vamos. Por aquí.

La anciana señaló la dirección con su bastón y no le quedó más remedio que ceder, después de sofocar la oleada de pánico. La ruta más corta hacia la libertad era seguirle la corriente a la dama. A la primera oportunidad, se escaparía..., y entonces nada, absolutamente nada, se interpondría en su camino.

Portia vio cómo lady O se alejaba con Simon a rastras y contuvo un suspiro, aunque no estaba muy segura si era de pesar o de alivio. No lo quería a su alrededor, revoloteando con esa arrogante desaprobación tan típica en él; sin embargo, tal vez no fueran ésas sus intenciones. A tenor de la expresión que había atisbado poco antes en sus ojos, su actitud hacia ella había cambiado, aunque no sabía exactamente cómo ni tampoco había tenido tiempo de adivinar la naturaleza de dicho cambio. Además, quería probar su nueva arma con él. Después de todo, era uno de los tres elegidos a «considerar» y si bien se le estaba dando bastante bien con Charlie y James, aún debía probarla con Simon.

Aun así, Charlie y el teniente Campion eran bastante interesantes y lo bastante susceptibles a sus encantos como para practicar.

Clavó la mirada en la cara del teniente Campion.

—Así que pasa la mayor parte del año en Dorset. Dígame: ¿hace mucho frío en invierno?

El hombre sonrió de oreja a oreja y procedió a contestarle. Sin más incentivo que su atenta mirada (no apartaba los ojos de su rostro y anotaba mentalmente cada dato que dejaba caer), el teniente estuvo encantado de hablarle largo y tendido sobre su vida, y dejó caer los suficientes detalles como para que pudiera hacerse una idea acerca de su riqueza, de la posición de su familia y de las propiedades que ésta poseía, así como de sus aficiones, tanto en el ámbito militar como en el personal.

Qué agradables eran los caballeros una vez que se les cogía el truco. Al hilo de esa idea recordó algunos comentarios de sus dos hermanas mayores acerca de lo complacientes que eran sus maridos.

Aunque eso no quería decir que el teniente Campion fuera su hombre ideal. No, le faltaba... algo. No era un reto. Estaba completamente segura de que podría manejarlo con el dedo meñique..., y eso, por extraño que pareciera, no la atraía en lo más mínimo.

Charlie, que los había dejado a solas un instante, regresó con otra copa de champán. Se la ofreció con una floritura.

—Aquí tiene... Debe de estar sedienta.

Cogió la copa y le dio las gracias antes de beber un sorbo. La temperatura comenzaba a aumentar en el salón de baile; la estancia estaba atestada y el calor corporal de los presentes se sumaba a la bochornosa noche.

La mirada de Charlie no se apartó de su rostro.

—La selección de obras del Teatro Real durante esta temporada ha sido magnífica... ¿Tuvo oportunidad de ver alguna? —le preguntó.

Ella esbozó una sonrisa antes de contestar:

—Las dos primeras obras, sí. Tengo entendido que el teatro ha cambiado de manos.

—Desde luego. —El teniente Campion fulminó a Charlie con la mirada—. He oído que...

Al escucharlo, cayó en la cuenta de que Charlie había esperado excluir al teniente de la conversación con su pregunta. No sabía que éste pasaba parte de la temporada social en Londres de permiso. Contuvo una sonrisa mientras el hombre continuaba con el tema y se explayaba al respecto.

Charlie afrontó el revés con elegancia, pero aprovechó la oportunidad y le pidió el siguiente baile en cuanto los músicos empezaron a tocar la siguiente pieza.

Aceptó y bailaron el vals con bastante brío y una buena dosis de risas. La renuencia que había mostrado Charlie en un principio había desaparecido; si bien se resistía a hablar demasiado acerca de sí mismo, sí que ponía más interés en averiguar todo lo que pudiera sobre ella.

Y sus intenciones. Sobre su objetivo.

Muy consciente de eso, Portia rió y le prestó toda su atención, pero en realidad puso mucho empeño en ocultarle lo que pensaba. Los hombres como Charlie y James parecían mucho más interesados en averiguar hacia dónde quería llevarlos (o más bien querían averiguar la naturaleza de lo que aprender) con la idea de echarle una mano en el proceso de aprendizaje... Esbozó una sonrisa y se aprestó a guardar muy bien ese secreto. No veía motivo alguno para perder innecesariamente lo que sospechaba que era una parte esencial de su recién descubierto atractivo.

El aspecto más peliagudo de batir su ingenio con caballeros como Charlie era que éstos conocían las reglas. Y cómo sortearlas.

Cuando los últimos acordes del vals se desvanecieron y se detuvieron entre carcajadas, acalorados y jadeantes, Charlie le sonrió con arrebatador encanto.

—Recuperemos el aliento en la terraza... Hace demasiado calor aquí dentro.

Ella mantuvo la sonrisa mientras se preguntaba si se atrevería a dar el paso.

«Quien no arriesga, no gana», pensó. Jamás lo descubriría si no lo intentaba.

—Muy bien. —Ensanchó ampliamente la sonrisa al aceptar el desafío—. Vamos.

Se giró hacia la terraza... y estuvo a punto de darse de bruces con Simon.

Se le disparó el pulso y, por un instante, se quedó sin respiración. Él la miró a los ojos y, aunque su expresión era tan adusta como de costumbre, no vio señales de su habitual desaprobación.

—Estábamos a punto de salir a la terraza. —La nota aguda de su voz sonó un tanto discordante. El champán, sin duda—. Hace mucho calor aquí dentro.

Utilizó la excusa para abanicarse con la mano. No cabía duda de que su temperatura corporal había subido.

La expresión de Simon no se suavizó. Desvió la vista hacia Charlie.

—Acabo de hablar con lady Osbaldestone... Quiere hablar contigo.

Charlie frunció el ceño.

—¿Lady Osbaldestone? ¿Qué demonios quiere esa vieja bruja de mí?

—¿Quién sabe? Aunque ha insistido bastante. La encontrarás cerca de la sala de refrigerios.

Charlie la miró.

Y la mano de Simon se cerró en torno a su codo.

—Yo acompañaré a Portia a la terraza... Con un poco de suerte, cuando hayas terminado con lady Osbaldestone, ya habremos vuelto.

Aunque la sugerencia parecía perfectamente inocente, Charlie no sabía si tragárselo o no. La mirada con la que fulminó a su amigo lo dejó muy claro. Claro que tampoco tenía alternativa, así que con una elegante reverencia hacia ella y una inclinación de cabeza hacia él, se marchó hacia el otro extremo del salón.

Simon la soltó. Al unísono, se dieron la vuelta y se encaminaron a las puertas francesas.

Lo miró a la cara.

—¿Es cierto que lady O quiere hablar con Charlie? ¿O sólo ha sido una muestra más de tu habitual prepotencia?

Simon la miró un instante a los ojos antes de hacerse a un lado para dejarla pasar.

—Hará un poco más de fresco fuera.

—Te lo has inventado, ¿verdad? —le preguntó al tiempo que salía a la terraza.

Cuando él la instó a continuar, se dio media vuelta para enfrentarlo. Simon estudió su rostro con detenimiento. Y lo que vio le hizo entrecerrar los ojos.

—Estás achispada. ¿Cuántas copas de champán has bebido?

Volvió a tirar de ella para que caminara y la tomó del codo mientras se adentraban en la penumbra de la terraza. Varias parejas y unos cuantos grupitos paseaban por allí y también por los jardines cercanos para disfrutar del respiro que proporcionaba el fresco aire nocturno.

—Eso no es de tu incumbencia. —Además, no hacía falta que se lo dijera—. Jamás he estado achispada antes... y es de lo más agradable. —Al darse cuenta de la verdad que encerraban esas palabras, se zafó de su mano y dio una vuelta—. Una experiencia nueva. Y de lo más inocua.

La expresión del rostro de Simon era extraña... Un tanto protectora, pero también había algo más. Como si lo hubiera cautivado. Un rayito de esperanza se abrió paso en su interior. ¿También funcionarían sus artimañas con él?

Clavó los ojos en su rostro y sonrió con dulzura. Después soltó una carcajada y se dispuso a caminar a su lado. El paseo los alejaba de la fiesta y del salón del baile hacia un lugar más tranquilo. Donde podrían conversar libremente.

Pero qué tontería, se dijo.

—No tiene sentido tirarte de la lengua para que me cuentes cosas sobre ti... Ya lo sé todo.

Se acercaban al extremo de la terraza. Sintió la mirada de Simon clavada en su rostro.

—A decir verdad —replicó él con un murmullo ronco—, sabes muy poco sobre mí.

Sus fascinantes palabras le erizaron la piel. Ella se limitó a sonreír y compuso una expresión de genuina incredulidad.

—¿Eso es lo que estás tramando? ¿Quieres aprender sobre los hombres?

No recordaba que él le hubiera hablado con ese incitante tono nunca; ladeó la cabeza y meditó la respuesta. Aunque debía admitir que su mente no estaba en plenas facultades.

—No sobre los hombres en general... y no sólo sobre ellos. —Doblaron la esquina al llegar al final de la terraza y continuaron paseando; no había nadie en ese lado de la casa. Inspiró hondo antes de soltar el aire lentamente—. Quiero aprender todas las cosas que no he aprendido antes.

Ya estaba dicho... Eso debería bastarle.

—¿Qué cosas?

Se giró para enfrentarlo y quedó de espaldas a la pared. El instinto le advertía de que se estaban alejando demasiado del salón de baile. A pesar de eso, lo miró con una sonrisa deslumbrante y dejó que la confianza que se había apoderado de ella aflorara a su rostro.

—En fin, pues todas las cosas que no he experimentado antes. —Abrió los brazos sin apartar la vista de sus ojos—. La emoción, la pasión. Todas esas cosas que los hombres podrían enseñarme pero a las que no he dedicado ni un solo pensamiento... hasta ahora.

Simon se había detenido frente a ella y tenía la mirada clavada en sus ojos. Las sombras le ocultaban el rostro.

—¿Por eso tenías tantas ganas de salir con Charlie?

Algo en su voz la puso sobre aviso, algo que la instó a retomar el sentido común. Sostuvo su mirada sin flaquear y respondió con la verdad:

—No lo sé. No fui yo quien lo propuso, fue él.

—Poco sorprendente dado tu deseo de aprender. Y, además, has acabado en la terraza.

El tono reprobatorio de su voz acabó por devolverle el sentido común de golpe. Levantó la barbilla.

—Contigo. No con él.

Silencio.

El desafío estaba lanzado, por más que fuera implícito; ambos entendían la situación.

Ninguno de los dos apartó la vista, ninguno se movió ni hizo nada por romper el hechizo. La temperatura de la noche aumentó hasta casi asfixiarlos. Portia habría jurado que todo a su alrededor comenzó a dar vueltas. Sentía la sangre corriendo bajo la piel y le palpitaban las sienes.

Simon estaba apenas a un paso de ella. De repente, deseó que se acercara, como si fuera una especie de anhelo atávico. Él pareció sentir lo mismo. Se acercó un tanto antes de quedarse muy quieto. Su rostro siguió oculto entre las sombras, de modo que fue incapaz de interpretar su mirada.

—Si te hubiera acompañado Charlie, ¿qué querrías aprender?

Tardó un instante en responder. Tuvo que humedecerse los labios antes de hablar.

—Tú lo conoces mucho mejor que yo... ¿Qué crees tú que habría aprendido, dado el entorno y las circunstancias?

El silencio se alargó hasta lo que le pareció una eternidad. Sin dejar de mirarla a los ojos, Simon se acercó a ella. E inclinó la cabeza muy despacio.

Alzó una mano hasta su rostro. Los largos dedos acariciaron la piel antes de posarse sobre su mentón y obligarla a levantar la barbilla.

Para que sus labios, cálidos y firmes, se posaran sobre los suyos con facilidad.

Portia cerró los ojos y se quedó sin aliento. Sus sentidos cobraron vida cuando su cuerpo descubrió ese placer sensual.

No tenía nada con lo que comparar ese maravilloso primer beso. Ningún otro hombre se había atrevido jamás a acercarse tanto, a tomarse semejantes libertades. Si alguno lo hubiera intentado, le habría dado un buen guantazo.

Los labios de Simon se movieron, indagadores, sobre su boca, rendida y más que dispuesta, mientras ella clavaba los dedos en la piedra que tenía a su espalda.

Sus sentidos se concentraron en el beso hasta que en su mente sólo existió esa dulce e incitante presión; hasta que el beso se convirtió en lo único que importaba. Le palpitaban los labios por el deseo. Le daba vueltas la cabeza... y no era por el champán.

Había olvidado respirar, ni siquiera le importaba. Le devolvió el beso, en un principio insegura, indecisa...

Simon volvió a cambiar de postura, pero no para alejarse, sino para acercarse más a ella. Los dedos que le sujetaban el mentón se cerraron sobre ella con más fuerza y la presión de esos incitantes labios aumentó.

Separó los labios tal y como él parecía desear; al punto, Simon deslizó la lengua entre ellos... y la sensación hizo que se le doblaran las rodillas. Tuvo la impresión de que él era consciente de ese hecho, aunque no sabía cómo. El cariz del beso se tornó más pausado, hasta que cada caricia pareció estar impregnada de languidez, de calmada apreciación, de placer compartido. La vertiginosa sorpresa de la novedosa y sensual experiencia se desvaneció.

La certeza de que jamás la habían besado emocionó a Simon sobremanera. Y se quedó perplejo ante el súbito apremio de apoderarse de ella. Reprimió el anhelo y se negó a demostrarlo; ni con los labios, ni con los dedos ni, muchísimo menos, con las lentas y embriagadoras caricias de su lengua.

Sabía a ambrosía, a néctar y a miel. Dulce como el verano y fresca como la pureza. De buen grado la habría besado durante horas, sin embargo... quería mucho más que un mero beso.

La acorraló contra la pared. Apoyó el brazo sobre la fría piedra, con los músculos contraídos y el puño apretado mientras luchaba para reprimir el anhelo de aprovecharse del momento. De acercarse más todavía, de amoldarse contra ella, de sentir esas curvas cubiertas por la seda pegadas a su cuerpo.

Portia era alta y de extremidades largas; el impulso de comprobar lo bien que encajarían, el delirante deseo de calmar su excitado cuerpo frotándose apenas contra ella, lo estaba volviendo loco. Por no hablar de la acuciante necesidad de cubrirle los pechos con las manos, de inclinar la cabeza y de seguir con los labios el sendero de las perlas...

Aun así, se trataba de Portia. Ni siquiera olvidó de quién se trataba durante el embriagador momento en el que intentó poner fin al beso y ella se enderezó, renuente a separarse de sus labios. De modo que se vio obligado a apoderarse de nuevo de su boca; de esa boca que le ofrecía sin reservas.

El dilema estaba allí, y por primera vez lo veía claramente, burlándose del deseo que sentía por ella. Cada instante de abandono a ese deseo, por parte de los dos, aumentaba el precio que debería pagar cuando acabara ese interludio.

Pero debía ponerle fin. Llevaban demasiado tiempo fuera del salón de baile.

Y se trataba de Portia.

Le costó la misma vida poner fin al beso y levantar la cabeza. Apartó la mano de su rostro, bajó el brazo y se quedó allí parado, esperando que el deseo que le corría por las venas disminuyera hasta un nivel inofensivo. Mantuvo los ojos clavados en su rostro y vio cómo sus párpados se movían hasta que los abrió.

Esos ojos azul cobalto resplandecían; un ligero rubor teñía sus pálidas mejillas..., pero no era de vergüenza. Parpadeó unas cuantas veces mientras lo miraba a los ojos, intentando descifrar su expresión.

Sabía que no descubriría nada en su tensa expresión, al menos nada que reconociera. Él, en cambio, era capaz de seguir el hilo de sus pensamientos reflejado en su semblante.

No había estupefacción, ni tampoco la había esperado; pero sí había sorpresa, curiosidad y una sed insaciable de aprender más. Además de la recién descubierta percepción de la sensualidad.

Tomó una honda bocanada de aire y esperó hasta asegurarse de que podía mantenerse en pie por sí misma.

—Vamos, tenemos que regresar.

La cogió de la mano y tiró de ella para llevarla de vuelta a la terraza principal.

Salvo por las dos parejas que se encontraban en el extremo más alejado, el lugar estaba desierto. Se colocó la mano de Portia en el brazo y recorrieron el trayecto hacia el salón de baile en silencio.

Ya veían las puertas francesas. Estaba dándole las gracias a su buena suerte por el hecho de que estuviera lo bastante distraída como para no querer hablar (no estaba en condiciones de soportar una discusión) cuando escuchó voces.

Ella también las escuchó. Antes de que pudiera detenerla, se acercó a la balaustrada y echó un vistazo hacia el sendero que discurría por debajo.

Tiró de ella, pero no se movió. Su rígida inmovilidad lo puso sobre aviso, de modo que la imitó y miró hacia abajo.

Escucharon los quedos susurros de una acalorada discusión. Desmond estaba de espaldas a la pared de la terraza. Kitty estaba delante de él, colgada de su cuello. El caballero, con el cuerpo totalmente rígido, forcejaba para apartarla.

Simon miró a Portia y ésta le devolvió la mirada.

Se giraron al unísono y regresaron al salón de baile.

Portia no alcanzaba a imaginar siquiera qué estaba tramando Kitty o qué esperaba conseguir con su vergonzoso comportamiento; se le escapaba por completo. Se desentendió de ese asunto... Después de todo, tenía cosas más importantes en la cabeza.

Como el beso de Simon.

Su primer beso romántico... No era sorprendente que se hubiera sentido fascinada. Mientras paseaba por los jardines a la mañana siguiente, rememoró el momento y revivió las sensaciones; no sólo los labios de Simon sobre los suyos, sino todo lo que había experimentado en respuesta a sus caricias. Los nervios a flor de piel, la aceleración del pulso, el acuciante anhelo de recrearse con una cercanía física de otra índole. No era de extrañar que otras mujeres encontraran esa actividad adictiva; en ese momento se habría dado de tortas por su anterior desinterés.

Desde luego que había deseado mucho más la noche anterior. Y seguía deseándolo. A pesar de su inexperiencia, a pesar de toda la experiencia que Simon poseía, sospechaba, presentía, que él había sentido lo mismo. Si hubieran tenido la oportunidad... En cambio, se habían visto obligados a regresar al salón de baile.

Una vez de vuelta con el resto de los invitados, no habían intercambiado una sola palabra sobre su interludio, aunque tampoco habían hablado de ninguna otra cosa. Ella había estado demasiado distraída analizándolo mientras que él, al parecer, no había sentido la necesidad de decir nada. A la postre, se había retirado a su habitación, a su cama. Y la sensación de esos labios sobre los suyos la había perseguido en sueños.

Esa mañana se había levantado decidida a seguir experimentando, a ir más allá. No obstante, había preferido desayunar con lady O en la habitación de la anciana en lugar de enfrentarse a Simon durante el desayuno antes de haber tenido la oportunidad de decidir el camino a seguir.

Los joviales comentarios de lady O acerca de la promiscuidad de los hombres, salpicados de sutiles alusiones a los aspectos físicos de las relaciones entre hombres y mujeres, sólo habían servido para decidirse a aclarar su opinión al respecto, de modo que pudiera decidir su curso de acción.

Razón por la que estaba paseando a solas por los jardines en esos momentos.

Intentaba decidir la importancia que debía otorgar a un beso. La importancia que debía otorgar a su propia respuesta.

Simon no había dado el menor indicio de que besarla hubiera sido diferente de besar a cualquier otra mujer. Arrugó la nariz y prosiguió su camino por uno de los senderos. Era demasiado práctica como para no reconocer que era todo un experto, que debía de haber besado a un centenar de mujeres. Sin embargo... estaba casi segura de que volvería a besarla si se le presentaba la oportunidad.

Al menos se sentía segura al respecto, razonablemente segura. El sendero que llevaba al templete se abría ante ella; sin ser consciente de ello, sus pies tomaron esa dirección.

No obstante, su propio camino parecía mucho menos despejado. Cuanto más reflexionaba, más perdida se sentía. Literalmente, como si hubiera emprendido un viaje a un país desconocido sin brújula, ni mapa.

¿Sentiría lo mismo la próxima vez que la besaran? ¿O la reacción de la noche anterior se debió a que fue su primera vez? ¿Habría sentido lo mismo de haberla besado otro hombre? Si Simon la besaba de nuevo, ¿sentiría algo?

Y la pregunta más importante: ¿era relevante lo que sentía cuando un caballero la besaba?

Las respuestas se ocultaban tras su inmensa inexperiencia. Irguió los hombros y levantó la cabeza... Tendría que experimentar para averiguarlo.

Una vez tomada esa decisión, se sintió mucho más optimista. El templete apareció frente a ella; era una pequeña construcción de mármol con columnas jónicas. Estaba rodeado de parterres cuajados de flores. Mientras subía los escalones, se percató de la presencia de un jardinero, un joven de abundante cabello negro, que estaba desbrozando uno de los parterres. Cuando el muchacho levantó la vista, le sonrió y lo saludó con un gesto de cabeza. Él parpadeó asombrado y a todas luces incómodo, pero le devolvió el saludo con la cabeza.

Cuando subió las escaleras, comprendió de inmediato el porqué de la expresión del jardinero. En el templete reverberaban las voces de dos personas... Una discusión. Si hubiera estado prestando atención, se habría dado cuenta antes de subir los escalones. El jardinero estaría escuchando todas y cada una de las palabras, le sería imposible evitarlo en el silencio de los jardines.

—¡Tu comportamiento es inmoral! No te he educado para que te comportes de esta manera. ¡No acabo de imaginar el propósito de semejante despliegue de ordinariez!

El melodramático discurso procedía de la señora Archer. Por lo que suponía, la dama estaba sentada en un banco emplazado al otro lado del templete, el lugar con las mejores vistas. Las palabras reverberaban en el interior del edificio y el eco aumentaba su volumen.

—¡Quiero una vida emocionante! —declaró Kitty con voz estridente—. Me casaste con Henry y me dijiste que sería una dama... ¡Me describiste la vida como su esposa como un lecho de rosas! Me hiciste creer que conseguiría todo lo que siempre había deseado... ¡Y no ha sido así!

—¡No puedes ser tan ingenua como para creer que tu vida será tal cual la has soñado!

Portia se alegró de que alguien estuviera diciendo lo que Kitty necesitaba escuchar, pero ella no tenía ganas de inmiscuirse en el asunto. En silencio, dio media vuelta y bajó los escalones.

Cuando llegó al sendero, escuchó la réplica de Kitty con voz adusta y seca.

—Más ingenua si cabe, porque te creí. Ahora me enfrento a la realidad... ¿Sabes que quiere que vivamos aquí casi todo el año? ¿Y que quiere que le dé hijos?

Kitty pronunció la última palabra como si Henry le hubiera pedido que se cortara las venas; anonadada, Portia se detuvo.

—¡Hijos! —repitió Kitty con evidente desdén—. Perderé mi figura. ¡Me pondré gorda y nadie querrá mirarme! Y si lo hicieran, se echarían a temblar y apartarían la vista. ¡Antes prefiero la muerte!

Sus palabras destilaban algo muy próximo a la histeria.

Portia sintió un escalofrío. Al apartar la vista, vio al jardinero y sus miradas se encontraron. Al instante, apartó la vista e inspiró hondo. El jardinero regresó a sus flores. Y ella reanudó su camino.

Con el ceño fruncido.

Cuando salió al prado, vio a Winifred, quien, como ella, paseaba sin rumbo fijo. Al juzgar sensato que no se acercara al templete, cambió de dirección y echó a andar hacia ella.

Winifred le sonrió en cálida bienvenida y ella respondió al gesto. Al menos, podría aprender de ella.

Tras intercambiar los saludos de rigor y de mutuo acuerdo, enfilaron el camino que llevaba al lago.

—Espero que no me tome por una imperdonable descarada —comenzó—, pero no he podido evitar percatarme de... —La miró a la cara—. ¿Me equivoco al creer que hay cierta relación de índole sentimental entre usted y el señor Winfield?

Winifred sonrió antes de clavar la vista al frente. Pasado un instante, contestó:

—Tal vez sea más pragmático decir que estamos considerando la posibilidad de una relación. —Esbozó una sonrisa mientras la miraba—. Sé que suena un tanto timorato, pero supongo que yo soy así, al menos en lo tocante al matrimonio.

Portia vio la oportunidad y la aprovechó sin dilación.

—Sé perfectamente a qué se refiere... Ya que yo opino igual. —Miró a su interlocutora a los ojos—. En estos momentos estoy considerando la idea del matrimonio, de manera abstracta, y tengo que confesar que hay muchas cosas a las que no les encuentro sentido. He estado relegando la cuestión por razones puramente egoístas, ya que me interesaban otros temas, de modo que ahora mismo me encuentro perdida y no tan informada como me gustaría. Sin embargo, supongo que usted tiene mucha más experiencia...

Winifred hizo un mohín, pero la expresión de sus ojos no varió y su semblante siguió siendo afable.

—En cuanto a eso, la verdad es que sí tengo más experiencia en cierto sentido, pero me temo que servirá de poca ayuda para cualquier otra mujer que quiera comprender el asunto. —Gesticuló con las manos—. Tengo treinta años y sigo soltera.

Portia frunció el ceño.

—Perdóneme, pero es de buena familia, supongo que dispondrá de una dote generosa y no le faltan encantos. Supongo que ha recibido numerosas proposiciones.

Winifred inclinó la cabeza.

—Algunas, desde luego, pero no demasiadas. Hasta el momento, no he animado a ningún caballero.

Portia no la comprendía.

Winifred se dio cuenta y esbozó una sonrisa torcida.

—Ya que me ha concedido el honor de confiar en mí, yo actuaré en consecuencia. Debo suponer que no tiene una hermosa hermana menor. En concreto, una hermosa hermana menor muy codiciosa...

Portia parpadeó. Una imagen de Penélope, con sus anteojos y su expresión severa, acudió a su mente. Meneó la cabeza.

—Pero... si... En fin, Kitty lleva casada varios años, ¿no es así?

—Sí, por supuesto. Por desgracia, el matrimonio no ha aplacado su deseo de apoderarse de todo cuanto yo tenga o pueda tener.

—Ella... —Se detuvo para buscar la palabra adecuada—. ¿Ella le robaba sus pretendientes?

—Siempre. Desde pequeñas.

A pesar de la revelación, el rostro de la joven permaneció calmado y sereno... Resignado, comprendió.

—Aunque... —continuó Winifred mirándola fijamente a los ojos— no sé si debería estarle agradecida. No desearía casarme con un caballero que me fuera infiel a la primera oportunidad.

Portia asintió con la cabeza.

—Por supuesto que no. —Titubeó un instante antes de añadir—: He mencionado al señor Winfield. Parece que se ha mantenido constante en sus afectos pese a los insistentes intentos de Kitty.

La mirada que le dirigió Winifred estaba teñida de incertidumbre; por primera vez atisbó a la mujer que se ocultaba tras la fachada de serenidad y que había sufrido una decepción tras otra a manos de su hermana.

—¿Usted cree? —En ese momento, Winifred sonrió, otra vez esa sonrisa torcida; su serena máscara volvió a su lugar—. Voy a contarle nuestra historia. Desmond conoció a mi familia hace unos años en Londres. Al principio, se quedó prendado de Kitty, como la mayoría de los caballeros. Después descubrió que estaba casada y se fijó en mí.

—Vaya. —Habían llegado al final del camino. Contemplaron unos instantes el lago antes de dar la vuelta y emprender el camino de regreso a la casa—. Pero... —continuó Portia—, eso quiere decir que Desmond lleva varios años cortejándola, ¿no?

Winifred asintió con la cabeza.

—Unos dos años. —Tras un instante, añadió con cierta timidez—: Me dijo que se apartó de Kitty en cuanto la conoció lo suficiente como para adivinar su verdadera naturaleza. Fue después cuando averiguó que estaba casada.

Portia tenía muy presente la escena que había presenciado la noche anterior en la terraza.

—La verdad es que parece... bastante tenso con Kitty. No he visto indicio alguno de que quiera aprovechar la primera oportunidad para renovar su interés por ella... Más bien todo lo contrario.

Winifred la miró a los ojos y estudió su expresión.

—¿De verdad lo cree?

Portia sostuvo su mirada.

—Sí, sin lugar a dudas.

La emoción, la esperanza, que atisbó en los ojos de la otra mujer antes de que ésta apartara la vista hizo que se sintiera inexplicablemente bien consigo misma. Suponía que eso era lo que sentía lady O cuando sus tejemanejes daban buen resultado; por primera vez en la vida, Portia entendió su atractivo.

Continuaron caminando. Cuando alzó la vista y vio a los dos hombres que se acercaban a ellas, recordó de golpe su propia situación.

Simon y James se acercaron. Las saludaron con su habitual encanto. De reojo, estudió a Simon, pero no detectó cambio alguno en su comportamiento, no leyó nada concreto en su actitud hacia ella..., ningún indicio que le dijera qué pensaba de su beso.

—Nos han enviado a buscarlas —informó James—. Se está organizando un almuerzo campestre. La mayoría ha decidido que la comida será mucho más apetitosa si se sirve en las ruinas del antiguo monasterio.

—¿Dónde está el monasterio? —preguntó Winifred.

—Al norte del pueblo, no está lejos. Es un lugar precioso. —James hizo un gesto con la mano—. Un lugar ideal para comer, beber y relajarse en el corazón de la campiña.

5

Las palabras de James resultaron ser ciertas. El monasterio era tan maravilloso como les había asegurado. Situado en un collado, las ruinas ocupaban una gran extensión. Si bien las vistas no eran tan buenas como las que se disfrutaban desde el mirador, merecía la pena contemplarlas.

El almuerzo se sirvió en un extenso prado descuidado, desde donde se podía disfrutar de una magnífica vista del valle y de los campos de cultivo hasta donde se confundían con el horizonte. Aunque la temperatura era agradable, el sol estaba oculto por unas algodonosas nubes. Una ligera brisa agitaba las hojas de los árboles y mecía las flores silvestres.

Una vez que hubieron dado buena cuenta del vino y de la comida, los invitados de más edad se dispusieron a pasar la tarde sentados e intercambiando cotilleos sobre la alta sociedad y el mundo en general. El resto se dispersó para explorar las ruinas.

Eran la fantasía romántica de toda jovencita. Las piedras caídas estaban bien asentadas en el suelo y no representaban ningún peligro, y en algunos lugares estaban cubiertas por las enredaderas. Se conservaba algún que otro arco y algunos de los muros seguían en pie. Una parte del claustro ofrecía un encantador y soleado rinconcito donde descansar.

Desde que la vio pasear por los jardines esa mañana, Simon no había dejado de pensar en ella ni un instante. Incluso fuera de su campo visual, era consciente de su presencia, tan suave como la caricia de la seda sobre la piel desnuda. Sí, ésa era la reacción que Portia le provocaba. La contempló, incapaz de resistirse, aun cuando sabía que ella se había dado cuenta. Quería saber... Necesitaba saber. No podía sacarse de la cabeza las posibilidades que el inesperado beso de la terraza había abierto.

No había sido su intención; y bien sabía que la de ella tampoco. Pero había sucedido. Por qué semejante interacción, tan insignificante a simple vista, lo mantenía en vilo era un enigma que no estaba seguro de querer resolver.

No obstante, no podía olvidarlo, no podía zafarse de la desquiciada idea que se había adueñado de su mente con la fuerza de un torrente y que había echado raíces sin más. De hecho, esa idea lo había mantenido en vela la mitad de la noche.

Por más que su instinto lo instara a actuar de otra manera, sabía que no debía perseguirla ni airear ante los demás lo que estaban sintiendo. Cuando Portia se levantó junto con los otros para explorar los alrededores, los siguió a cierta distancia. Charlie y James eran los encargados de vigilar al grupo.

Las Hammond no tardaron en adelantarse a todos los demás e intentaron apresurarlos entre risillas. Oswald y Swanston, con un fingido aire de superioridad, las siguieron, aunque sin muchas prisas. Desmond paseaba junto a Winifred. La pareja se separó del resto y tomó una ruta distinta. Drusilla, Lucy y Portia continuaron su exploración; esta última llevaba el sombrero en las manos y lo mecía por las cintas.

Henry y Kitty se habían quedado con las personas mayores. La señora Archer, lady Glossup y lady O habían creído necesario entablar una conversación con Kitty. James, por tanto, estaba relajado y sonreía de oreja a oreja mientras traspasaba el arco de entrada a la que fuera la nave de la iglesia.

Él también sonreía.

A Simon le llevó quince minutos desembarazarse de James y dejarlo con Drusilla. Cuando ésta se detuvo a descansar junto a una de las piedras caídas e instó a Lucy y a Portia a que prosiguieran sin ella, él también se detuvo con el ceño fruncido y miró a su amigo, que entendió a la perfección sin necesidad de palabras. James se sintió obligado a quedarse con Drusilla y a entretenerla como buenamente pudiera.

Charlie era un obstáculo más difícil, sobre todo porque también se había fijado en Portia. Aunque estaba seguro de que su amigo no tenía muy claro ni el motivo ni el objetivo. Sopesó sus opciones mientras aceleraban el paso para alcanzar a las muchachas.

Portia y Lucy los recibieron con una sonrisa.

Se dirigió primero a Lucy.

—¿Son las ruinas tal y como se las esperaba?

—¡Y mucho más! —Lucy extendió los brazos a ambos lados del cuerpo, con el rostro animado y los ojos brillantes—. Es un lugar maravilloso. ¡Caray! No cuesta trabajo imaginarse a algún que otro fantasma merodeando por aquí. Incluso a toda una fila de monjes espectrales que se dirigen muy despacio hacia el altar, incensarios en mano. Tal vez un coro cuyos cánticos se elevan de entre una espesa niebla donde no se puede ver a nadie.

Portia se echó a reír y él la miró a los ojos; distraída, olvidó lo que había estado a punto de decir.

De modo que fue Charlie quien replicó.

—Pero hay muchísimas más posibilidades. —Regaló a Lucy su sonrisa más arrebatadora—. ¿Qué me dice de la cripta? Ése sí que es un lugar para imaginar visiones fantasmagóricas. Las tumbas siguen allí, así que tiene garantizado un par de escalofríos como poco.

Lucy lo miraba con los ojos desorbitados.

—¿Dónde? —Comenzó a mirar a su alrededor—. ¿Está cerca? —Su mirada, a caballo entre la impaciencia y la gratitud, volvió a Charlie, que respondió como era habitual en él.

—Está al otro lado de la iglesia. —Con un elegante gesto, le ofreció el brazo, distraído de su anterior presa por el sincero entusiasmo que mostraban los ojos de Lucy—. Vamos, la acompañaré. Si es una amante de lo gótico, no puede perdérsela.

Lucy se colgó de su brazo de buena gana. Charlie los miró con una ceja enarcada, por encima de la cabeza de la joven.

—¿Venís?

Simon le indicó que se fuera.

—Pasearemos por aquí un poco más. Nos veremos en el claustro.

Charlie parpadeó, sorprendido, y titubeó un instante antes de inclinar la cabeza.

—De acuerdo. —Se giró hacia Lucy y emprendieron la marcha—. Se dice que en las noches sin luna se escucha el lamento de...

Se volvió hacia Portia justo a tiempo de ver su sonrisa, aunque no tardó en desaparecer en cuanto lo miró a los ojos. Con la barbilla en alto, lo estudió con detenimiento. Él hizo lo mismo, pero no pudo adivinar lo que estaba pensando.

Señaló un viejo camino pavimentado que llevaba al huerto de la cocina del monasterio. Portia echó a andar en la dirección indicada.

—Tú ya sabías que hay una cripta, ¿verdad?

La siguió de cerca hasta que el camino se ensanchó lo bastante como para caminar a su lado.

—Charlie y yo hemos visitado la propiedad varias veces a lo largo de los años.

Portia contuvo una sonrisa y lo acompañó de buen grado. Simon tenía la costumbre de no dar respuestas claras a preguntas que prefería no responder; preguntas cuyas respuestas revelarían mucho más de su persona de lo que le gustaría que nadie supiera. Sin embargo, se conformaba con pasar un rato a solas con él; no le interesaban las ruinas, pero sí quería explorar otros asuntos.

Caminaron en un silencio extrañamente cómodo. El

sol aparecía de vez en cuando, pero sin demasiada fuerza, de manera que no vio la necesidad de ponerse el sombrero. Aparte de otros inconvenientes, un sombrero hacía que conversar con un hombre alto fuera muy difícil.

Sentía la mirada de Simon clavada en ella, sentía su presencia y algo más, una faceta de su comportamiento que había vislumbrado años antes, pero que sólo había visto con claridad en estos últimos días. El constante flirteo (de Kitty, de James, de Charlie, de Lucy e, incluso, de las hermanas Hammond) lo había puesto aún más de manifiesto, por el contraste que suponía. Simon jamás flirteaba, jamás se involucraba en ese tipo de relación a menos que tuviera algo en mente... A menos que tuviera un objetivo.

Caminaba a su lado con pasos lentos y largos, pero ese poder que mantenía oculto jamás había resultado más evidente. Estaban en un lugar antiguo, a solas. Cualquier cosa que dijeran, cualquier cosa que sucediera entre ellos, no estaría sometida a los requisitos sociales. Sólo a los suyos propios.

Cualquier cosa que desearan, cualquier cosa que quisieran.

Tomó una honda bocanada de aire, consciente de la tensión del corpiño, consciente de que él también se había percatado. La expectación le provocó un escalofrío en la espalda. Habían llegado al huerto de la cocina, que en su tiempo estuvo tapiado, pero cuyos muros estaban derruidos. Las ruinas de la cocina estaban a un lado y el monasterio se extendía más allá. Se detuvo y miró a su alrededor. Nadie podía verlos, estaban a solas. Se giró para enfrentarlo.

Estaban separados apenas por un paso. Simon se había detenido y la observaba, a la espera... A la espera de que ella marcara el rumbo, con la certeza de que no podría resistirse y daría un paso, haría algo.

Alzó la barbilla. Clavó los ojos en su rostro.

Y fue incapaz de encontrar las palabras adecuadas.

Simon la contempló a su vez con los ojos entrecerrados antes de levantar una mano muy despacio y colocarle un dedo en el mentón, justo debajo de la oreja. Desde allí fue descendiendo hasta llegar a la barbilla y alzarle el rostro. La sencilla caricia le provocó un estremecimiento y le erizó la piel.

Era alta, pero él le sacaba algo más de media cabeza; ese dedo bajo su barbilla hizo que sus rostros quedaran más cerca.

—¿Debo asumir que quieres seguir con tu aprendizaje? —Su voz era ronca, hipnótica.

Portia no apartó la vista de sus ojos.

—Por supuesto.

Le resultó imposible interpretar su expresión; sin embargo, la sensación de saberse observada, como si él fuera un depredador al acecho, se intensificó.

—¿Qué tienes en mente?

Era una flagrante invitación..., justo lo que ella quería. Arqueó las cejas con un gesto arrogante, consciente de que Simon captaría el desafío implícito... y lo aceptaría.

—Ya he imaginado el siguiente paso.

Sus labios esbozaron una sonrisa torcida; a sabiendas de las sensaciones que provocaban, los encontraba fascinantes... Clavó los ojos en ellos y la expectación creció en su interior

—¿Y qué has imaginado?

Observó cómo sus labios formaban las palabras; le llevó un momento entender su significado. Después, desvió la vista hacia sus ojos y parpadeó.

—Había imaginado... otro beso.

Un brillo cauteloso asomó a sus ojos y le indicó que debería haber respondido otra cosa, que había más cosas que habría podido aprender en ese instante... Si hubiera sabido hacer la petición adecuada.

—¿Otro beso? Que así sea... —replicó él al tiempo que bajaba la cabeza y sus párpados hacían lo propio—. Si eso es lo que realmente quieres.

Esas palabras se abrieron paso en su mente como una

tentación al mismo tiempo que los labios de Simon rozaban los suyos con delicadeza, pero también con mucha más firmeza que la vez anterior, con un cariz más exigente. Ya sabía cómo responder, y eso hizo al separar los labios en clara invitación. La mano que le alzaba el rostro se movió y esos largos dedos se posaron sobre su nuca, si bien el pulgar quedó bajo su barbilla para mantenerla alzada mientras él ladeaba la cabeza para profundizar el beso... tal y como ella le exigía.

Para trasladarse a un plano mucho más ardiente y excitante. Mucho más íntimo.

Lo sintió en los huesos, sintió cómo sus sentidos se abrían como una flor bajo un sol sensual. Y se dejó llevar, ansiosa y encantada.

Alzó un brazo y le recorrió la mejilla con la yema de los dedos. Bebió de su aliento y le devolvió el beso; al principio, con timidez probando e imitando sus movimientos hasta que fue cogiendo confianza a medida que se percataba no sólo de su beneplácito, sino también del anhelo esquivo y seductor oculto bajo su fuerza y su experiencia.

Atrapada en la creciente intimidad del beso, en los sutiles pero firmes avances de esa lengua que se hundía en su boca, era muy consciente del brazo que la rodeaba, de esa mano que la sujetaba por la espalda y la apretaba contra él, incitándola a que se acercara todavía más.

La fuerza de Simon era un ente palpable a su alrededor. Ella era alta y delgada, pero él era mucho más alto y más fuerte, e infinitamente más poderoso. Se sentía como un junco al lado de un roble. Aunque él no la tronchara, sí podría doblegarla a su voluntad si así lo deseaba...

Un escalofrío la recorrió de pies a cabeza, un eco de lo que debió de haber sentido otra mujer, siglos atrás, cuando se vio atrapada entre los brazos de uno de los primeros Cynster. El paso del tiempo no había cambiado nada; Simon era como uno de esos antiguos conquistadores, sólo que ocultaba su verdadera naturaleza bajo un manto de elegancia. Si se provocaba su malhumor, el rugido sería el mismo.

Aunque lo sabía, era incapaz de detenerse. De hecho, el desafío implícito sólo la instaba a ser más atrevida. Lo bastante como para acortar la distancia entre ellos hasta que su corpiño le rozó la chaqueta, hasta que sus faldas se arremolinaron en torno a sus piernas y ocultaron sus botas; lo bastante como para colocar el brazo sobre su hombro y deslizar los dedos, muy despacio, por su sedoso cabello.

Simon sintió que su autocontrol se desintegraba; tensó los músculos para luchar contra la acuciante necesidad de amoldarla a su cuerpo. De calmar sus exigentes sentidos con ese minúsculo alivio; de sentir su grácil cuerpo contra él. De reclamarla para sí, como haría a su debido tiempo...

Pero todavía no.

Sintió cómo crecía la compulsión en su interior y luchó por contenerla; hasta que sólo fue evidente en el ardor con el que devoraba su boca.

Cálida y dulce, Portia se entregaba y él lo aceptaba sin tapujos, mientras profundizaba el beso hasta que sus labios, su lengua y el dulce interior de su boca fueron completamente suyos para saborearlos a su antojo.

Quería mucho más. Quería la promesa que ofrecía el cuerpo que apresaba entre los brazos... Quería reclamarla, obligarla a rendirse. Quería ese cuerpo rendido para hundirse en él y saciar el deseo que lo embargaba.

Otro beso. Eso era lo que Portia había pedido. A pesar de que su alma de conquistador le decía que ella no se quejaría si iba más lejos, la conocía muy bien. Demasiado bien como para aprovecharse de su arrogante petición. Era una tonta por confiar en él, o en cualquier otro hombre, hasta ese punto; no obstante, la conocía demasiado bien como para intentar aprovecharse de su confianza.

Al contrario, su intención era la de fomentarla, porque de ese modo ganaría muchísimo más.

Retirarse a terreno más seguro conllevó un esfuerzo sobrehumano y tuvo que hacerlo poco a poco, a regañadientes. Cuando sus labios se separaron, dejaron que sus alientos se mezclaran un instante. Después, alzó la cabeza y ella lo imitó mientras parpadeaba para enfocar la vista. En cuanto sus miradas se cruzaron comprendieron que el paisaje que se abría ante ellos había cambiado. Se habían creado nuevas vistas; unas cuya existencia jamás habrían imaginado.

Portia estaba fascinada..., igual que lo estaba él.

En ese instante, ella se percató de que sus manos aún le rodeaban la cintura. Inspiró hondo y retrocedió un paso. Se lo permitió y sus dedos la soltaron muy a su pesar.

Seguía mirándolo a los ojos, pero sabía que su mente trabajaba a toda velocidad. No había recobrado el aliento y parecía insegura. Perdida.

Esbozó una sonrisa deslumbrante al tiempo que extendía un brazo para colocarle un mechón azabache tras la oreja.

—¿Satisfecha? —le preguntó, arqueando una ceja con sorna.

Portia no se dejó engañar, y reconoció su intención; su oferta de regresar con placidez al mundo que habían dejado atrás. Se lo decían sus ojos..., aunque a ellos también asomaba cierta inseguridad.

Sin embargo, no tardó en recobrarse, enderezarse e inclinar la cabeza con más arrogancia que nunca.

—Por supuesto. —Una fugaz sonrisa asomó a sus labios. De repente, dio media vuelta, hacia el camino que los llevaría con los demás—. Ha sido de lo más... satisfactorio.

Contuvo una sonrisa mientras la seguía. Un poco más adelante, la cogió de la mano para ayudarla a sortear unas piedras y no la soltó. Cuando se acercaron al claustro, se colocó esa mano en el brazo. Siguieron paseando con aparente normalidad, aunque en su fuero interno eran muy conscientes de su mutua presencia.

De tácito acuerdo, ocultarían al mundo ese hecho, si bien proseguirían su exploración en privado.

Al llegar al claustro escucharon las voces de los demás. La llevó hasta allí sin dejar de observarla, pero con un objetivo totalmente distinto en mente. Tenía que asegurarse de que se sintiera cómoda con él, de que no tuviera reparos en acudir a su lado, en estar con él y, a la postre, en pedirle más.

Estaba más que preparado para enseñarle cuanto quisiera..., cuanto necesitara aprender. Quería que recurriera a él para la siguiente lección. Y para todas las que le siguieran.

Estrecharla entre sus brazos y sentir la arrolladora compulsión que le provocaba, así como su respuesta, había sido suficiente para hallar la contestación a la pregunta que lo torturaba.

La que había tomado por una idea desquiciada e inconcebible, ya no lo era en absoluto.

Quería hacerla su esposa... La quería en su cama. La quería como madre de sus hijos. Por fin había caído la venda de sus ojos y se había hecho la luz. La quería a su lado. La quería y punto. No terminaba de comprender el porqué, por qué ella; aun así, jamás había estado tan seguro de algo en toda su vida.

A la mañana siguiente, apoyado contra el marco de las puertas francesas de la biblioteca, Simon vigilaba las puertas del comedor matinal, de los gabinetes de la planta baja y del vestíbulo del jardín; puertas por las que Portia podría salir de camino a los jardines.

La conocía desde hacía años, conocía su forma de ser, su carácter, su temperamento. Sabía cómo tratar con ella. Si la presionaba, guiándola en una dirección concreta, se plantaría en el sitio o iría en dirección contraria sin importar que lo hiciera por su bien.

Dado lo que quería de ella, dada la posición que quería que ocupase, la manera más rápida de conseguir su objetivo pasaba por hacerla creer que había sido idea suya. Que era ella quien mandaba y que él era quien obedecía, no al revés.

Un beneficio añadido de esa estrategia era que no requería de una declaración por su parte. No tendría que admitir su deseo compulsivo ni, muchísimo menos, los sentimientos que éste despertaba.

Una cuidada y solapada estrategia era su camino más rápido hacia el éxito.

Las puertas del comedor matinal se abrieron. Portia, ataviada con un vestido de muselina azul estampado en un azul más oscuro, apareció y cerró las puertas tras ella. Echó a andar hacia el extremo de la terraza, donde se detuvo unos instantes para contemplar el templete antes de bajar los escalones y encaminarse rumbo al lago.

Simon se apartó del marco de la puerta, sacó las manos de los bolsillos y salió tras ella.

Cuando llegó a los jardines situados sobre el lago, Portia aminoró el paso y, al presentir su presencia, echó un vistazo por encima del hombro y se detuvo a esperarlo.

La estudió a medida que se acercaba; los únicos indicios de que recordaba su anterior encuentro a solas eran la expresión de sus ojos, el leve rubor de sus mejillas y, por supuesto, el gesto altivo de su barbilla.

—Buenos días. —Lo saludó con una inclinación de cabeza, un gesto tan arrogante como de costumbre; pero sus ojos, que no se apartaban de él, tenían una expresión interrogante—. ¿Has salido a dar un paseo?

Se detuvo delante de ella y la miró a los ojos.

—He salido para estar contigo.

Portia abrió los ojos de par en par, pero jamás había sido una timorata. Para tratar con ella, lo mejor era hablar sin tapujos, con franqueza y sin atenerse a las sutilezas que exigían las buenas costumbres.

Señaló el lago con una mano.

—¿Vamos?

Ella siguió el movimiento con los ojos y titubeó un instante antes de asentir con la cabeza. Caminaron el uno junto al otro, en silencio, y descendieron la pendiente hacia el camino que bordeaba el lago. Por tácito acuerdo, prosiguieron hacia el mirador.

Portia se concentró en el paseo, admirando los árboles, los arbustos y el lago en un esfuerzo por parecer tranquila, aunque no estaba muy segura de poder conseguirlo. Eso era lo que quería, la oportunidad de aprender; sin embargo, no tenía experiencia alguna en ese ámbito y no quería dar un traspiés, no quería caerse de bruces y acabar perdida.

Además, entre ellos habían cambiado las cosas.

Ya sabía lo que era tener sus manos en la cintura, lo que era sentir su fuerza alrededor. Lo que era saberse a su merced... Su reacción aún la sorprendía. Jamás habría creído que le gustaría, mucho menos que ansiaría más.

A lo largo de los años, a pesar de su relación, jamás habían sentido una atracción física. No obstante, en esos momentos la sentía, y era increíblemente tentadora, incitante... Su mera existencia había llevado su interacción a un plano distinto.

Uno en el que jamás había estado, con nadie; un plano en el que todavía andaba a ciegas.

Llegaron al mirador y Simon hizo un gesto para que dejaran el sendero, cruzaran la breve extensión de césped y subieran los escalones. El tejado era a dos aguas, pero el interior se dividía en tres zonas, separadas por dos hileras de columnas que dejaban una parte central muy amplia; en ella se habían dispuesto dos enormes sillones y un sofá a juego alrededor de una mesita auxiliar. El sofá estaba orientado hacia la entrada y el lago, con un sillón a cada lado, y los tres muebles estaban cubiertos con cojines de cretona. Había periódicos en un mueblecito ideado a tal efecto. Un banco pegado a la pared recorría todo el perímetro que conformaban los arcos.

El suelo estaba limpio y los cojines, mullidos. Todo estaba dispuesto para agradar a cualquiera que deseara pasar un rato allí.

Se giró nada más traspasar la entrada y contempló la superficie ovalada del lago. El comentario que hiciera Simon acerca de la intimidad que ofrecía el mirador resonó en su mente. Desde allí no parecía que hubiera casa alguna en las cercanías, ni siquiera se veía un parterre de flores ni un prado de césped cuidadosamente atendido. Resultaba fácil olvidar, resultaba fácil creer, que no había nadie más a su alrededor. Que sólo estaban ellos.

Cuando miró a Simon, descubrió que la estaba observando. En ese instante supo que estaba esperando alguna señal, algún indicio por su parte que le comunicara su deseo de seguir aprendiendo; o, por el contrario, su conclusión de que ya había aprendido lo suficiente. Se limitaba a observarla con su habitual serenidad.

Desvió la vista hacia el lago e intentó desentenderse del súbito despertar de sus sentidos, de la extraña certeza de que se le había desbocado el corazón.

Las restantes damas se habían reunido en el saloncito matinal para charlar a placer; los caballeros se habían dividido en grupos para hablar de política y de negocios o habían salido a cabalgar.

Estaban solos, tan solos como el lugar prometía.

La oportunidad estaba allí. La llamaba. Aun así...

Frunció el ceño. Se acercó a uno de los arcos, colocó las manos en el alféizar y clavó la vista en el exterior. Pero sin ver nada.

Pasado un momento, Simon se acercó a ella. Aunque no miró, era consciente de la elegancia con la que se movía. Cuando llegó a su lado, se apoyó contra el arco. Su mirada no la abandonó en ningún momento.

Pasó otro instante antes de que él murmurara:

—Te toca.

Portia hizo un mohín y comenzó a tamborilear con los dedos sobre el alféizar; cuando se dio cuenta de lo que hacía, se detuvo.

—Lo sé. —Aunque el hecho de saberlo no facilitaba las cosas en absoluto.

—Pues dime...

Tendría que hacerlo. Estaba apenas a un paso de distancia, pero al menos no tenía que mirarlo a los ojos ni alzar la voz. Inspiró hondo e irguió los hombros. Se aferró al alféizar.

—Quiero aprender más, pero no quiero que te hagas

una idea equivocada de mí. Que malinterpretes mis intenciones.

Ése era el dilema con el que se había despertado esa mañana y que la había hecho salir a los jardines en busca de paz.

Simon guardó silencio un instante y supo que intentaba averiguar lo que estaba pensando.

—¿Por qué quieres aprender más?

Su tono era tan sereno que no le indicó nada. Si quería saber lo que pensaba, tendría que mirarlo a los ojos; sin embargo, si quería darle una respuesta a su pregunta, no podía hacerlo.

Mantuvo la mirada clavada en el lago.

—Quiero comprender, quiero experimentar lo bastante como para entender qué es lo que sucede entre un hombre y una mujer para que despierte en ella el deseo de casarse. Quiero saberlo, no quiero conformarme con imaginármelo. Sin embargo... —prosiguió, enfatizando la palabra—. Sin embargo, es un interés puramente académico. Ni más ni menos. No quiero que tú... que te lleves una impresión errónea.

Desde luego que se le había desbocado el corazón, pero al menos lo había dicho, había pronunciado las palabras. Le ardían las mejillas. Jamás se había sentido más insegura en toda la vida. Insegura e indecisa. Ignorante. Odiaba la sensación. Sabía lo que quería sin el menor asomo de duda; sabía lo que querría de él si su conciencia no hubiera hecho acto de presencia. No obstante, era incapaz de pedírselo si había la más mínima posibilidad de que malinterpretara su interés.

No creía ni por un instante que Simon fuera vulnerable; conocía de sobra su reputación, pero las cosas entre ellos habían cambiado y no estaba segura de cómo ni de por qué. Dado que iba a ciegas, no podía estar segura (con la certeza que su corazón y su honor exigían) de que Simon no desarrollase algún tipo de concepción extraña y esperase algo más de lo que ella estaba preparada para darle a cambio de sus lecciones.

De lo que sí estaba segura era de que no podría soportarlo llegado el caso.

Simon estudió su perfil. Su confesión, sus intenciones y su meta eran tan poco convencionales y tan impulsivas..., tan típicas de ella que no le provocaron la menor sorpresa. Hacía mucho tiempo que se había acostumbrado a su carácter. De haberse tratado de otra muchacha soltera, se habría quedado de piedra; pero siendo Portia... tenía sentido.

Había sido su coraje y su candor a la hora de asegurarse que él comprendía... que no quedaba expuesto a que le hiciera daño, lo que instigó sus emociones. Una mezcla extraña. Consideración, aprobación... e incluso admiración.

Y un ramalazo de algo mucho más profundo. Se preocupaba por él hasta ese punto...

Si elegía seguir adelante y afrontar el peligro, por pequeño que éste fuera, de no ser capaz de hacerla cambiar de opinión y de convencerla para que se casara con él, no podría decir que no iba advertido de antemano.

De la misma manera, ni se le pasaba por la cabeza decirle que había decidido que ella fuera su esposa. Al menos, de momento. Portia no pensaba en esos términos... Y precisamente ése era el desafío al que debía enfrentarse: vencer su férrea voluntad y su oposición al matrimonio. Dada la relación que habían mantenido hasta entonces, dado todo lo que sabía de él, si le decía en ese momento crucial que pretendía convertirla en su esposa, bien podría salir corriendo.

—Creo que tenemos que hablarlo, que tenemos que aclarar la situación. —Sus palabras sonaron demasiado tranquilas, casi distantes incluso a sus oídos.

Portia lo miró un instante, pero no a los ojos.

—¿Qué es lo que quieres aprender? Específicamente —preguntó antes de que ella pudiera replicar.

Una vez más, Portia clavó la mirada en el lago.

—Quiero saber... —dijo al tiempo que un intenso rubor le teñía las mejillas—. Quiero conocer los aspectos físicos. ¿Qué hacen las criadas con sus pretendientes en su tiempo libre para que luego se lo cuenten entre risillas a escondidas? ¿Qué obtienen las mujeres (las damas, específicamente) de esos encuentros que las hace repetir y, sobre todo, que las impulsa al matrimonio?

Todas preguntas muy lógicas y racionales, al menos desde su limitado punto de vista. A todas luces estaba ansiosa por averiguar las respuestas o jamás habría sacado el tema a colación. Se percató de la tensión que la embargaba.

Se devanó los sesos intentando discernir el camino más seguro.

—¿Hasta qué... punto quieres ampliar tus conocimientos? —Su voz no denotó censura alguna; bien podría estar debatiendo una estrategia de ajedrez.

Pasado un momento, ella giró la cabeza y enfrentó su mirada... echando chispas por los ojos.

—No lo sé.

La respuesta lo dejó atónito, pero de pronto vio el camino... y se lanzó por él.

—Muy bien. Como no sabes (algo de lo más comprensible) las paradas de ese camino, ya que nunca lo has recorrido... Si de verdad quieres saber... —Se encogió de hombros con toda la tranquilidad de la que fue capaz—. Bueno, si ése es tu deseo, podemos recorrer dicho camino paso a paso. —Sostuvo su mirada—. Y puedes decirme que me detenga en cualquier momento.

Portia lo contempló con detenimiento. Su expresión era más indecisa que recelosa.

—¿Paso a paso?

Asintió con la cabeza.

—Y si digo que paremos... —Frunció el ceño—. ¿Qué pasa si no puedo hablar?

Llegados a ese punto, titubeó, muy consciente de lo que estaba diciendo. Aun así, se sintió obligado a ofrecerle una salida.

—Te pediré permiso antes de comenzar cada lección y me aseguraré de que lo comprendes antes de que decidas la respuesta.

Portia enarcó las cejas.

—¿Esperarás a que te dé una respuesta?

—Esperaré a que me des una respuesta racional, meditada y definitiva.

A pesar de eso, vaciló.

—¿Me prometes...?

—Palabra de Cynster.

Portia sabía que no debía poner en duda semejante promesa. A pesar de que su rostro mantuvo la expresión altiva, sus labios se relajaron y su mirada se suavizó... Estaba considerando su oferta.

Contuvo el aliento, ya que la conocía demasiado bien como para presionarla de ninguna de las maneras... Entabló una batalla contra la compulsión de hacerlo.

Portia asintió con la cabeza, decidida.

—De acuerdo.

Se giró hasta quedar de frente a él y le tendió la mano.

La miró unos instantes antes de desviar la vista hacia su rostro. Después, le cogió la mano y se giró, tirando de ella hacia el interior del mirador.

—¿Qué...?

Se detuvo a unos pasos de una columna. La miró por encima del hombro y enarcó una ceja.

—He supuesto que querías proseguir con tu instrucción...

Portia parpadeó.

—Sí, pero...

—No podemos hacerlo junto al arco, a la vista de cualquiera que pasee por el lago.

Se quedó boquiabierta por la sorpresa mientras tiraba de ella para dejarla frente a él. Le soltó la mano y tomó su rostro con ternura al tiempo que se acercaba a ella e inclinaba la cabeza.

La besó y esperó hasta que relajó la espalda y le entregó sus labios. En ese momento la hizo retroceder, paso a paso, muy despacio, hasta que la tuvo acorralada contra una de las columnas. La sorpresa la tensó, pero al ver que no la arrinconaba, se fue relajando y se abandonó al beso.

Durante largo rato, no hizo nada más. Se limitó a besarla y a dejar que ella le devolviera el beso. Se hundió en la calidez de su boca y la acarició con la lengua, incitándola a que jugara. Incitando a sus sentidos a que se acostumbraran a la mutua entrega, a un ritmo más lento y menos exigente.

Al sencillo placer que ya conocía.

Era más alta que la media, algo de agradecer. No tenía que echarle la cabeza hacia atrás, sino que podía abrazarla cómodamente. La columna que tenía detrás no era más que un punto de referencia; más tarde, le serviría para mantener el equilibrio... asumiendo que quisiera dar el siguiente paso.

La mera idea le calentó la sangre. Ladeó la cabeza y profundizó el beso, obligándola a que se aferrara a él. Le soltó la cara y deslizó las manos hasta su cintura, donde las cerró sobre la delicada muselina de modo que sintió el roce de la seda de su camisola situada entre el vestido y su piel.

Portia dejó escapar un jadeo ahogado y se pegó más a él; sin dejar de besarla, de juguetear con su lengua, la fue echando hacia atrás, muy despacio, hasta que quedó recostada contra la columna. Ella se dejó hacer y se relajó. Sus manos, que antes habían estado inertes en sus hombros, comenzaron a ascender hasta que le enterró los dedos en el pelo.

Acto seguido, lo soltó para arrojarle los brazos al cuello y se puso de puntillas para buscar sus labios con renovado ardor, arqueándose hacia él.

Simon sonrió para sus adentros y dejó que sus manos vagaran por su esbelta espalda, arriba y abajo. La besó con frenesí mientras sentía el calor que irradiaba su piel, mientras sentía las voluptuosas curvas de sus pechos contra el torso.

Su aroma lo envolvió y le nubló la razón, le atormentó los sentidos. El cariz del beso se tornó más íntimo mientras sus manos se limitaban a acariciarle la espalda.

Mientras esperaba.

Más. Portia sabía que quería más. Los besos estaban bien, eran increíblemente placenteros y embriagadores, la excitaban mucho y hacían que su cuerpo cobrara vida. Por no mencionar el tacto fresco y firme de sus manos, la promesa implícita en sus hábiles caricias, que le provocaba un sinfín de deliciosos escalofríos de emoción en la espalda. Sin embargo, esa misma emoción le estaba crispando los nervios. Sus sentidos aguardaban con avidez. Esperaban algo más. Estaban listos para algo más.

Para dar el siguiente paso.

Simon le había dicho que le enseñaría. Y ella quería saber, quería aprender. En ese mismo instante.

Se apartó de sus labios, aunque le costó un esfuerzo sobrehumano. Cuando sus bocas por fin se separaron, no se alejó de él, sino que abrió los ojos lo justo para mirarlo con los párpados entornados.

—¿Cuál es el siguiente paso?

Sus miradas se encontraron. Los ojos de Simon parecían más oscuros, de un azul más intenso.

—Éste —le respondió.

Deslizó las manos hasta que sus pulgares le rozaron la cara externa de los pechos.

Las caricias le provocaron una sensación increíble y sus sentidos siguieron con avidez el movimiento de esos dedos cuando volvieron a tocarla. Le temblaron las piernas y, de pronto, entendió la utilidad de la columna que tenía a la espalda. Se recostó contra ella. Simon resiguió el contorno de sus labios con la lengua, apenas era un roce, mientras sus pícaros pulgares trazaban lentos e incitantes círculos sobre su piel..., lo justo para que comprendiera...

Levantó la cabeza para mirarla a los ojos.

—¿Sí o no?

Sus pulgares trazaron otro círculo, una caricia demasiado liviana... De haber tenido fuerzas, le habría dicho que era una pregunta de lo más estúpida.

—Sí —contestó con un hilo de voz.

Antes de que pudiera preguntarle si estaba segura, lo

obligó a besarla de nuevo, convencida de que necesitaría el contacto para seguir anclada al mundo.

Sintió que él esbozaba una sonrisa, pero en ese momento sus manos volvieron a moverse y dejó de pensar en otra cosa que no fuera el placer que le proporcionaban sus lánguidas caricias, unas caricias que iban de la firme presión al roce más sutil. Cada vez más explícitas, más sensuales, más posesivas.

Hasta que abarcó, muy despacio, sus pechos con las manos; hasta que encerró los endurecidos pezones entre los dedos y los pellizcó.

Una bocanada de fuego la abrasó.

Interrumpió el beso entre jadeos. La presión sobre sus pezones disminuyó.

—¡No! ¡No pares!

Su propia voz la sorprendió por la sensualidad de la orden. Entreabrió los ojos para observarlo y sus miradas se entrelazaron. Había algo en él, en su expresión, que no había visto antes. Su semblante estaba crispado. Sus labios, aunque apretados, tenían una mueca algo torcida.

Él la obedeció con presteza y volvió a pellizcar los pezones. Y una vez más, la sensación se apoderó de ella y el fuego le recorrió la piel hasta apoderarse de sus venas y llevarse todas las inhibiciones.

Cerró los ojos con un suspiro de placer.

—¿Te gusta? —le preguntó Simon.

Lo estrechó con fuerza y lo obligó a acercarse de nuevo a ella.

—Sabes que sí.

Por supuesto que lo sabía, pero no quería perderse esa admisión de sus labios. Le encantaba. Era un premio de consolación dadas las limitaciones de su encuentro.

Unas limitaciones muy restrictivas... La ardorosa respuesta de Portia lo había excitado sobremanera, aunque no podía responder en consecuencia.

Aún.

Sentía su piel enfebrecida bajo las palmas de las manos. Sus turgentes pechos, con los pezones enhiestos, le llenaban las manos. El deleite que le provocaban sus caricias estaba implícito en el beso, en la avidez que demostraba su cuerpo.

Cerró las manos con más fuerza y comenzó a acariciarla con más ímpetu. Portia gimió y le devolvió el beso en un exigente gesto que decía a las claras...

De repente, le costó la misma vida quedarse como estaba y no aplastarla contra la columna, amoldarla a él y calmar el palpitante deseo que lo atenazaba. Inspiró hondo, sintió cómo su torso se expandía y se aferró a su autocontrol...

El inesperado sonido del gong fue una distracción para ambos. Se separaron al instante.

Tomó una honda bocanada de aire mientras le quitaba las manos de los pechos y la tomaba por la cintura.

El gong resonó de nuevo.

—El almuerzo —le explicó mientras ella parpadeaba y lo miraba con los ojos un tanto vidriosos—. El gong suena en la terraza. Así que tiene que haber más invitados paseando por los jardines. —O eso esperaba. Esperaba que no los estuvieran llamando concretamente a ellos. Retrocedió un paso y buscó su mano—. Será mejor que volvamos.

Portia lo miró a los ojos un instante antes de asentir con la cabeza. Después, dejó que la cogiera de la mano y la precediera por los escalones.

Mientras se apresuraban a regresar a la mansión, se recordó que debía refrenar sus demonios durante la siguiente lección. Debía prepararse para combatir la tentación, para no caer en ella.

La observó disimuladamente. Caminaba a su lado con pasos rápidos y mucho más largos que la mayoría de las mujeres. Estaba ensimismada, pensando... Y él sabía en qué. Si cometía un error, si dejaba que su verdadero objetivo saliera a la luz, no podía contar con que su inocencia la cegara. Tal vez no comprendiera la verdad de inmediato, pero, a la postre, lo haría. Analizaría y estudiaría todo lo sucedido entre ellos. En aras del saber, por supuesto.

Clavó la mirada al frente, molesto consigo mismo. Iba a tener que asegurarse de que no aprendiera más de la cuenta.

Como, por ejemplo, el verdadero motivo por el que había accedido a instruirla.

6

Portia se sentó a la mesa del almuerzo y dejó que las conversaciones fluyeran sin participar en ellas. Tenía suficiente práctica como para asentir con la cabeza a un lado o murmurar algo al otro.

Ardía en deseos de hablar sobre lo que había descubierto, pero ninguno de los presentes cumplía los requisitos para ser su confidente. Si estuviera Penélope... Claro que teniendo en cuenta la opinión de su hermana pequeña acerca de los hombres y del matrimonio, quizá fuera preferible que no estuviera.

Fue descartando a las restantes damas a medida que las evaluaba. Winifred no serviría, no quería escandalizarla, y Lucy o las Hammond, muchísimo menos. En cuanto a Drusilla... Kitty, que se empeñaba en perseguir sin compasión a James y a Ambrose, parecía la única posibilidad; una idea de lo más desalentadora...

Miró de soslayo a lady O, antes de clavar la vista en su plato. Albergaba la sospecha de que, lejos de escandalizarse, la anciana le diría que apenas había arañado la superficie y que aún le quedaban muchísimas cosas por descubrir.

No necesitaba más incentivos. Estaba muerta de curiosidad y no se atrevía a mirar a Simon por si éste lo descubría. Habían omitido la frecuencia con la que tendrían lugar sus «lecciones»; no quería parecer demasiado...

«atrevida». Ésa fue la única palabra que se le ocurrió. Tenía la profunda convicción de que no sería inteligente hacerle saber hasta qué punto estaba fascinada. Ya era bastante orgulloso de por sí; no necesitaba alentar su arrogancia.

Así pues, abandonó la mesa con el resto de las damas y las acompañó al prado, donde se sentaron al sol para intercambiar cotilleos. Simon se percató de que se marchaba, pero no hizo señales de detenerla ni ella le dio pie a que lo hiciera.

Una hora después, lady O le envió el recado de que la ayudara a subir a su habitación.

—Bien, a ver... ¿Cómo van tus meditaciones? —Lady O se dejó caer en el colchón y Portia se apresuró a ordenarle las faldas.

—Por buen camino, pero aún no he llegado a una conclusión definitiva.

—¿Y eso? —Los ojos negros de la anciana siguieron clavados en su rostro mientras refunfuñaba—: Simon y tú debéis de haber paseado varios kilómetros.

Le restó importancia al comentario encogiéndose de hombros.

—Fuimos hasta el lago.

Lady O frunció el ceño antes de cerrar los ojos.

—Bueno, si eso es todo lo que tienes que contarme, lo único que puedo sugerirte es que espabiles. Después de todo, sólo estaremos aquí unos cuantos días más.

Portia aguardó. Al ver que la anciana no decía nada más, se despidió con un murmullo y salió de la habitación.

Siguió haciéndose preguntas mientras deambulaba por la enorme mansión... ¿Cuántos días le harían falta para aprenderlo todo? O, al menos, para aprender lo suficiente. Cuando llegó a la larguísima galería, se detuvo junto a una de las ventanas y tomó asiento en el alféizar acolchado. Con la mirada perdida en las figuras que la luz del sol proyectaba sobre los paneles de madera, dejó que los recuerdos afluyeran a su memoria y dio rienda suelta a sus sentidos... Revivió las sensaciones y trazó con cuidado los límites de su aprendizaje, la frontera tras la cual residía todo aquello que le quedaba por sentir. Por descubrir.

No supo cuánto tiempo pasó sumida en sus pensamientos ni tampoco cuánto tiempo estuvo observándola Simon. Cuando volvió a la realidad, percibió su presencia, desvió la vista y se lo encontró allí, apoyado en la esquina. Sus miradas se encontraron.

Pasó un instante, tras el cual él enarcó una ceja.

—¿Estás lista para la siguiente lección?

¿Tanto se le notaba? Alzó la barbilla.

—Si no estás ocupado...

Llevaba desocupado una hora. Pero se mordió la lengua. En cambio, inclinó la cabeza con un gesto comedido y se enderezó.

Portia se puso en pie y la delicada tela de sus faldas cayó a su alrededor, delineando el contorno de sus largas piernas. Extendió un brazo, la tomó de la mano y luchó contra el impulso de aferrarla con fuerza. Tuvo que echar mano de toda su experiencia, pero al final logró contenerse y entrelazó sus brazos mientras enfilaban el pasillo.

Sintió que ella observaba su rostro, tenso por el esfuerzo. Al instante, le preguntó:

—¿Adónde vamos?

—A algún lugar donde no nos molesten. —Fue consciente de la brusquedad de su voz y supo que ella también la había notado. De todas formas, no pudo resistirse y añadió—: Por cierto, deja que te diga que si quieres ir superando las distintas fases para llegar a una conclusión razonable, tienes que estar disponible para ello.

Ella parpadeó y miró al frente.

—Suelo ir a la sala de música por las tardes... para practicar. Tenía intención de ir dentro de un rato.

—Ya tocas el piano con soltura. No pasa nada porque no practiques un día. O dos. No estaremos mucho tiempo aquí.

Se detuvo para abrir una puerta. La sostuvo mientras le indicaba a Portia que lo precediera y entraron en un pequeño gabinete conectado con un dormitorio, ambos desocupados. Había elegido la estancia a propósito, a sabiendas del mobiliario que contenía.

Portia se detuvo en el centro de la habitación y echó un vistazo a los muebles, cubiertos por sábanas. Entretanto, él cerró la puerta con llave y se acercó a ella. La tomó de la mano y la condujo hasta una de las ventanas, cuyas cortinas estaban corridas. La habitación estaba orientada al oeste y ofrecía una vista magnífica del pinar. Descorrió las cortinas y el sol entró a raudales.

Se dio la vuelta y agarró la sábana que cubría el mueble más grande, situado justo enfrente de la ventana. Dio un tirón y descubrió una amplia y cómoda otomana que quedó bañada por la dorada luz del sol.

Ella parpadeó. Sin darle tiempo a pensar, soltó la sábana y la cogió en brazos; acto seguido, se dejó caer sobre la espléndida otomana, arrastrándola con él. El súbito movimiento los hizo rebotar y le arrancó a ella una carcajada que se desvaneció en cuanto lo miró a los ojos. Sin soltarla, se movió hasta quedar recostado contra el brazo acolchado, de modo que Portia quedó prácticamente tendida sobre él.

Estaban bañados por la luz del sol. Portia le miró los labios. Sacó la punta de la lengua para humedecerse los suyos y, acto seguido, desvió la vista hacia sus ojos.

—Y ahora ¿qué? —le preguntó al tiempo que enarcaba una ceja sin apartar la mirada.

Simon supo sin la menor duda que estaba más que dispuesta. Sonrió, no sin cierto alivio. Le tomó el rostro con una mano y la atrajo hacia él.

—Ahora, jugamos.

Y eso hicieron. No recordaba haber sido partícipe jamás de un interludio semejante. No supo si fue su comentario o si se debió al sol que los calentaba, al silencio de la habitación o a la sensación de estar rodeados por objetos informes, pero ambos se abandonaron al momento con un vertiginoso e imprudente entusiasmo que los transportó a un mundo propio en el que no existía el decoro, sólo el ardiente deseo de su mutua entrega.

Sus labios apenas la habían rozado cuando sintió que ella se entregaba al beso, aunque siguió tensa entre sus brazos, como una cervatilla insegura, presta a huir. Profundizó el beso y ella lo siguió, ofreciéndole su boca y entregándole gustosa todo cuanto le reclamaba. Sin embargo, se mantuvo a raya. Se limitó a esperar y a dejar que fuera aprendiendo por sí misma. Que llegara a sus propias conclusiones.

Hacía mucho tiempo que había aprendido que ése era el mejor método para aliviar los miedos de las amantes más asustadizas: abrazarlas y protegerlas con su cuerpo sin que su peso o su fuerza las agobiaran. Hacerlas pensar que eran ellas las que controlaban la situación. Y, tal y como había ocurrido con el resto, con Portia también funcionó. La tensión la abandonó de forma paulatina, y ese cuerpo cálido, esbelto y maravillosamente vivo se relajó contra él.

Comenzó a acariciarle la espalda con delicadeza y, poco después, fue ella quien se apartó por propia iniciativa y le dio acceso a sus pechos, invitándolo sin pudor alguno a que los acariciara.

Fue ella quien, poco a poco, fue echando más leña al fuego.

Tal y como sucediera la vez anterior, fue ella quien puso fin al beso y apartó la cabeza para respirar de forma entrecortada mientras él seguía acariciándole los pechos. Sin embargo, en esa ocasión no se detuvo, sino que dejó que sus dedos continuaran la diestra tortura.

Portia abrió los ojos y bajó la vista. Tomó otra bocanada de aire mientras observaba cómo sus manos la tocaban. Al punto, abrió los ojos de par en par, enfrentó su mirada y con su habitual franqueza le preguntó:

—Y ahora ¿qué?

Simon sostuvo su mirada, le pellizcó los pezones con más fuerza y observó cómo el placer la invadía de nuevo, rompiendo su concentración y haciendo que cerrara los ojos.

—¿Estás segura de que quieres saberlo?

Abrió los ojos y lo atravesó con una mirada que habría considerado imperiosa de no ser por su sonrisa.

—Mucho. —Intentó componer una expresión seria, pero fue incapaz.

Aunque se lo hubiera propuesto, no podría haberse mostrado pícara ni coqueta... Era superior a sus fuerzas. No obstante, la alegría que bullía en su interior, la emoción, la excitación, eran prácticamente palpables.

Parecía que estuvieran explorando algo, una dimensión desconocida que había surgido entre ellos a modo de desafío. Portia no mostraba el menor asomo de miedo; estaba ansiosa y confiada, entregada al momento aunque no supiera lo que le aguardaba en el camino...

Confiaba en él.

La idea lo sobrecogió. Y no sólo por el hecho en sí mismo, sino por lo importante (una importancia de la que acababa de darse cuenta) que era para él.

Por los sentimientos tan especiales que despertaba en su interior.

Respiró hondo y luchó contra el nudo que le oprimía el pecho. Portia había bajado la vista para observar sus dedos mientras le acariciaba los pezones, ya enhiestos, pero en ese momento lo miró a los ojos y enarcó las cejas. Se vio obligado a aclararse la garganta y a cambiar de postura bajo ella...

—Si estás tan segura...

La expresión que asomó a esos ojos azul cobalto le indicó que continuara. Le fue imposible contener la sonrisa. El corpiño de su vestido se cerraba con una hilera de diminutos botones que se extendía desde el escote hasta la cintura. Apartó las manos de sus pechos y se dispuso a liberar los botones de sus ojales.

Portia parpadeó, pero no hizo ademán de detenerlo. Sin embargo, a medida que sus manos continuaban con la labor y el vestido se iba abriendo, frunció el ceño y un leve rubor cubrió sus mejillas.

En cuanto hubo liberado el último botón, alzó una mano, se la colocó en la nuca y tiró de ella hacia abajo.

Atrapó su mirada justo antes de que cerrara los párpados.

—Deja de pensar.

Le dio un largo y apasionado beso, hechizando sus sentidos por primera vez, cosa que hasta ese momento se había cuidado mucho de no hacer. Lo último que necesitaba saber era que podía hacerle perder la razón con un beso, pero si en ese instante no la privaba del uso de su considerable sentido común aunque sólo fuera por unos minutos, era posible que se echara atrás...

Y no estaba de humor para engatusarla y mucho menos para discutir. Su habitual serenidad lo había abandonado, al menos en lo que a ella se refería, y, por tanto, no podría aliviar sus temores con palabras. Y de eso se trataba, de temor, que no de miedo. El temor a lo desconocido.

De forma implacable, pero con las más tiernas caricias, la instó a continuar, a traspasar el umbral de su siguiente descubrimiento. Un descubrimiento mutuo.

La liberó del hechizo sin apartarle las manos de los pechos. Piel contra sedosa piel. Sus labios se separaron, pero ella no se alejó. Con los párpados entornados, lo miró a los ojos. Él siguió acariciándola y sintió que se estremecía. Algo en su interior se estremeció en respuesta.

Tenía una dolorosa erección. La deseaba con un apremio que le robaba el aliento. Alzó la cabeza para acortar la escasa distancia que los separaba y se apoderó otra vez de sus labios. Lo necesitaba para saciar el deseo.

Y ella se lo permitió. No supo cómo lo había percibido, pero lo besó en respuesta, le rodeó la cara con las manos y ladeó la cabeza para incitarlo..., para retarlo a que tomara un poco más. A que la devorara si se atrevía. Se ofreció, se dejó llevar, siguió su ejemplo y, al instante, se hizo con el control.

A la postre fue ella quien se apartó y el súbito asalto de la pasión se desvaneció. Le abrió el vestido un poco más para poder acariciarla con las dos manos a placer y ella no puso objeción alguna. El calor que desprendía su piel le abrasó las manos.

Portia deliraba... de placer. La certeza de estar haciendo algo ilícito era tan emocionante que apenas la dejaba respirar. Las caricias de Simon eran divinas, mucho más placenteras que el sol que los bañaba; mucho más cálidas; mucho más reales.

Infinitamente más íntimas.

Debería estar escandalizada. Sí. La idea se le ocurrió de repente. Y la descartó al punto.

Había muchas cosas que sentir, que absorber, que aprender. Ni el decoro ni el temor eran lo bastante poderosos como para distraerla del sensual deleite que le proporcionaban esos dedos, de la fuerza de esas manos y del placer que conjuraban.

La palabra «fascinación» ni siquiera se acercaba a describir lo que sentía.

Lo miró con los párpados entornados y sintió que algo cambiaba en su interior. Que la invadía el deseo de proporcionarle tanto placer como él le estaba ofreciendo. ¿Así era como ocurría? ¿Ése era el motivo de que las mujeres sensatas decidieran aceptar las necesidades de un hombre y acudir en busca de más?

Su mente fue incapaz de ofrecerle una respuesta. Así que dejó que la pregunta se desvaneciera.

Simon le estaba mirando los pechos. Estaba mirando sus manos sobre ellos. En ese momento, alzó la vista y sus miradas se encontraron.

La pasión estalló a su alrededor y una oleada de emoción la recorrió. Esbozó una sonrisa deliberada y, también deliberadamente, se inclinó haciendo caso omiso de las manos que le rodeaban los pechos y lo besó.

Sintió que él inspiraba hondo... antes de apartarla y moverse hasta quedar de costado sobre la otomana, con una mano aún sobre un pecho y la otra en una de sus mejillas. La besó. O más bien la devoró. Volvió a hechizar sus sentidos una vez más, antes de devolverla a la realidad muy lentamente.

Cuando él apartó la cabeza, ambos jadeaban. Sus miradas se encontraron. El deseo palpitaba en sus labios. Lo tenía aferrado por los hombros con fuerza. Se mantuvieron inmóviles un momento, atrapados en ese instante. Conscientes de la pasión, del latido de sus corazones, del abrumador deseo.

Hasta que pasó.

Despacio, muy despacio, Simon inclinó la cabeza y sus labios volvieron a encontrarse en un beso tierno, lento y reconfortante. Apartó las manos de ella, le cerró el corpiño y la rodeó con los brazos. Y así se quedaron un rato, abrazados.

Más tarde, mientras salían del gabinete, Portia miró por encima del hombro. La sábana cubría nuevamente la otomana. No había rastro de que la habitación hubiera sido el marco de su apasionante interludio.

Sin embargo, había sucedido. Algo había cambiado.

O, tal vez, algo les había sido revelado.

Simon la invitó a salir y cerró la puerta tras él. Su semblante era impasible, pero estaba segura de que sentía lo mismo que ella. Sus miradas se encontraron y se entrelazaron un corto instante mientras él la tomaba del brazo. Después, clavaron la vista al frente y regresaron a la galería.

Portia necesitaba pensar, pero la mesa de la cena y la compañía no se prestaban a ello. Lanzó una mirada irritada a Kitty. Y no era la única que lo hizo. Era una estúpida redomada, impredecible en sus cambios de humor. Ésa era la conclusión más benévola que pudo alcanzar.

—He oído que mañana se celebrará un almuerzo de gala —le dijo Charlie con las cejas enarcadas antes de mirar de reojo a Kitty, sentada al otro extremo de la mesa—. Al parecer, ha sido ella la organizadora.

Su voz tenía un deje de desconfianza, de recelo.

—Tal vez no deberíamos preocuparnos —sugirió—. Hoy ha estado muy comedida durante el almuerzo. ¿Quién sabe? Quizá sean las noches las que...

—¿La transforman en una *femme fatale,* especialmente indiscreta además?

Portia estuvo a punto de atragantarse. Se llevó la servilleta a los labios y le lanzó una mirada ceñuda a Charlie. Éste sonrió, en absoluto arrepentido, si bien el gesto no denotaba humor alguno.

—Me apena decepcionarla, querida, pero Kitty es capaz de comportarse de modo atroz a cualquier hora del día. —Volvió a mirar hacia el otro extremo de la mesa—. Su actitud es totalmente impredecible.

El ceño de Portia se acentuó.

—James dice que va a peor.

Charlie meditó un instante antes de asentir con la cabeza.

—Sí, es cierto.

Kitty había comenzado la noche de mala manera, coqueteando (o más bien intentando coquetear) sin disimulo con James en el salón. Charlie había intentado intervenir, pero sólo había logrado que la ira de la joven recayera sobre él. En aquel instante, Henry intentó aplacar los ánimos y, como resultado, su esposa acabó alejándose enfurruñada.

Se habían sentado a la mesa con la señora Archer visiblemente agitada, como si estuviera al borde de un ataque de nervios. Otros invitados mostraban también signos de estar molestos, de ser conscientes de lo que sucedía; signos que, en circunstancias normales, habrían ocultado con consumada naturalidad.

Parecía, concluyó mientras las damas se levantaban de la mesa para reunirse en el salón, que el ambiente cordial de la fiesta se estuviera resquebrajando. Aún no se había roto del todo, no se había desmoronado, pero pasar por alto el comportamiento de Kitty estaba resultando arduo para algunos.

Como para las Hammond. Las muchachas, confusas por los acontecimientos (algo lógico, porque nadie entendía lo que estaba sucediendo) se pegaron a ella, ansiosas por charlar y olvidar las torvas miradas de la concurrencia. Hasta Lucy Buckstead, que por regla general se comportaba con sensatez y seguridad en sí misma, parecía un tanto subyugada. Se compadeció de ellas y las animó a explayarse sobre el almuerzo: que si asistirían los oficiales con los que habían bailado la otra noche, que si el apuesto y callado vecino, George Quiggin, aparecería o no...

Aunque sus esfuerzos consiguieron distraer a las tres jóvenes, ella misma fue incapaz de olvidar la irritación que Kitty le provocaba. Echó un vistazo al otro extremo del salón y vio que Kitty hablaba animadamente con la señora Buckstead y con lady Hammond. A pesar de ello, sus ojos estaban clavados en la puerta.

La puerta por la que los caballeros entrarían en breve.

Contuvo un resoplido asqueado. Kitty parecía irradiar una especie de mal presagio desde el punto de vista social. En lo que a ella se refería, ya había tenido más que suficiente. Necesitaba encontrar el tiempo y el lugar apropiados para pensar.

—Si me disculpáis... —les dijo a las muchachas antes de echar a andar hacia las puertas francesas que daban a la terraza.

Con la vista clavada al frente, las atravesó y se internó en la agradable frescura de la noche.

Una vez que dejó atrás el resplandor del salón, se detuvo y tomó una profunda bocanada de aire. Le resultó delicioso, como si fuera el primer soplo de aire fresco del que disfrutara en horas. La frustración la abandonó, como una capa que acabara de resbalarle por los hombros. Esbozó una sonrisa y cruzó la terraza en dirección a la escalera que bajaba al prado, y de allí, al lago.

No debería ir a aquel lugar; al menos, no sola. No obstante, la luna llena brillaba con fuerza en el cielo, bañando el prado con su luz plateada. Le pareció bastante seguro pasear por allí. Además, no era muy tarde.

Necesitaba pensar en todo lo que había aprendido. Sacar una conclusión de los acontecimientos que se habían sucedido hasta ese punto. Las horas que había pasado a solas con Simon le habían abierto los ojos sin el menor asomo de duda. Y lo que estaba viendo era mucho más sorprendente de lo que había imaginado, por no decir que totalmente distinto. Había supuesto que la atracción, el vínculo físico, aquello que ocurría entre un hombre y una mujer, sería algo parecido al chocolate: lo bastante agradable como para desear darse el gusto cuando se presentara la oportunidad, pero sin llegar a ser un anhelo compulsivo.

Pero lo que había compartido con Simon hasta ese momento...

Sintió un escalofrío a pesar de la calidez de la noche. Siguió caminando con los ojos clavados en el césped mientras intentaba encontrar las palabras que explicaran lo que sentía. ¿Sería deseo ese apremio por repetir los encuentros? No, no de repetirlos. De ir más allá. Mucho más allá.

Era posible, pero se conocía lo bastante como para reconocer que, mezclada con esa compulsión puramente sensual, había una enorme dosis de curiosidad, de su habitual ansia de saber.

Que se había avivado, al igual que el deseo.

Sabía lo que quería aprender. Sabía que, una vez descubierta su existencia, no sería capaz de darle la espalda hasta haberlo examinado a fondo, hasta comprenderlo todo.

Había algo, algo muy sorprendente, entre Simon y ella.

Sopesó la conclusión mientras atravesaba despacio el prado y no pudo refutarla. Aun con su total inexperiencia en ese ámbito, confiaba en sus habilidades innatas. Si su instinto le decía que había algo que perseguir, estaba en lo cierto.

La naturaleza de ese «algo», sin embargo...

No atinaba a identificarla. Ni siquiera era capaz de formular una suposición. Y gracias a la vida protegida que había llevado, ni siquiera sabía si era normal.

Para ella, no lo era en absoluto.

Pero ¿lo sería para él? ¿Le ocurría con todas las mujeres?

No lo creía. Lo conocía lo bastante como para percibir sus cambios de humor. Esa tarde, cuando su encuentro en la otomana llegaba a su fin y percibió ese curioso cambio entre ellos, tuvo la impresión de que Simon estaba tan perplejo como ella.

Por más que se devanó los sesos, no encontró una razón específica que precipitara ese momento concreto. Tal parecía que hubieran abierto los ojos a la par y se hubieran descubierto en un lugar donde jamás habían esperado encontrarse. Ambos estaban disfrutando del momento, por decirlo someramente; ninguno estaba prestando atención, ni dirigiendo el interludio...

Era algo especial porque él no había esperado que sucediera.

Sin duda, tenía que averiguar mucho más. Descubrir y ahondar sobre el tema, a toda costa. El lugar más apropiado donde empezar era el mismo donde había comenzado todo. Esa dimensión en la que sólo existían las sensaciones.

Por suerte, tenía una ligera idea de cómo regresar a ese lugar. Habían estado inmersos en el deleite físico, absortos como sólo dos personas que se conocen a fondo podrían llegar a estar. Ninguno de los dos había estado pendiente del otro con el fin de evaluar su honestidad o su carácter. Si Simon hubiera querido hacer algo, decir algo, sabía a ciencia cierta que lo habría hecho. Y él la conocía en la misma medida, no le cabía duda.

Ésa era la clave. No habían estado pensando en nada. No tenían por qué hacerlo cuando estaban juntos. Podían concentrarse en lo que hacían.

En lo que estaban compartiendo.

Llegó hasta el extremo del prado que se alzaba sobre el lago. A sus pies se extendían sus aguas, negras e insondables.

Sin importar lo mucho que expandiera los límites de su imaginación, resultaba imposible (totalmente imposible) imaginarse que compartía con otro hombre lo mismo que había compartido con Simon.

Sintió su presencia como si de una caricia se tratara. Su mirada. Se dio la vuelta y atisbó su silueta de hombros anchos a lo lejos, mientras atravesaba el prado con las manos en los bolsillos y la vista clavada en ella.

Se detuvo a su lado y contempló el lago un instante antes de volver a mirarla.

—No deberías estar aquí sola.

Lo miró a los ojos.

—No lo estoy.

Simon apartó la mirada pero no antes de que ella se percatara de la media sonrisa que le curvó los labios.

—¿Qué tal ha ido? —Señaló hacia la mansión.

—Ha sido espantoso. Kitty está en la cuerda floja. Parece empecinada en ganarse los favores de Winfield aunque éste corra despavorido en cuanto la ve. Después del fracaso del salón, Henry decidió desaparecer de la escena y fingir que no se enteraba de nada más. La señora Archer está horrorizada, pero no es capaz de hacer nada. Lord y lady Glossup están cada vez más molestos. El único alivio de la noche ha venido de manos de lord Netherfield. Le ha dicho a Kitty que madure.

Portia dejó escapar un resoplido muy poco femenino. Pasaba demasiado tiempo con lady O...

Simon la miró pasados unos instantes.

—Será mejor que regresemos.

La idea no le resultó atractiva en lo más mínimo.

—¿Por qué? —Lo miró de soslayo—. Aún es demasiado temprano para irse a la cama. ¿De verdad que quieres regresar a la casa y tener que aguantar con una sonrisa el bochornoso comportamiento de Kitty?

La arrogante repulsión que asomó a sus ojos fue suficiente respuesta.

—Vamos, bajemos a la orilla. —Tenía la intención de pasarse por el mirador, pero no se sintió obligada a mencionarlo.

Simon titubeó, con la vista clavada precisamente en el mirador que se vislumbraba apenas en la otra orilla del lago. La conocía muy bien, no cabía duda...

Alzó la barbilla y lo tomó del brazo.

—El paseo te aclarará las ideas.

Tuvo que darle un tirón del brazo para que se pusiera en marcha, ya que parecía renuente a obedecerla, pero al final accedió y echó a andar con ella hacia el camino que bordeaba el lago. Sin embargo, la guió hasta el pinar, en la dirección contraria al mirador. Con la cabeza bien alta, lo siguió sin rechistar.

El camino rodeaba todo el perímetro del lago. Para regresar a la casa sin retroceder sobre sus propios pasos, tendrían que pasar por el mirador.

Como siempre, lady O había estado en lo cierto. Todavía quedaba muchísimo por aprender, por explorar, y no contaba con muchos días para hacerlo. En otras circunstancias, tres lecciones el mismo día podía considerarse algo imprudente; pero, tal y como estaban las cosas, no veía razón alguna para desaprovechar la oportunidad de ahondar en su objetivo.

Y de saciar su curiosidad.

Simon sabía lo que estaba pensando Portia. Su alegre comportamiento no lo engañaba en absoluto. Estaba fantaseando acerca de su siguiente paso.

Igual que él.

La única diferencia radicaba en que él era mucho más versado y estaba experimentando sentimientos contradictorios al respecto. No le extrañaba en absoluto que ella quisiera apresurar los acontecimientos. De hecho, contaba con su impulsivo entusiasmo para hacerla ir más allá. Sin embargo...

Le habría ido de perillas contar con un poco más de tiempo para reflexionar sobre lo ocurrido esa tarde.

Contar con un poco más de tiempo para redirigir sus pasos.

Y para descubrir el modo de mantener el control a pesar de la tentación que ella representaba. Una tentación mucho más irresistible porque sabía que Portia no era en absoluto consciente de ella.

Y no era tan tonto como para comentárselo. Lo único

que le hacía falta era que ella decidiera utilizarla a su favor...

—No entiendo a qué está jugando Kitty. Da la impresión de que no piensa en los demás, de que no tiene en cuenta sus sentimientos —le dijo.

Pensó en Henry y en lo que estaría sintiendo con todo aquello.

—¿Tan ingenua es?

Portia tardó un poco en responder.

—Me parece que no es tanto cuestión de ingenuidad como de egoísmo..., como si fuera totalmente incapaz de considerar los sentimientos de los demás. Actúa como si fuera la única persona real, como si los demás fuéramos... —Hizo un gesto con la mano—. Figuras de un carrusel que giramos a su alrededor.

—Ni siquiera parece estar muy unida a Winifred —refunfuñó él.

Portia meneó la cabeza.

—No lo están. De hecho, creo que Winifred preferiría estar aún más distanciada de ella. Sobre todo por lo de Desmond.

—¿Crees que hay algo definitivo entre ellos?

—Lo habría si Kitty los dejara.

Caminaron un rato en silencio.

—Debe de sentirse muy sola en el centro de su carrusel —murmuró él a la postre.

Pasaron unos instantes antes de que Portia le diera un apretón en el brazo y reconociera sus palabras con un gesto de cabeza.

Habían recorrido casi todo el perímetro del lago. El mirador se alzaba a poca distancia en la oscuridad. Dejó que ella lo condujera hasta los escalones de entrada. No puso objeción alguna cuando le soltó el brazo, se recogió las faldas y empezó a subir. Tras echar un vistazo al camino, la siguió.

Lo aguardaba en la penumbra. Su rostro ovalado parecía muy pálido entre las sombras. No podía leer la expresión de sus ojos. Ni ella la suya.

Se detuvo frente a ella. Portia alzó una mano, le acarició la mejilla y alzó el rostro para besarlo. Un beso que resultó una invitación flagrante. Aceptó tras rodearle la cintura con las manos, encantado de sentir ese cuerpo esbelto entre ellas, y a cambio le exigió que se rindiera. No le dio cuartel.

Cuando por fin alzó la cabeza, ella suspiró y le preguntó con serenidad:

—Y ahora ¿qué?

Había utilizado la última media hora para encontrar la respuesta. Sonrió, aunque en la oscuridad ella no pudiera verlo.

—Algo un poco distinto. —Siguió internándose en el mirador muy despacio, haciéndola retroceder de modo deliberado.

Percibió el ramalazo de excitación y nerviosismo que se apoderó de ella. Portia ardía en deseos de echar un vistazo a su alrededor para ver adónde la llevaba, pero el instinto de protección fue más poderoso..., así que no le quitó los ojos de encima.

Siguió avanzando hasta que ella se topó con uno de los sillones y se detuvo. En ese momento la soltó, la tomó de la mano y pasó a su lado para sentarse en el sillón. Después, tiró de ella para que se sentara en sus rodillas, casi de frente a él.

Su sorpresa le resultó evidente. En ese punto del mirador reinaban las sombras, ya que la luz de la luna no lo alcanzaba. Sin embargo, Portia superó su sorpresa al punto, puesto que no tuvo que incitarla para que se pegara a él. Se inclinó hacia delante de forma inesperada y lo besó.

Seductoramente. Antes de darse cuenta, estaba atrapado, cautivado y hechizado por el beso. Aunque no se mostrara pícara ni coqueta, al parecer era capaz de mostrarse seductora de un modo muy distinto.

Uno que le resultaba muchísimo más irresistible.

Sintió que el deseo se avivaba y rezó para que ella jamás se diera cuenta de la facilidad con la que lo conjuraba. El deseo que provocaba en él le bastaría para hacerlo comer de su mano.

Como una bestia a punto de darse un festín.

Apartó las manos de su espalda, cubierta por la delicada seda de su vestido de noche, y las colocó a ambos lados de su cintura. Ella se enderezó un poco y creyó que le estaba facilitando el acceso a sus pechos. No obstante, Portia interrumpió el beso y alzó la cabeza.

—Tengo una sugerencia.

El recelo se apoderó de él, en parte porque el tono de su voz había cambiado. Era mucho más ronco, más sugerente y tan sensual como la noche que los envolvía, ocultando su mirada y su expresión. No podía leer ninguna de ellas. No le quedó más remedio que adivinar sus intenciones por otros indicios.

Mucho menos precisos.

—¿Cuál?

Atisbó el asomo de una sonrisa en sus labios. Portia apoyó las manos en su pecho y se inclinó para darle un beso fugaz.

—Un apéndice que añadir a nuestra última lección.

¿Qué demonios estaba tramando?

—Explícate.

Soltó una suave carcajada que le caló hasta lo más profundo.

—Prefiero enseñártelo. —Lo miró a los ojos—. Es de lo más razonable... y justo.

En ese momento, se percató de que le había desabrochado el chaleco. La chaqueta ya estaba desabotonada cuando llegaron al mirador. Antes de que pudiera reaccionar, ella cambió de postura y le pasó los dedos por debajo del nudo de la corbata.

—Portia.

—¿Sí? —murmuró.

Discutir no le serviría de nada. Así que alzó las manos y la ayudó a deshacer el nudo. Con un gesto triunfal, ella se enderezó en su regazo y tiró de la prenda. Su mente conjuró al instante una imagen muy precisa y, sin pérdida de tiempo, le quitó la corbata de las manos y la dejó sobre el brazo del sillón.

Portia ya había perdido todo el interés en ella, concentrada como estaba en esos momentos en los botones que le cerraban la camisa. Se movió un poco para que pudiera sacarle los faldones por la pretina de los pantalones y, en cuanto hubo desabrochado todos los botones, la abrió, dejando su torso al descubierto. Se detuvo para observar lo que había dejado a la vista.

Simon habría vendido su alma al diablo por ver su rostro con claridad. Dadas las circunstancias, se conformó con su inmovilidad, con su ensimismamiento, con la evidente fascinación que se apoderó de ella cuando soltó la camisa muy despacio y extendió los dedos sobre su piel.

Por un instante, se limitó a seguir los contornos de sus músculos, a explorar, a aprender. Después, lo miró a la cara, absorbió su reacción y se percató de que había contenido el aliento. Sus manos se detuvieron al punto, sólo para retomar el asalto de un modo mucho más audaz.

—Te gusta. —Lo acarició con lentitud, trazando el relieve de los músculos del pecho con sensualidad antes de descender un poco y volver a ascender, rozándolo apenas con la yema de los dedos, hasta detenerse sobre la rizada mata de vello castaño que lo cubría.

Simon tomó una bocanada de aire.

—Si a ti te gusta, sí.

Ella soltó una carcajada.

—¡Claro que me gusta! Mucho más porque a ti también.

El asalto del deseo resultó increíblemente doloroso. El timbre de su voz, esa nota ronca, sensual y tan extrañamente madura (que parecía decir que lo conocía a la perfección y que en esa arena estaba la mar de segura) fue el afrodisíaco más potente con el que jamás se había encontrado. El peso de ese cuerpo cálido y excitante sobre sus muslos empeoró su tormento.

Portia acarició y se entregó gustosa al delicioso placer de tocarlo y de saber que, al menos durante esos minutos, lo tenía bajo su hechizo. Le encantaba sentir esa piel cálida, o más bien ardiente, bajo las manos y le fascinaba el tacto acerado de sus músculos. Ella también estaba hechizada; aunque lo más abrumador era la sensación que le provocó el descubrimiento de que sus caricias podían darle placer en la misma medida que él se lo había dado a ella.

Eso era lo justo, tal y como le había dicho. Justo para los dos.

Instantes después, Simon respiró hondo, aunque de forma entrecortada, y extendió los brazos hacia ella. No la apartó, sino que la acercó. Se apoyó sobre su torso y se inclinó hacia delante, más que dispuesta a entregarle sus labios, su boca y su lengua.

El cariz del beso cambió hasta convertirse en algo mucho más íntimo e internarse en un plano que todavía no habían explorado. Le clavó los dedos en los músculos del pecho y presionó las palmas sobre esa piel desnuda. Entretanto, las manos de Simon estaban ocupadas desabrochándole la larga hilera de botones que le llegaba hasta la base de la espalda.

En el calor de la noche, el aire apenas se agitó a su alrededor cuando Simon la instó a incorporarse para poder bajarle el vestido.

La recorrió un estremecimiento, no a causa del pudor, sino por la certeza de lo que iba a ocurrir. Ya le había acariciado los pechos antes sin el impedimento de la ropa, pero el vestido había estado allí, ocultando a sus ojos la piel desnuda que tocaba. Sin embargo, en esos momentos se lo bajó y, tras un breve instante de indecisión, le permitió que le bajara las mangas y se las sacara por los brazos. El vestido cayó en torno a su cintura. Acto seguido, se dispuso a desatarle las cintas de la camisola con una actitud casi indiferente. Lo miró a la cara. Él ni siquiera le devolvió la mirada para pedirle permiso. Desató la lazada como si tuviera todo el derecho a hacerlo.

Portia agradeció que no pudiera verle la expresión. Si seguía sentada, permitiéndole que la desnudara, era gracias a la oscuridad que los envolvía.

El aire era cálido, aunque tenía la piel enfebrecida y los pezones duros y muy sensibles. Sintió que la mirada de

Simon la recorría y la evaluaba. Creyó ver que esbozaba el asomo de una sonrisa carente de humor. En ese instante, alzó una mano y la tocó. Ella cerró los ojos, ya que tuvo la repentina sensación de que le pesaban mucho los párpados, y ladeó el cuerpo. Simon aprovechó para cubrirle ambos pechos con las manos, provocándole un estremecimiento.

Se entregó a las sensaciones sin abrir los ojos. Dejó que sus sentidos se centraran en cada caricia, en cada roce, en esa creciente tortura. Parecía tener la piel mucho más sensible que antes. Tenía los pezones tan duros que resultaba doloroso. Aunque era un dolor extraño, porque cada vez que él los pellizcaba, se transformaba en placer, en una oleada de sensaciones que la bañaba de la cabeza a los pies y se concentraba en su entrepierna.

Abrió los ojos lo justo para poder mirarlo a la cara. ¿Sabría él lo que le estaba haciendo? Con una mirada bastó. Por supuesto que lo sabía. ¿Habría planeado lo de la oscuridad para que ella se sintiera más predispuesta? No. Había sido ella quien lo había guiado hasta el mirador, pero estaba claro que estaba sacándole el mejor partido a su plan.

La idea la complació. Uno hacía un movimiento y el otro lo continuaba. Parecía correcto. Estimulante.

Como sus caricias; como el roce de sus manos sobre la piel. Contuvo el aliento y bajó la vista; observó sus manos, mucho más oscuras sobre la blancura de sus pechos, mientras jugueteaban con afán posesivo.

La pasión se avivó.

—¿Quieres que demos el siguiente paso?

Lo miró a los ojos. No sabía cuál podía ser ese siguiente paso, ni alcanzaba a imaginarlo. Aunque no le importaba.

—Sí.

Simon distinguió la nota resuelta de su voz y detectó el fugaz gesto decidido de su mentón. Suficiente para hacerlo suspirar de alivio.

Se obligó a alejar los dedos de su piel excitada y buscó

la corbata. Portia parpadeó y lo observó mientras él plegaba el largo rectángulo de seda hasta convertirlo en una estrecha cinta. Se lo enrolló en torno a las manos y lo estiró al tiempo que enfrentaba su mirada.

—Una sugerencia de mi cosecha.

Había accedido a su sugerencia, así que ella no podía negarse a la suya. No obstante, lo hizo con el ceño fruncido..., si bien le colocó las manos en el pecho, se inclinó hacia delante y le permitió que le pasara la corbata alrededor de la cabeza para vendarle los ojos.

—¿Es necesario?

—No del todo, pero creí que lo preferirías así.

Su silencio le dijo a gritos que no estaba segura de cómo interpretar su respuesta. Aseguró la corbata con un nudo mientras sonreía. Cuando apartó las manos, Portia hizo ademán de incorporarse.

—No. —Se lo impidió poniéndole las manos sobre la espalda desnuda y, en ese momento, sintió que algo en su interior se tensaba en respuesta—. Quédate como estás. —Le llevó una de las manos al rostro y la acercó para besarla—. No tienes que hacer nada, limítate a sentir.

Sus labios se encontraron y volvió a sumergirla en la pasión, en esa intimidad que ya les resultaba familiar. Sus manos siguieron apoyadas en su torso, manteniéndolos separados, cosa que en ese punto no importaba demasiado. Profundizó el beso para atrapar sus sentidos y, entretanto, aprovechó el momento para asimilar que la tenía desnuda de cintura para arriba sobre las rodillas, aguardando. Se dispuso a dar los últimos toques a los preparativos.

La oscuridad inherente al plan de Portia le había supuesto una ventaja inesperada y la venda de los ojos servía para incrementar su efecto. De otro modo, habría tardado mucho más tiempo en encontrar el lugar idóneo para avanzar en el camino y dar el siguiente paso sin correr el riesgo de que ella reaccionara de modo instintivo y saliera a la superficie su reticencia a someterse a la voluntad de un hombre. Un instinto que en Portia estaba muy desarrollado. Gracias a su plan, ella misma se había entregado en bandeja de plata y estaba más que dispuesto a darse un festín.

La apartó un poco hasta que estuvo de nuevo sentada con la espalda recta y él hizo lo mismo mientras deslizaba las manos por esa piel suave, dándose el gusto de volver a cubrirle los pechos. La intensidad del beso se agudizó y la pasión los abrasó. Dejó que siguiera su curso, a sabiendas de lo que estaba por llegar. Cuando los besos de Portia se tornaron más apremiantes, la apartó y le echó la cabeza hacia atrás para besarle la garganta.

Ella le apartó las manos del pecho. Una de ellas le agarró un hombro, por debajo de la camisa, y la otra le acarició la nuca antes de enterrarse en su pelo mientras él se inclinaba para lamer y besar en el punto donde le latía el pulso.

Aún con la cabeza inclinada hacia atrás, Portia jadeó, sorprendida.

Se apartó de su cuello al mismo tiempo que le alzaba un pecho y, tras acariciarle el pezón, inclinó la cabeza y lo besó.

De la garganta de Portia brotó un entrecortado grito de deleite; el sonido lo sacudió por entero y lo instó a continuar. Lamió el endurecido pezón y lo chupó hasta que logró arrancarle otro grito. Se detuvo lo justo para cambiar sus atenciones al otro pecho. Se dio un festín semejante al que disfrutaría un conquistador con una esclava sometida que se le ofrecía. Al igual que hacía Portia en esos momentos. No retrocedió ni una sola vez; al contrario, lo exhortó a continuar sin necesidad de palabras, aunque no por ello fue menos efectivo. Él conocía cada reacción, podía interpretar y entender hasta el menor de sus gemidos, de sus jadeos.

Sintió que le clavaba los dedos en el hombro mientras que con la otra mano se aferraba a su nuca. Lo acercó a ella y le pidió que tomara más. Y se entregó a cambio.

La obedeció, avivando la hoguera sin piedad. La dejó sentir y aprender todo lo que quisiera, pero en un momento dado y sin demostrar piedad alguna, tiró de las riendas con decisión a pesar de que ella se mostraba reticente, y los alejó poco a poco de las abrasadoras llamas del deseo.

Aún no había llegado ese momento.

Cuando se reclinó en el sillón, ambos jadeaban. Portia lo siguió y se desplomó sobre su pecho. Musitó algo antes de removerse y frotarse sensualmente contra el áspero vello de su torso. No la apartó; al contrario, le alzó la cabeza para darle un tierno beso y dejó que regresara a la normalidad a su propio paso.

Cuando por fin aceptó la situación, suspiró y se acomodó contra él. Alzó los brazos y se quitó la venda. Lo atravesó con la mirada y, aun en la oscuridad, habría jurado que esos ojos azul cobalto refulgían. Le clavó la mirada en los labios, se lamió los suyos y devolvió la vista a sus ojos.

—Más.

No era una pregunta. Era una orden.

—No. —Negarse le resultó doloroso. Tomó aire y sintió que el deseo le oprimía el pecho—. Sé paciente.

Craso error haber dicho esas palabras. Lo supo en cuanto las pronunció y vio el destello de decisión en sus ojos. Reaccionó al instante, antes de que ella tuviera opción de hacerlo. La besó. La movió hasta colocarla bien entre sus brazos y le devoró la boca. Mientras tanto y de forma deliberada, sus manos descendieron por esa espalda desnuda hasta deslizarse bajo el vestido y trazar la curva de su trasero. Quería conocer centímetro a centímetro lo que un día sería suyo.

Portia murmuró algo, no con afán de protesta, sino como incentivo. Hizo caso omiso, pero se negó a apartar las manos de ella todavía. No hasta que hubiera saciado ese innegable anhelo que lo instaba a explorar su cuerpo. Que lo instaba a asimilar que la haría suya... algún día.

Pronto.

Cuando alzó la cabeza, ella abrió los ojos y sus miradas se entrelazaron. No había rastro de temor en sus ojos, de remordimientos ni de engaño.

Descansaba entre sus brazos, desnuda hasta la cintura y con los pechos amoldados a su torso mientras él le acariciaba el trasero.

El deseo crepitaba entre ellos.

Ambos lo sabían.

Le costó un enorme esfuerzo respirar, pero lo hizo.

—Tenemos que regresar.

Ella estudió su rostro y comprendió el trasfondo de sus palabras. A la postre, asintió con la cabeza.

Les llevó su tiempo emprender el camino de regreso. Tuvieron que dejar que sus sentidos recobraran la normalidad; tuvieron que componerse y que volver a vestirse. Simon no se molestó en anudarse la corbata, la dejó que cayera alrededor del cuello y rezó para no encontrarse con nadie en el camino de vuelta a la mansión.

Se pusieron en marcha tomados de la mano y se internaron en la creciente oscuridad de la noche. La luna había descendido en el horizonte y los jardines estaban en completa penumbra.

La mansión se vislumbraba a lo lejos. Portia frunció el ceño.

—No hay luz... Lo normal sería que la mayoría de los invitados estuviera aún en el salón. No puede ser muy tarde.

A decir verdad, no tenía ni idea de la hora que era.

Simon se encogió de hombros.

—Tal vez hayan huido del carrusel de Kitty, igual que nosotros.

Siguieron caminando. Simon la guió en una dirección que no era la habitual y supuso que quería entrar en la casa sin que los vieran. Aún estaban a cierta distancia cuando escucharon unas pisadas que se acercaban a ellos, acompañadas por el susurro de las hojas de los arbustos.

Simon se detuvo al abrigo de un árbol y ella se vio obligada a imitarlo. Aguardaron en silencio e inmóviles.

Una figura apareció a cierta distancia, procedente del

camino de acceso a la mansión. No se percató de su presencia, pero a medida que se movía de sombra en sombra, ellos sí lo vieron.

Lo reconocieron al instante. Al igual que en la otra ocasión, el gitano atravesó los jardines como si se los conociera al dedillo.

Cuando se marchó y Simon la instó a continuar, susurró:

—¿Quién demonios es? ¿De verdad es un gitano?

—Al parecer, es el líder del grupo que suele acampar todos los veranos aquí cerca. Se llama Arturo.

Casi habían llegado a la mansión cuando Simon volvió a detenerla. Echó un vistazo al frente y vio lo que él: al joven jardinero apostado al abrigo de un árbol, cerca de una de las esquinas de la mansión. No estaba mirando en su dirección, sino en la opuesta, la que quedaba fuera de su vista. Por la que el otro gitano, Arturo, debía de haber abandonado la casa.

Estaba observando el ala que albergaba las estancias privadas de la familia.

Portia miró a Simon. Él le devolvió la mirada y le hizo un gesto para que continuara. El camino que habían tomado estaba cubierto de césped, al igual que la mayoría de los senderos que se internaban en los jardines, lo que les permitía moverse en silencio.

Tras doblar una esquina, él abrió una puerta y la hizo pasar al pequeño vestíbulo del jardín. En cuanto hubo cerrado, le preguntó:

—¿Por qué crees que está ahí el jardinero?

Simon la miró y torció el gesto.

—No es oriundo del condado. Es uno de los gitanos. Según me han contado, es excelente en su trabajo y suele trabajar aquí todos los veranos, ayudando con los parterres.

Portia frunció el ceño.

—Pero si estaba vigilando la salida de Arturo, ¿por qué sigue ahí?

—Sé tanto como tú. —La tomó del brazo y la guió hacia la puerta—. Vamos, tenemos que llegar a la planta alta.

La puerta daba acceso a uno de los pasillos secundarios. No había nadie por los alrededores. Atravesaron la mansión con actitud despreocupada, pero en silencio. Dado que ambos estaban muy acostumbrados al ritmo de vida de las casas señoriales, reconocían las señales que indicaban la presencia de otras personas, tales como el murmullo distante de las conversaciones. Todo estaba desierto y en silencio.

En uno de los pasillos había una vela encendida, situada sobre una consola. Simon se detuvo.

—Vigila.

Se anudó la corbata con presteza de modo que pasara la prueba si se encontraban con alguien en la penumbra de los pasillos. Reanudaron la marcha, pero no se toparon con nadie. Cuando llegaron al vestíbulo principal, murmuró:

—Parece que todo el mundo se ha retirado.

Lo que era extraño. Según el reloj que acababan de dejar atrás, ni siquiera era medianoche.

Simon se encogió de hombros y le hizo un gesto en dirección a la escalinata. Habían subido la mitad cuando escucharon que alguien hablaba.

—Causará un escándalo, por supuesto.

Se detuvieron e intercambiaron una mirada. Era Henry.

Simon se acercó a la balaustrada y miró hacia abajo. Ella se acercó e hizo lo mismo.

La puerta de la biblioteca estaba entornada. Desde la posición que ocupaban, veían la espalda de un sillón y la coronilla de James. Su mano, que descansaba sobre el brazo del sillón, hacía girar el contenido ambarino de una copa de cristal.

—Por el cariz que están tomando las cosas, el escándalo al que te enfrentas será infinitamente mayor si no lo haces.

Henry refunfuñó. Un momento después, replicó:

—Tienes razón, por supuesto. Aunque me gustaría que no la tuvieras, que hubiera algún otro modo de...

El tono de su voz les dijo cuál, o mejor «quién», era el

objeto de su discusión. Dieron media vuelta al unísono y continuaron subiendo en silencio.

Una vez en la galería, Simon le besó la punta de los dedos antes de separarse, sin necesidad de decirse nada.

No se encontró con nadie de camino a su habitación. Se preguntó qué se habrían perdido. Qué habría hecho Kitty para que todos se hubieran ido a la cama tan temprano y hubiera obligado a James y Henry a discutir las posibles ventajas de un escándalo.

De todas formas, no quería saberlo. Ya tenía más que suficiente con sus propios problemas como para preocuparse y tener que cargar con los deslices de Kitty. Que cada palo aguantara su propia vela... O, según decía otro refrán: «Vive y deja vivir.»

En cuanto a ella, estaba decidida a vivir la vida... al máximo. Hasta un grado, hasta un punto, del que jamás había sido consciente. Lo sucedido la noche anterior debería haberla escandalizado. No había sido así. Ni muchísimo menos. Se sentía alborozada, ansiosa y más que dispuesta a proseguir con su aprendizaje, a beber de nuevo de la copa de la pasión, a saborear nuevamente el deseo..., pero, en esa ocasión, apuraría hasta el último trago.

Las preguntas que la consumían eran cuándo y dónde. Ni se le pasó por la cabeza cuestionarse con quién.

Se abrió paso entre la multitud que ocupaba los jardines. El almuerzo al aire libre de Kitty estaba en pleno apogeo. A juzgar por la presteza con la que las familias vecinas habían respondido a la invitación, dedujo que los Glossup no habían dado muchas fiestas en los últimos tiempos.

Se mantuvo apartada a conciencia del resto de los invitados a la fiesta campestre para internarse en la multitud y charlar con los que había conocido en el baile y con otras personas que le fueron presentando poco a poco. Dado que estaba acostumbrada a asumir el papel de anfitriona en esos eventos (su hermano Luc celebraba sus propias fiestas en la propiedad de Rutlandshire), se sentía a sus anchas charlando con aquellos que, de encontrarse en Londres, habrían estado por debajo de ella en el escalafón social. Siempre le había interesado que los demás le contaran su vida; había sido el único modo de aprender a apreciar la comodidad de la suya propia. Cosa que habría dado por sentada de otro modo, como solían hacer la mayoría de las damas de su posición.

Para ser justos, Kitty tampoco se daba aires y, en cambio, se mezclaba con alegría con sus invitados. Mientras buscaba nuevas posibilidades, o algún asomo de posibilidad, para lograr su ya truncado objetivo Portia se percató de que las ansias de vivir que mostraba Kitty, su alegría, parecían de lo más genuinas. Con sus deslumbrantes sonrisas, sus vivaces carcajadas y el entusiasmo que demostraba, bien podría haber sido, no una novia en el día de su boda, pero sí una recién casada en su primer éxito como anfitriona.

Meneó la cabeza mientras la observaba saludar a una oronda dama con evidente buen humor antes de detenerse a conversar brevemente con su hija y su desgarbado hijo.

—Increíble, ¿verdad?

Al darse media vuelta se topó con la cínica mirada de Charlie.

El recién llegado señaló a Kitty con un gesto de cabeza.

—Si puede explicármelo, le estaré eternamente agradecido.

Portia desvió la vista hacia Kitty.

—Demasiado difícil para mí. —Tomó el brazo de Charlie y lo obligó a girarse; con una sonrisa torcida, el hombre aceptó sus órdenes y caminó a su lado.

—Tal vez sea como el juego de las charadas: se comporta como cree que debería comportarse... No, no constate lo evidente... Quiero decir que tiene una imagen mental de cómo cree que debería comportarse y actúa en consecuencia. Dicha imagen tal vez no sea la más adecuada en todas las situaciones, o no sea la que el resto creemos que es la adecuada. No sabemos qué piensa Kitty al respecto.

Mientras tiraba de él, Portia lo miró con el ceño fruncido.

—Simon se preguntaba si no sería una ingenua... Y yo empiezo a creer que tal vez tenga razón.

—Sin duda su madre ya la habría corregido, ¿no? ¿Acaso no es ésa la labor de las madres?

Portia pensó en su madre y luego en la señora Archer.

—Sí, pero... ¿Cree que la señora Archer...? —Dejó la pregunta a medias, sin saber muy bien cómo expresar con palabras lo que opinaba de la madre de Kitty.

Charlie resopló.

—Tal vez tenga razón. Estamos acostumbrados a hacer las cosas a nuestra manera..., a interactuar con personas muy parecidas a nosotros y nuestro comportamiento. Esperamos que sepan lo que es adecuado y lo que no. Tal vez vayan por ahí los tiros... —Miró a su alrededor—. Y ahora, señorita, ¿adónde me lleva?

Portia clavó la vista al frente y se puso de puntillas para ver por encima de los invitados.

—Por allí delante hay una dama que conoce a su madre... Estaba impaciente por hablar con usted.

—¿¡Qué!? —Charlie la miró con los ojos como platos—. ¡Por todos los infiernos! No quiero pasar el rato adulando a una vieja arpía...

—Pero sí que quiere... —Una vez localizado su objetivo, le dio un tirón del brazo—. Piense de este modo: si habla con ella ahora, en medio de este tumulto, no le costará nada intercambiar los saludos de rigor y luego alejarse. Eso contentará a la buena mujer. Pero si retrasa el inevitable momento y ella lo acorrala más tarde, cuando ya no haya tanta gente, tal vez lo retenga durante al menos media hora. —Lo miró a la cara con las cejas enarcadas—. ¿Qué prefiere?

Charlie la miró con los ojos entrecerrados.

—Simon tenía razón: es peligrosa.

Portia esbozó una sonrisa mientras le daba unas palmaditas en el brazo, y lo arrastró hacia su destino.

Una vez realizada la buena obra del día, retomó su obsesión: localizar un lugar e identificar el momento en el que pudiera, con una buena excusa o de modo que no llamara demasiado la atención, tener a Simon durante un par de horas para ella sola. Mejor, durante unas tres. No tenía ni idea de cuánto tiempo le llevaría la siguiente parada en su camino.

Tras librarse gracias a una sonrisa distante de un grupo de soldados ataviados con sus resplandecientes uniformes, meditó esa cuestión. A su edad, las normas sociales no consideraban que veinte minutos a solas con un caballero fuera un escándalo, pero más de media hora sería su ruina. Al parecer, esa media hora era más que suficiente. Sin embargo y a juzgar por los rumores, Simon era todo un experto, y a los expertos no les gustaba que los apresuraran.

La opción de las tres horas era sin duda la mejor.

Escudriñó la multitud. Hasta que no se le ocurriera un plan, no tenía sentido que buscara a Simon, no tenía sentido que pasara mucho tiempo a su lado. No estaban, precisamente, inmersos en un cortejo...

Charló con un mayor y después con un matrimonio residente en Blandford Forum. Tras despedirse de ellos, rodeó a los invitados manteniéndose pegada al altísimo seto. Estaba a punto de mezclarse de nuevo con la multitud cuando, de repente, vio a Desmond y a Winifred a su izquierda.

Estaban junto a un recoveco en el seto que albergaba una estatua sobre su pedestal. Sin embargo, ninguno de los dos le prestaba atención a la estatua; ni tampoco a los invitados. Desmond sostenía la mano de Winifred y la miraba a la cara mientras le hablaba apasionadamente en voz baja.

Winifred tenía los párpados entornados y miraba hacia el suelo, con una dulce sonrisa que le curvaba los labios.

De pronto, Kitty apareció junto a ellos. Como un torbellino que hubiera salido de entre la multitud, se colgó del brazo de Desmond. La mirada con la que obsequió a su hermana cuando ésta levantó la cara fue triunfal. Acto seguido, desvió los ojos hacia Desmond.

Incluso a varios metros de distancia, percibió cuán deslumbrante era la sonrisa que le dedicó Kitty al hombre. Y cómo comenzó a engatusarlo, con la seguridad de poder apartarlo de su hermana.

No obstante, se había equivocado. Eso quedó patente por la seca y cortante respuesta que Desmond, con expresión pétrea, le espetó.

Tan sorprendida como Kitty, Winifred lo miró con nuevos ojos, o eso sospechaba Portia.

Por un instante, el rostro de Kitty fue la viva imagen de la sorpresa; pero, pasados unos momentos, soltó una carcajada y retomó las zalamerías.

Desmond se interpuso entre las hermanas, obligando a Kitty a retroceder. Tras volver a colocarse la mano de Winifred en el brazo, dijo algo... descortésmente breve. Y, con un seco gesto de cabeza hacia Kitty, se alejó del lugar con una estupefacta Winifred del brazo.

Portia los perdió de vista cuando se internaron en la multitud; después, se concentró de nuevo en Kitty. En la anonadada y algo perdida expresión que le cruzó el rostro. Sin embargo, en un abrir y cerrar de ojos, la sonrisa regresó a sus labios. Y, con una carcajada, ella también se perdió entre los invitados.

Muerta de curiosidad, Portia se dispuso a seguirla, pero la interceptó un amigo de lord Netherfield. Tardó al menos veinte minutos en atisbar a Kitty.

Ataviada con su brillante vestido amarillo, resaltaba como una margarita en un prado de amapolas: estaba rodeada de casacas rojas con sus borlas doradas. Su vivaracho encanto y su chispeante risa estaban en plena efervescencia; sin embargo, para ella, que se encontraba a unos cuantos metros con un grupo de damas ya mayores, semejante actuación le pareció algo forzada.

Se hacía evidente por momentos que era Kitty quien daba alas a los oficiales. Éstos, a su vez y tal como era de esperar en ellos, devolvieron el coqueteo de un modo alegre y bastante ruidoso.

Portia se percató de las miradas de las que Kitty era objeto y de la silenciosa comunicación entre las damas de la localidad.

Lady Glossup y la señora Buckstead, que se encontraban varios metros más allá, también se percataron. Se disculparon con la pareja con la que estaban charlando y, cogidas del brazo, se lanzaron en línea recta hacia Kitty.

A Portia no le hizo falta mirar para conocer el resultado. Pocos instantes después, Kitty se alejaba de los oficiales entre su suegra y la amiga de ésta.

Algo más relajada después de ver cómo habían evitado el inminente desastre, Portia se concentró en la menuda y dulce anciana que tenía a su lado.

—Tengo entendido que se aloja en la casa, querida. —Los ojos de la anciana la miraban con cierto brillo—. ¿Es la dama que le ha robado el corazón a James?

Ocultó su sorpresa tras una sonrisa y corrigió la errónea impresión a la anciana. Pasados unos minutos, continuó con su paseo. La multitud estaba ya dando buena cuenta de unos delicados emparedados y pastelitos que un batallón de sirvientes hacía circular. Cogió una copa de licor de la bandeja que sostenía uno de los criados y se alejó dando pequeños sorbos.

¿Se le presentaría la oportunidad de escabullirse con Simon?

Decidida a comprobar hasta qué punto se habían dispersado los invitados, se encaminó al extremo más alejado de los jardines. Si algunos habían decidido pasear hasta el templete...

Cuando llegó al borde del gentío, miró hacia el sendero. Alguien lo bloqueaba. James.

Kitty estaba delante de él.

Se detuvo, renuente a dejar la multitud.

Le bastó una mirada al rostro de James para percatarse de su estado. Tenía la mandíbula apretada, al igual que los puños, pero no cesaba de mirar con disimulo al resto de los invitados. Estaba furioso con Kitty, pero se estaba mordiendo la lengua, ya que era demasiado educado como para provocar un escándalo, al menos delante de medio condado.

De pronto, se preguntó si Kitty no sería consciente de que ésa era la única razón por la que James no rechazaba abiertamente sus avances; de que su renuencia a mandarla a paseo no era un indicio de su predisposición hacia ella.

Fuera como fuese, James necesitaba que lo rescatasen. De modo que se irguió y...

Lucy apareció desde el otro lado. Con una dulce sonrisa, se acercó hasta la pareja y saludó primero a Kitty y luego a James.

La respuesta de Kitty fue educada pero a todas luces cortante. Y un tanto desdeñosa. Tras ella, se concentró de nuevo en James.

Un ligero rubor cubrió las mejillas de Lucy, pero la muchacha levantó la barbilla, irguió los hombros y aprovechó la primera pausa en la conversación para preguntarle algo a James.

Con una impaciencia que ninguna anfitriona que se preciara demostraría, Kitty se giró para decir algo y...

James inspiró hondo, le sonrió a Lucy y accedió a enseñarle lo que fuese. Le ofreció su brazo.

Portia sonrió.

Lucy aceptó con una sonrisa deslumbrante.

Y Kitty compuso una expresión de total... estupefacción. De total incredulidad.

De una decepción casi infantil.

La alegría de Portia se esfumó. Cambió de rumbo entre la multitud, ya que no deseaba que la incluyeran en ninguna conversación. El punto de vista de Kitty parecía erróneo, dadas sus percepciones, sus expectativas y sus aspiraciones.

Creía que se estaba alejando de ella, pero Kitty debía de haber dado media vuelta para alejarse a toda prisa. Y seguía caminando con presteza cuando estuvo a punto de darse de bruces con ella; por suerte, la vio justo a tiempo y cambió la dirección de sus pasos.

Un rubor excesivo cubría su rostro; sus ojos azules echaban chispas. Un rictus desabrido desfiguraba sus carnosos labios y caminaba con un ímpetu poco apropiado para una dama.

Portia apartó la vista de ella y observó que Henry se alejaba de un grupo de caballeros para interceptarla. Con la misma sensación de alguien que estuviera a punto de presenciar un accidente pero que fuese incapaz de evitarlo, dio unos pasos hacia ellos.

A unos metros de distancia, Kitty se dio prácticamente de bruces con su marido. Había varias personas cerca, pero estaban enzarzados en sus conversaciones. Henry la cogió del brazo con firmeza, pero sin el menor asomo de ira, como si quisiera tranquilizarla y, a la vez, instarla a recordar dónde se encontraban.

Con el rostro crispado, Kitty levantó la vista hacia él. Sus ojos echaban chispas mientras le hablaba. Aunque no podía oír las palabras, Portia supo que eran crueles, cortantes e hirientes a propósito. Henry se tensó y, muy despacio, soltó a su esposa. Acto seguido, le hizo una reverencia y le dijo algo en voz baja mientras se enderezaba. Kitty guardó silencio un instante. Henry inclinó la cabeza y se alejó con la espalda muy rígida.

El rostro de Kitty quedó demudado por la furia, igual que una niña que no se hubiera salido con la suya; después, como si se colocara una máscara, cambió de expresión. Inspiró hondo y se giró para enfrentarse a sus invitados antes de esbozar una sonrisa e internarse en la multitud.

—Un espectáculo nada edificante.

El comentario provino de su espalda.

Miró por encima de su hombro.

—Vaya, aquí estás.

Simon contempló su rostro, en especial la expresión de sus ojos.

—Así es. ¿Adónde ibas?

Debía de haberla visto antes mientras iba de un lado a

otro; era una de las desventajas de ser más alta que la media. De modo que sonrió, se dio la vuelta y se colgó de su brazo.

—No iba a ninguna parte, pero ahora que estás aquí, me gustaría dar un paseo por los jardines. Llevo más de dos horas hablando.

Otros invitados habían tenido la misma idea y ya enfilaban los innumerables senderos. Sin embargo, en lugar de dirigirse hacia el lago como la mayoría, ellos se encaminaron hacia los tejos y los jardines que había detrás.

Habían llegado al prado que se extendía tras la primera hilera de árboles cuando Simon volvió a hablar.

—Una guinea por tus pensamientos.

La había estado observando, había estado estudiando su rostro. Lo miró de reojo.

—¿Crees que son tan valiosos?

Se detuvieron; la mirada de Simon siguió clavada en sus ojos, pero el mechón que se le había soltado del recogido y le caía junto a la oreja lo distrajo. Alzó la mano para colocárselo tras la oreja y sus dedos le rozaron la mejilla.

Sus miradas volvieron a encontrarse.

La había tocado de forma mucho más íntima, pero esa caricia tan inocente transmitía algo muy profundo.

—Es el precio de mi deseo por conocerlos —respondió, sin apartar los ojos de ella.

Mientras intentaba interpretar su mirada, Portia sintió que algo se tambaleaba en su interior. Era una especie de admisión, una que jamás habría esperado. Una que no estaba segura de saber interpretar. Aun así... Dejó que sus labios esbozaran una sonrisa y ladeó la cabeza.

Tomados del brazo, reanudaron su lento paseo.

—Tenía la intención de perder de vista a Kitty y sus ardides... Pero no he hecho más que tropezarme con ella a cada paso. —Suspiró y clavó la vista al frente—. Ha traicionado a Henry, ¿verdad?

Percibió que Simon estaba a punto de encogerse de hombros, pero que recapacitaba en el último momento. Asintió con un gesto brusco de cabeza.

—Parece que sí.

Habría apostado su mejor bonete a que ambos estaban pensando en Arturo y en sus visitas nocturnas a la mansión.

Siguieron caminando y la mirada de Simon regresó a su rostro.

—No estabas pensando en eso.

El comentario le arrancó una sonrisa.

—No. —Había estado meditando acerca de los conceptos básicos del matrimonio..., la diferencia que debía de existir entre la teoría y la práctica en una relación. Hizo un gesto con la mano—. No concibo cómo... —Había estado a punto de decir que no concebía cómo Kitty y Henry eran capaces de continuar con su matrimonio, pero semejante confesión habría sido muy ingenua. Muchos matrimonios se mantenían juntos sin nada más que respeto entre los cónyuges. Inspiró hondo e intentó expresar lo que quería decir de verdad—. Kitty ha traicionado la confianza de Henry... Parece creer que la confianza no significa nada. Lo que no concibo es un matrimonio sin confianza. No entiendo cómo podría funcionar sin ella.

Era consciente de la ironía mientras pronunciaba las palabras; ninguno de los dos estaba casado. Además, ambos habían eludido el tema durante años.

Miró a Simon. Éste tenía la vista clavada en el suelo, pero su expresión era seria. Estaba reflexionando sobre lo que había dicho.

Pasado un momento, se percató de que lo miraba y levantó la vista; primero la miró a ella, pero después desvió los ojos al frente, hacia el prado.

—Creo que tienes razón. Sin confianza... No puede funcionar. No para nosotros. Quiero decir, para gente como nosotros. No con la clase de matrimonio que tú, o que yo, querríamos.

Si le hubieran dicho una semana antes que mantendría semejante conversación sobre el matrimonio con Simon Cynster, se habría desternillado de la risa. No obstante, en ese momento se le antojaba lo más natural del mundo.

Había deseado aprender lo que sucedía entre hombres y mujeres, en especial en el ámbito del matrimonio; el alcance de su estudio se había ampliado más allá de sus expectativas.

Confianza. Gran parte del matrimonio consistía en ella.

También se encontraba en el centro de lo que estaba naciendo entre Simon y ella. Sin embargo, fuera lo que fuese había crecido (era el efecto, al parecer, lógico) porque previamente existía un enorme grado de confianza entre ellos, una confianza que hasta entonces no se había puesto a prueba.

—Ella... Kitty, me refiero, jamás encontrará lo que busca. —Lo supo de repente y sin el menor asomo de duda—. Está buscando algo, pero quiere obtenerlo primero y después decidir si vale la pena o no..., si está dispuesta a pagar el precio. Pero, dada la naturaleza de lo que busca, su estrategia no funcionará porque está empezando la casa por el tejado.

Simon meditó el asunto; no sólo las palabras, sino las ideas que subyacían tras éstas. Percibió la mirada de Portia y asintió con la cabeza. Comprendía a la perfección lo que intentaba explicarle; no tanto el comportamiento de Kitty como lo que estaba diciendo. Porque era ella quien dominaba sus pensamientos, quien moraba en sus sueños.

Su opinión acerca del matrimonio era de vital importancia para él. Y estaba en lo cierto al afirmar que la confianza estaba por encima de todo. Lo demás, lo que quería de ella, lo que quería que ella quisiera de él, todas esas cosas que descubría poco a poco, eran como un árbol que crecería, robusto y fuerte, si estaba firmemente arraigado en la confianza.

La observó mientras caminaba, pensativa, a su lado. Tenía una confianza ciega en ella; confiaba más en ella que en cualquier otro ser humano. No se trataba sólo de la familiaridad, ni del hecho de saber que podía contar con ella, ni de la certeza con la que podía anticipar sus opiniones, sus reacciones y su comportamiento. Incluso sus sentimientos.

Era el hecho de saber que Portia jamás le haría daño premeditadamente.

Le había machacado el ego sin compasión, lo había desafiado e irritado, habían discutido, pero jamás había querido causarle mal alguno... Eso se lo había demostrado con creces.

Respiró hondo y clavó la vista al frente, consciente por primera vez de cuán valiosa era esa confianza.

¿Confiaba Portia en él? Debía de hacerlo en cierta medida, pero aún no estaba seguro de hasta dónde.

Una suposición discutible. Si la convencía... No, se corrigió. Cuando la convenciera de que confiara ciegamente en él, porque iba a convencerla, ¿soportaría esa confianza el descubrimiento de que no había sido del todo sincero con ella?

¿Comprendería el motivo? ¿Lo comprendería lo bastante como para ser magnánima?

Portia era como un libro abierto; siempre había sido, y siempre sería, demasiado directa, demasiado segura de sí misma, de su posición, de su capacidad y de su indomable voluntad como para andarse con subterfugios. No estaba en su naturaleza.

Sabía a la perfección lo que ella buscaba, lo que pretendía conseguir con su relación. Lo que no sabía era cómo reaccionaría cuando comprendiera que, además de proporcionarle todo lo que había estado buscando, estaba decidido a darle muchísimo más.

¿Creería que intentaba atraparla, cargarla con responsabilidades, someterla y coartar su libertad? ¿Reaccionaría en consecuencia?

A pesar de todo lo que sabía de ella... No, volvió a corregirse, precisamente por lo que sabía de ella, su reacción era impredecible.

Llegaron a un largo sendero, al abrigo de unas glicinias, que llevaba de vuelta a la casa. Dieron media vuelta al llegar bajo el emparrado y continuaron el paseo en un agradable silencio. Hasta que Portia aminoró el paso.

—Ay, Dios mío.

Siguió su mirada hasta el prado adyacente. Kitty estaba plantada en el centro de un grupo de oficiales y caballeretes, con una copa en la mano y una sonrisa en los labios. Hablaba y gesticulaba con excesiva hilaridad. No alcanzaban a escuchar sus palabras, pero su tono era estridente, al igual que su risa.

Uno de los oficiales hizo un comentario y todos se rieron. Kitty comenzó a gesticular como una loca mientras replicaba. Dos caballeros evitaron que se cayera y las carcajadas se redoblaron.

Simon se detuvo. Portia también.

Por el rabillo del ojo captaron un destello lavanda y desviaron la vista en esa dirección. La señora Archer se acercaba a toda prisa.

Observaron la escena y vieron cómo, con bastante dificultad y un buen número de apocadas sonrisas, consiguió rescatar a su hija. Tomadas del brazo, devolvió a Kitty hacia el prado principal, donde se encontraba el grueso de los invitados.

Los oficiales y los restantes caballeros se dividieron en grupos y reanudaron su charla. Simon tiró de Portia.

Se cruzaron con varias parejas que paseaban en dirección contraria y se detuvieron a charlar con ellas. A la postre, cuando regresaron al prado principal y se internaron en la considerable multitud de invitados, escucharon la voz de Kitty de inmediato.

—¡Ay, muchísimas gracias! ¡Es justo lo que necesitaba! —Hipó—. ¡Estoy muerta de sed!

A su derecha se encontraba el joven jardinero, ataviado con el uniforme de los camareros y con una bandeja de copas de champán en las manos. Con su uniforme prestado, que lo hacía parecer muy alto y desgarbado, su pelo negro y sus ojos oscuros, poseía un encanto de lo más llamativo.

Desde luego, Kitty era de esa opinión. Estaba delante de él, comiéndoselo con los ojos por encima del borde de la copa que no tardó en apurar.

Portia decidió que ya había visto y escuchado suficiente; tiró del brazo de Simon y éste la complació al continuar su paseo y mezclarse con los invitados.

Pasaron los siguientes veinte minutos en una agradable conversación, ya que primero se toparon con Charlie y después con las Hammond, que mostraron un desbordante entusiasmo por los jóvenes a los que habían conocido. Todos se relajaron con la charla y las bromas ya que el buen humor pareció contagiarlos, cuando un tumulto que tuvo lugar cerca de los escalones de la terraza los hizo mirar en esa dirección.

Como al resto de los presentes.

Y lo que vieron los dejó perplejos.

Al pie de las escaleras se encontraba Ambrose Calvin con Kitty colgada de su cuello mientras lo miraba con una expresión risueña y abiertamente sensual.

Nadie acertó a entender lo que decía. Estaba intentando susurrar, pero en realidad pronunciaba las palabras en voz alta y se le trababa la lengua.

Estaba totalmente apoyada contra Ambrose mientras éste forcejeaba por alejarla de él con ademanes rígidos y el rostro lívido.

Las conversaciones cesaron. Todos se limitaron a mirar.

Se hizo el silencio más absoluto. No se movía ni una mosca.

En ese momento, una risotada, contenida al punto, rompió el hechizo. Drusilla Calvin salió de entre los invitados y se colocó detrás de Kitty, mucho más baja que ella, para cogerla por los brazos y ayudar a su hermano a soltarse.

En cuanto Ambrose quedó libre, lady Hammond y la señora Buckstead se sumaron al trío. Kitty desapareció de la vista en el consecuente forcejeo. Alguien pidió agua fría y se impartieron órdenes a los criados; pronto quedó claro que estaban diciendo que Kitty se encontraba mal y que se había desmayado.

Portia miró a Simon a los ojos antes de darle la espalda al lamentable espectáculo y retomar la conversación con las Hammond justo donde la habían dejado. Las muchachas, aunque distraídas en un primer momento, eran demasiado educadas como para no seguir su ejemplo. Simon y Charlie hicieron lo propio.

Todo el mundo intentaba mantenerse al margen del grupo de la terraza, al que se habían sumado lord y lady Glossup, Henry, lady Osbaldestone y lord Netherfield. Lady Calvin también había acudido sin más dilación. Las cabezas se volvieron de nuevo hacia la terraza cuando reapareció Kitty, empapada de la cabeza a los pies, mientras lady Glossup y la señora Buckstead la obligaban a entrar en la mansión. La señora Archer las seguía, gesticulando inútilmente.

Al pie de las escaleras, los invitados que no habían entrado en la mansión intercambiaron una mirada antes de girarse sonrientes hacia la multitud y retomar las conversaciones con los distintos grupos.

Por supuesto, la incomodidad era palpable en el aire y también era innegable que todos se preguntaban el porqué del indecoroso comportamiento o más bien del escándalo en toda regla. Sin embargo...

Lady O apareció en escena con el rostro relajado y sin el menor asomo en su mirada ni en su comportamiento de que hubiera presenciado algo escandaloso.

Cecily Hammond, en un arranque de temeridad, preguntó:

—¿Está bien Kitty?

—Esa muchacha tonta se ha puesto enferma... Sin duda, a causa del esfuerzo para que todo saliera hoy bien. Y por la emoción, claro. Se ha mareado un poco... Y el calor no ha ayudado en nada. Seguro que se pondrá bien, sólo necesita echarse un ratito. Después de todo, es una joven casada. Debería tener más sentido común.

Lady O miró a Portia con una sonrisa deslumbrante antes de desviar la vista hacia Simon y Charlie.

Todos comprendieron al punto: ésa era la historia que tenían que difundir.

Tampoco hizo falta explicárselo a las Hammond. Cuando Portia sugirió que se separaran para mezclarse con el resto de los invitados, tanto Cecily como Annabelle estaban más que dispuestas a correr la voz. Charlie se fue por un lado y Simon y ella por otro. Tras intercambiar una mirada, se dispusieron a hacer cuanto pudieran para controlar los daños.

Los otros invitados de la familia estaban haciendo lo mismo. Lady Glossup asumió el papel de anfitriona y dispuso que los criados se mezclaran con los invitados llevando helados, sorbetes y pastas.

Gracias a los esfuerzos conjuntos, fue todo un éxito. El resto de la tarde, más o menos una hora, pasó con bastante tranquilidad. Por supuesto, todo era pura apariencia, una máscara que todos llevaban para enfrentarse a los demás. Por debajo de esa máscara... los amigos intercambiaban miradas cómplices, aunque nadie se atrevía a poner en palabras sus pensamientos.

En cuanto lo permitieron las buenas maneras, los vecinos comenzaron a marcharse. Estaba bien entrada la tarde cuando los últimos invitados se perdían por el camino.

Lady O se acercó a ellos. Le dio unos golpecitos a Simon con el bastón.

—Tú, ayúdame a subir a mi habitación. —Clavó sus ojos negros en ella—. Tú también puedes venir.

Simon obedeció y, juntos, se encaminaron a la casa. Ella tomó a la anciana del brazo libre cuando llegaron a la escalinata. Lady O ya no era joven y, a pesar de sus modales ariscos, ambos le tenían un gran cariño.

Llegó a la habitación casi sin resuello. Señaló la cama y la ayudaron a acostarse. Acababan de dejarla en el colchón, bien sentada con la espalda apoyada contra los almohadones tal y como les había ordenado, cuando alguien llamó a la puerta.

—¡Adelante! —exclamó lady O.

La puerta se abrió y apareció el rostro de lord Netherfield, que se apresuró a entrar.

—Estupendo... Una confabulación. Justo lo que necesitamos.

Portia contuvo una sonrisa. Simon buscó su mirada

antes de colocar un sillón para el recién llegado junto a la cama. Lord Netherfield aceptó la ayuda de Simon para sentarse; al igual que lady O, caminaba con la ayuda de un bastón.

Eran primos, o eso le habían dicho, aunque bastante alejados; también eran de la misma edad y viejos amigos.

—¡En fin! —exclamó lady O en cuanto el anciano estuvo sentado—. ¿Cómo vamos a solucionar esta estupidez? Es un lío espantoso, pero no tiene sentido que todos los invitados lo suframos.

—¿Cómo se lo ha tomado Ambrose? —preguntó lord Netherfield—. ¿Crees que creará problemas?

Lady O resopló.

—Yo diría que estaría encantado de que no se removiera este asunto. Está espantado... Se quedó blanco como un fantasma. Fue incapaz de articular palabra. Jamás he visto que un futuro político se quede sin palabras.

—A mi parecer —intervino Simon, que estaba apoyado contra uno de los postes de la cama—, en este asunto deberíamos seguir el dicho. En boca cerrada no entran moscas.

Portia se sentó al borde del colchón mientras lord Netherfield asentía con la cabeza.

—Sí, sin duda tienes razón. Pobre Calvin, no es de extrañar que esté en semejante estado. Lo único que le hacía falta en este momento es provocar un escándalo con una mujer como Kitty... Está aquí para intentar conseguir el apoyo de su padre para su campaña y ella se le lanza al cuello.

La mirada de lady O los recorrió antes de asentir con la cabeza.

—En ese caso, todos estamos de acuerdo. No ha sucedido nada de relevancia y por tanto no hay nada que decir... Todo va bien. Sin duda alguna, si nosotros adoptamos esa postura, el resto nos imitará. No hay motivos para que la fiesta de Catherine acabe siendo un desastre por el hecho de que su nuera haya perdido la cabeza. Ahí está su madre para enderezarla.

Una vez tomada la decisión y emitido el veredicto, lady O se recostó en los almohadones. Despachó a los hombres con las manos.

—Vosotros dos podéis marcharos. Tú te quedas —le dijo a ella—. Quiero hablar contigo.

Simon y lord Netherfield se fueron. Cuando la puerta volvió a cerrarse, Portia se giró hacia la anciana, pero descubrió que tenía los ojos cerrados.

—¿De qué quería hablarme?

Lady O abrió un solo ojo que la miró echando chispas.

—Creo que ya te he advertido que no se debe pasar todo el tiempo colgada del brazo del mismo caballero, ¿no es así?

Portia se ruborizó.

La anciana resopló y cerró el ojo.

—La sala de música debería ser lo bastante segura. Ve a practicar las escalas.

Un imperioso gesto de la mano acompañó la orden. Portia meditó un instante antes de obedecer.

El plan de hacer que la fiesta campestre siguiera su curso normal como si tal cosa debería haber funcionado. De hecho, habría funcionado si Kitty se hubiera comportado como todos esperaban. Sin embargo, en lugar de estar mortificada y de comportarse con el mayor de los decoros, temerosa por la posibilidad de hacer una nueva transgresión, apareció en el salón y les ofreció una magistral actuación en el papel de «la ofendida».

No pronunció palabra alguna sobre el desastre acontecido por la tarde en el jardín; fue la expresión de su rostro, la altivez con la que sostenía la cabeza y la arrogancia con la que los miraba a todos lo que transmitió sus sentimientos. Su reacción.

Se acercó a Lucy y a la señora Buckstead y le colocó la mano en el brazo a la primera para preguntarle, solícita:

—¿Has conocido a algún caballero agradable esta tarde, querida?

Lucy compuso una expresión sorprendida y balbuceó una vaga respuesta. La señora Buckstead, mucho más acostumbrada a esas lides, le preguntó por su salud.

Kitty hizo un gesto con la mano, restándole importancia al asunto.

—Por supuesto que me sentí un poco mal. Sin embargo, creo que nadie debería dejar que semejante comportamiento por parte de los demás lo humille, ¿no le parece?

Ni siquiera la señora Buckstead supo cómo responder a eso. Con una sonrisa y una mirada deslumbrante, Kitty se alejó de ellas.

Su comportamiento arrogante y altanero molestó a todos los presentes, los descolocó y los dejó sin saber qué estaba pasando. ¿Qué habían presenciado? Desde el punto de vista social, no tenía ningún sentido.

La cena estuvo lejos de ser un evento agradable que apaciguara las aguas como todos habían esperado, se convirtió en un momento de suprema incomodidad, sin risas y sin conversación: nadie sabía qué decir.

Cuando las damas se trasladaron al salón, Cecily, Annabelle y Lucy, a instancias de sus respectivas madres, se retiraron, aduciendo que estaban cansadas tras la larga jornada. A Portia también le habría gustado hacerlo, pero se sentía obligada a quedarse junto a lady O.

La conversación fue bastante tensa. Kitty siguió haciéndose la mártir; lady Glossup no sabía cómo tratarla y la señora Archer, a quien sólo le faltaba retorcerse las manos sobre el regazo, no servía de ninguna ayuda y se sobresaltaba cada vez que alguien se dirigía a ella.

No tardó en quedar patente que, lejos de acudir en su ayuda, los caballeros habían decidido dejarlas a merced de la suerte. Y a la de Kitty.

Aunque no se les podía culpar; si las damas, incluida lady O, que miraba a Kitty con el ceño fruncido, no eran capaces de dilucidar qué estaba pasando, los hombres debían de estar completamente confundidos.

Una vez que aceptó lo inevitable con elegancia, lady

Glossup ordenó que llevaran la bandeja del té. Se quedaron el tiempo justo para tomarse una taza, tras lo cual se pusieron en pie y se retiraron todos a sus respectivas habitaciones.

Tras ayudar a lady O a meterse en la cama, Portia fue a su propio dormitorio, que estaba situado en el extremo más alejado del ala este. Comenzó a pasearse frente a la ventana, que daba a los jardines, con la mirada clavada en el suelo y sin prestarle atención al paisaje bañado por la plateada luz de la luna.

Le había comentado a Simon que creía que Kitty no comprendía ni valoraba la confianza; había hablado de confianza entre dos personas, pero la escena que acababan de presenciar servía para confirmar su opinión, aunque trasladada a otros ámbitos.

Todos sentían que Kitty había roto la confianza social, como si los hubiera traicionado al negarse a seguir los patrones de conducta que todos conocían. Los patrones de comportamiento social, de educación..., la estructura subyacente que daba cuerpo a sus relaciones.

Su reacción había sido bastante extrema; y la negativa de los caballeros a regresar al salón había sido toda una declaración de principios.

Una declaración emocional. Desde luego, todos habían reaccionado de una manera emocional, instintiva; muy profundamente perturbados por la forma en la que Kitty había transgredido el código social por el que se regían.

Se detuvo y clavó la mirada en la penumbra del jardín sin ver nada.

La confianza y la emoción estaban relacionadas íntimamente. La primera conducía a la segunda. Si una resultaba perturbada, la otra actuaba en consecuencia.

Con el ceño fruncido, se sentó en el alféizar acolchado de la ventana, apoyó los codos en los muslos y descansó la barbilla en las manos.

Kitty quería amor. En su fuero interno, sabía que así era. Buscaba lo que tantas otras mujeres buscaban; sin embargo, dadas sus utópicas expectativas, debía de pensar que el amor era una emoción poderosa y muy pasional que aparecía de la nada para arrastrarla bien lejos.

A menos que estuviera equivocada, Kitty albergaba la idea de que lo primero era la pasión; de que una intensa relación física era el medio para conseguir una relación emocional más profunda y estable. Debía de suponer que si la pasión no era lo bastante intensa, el amor que derivaría de dicha pasión tampoco sería lo bastante poderoso... Lo bastante poderoso como para mantener su interés y satisfacer sus anhelos.

Eso explicaría por qué no valoraba la tierna adoración de Henry, por qué estaba tan decidida a provocar semejante lujuria, totalmente ilícita, en otros hombres.

Portia hizo un mohín.

Kitty estaba equivocada.

Ojalá pudiera explicárselo...

Pero era imposible, por supuesto. Kitty jamás aceptaría un consejo de una marisabidilla solterona y virgen acerca del amor y de cómo retenerlo.

Una suave brisa entró por la ventana y refrescó el caldeado interior. El silencio reinaba más allá de las ventanas y la oscuridad no era impenetrable. Los jardines serían mucho más frescos que el interior de la casa.

Se levantó, se sacudió las faldas y echó a andar hacia la puerta. Aún no podía dormir; el ambiente de la casa era opresivo, intranquilo, desasosegado. Un paseo por los jardines la calmaría, le serviría para ordenar las ideas.

Las puertas del saloncito matinal que daban a la terraza seguían abiertas. Salió por allí al agradable frescor de la noche. El perfume de las plantas estivales la envolvió cuando puso rumbo al lago; las damas de noche, los jazmines y otras flores de aroma más intenso le obnubilaron los sentidos.

Mientras se movía entre las sombras, vislumbró la silueta de un hombre en el prado, de uno de los caballeros. Estaba cerca de la mansión. Tenía la vista clavada en la oscuridad, al parecer ensimismado. El camino del lago la acercó más a él; reconoció a Ambrose, pero éste no pareció percatarse de su presencia.

Como no estaba de humor para mantener una conversación civilizada y estaba convencida de que Ambrose tampoco, se mantuvo entre las sombras y lo dejó con sus pensamientos.

Un poco más adelante, cuando cruzaba una de las intersecciones, miró a la derecha y vio al jardinero gitano. Dennis, así lo había llamado lady Glossup. Estaba totalmente inmóvil al amparo de las sombras, en uno de los senderos secundarios.

Prosiguió su camino sin detenerse, segura de que Dennis no se había dado cuenta de que ella estaba allí. Al igual que en la anterior ocasión, estaba muy pendiente del ala privada de la casa. Era probable que la presencia de Ambrose lo hubiera llevado a retroceder hasta ese punto de los jardines.

Se negó a meditar al respecto y se desentendió del asunto, ya que le dejaría un desagradable sabor de boca. No quería reflexionar sobre el significado de la vigilia nocturna de Dennis.

La idea le recordó de nuevo a Kitty... La expulsó de sus pensamientos. ¿En qué había estado pensando antes de eso?

En la confianza, en las emociones y en la pasión.

Y en el amor.

En el objetivo de Kitty y en los escalones que estaba convencida de que había debido ascender. Sin embargo, y a su parecer, había tomado la dirección contraria.

Pero ¿cuál era la adecuada?

Dejó que sus pies atravesaran el prado que se extendía hasta la orilla del lago mientras meditaba el asunto. La confianza y la emoción estaban vinculadas, cierto, pero dada la naturaleza de las personas, la confianza era lo primero que se forjaba.

Una vez que la confianza estaba afianzada, la emoción crecía... siempre que uno se sintiera lo bastante seguro como para dejar que dichos lazos emocionales se establecieran, con la consecuente vulnerabilidad que éstos creaban.

En cuanto a la pasión, a la intimidad física, era sin lugar a dudas una expresión de esa emoción; la expresión física del vínculo emocional. ¿Cómo podía ser de otro modo?

Ensimismada, enfiló el camino que llevaba al mirador.

Su mente la condujo inexorablemente un poco más allá, siempre según los dictados de la lógica. Y ella siguió caminando entre las sombras con la vista clavada en el suelo y el ceño fruncido. Según su razonamiento, al que no le encontraba fallo alguno, la compulsión que conducía a la intimidad física nacía de un vínculo emocional que, según el razonamiento lógico, debía de existir previamente.

Había llegado a los escalones del mirador. Alzó la vista... y en la penumbra del interior vio cómo una alta figura descruzaba sus largas piernas y se ponía de pie muy despacio.

«Para sentir la compulsión que conduce a la intimidad física, el vínculo emocional ya debe existir», pensó.

Se quedó largo rato mirando el interior del mirador. Mirando a Simon, que se mantenía a la espera y en silencio al amparo de la oscuridad. Después, se recogió las faldas, subió los escalones y entró en el mirador.

8

El quid de la cuestión, por supuesto, era la naturaleza de esa creciente emoción que había nacido entre Simon y ella. ¿Era lujuria, deseo o algo más profundo?

Fuera lo que fuese, la sentía crecer como la marea a medida que atravesaba la distancia que los separaba para acabar rodeada por sus brazos.

Unos brazos que la estrecharon con fuerza mientras alzaba el rostro para que sus labios se encontraran.

El beso puso de manifiesto la intensidad de esa emoción, aunque ambos la mantuvieron a raya.

Se apartó para mirarlo a la cara.

—¿Cómo sabías que vendría aquí?

—No lo sabía. —Esbozó una sonrisa, tal vez un poco irónica; en las sombras no podía estar segura—. James y Charlie se han escabullido a la taberna de Ashmore. Yo no estaba de humor para beber cerveza y jugar a los dardos; les dije que no y vine aquí.

La acercó un poco más, hasta que sus muslos se rozaron. Ella no se resistió, pero se mantuvo un tanto distante, observando, analizando...

Inclinó la cabeza y se apoderó de sus labios. Jugueteó con ellos hasta que la sintió abandonar el distanciamiento y responder al beso, provocadora. De todos modos, no tardó en rendirse cuando él decidió entregarse de lleno y le arrojó los brazos al cuello mientras la devoraba.

Y de nuevo se encontraron en el ojo del huracán. El deseo y la pasión más abrasadora amenazaron con consumirlos. Sus llamas les lamían la piel y avivaban ese anhelo que nacía de lo más recóndito de sus almas.

Interrumpieron el beso lo justo para calibrar las intenciones del otro. Sus miradas se encontraron brevemente, aunque ambos tenían los párpados entornados. Si bien ninguno podía ver bien en la oscuridad, esa mirada les bastó. A Simon le bastó para reafirmarse, para estrecharla aún más, para encerrarla entre sus brazos antes de inclinar la cabeza y buscar sus labios de nuevo.

Se lanzaron juntos a la hoguera. De buena gana. No necesitó convencerla de que lo siguiera. Tomados de la mano, cruzaron el umbral. Y recibieron el asalto de las llamas con los brazos abiertos; unas llamas que se avivaban por momentos.

Hasta que la pasión los abrasó y el deseo los consumió.

Comenzó a retroceder muy despacio, arrastrando a Portia consigo. Cuando rozó el borde del sofá con las piernas, se sentó y tiró de ella para sentarla en su regazo. Sus labios se separaron apenas un instante antes de volver a encontrarse.

Sintió la mano de Portia en la mejilla, acariciándolo con delicadeza mientras se entregaba sin paliativos. Donde otras se mostrarían reticentes, ella se mostraba audaz y directa. Decidida.

Segura. Dejó escapar un suspiro satisfecho cuando le quitó el vestido de los hombros y desnudó sus pechos. Incluso lo instó a continuar cuando inclinó la cabeza y acercó las manos y la boca a esos turgentes montículos para darse un festín.

Su piel era increíblemente sedosa, tan blanca que casi relucía, tan delicada que le provocaba un hormigueo en las puntas de los dedos mientras la rozaba. Sus enhiestos pezones eran toda una tentación. Se llevó uno a la boca y succionó con fuerza hasta que le arrancó un grito y sintió cómo le clavaba los dedos en la nuca.

Cuando apartó la cabeza, Portia respiraba de forma

entrecortada. La besó en los labios, acariciándolos con delicadeza. Sus miradas se encontraron un instante mientras sus alientos se mezclaban y la pasión los envolvía.

—Más. —El susurro fue como el roce de una llama en sus labios, en su mente.

El deseo había hecho mella en su cuerpo, que ya estaba duro y tenso por el esfuerzo que le suponía luchar contra la abrumadora necesidad de tomarla. De reclamarla.

Pero aún no.

Ni siquiera se molestó en preguntarle si estaba segura. Capturó sus labios y la estrechó contra su cuerpo al tiempo que se reclinaba en el sofá y la arrastraba con él. Portia quedó sentada de lado en su regazo, con las rodillas sobre uno de sus muslos. Él se tendió en el sofá sin interrumpir el beso mientras le acariciaba la espalda con una mano, que fue descendiendo hasta trazar la curva de una cadera y sus largas piernas.

La sumergió paso a paso en los misterios de la pasión. La sumergió paso a paso en ese reino donde sólo existían el deseo y los anhelos más básicos. Un reino donde la necesidad de ser acariciado crecía libremente hasta convertirse en una compulsión, y donde la compulsión de entregarse a la unión más íntima crecía hasta llegar a ser una necesidad imperiosa.

Cuando le alzó las faldas e introdujo una mano bajo ellas, Portia no protestó; al contrario, murmuró algo en señal de aprobación. Tuvo que luchar contra el impulso de nublarle el sentido, de aturdirla hasta haberla hechizado por completo; con ella, el libreto era otro. Era un libreto diseñado para conquistar algo más que su cuerpo. También quería su mente y su alma.

Así que siguió besándola con delicadeza, lo justo para que estuviera muy pendiente no sólo de lo que hacían sus labios, sino también de cada caricia, de cada roce, de cada libertad que se tomaban sus manos. Y para que fuera consciente de que él también estaba pendiente de ellos.

Llevaba medias de seda. Trazó el contorno de una pantorrilla con la yema de los dedos y fue ascendiendo hasta detenerse en la parte posterior de la rodilla. Desde allí, fue subiendo poco a poco hasta que encontró el borde de una liga, el cual se dispuso a rodear.

Sintió el repentino estremecimiento que la recorrió cuando siguió ascendiendo y le tocó la piel desnuda. Al igual que la de sus pechos, era sedosa, delicada y estaba enfebrecida por el deseo. La acarició con ternura y supo que Portia estaba siguiendo cada uno de los movimientos de sus dedos. Supo que toda su atención estaba puesta allí donde sus dedos le rozaban la piel.

Se topó con el bajo de la camisola. Introdujo los dedos bajo la seda y de allí se movió hasta tocar una cadera desnuda y trazar la ardiente curva de su trasero.

Portia volvió a estremecerse y, aunque siguió besándolo, supo que estaba un tanto asustada. De modo que se dispuso a tranquilizarla con los labios, con la lengua y con las lentas y posesivas caricias de su mano, y no reanudó su atrevida exploración hasta notar que ella se relajaba. A pesar de todo y aunque no hizo ademán de apartarse, sintió que un escalofrío le erizaba la piel mientras lo dejaba explorar a placer, mientras la excitación se apoderaba de ellos a medida que daban el siguiente paso.

Cuando estuvieron saciados de caricias, su mano se trasladó al frente moviéndose por encima de la cadera; extendió los dedos sobre su vientre desnudo. Un nuevo estremecimiento la sacudió al tiempo que se tensaba.

Así que se vio obligado a murmurar sobre esos labios hinchados:

—¿Estás segura?

Ella tomó una bocanada de aire y el movimiento hizo que sus pechos le rozaran el torso.

—Tócame... tócame ahí.

No necesitó más indicaciones, ni tampoco instrucciones más precisas. Se apoderó de sus labios y de su boca, y esperó hasta que la sintió entregarse de nuevo al beso antes de bajar la mano por la suave curva de su vientre y alcanzar los delicados rizos de su entrepierna.

Comenzó a acariciarla con deliberada lentitud, enterrando los dedos en los rizos hasta tocar la parte más suave de su cuerpo, que procedió a explorar. Y Portia siguió con él, compartiendo la sensualidad del momento y cada una de sus indagadoras caricias. Jamás había sido tan consciente de las reacciones de una mujer.

Saber que así se comportaría cuando estuviera desnuda bajo él, piel contra piel, le tensó aún más la entrepierna. La deseaba hasta un punto rayano al dolor, y llevaba en ese estado desde que llegó hasta él y se dejó abrazar sin el menor asomo de duda. Era una tortura casi imposible de soportar.

No obstante, el momento era tan intenso que su poder lo controlaba y, por primera vez desde que comenzaran sus lecciones, ese poder jugó a su favor a la hora de mantener el imperioso deseo a raya. Aquello era demasiado importante. Portia era demasiado importante. Su conquista, por encima de todas las demás, era cuestión de vida o muerte para él.

El deseo palpitaba en las yemas de sus dedos, cuya sensibilidad se había agudizado de forma notable. Le separó un poco más los muslos e hizo lo mismo con su sexo. Y procedió a torturarla y a excitarla hasta que ella comenzó a moverse con abandono contra su mano, exigiendo más con su habitual determinación. Hasta que le enterró los dedos en el pelo, como si ésa fuera su tabla de salvación.

Sus caricias fueron descendiendo, separándola con delicadeza hasta que introdujo un dedo en su ardiente humedad. Una humedad que lo abrasó y lo consumió, tentándolo más allá de todo límite. Apenas podía respirar; ni siquiera podía pensar en otra cosa que no fuera el súbito asalto de la pasión, la acuciante necesidad de enterrarse en esa suave feminidad que torturaba con sus hábiles caricias.

Sin embargo, se contuvo y refrenó ese atávico deseo sin miramientos. Aunque no menguó; al contrario, se avivó y se solidificó, convirtiéndose en una dolorosa realidad que se asentó en lo más hondo de su alma.

Y eso bastó para que continuara, para que siguiera por

el camino que había trazado de antemano, ajeno al precio que tendría que pagar.

Atrapada en las garras de la pasión, entregada hasta un punto que jamás habría imaginado posible, Portia fue apenas consciente de ese breve hiato, de esa minúscula pausa en la que la atención de Simon se desvió justo antes de regresar a la carga. Antes de que su atención regresara a ese lugar que acariciaba y torturaba con una insistencia que no atinaba a comprender.

No obstante, su cuerpo parecía entenderlo, parecía reconocer la cadencia de esas caricias, por más que su mente no pudiera interpretarlas. De modo que se dejó guiar por él y también dejó que su mente lo siguiera, que aprendiera, viera y comprendiera.

Se limitó a sentir. Nunca había imaginado que se pudieran experimentar sensaciones físicas tan poderosas, tan absorbentes. Los labios de Simon no se apartaron de los suyos en ningún momento. Uno de sus brazos la sostenía. El sólido muro de su torso estaba muy cerca y la reconfortaba mientras se enfrentaba a ese torbellino de sensaciones que la atravesaba de pies a cabeza, sacudiendo su mente y hechizando sus sentidos.

El hecho de tener una de sus manos entre los muslos, de que le hubiera separado las piernas y la estuviera acariciando allí, en ese lugar que parecía estar empapado, hinchado y muy caliente, debería abrumarla, pero no lo hacía. Sintió el calor que abrasaba su cuerpo, la intensa pasión que se apoderó de ella cuando su dedo la penetró un poco más.

Contuvo la respiración al sentir algo que amenazó con consumirla. Una tensión desconocida hasta entonces se apoderó de ella y de sus músculos. Le devolvió los besos entre jadeos al tiempo que la sensación que había comenzado en su entrepierna se iba extendiendo por todo el cuerpo.

Sabía que Simon la estaba incitando de forma deliberada. Sabía que a eso exactamente era a lo que había accedido. Y eso era también lo que había necesitado aprender, lo que siempre quiso experimentar.

Se entregó al momento, abandonó todas las inhibiciones y dejó que la marea la arrastrara. Que se la llevara lejos.

Que se la llevara a un lugar conformado por las sensaciones. A un pináculo de placer devastador.

Sus sentidos se expandieron hasta que le inundaron la mente. Su cuerpo estalló en llamas. El dedo de Simon se hundió aún más en su interior y el placer le inundó las venas, se deslizó bajo su piel, aumentando la tensión y confundiendo sus sentidos...

Hasta que se hicieron añicos. Hasta que estallaron.

Un intenso deleite, casi insoportable, se adueñó de ella mientras su cuerpo se estremecía, sacudido por oleadas de placer.

La ola la atravesó y dejó a su paso una profunda satisfacción. La sensación de estar flotando en la gloria, en un mar de contento.

Los estremecimientos remitieron poco a poco. La sensación se desvaneció y sus sentidos recobraron la normalidad. Simon apartó la mano.

Para su sorpresa, se sintió vacía. Incompleta.

Insatisfecha.

Cuando recobró el sentido común, lo comprendió. Comprendió que ése era un acto en el que participaban dos y que Simon se había detenido en los preliminares.

Y que no tenía intención de continuar.

Lo supo sin necesidad de preguntarle. Su determinación quedaba patente en la rigidez de sus músculos, en la tensión que se había apoderado de su cuerpo.

En ese instante y como si fuera el telón que pusiera fin a la obra, le bajó las faldas y colocó la mano en la cadera.

Sabía que su autocontrol era una fuerza a tener en cuenta. Interrumpió el beso y bajó una mano hacia su erección, ese rígido bulto que sentía contra el muslo.

Lo rodeó por encima del pantalón y sintió que Simon daba un respingo. Sintió que siseaba y tomaba aire.

Se acercó a él y le susurró contra los labios:

—Me deseas.

De su garganta brotó un gruñido ronco, una especie de carcajada estrangulada.

—Creo que es evidente...

Y lo era, sin ningún género de dudas, habida cuenta de que la evidencia estaba abrasándole la mano. Aun así, la magnitud de ese deseo, la intensidad de su poder, la sorprendió..., la sobresaltó.

Y la tentó más allá de la razón.

Sin embargo, saberlo (tener en la mano la prueba física que demostraba la conclusión abstracta a la que acababa de llegar su mente) le provocó un estremecimiento y la obligó a mostrarse más cautelosa. La sensación de peligro elemental que irradiaba era innegable.

Simon tomó una entrecortada bocanada de aire. Con los ojos cerrados, colocó una mano sobre la suya y presionó. De modo que sus dedos se cerraron aún más en torno a su miembro.

Al instante y con renuencia, él apartó la mano, llevándose la suya al mismo tiempo. Soltó el aire poco a poco.

No podía verlo en la oscuridad, pero habría jurado que los ángulos de su rostro parecían un poco más afilados.

Sin apartar los labios de los suyos, le preguntó:

—¿Por qué?

No necesitó elucubrar más. Sin duda alguna, él sabía incluso mejor que ella que podría haberla hecho suya de haber querido.

Simon observó su rostro mientras alzaba una mano y recorría el contorno de sus labios con un dedo. En él estaba impregnada la fragancia de su propio cuerpo. La olió y la probó. Al instante, él se inclinó y la besó, lamiendo ese aroma de sus labios.

—¿Estás preparada para eso?

Su mente registró el significado de una pregunta que en realidad no era tal.

Se separó un poco de él para mirarlo a los ojos. Su expresión era sombría, misteriosa, insondable. Todavía sentía su deseo, la poderosa necesidad que lo embargaba. Le contestó con sinceridad.

—No. Pero...

Su beso la acalló. Titubeó un instante al comprender que no deseaba escuchar lo que había estado a punto de decir. Y no lo deseaba porque él ya sabía de antemano lo que era. Así que le devolvió el beso. Profundamente agradecida.

En ese momento percibió que la pasión comenzaba a desvanecerse. Dejó que lo hiciera. Que menguara hasta...

Que sus labios se apartaron, si bien no se alejaron demasiado. Sus miradas se entrelazaron. Alzó una mano y le acarició un pómulo. Eligió ese momento para expresar sus pensamientos en voz alta.

—La próxima vez.

Simon tomó aliento y su torso se expandió. La aferró por la cintura para apartarla.

—Como desees.

«Como desees.»

La frase que más trabajo le había costado decir en toda su vida, pero no le había quedado otro remedio.

Regresaron a la mansión cogidos de la mano. Una breve discusión acerca de si era necesario o no que la acompañara a su habitación (que, por cierto, ganó él) los había ayudado a retomar, más o menos, sus respectivas posiciones.

Aunque no eran las mismas que las que ocupaban una semana atrás. Ese cambio era, en definitiva, un avance; pero el deseo que lo embargaba desde entonces era demasiado poderoso. Nunca había experimentado ese anhelo por una mujer, y mucho menos por una en concreto. Jamás se había visto consumido por el deseo de ese modo. Nunca había tenido que disimular, que ocultar su instinto hasta ese punto.

Verse obligado a separarse de ella esa noche, permitirle que escapara de él, no era un libreto que aprobara su instinto de guerrero, sus inclinaciones naturales. Verse obligado a luchar contra ese instinto, verse obligado a mantener la cabeza fría cuando todo su cuerpo ardía de deseo, no agradaba a su temperamento en lo más mínimo.

Y ella lo sabía. Llevaba mirándolo de reojo desde que salieron del mirador. Su semblante, crispado y adusto, era un fiel reflejo de sus sentimientos. Y Portia lo conocía tanto que no le habría costado trabajo percatarse de ellos.

De todos modos, dudaba mucho de que los entendiera por más que se percatara de su presencia. Dudaba mucho de que, a pesar de toda esa charla acerca de aprender sobre el sexo, la confianza y el matrimonio, se hubiera percatado de la posición en la que se encontraban. Dudaba mucho de que entendiera las consecuencias derivadas del siguiente paso; el destino al que acabaría abocada si seguía jugando.

Un destino que se cumpliría. Razón por la cual debía prepararse para jugar una partida larga. Si quería conseguir su objetivo, asegurarse de que todos sus deseos se realizaran, necesitaba la confianza ciega e implícita de Portia.

Y el único modo de conseguirla era ganándosela.

Nada de atajos ni de trucos de ilusionista.

Nada de presiones. De ningún tipo.

Sentía deseos de gruñir.

«Como desees.»

Si Portia se detenía a analizar el trasfondo de sus palabras, estaría metido en un buen problema. El pasado que compartían no iba a ayudarla a enfrentarse al futuro con una sonrisa, sino que la llevaría a sopesarlo todo seria y detenidamente. Sus fuertes temperamentos no le serían de ayuda a la hora de tomar la decisión final y de dar el último paso. Su inteligencia, su terquedad y, lo que era mucho peor, su independencia se alzaban en contra de la panoplia que conformaba su personalidad (una personalidad que Portia conocía muy bien) y harían que convencerla para que se entregase a él se convirtiera en una ardua batalla.

Necesitaba toda la ventaja que pudiera conseguir.

Siguió reflexionando mientras caminaba rodeado por la templada oscuridad de la noche. Portia seguía su ritmo sin dificultad.

Al menos, podía consolarse con un detalle en concreto: jamás había sido dada a la cháchara. Hablaba cuando lo deseaba. Y con él jamás parecía sentir esa necesidad que embargaba a otras mujeres de rellenar los silencios. Entre ellos se sucedían largos y cómodos silencios, como si fueran un par de zapatos usados.

Esa familiaridad, sumada a su forma de pensar, podría jugar a su favor si se mostraba astuto. Portia era una mujer dada al razonamiento lógico en mayor medida que cualquier otra mujer que hubiera conocido. Por tanto, tenía la oportunidad de adelantarse a sus reacciones, de predecir sus movimientos y de llevarla en la dirección que él deseara, siempre y cuando utilizara la lógica para acicatearla.

Siempre y cuando ella no adivinara cuál era su verdadera intención.

Si lo hacía...

¿Qué malévolo hado había decretado que eligiera como esposa a la única mujer que jamás sería capaz de manipular?

Contuvo un suspiro y miró al frente. Justo cuando Portia se tensaba.

Le dio un apretón en la mano cuando atisbó al jardinero vigilando de nuevo el ala privada de la mansión. Portia le dio un tirón. Él asintió con la cabeza y siguieron caminando hasta internarse en las sombras del vestíbulo del jardín.

La oscuridad reinaba en la mansión. No había nadie levantado. Dejaron atrás la vela que siempre se quedaba encendida al pie de la escalinata y, en ese momento, se percató de su expresión ceñuda.

—¿Qué pasa?

Ella parpadeó antes de contestar:

—Dennis, el jardinero, ya estaba ahí cuando salí.

Simon torció el gesto y le indicó que subiera la escalinata. Cuando llegaron a la galería superior, murmuró:

—Esa fijación parece insana. Se lo comentaré a James.

Portia asintió con la cabeza y tuvo que morderse la lengua para no decirle que también había visto a Ambrose, aunque no estuviera allí a su regreso. No había motivos para que Simon se lo comentara también a James.

Cuando llegaron a la puerta de su habitación, tiró de su mano para que se detuviera. Señaló la puerta con la cabeza.

Simon la miró antes de entrelazar los dedos con los suyos y alzarlos para depositar un beso en sus nudillos.

—Que duermas bien.

Lo miró a los ojos, que la observaban con los párpados entornados, y se acercó a él. Se puso de puntillas y lo besó en los labios.

—Tú también.

Le soltó la mano antes de abrir la puerta y entrar, tras lo cual cerró con mucha suavidad.

Pasó un buen rato antes de que lo escuchara alejarse.

La faceta física y más que real del deseo que Simon sentía por ella la había dejado totalmente impresionada. Una impresión muchísimo más reveladora que cualquier otra cosa que hubiera descubierto hasta entonces.

Y también había supuesto una tentación. Una tentación muchísimo más irresistible que cualquier otra cosa, que la instaba a continuar, a descubrir lo que la aguardaba si seguía. A descubrir qué era en realidad esa emoción que los empujaba a consumar su relación en el plano físico. Una emoción que con cada mirada, con cada momento compartido, parecía hacerse más fuerte, más nítida.

Más real.

Y eso también era sorprendente.

Portia se detuvo al llegar a la terraza y miró a su alrededor. Después de desayunar con lady O, había dejado a la anciana para que se arreglara y había aprovechado el momento para disfrutarlo en soledad. Para pasear y meditar.

Después de todo lo acaecido la noche anterior en el mirador, meditar era una necesidad prioritaria en su lista personal de cosas pendientes.

El rocío aún mojaba la hierba, aunque no tardaría mucho en evaporarse. El sol ya comenzaba a calentar. Prometía ser otro día caluroso. Según lo previsto, esa mañana irían en carruaje a Cranborne Chase, tras lo cual almorzarían en una posada antes de regresar. Todos albergaban la esperanza de que un día lejos de la mansión disipara el ambiente opresivo y ayudara a enterrar los sucesos del día anterior.

Todavía no había explorado el jardín de los setos, así que bajó la escalera que partía de la terraza y se encaminó hacia el arco de entrada. Al igual que los restantes jardines de Glossup Hall, ése era muy extenso; si bien apenas se había adentrado cuando escuchó voces.

Aminoró el paso.

—¿No te intriga ni un poquito la cuestión de la paternidad de este hijo?

«¡¿Paternidad!?», pensó Portia. Una palabra que la detuvo en seco. Era Kitty quien había hablado.

—En realidad, no creo que me incumba especular a ese respecto. No me cabe duda de que lo revelarás cuando llegue el momento.

Winifred. Las dos hermanas estaban al otro lado del seto junto al que ella se encontraba. El sendero de césped por el que paseaba giraba un poco más adelante, presumiblemente para dar acceso a algún patio con una fuente o un estanque.

—¡Vaya! Creí que estarías interesada. Te incumbe muchísimo, no sé si me entiendes...

El tono de Kitty le recordó al de una niña rencorosa que guardara un secreto horrible y que estuviera tomándose todo el tiempo necesario para provocar el mayor sufrimiento posible. No cabía duda del hombre que quería que Winifred identificara como el padre de su hijo.

Se escuchó el frufrú de la seda antes de que Winifred volviera a hablar.

—Querida, hay ocasiones en las que te miro y me pregunto si mamá engañaría a papá con otro hombre. —El desprecio que destilaban esas palabras resultó mucho más poderoso por la serenidad de la voz que las pronunciaba. Lo que era peor, había algo más en ellas, más profundo que el desprecio, que las hacía mucho más desagradables—. Y, ahora, si me disculpas —prosiguió—, debo prepararme para el paseo en carruaje. Desmond quiere que lo acompañe en su tílburi.

Portia dio media vuelta y salió a toda prisa del jardín. Se internó en la rosaleda y fingió oler las flores más grandes mientras miraba de soslayo hacia el prado hasta que vio que Winifred lo atravesaba y entraba en la casa. Al ver que su hermana no la seguía, ella también echó a andar hacia la mansión.

Echó un vistazo por encima del hombro en dirección a los setos y atisbó a Dennis, que desbrozaba un parterre que había al pie de uno de los arbustos. Uno de los que rodeaba el patio donde había escuchado a las hermanas. El muchacho la miró. Su rostro denotaba unas profundas ojeras.

Cosa que no era de extrañar.

Subió los escalones y entró en la casa.

Le había prometido a lady O que iría a ayudarla. Cuando llegó a su habitación, la anciana ya estaba lista y la esperaba sentada en el sillón que había delante de la chimenea. Una mirada a su rostro le bastó para despedir a la doncella con un gesto. En cuanto la puerta se hubo cerrado, le dijo con voz imperiosa:

—¡Bien! Háblame de tus progresos.

Portia parpadeó.

—¿De mis progresos?

—Precisamente. Cuéntame qué es lo que has aprendido. —Hizo un gesto con su bastón—. Y, por el amor de Dios, ¡siéntate! Eres casi tan horrenda como los Cynster, que se empeñan en mirarme desde arriba.

Con el asomo de una sonrisa en los labios, se sentó y se devanó los sesos para decidir qué le contaba.

—¡Vamos! —exclamó lady O al tiempo que se inclinaba sobre su bastón y sus ojos negros la taladraban—. Cuéntamelo todo.

Portia enfrentó su mirada. No encontraba las palabras que explicaran la mitad de lo que había sucedido.

—He aprendido cosas que no son tan... obvias como había supuesto.

La anciana enarcó las cejas.

—Ajá. ¿Qué cosas?

—Todo tipo de cosas. —Hacía mucho tiempo que había aprendido a no dejarse amedrentar por la vieja bruja—. Pero eso no es lo importante. Hay algo más... Algo que acabo de descubrir y que creo que usted debería saber.

—¡Caray! —Lady O era lo bastante ladina como para identificar una táctica disuasoria al instante, pero tal y como había supuesto, pecaba de un exceso de curiosidad—. ¿Qué es?

—Estaba paseando por el jardín de los setos...

Hizo un relato tan preciso como pudo de la conversación que había escuchado. Cuando acabó la explicación, observó el semblante de lady O. Si bien no supo cómo se las ingenió, la anciana mostró su profundo desagrado aun cuando sus facciones permanecieron inmutables.

—¿Cree que Kitty está embarazada de verdad? ¿O que es un bulo para herir a Winifred?

Lady O resopló.

—¿Es tan estúpida y tan inmadura, como para llegar a hacerlo?

Portia no contestó. Se limitó a observar con detenimiento la expresión de la anciana, las posibilidades que sopesaban las profundidades de esos ojos negros.

—He estado repasando los sucesos de los últimos días... Desde que la fiesta comenzó, no ha bajado a desayunar ni una sola vez. Hasta ahora lo había pasado por alto, pero dado lo mucho que le gusta la compañía masculina y el hecho de que los caballeros se reúnen todas las mañanas en el comedor matinal, tal vez sea un indicio revelador, ¿no cree?

—¿Cómo era la voz de Kitty? —refunfuñó lady O.

—¿De Kitty? —Portia rememoró la conversación—. La segunda vez que habló parecía una niña malcriada. Pero ahora que me lo pregunta, la primera vez daba la impresión de estar al borde de la desesperación.

Lady O compuso una mueca.

—Eso no parece alentador. —Golpeó el suelo con el bastón y se puso en pie.

Portia la imitó y se acercó para tomarla del brazo.

—¿Qué opina de todo esto?

—Si tuviera que arriesgarme, diría que la muy tonta está encinta. De todas maneras y dejando a un lado el tema de la paternidad del bebé, tiene tan poco seso que es capaz de utilizarlo en sus tejemanejes. —Se detuvo mientras ella abría la puerta. Cuando volvió a tomarla del brazo, la miró a los ojos—. Recuerda lo que te digo, esa muchacha va a acabar muy mal.

Era imposible no estar de acuerdo con ella. Asintió brevemente con la cabeza y echó a andar hacia la escalinata con ella tomada de su brazo.

Cranborne Chase, con sus imponentes robles y hayas, supuso un respiro para los invitados, tanto para el calor como para la tensión que se había instaurado entre ellos.

—En otras circunstancias, estoy segura de que lady Calvin se marcharía de buena gana —dijo Portia, que caminaba del brazo de Simon por una alameda.

—No puede. Ambrose está aquí... podría decirse que por negocios. Está muy ocupado buscando el apoyo de lord Glossup y del señor Buckstead. Y también el del señor Archer.

—Y lady Calvin siempre hará aquello que beneficie a su hijo. A eso me refería.

Estaban bastante alejados del resto del grupo, que deambulaba bajo las frondosas copas de los árboles, disfrutando del fresco ambiente, de modo que podían hablar sin tapujos. Repartidos en unos cuantos carruajes, los invitados habían pasado la mañana recorriendo los serpenteantes caminos que atravesaban el antiguo bosque y después habían hecho un alto en una diminuta aldea que se jactaba de contar con una posada en la que servían una excelente comida. El establecimiento estaba situado en el otro extremo del sendero por el que paseaban, según el posadero, en dirección a una hondonada desde la que partían numerosos caminos. Un lugar ideal por el que pasear para bajar la comida.

Lord Netherfield y lady O habían declinado las delicias del bosque y se habían quedado en la posada. El resto estaba estirando las piernas antes de volver a subir a los carruajes y emprender el regreso.

Portia se detuvo, dio media vuelta y echó un vistazo a la cuesta que acababan de subir. Habían elegido el camino más abrupto. Uno que nadie más había tomado. Todos estaban a la vista, desperdigados por la hondonada que se extendía a sus pies.

Hizo un mohín cuando localizó a Kitty, que paseaba flanqueada por su madre y su suegra.

—No creo que sirva de nada.

Simon siguió su mirada hasta las tres mujeres.

—¿Secuestrarla?

—Aquí no puede hacer nada, pero estoy seguro que la cosa empeorará cuando regresemos a la mansión.

Simon refunfuñó algo, guardó silencio un instante y después le preguntó:

—¿Cuál es el problema?

Alzó la vista y lo descubrió mirándola a la cara. Había estado analizando su expresión mientras ella observaba a Kitty y estudiaba su semblante malhumorado, su evidente resentimiento. Había intentado imaginar cómo afrontaría ella misma la situación de encontrarse en su piel. Esbozó una escueta sonrisa, meneó la cabeza y apartó a Kitty de su mente.

—Nada, sólo se me había ido el santo al cielo.

Los ojos de Simon siguieron clavados en su rostro. Antes de que pudiera insistir, lo tomó del brazo.

—Vamos, sigamos hasta allí arriba.

Él la complació y siguieron ascendiendo. Una vez en la parte más alta, descubrieron que el camino continuaba hacia otra hondonada más pequeña y menos accesible, donde pastaba un grupo de ciervos.

Alguien gritó para avisarlos de que debían regresar. Cuando llegaron a la posada, se produjo un leve altercado hasta que se decidió quién ocupaba qué lugar para el trayecto de vuelta. Todo el mundo hizo oídos sordos a las exigencias de Kitty de ir en el tílburi de James. Lucy y Annabelle se apretujaron en el asiento a su lado, tras lo cual él azuzó a los caballos. Desmond partió tras ellos, acompañado por Winifred. Simon fue el siguiente, con ella al lado y con Charlie en el lugar del lacayo, y tras ellos partieron todos los demás en los carruajes más lentos y pesados.

Los tílburis llegaron a Glossup Hall mucho antes que los demás vehículos. Fueron directos a los establos. Los caballeros ayudaron a bajar a las damas. Winifred, bastante pálida, se disculpó y se marchó hacia la casa a toda prisa. Los caballeros se enzarzaron en una discusión sobre la carne de caballo. Portia se habría unido con gusto, pero Lucy y Annabelle la aguardaban para que tomara la iniciativa de lo que hacer a continuación.

Suspiró para sus adentros y se resignó a pasar el resto de la tarde en el interior de la casa. De modo que abrió la marcha hacia la mansión.

Estaban aguardando en el saloncito matinal cuando por fin llegaron los demás carruajes. Lucy y Annabelle, que estaban bordando con mucha diligencia, alzaron las cabezas y miraron en dirección al vestíbulo principal.

Portia distinguió las desabridas voces incluso antes de que entraran en la mansión. Reprimió la mueca de fastidio que estaba a punto de hacer y se puso en pie.

Las dos muchachas la miraron de reojo. En ese momento, escucharon la voz de Kitty, estridente y airada. Abrieron los ojos como platos.

—Quedaos aquí —les dijo—. No hace falta que vayáis. Les diré a vuestras madres dónde estáis.

Ambas se lo agradecieron con la mirada y, tras esbozar una sonrisa reconfortante, Portia echó a andar hacia la puerta. Una vez en el vestíbulo, se acercó directamente a la señora Buckstead y a lady Hammond para informarles del paradero de sus hijas y, sin prestar atención a nadie más, fue en busca de lady O. Ésta le dio las gracias con un brusco movimiento de cabeza y la tomó del brazo. La fuerza de esa mano que se agarraba a ella fue suficiente indicativo del humor de la anciana, de lo molesta que se sentía. Lord Netherfield, que hasta ese momento estaba acompañando a lady O, hizo un gesto para expresar su aprobación, lanzó una mirada reprobatoria a su nieta política y se marchó a la biblioteca.

Portia ayudó a la anciana a subir a su habitación. En cuanto la puerta estuvo cerrada, se preparó para la diatriba que estaba a punto de escuchar. Lady O era cualquier cosa menos timorata a la hora de hablar.

Sin embargo, la anciana parecía demasiado cansada en esa ocasión. Preocupada, Portia la ayudó a recostarse en la cama sin pérdida de tiempo.

Mientras se enderezaba, lady O la miró a los ojos. Y contestó la pregunta que le rondaba la mente.

—Sí. Fue horrible. Peor de lo que me había imaginado.

Portia enfrentó esa sabia mirada.

—¿Qué dijo?

La anciana refunfuñó algo antes de contestar:

—Precisamente eso fue lo peor. No fue tanto lo que dijo como lo que se calló. —Clavó la vista en el otro extremo de la habitación un instante, tras el cual cerró los ojos y suspiró—. Déjame, niña. Estoy cansada.

Portia dio media vuelta para obedecerla, pero la anciana la detuvo.

—Se está cociendo algo desagradable.

Decidió utilizar las poco frecuentadas escaleras del ala oeste, ya que no quería toparse con nadie. Necesitaba estar un tiempo a solas.

Se estaba fraguando una tormenta sobre Glossup Hall, tanto de forma figurada como literal. El sol había desaparecido tras unos nubarrones grises y el ambiente se había tornado opresivo.

Aunque el que reinaba en la casa era aún peor. Contrariado, o más bien sombrío. Lo notaba a pesar de no ser una persona muy perceptiva. El efecto que tenía sobre las Hammond, incluso sobre la madre, y sobre la señora Buckstead era obvio.

Dos días más; los invitados se quedarían dos días más, tal y como se había previsto desde un principio. Marcharse antes sería un claro insulto hacia lady Glossup, que no había hecho nada para merecérselo. Sin embargo, ninguno de los invitados demoraría más su partida. Lady O y ella habían planeado regresar a Londres.

Se preguntaba adónde iría Simon.

Cuando llegó a la planta baja, escuchó el sonido de las bolas de billar. Echó un vistazo en dirección al pasillo que conducía al ala oeste. La puerta de la sala de billar estaba abierta y desde ella le llegaba el murmullo de las voces masculinas, entre ellas la de Simon.

Siguió caminando, atravesó el vestíbulo del jardín y de allí salió al prado.

Alzó la vista hacia las nubes. A pesar de ser bajas, no parecía que la tormenta fuera a desatarse de forma inminente. Todavía no había relámpagos ni truenos, ni se percibía el distante olor a tierra mojada. Sólo la opresiva quietud.

Hizo un mohín y echó a andar en dirección al jardín de los setos. Ése sería, sin duda alguna, el mejor lugar para evitar conversaciones reveladoras. Después de todo, los rayos no caían dos veces en el mismo sitio.

Atravesó el arco de entrada y enfiló el camino. Había alcanzado el mismo punto que la vez anterior cuando descubrió que la teoría no siempre quedaba demostrada con la práctica.

—¡Eres una estúpida! ¡Por supuesto que el niño es de Henry! No puedes ser tan tonta como para sugerir otra cosa.

Era la señora Archer, al borde de un ataque de nervios.

—Yo no soy la tonta —contraatacó Kitty—. Y puedes estar segura de que no pienso tenerlo. Pero no hace falta que te preocupes. Sé quién es el padre. Sólo es cuestión de persuadirlo para que vea las cosas como yo y después todo irá bien.

Sus palabras fueron recibidas por un silencio sepulcral. Poco después, la señora Archer (a la que Portia imaginó respirando hondo) prosiguió con la voz quebrada:

—Para que vea las cosas como tú. Las cosas siempre tienen que ser como tú quieres. Pero ¿qué es lo que quieres ahora?

Portia quiso dar media vuelta y marcharse, pero comprendió lo que implicaba la pregunta, lo que la señora Archer temía que sucediera. Era un asunto que a ella le tocaba muy de cerca y necesitaba saber...

—Ya te lo he dicho. —La voz de Kitty parecía más segura—. Quiero emociones. ¡Quiero pasión! No pienso sentarme a esperar y tener un niño... Y ponerme gorda y fea...

—¡Eres una cabeza de chorlito! —exclamó la señora Archer, horrorizada—. Te casaste con Henry. Estuviste encantada de hacerlo...

—Sólo porque tú me dijiste que tendría un título y todo lo que deseara...

—¡Pero no esto! No de este modo. No puedes...

—¡Sí que puedo!

Portia dio media vuelta y se encaminó hacia la salida; por suerte, el césped amortiguaba sus pisadas. Sus emociones se habían convertido en un torbellino. No podía pensar... No quería pensar en lo que Kitty estaba a punto de hacer. Caminó deprisa, con furiosas zancadas que le agitaban las faldas alrededor de las piernas y con la vista clavada en el suelo.

Hasta que se dio de bruces con Simon.

Sus brazos la sostuvieron. La miró a la cara antes de desviar la vista hacia el jardín de los setos.

—¿Qué ha pasado?

Una mirada a su rostro, a ese pétreo semblante, junto con la tensión de los músculos de su antebrazo le bastó para tragar saliva y tranquilizarlo.

—Tengo que salir de aquí. Una hora o dos al menos.

Simon observó su rostro con detenimiento.

—Podemos ir al mirador de Ashmore.

—Sí —replicó antes de tomar otra bocanada de aire—. Vamos.

9

Caminaron codo con codo por los jardines, de regreso al sendero que se internaba entre los árboles. No tomó el brazo de Simon ni éste se lo ofreció, y a pesar de la falta de contacto, era más que consciente de que él estaba a su lado. Junto a ella, pero sin avasallarla. Dado el torbellino de emociones que estaba sintiendo, agradeció sobremanera ese hecho.

En cuanto a Simon, él era, cómo no, la última persona con la que habría querido encontrarse, sobre todo por el tema acerca del que había querido reflexionar, acerca del que necesitaba reflexionar. Diseccionar, examinar y, en última instancia, comprender. Dada la naturaleza de ese tema, dada la íntima implicación de Simon, tanto literal como figuradamente, había esperado sentir cierta... Bueno, si no timidez, desde luego que cierta incertidumbre al estar a solas con él. Al estar tan cerca de él.

Sin embargo, se había sentido segura, tanto en ese momento como a lo largo de todo el día. No totalmente cómoda, pero sin el menor rastro de nerviosismo. Estaba convencida de que Simon siempre se comportaría de manera predecible; de que él, su manera de ser, jamás cambiaría; de que jamás sería, jamás podría ser, una amenaza para ella.

No físicamente. En el aspecto emocional era otro cantar.

Se reprendió para sus adentros y mantuvo la vista en el suelo mientras continuaba el paseo. Consciente en todo momento de la presencia de Simon.

Consciente de que le reconfortaba tenerlo allí.

Había sido Kitty, y su comportamiento, quien la había perturbado, y en esa ocasión mucho más que antes. Por tanto, era comprensible que se hubiera acercado a aquellos a quienes comprendía y en quienes confiaba. Como lady O.

Como Simon.

El camino los llevó hasta la cima de la loma, una estrecha extensión de tierra donde se alzaba la linde del bosque y que sufría el azote del viento procedente del distante mar. Les llegó una bocanada de ese frescor, aunque la tormenta aún estaba lejos. El viento le levantó los mechones de la nuca y le alborotó el cabello frente al rostro.

Se detuvo y se apartó los rebeldes mechones mientras levantaba la cabeza.

Simon se detuvo junto a Portia, levantó la cabeza y clavó la vista más allá de los campos, en los nubarrones que se veían en el horizonte. Después, la miró a la cara.

No le había sorprendido encontrarla en los jardines. Cualquier otra mujer habría estado descansando para recuperarse de los rigores del día. Portia no.

Esbozó una fugaz sonrisa al imaginársela apática y somnolienta en su cama. Era la mujer más activa que conocía, más inquieta, como si fuera inagotable, y esa faceta siempre le había atraído de un modo innegablemente físico.

Nunca la había visto fingir una debilidad. Su infatigable entusiasmo siempre la había mantenido a la par que él... Probablemente en cualquier campo.

Recorrió con la mirada su esbelta y ágil figura, empezando por la cabeza y acabando por sus interminables piernas. En esos momentos, vibraba de vitalidad, rebosaba de vida.

Todo un punto a su favor.

Sin embargo, nunca la había visto tan distraída.

—¿Qué sucede?

Portia lo miró y estudió su rostro para confirmar que había escuchado un matiz extraño... que dejaba bien claro que sólo se conformaría con la verdad.

Sus labios esbozaron una media sonrisa mientras devolvía la vista al paisaje.

—Kitty está embarazada. Esta mañana escuché cómo se lo contaba a Winifred... Cómo intentaba que creyera que el bebé es de Desmond.

Simon no intentó ocultar su desprecio.

—Qué desagradable.

—El bebé no es de Henry.

—Ya lo había supuesto.

Ella lo miró con el ceño fruncido.

—¿Por qué?

Enfrentó su mirada y torció el gesto.

—Tengo entendido que Henry y Kitty llevan cierto tiempo distanciados. —Titubeó antes de continuar—: Sospecho que la conversación que escuchamos la otra noche entre Henry y James trataba de un posible divorcio.

—¿Divorcio? —Portia lo miró sin dar crédito.

No era necesario que le explicara lo que eso implicaba. Un divorcio sería un escándalo y, en el caso que los ocupaba, supondría el ostracismo más absoluto para Kitty.

Portia apartó la mirada.

—Me pregunto si Kitty lo sabe. —Guardó silencio un instante antes de proseguir—: Acabo de escuchar cómo la señora Archer y Kitty discutían el asunto. Acabo de escuchar lo que Kitty quiere hacer.

Aunque no era hijo suyo, Simon sintió un nudo en el estómago.

—¿Qué tiene en mente?

—No quiere al niño. No quiere engordar y... Creo que, sencillamente, no quiere que nada se interponga en lo que ella llama «una vida emocionante»... Algo que cree que se merece.

Simon estaba totalmente perdido. Después de haber crecido con un buen puñado de hermanas, tanto mayores como menores que él, creía poseer unas nociones mínimas sobre la psique femenina; sin embargo, la mente de Kitty se le escapaba por completo. Portia se giró y reanudó la marcha. Él se apresuró a alcanzarla.

Sabía que seguía meditando acerca de ese tema que la tenía preocupada. La dejó con sus pensamientos mientras coronaban la subida y atravesaban la siguiente zona boscosa. Se detuvo cuando salieron a campo abierto, por encima del pueblo de Ashmore. Portia seguía ceñuda. Esperó a que se diera cuenta de que no estaba a su lado y a que se volviera para mirarlo.

—¿Qué pasa? —Lo miró a los ojos un instante, tras lo cual hizo un mohín y apartó la vista.

Simon esperó en silencio y, tras un momento, Portia volvió a mirarlo.

—Tienes que prometerme que no te reirás.

Esas palabras lo sorprendieron.

Ella apartó la mirada y reanudó la marcha. Se detuvo lo justo para que la alcanzara y continuó caminando sin que su expresión variara un ápice.

—He estado pensando si... Bueno, si con el tiempo... me convertiría... podría convertirme en alguien como Kitty.

—¿Como Kitty? —Le llevó un cierto tiempo saber a qué se refería.

Ella lo miró a la cara y su ceño se acentuó.

—Como Kitty, adicta a las emociones.

Cuando se detuvo, Portia hizo lo mismo.

Fue superior a sus fuerzas. Se echó a reír. Ni el rictus airado de sus labios ni las chispas que lanzaban sus ojos consiguieron refrenarlo.

—¡Lo has prometido! —exclamó ella, dándole un guantazo.

Lo que hizo mucho más difícil que dejara de reírse.

—¡Tú...! —Portia hizo ademán de volver a golpearlo.

Le atrapó las manos y se las sujetó.

—No... Estate quieta. —Inspiró hondo sin apartar la vista de su cara. La preocupación y la confusión que vio en sus ojos, dos emociones claras después del estallido de temperamento, le devolvieron la seriedad al punto. ¿No creería de verdad que...? Enfrentó su mirada—. Es totalmente imposible que llegues a ser como Kitty. Que te conviertas en algo remotamente parecido. —No parecía convencida—. Créeme, ni de lejos. No hay la más mínima posibilidad.

Portia estudió su rostro con los párpados entornados.

—¿Cómo lo sabes?

Porque la conocía.

—No eres Kitty. —Escuchó su propio tono de voz, inspiró hondo y recalcó las siguientes palabras para que no le quedara la menor duda al respecto—. Jamás te comportarás como ella. Jamás podrías hacerlo.

Ella enfrentó su mirada con evidente incertidumbre.

De repente, comprendió aquello de lo que estaban hablando. Sintió una opresión en el pecho y se le hizo un nudo en la garganta al percatarse de que Portia (de que ambos, en realidad) estaba al borde de un precipicio. Lo había sabido de antemano y habría sido de lo más sorprende que ella no albergara ninguna duda, que se hubiera entregado a él sin haberlo meditado en profundidad.

Puesto que la conocía como la palma de su mano, conocía su curiosidad y sus ansias de conocimiento, había estado convencido de su decisión final. Jamás se le había pasado por la cabeza que Kitty supusiera un obstáculo en su camino y mucho menos de ese calibre.

Estudió la mirada de Portia mientras ella hacía lo mismo. Sus ojos se habían oscurecido mucho; tanto que sólo era capaz de discernir las emociones más fuertes. En ese momento, eran menos perspicaces, parecían nublados por la incertidumbre; una incertidumbre que estaba dirigida contra ella misma, no contra él como había creído en un principio.

Portia parpadeó. La sintió retroceder y reaccionó instintivamente.

—Confía en mí. —Le apretó las manos con fuerza y volvió a capturar su mirada. Sin apartar la vista de sus ojos, se llevó una mano a los labios, después la otra—. En serio, confía en mí.

Ella lo miraba con los ojos desorbitados. Pasado un momento, le preguntó:

—¿Cómo estás tan seguro?

—Porque... —Perdido como estaba en sus ojos y aun siendo consciente de que debía decir la verdad, le resultó imposible encontrar las palabras necesarias para describir el tema que los ocupaba—. Porque esto..., lo que tenemos entre nosotros, lo que podría llegar a ser, jamás será lo bastante fuerte como para cambiarte. Para convertirte en alguien que no eres.

Portia frunció el ceño, pero con actitud pensativa, no de rechazo. La dejó zafarse de sus manos y darle la espalda para clavar la vista en los campos, aunque en realidad su mirada estaría perdida en el horizonte sin ver nada.

Tras un momento, se giró y se encaminó al mirador. La siguió a corta distancia. Cuando entraron, Portia clavó la vista en el Solent. Simon aguardó a cierta distancia, con las manos en los bolsillos.

No se atrevía a tocarla, a presionarla de ninguna manera.

Portia lo miró a la cara antes de recorrerlo con la mirada, como si presintiera la tensión que se había apoderado de sus músculos. Cuando levantó la vista de nuevo, enarcó una ceja.

—Creía... Esperaba que fueras más persuasivo.

Con la mandíbula apretada, negó con la cabeza.

—La decisión es tuya. Tú tienes que tomarla.

Iba a preguntarle por qué, lo vio en sus ojos, pero algo la hizo titubear y apartar la vista.

Poco después, le dio la espalda al paisaje. La siguió al exterior para emprender el camino de vuelta a la mansión.

Caminaron en silencio; ese silencio cómodo y que parecía unirlos de un modo extraño. Eran muy conscientes de la presencia del otro, pero prefirieron sumirse en sus pensamientos con la certeza de que ninguno esperaría que el otro entablara conversación.

Sus pensamientos estaban dedicados por completo a Portia. Y también a su relación. Lo que tenían entre ellos, ese creciente vínculo. Se estaba desarrollando de un modo que no había previsto; sin embargo y una vez consciente de ello, en lugar de echarse para atrás (cosa que su alma de libertino le estaba pidiendo a gritos que hiciera) se veía arrastrado por una serie de sentimientos e instintos muy profundos a presionarla, a hacerla suya, a reclamarla para sí mismo. Esos instintos le decían que debía estar encantado con la fuerza de ese vínculo emocional, con los hilos que se estaban entretejiendo entre ellos, que nada tenían que ver con su relación física pero que, aun así, los unían de un modo que ninguno de los dos había anticipado.

Había sabido desde el principio que conseguir que Portia confiara en él para aceptarlo como marido sería una tarea bastante difícil. Sin embargo, hacerlo bajo la sombra de un posible divorcio entre Henry y Kitty creaba escenarios que no había previsto y lo obligaba a considerar cuestiones, a sopesar elementos, sentimientos y expectativas que en otras circunstancias habría dado por sentado.

Como el hecho de que confiaba plenamente en ella... y el porqué. El porqué de la idea de que se convirtiera en otra Kitty era tan ridícula, el porqué de que se hubiera reído.

Era imposible que se convirtiera en alguien como Kitty y siguiera siendo Portia.

Su carácter, esa férrea voluntad que también poseían sus hermanas y que en Portia era mucho más intensa, no lo permitiría. En ese aspecto, la conocía mucho mejor de lo que ella misma se conocía.

Tenía una fe ciega en su carácter.

Jamás había considerado ese rasgo como una característica indispensable en una esposa.

En esos momentos, sin embargo, se percataba de lo valioso que era.

Reconocía en él una garantía que aplacaba esa parte tan profunda de sí mismo que, incluso en ese instante y a pesar de la decisión que había tomado, evitaba la mera idea de aceptar el talón de Aquiles de los Cynster; evitaba el compromiso emocional que, para los hombres de su familia, era una parte esencial del matrimonio.

Llegaron a los jardines y al camino cubierto por el emparrado de glicinias. La casa se alzaba frente a ellos.

Le puso una mano en el brazo para detenerla. Cuando lo hizo, se giró hacia él. Sin apartar la mirada de sus ojos, Simon bajó la mano hasta que sus dedos se entrelazaron.

—Te puedo prometer una cosa. —Se llevó la mano a la boca y le besó la palma sin dejar de mirarla—. Jamás te haré daño. De ninguna manera.

Portia no parpadeó, ni siquiera se movió. Sus miradas se quedaron entrelazadas largo rato. Después, inspiró hondo y respondió con una inclinación de cabeza.

Tras colocarse la mano en el brazo, Simon se encaminó hacia la casa.

Desde luego que era decisión suya. Era todo un alivio que Simon se diera cuenta y lo aceptara.

Claro que tampoco tenía muy claro cómo interpretar tanta magnanimidad por su parte. Algo de lo más inusual. Simon la deseaba y eso era evidente... Conociendo al tirano que se ocultaba tras esa máscara de elegancia, se veía obligada a buscar un motivo que explicara su contención, su paciencia.

Estaba meditando al respecto delante de su ventana y sopesaba los acontecimientos de la tarde. Se preguntaba a qué se debía esa actitud y en qué medida debía afectar a su propia decisión.

Durante la media hora que había pasado en el salón, Simon encontró el momento para susurrarle al oído el emplazamiento de su dormitorio, por si acaso necesitaba la información. De haber creído que la estaba presionando, lo habría fulminado con la mirada; pero le bastó un vistazo a sus ojos azules para darse cuenta de que, en realidad, estaba luchando contra su instinto y de que, de momento, lo mantenía a raya.

Había respondido con una inclinación de cabeza justo antes de que se les unieran más personas y el momento de intimidad se esfumara. Con todo, había pasado el resto de la velada siendo consciente de que Simon esperaba algún indicio de su decisión.

Durante la cena y sentada en la otra punta de la mesa, lo había observado con mucho disimulo. Aun así, si los demás invitados no hubieran estado tan empecinados en controlar la conversación y mantenerla dentro de los límites aceptados, alguien habría acabado por darse cuenta.

Por primera vez, Kitty había demostrado ser de utilidad; aunque de forma totalmente inconsciente. Había retomado su anterior papel, aunque con mucho más dramatismo. Esa noche era una dama a la que habían juzgado mal y que mantenía su orgullo intacto a pesar de las pullas que le lanzaban las personas que deberían conocerla y apoyarla.

Tras la cena, las damas se retiraron al salón y los caballeros se demoraron en el comedor. Nadie había tenido deseos de alargar la velada. El ambiente que se respiraba era tenso y las emociones giraban en torno a Kitty y varios invitados. La bandeja del té llegó pronto. Tras una taza, todas las damas se retiraron a sus habitaciones.

De ahí que se encontrara en esos momentos con la vista clavada en la oscuridad de la noche mientras meditaba su decisión; una decisión que ella y sólo ella podría tomar.

Aunque, en el fondo, su decisión dependía de Simon.

A pesar de su pasado común, o a decir verdad más bien a causa de ese pasado, no le había resultado sorprendente que Simon se ofreciera voluntario para guiarla en su exploración de las relaciones físicas entre hombres y mujeres. No había aprobado su deseo, al menos en un principio, pero no había tardado en capitular al ver que estaba decidida a continuar con su investigación. Había sido consciente de que si él se negaba, habría buscado la ayuda de otro hombre. Desde ese punto de vista tan protector que lo caracterizaba, el hecho de que fuera él quien la acompañara en su proyecto, a pesar de las implicaciones, era muchísimo mejor que verla acompañada de otro.

Aunque nada de eso mitigaba el hecho de que fuera un Cynster y ella, una Ashford. Ambos pertenecían a la alta sociedad. De haber sido algo más joven, más inocente y también más delicada, o de haberse tratado de una joven a la que Simon no conocía tan bien, apostaría su collar de perlas a que cualquier intimidad habría acabado con un decreto del tipo «te he seducido y ahora tenemos que casarnos».

Por suerte, no era el caso. Porque Simon la conocía... muy bien. No la habría ayudado en su búsqueda de conocimientos de creer que, al hacerlo, cometía un acto deshonroso. Por absurdo que pareciera, le complacía mucho que hubiera aceptado que ella tenía tanto derecho a la exploración sexual como él.

Y dicho derecho, o eso creía, bastaba para absolverlo de cualquier responsabilidad moral; para evitar que se comportara con arrogancia y desaprobación paternalista. Simon siempre había acatado sus deseos y había esperado que ella le diera su consentimiento.

No la estaba seduciendo en el sentido estricto; en realidad, se había prestado voluntario, se había puesto a su disposición, en caso de que quisiera ser seducida.

Debía entender que su sempiterna reticencia, que su determinación a no presionarla, era reflejo de ese hecho; que algún enrevesado código masculino dictaba lo que era honorable en semejantes circunstancias. Tal vez así era como se llevaba a cabo una seducción consentida.

Todo lo que había sucedido entre ellos hasta el momento había sido con su expreso consentimiento y según su expreso deseo. La decisión que debía tomar era si quería más, si de verdad quería dar el paso final, desvelar el último secreto y aprenderlo todo.

La erudita que llevaba dentro quería lanzarse de cabeza; su lado más pragmático insistía en que sopesara los pros y los contras.

En su fuero interno, tanto su edad como su estado de solterona confirmada la liberaban de cualquier noción timorata sobre la virginidad y eso mismo debían de pensar los demás. Si no se lanzaba al agua para aprender lo que creía necesario, tal vez nunca llegaría a casarse; en ese caso, ¿qué importaba? Para ella, la virginidad era un concepto atrasado.

El riesgo de embarazo existía, pero era aceptable; era un riesgo al que no le importaba enfrentarse. A diferencia de Kitty, quería tener hijos. Dado que contaba con una familia cariñosa y comprensiva, y que las reglas sociales le importaban un comino, podría manejar la situación llegado el caso. Siempre que no dijera quién era el padre. Su instinto de supervivencia estaba demasiado desarrollado como para cometer semejante error.

Por si fuera poco, la certeza de Simon había borrado el temor de que podría acabar enganchada a las emociones físicas, tal y como le sucedía a Kitty, si se demostraba que la emoción predominante entre ellos era lujuria. Había sido honesto y contundente al respecto, y su actitud había despejado todas sus dudas; además, su reputación aseguraba que tenía experiencia de sobra como para fiarse de su opinión.

Una vez considerado todo, llegó a la conclusión de que no había contras insuperables, al menos no desde una perspectiva personal.

En cuanto a los pros, sabía lo que quería, lo que deseaba. Quería aprender todo lo que pudiera del matrimonio antes de dar semejante paso; necesitaba comprender los aspectos físicos inherentes al estado matrimonial antes de aceptarlo. El desastroso estado del matrimonio de Kitty había puesto de manifiesto su necesidad de comprender a la perfección en qué consistía antes de llegar al altar. Si después de todo lo que había visto esa semana tomaba decisiones precipitadas, no se lo perdonaría jamás.

Comprender todos los aspectos del matrimonio había sido el objetivo inicial... Sin embargo, en esos momentos quería más. También quería averiguar qué era ese vínculo emocional que se había desarrollado entre ellos... Una emoción que no sólo la ayudaba a enfrentarse a la idea de meterse en su cama, sino que la impulsaba a hacerlo.

A tenor del comportamiento de Kitty, aprender eso también se le antojaba sensato.

Tal y como estaban las cosas, meterse en la cama de Simon sólo le suponía un riesgo emocional. Y era hipotético, algo que no terminaba de ver por la sencilla razón de que aún desconocía cuál era la emoción que la instaba a entregarse a él.

Dicha emoción y sus efectos eran muy reales. De igual forma, el riesgo también lo era. Y sabiendo lo que sabía de él no podía cerrar los ojos ni pretender que no existía.

¿Qué ocurriría si la emoción que había entre ellos era amor?

No lo sabía con certeza. Además de los hombres y del matrimonio, el amor era otro tema que jamás había figurado en su lista de estudio.

No lo había buscado; el amor no había sido la razón por la que se había aprovechado de la oferta de Simon para enseñarle lo que quería saber. Aun así, no era tan estúpida ni tan arrogante como para no preguntarse, para no darse cuenta de que, por extraño que pareciera, podría tener la posibilidad delante de las narices.

Una vez que se dieran el gusto (una vez, dos, las que hicieran falta para aprender todo lo que quería y para poner un nombre a esa emoción), si no era amor, se irían cada uno por su lado y su experimento habría concluido, habría descubierto lo que quería. Eso estaba muy claro. No era ahí donde residía el peligro.

El peligro estaba en la otra cara de la moneda. ¿Qué ocurriría si lo que había entre ellos era amor?

Conocía la respuesta. Si era amor, tanto por su parte o por la de él, o por ambas partes, y Simon se daba cuenta... insistiría en que se casaran. Y ella no se zafaría tan fácilmente de la situación.

Después de todo, era un Cynster. Sin embargo, en el caso de que Simon se saliera con la suya, ¿dónde la dejaría eso a ella?

Casada con un Cynster. Vinculada, posiblemente, por amor... y casada con un Cynster. Y eso era peliagudo. Si el amor los motivaba a ambos, la situación tal vez sería más o menos llevadera, tampoco estaba segura del todo. Sin embargo, si el amor sólo motivaba a uno de ellos, el resultado sería un completo desastre.

Y ahí residía el peligro.

La pregunta a la que se enfrentaba era si se atrevería a arriesgarse. En definitiva, si apostaba o no.

Dejó escapar el aire muy despacio y clavó la vista en las siluetas de los árboles.

Si no buscaba la respuesta en ese momento, si no aceptaba la oportunidad de ser seducida, cada uno seguiría su camino en unos días. Ella regresaría a Rutlandshire, muerta de curiosidad. ¿Quién podría satisfacer su necesidad de conocimientos? ¿En qué otra persona podría confiar?

Las posibilidades de que volvieran a encontrarse ese verano, en las condiciones apropiadas, eran nimias. Además, no tenía la certeza de que Simon quisiera seguir enseñándole todo lo que ella quería aprender dentro de un mes, mucho menos de tres.

¿Sería capaz de darle la espalda a esa posibilidad y quedarse siempre con la duda de lo que pudo ser? ¿Podría vivir sin descubrir lo que la intimidad física habría representado para ellos? ¿Sin averiguar qué los había llevado a esa intimidad? ¿A no saber si era amor, si ambos lo sentían, y a no saber qué habría resultado de todo?

Torció el gesto en una mueca de autodesprecio. A decir verdad, no había nada que cuestionarse. Dada su naturaleza imprudente, a menudo incauta en su arrogancia, y voluntariosa a más no poder, era incapaz de darle la espalda. A pesar del riesgo.

Tal y como estaban las cosas, tal vez lo más sensato y lo más lógico fuera acudir al dormitorio de Simon esa noche. Sin duda, algunas personas la tacharían de imprudente y alocada, pero su razonamiento tenía sentido para ella.

No tenía sentido perder el tiempo.

Para llegar a la habitación de Simon, tenía que rodear la galería que pasaba por encima de la escalinata. Por suerte y dado que el resto de las damas se había retirado ya, no se cruzó con nadie mientras se escabullía entre las sombras y enfilaba el pasillo que llevaba al ala oeste.

En la confluencia del ala central con el ala oeste, se vio obligada a cruzar el distribuidor. Acababa de salir al descubierto cuando escuchó unas pisadas que subían las escaleras.

Retrocedió a toda prisa hacia las sombras del pasillo que acababa de dejar. Las pisadas, pertenecientes a dos personas, fueron aumentando de volumen hasta que distinguió también la voz de Ambrose; Desmond le contestó. Dio gracias en silencio porque sus habitaciones estuvieran en el ala oeste y no en la central, donde ella se encontraba.

Aguzó el oído. Los hombres llegaron a la parte superior de las escaleras, charlando sobre perros, nada menos. Sin perder tiempo, continuaron su camino.

Por el ala oeste.

Aliviada inmensamente, pero indecisa, aguardó un instante, pero a la postre decidió que saber en qué habitaciones estaban le resultaría útil. De manera que, sin abandonar el amparo de las sombras, pegó la espalda a la pared y asomó la cabeza para echar una miradita.

Los dos hombres habían recorrido casi todo el pasillo. Se despidieron casi al llegar al final del mismo. Uno entró en una habitación situada a la izquierda y el otro, en una situada a la derecha.

Dejó escapar el aire que había estado reteniendo y se enderezó. Simon le había dicho que su puerta era la tercera a partir de las escaleras, de modo que no tendría que pasar por delante de las habitaciones de Ambrose y de Desmond.

Cruzó el distribuidor. Cuando pasó por las escaleras, le llegó el ruido de las bolas de billar. Se detuvo, echó un vistazo a su alrededor y se acercó al hueco de las escaleras. Agudizó el oído y alcanzó a escuchar un murmullo de voces procedentes de la sala de billar.

La voz más aguda de Charlie, la carcajada de James... y la voz ronca de Simon.

Se quedó allí parada un instante, con los ojos entrecerrados y los labios apretados, antes de dar media vuelta y continuar hacia su habitación.

Abrió la puerta y entró, y se contuvo justo a tiempo para cerrarla suavemente. Dado el número de habitaciones libres, no parecía probable que hubiera alguien en los dormitorios contiguos, pero no tenía sentido correr un riesgo innecesario.

Recorrió la habitación con la mirada, medio oculta entre las sombras y muy irritada por que Simon no la estuviera esperando para darle la bienvenida. Para ayudarla a no pensar en lo que estaba haciendo. De todos modos, ¿cuánto podía durar una partida de billar? Pensó un instante y acabó por resoplar. Era de esperar que, al menos, tuviera el tino de subir para averiguar si había utilizado la información que con tanto secretismo le había ofrecido.

Se internó en la estancia, aplastando sin compasión las mariposas que revoloteaban en su estómago. Había tomado una decisión, y ni loca cambiaría de opinión. Se había armado de valor para enfrentarse al desafío.

Las habitaciones del ala oeste eran algo más pequeñas que las del ala este. Esa zona de la mansión parecía más antigua. Los techos eran igual de altos, pero las habitaciones eran más estrechas. No había ningún sillón junto a la chimenea, ni alféizar acolchado bajo la ventana, ni tampoco un tocador con su correspondiente taburete. Sólo una cómoda alta, flanqueada por dos sillas en absoluto cómodas.

Desvió la mirada hacia la cama. Era el único lugar apropiado para sentarse a esperar. Avanzó hacia ella y se sentó. Acto seguido, comprobó el grosor y la comodidad del colchón con unos botecitos. Perfecto.

Subió por la cama hasta recostarse sobre los almohadones apilados en el cabecero, cruzó los brazos a la altura del pecho y clavó la vista en la puerta. Por supuesto, había otra explicación plausible al hecho de que Simon no se encontrase allí. Era evidente que no la esperaba, que no tenía muy claro que acabara por aceptar su proposición.

A tenor de su arrogancia, por otro lado tan característica de los Cynster, y de su reputación, semejante posibilidad era digna de mención.

La ventana estaba abierta y por ella entraba una fresca brisa. La tormenta se había alejado sin arreciar, dejando a su paso un ambiente mucho más fresco.

Sintió un escalofrío y cambió de postura. No tenía frío, pero...

Miró la colcha, después levantó la vista y la clavó en la puerta nuevamente.

Tras despedirse de Charlie delante de su puerta, Simon entró en el dormitorio. Cerró la puerta y, acto seguido, desvió la vista hacia la ventana. Al ver la luz de la luna que se filtraba por ella, no se molestó en encender una vela.

Contuvo un suspiro mientras se quitaba la chaqueta. Después, pasó a desabrocharse el chaleco y dejó ambas prendas en una de las sillas que había junto a la cómoda. Se quitó el alfiler de corbata y lo dejó sobre el mueble justo antes de tirar del intrincado nudo para soltarlo... En un intento muy consciente por mantener ocupada su mente con esas insignificancias en lugar de pensar en las horas que pasaría dando vueltas en la cama esa noche.

En lugar de pensar en el tiempo que le llevaría a su obsesión tomar una decisión.

En lugar de pensar en cuánto más podría interpretar el papel de seductor indiferente. Jamás en su vida había intentado asumir un papel tan diferente a su verdadera naturaleza. Claro que jamás había intentado seducir a Portia...

Tras soltar los extremos de la corbata, se la quitó del cuello y fue a dejarla sobre la otra silla...

Un vestido de seda de color claro estaba pulcramente colocado sobre ella. Seda verde manzana... Su mente rememoró el tono exacto del vestido que Portia había llevado esa noche. El color había resaltado su piel de alabastro en contraste con su pelo negro; y había hecho que sus ojos azul cobalto brillaran aún más.

Bajó la mano y acarició la tela con los dedos... En realidad, lo hizo para cerciorarse de que no eran imaginaciones suyas. Sus dedos se toparon con un par de diáfanas medias de seda, dispuestas sobre unas ligas de seda fruncida y ribeteadas de encaje.

Su mente conjuró la imagen de Portia... ataviada únicamente con su camisola de seda.

Muy despacio, sin atreverse a creer lo que le decía su mente, se giró.

Portia estaba dormida en su cama, con el cabello negro extendido sobre los almohadones.

Se acercó a la cama con sigilo. Estaba tendida de costado, de cara a él, con una mano bajo la mejilla. Tenía los labios entreabiertos. La sombra de sus largas pestañas oscurecía la piel de alabastro de sus mejillas.

Su perfume flotaba en el aire. Un sutil aroma floral que le nublaba la mente y lo envolvía en un hechizo sensual.

Los estímulos que sus sentidos absorbían lo embriagaron.

Una sensación de triunfo lo inundó..., pero se apresuró a refrenarla. Apretó los dientes y contó hasta diez mientras sentía cómo se le aceleraba el pulso. Había pasado toda la tarde diciéndose que no esperara ese momento, que con Portia nada era sencillo y directo.

Aun así, allí estaba ella.

No terminaba de asimilarlo. Le costaba respirar. Inspiró hondo y dejó escapar el aire muy despacio, recordándose que no debía leer entre líneas, que no debía sacar conclusiones precipitadas de su presencia en la cama. Desde luego, no era el momento apropiado para dejar que sus instintos se hicieran con el control y la reclamaran.

Aun así, requería coraje haber acudido a su cama.

Portia sabía cómo era... Ninguna mujer con la que se había acostado lo conocía tan bien como ella. Sabía qué carácter tenía, conocía su personalidad... y también sabía cómo sería en el papel de marido. O se hacía una idea bastante acertada.

Él había accedido a enseñarle todo cuanto quisiera saber, aunque jamás habían hablado de nada más. De nada más vinculante. A pesar de eso, Portia debía de saber que al acudir a él, al aceptar su proposición para iniciarla en las relaciones íntimas, le estaba confiando (estaba arriesgando) algo bastante más importante que la virginidad.

La independencia era algo esencial para Portia, formaba parte de ella; poner algo tan fundamental en la balanza requería el tipo de arrojo característico en ella. No obstante, no habría tomado esa decisión a la ligera. Portia no.

No le cabía duda de que habría visto el peligro, aunque él se había encargado de ocultarlo en la medida de lo posible.

Todavía no sabía cómo podían lograr que su matrimonio funcionara; sabía que no sería sencillo ni mucho menos. Pero eso era lo que quería.

Lo único que tenía que hacer era conseguir que Portia llegara a la conclusión de que ella también lo quería.

Todo ello, sin desvelar que el matrimonio siempre había sido su objetivo.

Por más que confiara en ella, no necesitaba conocer ese detallito; no tenía por qué averiguar una debilidad que él no estaba dispuesto a revelarle.

Se demoró observándola mientras el tiempo pasaba, mientras tramaba y planeaba su estrategia, ya que la conocía demasiado bien como para acelerar las cosas. Una vez que supo cómo acercarse a ella, se armó de valor y se sentó en el borde del colchón.

Portia no se despertó.

Le enterró los dedos en el pelo y comenzó a acariciar los sedosos mechones, dejando que se deslizaran por su mano. Contempló la expresión inocente que el sueño confería a su rostro antes de inclinarse para despertarla con un beso.

Se despertó muy despacio, de una forma muy dulce y femenina; después, murmuró algo ininteligible mientras se colocaba de espaldas, le enterraba los dedos en el pelo y le devolvía el beso.

De la forma más seductora.

Simon se apartó y la miró a los ojos, más oscuros que la noche, tras las sombras de las largas pestañas. Miró sus labios.

—¿Por qué estás aquí?

Sus labios, carnosos y sensuales, esbozaron una lenta sonrisa. Tiró de él.

—Lo sabes perfectamente. Quiero que me enseñes... que me lo enseñes todo.

Lo besó tras pronunciar esa última palabra; le introdujo la lengua en la boca para buscar la suya y comenzó a acariciarla en franca provocación. La pasión estalló entre ellos y se extendió por su piel como una llamarada.

Su control comenzó a resquebrajarse, pero se recuperó enseguida. Se apartó y la miró a la cara.

—¿Estás segura? ¿Completamente segura? —Al ver que ella enarcaba las cejas en gesto burlón, gruñó—: ¿Estás segura de que no te arrepentirás por la mañana?

Nada más salir de sus labios, se dio cuenta de la estupidez que estaba diciendo. Estaba hablando de Portia, y ella jamás se arrepentía de nada.

Y bien sabía Dios que no quería que lo hiciera.

—No importa. Olvida lo que he dicho. —Le sostuvo la mirada—. Sólo dime una cosa: ¿significa esto que confías en mí?

Portia no respondió de inmediato. De hecho, meditó la respuesta un instante antes de asentir con la cabeza.

—En esto, sí.

Simon soltó el aire que había estado reteniendo.

—Gracias a Dios.

Se apartó de sus brazos para ponerse en pie. Se sacó la camisa de los pantalones y se la pasó por encima de la cabeza.

10

Portia contempló el repentino despliegue de piel desnuda y puro músculo que quedó delante de ella. Se le secó la boca. La parte lógica de su mente se esforzaba por prestar atención a lo que Simon le había preguntado..., a por qué se lo había preguntado... Pero la otra parte de su mente ni siquiera se molestó en hacerlo.

Después de todo, eso era lo que había querido experimentar. Aprender.

La súbita incertidumbre, la punzada de temor que sintió cuando él se llevó las manos a la pretina del pantalón y lo desabrochó, era de lo más lógica, se reprendió. Si bien parecía más sensato concentrarse en otras cosas..., como en lo a gusto que se encontraba. Comprenderlo hizo que diera un pequeño respingo y al punto notó el suave roce de la camisola sobre la piel. En comparación, el tacto de las sábanas le resultó áspero.

Simon se dio media vuelta y se sentó en la cama. El colchón se hundió bajo su peso mientras se quitaba las botas y las dejaba caer al suelo. Su rostro parecía un boceto artístico que estudiara la determinación, la concentración más absoluta.

Una concentración que en breve estaría en...

Sintió un escalofrío en la espalda. Sus sentidos se sobresaltaron cuando él se puso en pie para quitarse los pantalones y se giró.

Clavó la vista en él... y no precisamente en sus ojos. Fue consciente de que se quedaba boquiabierta. De que lo miraba con los ojos como platos.

Lo había tocado, pero nunca lo había visto.

Y verlo era mucho más impresionante que tocarlo. Al menos para su mente. A decir verdad, su mente no estaba muy segura de...

—¡Por el amor de Dios, deja de pensar!

Parpadeó mientras él apartaba las sábanas y se metía en la cama. Volvió a mirarlo a la cara cuando le tendió los brazos y la acercó a él.

—Pero Sim...

La besó... con ardor. Con arrogante exigencia. Con afán dominante. Agraviada, respondió en consecuencia de forma instintiva y él cambió de inmediato el cariz del beso. La besó con ternura mientras ella se tensaba, sobresaltada de repente al sentir el calor que irradiaba su cuerpo. Al percibir lo real que era ese cuerpo musculoso, excitado, desnudo y resuelto que de repente la había rodeado y parecía muy capaz de avasallarla.

Pese a todo, fue toda una conmoción. Una conmoción de lo más real y, en cierto sentido, aterradora. También en ese ámbito, la teoría era una cosa y la práctica otra.

Siguió besándola, de modo que sólo podía respirar mediante el aliento que él le daba. Intentó alejarse, liberar su mente lo suficiente como para pensar. Pero él no se lo permitió. Y entonces, del modo más inesperado, descubrió que se hundía, que la arrastraba hacia el fondo de un mar de sensualidad.

Tendido a medias sobre ella, con las piernas entrelazadas con las suyas y las manos sobre su piel, hechizó sus sentidos y los arrastró sin piedad hasta el fondo mientras todo vestigio de resistencia se desvanecía. Hasta que su mente estuvo inundada no por el placer, sino por la expectación, por el deseo. Y no le permitió regresar a la superficie; la besó de forma aún más apasionada, devorando su boca sin molestarse en ocultar en ningún momento su verdadera intención, su afán conquistador.

Portia se rindió con un jadeo. Una rendición que fue más allá del beso y estuvo impulsada por el deseo de apaciguarlo, de entregarse, de rendirse. De aplacarlo mediante la ofrenda de su cuerpo, de todo su ser.

Y él lo tomó todo. Hasta ese momento, nunca había comprendido hasta qué punto la deseaba. Lo que en realidad deseaba de ella. Cuando comprendió la magnitud de la realidad, se estremeció de la cabeza a los pies.

El asalto a sus labios se suavizó, pero no cesó.

Porque Simon desvió su atención hacia otras conquistas.

Como sus pechos. Excitados y doloridos por el deseo, notó cómo sus caricias le endurecían los pezones. Más diestros que nunca, sus dedos torturaron, mimaron... y pellizcaron.

La pasión la tomó por asalto y se deslizó bajo su piel. Gimió, aunque el sonido quedó sofocado por un beso. Simon no se detuvo, no interrumpió sus abrumadoras caricias.

Sólo se apartó de sus labios cuando ella arqueó la espalda y gritó. Apartó las manos de sus pechos y comenzó a subirle la camisola sin muchos miramientos.

—Levanta los brazos.

Lo obedeció al mismo tiempo que respiraba hondo. Él le quitó la camisola y, antes de que pudiera bajar los brazos, atrapó una de sus muñecas con una mano y luego la otra. Le bajó los brazos hasta que quedaron apoyados en los almohadones, sobre su cabeza. La posición le elevó los senos y los aplastó contra su torso, arrancándole un jadeo.

Sintió una oleada de sublime placer. Simon inclinó la cabeza y volvió a capturar sus labios con avidez. Acto seguido, comenzó a mover el torso de un lado a otro. El movimiento hizo que el vello de su pecho le rozara los enhiestos pezones y la sensación fue tan placentera que rayó en el dolor.

Ni siquiera era capaz de jadear cuando él se apartó por fin de sus labios para dejar un abrasador y húmedo reguero de besos por su cuello. Descendió hasta llegar al hueco de la garganta y, desde allí, trazó el contorno de una clavícula con afán posesivo antes de bajar un poco más y capturar un pezón con el que se dio un festín.

Atrapada como estaba con las manos sobre la cabeza y el cuerpo arqueado, expuesto para que saciara su voracidad, no pudo evitar, no pudo contener la miríada de estímulos que Simon le provocó.

Unos estímulos que la atraparon y la elevaron, que expandieron todos sus sentidos de modo que la realidad caló hasta lo más hondo de su ser. Una realidad protagonizada por la ardiente calidez de esa boca que le chupaba un pezón; por el peso de esos poderosos músculos que la mantenían atrapada; por la evidente erección que le presionaba la cadera, lista para tomarla.

La promesa, la certeza de lo que estaba por llegar la abrumó..., y ella lo permitió de buena gana.

Dejó de forcejear. Dejó que él le enseñara. Que se lo mostrara todo.

Simon percibió el momento exacto en el que Portia se rindió, en el que dejó de analizar, de pensar. De resistirse. Su cuerpo, más débil que el suyo pese a poseer una fuerza muy femenina, se relajó. Una señal que su naturaleza conquistadora reconoció y apreció en su justa medida. Alzó la cabeza, la besó en los labios, capturó su boca para saborearla a placer y se colocó sobre ella.

Dejó que sintiera todo su peso, dejó que lo conociera y que lo aprendiera, porque era imperativo que así fuera. Cuando la sintió forcejear para liberar los brazos, la soltó y colocó las manos sobre sus pechos. Desde allí fueron descendiendo, siguiendo sus curvas hasta introducirse entre la sabana y su espalda para aferrarla por las nalgas y alzarle las caderas.

Ella musitó algo, un sonido gutural e ininteligible. Encantado con la situación, aunque no dio muestras de ello, subyugó sus sentidos y la sumergió en el beso.

Cuando se apartó de sus labios y descendió hasta sus pechos, lamiéndola y besándola en el trayecto, ella no opuso la menor resistencia. Lo aferró por los hombros y le clavó los dedos mientras él daba buena cuenta de su entrega. Respiraba de forma entrecortada, y cuando la miró a la cara vio que tenía los ojos cerrados. Fruncía el ceño como si estuviera concentrada al máximo.

En ese momento, lamió un enhiesto pezón. Lo rodeó con la lengua antes de atraparlo con los labios y succionar con fuerza, lo que rompió su concentración a juzgar por el jadeo que escapó de su garganta.

Descendió un poco más y decidió dar rienda suelta a su deseo. Sabía sin ningún género de dudas que no sería capaz de controlar sus instintos más básicos. Esa noche no. Con ella no. Había admitido días atrás que la deseaba desde mucho antes de la fiesta. Desde muchísimo antes. Su cuerpo era un tesoro que su alma de libertino había codiciado desde siempre, aunque no lo hubiera admitido.

Pero esa noche sería suya. Más aún, esa noche ella se entregaría por entero, sin reservas. Si iban a tener un futuro juntos, no tenía sentido fingir ser alguien que no era; fingir que no iba a mostrarse exigente, que no iba a hacerle demandas en ese terreno.

La reacción que ella mostrara era otro cantar, aunque era bien cierto que nunca la había visto acobardarse ante nada.

En lo profundo de su corazón, supo que podía pedirle cualquier cosa y que ella se lo entregaría, de forma consciente y a manos llenas. Además, en última instancia, él jamás podría hacerle daño. Y Portia lo sabía tan bien como él.

Recorrió con los labios la tersa piel de su vientre y notó cómo ella contenía la respiración y se removía, inquieta. Le inmovilizó las caderas con las manos y siguió descendiendo al tiempo que le separaba los muslos con los hombros.

Y ella imaginó cuál era su destino. Le enterró los dedos en el pelo. La sintió tomar aire mientras bajaba la cabeza y rozaba esa suave carne con los labios.

—¡Simon!

Pronunció su nombre con un grito desgarrado que le

abrasó el alma. Comenzó a lamer, a explorar y a saborearla. En un principio, se mostró cauto y chupó con delicadeza, pero no pasó mucho antes de que su exploración se hiciera más y más explícita. Se fue mojando mientras él disfrutaba del festín. El sabor de su deseo era como miel para su paladar, dulce pero con un toque excitante. Localizó el punto que le daría más placer, tenso ya por el deseo, y succionó con suavidad. Estaba totalmente entregado a ella, pendiente de la menor reacción que mostrara.

Fue guiándola paso a paso. La llevó al límite con paciencia hasta que notó que lo aferraba con fuerza del pelo, alzaba las caderas y se rendía sin necesidad de palabras. Bajó un poco y la abrió para explorar la entrada de su cuerpo. Acto seguido y con total deliberación, la penetró muy lentamente con la lengua.

El placer la atravesó en ese instante y le arrancó un grito. Un grito que a él le supo a gloria. Saboreó cada uno de sus estremecimientos, pero en cuanto llegaron a su fin, se movió para quedar sobre ella. Tras separarle los muslos aún más, apoyó todo el peso en las manos que había colocado a ambos lados de su cabeza y llevó la punta de su miembro hasta los húmedos pliegues de su sexo.

Buscó la entrada, probó un poco... y se hundió definitivamente en su interior.

Portia gritó y se arqueó bajo él. No se detuvo, sino que la penetró aún más al tiempo que intentaba asimilar las sensaciones que lo asaltaban. La abrasadora humedad que se rendía bajo su asalto y lo iba rodeando poco a poco, estrechándolo con fuerza. La estrechez de esa carne que se cerraba en torno a él con su delicioso calor. Luchó denodadamente para saborearlo todo, pero sin dejarse llevar, sin dejar que sus instintos más atávicos se salieran con la suya. Más tarde podría tomar a su antojo, una vez que ella lo comprendiera, una vez que ella accediera.

Portia estaba muy quieta bajo él. Puesto que tenía la cabeza apoyada contra la suya, sentía cada uno de sus jadeos junto a la oreja. Su cuerpo se había cerrado en torno a su miembro y escuchaba los desbocados latidos de su corazón. Con todos los músculos tensos por el abrumador impulso de moverse en su interior, alzó la cabeza y la miró a la cara.

Tenía los párpados entornados y, bajo ellos, bajo el negro encaje de sus pestañas, le brillaban los ojos. Lo miraban echando chispas. Sus labios, hinchados y entreabiertos, se crisparon un poco. La vio tomar aire.

—Creí que habías prometido que nunca me harías daño.

No fue una acusación en toda regla, si bien estuvo acompañada de una leve mueca de dolor. Para su inmenso alivio, notó que comenzaba a relajarse bajo él y que la tensión provocada por la instintiva reacción defensiva ante su invasión remitía.

Inclinó la cabeza, le rozó los labios con los suyos y le dio un beso fugaz.

—Creo que... —murmuró al tiempo que se movía un poco en su interior— no tardarás en descubrir que es un dolor efímero.

Volvió a alzarse sobre ella y, sin dejar de mirarla a los ojos, se retiró un poco antes de volver a introducirse en ella.

Portia parpadeó.

—Haz eso otra vez.

Habría sonreído de buena gana, pero no podía. Tenía los músculos de la cara demasiado tensos a causa del deseo. La obedeció mientras dejaba escapar el aire al ver que ni su expresión ni su cuerpo volvían a tensarse.

Mientras lo miraba a la cara, Portia luchaba por asimilar la sensación de tenerlo en su interior, la sensación de plenitud que la embargaba. Ni en sus sueños más atrevidos había imaginado que la intimidad, la entrega de su cuerpo, la sensación de que él la poseyera, sería tan poderosa.

Ni que sería tan trascendental y devastadora en un sentido mucho más elemental.

Aunque en esos momentos no podía pararse a examinarlo. Ni su cuerpo ni el de Simon se lo permitirían. Ambos estaban listos y tensos. Aunque no tenía ni la menor idea de para qué...

Le había quitado las manos de los hombros para aferrarlo con todas sus fuerzas por los brazos. Apartó una y la alzó hasta su rostro para apartarle un mechón de cabello que le caía sobre una mejilla. Lo instó a inclinar la cabeza hacia ella.

Separó los labios, en clara invitación a que la tomara, a que le enseñara más, de la única forma que sabía.

Simon se apoderó de su boca y le acarició la lengua con la suya. La retiró al mismo tiempo que lo hacía su miembro y volvió a introducirla justo cuando se hundía en ella, imitando los movimientos.

El ritmo prosiguió hasta atraparla, hasta que llegó la marea de sensaciones que ya conocía, pero en esa ocasión él la acompañaba. Su cuerpo, que a esas alturas había escapado a su control, lo siguió por instinto y se movió hasta que el fuego la rodeó; hasta que las llamas le rozaron la piel; hasta que se le derritieron los huesos y su cuerpo se convirtió en una hoguera donde él se hundía cada vez más rápido, más hondo, con más ímpetu, avivando las llamas y marcándola con su impronta.

Sus sentidos se desbocaron y se dejó llevar por el momento. Jamás se había sentido tan viva. Jamás había sido tan consciente de sí misma, ni de él. De sus cuerpos unidos, entregándose y recibiendo a la vez. Sudorosos y enfebrecidos mientras se frotaban, se acariciaban, se rozaban. De sus alientos mezclados, mientras sus corazones latían al unísono. De sus cuerpos entregados plenamente hacia el mismo fin.

Se lanzó a las llamas y dejó que la pasión la bañara, encantada de verse inmersa en el infierno de su mutuo deseo. Jadeante y aferrada a él, se atrevió a atizar la hoguera hasta que las llamas se alzaron un poco más. Hasta que se convirtieron en una columna de fuego que los arrastró a las alturas mientras los consumía y reducía a cenizas cualquier asomo de pensamiento racional. La abrasadora sensación los recorrió por entero mientras las llamas les lamían la piel. Siguieron inmersos en la danza, desesperados y jadeantes, con los corazones desbocados.

Le clavó los dedos con fuerza. Simon alzó la cabeza, inspiró hondo, como ella, y la miró a los ojos.

—Hazme un favor.

Descubrió que apenas podía hablar.

—¿Cuál?

—Rodéame las caderas con las piernas.

Quiso saber la razón, pero decidió limitarse a obedecerlo y conocer la respuesta de primera mano.

La nueva posición le permitió hundirse en ella aún más e hizo que sus movimientos ganaran en ritmo y en fuerza. Hasta el punto que creyó sentirlo en el corazón. Se arqueó bajo él, lo apretó con fuerza con los muslos y se escuchó gritar mientras sus sentidos se fragmentaban; no como antes, sino de una forma más poderosa que los convirtió en destellantes pedacitos de gloria.

Sintió que Simon se detenía, aún enterrado en ella, y al instante estuvo a su lado en ese torbellino de placer que los inundó con su energía, y que resultaba agotador y estimulante. Y que a la postre acabó por derretirlos.

Sus cuerpos, acalorados y sudorosos, se derritieron al tiempo que la tremenda explosión de deleite les derretía el alma.

Se había preguntado en muchas ocasiones por lo que sucedía, pero ninguna conjetura la había preparado para algo así.

Para el peso de Simon sobre ella; para los atronadores latidos de sus corazones; para el goce que aún les corría por las venas; para la pasión que aún palpitaba bajo la piel.

Por fin pasó. La violenta tormenta amainó y los dejó exhaustos, flotando en las olas de alguna isla desierta.

Sólo ellos eran reales. El resto del mundo dejó de existir.

Extenuada, siguió tendida bajo él. Estaba atónita, pero contenta. Simon giró la cabeza. Sus alientos se mezclaron y, al momento, se besaron. Lentamente. Sin apartarse el uno del otro ni un milímetro.

—Gracias.

Su aliento le rozó la mejilla. Alzó una mano para apartarle el pelo de la cara y lo acarició. Pasó la mano por los poderosos músculos de su torso, por los estilizados músculos de su espalda.

—No, soy yo la que tiene que darte las gracias.

Por instruirla. Por dejarla ver... tal vez más de lo que a él le habría gustado.

Había estado en lo cierto. Había algo especial entre ellos, algo por lo que merecía la pena luchar. Aunque todavía le quedaba muchísimo por aprender...

Simon la besó en los labios antes de respirar hondo y salir de ella. El cambio fue impactante. La diferencia de las sensaciones, de lo que sentía teniéndolo dentro y lo que sentía cuando la dejó, fue tremenda.

Él se apartó y se dejó caer en el colchón, a su lado. Alzó un brazo con evidente esfuerzo y la acercó a su costado antes de abrazarla.

—Duérmete. Tendrás que regresar a tu habitación antes de que amanezca. Te despertaré a tiempo.

Sonrió y se mordió la lengua para no confesarle que estaba deseando que llegara ese momento, que la despertara... Dio media vuelta y se acurrucó contra él, de espaldas a su costado. Nunca había dormido con un hombre, pero dormir con él le pareció lo más natural del mundo. Lo más normal.

Lo que estaba escrito.

El amanecer llegó demasiado pronto.

Fue ligeramente consciente del momento en el que Simon se apartó de su lado y su peso abandonó el colchón. Refunfuñó mientras se daba la vuelta y aferraba las sábanas y la colcha para arrebujarse entre ellas, rodearse con su calor, y volver a zambullirse en el delicioso sueño.

Estaba flotando, exhausta y contenta, en un mar cálido y plácido cuando una mano se cerró con fuerza sobre su hombro y la zarandeó.

—Vamos... Despierta. Está clareando.

Abrir un ojo supuso un considerable esfuerzo. Lo miró y vio que se inclinaba sobre ella completamente vestido. Había luz suficiente como para distinguir el color de sus ojos y percatarse de su semblante preocupado.

Sonrió, cerró el ojo y alzó una mano para agarrarlo por la solapa.

—Nadie se levantará hasta dentro de unas horas. —Tiró de él—. Vuelve aquí. —Esbozó una sonrisa mientras los recuerdos acudían en tropel a su mente—. Quiero aprender más.

Él dejó escapar un suspiro. Un largo suspiro. Acto seguido, le cogió la mano que lo tenía sujeto por la solapa... y, sin muchos miramientos, le dio un tirón que la sacó de su cálido refugio.

—¿¡Qué...!? —exclamó, abriendo los ojos de par en par.

Simon la tomó por ambas muñecas y tiró de ella hasta dejarla de rodillas sobre el colchón.

—Tienes que vestirte y regresar a tu habitación antes de que los criados estén por todas partes.

Sin darle tiempo a protestar, le pasó la camisola por la cabeza. Ella alzó los brazos para que se la pusiera sin que los delicados tirantes sufrieran daño en el proceso y después tiró del bajo hasta que estuvo en su sitio. No le extrañó que frunciera el ceño y lo mirara echando chispas por los ojos.

—Esto no es lo que esperaba.

La observó sin hacer nada, aunque le costó la misma vida contener una sonrisa.

—Ya me he dado cuenta. —Tensó la mandíbula—. De todos modos, nuestra estancia aquí sólo durará dos días más y no vamos a causar ningún escándalo mientras tanto. —Le arrojó el vestido.

Ella lo cogió, ladeó la cabeza y lo observó con detenimiento.

—Ya que sólo nos quedan dos días, ¿no sería más sensato...?

—No. —Titubeó un instante mientras estudiaba su

expresión antes de añadir—: Podremos continuar con tus lecciones esta noche. —Dio media vuelta y se sentó en la cama para ponerse las botas—. No esperes aprender nada nuevo hasta entonces.

Se puso el vestido mientras meditaba, a todas luces, acerca de sus palabras. Gateó por la cama hasta llegar al borde, donde se sentó para ponerse las medias.

—¿Por qué tenemos que esperar hasta la noche? —le preguntó por fin.

Su tono denotaba una curiosidad genuina, pero también encerraba cierta inseguridad. Emociones que no le pasaron desapercibidas. Sus ojos se clavaron en ella y su cuerpo se tensó cuando la vio extender sin atisbo de malicia una larguísima pierna que quedó cubierta por una media.

Parpadeó al tiempo que se esforzaba por recordar la pregunta. Lo consiguió a duras penas. Alzó la vista hasta su rostro y buscó su mirada. Sus instintos le decían que sorteara la pregunta, que diera un rodeo.

Ella enarcó las cejas, a la espera de una respuesta.

Con la mandíbula apretada, se puso en pie y le tendió la mano para ayudarla a bajar de la cama. Ella se inclinó para ponerse los escarpines.

—Tu cuerpo... —Comenzó mientras le miraba la coronilla—. Necesitas un poco de tiempo para recuperarte. —Portia alzó la cabeza y parpadeó, decidida a refutar sus palabras—. Confía en mí, lo necesitas. —La empujó hasta la puerta.

Para su inmenso alivio, se dejó llevar, aunque todavía seguía meditando. Se detuvo al llegar a la puerta. La rodeó con un brazo para aferrar el picaporte, pero en ese instante ella se giró, apoyó el hombro contra su pecho y le acarició un pómulo con la yema de un dedo.

Sus miradas se encontraron.

—No soy lo que se dice una delicada florecilla. No voy a romperme.

Sin dejar de mirarla, él replicó:

—Y yo no ando lo que se dice corto de atributos y

tampoco voy a mostrarme delicado. —Inclinó la cabeza y le dio un beso fugaz—. Confía en mí. Esta noche, pero no antes.

Ella lo besó en respuesta y suspiró contra sus labios.

—De acuerdo.

Simon aferró el picaporte y abrió la puerta.

E insistió en acompañarla hasta su habitación. Para llegar hasta ella tendrían que atravesar el ala principal de un extremo a otro. Era la parte más antigua de la mansión y albergaba numerosos gabinetes, muchos de los cuales servían de antesala a otras estancias. Utilizó esa ruta para evitar la presencia de las fregonas, las criadas de menor rango, que a esa hora se afanaban de un lado a otro por los pasillos principales.

Estaban a punto de llegar al ala este a través de un pasillo rara vez usado, cuando Portia echó un vistazo al exterior a través de un ventanal emplomado y se detuvo. Le dio un tirón para detenerlo cuando hizo ademán de proseguir y se acercó aún más a la ventana.

Miró por encima de su cabeza y vio lo que le había llamado la atención.

Kitty, ataviada con un salto de cama que hacía bien poco por ocultar sus encantos, estaba de pie en el prado a plena vista, hablando con Arturo y Dennis mientras gesticulaba.

Tiró de Portia para alejarla del ventanal. Kitty estaba de espaldas a ellos, pero cualquiera de los dos hombres podría verlos si alzaba la vista.

Ella lo miró a los ojos y meneó la cabeza como si el comportamiento de Kitty le resultara incomprensible, tras lo cual se dejó llevar a su habitación.

Cuando llegaron a la puerta, le dio un beso fugaz en los nudillos a modo de despedida y la instó a entrar. En cuanto hubo cerrado la puerta, emprendió el regreso a su habitación.

Las risillas sofocadas de un par de doncellas lo obligaron a tomar las escaleras del ala este. Un camino hasta cierto punto seguro porque podría acortar por la planta baja del ala principal y llegar al ala oeste por la escalinata. Cuando dobló la esquina tras bajar las escaleras...

—Vaya, vaya... ¿Qué tenemos aquí?

Se detuvo en seco y dio media vuelta. Kitty estaba tras él, aferrándose el escote de la bata mientras lo atravesaba con su mirada. Abrió los ojos de par en par cuando comprendió lo que sucedía y, después, lo recorrió de arriba abajo con expresión maliciosa.

Simon soltó un juramento para sus adentros. Llevaba la misma ropa que la noche anterior.

Kitty alzó la vista. A su rostro asomaba una expresión ladina y un tanto desabrida.

—Un poquito tarde para abandonar la cama de la señorita Ashford, pero no hay duda de que estabas tan entretenido que te distrajiste por completo.

Su voz destilaba la furia de una mujer despechada. La había rechazado en numerosas ocasiones, y el malévolo brillo de su mirada sugería que recordaba muy bien cada una de ellas.

—No tanto como para creer que la visita de los gitanos a la señora de la casa al amanecer es producto de mi imaginación.

Kitty se quedó lívida antes de ruborizarse. Por la furia, que no por la culpabilidad. Abrió la boca, lo miró a los ojos... y decidió que sería mejor no decir lo que tenía en la punta de la lengua. Con una mirada furibunda, se arrebujó con la bata y comenzó a subir las escaleras.

Con los ojos entrecerrados, Simon la observó mientras se alejaba. Sus instintos le advirtieron del peligro con un escalofrío que le recorrió la espalda. Las pisadas se desvanecieron. Dio media vuelta y echó a andar hacia el ala oeste.

—¿Les apetecería cabalgar esta mañana? —preguntó Cecily Hammond mientras observaba a los comensales reunidos en torno a la mesa del desayuno con una expresión esperanzada en sus ojos azules.

Todos los presentes sabían cuál era su deseo en realidad: que el improvisado plan, trazado en ausencia de Kitty, los ayudara a evitar su presencia al menos durante la mañana.

James miró a Simon.

—No veo por qué no.

—Una idea estupenda —replicó Charlie. Su mirada recorrió a todos los presentes: Lucy, Annabelle, Desmond, Winifred, Oswald, Swanston y ella—. ¿Adónde podríamos ir?

Se hicieron numerosas sugerencias. En el fragor de la discusión, Portia bajó la vista al plato. Y observó la ingente cantidad de comida que estaba devorando. Por regla general, tenía un apetito excelente; esa mañana estaba tan famélica que podría comerse un caballo.

Aunque no se veía capaz de subirse a lomos de uno... Al menos, no durante una buena temporada.

Aparte de las molestias (los pequeños pinchazos y dolorcillos que había pasado por alto en un primer momento, pero que habían empeorado hasta hacerse notar), si cabalgar iba a empeorar su estado hasta el punto de verse obligada a posponer su cita nocturna... Prefería no cabalgar a verse privada de la lección que la aguardaba esa noche.

De la oportunidad que le brindaba para ahondar en su investigación. Cosa que estaba decidida a hacer.

Los demás acordaron cabalgar rumbo al sur, por la antigua vía romana que llevaba a Badbury Rings donde podrían ver los restos del castro de la Edad de Hierro. Jugueteó con lo que quedaba de su desayuno (arroz cocido, pescado ahumado y huevos duros) mientras buscaba una excusa plausible.

—Quiero sacar mis caballos para que den una vuelta —estaba diciéndole Simon a James—. Están a punto de comerse el uno al otro; después del ajetreo de estos últimos meses, la inactividad no les sienta bien. —La miró desde el otro lado de la mesa—. ¿Te gustaría acompañarme en el tílburi?

Parpadeó y se dio cuenta (como ya lo había hecho él) de que aparte de lady O, quien no estaba presente para escucharlos, nadie sabía que adoraba cabalgar. Por tanto, a nadie le extrañaría que eligiera el tílburi en lugar de un caballo.

—Sí, gracias. —Se removió en la silla y comprendió que Simon debía de saber lo que le sucedía. Bajó la vista al plato antes de que la viera ruborizarse—. Prefiero ir sentada y contemplar el paisaje.

No lo miró para comprobar si sonreía. Notó el momento exacto en el que su mirada la abandonaba antes de entablar una conversación con James.

Un cuarto de hora más tarde, se reunieron en el vestíbulo del jardín desde donde partieron en dirección a los establos. Decidir las monturas y las guarniciones les llevó un buen rato. Ella se entretuvo tranquilizando a la pequeña yegua castaña mientras enganchaban los bayos de Simon al tílburi.

Cuando estuvieron preparados, fue a por ella. De camino a la salida, la miró con una ceja enarcada.

—¿Estás lista?

Lo miró a los ojos y se percató de la preocupación que había en ellos. Le dio la mano al tiempo que le ofrecía una fugaz sonrisa.

—Sí.

Una vez que salieron, la acompañó hasta el tílburi y la ayudó a subir. Después, hizo lo propio antes de sentarse a su lado y gritarle a James:

—¡Os veremos por el camino!

James, que todavía estaba supervisando las monturas de las damas, les hizo un gesto de despedida con la mano. El mozo que sostenía las riendas de los bayos se retiró de un salto. Simon hizo restallar el látigo con un florido movimiento y los caballos se pusieron en marcha.

No hablaron. No necesitaban hacerlo. Se entregó de buena gana a la contemplación del paisaje, ávida por conocer una parte del condado que hasta entonces no había visto. Más allá de los inmensos árboles de Cranborne

Chase, el camino estaba flanqueado por algún que otro hayal que rompía la monotonía de los brezales. Simon permitió que los caballos avanzaran a placer durante un trecho antes de refrenarlos hasta que adoptaron un agradable trote. El resto del grupo, que cabalgaba campo a través, los alcanzó cuando estaban a punto de llegar a su destino. Rodearon el tílburi y siguieron en grupo, charlando e intercambiando bromas y chistes.

A su alrededor, la mañana era gloriosa. El cielo era de un azul intenso y el sol brillaba con fuerza. La ligera brisa bastaba para despejar a cualquiera. Disfrutaron mucho explorando las ruinas, trepando y descendiendo por las tres murallas concéntricas de tierra apisonada que conformaban el antiguo castro. Todos se mostraron encantados de haberse librado de la tensión que se respiraba en Glossup Hall. Todos y cada uno de ellos hicieron un gran esfuerzo por mostrar su faceta más afable y encantadora..., incluso Oswald y Swanston.

Entretanto, era muy consciente del hecho de que Simon observaba, de que estaba muy pendiente de ella. Ya estaba acostumbrada a ese tipo de comportamiento por su parte. Antes siempre la había sacado de quicio, pero en esa ocasión... mientras paseaba junto a Winifred y Lucy, disfrutando de la brisa procedente del lejano mar y consciente de su mirada a pesar de que él se encontraba a cierta distancia, se sintió cuidada, para su total asombro. Protegida.

Había algo muy distinto en su actitud.

Intrigada, se detuvo y dejó que las otras dos mujeres se adelantaran antes de darse la vuelta y mirar en dirección al lugar donde se encontraba Simon, que escuchaba la discusión que mantenían James y Charlie. Él enfrentó su mirada desde el otro lado de las dos murallas. Se sacó las manos de los bolsillos y echó a andar hacia ella.

Sabía que estaba estudiando su expresión mientras se acercaba. Se detuvo al llegar a su lado, ocultándola a los ojos de los demás, y sin apartar la mirada de sus ojos le preguntó:

—¿Estás bien?

Tardó un momento en contestarle. Estaba demasiado ocupada interpretando, o más bien saboreando, la expresión que asomaba a sus ojos. No a su rostro, que como siempre mostraba una expresión arrogante. Su mirada era más tierna, su preocupación había tomado un cariz diferente, se había transformado en algo distinto a lo que había sido hasta el momento.

La imagen la enterneció. La alegría brotó desde el fondo de su corazón hasta inundarla por completo.

Sonrió al tiempo que asentía con la cabeza.

—Sí. Perfectamente.

Escucharon un grito procedente del lugar donde Oswald y Swanston se habían enzarzado en una fingida lucha para divertimento de las Hammond. Colocó una mano en el brazo de Simon y ensanchó la sonrisa antes de decirle:

—Vamos, demos un paseo.

Él la complació y adaptó el paso al suyo. Las palabras eran superfluas. Ni siquiera necesitaban de las miradas para mantener el vínculo que los unía. Con la vista clavada en el horizonte, percibió el delicado roce de ese vínculo, sintió que su corazón se henchía como si quisiera acomodarlo. ¿Eso era lo que sucedía? ¿Un vínculo que crecía entre dos personas y que se convertía en un canal de entendimiento ajeno al plano físico?

Fuera lo que fuese, era especial, precioso. Lo miró de soslayo, a sabiendas de que él también lo sentía. Y no parecía estar luchando contra él ni negándolo. Se preguntó en qué estaría pensando.

Tras una hora de placeres sencillos y de mutuo y cordial acuerdo, regresaron a por los caballos y el tílburi con evidente renuencia y emprendieron el camino de regreso a la mansión.

Llegaron a tiempo para el almuerzo. A tiempo para presenciar una nueva muestra de la petulancia de Kitty. El distendido ambiente matinal se desvaneció en un abrir y cerrar de ojos.

Los lugares que debían ocupar los comensales no se habían fijado, de modo que Simon reclamó la silla contigua a la de Portia, se sentó, comió y observó. La mayor parte de los invitados hizo lo mismo. Si Kitty hubiera tenido dos dedos de frente, habría notado el distanciamiento, el recelo, y habría actuado en consonancia.

En cambio, su estado de ánimo parecía uno de los peores hasta el momento y su actitud oscilaba entre el enfurruñamiento por no haber participado en la excursión matinal y la chispeante alegría que le iluminó los ojos... Como si estuviera a punto de suceder algo importantísimo que sólo ella sabía.

—¡Caray! Hemos estado muchas veces en las ruinas, querida —le recordó su madre—. No me cabe duda de que habría sido agotador verlas de nuevo.

—Cierto —convino Kitty—, pero...

—Claro que —la interrumpió la señora Buckstead, que miraba a su hija, sentada al lado de las Hammond, con una sonrisa— las más jóvenes necesitan disfrutar del aire libre.

Kitty la miró echando chispas por los ojos.

—Winifred...

—Y, por supuesto, una vez casada, las excursiones matinales pierden todo su atractivo. —Imperturbable, la señora Buckstead se sirvió un poco más de sorbete de espárragos.

Kitty se quedó sin palabras por un instante, aunque no tardó en dirigir su mirada al otro extremo de la mesa. Hacia Portia. Ajena a ello, ésta siguió comiendo con la vista clavada en su plato y una sonrisa velada (a pesar de su sutileza dejaba bien claro que había entendido las palabras de la señora Buckstead) pero innegable en los labios.

Kitty abrió la boca y entrecerró los ojos.

En ese instante, él extendió un brazo hacia la copa de vino. Kitty se distrajo y enfrentó su mirada. Se retaron el uno al otro mientras él bebía y volvía a dejar la copa en la mesa... permitiendo que Kitty leyera en sus ojos lo que haría en caso de que se atreviera a pagar con Portia los celos que la invadían. En caso de que hiciera la menor alusión a los placeres nocturnos que sospechaba que habían disfrutado Portia y él.

A punto estuvo de decir algo, aunque la cordura acabó ganando la batalla. Inspiró hondo y bajó la vista a su plato.

En otro lugar de la mesa, la señora Archer, ajena al parecer al desliz de su hija menor, hablaba con el señor Buckstead. Lord Glossup estaba enzarzado en una conversación con Ambrose mientras que lady O charlaba con su esposa mostrando un absoluto desinterés por el resto de la concurrencia.

Otras conversaciones comenzaron a surgir poco a poco, a medida que el silencio de Kitty se alargaba. Lady Calvin reclamó la atención de James y Charlie; Desmond y Winifred intentaron entablar conversación con Drusilla.

Él intercambió un par de comentarios intrascendentes con Annabelle Hammond, sentada a su otro lado; sin embargo, su mente trabajaba a toda prisa. Kitty carecía de discreción. ¿Quién sabía en qué momento se sentiría lo bastante amenazada como para decir algo? Si lo hacía...

Acabó de comer, pero se demoró en la mesa. En cuanto Portia soltó el tenedor, extendió una mano y le acarició la muñeca con un dedo.

Ella lo miró de reojo, con la ceja alzada.

—Vamos a dar un paseo. —La expresión de perplejidad de Portia se hizo más evidente. Comprendió al punto el rumbo que habían tomado sus pensamientos. Esbozó una sonrisa mientras le dejaba clara su intención—: Quiero hablar contigo.

De un tema que, gracias a Kitty, no podía dejar en el aire por más tiempo sin correr riesgos.

Portia estudió su expresión y comprendió que hablaba en serio. Con franca curiosidad, asintió con la cabeza. Se llevó la servilleta a los labios y murmuró:

—No creo que sea nada fácil poder escabullirnos sin que se den cuenta.

En eso estaba en lo cierto. Aunque gran parte de los

invitados había abandonado la mesa a esas alturas y se había dispersado para pasar la tarde cada cual a su placer, Annabelle, Cecily y Lucy esperaban que Portia tomara la iniciativa para seguir su ejemplo. Musitó una disculpa para zafarse de jugar una partida de billar con James y Charlie y siguió a las cuatro jóvenes hacia la terraza mientras se preguntaba cómo despistar a tres de ellas.

Se había detenido en el vano de la puerta para considerar varias opciones que no tardó en descartar, cuando escuchó un golpe a su espalda. Se giró al tiempo de ver que lady O llegaba a su lado. Lo tomó del brazo que le había ofrecido de forma instintiva.

La anciana alzó la vista hacia las cuatro jóvenes reunidas junto a la balaustrada. Meneó la cabeza.

—No lo conseguirás.

Antes de que pudiera encontrar una réplica adecuada, ella le zarandeó el brazo.

—Acompáñame... Quiero sentarme en el jardín de los setos. —Sus labios esbozaban una sonrisa particularmente maliciosa—. Parece ser el lugar indicado para enterarse de un sinfín de cosas.

Asumiendo que tenía algún plan en mente, Simon la complació. Atravesaron la terraza y la ayudó cuando llegaron a los escalones. Lady O se detuvo en seco al llegar al prado. Dio media vuelta e hizo un gesto en dirección a Portia y sus acompañantes.

—¡Portia! ¿Podrías traerme mi sombrilla, querida?

Los ojos de Portia habían estado clavados en ellos todo el tiempo.

—Sí, por supuesto.

Se disculpó con las demás y entró en la mansión.

Lady O dio media vuelta y reanudó el paseo.

Estaba ayudándola a acomodarse en un banco de hierro forjado emplazado bajo las extensas ramas de un magnolio cuando Portia se acercó a ellos.

Miró hacia la copa del árbol.

—No creo que necesite esto después de todo.

—Da igual. Ha cumplido su propósito. —La anciana

cogió la sombrilla, se arregló las profusas faldas y se reclinó en el banco con los ojos cerrados—. Podéis marcharos, los dos.

Simon miró a Portia, que abrió los ojos de par en par mientras se encogía de hombros.

Dieron media vuelta.

—Da la casualidad —dijo lady O— de que el jardín tiene otra salida. —Cuando se giraron, vieron que había entreabierto los ojos y que señalaba con el bastón—. Ese sendero. Si no me falla la memoria, llega hasta el lago después de rodear la rosaleda.

Volvió a cerrar los ojos.

Y él volvió a mirar a Portia.

Ella sonrió y regresó hasta el banco para darle un beso a la anciana en la mejilla.

—Gracias. Volveremos den...

—Soy perfectamente capaz de regresar sola a la casa si me apetece. —Abrió los ojos un poco y los fulminó con su mirada de basilisco—. Marchaos... No tenéis por qué apresurar vuestro regreso. —Al ver que no la obedecían de inmediato, alzó el bastón y la sombrilla al mismo tiempo y los ahuyentó sin miramientos—. ¡Fuera! ¡Fuera!

La obedecieron conteniendo la risa.

—Es incorregible —dijo Portia.

Sus miradas se entrelazaron mientras se agachaban para pasar bajo el arco que llevaba a la rosaleda.

—Tengo la sensación de que siempre lo ha sido.

Extendió un brazo para tomarla de la mano y entrelazar los dedos. No tardaron en dejar atrás la rosaleda e internarse en los jardines más agrestes situados sobre el lago. Poco después, se detuvieron cuando el sendero llegó a la cima de la pequeña loma que dominaba el lago. Echó un vistazo. No había un alma a la vista.

—Vamos. —La guió camino abajo en dirección al otro camino, bastante más ancho, que bordeaba el lago.

Ella se acomodó a su paso. Caminaban con las manos entrelazadas. Estaba bastante seguro de que nadie elegiría ese camino en concreto, al menos durante un buen rato.

Cuando dejaron atrás el mirador, ella lo miró de reojo. No le fue complicado adivinar la pregunta que le rondaba la cabeza, pero ella, en lugar de preguntarle adónde iban, fue directa al grano.

—¿De qué quieres hablar?

El momento de la verdad había llegado, para los dos. Aunque sabía lo que debía decir, no estaba seguro de cómo hacerlo. Gracias a Kitty, no había tenido tiempo para planear lo que, en realidad, era el acontecimiento crucial en su campaña para conseguir que Portia fuera su esposa.

—Me encontré con Kitty esta mañana, cuando te dejé en tu habitación. —La miró de reojo y ella lo miró a su vez, con los ojos desorbitados—. Se puede decir que ha sumado dos más dos.

Portia arrugó la nariz antes de adoptar una expresión pensativa. Frunció el ceño.

—De modo que puede ocasionarnos problemas.

—Eso depende. Está tan absorta en sus juegos que sólo atacará y nos mencionará si se siente provocada.

—Quizá debería hablar con ella.

Se detuvo.

—¡No! Eso no es lo que...

Ella también se detuvo mientras su expresión se tornaba interrogante.

Simon apartó la mirada hacia el camino y escuchó una voz femenina muy aguda que flotaba desde los jardines situados justo encima. Habían llegado al pinar. Desde allí partía un serpenteante sendero que se internaba entre los pinos. La agarró con más fuerza de la mano y la instó a reanudar la marcha.

Sólo se detuvo cuando estuvieron rodeados por los altos árboles, ocultos por la delicada sombra de sus copas. Totalmente resguardados de cualquier mirada curiosa.

En ese momento, la soltó y se giró para enfrentarla.

Ella lo observó y aguardó con evidente curiosidad.

Pasó por alto la opresión que sentía en el pecho, tomó aire y buscó esa mirada azul cobalto.

—Quiero casarme contigo.

11

Portia parpadeó antes de mirarlo con los ojos desorbitados.

—¿Qué has dicho?

Su voz sonaba un tanto extraña.

Simon apretó los dientes.

—Ya me has oído. —Cuando ella continuó mirándolo totalmente perpleja, repitió—: Quiero casarme contigo.

Portia parecía no dar crédito.

—¿Cuándo tomaste la decisión? ¿Y por qué? ¡Por el amor de Dios!

Simon titubeó un instante mientras intentaba responder.

—Kitty. Estuvo a punto de irse de la lengua durante el almuerzo. En algún momento, lo hará... Será incapaz de resistirse. Ya había estado considerando la idea de casarme y si espero a que Kitty hable, lo verás como una salida al escándalo y no quiero que eso suceda.

Con cualquier otra mujer, dejar que Kitty creara un escándalo y proponerle matrimonio después habría sido una manera más que aceptable de afrontar la situación, pero no con Portia. Ella jamás aceptaría una proposición nacida de la imposición social.

—¿Que ya estabas pensando en casarte? ¿Conmigo? —Aún tenía esa expresión estupefacta en el rostro—. ¿Por qué?

La miró con el ceño fruncido.

—A estas alturas creía que era más que evidente.

—Para mí no. ¿De qué, exactamente, estás hablando?

—Estoy seguro de que no se te ha olvidado que has pasado toda la noche en mi cama.

—Tienes toda la razón, no se me ha olvidado. Como tampoco se me ha olvidado que te expliqué, de modo que no te quedara la menor duda al respecto, que mi interés en tales menesteres era puramente académico.

—Eso era antes —replicó él, sin dejar de mirarla—. Esto es ahora. Las cosas han cambiado. —Pasó un instante antes de que le preguntara—: ¿Vas a negarlo?

No podía hacerlo; sin embargo, ese repentino interés por el matrimonio, como si la cuestión siempre hubiera estado allí, implícita, hizo que se sintiera acorralada. Paralizada, sin saber hacia dónde correr, estupefacta, sorprendida, totalmente fuera de sí.

Como no respondió de inmediato, Simon prosiguió:

—Aparte de todo eso, tu participación en los... menesteres de la noche no tenía nada de académica.

Se ruborizó y levantó la cabeza. ¿Por qué diantres había elegido esa táctica? Intentó poner en orden sus caóticas ideas.

—Ésa no es razón suficiente para creer que debamos casarnos.

Fue el turno de Simon de abrir los ojos de par en par.

—¿¡Qué!? —exclamó con tanta fuerza que dio un respingo. Después, se acercó a ella con paso amenazante—. Viniste a mi cama..., te entregaste a mí y ¿ni siquiera se te había pasado por la cabeza que tuviéramos que casarnos?

Sus rostros estaban apenas a un palmo; la perplejidad de Simon era genuina. Sostuvo su mirada sin flaquear.

—No, no lo esperaba. —No había profundizado tanto en sus deliberaciones.

Simon no respondió al punto, pero algo cambió en su expresión. Sus ojos se oscurecieron y sus facciones se endurecieron. Un músculo comenzó a palpitarle en la mandíbula.

—No esperabas... Pero ¿qué clase de hombre crees que soy?

Su voz se había convertido en un gruñido..., un gruñido furioso. Se acercó todavía más a ella, que a duras penas contuvo el impulso de retroceder. Con la espalda muy recta, le sostuvo la mirada mientras se preguntaba por qué se había enfurecido tanto de pronto; mientras se preguntaba si estaría fingiendo... Y mientras sentía que su temperamento estaba a punto de estallar.

—Eres un libertino —comenzó, enfatizando la última palabra—. Seduces a las mujeres; es algo inherente al oficio. Si te hubieras casado con cuanta mujer has seducido, tendrías que vivir en Arabia porque tendrías un harén. —Su voz sonaba con más fuerza y había adquirido el mismo tono beligerante que la de Simon—. Dado que sigues viviendo aquí, en esta civilizada isla, debo llegar a la correcta conclusión de que no te casas con cuanta mujer seduces.

Simon sonrió, aunque fue una mueca feroz.

—Tienes razón, no lo hago. Pero deberías revisar tus ideas acerca del... oficio, porque al igual que la mayoría de los libertinos jamás seduzco a vírgenes solteras de buena cuna. —Dio otro paso hacia ella y en esa ocasión Portia sí retrocedió—. Como es tu caso.

Tuvo que esforzarse para apartar la vista y era muy consciente de que respiraba de forma alterada.

—Pero sí me sedujiste.

Simon asintió con la cabeza y acortó la distancia que los separaba.

—Y tanto que te seduje... Porque tenía toda la intención de casarme contigo.

Su confesión la dejó boquiabierta y le arrancó un jadeo incrédulo. Sin embargo, no tardó en recuperar la compostura, levantar la barbilla y entrecerrar los ojos para fulminarlo con la mirada.

—¿Me has seducido porque tenías la intención de casarte conmigo?

Simon parpadeó y guardó silencio.

Y ella lo vio todo rojo.

—¿Qué me estás ocultando? —Le clavó un dedo en el pecho y él se apartó un poco—. ¿Tenías la intención de casarte conmigo? ¿Desde cuándo? —Extendió los brazos en un gesto de incredulidad—. ¿Cuándo lo decidiste exactamente?

Ni siquiera a ella se le escapaba la nota algo histérica y más que espantada de su voz. Había evaluado la amenaza, había sopesado el riesgo que suponía meterse en su cama, pero no había visto, ni reconocido, la verdadera amenaza, el verdadero riesgo.

Porque Simon se lo había ocultado.

—¡Tú...! —Intentó abofetearlo, pero él le aferró la mano—. ¡Me has engañado!

—¡No te he engañado! Fuiste tú la que se engañó a sí misma.

—¡Ja! Sea como sea... —dijo mientras forcejeaba para liberar su mano. Simon la soltó—. La verdad es que no me sedujiste: ¡fui yo quien se dejó! Quería hacerlo. Eso supone una gran diferencia.

—Tal vez, pero no cambia el resultado. Mantuvimos relaciones íntimas, fuera cual fuese el desencadenante.

—¡Tonterías! No voy a casarme contigo por eso. Tengo veinticuatro años. El hecho de que fuera una virgen de buena cuna no tiene la menor relevancia.

Simon la miró a los ojos.

—Sí que la tenía... y la tiene.

No le hizo falta decir que creía que el hecho en sí le otorgaba ciertos derechos. La verdad quedó suspendida entre ellos y su presencia resultó casi tangible.

Portia alzó la barbilla.

—Siempre supe que eras un déspota salido de la Edad Media. Me da igual, no pienso casarme contigo por esa razón.

—Y a mí me da igual la razón por la que te cases conmigo siempre que lo hagas.

—¿Por qué? —Ya lo había preguntado, pero él no le había dado una respuesta—. ¿Y cuándo decidiste que querías casarte conmigo? Quiero la verdad y la quiero ahora mismo.

Los ojos de Simon no se habían movido de su rostro; inspiró hondo y después soltó el aire muy despacio. Aparte de eso, ni su cara ni su cuerpo se relajaron un ápice.

—Lo decidí después del almuerzo campestre en el monasterio. Empecé a pensar en ello después de nuestro primer beso en la terraza.

Deseó no tenerlo tan cerca para poder rodearse el cuerpo con los brazos.

—Debes de haber besado a un millón de mujeres.

Sus labios esbozaron una sonrisa.

—A miles.

—Y ¿se supone que tengo que tragarme que después de un beso..., no, de dos besos, decidiste casarte conmigo?

Simon estuvo a punto de decirle que le importaba un comino lo que ella creyera, pero percibía que detrás de su furia se ocultaba un creciente pánico, un miedo atávico que comprendía a la perfección y que había intentado por todos los medios no despertar.

Estaba a un paso de estropearlo todo; podría llevarle meses, incluso años, recuperar a Portia.

—No sólo por eso.

Ella había apretado los dientes y lo miraba con la barbilla en alto.

—Entonces ¿por qué? —Sus ojos lo miraban con una expresión indescifrable.

Se apartó un poco más y no le sorprendió en absoluto que Portia aprovechara la oportunidad para cruzar los brazos por delante del pecho.

—Ya había decidido que quería esposa e hijos antes de abandonar Londres. Cuando te encontré aquí, me di cuenta de que nos complementamos a la perfección.

Ella parpadeó.

—¿Que nos complementamos? ¿Estás loco? Si somos... —Gesticuló mientras buscaba las palabras adecuadas. Bajó los brazos.

—¿Demasiado parecidos? —la ayudó.

—¡Exacto! —Abrió los ojos de par en par—. No somos lo que se dice compatibles...

—Piensa en lo que ha sucedido durante los últimos días. Piensa en lo de anoche. En lo que respecta al matrimonio, somos perfectamente compatibles. —Clavó los ojos en su rostro—. En cualquier aspecto que se te ocurra.

Portia se negó a ruborizarse. Simon lo estaba haciendo a propósito.

—Una noche... No puedes decir que sea una base sólida sobre la que cimentar semejante decisión. ¿Cómo puedes saber que la próxima vez no será... aburrida? —preguntó con un gesto de la mano.

Los ojos azules de Simon la atravesaron.

—Confía en mí. No lo será.

Había algo en su rostro, cierta acritud, cierta crueldad, desconocidas en él hasta ese momento. Sin apartar los ojos de su rostro, intentó desentenderse del aura de peligro que irradiaba.

—Tú... estás hablando en serio.

Le estaba costando un gran esfuerzo asumirlo. Un momento antes estaba siguiendo su meticulosa investigación sobre la atracción física del matrimonio y, en un abrir y cerrar de ojos, todo había cambiado y se encontraban discutiendo la posibilidad de casarse.

Simon alzó la cabeza y expulsó el aire entre dientes.

—¿Por qué te cuesta tanto creer que quiera casarme contigo? —Le preguntó mirando al cielo. Bajó la vista y preguntó con un gruñido malhumorado—: ¿Qué tiene de malo la idea de casarte conmigo?

—¿¡Que qué tiene de malo la idea de casarme contigo!? —Cuando se dio cuenta de que estaba gritando, intentó bajar el tono—. ¡Pues que nos haríamos la vida imposible! Tú eres un déspota, un tirano —dijo al tiempo que le daba un manotazo en el pecho—. ¡Un Cynster! Tú ordenas y esperas que todo el mundo te obedezca... ¡No, eso no es verdad! Tú asumes que todo el mundo va a obedecerte. Y ya sabes cómo soy yo. —Lo miró a los ojos en actitud desafiante—. No me avendré sin más a lo que dispongas... ¡No acataré tus órdenes sin rechistar!

Él la contemplaba con los labios apretados y los ojos entrecerrados. Esperó un instante antes de replicar:

—Y ¿qué?

Lo miró con los ojos como platos.

—Simon... No va a funcionar.

—Claro que sí. Funcionará.

Ése fue su turno de levantar la vista al cielo.

—¿Lo ves?

—Eso no es lo que te preocupa.

Bajó la cabeza para observarlo. Parpadeó. Esos tiernos ojos azules, tan engañosos como bien sabía ella, no ocultaban una naturaleza tierna, sólo una férrea determinación, una resolución inflexible, la acerada voluntad de un conquistador...

—¿A qué... a qué te refieres?

—Siempre he sabido lo que te preocupa de mí.

Portia sintió que algo se agitaba en su interior. Algo que se sacudió con fuerza. Sostuvo su mirada largo rato antes de animarse a preguntar:

—¿El qué?

Simon titubeó y ella supo que estaba pensando hasta dónde podía revelarle, hasta qué punto podía confesarle lo que sabía. Cuando habló, lo hizo en voz baja y controlada, aunque cortante.

—Tienes miedo de que intente controlarte, de que intente coartar tu independencia para convertirte en una mujer que no eres. Y de que sea lo bastante fuerte como para lograrlo.

Sus palabras le secaron la boca.

—Y ¿lo harás? ¿Lo intentarás, lo conseguirás?

—Desde luego que lo intentaré, al menos intentaré refrenar tus impulsos más alocados, pero no porque quiera hacerte cambiar, sino para protegerte. Te quiero por lo que eres, no por lo que no eres.

El peligro emocional al que se enfrentaba con él le provocó un nudo en la garganta.

—¿No lo dices por decir?

Simon era capaz de eso y de mucho más; acababa de demostrar que sabía más de lo que ella había creído, que la comprendía muchísimo mejor que ninguna otra persona. Y era cruel e implacable a la hora de conseguir lo que quería.

Y la quería a ella.

Tenía que creerlo, no le quedaba más opción.

Simon soltó el aire muy despacio y la miró a la cara. Su crispado semblante era un signo de que su temperamento era un ente muy real. Pero aún lo era más su deseo de reclamarla, de capturarla, de hacerla suya.

Desde las profundidades de esos ojos azules la miraba un conquistador.

Simon extendió una mano muy despacio.

—Arriésgate. Ponme a prueba.

Portia miró la mano que le ofrecía antes de alzar la vista hasta su rostro.

—¿Qué estás sugiriendo?

—Que seas mi amante hasta que estés segura de que deseas convertirte en mi esposa. Al menos, durante los días que estemos aquí.

Inspiró hondo. La cabeza le daba tantas vueltas que no podía pensar. El instinto le decía que había más, que aún no sabía qué lo había llevado a pensar contra toda lógica que se complementarían, y que tal vez nunca lo supiera. Aunque había otros modos de enfocar ese tema, había maneras de averiguar lo que Simon no diría con palabras.

Pero si deseaba averiguarlo... tendría que arriesgarse.

Arriesgarse mucho más de lo que había creído.

Había pensado en abordar el matrimonio paso a paso, segura del terreno que pisaba. Pero ¿quién sabía? Tal vez habría llegado un momento en el que lo hubiera considerado como marido. Si hubiera seguido el cauteloso camino de la lógica, habría sabido qué hacer. No se habría sentido insegura.

No obstante, Simon había pasado a un nivel que ella ni siquiera había previsto, sin darle tiempo a adaptarse a las nuevas circunstancias. La cabeza seguía dándole vueltas, pero él esperaba una respuesta, no cejaría hasta obtenerla; y la verdad era que merecía recibir una. Debía confiar en su instinto para decidir qué hacer.

El corazón le dio un vuelco, pero irguió la espalda.

Alzó la mano y aferró la que él le había ofrecido.

Simon cerró su mano y la apretó con firmeza.

El gesto posesivo la sobresaltó. Levantó la barbilla y enfrentó su mirada.

—Esto no quiere decir que haya aceptado casarme contigo.

Sin apartar la vista de ella, él se llevó su mano a los labios.

—Has accedido a darme la oportunidad de convencerte.

Reprimió el escalofrío provocado por su beso y por el brillo decidido de sus ojos e inclinó la cabeza.

Simon dejó escapar el aire que había estado conteniendo y sintió que el nudo que le había cerrado la garganta se deshacía. Jamás había imaginado que tratar con su futura esposa sería tratar con Portia. Era la única persona que lo sacaba de quicio.

Sin embargo, ya había pasado lo peor, había logrado dejar atrás el tema de su reciente engaño y había centrado la conversación en lo que realmente importaba: el futuro. No iba a darle más vueltas al hecho de que Portia creyese que pensaba seducirla y dejarla marchar sin más; no tenía sentido discutir su error de cálculo.

Ella lo miró un instante antes de girarse para continuar por el sendero. La dejó reanudar la marcha, pero no le soltó la mano, sino que caminó despacio a su lado.

Sabía lo que estaba pensando, lo que estaba analizando y diseccionando. Y no tenía manera de evitarlo.

Bajo la copa de los árboles todo estaba en silencio, tranquilo. Escucharon los lejanos trinos de un pájaro. El sendero se internaba entre los pinos. Tenían el patio principal justo enfrente cuando Portia se detuvo. Y se giró para enfrentarlo.

—¿Qué pasa si no acepto casarme contigo?

Una mentira facilitaría su vida en gran medida. Pero ésa era Portia. La miró a los ojos.

—Que hablaré con Luc.

Ella se tensó y su mirada se tornó furibunda.

—Si lo haces, puedes estar seguro de que no me casaré contigo.

Dejó que el silencio se extendiera un momento.

—Lo sé. —Tras un instante, frunció los labios y prosiguió—: Si llegamos a ese punto, estaremos en tablas. Pero no llegaremos a ese punto, así que no tiene sentido que nos preocupemos.

Ella lo miró con los ojos entrecerrados antes de hacer un mohín y reanudar la marcha.

—Pareces muy seguro de ti mismo.

Cuando salieron al patio, Simon alzó la vista hacia la mansión.

—De cómo deberían ser las cosas, sí, lo estoy. —De lo que se avecinaba... Bueno, eso era otro cantar.

Subieron los escalones de la entrada principal y transpusieron la puerta, abierta de par en par.

Portia se detuvo en el vestíbulo.

—Necesito pensar.

Por decirlo de alguna manera. Aún tenía la sensación de que estaba soñando, de que nada de lo sucedido era real. No tenía claro en qué se había metido, a qué se enfrentaba.

Dónde se encontraban.

Se zafó de su mano y él la dejó ir a regañadientes. Le bastó un vistazo a su rostro para tener la certeza de que Simon preferiría que no pensara y el presentimiento de que estaba sopesando la idea de distraerla. Pero entonces la miró a los ojos y se percató de que había adivinado sus intenciones.

Inclinó la cabeza a modo de despedida.

—Estaré en la sala de billar.

Portia le devolvió el gesto y se giró para entrar en la biblioteca. La enorme estancia estaba desierta. Aliviada, cerró la puerta tras ella y se apoyó contra la hoja de madera. Un instante después, escuchó las pisadas que se alejaban por el vestíbulo.

Con la espalda pegada a la puerta, esperó a que la cabeza dejara de darle vueltas y a que sus emociones se calmaran.

¿Estaba Simon en lo cierto? ¿Podría funcionar un matrimonio entre ellos?

No parecía tener mucho sentido repasar el pasado. A sabiendas de que su objetivo siempre había sido el matrimonio, el comportamiento de Simon cobraba sentido. Incluso el hecho de que no lo mencionara hasta que Kitty lo obligó a hacerlo; conociéndola como la conocía, era la única opción. Hasta ella habría hecho lo mismo de estar en su lugar.

Nunca había sido una persona vengativa. El pasado... pasado estaba. Era el futuro lo que debía importarle. El futuro que Simon le había impuesto.

A pesar de todo, tenía la sensación de que el control de su vida se le había escapado de las manos, como un par de caballos desbocados. Había estado tan pendiente del vínculo emocional entre ellos que no se había parado a pensar adónde podría llevarlos. Era evidente que él sí había reparado en el desenlace; pero ¿habría considerado la naturaleza de esa emoción?

Mientras que ella analizaba ese vínculo paso a paso, guiada por la lógica, Simon había dado un impulsivo salto hacia una de las posibles conclusiones... y estaba convencido de que dicha conclusión era la correcta. Que era la que debía ser.

Por regla general, era ella la impulsiva y él era el hombre circunspecto. No obstante, en el caso en el que se encontraban, Simon estaba convencido de su posición mientras que ella seguía buscando indicios que calmaran sus dudas.

Hizo un mohín y se apartó de la puerta. Sin duda, su precaución se debía a todo lo que estaba en juego; era ella quien se ponía en peligro al concederle su mano. Al concederle derechos sobre su persona. Cualquier derecho que Simon quisiera ejercer sobre ella.

Le había dicho que funcionaría, que comprendía sus miedos y que la quería como era. Una vez más, su decisión dependía de la confianza. ¿Confiaba en él hasta el punto de creer que cumpliría su palabra día tras día durante el resto de sus vidas?

Ésa era la pregunta para la que debía encontrar respuesta.

Aunque una cosa sí tenía clara. Su conexión, ese vínculo emocional que intentaba comprender, que había nacido de un pasado compartido y que se había fortalecido con las relaciones íntimas de los últimos días, era muy real; era un ente casi tangible.

Y seguía creciendo, seguía fortaleciéndose.

Simon era muy consciente. Lo sentía y lo reconocía al igual que ella misma; de hecho, se estaba aprovechando de ese vínculo, utilizándolo en su propio beneficio. Lo usaba en conjunción con su férrea voluntad (algo que ella no había previsto) para encauzarlo por el camino que deseaba que tomase.

Todo eso la conducía a la pregunta más pertinente. ¿El sentimiento que los unía era real o era una ilusión creada por la férrea voluntad de Simon y su enorme experiencia con el objetivo de que se casara con él?

Rememoró su reacción a la preocupación que él le había demostrado esa mañana. ¿Era tan implacable como para haberla fingido? Conocía la respuesta: sí.

Pero ¿lo habría hecho?

Percibía las emociones, la pasión y el deseo que Simon controlaba con mano de hierro, que refrenaba pero que no conseguía ocultar del todo. Aún sentía el impulso de huir, de alejarse de él y de esas emociones; de alejarse del poder que éstas tenían y de la amenaza implícita que suponían para ella; sin embargo, ese impulso se contrarrestaba con la curiosidad, con la poderosa fascinación que evocaban esas mismas emociones, ese sentimiento que existía entre ambos y la promesa de lo que podría llegar a ser.

Simon leía sus pensamientos y sus emociones como si fueran un libro abierto. En circunstancias normales, jamás se molestaba en ocultarle lo que sentía o pensaba. El hecho de que hubiera averiguado el único secreto que creía haberle ocultado evidenciaba que estaba más unido a ella de lo que había creído en un principio. Que era mucho más consciente de lo que ella lo era de él.

Hasta ese momento había pensado en el matrimonio de modo abstracto, aunque desde luego jamás había tenido en mente a Simon ni a nadie como él. Había acabado atrapada en su red por culpa de las circunstancias y de su propia curiosidad. Simon acababa de convertir la posibilidad de casarse con un tirano en algo muy real.

Si estuviera en su sano juicio, lo rechazaría... y saldría corriendo. Muy rápido. Y muy lejos.

No obstante, la idea de huir de lo que podría llegar a existir entre ellos le provocaba tal rechazo que sabía que jamás lo haría, que jamás le daría la espalda a esa posibilidad y la dejaría pasar. Si lo hiciera, jamás sería capaz de volver a mirarse en un espejo. Las posibilidades que la aguardaban a lo largo del camino que Simon le proponía eran incontables, emocionantes y suponían una peligrosa tentación. Diferentes, únicas. Estimulantes.

Todo lo que siempre había deseado que existiera en su vida.

La idea de casarse con un Cynster sin el amor para allanar el camino, algo que había dejado de ser una hipótesis para convertirse en realidad, era como una espada que pendía sobre su cabeza y amenazaba su verdadero ser. A pesar de eso, seguía sin sentirse amenazada por él, por el hombre. Simon había sido su indeseado y renuente protector durante años; y una parte de ella se negaba en redondo a modificar su papel a esas alturas.

Suspiró. Por más cosas que pensara, sólo se encontraba con contradicciones y su mente seguía ofuscada. La única certeza que albergaba era el hecho de que Simon, por sorprendente que pareciera, estaba decidido a casarse con ella, aunque ella aún no se hubiera decidido al respecto.

La magnitud del cambio que se había producido en su vida en apenas una hora la dejó aturdida.

Miró a su alrededor mientras se obligaba a respirar con calma. Tenía que tranquilizarse y recuperar el equilibrio para que su mente funcionara con su habitual precisión.

Su mirada vagó por las pulcras hileras de libros encuadernados en piel al tiempo que comenzaba a pasear por el perímetro de la estancia. Se obligó a concentrarse, a leer los títulos, a pensar en otras cosas. A reconectar con el mundo en el que solía vivir.

Llegó a uno de los extremos de la estancia y pasó frente a la inmensa chimenea. Las puertas francesas que daban al jardín estaban abiertas; paseó por su lado, admirando los bustos que había entre cada puerta e intentando no pensar en nada más hasta que volvió a llegar a las paredes cubiertas por las estanterías.

En ese extremo de la biblioteca se emplazaba un escritorio, colocado en perpendicular a la chimenea. Tras él había otra chimenea más pequeña. Su mirada reparó en el intrincado diseño de la repisa...

Y desde donde se encontraba, atisbó un pie pequeño y ataviado con un escarpín que yacía en el suelo, junto al escritorio.

Cómo no, el pie estaba unido a una pierna.

—¡Válgame Dios! —Se acercó a toda prisa al escritorio y lo rodeó...

Se detuvo, temblando. Con los ojos desorbitados.

Y se aferró al borde del escritorio con una mano mientras se llevaba la otra a la garganta.

Era incapaz de apartar la vista del rostro de Kitty. Un rostro hinchado, enrojecido, con la lengua ennegrecida asomando entre los labios y una mirada vidriosa en esos ojos azules... Era incapaz de apartar la vista del cordón de seda que le rodeaba el cuello y se hundía en su delicada piel...

—¿Simon? —Su voz apenas fue un susurro. Le costó un esfuerzo sobrehumano tomar el aire suficiente para poder gritar—. ¡Simon!

Pasó un momento. Escuchaba el tictac del reloj que había en la repisa de la chimenea. Estaba demasiado mareada como para soltar el escritorio y comenzaba a preguntarse si tendría que ir en busca de ayuda...

Escuchó las pisadas que se acercaban por el pasillo.

La puerta se abrió de par en par.

En un abrir y cerrar de ojos, Simon estuvo a su lado, cogiéndola por los brazos mientras contemplaba su rostro. Cuando siguió su mirada, soltó un juramento, se interpuso entre ella y el escritorio y la estrechó entre sus brazos para alejarla de la espantosa imagen.

Portia se aferró a las solapas de su chaqueta y, temblando, enterró la cara en su hombro.

—¿Qué pasa? —preguntó Charlie desde la puerta.

Simon señaló con la cabeza la zona situada tras el escritorio.

—Kitty...

Abrazó a Portia con fuerza, consciente de los escalofríos que la recorrían, de los temblores que la sacudían. Al diablo con el decoro. La estrechó un poco más, amoldándola a su cuerpo para darle calor y bajó la cabeza para besarle la sien.

—No pasa nada.

Portia tragó saliva y se acercó aún más a él. Comprendió que intentaba luchar contra su reacción, contra la fuerte impresión. A la postre sintió que enderezaba la espalda y levantaba la cabeza, pero no se apartó de él. En cambio, miró hacia el escritorio.

Miró a Charlie, que se había acercado para echar un vistazo y que, en esos momentos, estaba lívido y apoyado en el borde del escritorio mientras se aflojaba la corbata. Soltó una maldición antes de mirarlo.

—Está muerta, ¿verdad? —le preguntó su amigo.

Fue Portia quien respondió con voz quebrada:

—Sus ojos...

Simon desvió la mirada hacia la puerta. No había acudido nadie más. Miró a Charlie.

—Busca a Blenkinsop. Y cierra la puerta al salir. Cuando hayas dado con él, busca a Henry.

Charlie parpadeó antes de asentir con la cabeza. Se enderezó, inspiró hondo, se arregló la chaqueta y echó a andar hacia la puerta.

Los temblores de Portia estaban empeorando. En cuanto se cerró la puerta, la cogió en brazos. Ella siguió aferrada a su chaqueta, pero no protestó. La llevó hacia los sillones emplazados frente a la chimenea principal y la dejó en uno.

—Quédate aquí. —Recorrió la estancia con la mirada y localizó la licorera. Se acercó al mueble y sirvió una generosa cantidad de *brandy* en una copa de cristal. Regresó junto a Portia y se arrodilló a su lado mientras estudiaba su semblante—. Toma, bébete esto.

Ella extendió una mano pero comprendió que necesitaría las dos. La ayudó a llevarse la copa a los labios y a sostenerla para que pudiera beber. Permaneció arrodillado en el suelo, ayudándola a beber; un rato después, sus mejillas habían recuperado un poco de color y a sus ojos asomaba un atisbo de su habitual fuerza.

Se apartó un poco para mirarla a la cara.

—Espera aquí. Voy a echar un vistazo antes de que el caos se desate.

Portia tragó y asintió con la cabeza.

Se levantó y cruzó la estancia sin dilación hasta llegar al cadáver, que examinó con cuidado. Kitty estaba de espaldas, con las manos a la altura de los hombros, como si hubiera forcejeado con todas sus fuerzas para librarse del asesino hasta su último aliento.

Por primera vez sintió verdadera lástima por ella; tal vez hubiera sido un completo desastre desde el punto de vista social, pero nadie tenía derecho de acabar con su vida de ese modo. A la zaga de esa emoción llegó la furia; aunque era algo mucho más complejo y no sólo por lo que le había sucedido a Kitty. Refrenó su ira y procedió a catalogar cuanto veían sus ojos.

El asesino se había colocado detrás de Kitty y la había estrangulado con el cordón de una cortina de las puertas francesas, comprobó cuando se agachó. Kitty era la mujer más baja de toda la casa, apenas llegaba al metro cincuenta de estatura; no debió de resultar muy difícil matarla. Recorrió el cuerpo con la mirada y le estudió las manos, pero no encontró nada fuera de lo normal salvo el hecho de que se hubiera cambiado de ropa después del almuerzo. Antes llevaba un vestido mañanero bastante sencillo; el que tenía puesto era mucho más bonito, un vestido de tarde diseñado para mostrar sus voluptuosas curvas, si bien totalmente aceptable para una mujer casada.

A continuación, examinó el escritorio, pero tampoco allí vio nada fuera de lugar; no había cartas a medio escribir ni manchas de tinta en el papel secante. Las plumas estaban bien ordenadas en su lugar y el tintero, bien cerrado.

Aunque tampoco creía que Kitty se hubiera retirado a la biblioteca para escribir una carta.

Regresó junto a Portia y meneó la cabeza al ver su expresión interrogante.

—No hay pistas.

Cogió la copa que Portia le ofreció. Seguía medio llena. Se la bebió de un trago y agradeció el calor que el licor extendió por su cuerpo. Si las consecuencias de la discusión que había mantenido con Portia le habían dejado los nervios a flor de piel, aquello era la gota que colmaba el vaso.

Inspiró hondo y la miró a los ojos. Portia sostuvo su mirada. Pasó un instante antes de que ella le tendiera la mano. Se la cogió y entrelazó sus dedos con fuerza.

Portia desvió la vista hacia la puerta. En ese preciso momento, ésta se estampó contra la pared; Henry y Blenkinsop entraron en tromba seguidos de Ambrose y un criado.

Las siguientes horas fueron las más espantosas que Simon había pasado en toda su vida. Una fuerte impresión era una manera muy suave de describir lo que la muerte de Kitty les había provocado. Todos estaban anonadados, eran incapaces de asimilar lo ocurrido. A pesar de lo que había estado sucediendo delante de sus narices durante los últimos días, a nadie se le había ocurrido que todo acabara de ese modo.

—Puede que haya pensado estrangularla alguna que otra vez —afirmó James—. Pero jamás creí que alguien fuera capaz de hacerlo.

Pero los hechos eran los hechos.

En cuanto a las damas, casi todas estaban desconcertadas. Incluso lady O. Se olvidó de apoyarse en su bastón y ni se le pasó por la cabeza golpearlo contra el suelo. Drusilla era la menos afectada; pero incluso ella se echó a temblar, se quedó lívida y tuvo que sentarse cuando se enteró de la noticia. Muerta, Kitty despertaba muchas más simpatías que viva.

En cuanto a los hombres, una vez que superaron la primera impresión, la confusión fue la nota imperante. Junto con una creciente preocupación por lo que estaba por llegar, por cómo acabaría todo.

Simon estuvo pendiente de Portia y nada más. Horas más tarde, seguía bajo los efectos de la terrible impresión y seguía estremeciéndose de vez en cuando. Tenía los ojos desorbitados y las manos, sudorosas. Quería cogerla en brazos y llevársela muy lejos de allí; pero era del todo imposible.

Habían mandado llamar a lord Willoughby, el magistrado local. Llegó en poco tiempo y, tras intercambiar las cortesías de rigor y examinar el cuerpo (que seguía tal como lo encontraron en el suelo de la biblioteca), se retiró al despacho de lord Glossup. Interrogó primero a los caballeros y, después, llamó a Portia para que le contara lo sucedido.

Simon la acompañó como si estuviera en su derecho. Portia no se lo había pedido, ni él a ella; no obstante, desde que entrelazaran sus manos en la biblioteca, sólo las habían separado lo estrictamente necesario. Hundida en un sillón colocado junto a la chimenea (la cual habían encendido a toda prisa) y con él a su lado, relató como pudo su macabro hallazgo.

Lord Willoughby tomaba notas con los anteojos en la punta de la nariz.

—De manera que antes de que encontrara a la señora Glossup sólo estuvo en la biblioteca unos... ¿cinco minutos?

Portia meditó un instante antes de asentir con la cabeza.

—Y no vio a nadie ni escuchó que nadie saliera de la estancia, ni cuando entraron en la casa ni cuando pasó a la biblioteca. ¿Es correcto?

Volvió a asentir.

—¿A nadie en absoluto?

Simon se removió inquieto en el sillón ante tantas preguntas, pero el magistrado sólo estaba haciendo su trabajo y, además, con bastante tacto. Era un hombre mayor, de aspecto paternal, pero de mirada penetrante. Parecía haberse percatado de que la falta de respuesta de Portia no se debía a que intentara ocultarle algo.

Ella se aclaró la garganta.

—A nadie.

—Tengo entendido que las puertas de la terraza estaban abiertas. ¿Miró al exterior?

—No, ni siquiera me acerqué demasiado a ellas... Sólo pasé por delante.

Lord Willoughby esbozó una sonrisa alentadora.

—Y entonces fue cuando la vio y llamó al señor Cynster. ¿Tocó usted algo?

Cuando Portia negó con la cabeza, el hombre se giró hacia él.

—No vi nada extraño... Eché un vistazo, pero no vi nada que estuviera fuera de lugar.

El magistrado asintió con la cabeza y siguió con sus notas.

—Muy bien. Creo que eso es todo. —Sonrió con amabilidad y se puso en pie.

Portia, aún cogida de su mano, también se levantó.

—¿Qué va a pasar ahora?

Lord Willoughby miró a Simon y después a ella.

—Me temo que me veo en la obligación de recurrir a uno de los caballeros de Bow Street. Enviaré mi informe esta noche. Con suerte, tendremos aquí a uno de ellos mañana por la tarde. —Volvió a sonreír, en esa ocasión con ánimo reconfortante—. Han mejorado muchísimo, querida, y en este caso... —Se encogió de hombros.

—¿Qué quiere decir con eso? —quiso saber él.

El magistrado lo miró de nuevo y frunció los labios.

—Por desgracia, ninguno de los caballeros, salvo el señor Cynster aquí presente y el señor Hastings, tiene coartada para el momento del crimen. Por supuesto, no debemos olvidar que hay gitanos en las cercanías; pero, en los tiempos que corren, es mejor seguir el procedimiento.

Portia lo miró y a él no le cupo duda de lo que estaba pensando. Quería atrapar al asesino, fuera quien fuese.

Se despidió del magistrado con un gesto de cabeza y acompañó a Portia fuera de la estancia.

Lord Willoughby habló por último con lord Glossup y después se marchó.

La cena, compuesta por una selección de platos fríos, se sirvió temprano. Y todos se retiraron a sus habitaciones antes del crepúsculo.

Sentada en el alféizar de la ventana, con la barbilla apoyada en los brazos, Portia observaba cómo el sol iba desapareciendo poco a poco por el horizonte.

Y pensaba en Kitty. En las múltiples facetas de la misma mujer que había conocido en esos últimos días. Había sido una mujer hermosa y vivaz, capaz de ser encantadora y agradable; pero también de ser vengativa, caprichosa y cruel con los demás. Exigente... Ése tal vez fuera su mayor pecado, y, tal vez, su última estupidez. Había exigido ser el centro de atención de todos los que compartían la vida con ella.

A pesar de lo mucho que la había observado, jamás había visto que tuviera en cuenta los sentimientos de otra persona.

Sintió un escalofrío. Había algo que no podía sacarse de la cabeza. Kitty había confiado en alguien, alguien con quien se había encontrado en la biblioteca, un lugar al que jamás acudiría de otro modo. Se había cambiado de vestido. Recordó la expectación de la que había hecho gala durante el almuerzo al aire libre.

Había depositado su confianza a ciegas en alguien. Un error que había acabado siendo fatal.

Aunque había más de un modo de perder la vida.

Se concentró un instante a fin de comprobar si ya se encontraba preparada para desentenderse unos momentos de la muerte de Kitty y enfrentarse a las preguntas que la acosaban. Las preguntas de índole personal y muy emocional que afectaban a su futuro, a su vida y a la de Simon... Las vidas que tendrían que vivir a pesar de la muerte de Kitty.

Siempre había sabido que una dama que no era cuidadosa podría enfrentarse a una muerte en vida. ¿Cuánto tiempo hacía que sabía que esa noción también se aplicaba a ella? Bueno, no tenía ni idea. Tal vez ése fuera el motivo de que su subconsciente la hubiera instado a evitar a los hombres, y al matrimonio, durante tantos años y con tanto ahínco.

Para ella, el matrimonio siempre sería un riesgo, de ahí que buscara al marido ideal: uno que pudiera proporcionarle lo que ella necesitaba y permitirle manejarlo, dictar su relación y, en última instancia, vivir su vida. Su temperamento jamás la dejaría vivir en los confines de una relación asfixiante. En ese caso las opciones serían claras: o acababa con dicha relación o la relación acabaría con ella.

Y allí estaba, enfrentada a la posibilidad de casarse con un hombre lo bastante fuerte como para someterla a su entera voluntad. Un hombre al que no podría dominar y que, de aceptar su proposición, podría doblegarla si se lo proponía.

Siempre había sabido cómo era Simon; ni una sola vez, ni siquiera a los catorce años, había malinterpretado su naturaleza ni lo había visto como otra cosa que el tirano que era. Aunque tampoco había creído jamás que se le metería en la cabeza casarse con ella..., a ella desde luego que no se le había ocurrido. Sin embargo, así estaban las cosas y ella, con la curiosidad que había despertado su deseo de encontrar un marido (algo que, por suerte, Simon desconocía) había caído en sus redes de cabeza.

Y él se lo había permitido.

No era sorprendente, por supuesto; no era, ni más ni menos, que lo que su naturaleza le dictaba.

Clavó la mirada en la oscuridad de la noche y dejó que sus pensamientos se centraran en él, en todo lo que habían compartido. En todo lo que aún desconocía.

En todo lo que aún deseaba aprender.

¿Sería amor lo que estaba naciendo entre ellos? ¿O algo que Simon había fraguado para atarla a él?

Y en otro orden de cosas, ¿sería Simon capaz de darle rienda suelta dentro de unos límites aceptables, le permitiría ser de verdad como realmente era? ¿O sería su oferta una estratagema para que aceptara casarse con él?

Dos preguntas. Sus interrogantes se habían reducido a dos preguntas muy claras.

Sólo había un modo de averiguar las respuestas.

«Ponme a prueba.»

Tendría que ponerlo a prueba, sí.

Permaneció sentada en el alféizar de la ventana mientras las sombras se alargaban y se oscurecían en el exterior. Mientras contemplaba caer la noche y, con ésta, el silencio sobre los jardines.

Pensó de nuevo en Kitty, que yacía muerta en la caseta del hielo.

Sintió que la sangre seguía corriendo por sus venas.

Ella tenía que seguir adelante con su vida, y eso significaba labrarse su propio futuro. Jamás le había faltado el valor y jamás en su vida había rehuido un desafío.

Claro que jamás se había enfrentado a un desafío semejante...

Debía hacerse con el control de la situación en la que él los había metido y convertirla en la vida que ella deseaba; debía obtener de Simon (de Simon, nada más y nada menos) las respuestas..., las garantías que necesitaba para sentirse segura.

La verdad era que no había marcha atrás. No podían fingir que no había pasado nada entre ellos ni que el vínculo que se había establecido, y que se fortalecía con cada día que pasaba, no existía.

Como tampoco podía alejarse sin más, de su relación y de él... Entre otras cosas, porque él no se lo permitiría.

No tenía sentido fingir.

Tras quitarse la chaqueta, Simon se había colocado delante de la ventana de su habitación para observar cómo las sombras iban reclamando las aguas del lago.

Y sentía cómo su humor se iba ensombreciendo a la par.

Quería estar con Portia. En ese mismo instante, esa noche. Quería estrecharla entre sus brazos y saber que estaba a salvo. Quería, con un anhelo tan novedoso y tan diferente de la pasión que casi no daba crédito a su fuerza, hacerla sentirse segura.

Ése era el impulso que corría por sus venas; un impulso que no podía saciar.

Y ese hecho sólo incrementaba su inquietud.

Portia estaba en su dormitorio, sola. Pensando.

No podía hacer nada por cambiarlo... Nada por influir en las conclusiones a las que llegara.

No recordaba haberse sentido más inseguro con una mujer en toda su vida; desde luego, nunca había puesto en duda su capacidad para doblegar la voluntad de una mujer.

No podía hacer nada. A menos que ella lo buscara, no podía proseguir con su persuasión. No podía convencerla para que continuara a su lado y juntos exploraran el modo de que su matrimonio funcionara... Y estaba decidido a lograrlo. Había hablado en serio cuando le prometió encontrar el modo de dejarla hacer y deshacer a su antojo, siempre que le fuera posible.

Haría cuanto hiciera falta para casarse con ella; ni siquiera se planteaba otra alternativa.

Sin embargo, no podía hacer nada en ese momento. Estaba acostumbrado a controlar su vida, a manejar los asuntos que realmente importaban. Pero en eso, en ese asunto que le importaba más que nada en el mundo, no podía hacer nada hasta que ella le diera la oportunidad.

Su vida y su futuro estaban en manos de Portia.

Si le diera la menor oportunidad de persuadirla para después rechazarlo, la perdería aunque él fuera más fuerte que ella en lo esencial. Ya podría amenazarla con echarle encima a toda la alta sociedad que Portia no se doblegaría. No se sometería. Él mejor que nadie sabía que era cierto.

No tenía la menor idea de por qué se había fijado en una mujer tan indomable, pero ya era demasiado tarde para cambiar ese hecho.

Tomó una honda bocanada de aire que le ensanchó el pecho. Años atrás, se había reído de sus cuñados cuando les salió el tiro por la culata. Pero ya no se reía. Se encontraba en el mismo atolladero.

Escuchó el ruido del picaporte y se giró al mismo tiempo que se abría la puerta. Portia entró en el dormitorio y se dio la vuelta para cerrar la puerta.

Echó el pestillo y se detuvo para observarlo con detenimiento. Después, levantó la barbilla y se encaminó hacia él.

Aguardó totalmente inmóvil. Renuente incluso a respirar.

Se sentía como un depredador que observara a su presa mientras ésta se acercaba sin ser consciente del peligro.

La tenue luz de la luna la iluminó cuando se acercó a la ventana; vio la expresión de su rostro, su mirada seria y la determinación que ambas traslucían.

Fue directa hacia él, le colocó una mano en la nuca y le bajó la cabeza.

Para besarlo.

El fuego seguía allí, entre ellos; cobró vida en cuanto

ella separó los labios, en cuanto él respondió de forma instintiva.

Muy despacio a fin de darle todo el tiempo del mundo para apartarse si ése era su deseo, Simon le rodeó la cintura con las manos y, después, al ver que no protestaba, la envolvió con los brazos hasta amoldarla a su cuerpo.

Portia se apoyó en él y eso hizo que algo se rompiera en su interior, algo helado que acabó por derretirse. Le devolvió el beso, ansiando más, y ella se lo entregó. A manos llenas y sin el menor asomo de duda.

Aún no sabía qué había decidido, qué nuevo plan estaba poniendo en práctica; sólo era consciente del inmenso alivio que sentía al tenerla entre sus brazos. Al tenerla allí, muriéndose de deseo por él.

Porque lo deseaba. Lo había dejado bien claro en cuanto se amoldó sin temor alguno a su cuerpo. Sus lenguas se rozaban cambiando poco a poco el cariz del beso. Deseando más, reclamando más, dando más. Portia lo besaba con su habitual concentración, con la misma devoción de la que siempre hacía gala.

Sabía que era algo deliberado... Que había decidido seguir por ese camino.

Con la misma deliberación, se desentendió de sus argumentos, de su afán de persuasión, y se limitó a emularla.

Se inclinó para aferrarla por la parte trasera de los muslos y alzarla sin apartarla de él. Portia respondió con un ardiente murmullo antes de arrojarle los brazos al cuello y, una vez que le bajó la cabeza, darse un festín con sus labios. Semejante despliegue de pasión lo distrajo por un instante mientras luchaba por aplacar las ansias de Portia. Acto seguido reclamó sus labios con renovado ardor y recuperó el control mientras la llevaba a la cama.

Cayeron sobre el colchón y rodó de forma instintiva para atraparla bajo su cuerpo. Ella jadeó y se aferró a su pelo, a sus hombros..., a cualquier parte que tuviera a su alcance. Se entregó al beso y comenzó a forcejear bajo él hasta que cedió y rodó sobre el colchón, de modo que quedó tendida sobre él, libre de su peso.

En ese instante recordó que le tocaba asumir el papel de suplicante y que Portia no lo olvidaría. Así que decidió sosegarla, hechizarla y seducirla una vez más.

Dedicó su mente, sus manos, sus labios y su lengua a esa tarea. A entregarse a ella en cuerpo y alma.

En cuanto esa idea tomó forma, en cuanto por fin la aceptó y asimiló, sintió que había dado el paso correcto. Y esa inmensa sensación inspiró sus caricias mientras le acariciaba la nuca, y se apoderó de su cuerpo mientras permanecía inmóvil bajo ella.

Preparado para que ella tomara las riendas en ese momento.

Portia vaciló, recelosa de sus motivos, pero aceptó la invitación implícita y se incorporó un poco para saborear mejor su boca. Le tomó la cara entre las manos y lo inmovilizó mientras suspiraba de placer. Después, liberó sus labios y, con una mirada resplandeciente bajo los párpados entornados, le enterró los dedos en el cabello.

Simon interpretó el gesto como una señal y comenzó a acariciarle la espalda, enderezando el vestido antes de proceder a desabrocharle los botones.

Ella emitió un gemido de protesta y se apoyó sobre su pecho para incorporarse hasta que quedó sentada a horcajadas sobre su cintura; desde esa posición, observó su rostro.

No tenía ni idea de lo que podía ver en su cara, pero se quedó inmóvil, con las manos sobre sus costados, observándola mientras ella lo estudiaba, a la espera de que dictara el camino a seguir.

Portia lo miró a la cara, iluminada por la luz de la luna que se filtraba por la ventana. Leyó su conformidad, su predisposición para, al menos por esa noche, ser lo que ella quería que fuese. Para comportarse tal y como ella quisiese.

Ella así lo quería. Lo necesitaba.

—Me sugeriste que te pusiera a prueba. ¿Lo decías en serio?

Sus respectivas posiciones impedían que Simon leyera su expresión. Percibió que estaba intentando hacerlo y que, al verse incapaz, titubeaba antes de contestar.

—Me refería a que deberíamos comportarnos como si estuviéramos casados para que vieras, para que te convencieras, que es posible. Que estar casada conmigo no será el desastre que tú crees.

—¿Seguro que no empezarás a dar órdenes a diestro y siniestro? —Gesticuló con la mano—. ¿Que no te harás con el control?

—Intentaré no hacerlo. —Apretó los dientes—. Estoy dispuesto a amoldarme cuanto me sea posible, a complacerte dentro de unos límites razonables, pero no puedo...

Al ver que no terminaba la frase, lo hizo ella en su lugar.

—¿Cambiar tu forma de ser?

Lo sintió soltar el aire.

—No puedo ser alguien que no soy, de la misma manera que tú no aceptas que te obliguen a ser alguien que no eres. —Sus miradas se entrelazaron—. Lo único que podemos hacer es intentarlo y sacar el máximo partido.

La sinceridad de su voz se deslizó bajo sus defensas y la conmovió. De momento, eso bastaba... Era una invitación más que adecuada para ponerlo a prueba y ver qué pasaba.

—Muy bien. Intentémoslo y veamos adónde nos lleva.

Sus manos, grandes y fuertes, seguían inertes en sus costados, sin exigir nada..., a la espera.

Portia sonrió, inclinó la cabeza y lo besó en los labios. Lo incitó y, cuando sintió que tensaba los dedos, se retiró. Lo dejó inmovilizado con una mirada.

Y se dispuso a soltarle la corbata. Le quitó el alfiler de diamantes, lo clavó en el borde del chaleco antes de desatar el nudo y, a la postre, soltó el largo trozo de tela. Lo sostuvo en alto con una mano mientras sopesaba una miríada de posibilidades; después, sonrió.

Cogió la corbata con ambas manos y la convirtió en una venda para los ojos.

Sus miradas se encontraron por encima de la prenda.

—Te toca.

La expresión de su rostro fue un poema, aunque le resultara imposible negarse. Se incorporó sobre los codos con la cabeza inclinada para que pudiera colocarle la venda sobre los ojos.

—Espero que sepas lo que estás haciendo —murmuró.

—Creo que me las apañaré.

Si tenía los ojos vendados, podía olvidarse de la necesidad de controlar su propia expresión y concentrarse por completo en él, en conseguir todo lo que quería de él.

Le llevó las manos a los hombros y lo empujó para que volviera a tenderse en el colchón, bajo ella. El cabecero y los almohadones estaban a su derecha. A su espalda, la luna brillaba y derramaba su luz plateada sobre Simon.

Portia se dispuso a recrear la escena que tenía en mente, el escenario donde lo pondría a prueba esa noche.

12

La idea era demasiado fascinante como para dejar pasar la oportunidad. Tras abrirle el chaleco, se lo fue bajando poco a poco por los brazos. Una vez que lo tuvo en la mano, lo arrojó al suelo sin muchos miramientos.

Simon se recostó en el colchón y ella se afanó en la hilera de botones de la camisa. Mientras sus dedos trabajaban, observó su rostro. Con los ojos vendados, no podía verla mientras lo miraba, así que no guardaba su expresión con tanto celo como de costumbre. Por lo que veía, Simon había adivinado sus intenciones al menos en parte y no estaba muy seguro de cómo debía reaccionar.

Su sonrisa se tornó más decidida cuando liberó el último botón, tiró de la camisa para sacársela del pantalón y la abrió para descubrirle el torso. Simon no tendría más remedio que poner buena cara y aguantarse con lo que había.

—Piensa en Inglaterra —le dijo, antes de colocarle las manos en el pecho.

Dejó que sus sentidos disfrutaran de la belleza de ese torso que parecía esculpido. El contraste entre la suavidad y la firmeza de su piel y el tacto áspero del vello la hechizó. Se dio un festín con los poderosos músculos. Lo veneró en toda su amplitud, bebió de su fuerza inherente y se deleitó con los placeres que prometía.

Simon se removió, inquieto.

—Sobreviviré.

Su sonrisa se tornó maliciosa. Le quitó la camisa y la arrojó al suelo antes de inclinarse hacia delante y rozarle un hombro con la punta de la lengua. Simon tomó aire e intentó encubrir su reacción mientras los músculos de su abdomen se tensaban por el esfuerzo. Totalmente concentrada, ella prosiguió la exploración de ese pecho desnudo y se dispuso a atormentarlo y torturarlo a placer.

A lamerlo, besarlo y mordisquear los tensos pezones antes de succionar con fuerza.

Hasta que él no pudo aguantarlo y comenzó a removerse; hasta que sus manos, que habían estado quietas aferrándola por las caderas, comenzaron a tensarse; hasta que los músculos de sus brazos se abultaron por el esfuerzo de contenerse.

Tras un último lametón, Portia se incorporó.

Se puso de rodillas y se echó hacia atrás para sacarse la falda de debajo de las piernas antes de sentarse a horcajadas sobre sus fuertes muslos. Se inclinó hacia delante, volvió a apoyar las manos en su pecho y fue bajándolas muy despacio, centímetro a centímetro. Deslizándolas por el delicioso relieve de sus abdominales y por su cintura.

Bajo sus palmas, los músculos se tensaron. Se endurecieron.

Satisfecha, se echó hacia atrás y esperó. Lo observó mientras se relajaba de nuevo. Mientras tomaba aliento.

Extendió las manos hacia la pretina de sus pantalones.

Los desabrochó, le abrió la bragueta y rodeó su miembro con ambas manos. Simon se tensó de la cabeza a los pies. Todos sus músculos se endurecieron. Y durante esos primeros instantes, mientras sus manos se aflojaban en torno a él y volvían a apresarlo con fuerza antes de acariciarlo y explorarlo a conciencia, él contuvo la respiración. Hasta que tomó una entrecortada bocanada de aire.

—¿Me permites una sugerencia?

Portia lo meditó antes de responder con su voz más sensual:

—Sugiere lo que quieras.

Las manos de Simon se apartaron de la colcha y se cerraron en torno a las suyas.

Para mostrarle exactamente lo que ella quería saber. Cómo tocarlo, cómo proporcionarle placer, cómo inundarlo de deleite hasta hacerlo jadear y soltar un suspiro entrecortado. En ese momento, se zafó de sus manos y comenzó a moverse bajo ella para quitarse los pantalones.

Portia se apartó para ayudarlo, se los bajó por las piernas y lo desnudó.

Por completo.

Tendido de espaldas y sin nada que cubriera su cuerpo salvo los escasos centímetros de corbata blanca que le tapaban los ojos, era una estampa que le robó el aliento.

Y todo lo que apreciaba su vista era suyo.

Si se atrevía a reclamarlo.

Se humedeció los labios y se colocó de nuevo sobre sus muslos. Volvió a sacarse las faldas de debajo de las piernas y las dejó caer a su alrededor, cubriendo las piernas de Simon y las suyas. De ese modo, él podría sentir el calor que irradiaba su cuerpo desde ese lugar que palpitaba de deseo y que quedó muy cerca de él al sentarse.

Entretanto, no le quitó los ojos de encima. Evaluó el estado en el que él se encontraba mientras afianzaba su posición y se alzaba la camisola. Cuando estuvo lista, su otra mano volvió a cerrarse sobre su rígida erección.

Se percató al instante de que lo asaltaba una abrumadora oleada de estímulos. Sin embargo y pese al asalto sensorial, su férreo autocontrol resistió. Siguió inmóvil bajo ella mientras su respiración se aceleraba.

Portia sonrió. Todavía no había acabado con él.

Bajó la vista para admirar el premio que tenía entre las manos. Acto seguido, inclinó la cabeza y rozó con los labios esa piel ardiente y suave como la de un bebé.

Él dio un respingo y contuvo el aliento.

Con mucho cuidado, se dispuso a acariciar la punta con los labios antes de lamerlo desde allí hasta la base... sin apartar la mirada de su rostro. Tenía la mandíbula tensa. Más que nunca.

En un arranque de audacia, se lo metió en la boca.

Él soltó un gemido estrangulado. Extendió una mano hacia ella y le enterró los dedos en el pelo.

—No. No lo hagas —farfulló, aunque apenas logró entenderlo.

Lo soltó y observó su expresión con más detenimiento.

—¿Por qué? Te gusta...

Por lo poco que había visto, llevarse su miembro a la boca había sido la tortura más exquisita que se le había ocurrido hasta el momento.

—Ésa no es la cuestión. —Tomó una entrecortada bocanada de aire—. Al menos, no ahora mismo.

—Vaya... —Le dio un lametón, encantada con la sensación de tenerlo bajo su poder.

—¡Por el amor de Dios! ¡Ten piedad de mí! —Sus manos la habían aferrado por los brazos, de modo que tiró de ella hasta alzarla—. Luego... En otra ocasión.

Portia sonrió.

—¿Me lo prometes?

—Palabra de Cynster.

Soltó una carcajada. Se puso de rodillas y se movió hasta quedar sentada sobre sus caderas, sin nada entre sus cuerpos salvo los escasos centímetros de aire que separaban su erección de su palpitante entrepierna.

Simon había dejado de tirar de ella desde el mismo instante en que se alejó de su miembro. Parecía estar conteniendo el aliento.

Lo miró un instante y después se inclinó para besarlo con ternura. No le sorprendió que él la agarrara y devorara su boca con avidez.

La tensión volvió a apoderarse de ese poderoso cuerpo que tenía entre los muslos.

Se alejó de sus labios. Él no la detuvo, se limitó a aguardar, mientras su pecho subía y bajaba con cada respiración...

Al ver que ella no se movía, preguntó entre dientes:

—¿Sabes lo que estás haciendo?

No era tan inocente. Al menos en ese ámbito. Había un

buen número de libros en la biblioteca de Calverton Chase que su hermano Luc siempre había insistido en colocar en la balda superior de las estanterías. Se había negado a bajarlos. En consecuencia, ella y Penélope habían aprovechado la primera oportunidad para subirse a la escalera y bajar los volúmenes censurados. Habían descubierto que muchos eran libros ilustrados... con grabados muy esclarecedores. Las imágenes jamás se le habían borrado de la memoria.

—Podría decirse que sí. —Movió las caderas hacia atrás un poco más—. Sé que es posible, pero dime qué tengo que hacer. —Se inclinó hacia delante y lamió un endurecido pezón, saboreando el regusto salado de su piel—. ¿Cómo se hace exactamente?

La carcajada que escapó de la garganta de Simon fue ronca e inesperada. Como si le doliera algo. Su torso se expandió.

—Es muy fácil. —La agarró por las caderas—. Así.

Aunque no veía, la guió sin dificultad hacia abajo, hasta que su rígido miembro rozó la entrada de su cuerpo. En ese instante, alzó un poco las caderas, la penetró con la punta y se detuvo antes de que ella se lo ordenara.

Portia sonrió.

—Supongo que ahora tengo que erguir la espalda hasta quedar sentada. —Le colocó las manos en el pecho y se incorporó—. Así...

No necesitó que le respondiera. La facilidad con la que su miembro la penetró la dejó sin aliento y le provocó un escalofrío de lo más sensual en la espalda. Cerró los ojos a medida que su cuerpo lo acogía y se cerraba a su alrededor centímetro a centímetro. Todo bajo su control. Se sentó sobre él y lo sintió en lo más hondo. La experiencia le resultó abrumadora, devastadora. El calor que irradiaba, la plenitud, la realidad física del deseo con su patente dureza. Soltó el aire y alejó las rodillas de sus costados para acomodarse mejor y tomarlo por entero.

Y apretó los músculos.

—¡Dios! —exclamó Simon al tiempo que le clavaba

los dedos en las caderas y la inmovilizaba—. ¡Por el amor de Dios, quédate quieta un minuto!

Su voz sonaba demasiado tensa, como si estuviera a punto de llorar.

Lo miró a la cara. Su rostro estaba crispado por la pasión. Le concedió el minuto y lo aprovechó para absorber las sensaciones del momento. La plenitud de tenerlo dentro y la generosidad de su cuerpo al recibirlo. Todos sus sentidos estaban en alerta, excitados y muy pendientes de lo que sucedía, listos y en espera de lo que estaba por llegar.

Bajo ella, Simon se aferraba a la escasa cordura que le quedaba. Le había asegurado que sobreviviría..., aunque ya no estaba tan seguro. La ardiente sensación de la carne femenina que lo rodeaba, tan suave como la seda, a sabiendas de que estaba completamente vestida mientras que él notaba la fresca caricia del aire sobre la piel, el roce de las medias en sus costados... A sabiendas de que Portia tenía toda la intención de montarlo hasta hacerlo caer en el olvido y sin saber realmente lo que había planeado para después... Lo habría postrado de rodillas de no haber estado acostado.

Al parecer, ya le había llegado la hora. Portia lo agarró por las muñecas y le apartó las manos de las caderas. Entrelazó sus dedos y se apoyó en él mientras sus músculos internos lo acariciaban, se relajaban en torno a su miembro y comenzaba a alzarse. Hasta que estuvo a punto de abandonarlo por completo. En ese instante comenzó a bajar, moviéndose mucho más despacio que antes.

Simon tensó la mandíbula y apretó los dientes. Su cuerpo estaba todavía tan estrecho que era un milagro que no hubiera sufrido una combustión espontánea con la simple fricción. Tal y como estaban las cosas, le fue imposible contener un respingo justo cuando ella volvía a sentarse.

—Ni hablar. Tienes que estar quietecito.

Contuvo una réplica mordaz y se abstuvo de comentarle que necesitaría un ejército completo para inmovilizarlo. Se dijo que él mismo se había metido en esa situación y que no le quedaba más remedio que aguantarse.

Portia volvió a experimentar con los movimientos. Se alzó y volvió a descender. Puesto que tenían las manos entrelazadas, Simon percibió la tensión de sus dedos y a partir de ese momento incrementó el ritmo de sus movimientos.

Contaba con una preparación excelente, si bien en otro ámbito muy distinto. Montaba a caballo desde que era muy pequeña y había pasado años galopando por los bosques de Rutlandshire. Era imposible que se cansara pronto...

El cuerpo de Simon decidió aceptar el desafío. Luchó por mantenerse inmóvil, por someterse a sus dictados. Portia lo acogía y se cerraba a su alrededor con todas sus fuerzas mientras lo montaba sin darle tregua, disfrutando del momento. Sus movimientos fueron ganando velocidad poco a poco.

Notó que se le aceleraba la respiración, al igual que a ella. Portia se aferró con más fuerza a sus manos, pero no aminoró el ritmo. En ese instante, sintió que se tensaba sobre él, percibió la tensión que se apoderaba de su cuerpo hasta condensarse.

Le soltó las manos al tiempo que jadeaba y lo agarró por las muñecas para indicarle que le acariciara los pechos. Sin apenas resuello, la obedeció y los tomó en sus manos antes de acariciarlos con sensualidad. Buscó los pezones, duros y enhiestos, los rozó con las yemas de los dedos y los pellizcó... hasta que ella volvió a jadear y se cerró en torno a su miembro con fuerza. Perdió el equilibrio y tuvo que apoyarse sobre su pecho. Una vez estabilizada, retomó el ritmo y prosiguió. Siguió haciéndole el amor cada vez más rápido, cada vez con más ímpetu, y separó las piernas para poder sentirlo más adentro.

El esfuerzo de mantenerse inmóvil estuvo a punto de matarlo. El pulso se le desbocó hasta acompasar el ritmo con el que ella se movía, atrapado en la creciente pasión, apresado en esa cadencia enloquecedora. La acompañó y la instó a ir más deprisa.

Siguió acariciándole los pechos, arrancándole gemidos con los dedos cada vez que le pellizcaba los endurecidos pezones.

Portia se inclinó hacia delante, haciendo que sus pechos se apretaran contra sus manos, y le ordenó con voz ronca:

—Tócame.

No necesitó preguntarle dónde. Abandonó sus pechos, le apartó las voluminosas faldas e introdujo las manos bajo ellas. Las colocó en los muslos y comenzó a ascender. Una de ellas se cerró en torno a una cadera. La otra acarició los húmedos rizos de su entrepierna. La escuchó jadear al tiempo que se cerraba a su alrededor de forma casi dolorosa.

Llevó un dedo hasta su perla.

Y comenzó a acariciarla con delicadeza.

Hizo una pausa y escuchó una elocuente súplica pronunciada con un hilo de voz.

Presionó.

Y ella explotó.

Dejó escapar un delicado grito cuando alcanzó el orgasmo. Sus rítmicos espasmos lo acariciaron mientras se apoyaba sobre su pecho.

Simon sintió la reacción de su cuerpo al instante.

La oleada de deseo visceral, de pasión enfebrecida, de anhelo y de mucho más estuvo a punto de hacer añicos su autocontrol. Echó la cabeza hacia atrás mientras jadeaba para poder llevar un poco de aire a sus pulmones. La aferró por las caderas de modo que no se moviera y la mantuvo así, con su miembro hundido en ella hasta el fondo. Entretanto, hizo todo lo posible por controlar sus demonios, que tras haber sido sometidos a una tortura tan placentera esperaban ser liberados para poder darse un festín con ese cuerpo lánguido, saciado y tan femenino.

Con la mandíbula tensa y los dientes apretados, esperó entre resuellos...

Portia se desplomó sobre su pecho. Alzó la cabeza, le tomó la cara entre las manos y lo besó.

De la forma más sensual. O eso creyó él. Rezó para que fuera una invitación.

La tensión que le hormigueaba bajo la piel y la rigidez que se había apoderado de su cuerpo eran tan intensas que ella lo notó y dudó por un instante. Sin embargo, no tardó en incorporarse de nuevo... para quitarle la venda de los ojos.

Lo observó parpadear y enfrentó su mirada abiertamente mientras se tendía de nuevo sobre su pecho con abandono. Sonrió cuando sus manos la aferraron por las caderas, manteniéndola donde estaba. Con expresión satisfecha y sin apartar la mirada de sus ojos, arrojó la corbata al suelo. Le llevó una mano hasta la cara y trazó el contorno de un pómulo mientras susurraba:

—Tómame cuando quieras.

Un estímulo inmediato para sus sentidos que lo llevó a dar un respingo antes de retomar las riendas de su control y volver a ser dueño de sus acciones. Ella lo miró con los ojos desorbitados, pero el cariz de su sonrisa (una sonrisa decididamente lasciva) no cambió.

Estudió esos ojos azul cobalto. Tenían una expresión soñadora a causa de la pasión satisfecha, pero también muy despierta. Estaba observando, esperando para ver lo que hacía...

Sus alientos se mezclaron. El suyo seguía siendo superficial y trabajoso; el de Portia, relajado tras el clímax.

Otro estímulo que no necesitaba.

Acababa de hacerle una invitación sin especificar nada. Se preguntó si podría imaginarse siquiera la profundidad del anhelo que sus jueguecitos habían despertado.

Quería tomarla desde atrás, colocarla de rodillas frente a él y alzarle el vestido hasta los hombros como si fuera una cautiva rendida, y hundirse en ella mientras sentía cómo su cuerpo se abría a su invasión.

Sentirla suya por completo.

Se humedeció los labios. Le apartó las manos de las caderas para desabrocharle los botones que le cerraban el vestido.

Sus miradas siguieron entrelazadas.

Se dijo a sí mismo que algún día la tomaría como deseaba... Algún día.

Pero todavía no. Ya llegaría el momento de soltar las riendas y demostrarle lo que significaba para él sin necesidad de contenerse. Siempre y cuando fuera capaz de jugar su baza esa noche de forma inteligente y se comportara con la cabeza fría durante los días restantes, o tal vez durante unas semanas.

Ya llegaría el momento de demostrarle exactamente lo que ella le provocaba.

La movió lo imprescindible y le sacó el vestido por la cabeza. Portia colaboró levantando los brazos y ayudándolo a alzar las faldas. Después le llegó el turno a la camisola.

La dejó desnuda salvo por las medias.

Rodó sobre el colchón para quedar sobre ella.

Estuvo a punto de perder la razón cuando sintió que le empujaba un hombro.

—Espera... —le dijo.

Su control estaba en un tris de hacerse añicos y, de hecho, comenzó a resquebrajarse...

Portia se movió en ese momento. Sin resuello, Simon separó los labios para asegurarle que no podía esperar y... contempló, estupefacto, cómo ella alzaba una de sus largas piernas para quitarse la media. Parpadeó mientras la observaba. Ella enfrentó su mirada mientras arrojaba la prenda al suelo.

—Me gusta sentir tu piel contra la mía.

No tenía intención de discutir ese punto. Dejó que se moviera lo justo para repetir la operación con la otra pierna, maravillándose durante el proceso al ver la facilidad con la que realizaba la tarea.

A su mente acudieron nuevas posibilidades...

Pero en ese momento ella se libró de la segunda media, le arrojó los brazos al cuello y le bajó la cabeza.

—Ya está. Ahora puedes...

La interrumpió con un beso abrasador.

Tomó su aliento, devoró su boca y le robó la razón. La besó con un ímpetu creciente, moviendo la lengua con frenesí hasta que ella arqueó la espalda y le suplicó sin palabras... Le inmovilizó las caderas y se hundió en ella.

Una vez. Y otra. Y otra más.

Sintió que las riendas se le escapaban de las manos, pero no pudo recuperarlas. Se vio obligado a rendirse a la tormenta. A rendirse a la incontrolable necesidad que lo instaba a hacerla suya.

Lejos de quejarse, ella se ofreció gustosa mientras le acariciaba la espalda con las uñas. Mientras le exigía sin tapujos que le diera más, movida por un deseo desesperado.

Le separó los muslos y Portia fue más allá, alzando las piernas para rodearle las caderas. La posición la abrió a sus embestidas y le ofreció la libertad de movimientos que ansiaba.

Con el corazón desbocado, la tomó y se entregó a ella.

Echó la cabeza hacia atrás y, sin soltarla, se dejó llevar. Cerró los ojos y dejó que el turbulento poder lo invadiera.

Sintió cómo lo rodeaba y lo alzaba hasta las alturas.

Hasta que lo hizo añicos.

Se percató de que Portia también se tensaba mientras él se estremecía y se percató del momento exacto en el que la traspasó el placer.

Sintió que el éxtasis los inundaba al unísono, corriendo por sus venas y alimentando sus corazones.

Portia descansaba sobre los almohadones donde Simon la había dejado una vez que el huracán hubo pasado.

Pasado, pero no desaparecido. La placentera satisfacción seguía ahí a pesar de que la pasión se iba desvaneciendo y la languidez se apoderaba de sus cuerpos.

Qué fácil sería acostumbrarse a eso, pensó. A esa sensación de intimidad, a la entrega, al ímpetu de la pasión. Al sublime deleite.

Dejó que uno de sus brazos reposara sobre el almohadón que tenía bajo la cabeza mientras que el otro jugueteaba con el cabello de Simon. Su suave textura era de lo más sensual. Estaba tendido en parte sobre ella y en parte sobre el colchón, con un brazo bajo su cuerpo y la cabeza apoyada sobre sus pechos. Su otra mano descansaba sobre su vientre en un gesto posesivo. Su cuerpo era muy pesado, irradiaba mucho calor y resultaba increíblemente real.

Había salido de ella poco antes, de modo que su cuerpo iba recobrando la normalidad poco a poco, iba volviendo a ser suyo solamente, iba acostumbrándose a no tenerlo dentro de sí. Sentía una curiosa vitalidad. Sus sentidos todavía estaban obnubilados por el éxtasis, su sexo aún estaba palpitante e inflamado y los latidos de su corazón seguían siendo frenéticos.

Kitty yacía, fría e inmóvil, en la caseta del hielo, incapaz de sentir nada.

Meditó durante un buen rato sobre lo que había compartido con Simon. Sobre todo lo que aún les quedaba por descubrir.

Y juró en silencio no cometer los errores de Kitty.

Valoraría la confianza y la devoción por encima de todo. Entendería el amor por lo que era, lo aceptaría tal y como había surgido, como también aceptaría a la persona que lo había inspirado.

Y se aseguraría de que él hiciera lo mismo.

Si lo que había entre ellos era amor, no iba a ser tan tonta como para luchar contra él. Al contrario. Si era amor, lucharía por él con uñas y dientes.

Bajó la vista hacia la cabeza de Simon y pasó los dedos por esos suaves mechones castaños, más sedosos que los de muchas mujeres.

Él alzó la cabeza y enfrentó su mirada.

Portia la sostuvo un instante y después dijo:

—No voy a casarme contigo a menos que esté convencida.

—Lo sé.

Deseó poder ver la expresión que asomaba a sus ojos,

pero la luz de la luna se había desvanecido y los había dejado sumidos en la oscuridad.

Simon soltó un suspiro, se apartó y se apoyó en los almohadones, llevándola consigo. Rodeada por sus brazos y exhausta, apoyó la cabeza sobre su pecho.

—Quiero aprender más. Necesito aprender más, pero no creas que eso es el primer paso de un sí.

Él alzó la cabeza pasado un momento y le dio un beso en la coronilla.

—Duérmete.

Su voz fue bastante tierna, si bien sospechaba que sus pensamientos no tenían un pelo de ternura. Su naturaleza no le permitía ser complaciente. No era el tipo de hombre que renunciaba a la lucha, que se alejaba de la liza al primer revés. Recuperaría fuerzas y volvería a la carga, implacable y dispuesto a lograr su objetivo.

Aunque no le serviría de mucho, porque ella no estaba dispuesta a rendirse.

Claro que ya se lo había advertido, al igual que había hecho él. Era una especie de tregua. Compleja y condicionada, pero que les permitía seguir adelante. No sólo a la hora de explorar la naturaleza del vínculo que había entre ellos, sino también a la hora de afrontar lo que los próximos días les depararan. El «caballero de Bow Street» y el desenmascaramiento del asesino de Kitty. Pasara lo que pasase, lo enfrentarían codo con codo, unidos por un acuerdo tan implícito que ni siquiera necesitaba de palabras.

Había sido un día muy largo, plagado de acontecimientos que habían provocado una inesperada conmoción.

El reloj fue marcando los minutos mientras los latidos del corazón de Simon, que resonaban bajo su oreja, la relajaban y tranquilizaban.

Cerró los ojos y se rindió al embrujo de la noche.

Simon la despertó exactamente como a ella le habría gustado que lo hiciera la vez anterior.

Siempre dormía como un tronco, de modo que su cuerpo respondió a sus caricias sin que fuera consciente de ello. Le separó los muslos, se colocó sobre ella y la penetró.

Sintió cómo arqueaba la espalda y contenía el aliento antes de suspirar y abrir los ojos. Unos ojos que lo miraron con un brillo cegador. Tan misteriosos que hechizaban. Mientras se hundía en ella, creyó ahogarse en esas profundidades azules.

Portia alzó las caderas y lo estrechó con fuerza al tiempo que cerraba los ojos y el éxtasis la consumía. Dejó escapar un grito ahogado.

Un grito que lo atravesó y se hundió en su cuerpo hasta asentarse en sus entrañas, en su corazón, en su alma, y lanzarlo sin remisión a la vorágine. Hasta arrojarlo por el confín del mundo hacia un dulce olvido.

Envueltos en el calor de las sábanas, se demoró un instante sobre ella mientras saboreaba la perfección de su unión, la perfección de la respuesta de Portia. Ella giró la cabeza y sus labios se encontraron en un beso lento y tierno. Lo rodeó con los brazos y con sus delgados muslos.

El amanecer se estaba acercando. No podía dejar que volviera a dormirse. La espabiló y la sacó de la cama para vestirla.

Sus gruñidos le dejaron muy claro que el amanecer no era su momento preferido del día para escabullirse por los pasillos.

Llegaron hasta su habitación sin que nadie los viera. Abrió la puerta, depositó un beso en sus nudillos y la hizo pasar antes de cerrar la puerta de nuevo.

Con los ojos clavados en la puerta y el ceño fruncido, Portia escuchó las pisadas de Simon mientras éste se alejaba. Habría preferido quedarse calentita y segura entre sus brazos, al menos durante una hora más. Lo suficiente como para recobrar las fuerzas. Unas fuerzas que él se había encargado de robarle. Mantenerse a su lado durante el recorrido por los pasillos le había costado la misma vida. Había tenido que concentrarse para que sus músculos siguieran moviéndose y pasaran por alto los extraños dolorcillos y las molestias.

Tenía la certeza más absoluta de que Simon no sabía lo... vigoroso que era en realidad.

Contuvo un suspiro, dio media vuelta y ojeó la habitación.

Estaba tal cual la había dejado la noche anterior: la ropa de la cama apartada, la ventana abierta y las cortinas descorridas.

Echó un vistazo a la cama y consideró la idea de acostarse. Ésa sería la opción más sensata dado el estado en el que se encontraba. El problema era que, en cuanto colocara la cabeza sobre la almohada, se quedaría dormida. Tendría que ponerse el camisón antes, o se vería obligada a inventarse una explicación que convenciera a la doncella.

El problema era irresoluble, al menos en su estado. No le quedaban fuerzas para desabrochar todos esos botones que Simon acababa de abrochar...

Lo cual dejaba el sillón situado junto a la chimenea o el alféizar acolchado de la ventana. La brisa del amanecer era demasiado fresca. Se decidió por el sillón, aunque una chimenea sin fuego era un poco deprimente. Arrastró el sillón de modo que mirara a la ventana y se dejó caer en su mullido asiento con un profundo suspiro.

Dejó que sus pensamientos vagaran. Ahondó en lo más profundo de su corazón y se preguntó qué sentiría Simon en el suyo. Repasó sus objetivos y reafirmó sus aspiraciones. Hizo un mohín al recordar la conclusión a la que había llegado y según la cual Simon era, de entre todos los caballeros presentes y pese a ser un Cynster, el epítome del hombre con el que casarse, por las cualidades que poseía. Lo que había querido decir, y en esos momentos lo veía muy claro y no le quedaba más remedio que admitirlo, era que las cualidades inherentes a su persona conseguirían convencerla de que se casara.

Aunque también se conociera al dedillo todos sus defectos. Su afán protector siempre le había resultado en exceso irritante, si bien era su talante posesivo y dictatorial lo que más la asustaba. Una vez que fuera suya, no habría escapatoria. Ésa era su naturaleza y no había vuelta de hoja.

Sintió un escalofrío y se abrazó, deseando haber cogido un chal. No tenía la fuerza suficiente como para ponerse en pie y hacerlo en ese momento.

El único modo de aceptar el cortejo de Simon, de ofrecerle su mano y aceptar todo lo que eso conllevaba, pasaba por estar totalmente segura de que siempre tendría en cuenta sus sentimientos y trataría con ella cada asunto sin imponer su opinión de forma arbitraria.

Toda una hazaña teniendo en cuenta que trataba con un tirano.

La noche anterior había acudido a su lado a sabiendas de que era ella quien llevaba las riendas de la situación, con la esperanza de que le permitiera manejarlas. Podría habérselas arrebatado en cualquier momento, pero no lo había hecho aunque le había costado la misma vida contenerse, según había podido comprobar.

Simon se había plegado a sus condiciones y ella había pasado la noche segura y convencida de su fuerza vital, de su capacidad para vivir y para amar. De su capacidad para confiar y ganarse la confianza de Simon en respuesta.

Él jamás habría permitido algo así antes, sin importar las circunstancias. No estaba en su naturaleza... No lo había estado nunca, pero en ese momento sí era una cualidad visible en él, al menos en lo concerniente a ella.

Lo percibía en la disponibilidad para compartir las riendas, para intentar acomodarse a sus deseos tal y como le había prometido. Lo había sentido en sus caricias, lo había leído en sus ojos... Los acontecimientos de esa noche confirmaban que estaba allí y que no era un fragmento de su ansiosa imaginación.

De modo que no les quedaba más remedio que seguir adelante y examinar las posibilidades.

Al otro lado de la ventana, el cielo adquirió un tinte rosáceo antes de convertirse en el azul pálido de un caluroso día de verano.

El clic de la cerradura la arrancó de sus reflexiones. Se

giró sin levantarse del sillón mientras le ordenaba a su mente que funcionara, y vio cómo entraba la menuda y alegre doncella que se ocupaba de su habitación.

La muchacha la vio y abrió los ojos como platos. A su rostro asomó una expresión compasiva.

—¡Ay, señorita! ¿Ha pasado la noche ahí?

—Yo... —Rara vez mentía, pero...—. Sí. —Miró hacia la ventana de nuevo e hizo un significativo gesto con la mano—. No podía dormir y...

—Bueno, no es de extrañar, ¿verdad? —Con actitud alegre y despreocupada, la doncella sacó un paño y comenzó a limpiar la repisa de la chimenea—. Nos hemos enterado de que fue usted quien encontró el cuerpo..., de que se tropezó con él.

Portia inclinó la cabeza.

—Cierto.

—Todos lo comentamos en las dependencias de la servidumbre. Estábamos muy asustados por que la hubiera matado uno de los caballeros, pero la señora Fletcher, el ama de llaves, nos dijo que segurito, segurito que han sido los gitanos.

—¿Los gitanos?

—Ese Arturo... Siempre anda por aquí, dándose aires... Es un diablo muy apuesto y tiene mucho éxito con las damas, ya me entiende usted...

Portia frunció el ceño para sus adentros. Luchó contra su conciencia un instante.

—¿Hay alguna razón que os haga creer que podría haber sido alguno de los caballeros?

—¡Qué va! Es que somos así, nos gusta imaginar cosas.

—¿La señora Glossup se había ganado la simpatía de la servidumbre?

—¿La señora? —repitió al tiempo que cogía un jarrón de peltre y lo frotaba con todas sus fuerzas mientras sopesaba la respuesta—. No era mala. Tenía mucho carácter, claro, y supongo que algunos podrían llamarla frívola. Pero, bueno, todas las damas recién casadas lo son, ¿no?

Portia se mordió la lengua.

La muchacha soltó el jarrón y se guardó el paño en el bolsillo.

—En fin, qué quiere que le diga... Es el día de la colada para las sábanas. —Atravesó la habitación hasta llegar junto a la cama mientras ella la observaba y envidiaba ese despliegue de energía—. Blenkinsop dice que vendrá un tipo de Lunnon. —Agarró las sábanas por el embozo y alzó la vista hacia ella—. Para preguntar por lo que ha pasado.

Portia asintió con la cabeza.

—Según parece, así es como deben hacerse estas cosas.

La doncella se quedó boquiabierta por la sorpresa. Tiró de las sábanas...

Y un siseo furioso se escuchó en la habitación.

La muchacha se alejó de la cama de un salto con los ojos clavados en las sábanas. Se quedó lívida.

—¡Ay, Dios mío! —la última palabra fue un auténtico chillido incontrolado.

Portia se levantó de un salto y corrió hacia ella.

El siseo se hizo más fuerte.

—¡Por el amor de Dios! —exclamó con los ojos clavados en la víbora que se retorcía furiosa en mitad de su cama.

Le dio un tironcito a la doncella de la manga.

La muchacha chilló.

Atravesaron la estancia al unísono como si les fuera la vida en ello, abrieron la puerta y la cerraron con fuerza a sus espaldas.

La doncella se dejó caer sobre la barandilla de la cercana escalera, jadeando en busca de aire.

Portia comprobó que la hoja de la puerta bajaba hasta el suelo sin dejar resquicio alguno para que se colara una víbora furiosa y, una vez segura, se dejó caer contra la pared.

Una hora después estaba sentada en la habitación de lady O, con una humeante taza de chocolate en las manos. Ni siquiera el chocolate era capaz de detener sus escalofríos y eso que estaba hirviendo.

Su habitación estaba emplazada al fondo del ala este. Blenkinsop, ocupado con las tareas matinales necesarias para poner en orden la gran mansión, estaba a los pies de la escalera cuando la doncella y ella salieron despavoridas de su habitación. El mayordomo había escuchado sus gritos y había subido corriendo para comprobar lo que pasaba, justo a tiempo de evitar que la doncella sufriera un ataque de nervios.

Por tanto, recayó sobre ella la tarea de explicarlo todo. Blenkinsop se quedó lívido antes de hacerse cargo de la situación sin pérdida de tiempo. La acompañó a un gabinete de la planta baja mientras ordenaba a unos cuantos criados que lo ayudaran, tras lo cual le encargó al ama de llaves que se hiciera cargo de la llorosa doncella.

Con voz quebrada, ella le pidió que avisaran a Simon. No se había detenido a considerar si era indecoroso o no. Lo único que sabía en aquel momento era que lo necesitaba y que él acudiría en su ayuda.

Así fue. Le bastó con una mirada para llevarla de nuevo escaleras arriba, a la habitación de lady O.

Recostada sobre sus almohadones, la anciana había escuchado la abreviada explicación de Simon justo antes de atravesarlo con una mirada furibunda.

—Ve en busca de Granny. —Cuando vio que él parpadeaba sorprendido, resopló y se explicó—: Granville. Lord Netherfield. Puede que ya esté un poco enclenque, pero siempre ha sabido mantener la cabeza fría en las crisis. Su habitación está en el centro del ala principal. La más cercana a las escaleras. —Simon asintió mientras la mirada de lady O caía sobre ella—. En cuanto a ti, muchacha... será mejor que te sientes antes de que te caigas al suelo.

La obedeció y se dejó caer en el sillón que había delante de la chimenea. Simon se marchó en cuanto la vio sentada.

Una vez que se quedaron a solas, lady O se bajó de la cama, se arrebujó con su chal, cogió su bastón y se acercó despacio hasta el otro sillón. En cuanto estuvo sentada, la observó con esos ojos tan perspicaces.

—Muy bien. Cuéntame lo que ha pasado y no dejes nada en el tintero.

Blenkinsop apareció justo cuando la curiosidad de la anciana quedaba satisfecha, y para ello tuvo que inventarse que se había quedado dormida en el sillón la noche anterior...

—Hemos sacado la víbora, señorita. Los criados han registrado la habitación y no hay peligro alguno.

Le dio las gracias con un murmullo mientras intentaba asimilar que hubiera ocurrido algo semejante. Que aquello no se había tratado de un mal sueño. Lady O mandó llamar a un par de doncellas para que la ayudaran a vestirse y otra más para que le trajera ropa limpia a ella. Junto con el chocolate.

Cuando los toquecitos en la puerta anunciaron la llegada de Simon y de lord Netherfield, ella ya estaba sentada, primorosamente ataviada con un vestido de sarga en tono magenta y bebiendo el chocolate al tiempo que trataba infructuosamente de asimilar que alguien había intentado matarla. O, al menos, darle un susto de muerte.

Lord Netherfield se mostró preocupado, pero práctico. Después de que le contara lo sucedido y mirara a Simon a los ojos al llegar a la parte en la que explicaba por qué había dormido en el sillón en lugar de hacerlo en la cama, el anciano, sentado en un taburete entre los dos sillones, se echó hacia atrás mientras su mirada los recorría.

—Esto es de lo más alarmante. Le he pedido a Blenkinsop que mantenga el asunto en secreto. Según parece, ninguna de las damas ha escuchado el alboroto y la servidumbre es de fiar. No dirán nada.

Simon, de pie y con un brazo apoyado en la repisa de la chimenea, frunció el ceño.

—¿Por qué?

Lord Netherfield alzó la vista hacia él.

—Para privar al enemigo de información, ¿para qué si no? —Su mirada regresó a ella—. Tal vez no sea mucho en cuanto a información, pero es un hecho que esa víbora no se ha colado en tu cama por sí sola. En estos momentos, alguien espera que estés muerta o, si no, que estés lo bastante alterada como para marcharte de inmediato.

—¿Antes de que llegue el caballero de Bow Street? —preguntó Simon, mirando de reojo al anciano, que asintió con la cabeza.

—Eso es lo que creo —contestó y su mirada regresó a ella—. ¿Cómo te sientes, querida?

Portia meditó la respuesta.

—Asustada, pero no tanto como para salir huyendo —admitió.

—Ésta es mi chica. Así que... —Lord Netherfield se golpeó los muslos con las palmas de las manos—. ¿Qué conclusión sacamos de todo esto? ¿Por qué desea el asesino o asesina de Kitty verte lejos de aquí, ya sea muerta o huyendo a toda prisa? Creo que debemos asumir que ha sido la misma persona, dadas las circunstancias.

Portia lo miró sin saber qué decir.

—Porque —contestó Simon— el asesino cree que viste algo que lo incrimina.

—O que escuchaste algo. O que sabes algo, algún otro detalle —convino lady O—. Sí, tiene que ser eso. —Su mirada la atravesó—. Así que, ¿qué es lo que sabes?

Portia los miró.

—Nada.

La sometieron a un interrogatorio que la obligó a repasar todo lo que había hecho; todo lo que había visto desde que entrara en el vestíbulo principal la tarde anterior. A la postre, soltó la taza vacía y dijo:

—No puedo decir algo que desconozco.

Los tres aceptaron la realidad con un resoplido, un suspiro y un ceño fruncido respectivamente.

—¡De acuerdo! —exclamó Netherfield, poniéndose en pie—. Sólo nos queda esperar la llegada del tipo de Bow Street. Cuando hables con él, cuéntale todo lo que sabes; sobre Kitty y sobre todo lo demás. No sólo los acontecimientos de ayer, sino lo que has presenciado desde que llegaste... No. Aún más. Cualquier cosa que supieras de antemano sobre los invitados. —Enfrentó su mirada—.

Quién sabe si tienes alguna información, por insignificante que parezca, que incrimina a ese canalla.

Ella parpadeó antes de asentir con la cabeza.

—Sí, por supuesto. —Comenzó a catalogar mentalmente a todos los invitados que conocía de antemano.

Lady O preguntó con voz desabrida:

—¿A qué viene eso de enviar a un hombre de Bow Street? ¿Por qué tienen que involucrarse?

—Así es como se hacen las cosas ahora. No es muy agradable, pero parece que tiene su función en aras de la justicia. No hace demasiado tiempo me contaron un caso muy peculiar en el club. Un caballero al que habían asesinado con un atizador en su propia biblioteca. Todas las sospechas recaían sobre el mayordomo, pero el investigador demostró que había sido el hermano del fallecido. Un escándalo impresionante, claro está. La familia quedó destrozada...

Las palabras del anciano quedaron flotando en el aire. Todos guardaron un respetuoso silencio mientras pensaban exactamente lo mismo.

Quienquiera que hubiese matado a Kitty o bien era uno de los invitados de los Glossup o bien era uno de los nietos de lord Netherfield, James o Henry. Si se desenmascaraba al asesino, habría un escándalo. Un escándalo potencialmente dañino. Para alguien, para una familia en concreto.

El anciano suspiró pasado un instante.

—No puedo decir que me gustara Kitty, ya lo sabéis. No la aprobaba. No aprobaba ese modo tan frívolo de comportarse con Henry. Era una muchacha tonta y de lo más desvergonzada, pero... —Frunció los labios—. A pesar de todo, no se merecía semejante muerte. —Los miró de uno en uno—. No me gustaría que su asesino quedara impune. La pobre muchacha se merece al menos eso.

Todos asintieron con la cabeza. El pacto estaba sellado. Se conocían demasiado bien como para no reconocer lo que tenían en común: su fe en la justicia, la reacción instintiva que los enfrentaba a aquellos que la despreciaban.

Juntos, trabajarían para desenmascarar al asesino, fuera quien fuese.

—¡De acuerdo! —exclamó de nuevo lord Netherfield dando una palmada. La miró a ella en primer lugar antes de desviar los ojos hacia lady O—. Bajemos a desayunar. Y veamos a quién le sorprende ver a la señorita Ashford fresca como una lechuga.

Se pusieron en pie. Se arreglaron las faldas, las chaquetas y los puños de las camisas, y bajaron la escalinata, listos para presentar batalla.

13

No les sirvió de mucho. Los comensales que se reunieron en torno a la mesa del desayuno estaban tan nerviosos (unos se sobresaltaban por el menor ruido y otros estaban sumidos en sus pensamientos) que les resultó imposible distinguir una reacción significativa a la presencia de Portia.

Todos estaban muy pálidos. Muchos parecían exhaustos, como si no hubieran dormido bien.

—Si juzgáramos por las apariencias, se podría tachar de sospechosa a la mitad de los invitados —murmuró Simon mientras caminaba con Portia por la terraza en dirección al prado, después de abandonar el comedor matinal.

—Creo que flota cierta sensación de culpabilidad en el ambiente. —Muchas de las damas de más edad habían abandonado por ese día la costumbre de desayunar en sus aposentos y se habían unido al resto del grupo en el comedor—. Si hubieran intentado hablar con ella para entenderla, en lugar de darle la espalda e intentar controlarla cuando vieron que pasar por alto sus transgresiones era inútil... No parecía tener amigos, ni siquiera un confidente. Nadie que pudiera aconsejarla. De haber contado con esa persona, tal vez alguien sabría por qué la han asesinado. O tal vez ni siquiera estaría muerta.

Simon enarcó las cejas, pero no hizo comentario alguno. Tanto en su familia como en la de Portia todas las mujeres estaban rodeadas de otras de gran carácter desde la más tierna infancia. Le costaba trabajo pensar que la vida fuera de otra manera.

Se encaminaron hacia el lago de tácito acuerdo. La vista era fresca y relajante. Reconfortante. Plácida.

—Las damas parecen ser de la opinión de que ha sido alguien ajeno a la propiedad, por lo que supongo que se refieren a los gitanos. —La miró de soslayo—. ¿Sabes si alguna de ellas tiene una razón sólida para sospechar de Arturo o de Dennis?

Portia negó con la cabeza.

—Lo piensan porque es la opción más segura para todos. La posibilidad de que el asesino sea un conocido, alguien con quien han compartido los últimos días..., les resulta aterradora.

Quiso preguntarle si ella tenía miedo, pero se mordió la lengua cuando la miró por el rabillo del ojo. Era demasiado inteligente como para no tenerlo. Aunque prefiriera mantenerla alejada del miedo, no podía impedir que viera cosas, las analizara y sacara sus propias conclusiones.

Aceptó de mala gana que entre ellos siempre sería así. Si tenía que tratar con ella tal y como era, eso no cambiaría. Tal vez se amoldara un poquito a sus deseos, pero sería él quien tendría que realizar el cambio más radical. Tendría que amoldar su forma de pensar y modificar sus reacciones si quería tener la opción de llevarla al altar.

—¡Esto no tiene sentido! —Habían llegado frente al mirador. Portia abandonó el camino y echó a andar hacia los escalones. Se agarró las faldas mientras daba media vuelta para sentarse en uno de ellos.

Mientras la observaba allí sentada, bañada por el sol, se preguntó si todavía tendría frío y se sentó a su lado, lo bastante cerca como para que se apoyara en él si lo deseaba.

Con los codos sobre las rodillas y la barbilla apoyada en las manos, Portia contemplaba el lago con semblante ceñudo.

—¿Cuál de los hombres podría haber matado a Kitty?

—Ya oíste lo que dijo Willoughby. Aparte de Charlie, que estaba con lady O, y de mí, cualquiera de ellos. —Un momento después, añadió—: Por lo que sabemos, también pudo ser cualquiera de las damas.

Portia giró la cabeza para mirarlo.

—¿Winifred?

—¿Drusilla? —apuntó él.

Ella hizo un mohín.

—Kitty era demasiado baja, podría haber sido cualquiera de ellas.

—O cualquiera de las otras. ¿Cómo vamos a descartarlas? —Apoyó el codo en el escalón que tenía a la espalda y se echó hacia atrás mientras ladeaba un poco el cuerpo para poder mirarla a la cara—. Tal vez Kitty hiciera algo en Londres durante la temporada que la enemistara con una de ellas.

Portia volvió a fruncir el ceño antes de menear la cabeza.

—No percibí nada de eso... Me refiero a que no he visto que ninguna le guardara rencor.

Pasó un instante de silencio antes de que él sugiriera:

—Hagamos una lista con aquellos que no han podido ser. Es imposible que haya sido una de las hermanas Hammond. Son demasiado bajas y me resulta del todo inconcebible. Y lo mismo se aplica a Lucy Buckstead.

—Aunque no a su madre. La señora Buckstead es bastante corpulenta y tal vez Kitty estuviera planeando algo que pudiera arruinar las posibilidades de Lucy. Es la única hija de los Buckstead, después de todo, y está enamorada de James.

Simon asintió con la cabeza.

—La señora Buckstead se queda en la lista de las posibles sospechosas. No es probable que haya sido ella, pero no la descartamos.

—Y por la misma razón tenemos que dejar al señor Buckstead.

—En mi opinión, los caballeros son todos sospechosos. Salvo Charlie y yo.

Ella parpadeó, pero siguió mirándolo.

—¿Y lord Netherfield?

Tras un instante en el que sus miradas siguieron entrelazadas, le contestó:

—Hasta que sepamos quién fue, asumo que ha podido ser cualquiera. Así que todos están en nuestra lista de sospechosos.

Portia apretó los labios y estaba a punto de protestar...

—No —la interrumpió sin miramientos, logrando con su tono que ella parpadeara, sorprendida. Al ver que no decía nada, se vio obligado a explicárselo—. El asesino trató de matarte. Dado que ahora eres su objetivo, no estoy dispuesto a correr ningún riesgo. —Sintió que se le crispaba el rostro mientras añadía, por si acaso Portia no lo había entendido—: Ninguno. No pienso excluir a nadie.

Sus ojos lo estudiaron un instante. Casi podía ver los pensamientos que se arremolinaban tras esas profundidades azul cobalto. Casi podía ver la balanza en la que pesaba su conclusión y su personalidad, junto con todo lo que ésta conllevaba. A la postre, acabó accediendo y asintió con la cabeza.

—De acuerdo. —Su mirada regresó al lago y él dejó escapar un silencioso suspiro—. Tampoco es lady O. Ni lady Hammond.

Lo meditó un instante antes de mostrarse de acuerdo.

—Cierto. Y creo que también podemos eliminar a la señora Archer.

—Pero no a su marido.

—No creo que fuese él, pero de acuerdo. Tampoco podemos olvidarlo.

—Si seguimos tu línea de razonamiento, cualquiera de los Glossup podría ser el responsable.

Simon titubeó un instante.

—¿Qué opinas de Oswald?

Ella frunció el ceño antes de hacer un mohín.

—Creo que evitaba a Kitty a toda costa. Supongo que porque lo consideraba un niño y lo trataba como a tal.

—Poco satisfactorio para su ego, pero... a menos que

haya algo que explique su transformación en un asesino rabioso, y no hay nada en su carácter que lo predisponga, no parece un candidato probable.

—Muy cierto. ¿Y Swanston? ¿Lo eliminamos por el mismo motivo?

Él frunció el ceño.

—No creo que debamos hacerlo. Es el hermano de Kitty. Tal vez hubiera rencillas entre ellos, y no es tan tranquilo como Oswald ni tiene un carácter tan moderado. Si Kitty lo hostigó demasiado, Swanston habría podido asesinarla. Desde luego, tiene el físico necesario para hacerlo. Si lo hizo o no...

—Lo que nos lleva a Winifred. —Portia hizo una pausa para meditar al respecto. A la postre, dijo—: ¿Crees que podría estar tan enfadada con su hermana por ese empeño en robarle los pretendientes? Recuerda que no dejaba en paz a Desmond.

La miró a la cara.

—Tú conoces a Winifred mejor que yo. ¿Crees que podría haberlo hecho?

Portia contempló las oscuras aguas del lago un buen rato antes de mirarlo y arrugar la nariz.

—Winifred tendrá que seguir en la lista.

—Y Desmond también, no cabe duda, algo que sólo refuerza el móvil de Winifred.

Portia hizo un mohín, pero no rebatió su conclusión.

—Ambrose también. Lo que significa que tanto lady Calvin como Drusilla deben estar en la lista.

Un momento después, Simon le preguntó:

—¿Por qué Drusilla? Entiendo lo de lady Calvin, ha invertido mucho tiempo y esfuerzo en el futuro de su hijo y, aunque es muy reservada, se nota que Ambrose es su preferido. Pero, tal y como yo lo veo, entre Drusilla y Ambrose no existe el menor vínculo fraternal.

—Cierto. Sin embargo, Drusilla tiene dos motivos. En primer lugar, de entre todos los invitados, ella era la que más resentía el comportamiento de Kitty. Aun teniendo todos los atributos de los que ella carece, Kitty no pare-

cía estar contenta con la vida. Estoy segura de que eso la
sacaba de sus casillas. No se conocían de antemano, así
que ésa es la única explicación que se me ocurre para justificar su reacción.

—¿Y el segundo motivo?

—Lady Calvin, por supuesto. El dolor que su madre
se vería obligada a sufrir si Ambrose acababa envuelto en
un escándalo. —Lo miró a los ojos—. Drusilla está dedi-
cada a su madre en cuerpo y alma.

Él enarcó las cejas, pero si se paraba a pensarlo...

—Eso nos deja a los gitanos o a uno de los criados.

Portia frunció el ceño.

—No me hace gracia que Arturo entrara a hurtadillas
por el jardín de los setos a todas horas, pero no veo razón
alguna que lo llevara a enfadarse con Kitty hasta el punto de matarla. Si el bebé era suyo... —Dejó la frase en el
aire—. ¡Caramba! ¿Crees que eso podría ser motivo suficiente? Que Kitty le dijera que estaba planeando deshacerse del bebé... ¿No tienen los gitanos unas leyes al respecto o algo por el estilo?

Simon sostuvo su mirada sin flaquear.

—Todos los hombres tienen unas leyes al respecto o
algo por el estilo.

Ella se ruborizó.

—Sí, claro. Pero ya sabes a lo que me refiero.

—Sí, pero creo que has pasado por alto una cosa.

Portia enarcó las cejas.

—La secuencia temporal. Kitty debió de concebir en
Londres, no aquí. Y Arturo no estaba en Londres.

—¡Ah! —Su expresión se aclaró—. Por supuesto. Así
que, en realidad, no hay razón alguna para que Arturo la
matara.

—Ninguna que se me ocurra. En cuanto a Dennis, aunque imaginemos un amor no correspondido y dado que
Arturo estaba cortejando a Kitty, no creo que él mismo se
viera como candidato a ganarse sus favores. ¿Por qué iba
a matarla?

—Le pregunté a la doncella acerca de la opinión que

el servicio tenía de Kitty. La chica nació en el condado y ha vivido en la propiedad toda su vida. Conoce a todo el mundo y tiene la edad suficiente como para haberse percatado de cualquier indicio de escándalo entre la señora y algún criado. No noté nada en sus palabras que pudiera llevar a la remota conclusión de que algo así estuviera sucediendo. De hecho, me aseguró que a las criadas les aterraba la posibilidad de que fuera uno de los caballeros, pero que el ama de llaves las había tranquilizado asegurándoles que, sin duda alguna, fue uno de los gitanos.

—Los gitanos —repitió con voz burlona—. Siempre son los chivos expiatorios más convenientes.

—Sobre todo si recogen su campamento y se marchan. —Hizo una pausa para meditar—. Me pregunto si el asesino, sea quien sea, lo tuvo en cuenta.

—Yo diría que contaba con ello. El hecho de que los gitanos marcharan en plena noche sería su salvación.

Ambos clavaron la vista en el lago y observaron las pequeñas olas que la brisa provocaba en su cristalina superficie. Pasaron varios minutos antes de que Portia suspirara.

—Los Glossup. Siguen todos en la lista salvo Oswald. Incluso lady Glossup. ¿Por qué crees que uno de ellos querría matar a Kitty? Llevaban aguantándola al menos tres años y los Archer eran sus invitados. ¿Por qué iban a matarla? ¿Y por qué en este preciso momento? Tendría que haber una razón de peso.

—Hay dos razones —replicó él, con voz firme—. En primer lugar, el divorcio. Un tema que Henry se ha visto obligado a considerar de un tiempo a esta parte. Y, en segundo lugar, un hecho fundamental: el bebé que Kitty llevaba no era de ninguno de ellos, pero de haber nacido, habría sido el heredero al título. Tal vez no sea tan preeminente como el de los Cynster o el de los Ashford, pero es un título que se remonta casi a los mismos tiempos que los nuestros. Su linaje es antiguo y, a su modo, son una familia distinguida.

—Pero Kitty no iba a tener el bebé. Estaba decidida al respecto.

—Tú la escuchaste mientras se lo contaba a su madre. ¿Cuántas personas más lo sabrían?

Ella se encogió de hombros y alzó las manos.

—¿Cuántos sabían que estaba embarazada?

—Sólo tú, aquellos a los que se lo dijo personalmente y, en consecuencia, todos aquellos con los que estos últimos hablaron.

Portia arrugó la nariz.

—Yo se lo he dicho a lady O. Y a ti.

—A eso me refería. Y no nos olvidemos de la servidumbre. Los criados se enteran de mucho más de lo que creemos.

—Y debían de saber que Kitty y Henry llevaban vidas separadas.

—Lo que significa que habría sido obvio para todos ellos que el hijo de Kitty no era...

Cuando dejó de hablar, Portia lo miró, espantada.

—Si el bebé no era un Glossup, y lo más probable es que no lo fuese, habría sido horrible. Pero ¿y si lo era?

—Peor aún, ¿y si no lo era, pero Kitty se empecinaba en afirmar lo contrario?

—No. Te olvidas de un detalle. No quería llevar el embarazo a término.

—No lo he olvidado. —Su tono de voz fue gélido—. Si quería persuadir al padre (o a alguien que pudiera ser el padre, o incluso a alguien que supiera a ciencia cierta que no lo era) de que lo más sensato era abortar... —La miró a los ojos—. ¿Qué mejor forma de persuadir a James, o a Harold, o incluso a lord Netherfield, de que la ayudaran que afirmar que el niño era un Glossup, pero no de Henry?

Portia lo miró con los ojos desorbitados.

—Quieres decir... que le habría dicho a James que era de Harold o a Harold que era de James. O a lord Netherfield que era de cualquiera de los dos... —Se llevó las manos al pecho y tragó saliva—. ¡Válgame Dios!

—Exacto. ¿Y si Henry lo descubrió? —Portia sostuvo su mirada un instante antes de apartarla. Él prosiguió tras una brevísima pausa—: Y eso sin tener en cuenta la amenazadora posibilidad de un divorcio en el horizonte. Para Harold y Catherine, la idea es de lo más chocante, no digamos ya para lord Netherfield. Mucho más que para nosotros. Son de otra generación, y supone un escándalo impensable que recaería sobre toda la familia.

»Sabemos cómo era Kitty, lo mucho que le gustaba irritar a la gente. Sabemos que fue a la biblioteca para encontrarse con alguien, pero no sabemos con quién ni por qué. No sabemos sobre qué discutieron..., el motivo que llevó al asesino a acallarla para siempre.

Portia no dijo nada, pero su comprensión y aquiescencia quedaron implícitas en su silencio. Pasados unos minutos, acercó una mano a la suya, entrelazó los dedos y apoyó la cabeza en su hombro. Simon se soltó de su mano para poder echarle el brazo por los hombros y tenerla más cerca de su cuerpo. Ella suspiró.

—Kitty estaba jugando con fuego en tantos frentes que no es de extrañar que acabara quemándose.

El almuerzo se celebró en un ambiente contenido. Lord Willoughby les había informado de que tendrían que quedarse hasta que llegara el investigador de Bow Street. Puesto que se esperaba la llegada del hombre a última hora de la tarde, muchos se entretuvieron hasta entonces haciendo discretos preparativos para marcharse esa misma noche.

Aparte de todo lo demás, la mayoría era de la opinión de que los Glossup deberían quedarse en familia para poder sobrellevar el disgusto con tranquilidad, sin la distracción de los invitados. Cualquier otra opción era impensable para todos ellos.

El investigador llegó como estaba previsto. Y no tardó en comunicarles que tendrían que reconsiderar su decisión.

El inspector Stokes era un tipo alto y corpulento, con ademanes decididos y enérgicos. Lo primero que hizo fue hablar con lord Glossup y lord Netherfield en el despacho antes de que lo acompañaran al salón para que todos lo conocieran a la vez. Inclinó la cabeza cortésmente cuando las presentaciones llegaron a su fin.

Portia se percató de que sus ojos, de un gris pizarra, estudiaban cada rostro a medida que escuchaba los nombres. Cuando llegó su turno, ella inclinó la cabeza con elegancia y observó cómo el hombre se fijaba en la posición que Simon ocupaba en el brazo de su sillón, con uno de sus brazos extendidos sobre el respaldo. Acto seguido, lo miró a la cara y lo saludó con un breve gesto antes de pasar al siguiente invitado.

A pesar de la situación en la que se encontraban, se sintió intrigada. No por el hombre en sí, sino por su papel de investigador. ¿Cómo pensaba desenmascarar al asesino?

—Supongo, señor Stokes, que ahora que nos conoce a todos, no pondrá objeción alguna a que nos marchemos, ¿cierto? —preguntó lady Calvin, imprimiendo a su voz toda la fuerza que le otorgaba el hecho de ser la hija de un conde.

Stokes ni siquiera parpadeó.

—Me temo, señora, que hasta que el asesino no pueda ser identificado o hasta que yo no haya llevado a cabo todas las pesquisas pertinentes, tendré que pedirles que... —Su mirada recorrió al grupo—. Tendré que pedirles que se queden en Glossup Hall.

Lady Calvin se ruborizó.

—¡Eso es ridículo!

—Ciertamente, señor —replicó lady Hammond, atusándose el chal—. Estoy segura de que tiene las mejores intenciones en mente, pero está fuera de toda cuestión...

—Por desgracia, señora, es lo que dicta la ley. —No había nada de ofensivo en su voz, pero tampoco nada reconfortante. Se inclinó en un gesto que recordaba vagamente a una reverencia—. Lo siento, señora, pero es un requisito fundamental.

Lord Glossup resopló antes de decir:

—Asumo que se trata del procedimiento habitual y

todo lo demás. No tiene sentido discutir. Además, no hay motivo alguno para dar por concluida la fiesta aparte de... En fin, aparte de eso.

Portia estaba sentada frente a los Archer. La señora Archer parecía seguir muy afectada. Era poco probable que hubiera prestado atención a lo que había acontecido a su alrededor desde que le comunicaron que su hija menor había muerto estrangulada. El señor Archer, en cambio, estaba pálido, pero mostraba una actitud firme. Estaba sentado al lado de su esposa, con una mano sobre su brazo. Al escuchar las palabras del señor Stokes, sus rasgos se crisparon momentáneamente por el dolor. En ese momento, carraspeó y dijo:

—Agradecería enormemente que todos ayudáramos al señor Stokes en la medida de lo posible. Cuanto antes identifique al asesino de Kitty, mejor será para todos.

Su voz sólo destilaba su dolor como padre, controlado pero genuino. Como era natural, su ruego fue aceptado con un coro de murmullos y de afirmaciones de que se haría todo lo posible, visto de ese modo el asunto.

El señor Stokes ocultó su reacción bastante bien, pero estaba aliviado. Esperó hasta que los murmullos se apagaron antes de decir:

—Según me han dicho, la señorita Ashford, el señor Cynster y el señor Hastings fueron los primeros en ver el cuerpo. —Su mirada se posó sobre ella y sobre Simon. Portia asintió con un breve gesto—. Si pudiera hablar con ustedes en primer lugar...

No era una pregunta ni mucho menos, por supuesto. Los tres se pusieron en pie y siguieron al investigador y a lord Glossup hasta la puerta.

—Puede utilizar la oficina del administrador. Les dije a los criados que la limpiaran a conciencia.

—A decir verdad... —El señor Stokes se detuvo al llegar al vano de la puerta—. Preferiría utilizar la biblioteca. Creo que fue allí donde se encontró el cuerpo, ¿no?

Lord Glossup frunció el ceño, pero asintió con la cabeza.

—Sí.

—En ese caso, es poco probable que sus invitados quieran asomar por el lugar. Será una ayuda para la investigación si puedo sacar ciertas conclusiones en el escenario del crimen, por decirlo de algún modo.

A lord Glossup no le quedó más remedio que acceder. Portia salió en primer lugar mientras el investigador sostenía la puerta del salón y se encaminó hacia la biblioteca. Cuando llegaron, Simon abrió la puerta e intercambiaron una mirada que le aseguró que él también creía que el requerimiento del señor Stokes tenía motivos ulteriores.

Fuera lo que fuese, le resultó de lo más extraño volver a entrar en la estancia donde había descubierto el cuerpo sin vida de Kitty. ¿Sólo habían pasado veinticuatro horas? Le daba la sensación de que habían pasado días...

Se detuvieron en grupo en la entrada. El señor Stokes cerró la puerta y los invitó a tomar asiento en los sillones emplazados frente a la chimenea, que se alzaba en el extremo opuesto al escritorio.

Ella se sentó en el diván y Simon lo hizo a su lado. Charlie eligió uno de los sillones. El investigador los observó un instante antes de tomar asiento en el otro sillón, frente a ellos.

Portia se preguntó si sería lo bastante perceptivo como para notar sus respectivas posiciones. Eran tres contra uno, al menos hasta que decidieran si podían confiar en él.

El hombre se sacó un cuaderno del bolsillo del abrigo y lo abrió.

—Señorita Ashford, si pudiera comenzar describiéndome exactamente lo que sucedió desde que entró en el vestíbulo principal ayer tarde... —Alzó la vista hasta ella—. ¿Estaba con el señor Cynster?

Ella inclinó la cabeza.

—Habíamos estado dando un paseo por el pinar.

El investigador echó un vistazo a un pliego de papel que se había colocado sobre una de sus rodillas.

—De modo que habían salido juntos por la puerta principal, ¿no?

—No. Salimos por la terraza, después del almuerzo, y rodeamos el lago por el camino que lleva al pinar.

El hombre trazó la ruta indicada en lo que claramente era un croquis de la propiedad.

—Entiendo. Así que entraron en el vestíbulo principal procedentes del patio principal. ¿Qué sucedió después?

Fue guiándola paso a paso mediante sus preguntas, logrando que le explicara sus movimientos con sorprendente precisión.

—¿Por qué se movió por la biblioteca de ese modo en concreto? ¿Buscaba algún libro?

—No. —Titubeó un instante y después, tras una fugaz mirada en dirección a Simon, se explicó—: Estaba un poco agitada después de la discusión con el señor Cynster. Vine aquí para pensar y estaba caminando para tranquilizarme.

El señor Stokes parpadeó. Su mirada, claramente curiosa, se trasladó a Simon. No había indicios de que la relación entre ellos fuera tensa. Todo lo contrario. De modo que se apiadó de él y se explicó.

—El señor Cynster y yo nos conocemos desde que éramos niños. Solemos discutir muy a menudo.

—¡Vaya! —Los ojos del investigador se clavaron en ella de nuevo con expresión respetuosa. Se había percatado de que le había leído el pensamiento con bastante precisión como para responder la pregunta que ni siquiera había llegado a formular. Volvió a mirar su cuadernillo—. Muy bien. Así que siguió paseando por el perímetro de la estancia...

Portia prosiguió su relato. Cuando llegó al punto en el que Simon entró corriendo por la puerta, el señor Stokes la detuvo y comenzó a interrogarlo a él.

Era mucho más fácil percatarse de su habilidad cuando no se era el objeto de ésta. Observó y escuchó mientras le arrancaba a Simon una descripción detallada y muy precisa de los hechos, antes de hacer lo propio con Charlie. Era muy bueno en su trabajo. Si bien los tres habían ido preparados para contárselo todo, había habido entre ellos cierta reticencia, una barrera que no cruzarían aunque hablaran. El señor Stokes no pertenecía a su clase social, no pertenecía a su mundo.

Habían entrado en la biblioteca sin haberse hecho una opinión sobre el hombre. Intercambió una mirada con Simon y se percató de la actitud relajada de Charlie. Ambos comenzaban a mirar al «caballero de Bow Street» con otros ojos.

El pobre hombre libraría una ardua batalla si no traspasaban esa barrera y lo ayudaban a entender lo que en realidad se cocía en la mansión. Las inquietudes que motivaban a los diferentes miembros del grupo. Las intrincadas redes que Kitty había tejido antes de su trágico final.

Y el señor Stokes era lo bastante inteligente como para saberlo. Lo bastante inteligente, una vez que los hubiera calado, como para no reconocer ese hecho. Los había llevado hasta el punto en el que los demás habían entrado en tromba en la biblioteca y la noticia de la muerte de Kitty comenzó a extenderse. Apartó el croquis y alzó la vista. Dejó que su mirada se demorara sobre ellos antes de preguntar con voz seria:

—¿Hay algo que puedan decirme, cualquier hecho del que sean conscientes, cualquier motivo que se les ocurra, que pudiera haber llevado a alguno de los invitados o a algún miembro del servicio, o incluso a alguno de los gitanos, a asesinar a la señora Glossup? —Al ver que ninguno de ellos reaccionaba de inmediato, se enderezó en el sillón—. ¿Tienen algún sospechoso en mente?

Ella miró a Simon. Charlie hizo lo mismo. Simon la miró, leyó su decisión, comprobó que Charlie accedía con un gesto casi imperceptible, y clavó los ojos en el señor Stokes.

—¿Tiene la lista de los invitados?

Una hora después, el investigador se pasaba los dedos por el pelo mientras ojeaba la maraña de notas que había ido escribiendo en torno al nombre de Kitty.

—¿Es que esa maldita mujer estaba buscando que la estrangularan?

—Si la hubiera conocido, lo entendería. —Tras mirarlo a los ojos, Simon continuó—: Parecía incapaz de entender el efecto que sus propias acciones tenían sobre los demás; la verdad es que no tenía en cuenta los sentimientos de nadie en absoluto.

—Esto no va a ser fácil —concluyó el señor Stokes con un suspiro mientras agitaba el cuadernillo en el aire—. Por regla general, siempre me centro en los motivos, pero aquí hay un sinfín de ellos, numerosas oportunidades para que cualquier persona presente en la mansión llevara a cabo el asesinato y muy pocas pistas que nos indiquen quién lo hizo de verdad. —Volvió a estudiar sus rostros—. ¿Están seguros de que nadie ha mostrado el menor indicio de culpabilidad desde...?

La puerta de la biblioteca se abrió en ese momento. El señor Stokes se giró en el sillón con el ceño fruncido. Cuando vio a los recién llegados, borró su expresión y se puso en pie para recibirlos.

Al igual que hicieron ellos cuando lady Osbaldestone y lord Netherfield, a todas luces una pareja de ancianos conspiradores, cerraron la puerta a sus espaldas y atravesaron toda la estancia hasta reunirse con ellos, tan silenciosamente como se lo permitieron sus respectivos bastones.

El señor Stokes intentó reafirmar su autoridad.

—Milord, señora... Si no les importa, necesito...

—¡Paparruchas! —exclamó lady O—. No van a cerrar el pico porque estemos aquí.

—Sí, pero...

—Hemos venido para asegurarnos de que se lo cuentan todo —declaró lady O, atravesando al hombre con su furibunda mirada de basilisco—. ¿Le han hablado de la serpiente?

—¿De la serpiente? —repitió el señor Stokes mientras su rostro permanecía tan inexpresivo como el de una estatua. Echó un vistazo en dirección a Simon y luego la miró a ella, con una súplica en los ojos para que lo rescataran. Al ver que nadie acudía en su ayuda, entrecerró los ojos, clavó la mirada en lady O y preguntó—: ¿De qué serpiente habla?

Simon suspiró.

—No habíamos llegado a ese punto todavía.

Como era natural, no hubo modo de librarse de lady O después de eso. Volvieron a sentarse. Simon les cedió su lugar en el diván a los recién llegados y permaneció de pie junto a la chimenea.

Le relataron el episodio de la víbora que había sido descubierta en la cama de Portia, quien por suerte, se había quedado dormida en un sillón antes de meterse en ella... El investigador aceptó la explicación sin parpadear. Ella miró a Simon, aliviada.

—¡Válgame Dios! ¡Menudo canalla! —exclamó Charlie, ya que era la primera noticia que tenía de lo sucedido con la víbora—. No me puedo creer que no se marchara presa de un ataque de nervios —le dijo.

—Sí, en fin... —lo interrumpió lord Netherfield—. Por si no os habéis dado cuenta, eso era precisamente lo que quería el rufián.

—Cierto —convino el señor Stokes con una mirada resplandeciente—. Eso significa que hay algo... algo que acabará por delatar al asesino. —La miró con el ceño fruncido—. Algo que cree que usted sabe.

Portia meneó la cabeza.

—No paro de darle vueltas al asunto desde entonces y no he olvidado nada, lo juro.

El gong que anunciaba la cena resonó desde las profundidades de la mansión. Era la segunda llamada, la que los llamaba a acudir al comedor. Habían hecho caso omiso de la primera, que indicaba que debían cambiarse de ropa porque la cena estaba lista. Esa noche no observarían las formalidades. Ayudar al señor Stokes les había parecido mucho más importante que aparecer en el comedor con sedas y oropeles.

El investigador cerró el cuadernillo.

—Está claro que el rufián, quienquiera que sea, no se ha percatado de ello.

—Tal vez no se haya percatado, pero cuando vea que he hablado con usted sin que hayamos logrado identificarlo, posiblemente lo comprenda. —Alzó las manos con impotencia—. Ya he dicho todo lo que sé.

Se pusieron en pie al unísono.

—Puede que así sea —replicó el señor Stokes mientras intercambiaba una mirada con Simon de camino a la puerta—. Pero el rufián tal vez esté convencido de que recordará ese detalle más adelante. Si es tan importante como para que haya intentado matarla en una ocasión, no hay motivo para que no vuelva a intentarlo.

—¡Válgame Dios! —exclamó Charlie con la vista clavada en el investigador antes de mirarla a ella—. Tendremos que tomar medidas para protegerla.

Ella se detuvo.

—No creo que eso sea neces...

—Día y noche —convino el señor Stokes con voz grave y firme.

Lady O golpeó el suelo con su bastón.

—Puede dormir en un catre en mi habitación. —Hizo un mohín mientras la miraba—. Supongo que incluso tú te lo pensarías dos veces antes de volver a acostarte en la misma cama en la que encontraste una serpiente.

Portia se las arregló para no estremecerse. En cambio, lanzó una mirada de lo más elocuente a Simon. Si dormía en la habitación de lady O...

Él enfrentó su mirada abiertamente y con expresión decidida.

—Día y noche —repitió al tiempo que miraba a Charlie—. Tú y yo nos turnaremos durante el día.

Atónita, y bastante irritada por el hecho de que la trataran de ese modo, como si fuera un objeto que pudiera ir de mano en mano, abrió la boca para protestar... y se dio cuenta de que todos los ojos estaban clavados en ella, convencidos de estar en lo cierto. Se dio cuenta de que no podría ganar.

—¡Está bien! —Agitó las manos en el aire y se encaminó hacia la puerta. Lord Netherfield se la abrió y le ofreció el brazo.

Ella lo aceptó y lo escuchó chasquear la lengua mientras la acompañaba hacia el pasillo. Le dio unas palmaditas en el brazo.

—Muy inteligente por tu parte, querida. Era una batalla imposible de ganar.

Hizo un enorme esfuerzo para contener un resoplido. Con la cabeza bien alta, enfiló el pasillo y entró en el comedor.

Simon y lady O los siguieron más despacio, tomados del brazo. Tras ellos iban Charlie y el señor Stokes, que se despidió al llegar a la puerta del comedor y se marchó en dirección a las dependencias del servicio, después de encomendarle a Charlie la tarea de comunicarles a los invitados que reanudaría el interrogatorio por la mañana.

Charlie entró para buscar el lugar que le había sido asignado en la mesa. Simon ayudó a lady O a entrar.

La anciana se detuvo en el vano para colocarse el chal con gran pompa mientras soltaba una risilla malévola.

—No te pongas tan serio. Mi vista ya no alcanza para ver en detalle al otro extremo de mi habitación. ¿Cómo voy a saber si Portia duerme allí o no? —Con la excusa de volver a tomarlo del brazo, le asestó un codazo en las costillas—. Y duermo como un tronco. Ahora que lo pienso, no sé para qué me he ofrecido a vigilarla por las noches.

Simon se las arregló para no quedarse boquiabierto. Hacía mucho que sabía que lady O era una casamentera incorregible, o más bien que era incorregible en todos los aspectos de su carácter, pero la idea de que lo ayudara abiertamente, de que apoyara sin tapujos su cortejo...

La anciana permitió que la ayudara a sentarse y después lo despachó con un gesto de la mano. Mientras se encaminaba al otro extremo de la mesa para ocupar el lugar vacío junto a Portia, reflexionó al respecto. Apartó la silla para sentarse, se demoró un instante para observar su cabello negro y el gesto de su cabeza (ladeada en un ángulo que no le costó trabajo alguno interpretar) y tomó asiento tras llegar a la conclusión de que tener a lady O de aliada era muy positivo.

Sobre todo en esos instantes. Sin tener en cuenta lo demás, la anciana era pragmática hasta decir basta. Podría contar con ella para que le recordara a Portia que debía comportarse con sensatez. Que no debía correr riesgos.

Extendió su servilleta y echó un vistazo a la expresión altanera del rostro de Portia antes de permitir que el criado le sirviera. Tal vez siguieran en la cuerda floja, tanto él como ella, pero se sentía mucho más seguro que nunca desde que le comunicara a Portia cuál era su verdadero objetivo.

Por consenso general, el cariz de la fiesta cambió de forma deliberada. Mientras tomaba el té en el salón, a Portia le resultó imposible pasar por alto el hecho de que Kitty no lo habría aprobado. El ambiente se asemejaba al de una concurrida reunión familiar, pero sin la alegría típica de esos acontecimientos. Los presentes se encontraban relajados en su mutua compañía y parecían haberse quitado las máscaras, como si consideraran que las circunstancias los eximían de mantener las apariencias sociales de rigor.

Las damas se habían congregado en el salón. Ninguna esperaba que los caballeros hicieran acto de presencia. Estaban diseminadas en diversos grupos por la enorme estancia, charlando tranquilamente y sin carcajadas ni salidas de tono. Sólo se escuchaban los suaves murmullos de las conversaciones.

Conversaciones que estaban destinadas a relajar, tranquilizar y dejar atrás el horror del asesinato de Kitty y de la investigación que se cernía sobre ellas.

Las hermanas Hammond estaban muy pálidas, pero parecía que comenzaban a asimilarlo. Lucy Buckstead estaba un poco mejor. Winifred, vestida de color azul marino (un color que no la favorecía en absoluto), parecía pálida y exhausta. La señora Archer no había bajado a cenar.

Tan pronto como se bebieron el té, todas se pusieron en pie y se retiraron a sus habitaciones. El sentimiento implícito de que necesitarían un buen descanso para enfrentarse a lo que el día siguiente y las preguntas del señor Stokes les depararan parecía flotar en el ambiente. Sólo a Drusilla se le había ocurrido preguntarle su opinión sobre el investigador, preguntarle si lo creía competente. Le respondió que así lo creía, pero que había tan pocas pistas que tal vez el crimen quedara sin resolver. Drusilla torció el gesto, asintió con la cabeza y se marchó.

Cuando entró con lady O en su habitación para ayudarla a acostarse, se percató de que el catre la esperaba frente a la chimenea, al otro extremo de la estancia, alejado de la cama. La doncella de la anciana estaba allí para ayudarla a desvestirse. Portia se apartó y se encaminó hacia el alféizar acolchado de la ventana. En ese momento, se dio cuenta de que habían sacado toda su ropa de su habitación. Sus vestidos estaban colgados en una cuerda que se había dispuesto en uno de los rincones del dormitorio. Su ropa interior y sus medias estaban primorosamente dobladas en su baúl, en ese mismo rincón. Alzó la cabeza y vio que sus cepillos y horquillas, así como su frasquito de perfume y sus peines, se encontraban en la repisa de la chimenea.

Se reclinó en el mullido alféizar y contempló los oscuros jardines mientras se devanaba los sesos tratando de encontrar una excusa que le permitiera salir de la habitación con la aprobación de lady O.

Todavía no se le había ocurrido nada útil cuando la doncella se acercó para preguntarle si deseaba ayuda para desvestirse. Negó con la cabeza, le dio las buenas noches a la muchacha y se puso en pie para acercarse a la cama.

La vela de la mesita de noche ya estaba apagada. Lady O estaba recostada contra los almohadones, con los ojos cerrados. Portia se inclinó para darle un beso en una de sus delicadas mejillas.

—Que duerma bien.

—Por supuesto que lo haré —replicó la anciana con tono burlón—. Aunque no puedo decir lo mismo de ti, de modo que tendrás que averiguarlo por ti misma. —Sus ojos seguían cerrados cuando alzó una mano y la despachó hacia la puerta con un gesto—. Vamos, vete... Fuera.

Portia se limitó a mirarla sin decir nada. Sin embargo, no pudo resistirse a preguntarle:

—¿Adónde quiere que me vaya?

Lady O abrió uno de sus ojos negros y su mirada la atravesó.

—¿Tú qué crees? —Al ver que se limitaba a quedarse allí plantada sin saber qué hacer exactamente, la anciana resopló y volvió a cerrar el ojo—. No tengo siete años, ¡por el amor de Dios, tengo más de setenta y siete! Me las sé todas, tengo la experiencia necesaria para darme cuenta de lo que pasa delante de mis narices.

—¿De veras?

—De veras. Aunque no se pueda decir lo mismo de ti. Ni de Simon, pero así deben ser las cosas. —Se acomodó mejor sobre los almohadones—. Y ahora vete, no tiene sentido que pierdas el tiempo. Tienes veinticuatro años y él... ¿cuántos tiene? ¿Treinta? Ya habéis perdido tiempo de sobra.

Portia no supo cómo replicar y al final decidió que sería más sensato seguir con la boca cerrada.

—En ese caso, buenas noches. —Se dio la vuelta y echó a andar hacia la puerta.

—¡Espera un momento!

Al escuchar la airada orden, se detuvo y se giró.

—¿Adónde vas?

—Acaba de decirme que... —respondió mientras señalaba la puerta con una mano.

—¡Válgame Dios, muchacha! ¿Es que tengo que enseñártelo todo? Antes deberías cambiarte de vestido.

Portia observó su vestido de sarga color magenta. Dudaba mucho de que a Simon le importara lo que llevara puesto. Conociéndolo, no tardaría en quitárselo... Alzó la cabeza, abrió la boca para preguntarle qué importancia tenía...

—Ponte el vestido mañanero que tengas pensado llevar mañana —le explicó lady O con un suspiro—. De ese modo, si alguien te ve regresar aquí por la mañana, creerá que te has levantado temprano para dar un paseo. Si te ven esta noche por los pasillos, pensarán que estabas a punto de acostarte cuando caíste en la cuenta de que se te había olvidado hacer algo, o que he sido yo quien te ha mandado a hacer un recado. —Soltó un resoplido exasperado y se dejó caer sobre los almohadones—. ¡Ay, la juventud! La de cosas que podría enseñarte... Pero, claro... —cerró los ojos al tiempo que esbozaba una sonrisa maliciosa—, si no recuerdo mal, el proceso de aprendizaje era parte de la diversión.

Portia sonrió, ¿qué otra cosa iba a hacer? Sin rechistar, se quitó el vestido color magenta y se puso uno mañanero de popelina azul. Mientras bregaba con los botoncitos que cerraban el corpiño, su mente voló hasta Simon..., que dentro de poco estaría bregando por desabrocharlos. De todos modos, el sabio consejo de lady O, fruto de la práctica, tenía sentido...

Se detuvo un instante y alzó la cabeza. Acababa de ocurrírsele una idea que la había dejado atónita. Una sospecha repentina... Cuando el último botón estuvo abrochado, regresó junto a la cama. Se detuvo para mirar a lady O y se preguntó si ya estaría dormida.

—¿Todavía estás aquí?

—Ya me voy, pero me preguntaba... ¿Sabía que Simon vendría a la fiesta campestre?

Un breve silencio precedió a la respuesta.

—Sabía que James y él eran muy amigos desde sus lejanos días en Eton. Me pareció lógico que se dejara caer por aquí.

Portia rememoró las discusiones que habían tenido lugar en Calverton Chase con su madre, Luc, Amelia y ella misma, todos empeñados en convencer a lady O de que debía llevar un acompañante durante el viaje. La anciana se había resistido en un principio, pero a la postre había cedido a regañadientes a llevarla con ella...

Con los ojos entrecerrados, contempló a la anciana que fingía dormir en la cama y se preguntó hasta qué punto Simon y ella debían agradecerle su situación a las astutas manipulaciones de la bruja más temida de la alta sociedad.

Decidió que no le importaba. Lady O tenía razón, ya habían perdido demasiado tiempo. Se enderezó y se giró hacia la puerta.

—Buenas noches. La veré por la mañana.

Y sería por la mañana. Una ventaja inesperada del plan de lady O, ya que puesto que estaba ataviada con un vestido mañanero, no tendría que abandonar la habitación de Simon antes de que amaneciera.

Simon estaba en su habitación, esperando mientras se preguntaba si Portia encontraría el modo de reunirse con él o si aprovecharía la tesitura para pensar, analizar y sopesar cada una de las razones por las que no quería casarse con él, a fin de alzar las barreras correspondientes.

De pie junto a la ventana, era muy consciente de la tensión que lo embargaba. Dio un sorbo a la copa de *brandy* que tenía en la mano desde hacía más de media hora y contempló los jardines bañados por la oscuridad de la noche.

No quería que Portia hiciera demasiadas conjeturas sobre su futuro comportamiento como marido. Pero al mismo tiempo sabía que, por muy sutil que fuese, si intentaba alejarla de su propio camino, estaría tirándose piedras a su propio tejado, ya que ella confirmaría su teoría de que no podía fiarse de que le permitiera tomar sus propias decisiones en el futuro.

Atado de pies y manos. Así estaba. Y no podía hacer nada, maldita fuera su estampa.

Portia seguiría su propio camino. Era demasiado perspicaz, demasiado sensata como para no enfrentarse a los hechos directamente: sus fuertes temperamentos y las dificultades que eso conllevaba. El único consuelo que le reportaba era la certeza de que si por fin... o mejor, cuando por fin, se decidiera a darle el sí, sabría sin lugar a dudas que se entregaba sin reservas, con los ojos abiertos y el corazón en la mano.

Titubeó un instante antes de apurar el *brandy*. Casi merecía la pena pasar por semejante tormento si finalmente llegaban a ese punto.

Escuchó el clic de la cerradura. Se giró y vio su elegante y delgada figura, ataviada con un vestido diferente. A medida que se acercaba, se percató de que sus labios esbozaban una sonrisilla satisfecha. Dejó la copa en el alféizar de la ventana a fin de tener las manos libres para rodearle la cintura cuando llegó, directa a sus brazos.

Inclinó la cabeza y sus labios se encontraron en un beso lento. Las ascuas que durante todos esos días parecían esconder en su interior se avivaron y las llamas los envolvieron.

Cuando se dio cuenta de que el vestido se abrochaba por la parte delantera, le quitó las manos de la cintura y las introdujo entre sus cuerpos. Sin embargo, los botones eran diminutos y los ojales muy pequeños; de modo que tuvo que apartarse de sus labios para mirar lo que estaba haciendo.

—¿Por qué te has cambiado? —Habría podido quitarle el otro vestido en un santiamén.

—Lady O.

Alzó la vista y ella le sonrió.

—Me señaló que así nadie sospecharía si me veían regresar a su habitación por la mañana.

Sus dedos se detuvieron.

—¿Sabe que estás aquí? —Contar con su apoyo era una cosa. Una ayuda semejante, otra muy distinta.

—Me sacó de la habitación a empujones, metafóricamente hablando, y me sugirió que dejásemos de perder el tiempo.

Sus ojos estaban clavados en los botones, pero captó la nota jocosa en la voz de Portia. Cuando la miró... maldijo para sus adentros porque la oscuridad no le permitía verle los ojos con claridad y así no podía interpretar su expresión.

—¿Qué? —Sabía que había algo más. Algo que ella había descubierto y que él ignoraba.

Confirmó sus sospechas cuando ella estudió su rostro, volvió a sonreír y meneó la cabeza.

—Es lady O... Es una anciana de lo más sorprendente. Creo que seré igual que ella cuando me haga mayor.

Simon soltó un resoplido burlón. El último botón por fin abandonó su ojal.

Ella alzó las manos y tiró de él para que volviera a besarla.

—Y ahora que has terminado, creo que deberíamos obedecerla al pie de la letra.

No perdieron tiempo, aunque tampoco permitió que Portia apresurara las cosas. En esa ocasión, por primera vez, se medían de igual a igual. Ambos sabían lo que querían y por qué. Ambos deseaban continuar, arrojarse de buena gana a la hoguera cogidos de la mano. Codo con codo.

Era un momento para saborear. Para recordar. Se veneraron con caricias, dejándose arrastrar por la pasión.

No sabía lo que ella esperaba de esa noche. No sabía qué más buscaba, qué podría darle que no le hubiera dado ya. Lo único que le quedaba era entregarse a sí mismo. Y rezar para que eso fuera suficiente.

No se apartaron de la ventana. Se quitaron la ropa allí de pie, prenda a prenda. Se demoraron en los descubrimientos previos, en cada curva, en cada hueco. Adoraron nuevamente cada centímetro de sus cuerpos.

Hasta que ambos estuvieron desnudos. Hasta que sus cuerpos estuvieron piel contra piel.

El fuego los rodeó. La pasión creció y los excitó.

Sus bocas se fundieron, avivando la conflagración, alimentando las llamas. Sus lenguas se acariciaron con ardor.

Se dieron un festín con las manos, tocándose y explorándose el uno al otro.

El apremio creció.

Simon la alzó y ella le arrojó los brazos al cuello antes de besarlo con un ansia voraz. Le rodeó la cintura con esas largas piernas y suspiró cuando la penetró. Cuando se introdujo en ella con delicadeza a medida que la hacía descender aferrándola por las caderas.

Portia lo abrazó mientras le hacía el amor. Enterró los dedos en su cabello, se agarró a sus mechones y tiró de él para que volviera a besarla. Lo devoró mientras la penetraba y se retiraba con una rítmica cadencia.

Se entregó por entero, no se reservó nada y tampoco pidió nada a cambio. Y Simon tomó lo que le ofrecía, reclamó su cuerpo, aunque le quedó claro que quería más. Que anhelaba más. Lo sabía, lo percibía en la tensión que se había apoderado de los músculos que la sujetaban y la movían. Supo que aún le quedaba mucho por aprender. Que él aún tenía mucho que ofrecerle.

Si ella quería.

Si se atrevía.

Si confiaba en él lo bastante como para...

Tenía la piel en llamas, su cuerpo se había convertido en fuego líquido y él todavía no se había hundido en ella hasta el fondo. Quería sentirlo muy adentro, quería que le hiciera el amor con desenfreno, quería volver a experimentar la maravillosa sensación de su peso sobre ella mientras le hacía el amor. Apartó los labios de los de Simon y se dio cuenta de que jadeaba.

—Llévame a la cama.

Volvió a besarlo mientras la obedecía. Cuando se inclinó para dejarla sobre los almohadones, se aferró a él con más fuerza, de modo que ambos cayeron a la par sobre el colchón. Simon soltó un juramento e hizo ademán de apartarse, temeroso de haberle hecho daño. Ella se lo impidió aferrándole las nalgas y acercándolo.

—Más.

Le clavó las uñas y él se plegó a sus deseos, hundiéndose un poco más en ella. Se apartó para apoyar su peso en los brazos y la miró a los ojos a medida que la penetraba lentamente... hasta que estuvo hundido en ella hasta el fondo.

Simon contemplaba a Portia mientras se afanaba por respirar. Mientras se afanaba por mostrar un atisbo de sofisticación, por contener aquella marea de deseo que amenazaba con consumirlo. Con consumirlos a los dos.

Ella también parecía sentirla, porque alzó los brazos para acariciarle las mejillas con las yemas de los dedos. Desde allí siguió hacia los hombros, descendió por el pecho y acabó colocándole las manos en los costados, exhortándolo a que apoyara todo su peso en ella.

Inclinó la cabeza para besarla, pero ella quería más. Le exigió que le diera más. De modo que acabó por rendirse y se dejó caer sobre ella poco a poco. Hasta que su peso la inmovilizó bajo él. Supuso que la posición la sofocaría y comenzaría a forcejear para liberarse. En cambio, ella le hundió la lengua en la boca y alzó las piernas un poco más para rodearle la cintura. Una vez que ajustó la posición, alzó las caderas y se abrió por completo a sus embestidas.

Le mordisqueó el labio inferior y le dio un tironcito antes de soltarlo.

—Ahora —jadeó, y su aliento le abrasó los labios—. Enséñame.

La miró con los párpados entornados.

Y la obedeció.

Comenzó a moverse con fuerza y frenesí sin dejar de mirarla a los ojos. Deseaba poder ver su color, ver cómo la pasión dilataba sus pupilas, asegurarse de que eran totalmente negros cuando llegara al clímax.

Ese anhelo siguió presente a pesar de que las llamas lo instaban a centrarse en otras cosas y de que poco a poco fue perdiendo contacto con cualquier realidad que no fuera la calidez de ese cuerpo que lo rodeaba con su maravillosa humedad y lo acogía con abandono, tan ansioso como él por alcanzar el clímax.

Se prometió que algún día los vería.

Que le haría el amor a plena luz del día para poder verla mientras la hacía suya.

Sus ojos y todo lo demás.

Quería ver su piel. Tan blanca e inmaculada que brillaba como la más fina de las perlas. En la penumbra, el sonrojo del deseo apenas era visible. Quería verlo. Necesitaba ver la evidencia física de lo que la hacía sentir.

Quería ver el color de sus rugosos pezones, de sus labios hinchados, de los húmedos pliegues de su sexo.

Era consciente de que Portia acompasaba sus movimientos. Se percató del vínculo que los complementaba, que los unía y que parecía fundirlos.

Y que los llevó a la par a la gloriosa cúspide donde sus sentidos se fragmentaron en una brillante lluvia de placer que se transformó en el éxtasis más sublime.

Lo que experimentaba con Portia era mucho más que la simple satisfacción sexual. Salió de ella y se dejó caer a su lado mientras el placer seguía corriéndole por las venas. La acercó y la abrazó. Quería tenerla cerca de su corazón.

Donde más la necesitaba.

Un inefable bienestar se adueñó de él y se dejó arrastrar por el sueño.

14

A la mañana siguiente, Kitty, o para ser más precisos, Catherine Glossup, Archer de soltera, fue enterrada en el panteón que los Glossup poseían junto a la pequeña iglesia de Ashmore.

Asistieron todos los residentes de Glossup Hall, salvo un puñado de criados que se quedó al cargo de los preparativos para la recepción posterior. En cuanto a los habitantes del condado, la nobleza local estuvo representada por los cabezas de familia. Ninguna de sus esposas asistió.

La ausencia llevaba implícito un mensaje que Portia, Simon y Charlie interpretaron con facilidad. Los tres se mantuvieron apartados, dispuestos para prestar ayuda a lady O o a lord Netherfield en caso de que alguno de ellos la necesitara. Observaron con atención cómo los otrora alegres vecinos, a la mayoría de los cuales conocieron durante el almuerzo de Kitty, se iban acercando con expresiones sombrías a la familia para murmurarles las condolencias antes de alejarse, a todas luces incómodos.

—Esto no pinta nada bien —musitó Charlie.

—Se reservan la opinión hasta saber por dónde van los tiros —replicó Portia.

—Lo que significa que creen que existe una posibilidad bastante factible de que haya sido uno de los Glossup quien... —Simon dejó la frase en el aire. Ninguno de ellos necesitaba escuchar la verdad.

El servicio había sido sobrio, como todos los funerales, aunque abreviado dadas las circunstancias y con un tono un tanto más lóbrego. Como si se cerniera sobre todos ellos un oscuro nubarrón; o, al menos, sobre Glossup Hall. Un nubarrón que sólo se desvanecería si se desenmascaraba al asesino de Kitty.

Cuando todo estuvo dicho, tanto las condolencias como los agradecimientos por la asistencia, la concurrencia comenzó a dispersarse. Una vez que ayudaron a lady O y a lord Netherfield a subir al carruaje que compartían, Simon ayudó a Portia a acomodarse en su tílburi y se sentó a su lado. Tomó las riendas mientras Charlie se encaramaba en el lugar que normalmente ocupaba el lacayo y, con un giro de muñeca, ordenó a los bayos que se pusieran en movimiento y enfilaran el camino.

Pasaron unos cuantos minutos en silencio y, después, escucharon que Charlie soltaba un juramento.

Portia se giró para mirarlo.

—Lo siento —dijo él con una mueca arrepentida—. Acabo de acordarme de la cara de James. Y de la de Henry.

—Por no mencionar a lord y lady Glossup —añadió Simon con voz tensa—. Todos intentan afrontar los hechos con valentía, pero saben lo que se les viene encima y no pueden hacer nada para evitarlo.

Portia frunció el ceño.

—No es justo. Ellos no son los únicos sospechosos de haber matado a Kitty.

—A tenor del comportamiento de Kitty durante el almuerzo, que sin duda ha sido adornado y exagerado a lo largo y ancho del condado, la supuestamente sociedad más civilizada no ve necesario buscar culpables más allá de la propia familia.

Charlie soltó otro juramento, en esa ocasión mucho más colorido.

—A eso me refería. Les da igual que fueran las víctimas de la desfachatez de Kitty, y que me aspen si no se han convertido también en las víctimas del asesinato.

Portia se sintió obligada a matizar algo:

—Podría haber sido uno de ellos.

—Cuando las ranas críen pelo... —refunfuñó Charlie.

Portia miró a Simon. Tenía los ojos clavados en el camino, pero a juzgar por el rictus de sus labios, supuso que estaba de acuerdo con su amigo. Comprensible, se dijo. Eran amigos íntimos de James. Y de la familia.

Se enderezó en el asiento y analizó sus sentimientos. No con la cabeza, sino con el corazón. Cuando la verja de Glossup Hall apareció frente a ellos, dijo:

—A decir verdad, todos los invitados, salvo nosotros tres, las muchachas más jóvenes, lady O, lady Hammond y la señora Archer están en la cuerda floja, aunque todavía no se hayan percatado de ello.

—Si tenemos en cuenta el silencio que cayó sobre la mesa del desayuno esta mañana, yo diría que la mayoría ya se ha dado cuenta... aunque intente pasarlo por alto —replicó Charlie, tras lo cual, añadió—: No todos los días va uno a una fiesta campestre y acaba enredado en un asesinato.

Simon refrenó a los caballos cuando llegaron al patio principal. Le entregó las riendas al lacayo que llegó corriendo hasta el tílburi, bajó y la ayudó a hacer lo mismo. El primero de los carruajes del grupo apareció por el camino, a un paso mucho más lento. Intercambiaron una mirada y los tres se alejaron por el sendero que llevaba al pinar.

Siguieron la ruta inversa a la que tomaron Simon y ella el día que descubrió el cuerpo de la pobre Kitty. Sus pensamientos la sobresaltaron. ¿La «pobre» Kitty?

Entrelazó el brazo con el de Simon. Él la miró de reojo, pero no dijo nada. Siguieron paseando bajo los árboles. Charlie los seguía, igualmente ensimismado en sus pensamientos.

En su indignación por las injustificadas sospechas que mancillaban el honor de sus amigos, habían olvidado, no sólo ellos sino también el resto de los invitados, que Kitty había sido, después de todo, la «pobre» Kitty. Kitty estaba muerta. Ya no podría pasear bajo los árboles tomada del brazo de un hombre, ni despertaría entre sus brazos presa de un dulce anhelo que no tardaría en convertirse en deleite.

Ella lo tenía todo, mientras que Kitty no tenía nada. Pobre Kitty, sí.

—Tenemos que descubrir al asesino. —Clavó la vista al frente—. Estoy segura de que podemos ayudar al señor Stokes de algún modo.

—¿Usted cree? —preguntó Charlie—. Me refiero a que no sé si nos lo permitirá. ¿Tú qué opinas? —le preguntó a Simon.

—Estaba en el funeral —le contestó él—. Estaba observando a todo el mundo, pero lo mueven simples suposiciones cuando nosotros nos basamos en hechos concretos. —La miró a los ojos—. ¿Qué te parece si le ofrecemos nuestra ayuda?

Ella asintió, decidida.

—Deberíamos hacerlo.

Ya habían llegado al camino que bordeaba el lago.

—Pero antes —dijo Charlie, poniéndose a su lado—, será mejor que regresemos a la mansión y hagamos acto de presencia.

Eso hicieron. Los asistentes al funeral se habían reunido en el salón, donde las cortinas estaban a medio correr. Tras despedirse de ellos con un breve asentimiento de cabeza, Charlie se alejó para hablar con James, que se encontraba un tanto alejado de los demás con una copa en la mano.

Ellos dos caminaron de grupo en grupo. Los representantes de la nobleza local se habían marchado en su mayor parte tras la misa, de modo que la concurrencia estaba formada, en su mayoría, por los invitados. Portia se detuvo para charlar con las Hammond, que parecían bastante afectadas. Simon la dejó y continuó hasta llegar al lado del señor Stokes.

El «caballero de Bow Street» se mantenía alejado de los demás y estaba apoyado contra la pared mientras daba buena cuenta de un pastelito. Enfrentó su mirada cuando se percató de que se acercaba a él.

—Lord Netherfield sugirió que asistiera —le explicó antes de darle otro bocadito al pastel y apartar la vista—. Un tipo agradable.

—Mucho. Y no, no creo que fuera él.

El señor Stokes sonrió y lo miró de nuevo a los ojos.

—¿Por algún motivo en concreto?

Simon se metió las manos en los bolsillos y echó un vistazo hacia el otro extremo de la estancia.

—Su forma de ser y la generación a la que pertenece lo obligan a considerar de muy mala educación el asesinato de una persona potencialmente indefensa como lo era Kitty, quiero decir, la señora Glossup.

El investigador dio otro bocado al pastelito y añadió en voz baja:

—¿Acaso continúa importando hoy en día «la buena educación»?

—No para todos, pero para los que son como él, sí. —Sostuvo la mirada curiosa del hombre antes de explicarse—: Para él sería una cuestión de honra, y eso es algo, se lo aseguro, vital para él.

El señor Stokes asintió con la cabeza un momento después. Acto seguido, se sacó un pañuelo del bolsillo y se limpió los dedos. Ni siquiera alzó la vista para decir:

—¿Debo suponer que está dispuesto a... ayudarme en mis pesquisas?

Simon titubeó antes de contestar.

—Tal vez en lo referente a la interpretación de cualquier evidencia que pueda encontrar o a darle la importancia adecuada a cualquier cosa que pueda escuchar.

—¡Vaya, ya entiendo! —Los labios del hombre esbozaron una sonrisa—. Tengo entendido que es usted amigo del señor James Glossup.

Simon inclinó la cabeza.

—Ése es el motivo de que la señorita Ashford, el señor Hastings y yo estemos ansiosos por que el asesino, sea quien sea, quede al descubierto. —Miró al investigador a los ojos—. Nos necesita para avanzar en su investigación. Y nosotros lo necesitamos a usted para atrapar al culpable. Creo que es un trato justo.

El señor Stokes meditó un instante la oferta mientras se guardaba de nuevo el pañuelo en el bolsillo.

—Estaré toda la tarde ocupado con los interrogatorios. Aún no he hablado con todas las personas que se encontraban en la mansión. Después iré al campamento de los gitanos. Dudo mucho que pueda regresar antes de la cena, pero ¿podríamos hablar cuando vuelva?

—En el mirador —le dijo—. Está junto al lago. No tiene pérdida. Es un lugar privado y nadie irá tan lejos de noche. Lo esperaremos allí.

—De acuerdo.

Tras despedirse del señor Stokes con una inclinación de cabeza, se alejó.

Los tres salieron de la mansión en dirección al mirador tan pronto el té, servido en cuanto los caballeros entraron en el salón, llegó a su fin. Una vez que se cumplieron las formalidades de rigor, la mayoría de los invitados se retiró a sus aposentos, aunque en la sala de billar aún había luz. Dado que la biblioteca se había convertido en el despacho del investigador, la sala de billar había pasado a ser el santuario masculino.

El señor Stokes había pasado toda la tarde interrogando al resto de los invitados y después había desaparecido. El ambiente se cargó de tensión, como si la fantasiosa posibilidad de que el asesino fuera uno de los gitanos se estuviera desvaneciendo poco a poco. La ausencia del investigador contribuyó a que la tensión se hiciera aún más palpable.

Portia caminaba al lado de Simon mientras enfilaban el camino que bordeaba el lago, preguntándose (tal y como llevaba haciendo desde que saliera de la cama de Simon esa mañana con su energía habitual) qué habría motivado el asesinato de Kitty.

—Debemos admitir que el señor Stokes se ha mostrado muy valiente al interrogar a lady O. —Charlie caminaba tras ellos.

—Parece muy minucioso —replicó Simon.

—Y decidido.

—Eso también.

—¿Tendrá éxito? —preguntó Charlie.

Simon lo miró.

—Espero que sí, por el bien de los Glossup. En realidad, por el bien de todos. —Al parecer, Charlie estaba preocupado por algo—. ¿Por qué lo preguntas?

Se dieron la vuelta para enfrentarlo.

—Estuve hablando con James después del funeral y esta tarde también. Está... raro —les explicó, haciendo una mueca.

Portia alzó las cejas.

—Yo también lo estaría si supiera que soy una de las principales sospechosas de un asesinato.

—Sí, bueno, pero no es sólo eso. —Charlie miró a Simon—. Ya sabes lo unidos que están James y Henry. Todo esto los ha unido más si cabe... —Se pasó una mano por el pelo—. Quiero decir que James se siente culpable por todo lo relacionado con Kitty. No porque le haya hecho daño, sino por la preferencia que ella mostraba hacia él. Aunque nunca le diera pie, claro. En fin, ya sabéis lo que sucedía. Una situación muy embarazosa cuando estaba viva..., así que ahora que está muerta, es un infierno.

Simon guardó silencio y ella percibió el cambio que se había obrado en él.

—¿A qué te refieres exactamente?

Charlie suspiró.

—Me preocupa la posibilidad de que cometa una estupidez. Sobre todo si las cosas se ponen feas para Henry. Bien sabe Dios que ya pintan muy mal. Creo que tal vez confiese que es el asesino para librar a su hermano.

—¡Maldita sea! —exclamó Simon.

Los ojos de Portia volaban del uno al otro.

—¿Sería capaz de hacerlo?

Simon asintió con la cabeza.

—Desde luego que sí. Si conocieras su pasado, lo entenderías. James hará cualquier cosa para proteger a Henry, porque su hermano se ha pasado media vida haciendo exactamente lo mismo por él.

—¿Qué podemos hacer? —preguntó Charlie—. Eso es lo que quiero saber.

—Lo único que podemos hacer... —le contestó Simon— es ayudar a desenmascarar al asesino lo antes posible.

Era bastante tarde cuando el señor Stokes llegó, visiblemente cansado.

—Tratar con los gitanos nunca es fácil —les comentó mientras se dejaba caer en uno de los sillones—. Siempre creen que estamos a punto de detenerlos. —Frunció los labios—. Algo comprensible, sobre todo por cómo solían ser las cosas hasta no hace mucho.

—Puesto que no ha arrestado a ninguno —le dijo Simon—, supongo que no cree que Arturo sea culpable, ¿verdad?

—No tiene sentido —respondió el hombre, enfrentando su mirada—. ¿Se lo ve usted?

—La verdad es que no —contestó—. Pero todos lo incriminarán, estoy seguro.

—Sí, ya lo han hecho, pero las sospechas son prácticamente infundadas. No tengo razón alguna que me lleve a pensar que él, o el otro más joven..., el tal Dennis, sea el asesino.

Portia se inclinó hacia delante.

—¿Tiene alguna teoría sobre el verdadero asesino?

—No es tanto una teoría como ciertas líneas de investigación que me gustaría seguir —respondió al tiempo que se reclinaba en el sillón.

Intercambiaron información. Ellos le contaron todo lo que sabían, desde las escaramuzas verbales de Kitty hasta sus comentarios mordaces más recientes. Mientras esperaban la llegada del señor Stokes habían decidido que no le ocultarían nada, porque confiaban en que la verdad en las manos del investigador no causaría daño alguno a los inocentes. Había demasiado en juego como para seguir ateniéndose a las estrictas normas sociales que dictaban guardar discreción al respecto.

Así que le contaron todo lo que ella había escuchado. Todas las conclusiones que habían sacado, tanto a título personal como en grupo, acerca de la tendencia de Kitty a interferir en las vidas de los demás.

El señor Stokes se quedó sorprendido. Y sobrecogido. Les hizo una serie de preguntas y los escuchó con atención, intentando comprender sus explicaciones.

Al final, llegaron a un punto en el que el investigador se quedó sin preguntas, aunque ni siquiera vislumbraban el asomo de una conclusión. Se pusieron en pie y regresaron a la mansión mientras meditaban sumidos en el silencio todo lo que habían dicho, como si se tratara de las piezas de un rompecabezas que hubiera que catalogar antes de comenzar a unirlas.

Portia aún seguía sumida en sus pensamientos cuando entró sigilosamente en la habitación de Simon una hora después.

De pie junto a la cama, él alzó la vista y continuó encendiendo las seis velas del candelabro que había tomado prestado de uno de los gabinetes sin ocupar. Escuchó el clic de la cerradura y después los pasos de Portia mientras cruzaba la habitación.

Supo el momento exacto en el que se dio cuenta.

Se detuvo para observar los candelabros con todas las velas encendidas. Echó un vistazo a su alrededor y cayó en la cuenta de que las cortinas estaban corridas, cosa inusual durante los meses más cálidos. Después miró hacia la cama, bañada por el resplandor dorado de las velas de los dos candelabros de seis brazos dispuestos en las mesitas de noche, de otro de siete brazos emplazado sobre la cómoda que había junto a una de las paredes y de otro más, uno de cinco brazos, colocado sobre el baúl en la pared opuesta.

—¿Qué...? —Lo miró desde el otro lado de la cama, envuelta en la cálida luz.

Simon apagó el cabo que había utilizado para encender las velas antes de ajustar el candelabro situado sobre la mesita de noche que tenía al lado de modo que iluminara los almohadones. Después alzó la cabeza. Y enfrentó su mirada.

—Quiero verte... esta vez.

Ella se ruborizó. No de forma intensa, pero la luz le permitió ver el tono rosado que adquirió su piel de alabastro. Contuvo una sonrisa depredadora. Con los ojos clavados en ella y evaluando su reacción, rodeó la cama para ponerse a su lado. Estaba contemplando la colcha, de un brillante carmesí a la luz de las velas.

Extendió los brazos, deslizó las manos por su esbelta figura y tiró de ella para abrazarla. Ella se dejó hacer; pero, cuando lo miró a los ojos, Simon descubrió que estaba frunciendo el ceño.

—No estoy muy segura de que ésta sea una de tus mejores ideas.

Inclinó la cabeza para besarla con ternura y una buena dosis de persuasión.

—Tú también podrás verme —le susurró sobre los labios antes de volver a apoderarse de ellos y demorarse con otro beso.

Portia se amoldó a él y se entregó sin reservas. Sin embargo, interrumpió el beso un instante. A sus ojos asomaba una clara indecisión. Él volvió a acercarla a su cuerpo, pegando sus caderas a las suyas.

—Confía en mí —le dijo—. Te va a encantar.

Y se frotó de forma sugerente contra ella.

Portia resopló para sus adentros y decidió no explicarle el motivo de sus temores: que sabía que le encantaría la desvergonzada aventura y que disfrutaría muchísimo adentrándose cada vez más en su red sensual. Una red que él había tejido con total deliberación.

De todas formas, ya había aceptado el desafío, había decidido cuál era el camino a seguir.

Sostuvo su mirada y le arrojó los brazos al cuello, que hasta entonces descansaban contra su pecho. Se estiró con abandono contra él y le dijo:

—De acuerdo.

Justo antes de que sus labios se encontraran, la indecisión volvió a apoderarse de ella. Ese instante le bastó para percatarse de la tensión que Simon se esforzaba por ocultar, por más que ésta creciera a pasos agigantados.

Con la vista clavada en su boca, murmuró con voz deliberadamente sensual:

—Enséñame más. —Y le ofreció los labios.

Simon aceptó la entrega con voracidad. Hechizó sus sentidos, se dio un festín con su boca y le robó la razón.

Su ardor los arrojó directos a la hoguera de la pasión, a las rugientes llamas del deseo.

Un deseo que los dos avivaron. Sentía las manos de Simon acariciándola por doquier con afán posesivo, excitándola con cada sugerente roce. Le enterró los dedos en el pelo y lo instó a proseguir... hasta que él decidió controlar las llamas que amenazaban con devorarlos. Se movió un poco y la inmovilizó contra la cama, apresándola con sus piernas.

Simon puso fin al beso y esperó con la cabeza inclinada hasta que ella se decidió a abrir los ojos y mirarlo.

—Esta noche vamos a tomarnos las cosas con calma —le advirtió. Su voz era ronca, muy seria... y un tanto dictatorial.

Portia sostuvo su mirada sin flaquear y enarcó una ceja.

—Creí que eso era lo que habíamos hecho hasta ahora.

Un brillo respetuoso iluminó los ojos de Simon.

—Tengo una propuesta: veamos hasta qué punto somos capaces de tomarnos las cosas con calma.

No sabía exactamente adónde quería llevarla, pero se encogió de hombros con fingida despreocupación.

—Como desees.

Él inclinó la cabeza.

—Eso es lo que deseo.

Simon volvió a tomar posesión de su boca con un beso largo, lento, sublime y de lo más excitante. Ya no pensaba ofrecer resistencia alguna, ni siquiera fingida, puesto que hacía un buen rato que había abandonado cualquier intento de seguir los dictados de la razón o de la voluntad. Habían quedado abandonados a un lado del camino, mientras él tejía su hipnótico hechizo.

Ni siquiera pensó en la reveladora luz de las velas cuando le desabrochó el vestido y se lo bajó por los hombros. Ni cuando le apartó los brazos del cuello y dejó que las mangas se deslizaran hasta que el corpiño cayó en torno a su cintura.

Con esos labios devorando los suyos y esa lengua que la acariciaba sin tregua prometiéndole un sinfín de deleites, ni siquiera se percató de los tirones que sufrían las cintas de su camisola.

Sin embargo, en ese instante, Simon se apartó, interrumpió el beso y bajó la vista mientras apartaba la liviana prenda de seda para dejar sus pechos al descubierto..., a merced de la ardiente mirada de sus ojos azules.

La expresión que adoptó su rostro la dejó sin respiración. Simon levantó una mano, le pasó el dorso de los dedos por el hombro y descendió hasta la curva de un pecho. Una vez allí, giró la mano y lo capturó con la palma, como si fuera un conquistador evaluando un obsequio que acabaran de ofrecerle. Al primer apretón, la razón la abandonó.

Incapaz de respirar, se limitó a mirar, atrapada sin remisión en el hechizo sensual mientras él se daba un festín con los ojos y la examinaba, acariciaba y torturaba sin prisa alguna, lánguidamente.

Cuando estuvo satisfecho, buscó su mirada, se movió un poco e inclinó la cabeza muy despacio. Llevó los labios hasta un enhiesto pezón y succionó con suavidad. Al escuchar su jadeo, se detuvo y comenzó a besarlo y lamerlo. No tardó en trasladar sus atenciones al otro pecho mientras que sus dedos se demoraban en el excitado pezón para continuar la tortura que sus labios habían comenzado.

Hasta que regresó, se lo metió en la boca y lo chupó con fuerza. Portia gritó y se aferró a su pelo mientras arqueaba el cuerpo y echaba la cabeza hacia atrás, instándolo a acercarse más. Intentó concentrarse en la cenefa bordada del dosel, pero fue incapaz.

Cerró los ojos cuando succionó de nuevo y se preguntó hasta cuándo la sostendrían las piernas. Como si le hubiera leído el pensamiento, él bajó las manos por sus costados y la aferró por el trasero en un gesto de lo más posesivo.

Se obligó a abrir los ojos y jadeó al tiempo que bajaba la vista y lo contemplaba en mitad de su festín. Sus miradas se entrelazaron y, con total deliberación, él le pasó la lengua por el pezón antes de mordisquearlo.

Portia se estremeció y volvió a cerrar los ojos.

Lo sintió enderezarse al tiempo que le quitaba las manos del trasero. Ella le soltó la cabeza y dejó las manos sobre su pecho.

Una vez más, se obligó a abrir los ojos a pesar del considerable esfuerzo que le supuso. Tenía que ver lo que iba a suceder a continuación. Tenía que verle el rostro mientras le bajaba el vestido y la camisola hasta las caderas, desde donde cayeron al suelo con un suave frufrú. En ese instante, se alejó un poco de ella, pero sus ojos no habían seguido el recorrido de la ropa. Estaban clavados en los oscuros rizos de su entrepierna.

Intentó adivinar sus pensamientos, pero no lo logró. La crispada expresión de su rostro quizás indicara que ni siquiera estaba pensando.

En ese instante, le apartó las manos de la cintura y fue bajándolas sobre la ligera curva de su vientre hasta llegar a las ingles. Alzó la cabeza y se acercó un poco más. El brillo que apareció en esos ojos azules hizo que contuviera el aliento.

Portia le colocó las manos en el pecho y lo apartó.

—No... Tu ropa. —Sus miradas se entrelazaron mientras ella se lamía los labios—. Yo también quiero verte.

—Y me verás. —Le rodeó la cintura con las manos e inclinó la cabeza para besarla—. Pero todavía no. Esta noche no vamos a apresurarnos. Tenemos tiempo para saborearlo todo. Cada paso. Cada experiencia.

La última palabra resultó una promesa imposible de resistir. De modo que volvió a hechizarla y se vio incapaz de impedirle que conquistara sus labios, su voluntad y su sentido común.

La estrechó entre sus brazos y la respiración le falló de nuevo. Todavía estaba vestido y su piel pareció cobrar vida con el roce de la chaqueta y de los pantalones. Con total deliberación, sus suaves curvas quedaron aplastadas contra los duros contornos de ese cuerpo masculino, de tal modo que fue muy consciente de su erección y del contraste entre su cuerpo desnudo y el suyo, aún vestido. Asimismo supo sin lugar a dudas que estaba a su merced. Que era suya para hacer lo que se le antojara.

Al menos, hasta donde ella se lo permitiera.

Esa afirmación era tan obvia que no albergaba la menor duda al respecto. Ni siquiera protestó cuando él la alzó del suelo y la colocó de rodillas en la cama, mirándolo de frente. Se aferró a sus hombros para guardar el equilibrio mientras él seguía devorando sus labios y la mantenía atrapada en el beso. Sus manos exploraban sin descanso: los pechos, los costados, la espalda... Desde allí descendieron hasta el trasero, al que dieron un seductor apretón antes de proseguir con su descenso y acariciar la cara posterior de sus muslos para después seguir con el recorrido hacia delante, hasta tocar con los dedos la cara interna de los muslos.

Desde allí, fue ascendiendo hasta que alcanzó ese lugar hinchado y palpitante de deseo.

Comenzó a jadear mientras él la exploraba con los dedos en busca de ese diminuto botón que le daba tanto placer. Acto seguido, se introdujo entre sus húmedos pliegues. Descubrió la entrada de su cuerpo y se demoró, rozándola con las yemas de los dedos, hasta que la sintió contener el aliento, hasta que le clavó los dedos en los hombros. En ese instante, la penetró con un dedo y comenzó a acariciarla con languidez. Después, lo siguió otro más, provocándole un estremecimiento. Echó la cabeza hacia atrás, interrumpiendo el beso.

Simon se lo permitió y entretanto la mantuvo erguida, aferrándole la cadera con una mano mientras que con la otra la acariciaba con movimientos deliberadamente lentos y controlados. Era maravilloso sentir la húmeda presión de su cuerpo en torno a los dedos.

La observó detenidamente mientras la llevaba al borde del clímax.

Observó el rubor del deseo extendiéndose sobre esa delicada piel, cuyo tono iba cambiando del alabastro al rosa más pálido. La pasión había borrado la habitual determinación de su rostro. Estaba entregada a sus caricias, a él, a sus deseos. A lo que deseaba hacerle. A lo que deseaba que hicieran juntos. Notó que se le aceleraba la respiración y separaba los labios por el esfuerzo de tomárselo con calma y no precipitarse. Cuando abrió los ojos, comprobó que el azul cobalto de sus iris se había oscurecido hasta el punto de parecer negro. Lo miró mientras él la observaba. Mientras disfrutaba al máximo del momento y la llevaba hasta el orgasmo lenta pero inexorablemente.

Su mirada se posó sobre sus pezones, enhiestos y rosados, y no pudo resistirse a tan suculento manjar.

Mientras la pasión se adueñaba de ella paso a paso y su cuerpo se movía al ritmo que él marcaba, el rubor del deseo fue intensificándose y llegó un punto en el que volvió a cerrar los ojos. Aprovechó el momento para inclinar la cabeza y rodear un pezón con los labios.

La torturó con las caricias de su lengua mientras sentía cómo el deseo crecía en ella y la marea de placer amenazaba con arrastrarla.

En ese instante, succionó con fuerza. La escuchó gritar al tiempo que sus manos lo aferraban por la cabeza cuando alcanzó el clímax. Siguió chupándole el pezón y dejó que los espasmos se desvanecieran hasta que se relajó por completo contra él. En ese momento, apartó la mano de su sexo y la alzó en brazos. Se arrodilló en el colchón y la dejó tendida.

Tenía los ojos abiertos y lo estaba observando. Siguió cada uno de sus movimientos, totalmente expuesta como un delicioso manjar sobre la colcha carmesí, mientras él se desvestía lentamente.

No había motivos para apresurarse, tal y como ya le había asegurado. Había planeado la noche como una sucesión de actos. Portia necesitaría unos minutos para recuperarse. Cuantos más, mejor. Mejor para el siguiente acto. Mejor para él.

Tenía sobrada experiencia a la hora de concentrarse en otras cosas y así olvidar el apremio que le corría por las venas. Y fue esa experiencia, junto con la certeza de que podría conseguir su propósito si se ceñía al libreto y a su férrea voluntad, lo que lo ayudó a no echarse sobre ella y hacerle el amor con desenfreno.

Tenía una piel muy delicada. Aunque el rubor del deseo se desvanecía, era tan pálida y translúcida que absorbía el tono de la luz de las velas hasta brillar como si estuviera cubierta por una pátina dorada. Las ondas de su abundante melena negra se esparcían sobre los almohadones, enmarcándole el rostro.

El rostro de una *madonna* inglesa, suavizado aún más por la pasión satisfecha e iluminado por un resplandor sensual.

Un rostro que poco a poco dejaba ver la intriga y la fascinación por lo que sucedería a continuación.

Rodeó la cama mientras se quitaba la chaqueta, el chaleco y la camisa. Como lo haría cualquier caballero que estuviera a punto de meterse en la cama para dormir, no para hundirse en el acogedor cuerpo de una hurí que ya había sucumbido a sus deseos.

Esos ojos azul cobalto siguieron todos sus movimientos.

Ninguno de los dos habló, pero la tensión que cayó

sobre ellos y que fue incrementándose a medida que rodeaba la cama resultaba prácticamente palpable. E hizo que se le desbocara el corazón. Cuando se quitó por fin los pantalones, lo invadió un alivio inmenso.

Los dejó pulcramente doblados sobre una silla antes de enderezarse y regresar junto a la cama.

Ella lo observaba con los párpados entornados, inmóvil sobre el colchón. Su mirada descendió por su rostro, su pecho y su rígido abdomen hasta clavarse con evidente placer sobre su erección.

Con afán posesivo.

Casi podía escuchar los pensamientos que pasaban por su cabeza mientras lo miraba y se aferraba a las sábanas con fuerza.

Se arrodilló en el colchón y se sentó sobre los talones, fuera del alcance de Portia. Alzó una mano y le ordenó:

—Ven aquí.

Ella lo miró a los ojos al escuchar la imperiosa y adusta orden. Se incorporó sobre un codo sin dejar de mirarlo. Estaba a punto de inclinarse para ayudarla a ponerse de rodillas cuando Portia se decidió.

Inclinó la cabeza hacia él y, antes de que se diera cuenta de sus intenciones, sintió el roce de su pelo en la entrepierna. Sintió el roce de su aliento sobre su miembro. Al instante, lo lamió. Muy despacio y con abandono.

Y comprendió que estaba perdido.

Olvidó el libreto por completo cuando ella cambió de postura para tener mejor acceso. Se apoyó sobre sus muslos y comenzó a acariciar su miembro con una mano, arriba y abajo, al mismo tiempo que su lengua recorría la punta, humedeciéndolo y excitándolo aún más. En un momento dado, se apartó un poco para observar su obra y, cuando se dio por satisfecha, se inclinó de nuevo para metérselo en la boca.

Simon le enterró los dedos en el pelo y se los clavó cuando ella succionó con fuerza. Se contuvo a duras penas mientras lo atormentaba y tuvo que echar mano de toda su fuerza de voluntad para apartarla cuando ella hizo una pausa para respirar. La agarró por los hombros y la alzó.

—Todavía no he acabado —protestó, mirándolo implorante a los ojos.

—Ya es suficiente —replicó él entre dientes—. Luego.

—Eso me dijiste la última vez.

—Por una buena razón.

—Me lo prometiste.

—Te prometí que podrías mirar. No dije nada de lamer.

Lo miró con los ojos entrecerrados mientras se plegaba a sus deseos y se colocaba sobre su regazo, irguiéndose sobre las rodillas. Se acercó a él hasta que sus rostros estuvieron a punto de rozarse y le dijo con el ceño fruncido:

—Creo que protestas demasiado. Te gusta. Mucho.

La aferró por las caderas.

—Me gusta demasiado, maldita sea.

Ella separó los labios y él detuvo sus palabras de la manera más eficiente que conocía: tiró de sus caderas hacia abajo y comenzó a penetrarla con lentitud, centímetro a centímetro, mientras la sentía cerrarse en torno a él. A la postre y ya olvidado lo que iba a decir, Portia soltó un jadeo, le rodeó la cara con las manos y tiró de él para besarlo.

Con más sensualidad que una hurí.

No necesitó más estímulos. Comenzó a embestir con las caderas al mismo tiempo que la movía a ella. Portia no tardó en hacerse con el ritmo. Se cerraba a su alrededor cuando se hundía en ella y se relajaba cuando salía. Aunque no salía del todo. A ella le gustaba sentirlo bien adentro, según parecía, y estaba encantado de complacerla, al menos en ese aspecto.

En su opinión, no había nada más satisfactorio desde el punto de vista sensual que sentir un cuerpo ardiente, húmedo y voluptuoso rodeando su miembro.

Sobre todo si se trataba de Portia.

Con ella, la satisfacción era mucho más intensa que la que proporcionaba el sexo por el sexo. Mucho más intensa que la gratificación sensual. Era una satisfacción que le calaba hasta el fondo del alma. Que lo aliviaba, lo alimentaba, lo incitaba y le creaba una poderosa adicción, como si fuera un elixir paradisíaco.

Cambió el *tempo* y dejó que el apremio los embargara. Ella lo rodeó con los brazos y lo estrechó con fuerza. El beso se intensificó.

El anhelo que corría por sus venas se avivó y creció hasta inundarlos por completo. Era mucho más básico que la mera lujuria. Mucho más poderoso que la pasión.

Se adueñó de ellos como si fuera una riada y ambos lo aceptaron mientras sus movimientos se hacían más rápidos, más urgentes, más bruscos.

Hasta que Portia estalló. Su cuerpo se cerró en torno a él sin piedad cuando alcanzó el orgasmo. Gritó, aunque el sonido quedó sofocado por el beso. La inmovilizó sosteniéndola por las caderas mientras los espasmos la sacudían y se desvanecían.

Cuando se relajó, se desplomó extenuada sobre él.

Fue entonces cuando Simon se atrevió a poner fin al beso. Respiró hondo y pensó. Sobre el siguiente acto.

Portia por fin pudo tomar una entrecortada bocanada de aire. Se dio cuenta de que él se había detenido, pero aún lo sentía duro y rígido en su interior. Sus manos la acariciaban con ternura, pero estaba tenso... a la espera.

Alzó la cabeza para mirarlo a los ojos. Y vio la bestia que merodeaba tras esos iris azules.

—Y ahora ¿qué?

Tardó un momento en contestarle. Cuando lo hizo, su voz apenas fue un gruñido gutural.

—El siguiente acto.

La apartó de él y la empujó con suavidad hacia los almohadones que había amontonados junto al cabecero de la cama.

Ella gateó hasta llegar allí y se dejó caer. Aguardó tendida sobre el vientre y esperó a que él le diera la vuelta. Al ver que no lo hacía, se incorporó sobre un codo y lo miró.

Seguía sentado sobre los talones, con una flagrante erección y los ojos clavados en su trasero. Al darse cuenta de que lo estaba observando, la miró a la cara.

—¿Qué? —le preguntó, mientras intentaba atisbar qué le llamaba tanto la atención.

Él titubeó, pero acabó meneando la cabeza.

—Nada. —Extendió los brazos para agarrarla por las piernas—. Date la vuelta.

Cuando lo hizo, le separó los muslos, se colocó sobre ella y, sin muchos más preámbulos, la penetró. Con una poderosa embestida que le hizo arquear el cuerpo con abandono y estuvo a punto de hacerla olvidar.

Pero no lo consiguió del todo.

Simon se apartó para embestir de nuevo y hundirse hasta el fondo. Tiró de él para instarlo a apoyar todo su peso en ella, pero tardó un poco en obedecerla.

Una vez que lo hizo, lo miró a los ojos.

—¿Qué me estás ocultando?

—Nada que necesites saber. —Introdujo una mano bajo ella y le alzó las caderas justo cuando volvía a embestir.

—No prestaré atención hasta que me lo digas.

Él soltó una carcajada.

—No me tientes...

Portia intentó fulminarlo con la mirada, pero su siguiente movimiento, mucho más brusco y devastador, se llevó por delante todo pensamiento. Se movió un poco sobre ella y la posición le permitió penetrarla más hondo que nunca.

—Si lo aprendieras todo de una sola vez, ya no me quedaría nada para enseñarte. No me gustaría que acabaras aburriéndote.

—No creo que...

«Que exista la más remota posibilidad de que eso ocurra, al menos en esta vida», pensó mientras cerraba los ojos. Intentó contener la apremiante marea de deseo que iba creciendo en su interior con cada profundo envite, con cada roce de su miembro en lo más hondo de su cuerpo.

No pudo.

Dejó que la inundara, que la traspasara, que la arrastrara.

Que la transportara hasta ese mar en el que ya se habían bañado lo suficiente como para apreciar el valor de esos momentos, para atesorarlos, para saborearlos al máximo.

Esos valiosos momentos de intimidad eran eso y mucho más. Porque trascendían el plano físico.

Lo sentía en la médula de los huesos y se preguntó, en lo más recóndito de su mente, si él también lo sentiría.

Si sentiría el poder de ese sentimiento que crecía entre ellos. Si sentiría cómo los iba uniendo mientras sus cuerpos se fundían. Cada vez más rápido y con más fuerza, en su camino hacia el pináculo donde encontrarían ese supremo y glorioso deleite. Porque no les cabía duda de que lo alcanzarían.

Y lo hicieron, como era inevitable. Hasta allí llegaron subidos en la cresta de la sublime ola antes de dejarse caer tomados de la mano a ese mar de dichosa satisfacción.

Había sido fácil. Tanto que no estaba segura de poder fiarse de su intuición. Algo tan importante no podía ser tan sencillo.

¿Era amor verdadero? ¿Cómo podía asegurarse?

Ciertamente, el vínculo que había entre ellos era algo mucho más poderoso que la lujuria. Aunque no tuviera experiencia alguna al respecto, de eso, al menos, estaba segura.

Abandonó la mesa del desayuno a la mañana siguiente con la esperanza de que nadie hubiera notado su portentoso apetito y se dirigió al saloncito matinal para salir a la terraza. Necesitaba pensar, reconsiderar y volver a analizar la situación en la que se encontraban y a la que podrían llegar. Los paseos al aire libre siempre la habían ayudado a reflexionar.

Pero no podía hacerlo con él a su lado.

Se detuvo al llegar a la terraza y se giró para enfrentarlo.

—Quiero pensar. Voy a dar un paseo.

Con las manos en los bolsillos, Simon la miró e inclinó la cabeza.

—De acuerdo.

—Sola.

El cambio que se produjo en su expresión no fue producto de su imaginación. Su semblante se endureció, tensó la mandíbula y entrecerró los ojos.

—No puedes deambular por ahí tú sola. Alguien ha tratado de matarte, ¿lo has olvidado?

—Eso fue hace días. Ya deben de haber comprendido que no sé nada sobre el crimen. —Alzó las manos—. Soy inofensiva.

—Eres tonta —replicó él con el ceño fruncido—. Si piensa que puedes recordar ese detalle que conoces, pero que has olvidado, no se detendrá... Ya oíste al señor Stokes. Hasta que no atrapemos al asesino, no irás a ningún lado sin protección.

Portia entrecerró los ojos.

—Si crees que voy a...

—No creo, lo sé.

Lo miró a los ojos y sintió cómo la ira la iba consumiendo hasta que la sangre comenzó a hervirle en las venas y estuvo a punto de entrar en erupción...

Recordó la conclusión a la que había llegado poco antes. ¿Fácil? ¿Había pensado que sería fácil? ¿Con él?

Le lanzó una mirada furibunda. Cualquier otra persona habría dado un respingo y se habría escabullido de inmediato. Simon ni siquiera parpadeó, su determinación no flaqueó en ningún momento. Contuvo un gruñido y refrenó su temperamento, ya que no quería volver al tira y afloja que había caracterizado su relación hasta hacía muy poco. Consciente de que no tenía otra salida, asintió con la cabeza.

—Muy bien. Puedes seguirme. —Se percató de su sorpresa y percibió que él había enarbolado sus defensas, dispuesto para enfrentarse en una batalla en toda regla. Sostuvo su mirada con un gesto desafiante—. Pero a cierta distancia.

Simon parpadeó y la tensión lo abandonó en parte.

—¿Por qué a cierta distancia?

No quería admitirlo, pero no cedería si ella no lo hacía antes.

—No puedo pensar, no soy capaz de llegar a una conclusión fiable, si te llevo pegado a los talones. O si estás cerca. —No esperó a ver su reacción, ya le bastaba con imaginársela. Se dio la vuelta y echó a andar hacia los escalones—. Mantén una distancia de al menos veinte metros.

Creyó escuchar una carcajada rápidamente sofocada, pero no miró atrás. Con la cabeza bien alta, se puso en marcha y atravesó el prado en dirección al lago.

Cuando estuvo a mitad de camino, miró hacia atrás y lo vio bajando los escalones sin ninguna prisa. No se detuvo a comprobar si estaba sonriendo o no. Devolvió la vista al frente y siguió caminando.

Se obligó a pensar en aquello que quería pensar.

En él. Y en ella. En su relación.

En el increíble giro que ésta había sufrido. Recordó su objetivo original, aquel que la había arrojado a sus brazos. Había deseado con todas sus fuerzas experimentar la atracción que unía a un hombre y una mujer. Esa atracción culpable de llevar a una mujer al matrimonio.

Y ya tenía la respuesta. Ya sabía muy bien el porqué.

Frunció el ceño y bajó la vista. Unió las manos tras la espalda y caminó sin prestar atención al rumbo que tomaban sus pasos.

¿De verdad estaba considerando la idea de casarse con Simon, un tirano en potencia cuya verdadera naturaleza salía de vez en cuando a la luz?

Sí.

¿Por qué?

No porque disfrutara muchísimo con él en la cama. Si bien ese aspecto era maravilloso, no resultaba convincente por sí solo. Movida por la ignorancia, había supuesto en un principio que el aspecto físico de una relación tenía bastante más peso. En esos momentos, aunque admitía que era una parte muy importante y de lo más adictiva (al menos con alguien como Simon), no podía imaginarse (ni siquiera tratándose de él) que aceptaría jamás un matrimonio basándose sólo en eso.

Era ese sentimiento indefinido que había crecido entre ellos lo que había añadido el peso suficiente para inclinar la balanza a favor del sí.

Ya era hora de que comenzara a llamarlo por su nombre. Porque tenía que ser amor. No tenía caso seguir dudándolo. Estaba allí, entre ellos y era casi tangible, jamás los abandonaba.

¿Sería un sentimiento nuevo para los dos? ¿Estaría Simon ofreciéndole algo que jamás le había ofrecido antes a nadie? ¿O sería la edad, y tal vez las circunstancias, lo que los había llevado a variar sus puntos de vista y a abrirles los ojos para que apreciaran mutuamente ciertos detalles que antes se les habían pasado por alto?

Ésa parecía la opción más lógica. Si echaba la vista atrás, debía admitir que entre ellos siempre había existido potencial, pero había estado oculto bajo el choque inevitable de sus personalidades.

Dichas personalidades no habían cambiado, pero tanto ella como aparentemente él... parecían haber llegado con la edad a un punto en el que se aceptaban el uno al otro tal y como eran; en el que estaban dispuestos a amoldarse y a cambiar para así optar al premio más gratificante de todos.

El prado se estrechaba a medida que se convertía en el sendero que llevaba al lago. Alzó la vista justo cuando doblaba en la curva...

Y estuvo a punto de caerse de bruces cuando tropezó con algo. Se alzó las faldas justo a tiempo y consiguió sortear el obstáculo con un salto. Una vez que recuperó el equilibrio, miró hacia atrás.

Y vio...

De repente, fue consciente de la ligera brisa que agitaba los mechones que habían escapado al recogido; del latido de su corazón; de la sangre que corría por sus venas.

Del escalofrío que acababa de erizarle la piel.

—¿Simon? —Había hablado demasiado bajo. Él estaba cerca, pero la curva lo había dejado fuera de su vista en ese instante—. ¡Simon!

Escuchó de inmediato sus pisadas cuando echó a correr. Extendió las manos para ayudarlo cuando tropezó, al igual que le había sucedido a ella.

Recuperó el equilibrio, miró al suelo y soltó una maldición. La agarró por los brazos y tiró de ella para acercarla a su cuerpo.

Volvió a maldecir de nuevo. La estrechó con más fuerza y la hizo girar para apartarla de la imagen que tenían a sus pies.

La imagen del joven jardinero, Dennis, que yacía estrangulado en el suelo... como Kitty.

Tan muerto como Kitty.

15

—No —respondió el señor Stokes a la pregunta de lord Netherfield; los seis, el propio lord Netherfield, así como el investigador, Charlie, lady O, Portia y él, estaban reunidos en la biblioteca, sopesando la situación—. A una hora tan temprana, nadie tiene una coartada sólida. Todos se encontraban en sus habitaciones, solos.

—Era muy temprano, ¿no?

—Al parecer, Dennis comenzaba su jornada al clarear el día. Hoy, el jardinero jefe se cruzó con él e intercambiaron unas palabras, no sabemos la hora exacta, pero fue bastante antes de que empezara la actividad en la casa. Sin embargo, hay una cosa que sí está clara. —El señor Stokes se detuvo en mitad de la estancia y los enfrentó a los cinco, que estaban repartidos por los dos sillones y el diván delante de la chimenea—. Quienquiera que matase a Dennis era un hombre joven. El muchacho se defendió con ferocidad..., eso ha quedado demostrado.

Sentado en el reposabrazos del sillón de Portia, Simon la miró a la cara. Aún seguía pálida por la impresión y demasiado callada, a pesar de que ya había pasado más de medio día desde el desagradable descubrimiento. Su segundo descubrimiento. Apretó los labios y desvió la vista hacia el investigador; al recordar las marcas que había en la hierba y la postura doblada del cuerpo, asintió con la cabeza.

—A Kitty pudo matarla cualquiera, pero Dennis es otra historia.

—Sí. Y ya podemos descartar que el asesino fuera una mujer.

Lady O pareció perpleja.

—No sabía que las mujeres fueran sospechosas.

—Todo el mundo lo era. No podemos permitirnos el menor error.

—¡Caray! Supongo que es cierto —refunfuñó mientras se atusaba el chal. La seguridad que la caracterizaba se desvanecía por momentos.

El segundo asesinato había descolocado a todo el mundo a un nivel muy profundo, y no sólo por el hecho de haber sido el segundo crimen. Era incuestionable que el asesino seguía entre ellos; tal vez alguno de los invitados hubiera comenzado a olvidarse del asunto, pero el asesinato de Dennis los había obligado a reconocer que ese horror no se podía ocultar tan fácilmente.

Apoyado contra la repisa de la chimenea, Charlie preguntó:

—¿Qué usó el rufián para estrangular al pobre desgraciado?

—Otro cordón de cortina. Aunque en esta ocasión provenía del saloncito matinal.

Charlie torció el gesto.

—Así que puede haber sido cualquiera...

El señor Stokes asintió con la cabeza.

—No obstante, si asumimos que una misma persona ha cometido los dos crímenes, podemos reducir la lista de sospechosos considerablemente.

—Sólo hombres —dijo lady O.

El investigador reconoció sus palabras con una inclinación de cabeza.

—Y sólo los que sean lo bastante fuertes como para someter a Dennis... Creo que el hecho de que se sintiera confiado es fundamental. Nuestro asesino no podía arriesgarse al fracaso, y tenía que proceder con presteza. Después de todo, debía de saber que había otras personas por los alrededores. —Titubeó un instante antes de continuar—: Creo que los sospechosos más probables son Henry Glossup, James Glossup, Desmond Winfield y Ambrose Calvin. —Se detuvo y, al ver que ninguno protestaba, prosiguió—: Todos tienen motivos para matar a la señora Glossup, todos tienen capacidad física para haberlo hecho, todos tuvieron la oportunidad y ninguno tiene coartada.

Simon escuchó el suspiro de Portia; bajó la vista y la vio estremecerse antes de levantar la cabeza.

—Sus zapatos. La hierba debía de estar húmeda a esas horas de la mañana. Tal vez si comprobamos...

Con expresión sombría, el señor Stokes negó con la cabeza.

—Ya lo hice. Quienquiera que sea nuestro hombre, es inteligente y muy cuidadoso. Todos los zapatos estaban limpios y secos. —Desvió la vista hacia lord Netherfield—. Le estoy muy agradecido, señor. Blenkinsop y el personal me han ayudado enormemente.

Lord Netherfield le restó importancia al agradecimiento.

—Quiero atrapar al asesino. No quiero que mis nietos, que mi familia se vea salpicada por este asunto. Y eso es lo que va a suceder a menos que atrapemos al criminal. —Miró al señor Stokes a los ojos—. He vivido demasiado como para esconderme de la realidad. No desenmascarar al asesino sólo conseguirá que los inocentes se vean arrastrados al fango con él. Tenemos que atrapar a ese rufián ahora, antes de que las cosas empeoren.

El señor Stokes vaciló antes de decir:

—Si me permite la observación, milord, parece usted muy seguro de que ninguno de sus nietos pudiera ser el culpable.

Lord Netherfield asintió con la cabeza mientras aferraba la empuñadura del bastón con ambas manos.

—Lo estoy. Los conozco suficientemente desde que nacieron y ninguno de ellos es un asesino. Pero como es lógico que usted no lo sepa, no voy a malgastar mi aliento intentando convencerlo. Debe investigar a los cuatro, pero recuerde lo que le digo: será uno de los otros dos.

El respeto con el que el señor Stokes inclinó la cabeza era, a todas luces, sincero.

—Gracias. Y ahora... —Recorrió a los presentes dirigiéndoles una mirada intensa—. Debo retirarme. Tengo que comprobar ciertos detalles, aunque mucho me temo que no espero encontrar ninguna pista fiable.

Tras hacer una reverencia, se marchó.

Una vez que la puerta se cerró tras el señor Stokes, Simon se percató de que lady O intentaba llamar su atención para que se fijara en Portia.

Aunque tampoco era necesario. Cuando la miró, extendió el brazo para cogerla de la mano.

—Vamos, salgamos a cabalgar un rato.

Charlie los acompañó. Se cruzaron con James y le preguntaron si quería unirse a ellos, pero rechazó la invitación, cosa extraña en él. Era evidente que se sentía incómodo al saberse sospechoso, lo que se traducía en que ellos también se sentían así. A regañadientes, lo dejaron en la sala de billar, jugando sin demasiado entusiasmo.

Encontraron a las restantes damas sentadas en silencio en el salón de la parte posterior de la mansión. Lucy Buckstead y las hermanas Hammond aceptaron la invitación al punto y sus madres les dieron permiso, aliviadas.

Cuando todos se hubieron cambiado de ropa y fueron a los establos en busca de los caballos, ya estaba bien avanzada la tarde. Una vez sobre la briosa yegua castaña, Portia encabezó el grupo y Simon la siguió de cerca.

Al contemplarla, se dio cuenta de que parecía muy distante. Sin embargo, controlaba la yegua con su habitual soltura. Tanto era así que no tardaron en dejar a los demás atrás. Cuando llegaron a los frondosos caminos de Cranborne Chase, dejaron que sus monturas eligieran el paso... hasta que estuvieron galopando a toda velocidad, cada vez más deprisa, codo con codo.

De repente, tan de repente que la adelantó sin darse cuenta, Portia tiró de las riendas. Sorprendido, Simon refrenó su caballo, dio media vuelta... y la vio desmontar a toda prisa y dejar a la yegua suelta. Acto seguido, echó a correr ladera arriba entre los crujidos de las hojas caídas que iba aplastando. Cuando llegó a la parte superior de la cuestecilla, se detuvo con la espalda muy derecha, la cabeza en alto y la vista clavada en los árboles.

Desconcertado, Simon detuvo su caballo junto a la yegua, desmontó y ató ambos animales a una rama cercana antes de seguirla.

Muy preocupado. El hecho de que se hubiera detenido de ese modo y hubiera soltado las riendas sin más... No era típico de ella.

Aminoró el paso conforme se fue acercando. Se detuvo a unos cuantos pasos de ella.

—¿Qué pasa?

Portia no lo miró, se limitó a menear la cabeza.

—Nada. Sólo que... —Se detuvo, hizo un gesto con la mano; tenía la voz llorosa y el gesto era de impotencia.

Acortó la distancia que los separaba y la apretó contra su pecho; hizo caso omiso de su resistencia y la rodeó con sus brazos.

La sostuvo mientras lloraba.

—¡Es tan espantoso! —dijo entre sollozos—. Están muertos. ¡Se han ido! Y él... era tan joven. Mucho más joven que nosotros.

Él se mantuvo en silencio y le dio un beso en la coronilla antes de apoyar la mejilla sobre su cabeza. Dejó que todo lo que sentía por ella se expandiera y los rodeara.

Y la tranquilizara.

La mano de Portia se cerró sobre su chaqueta y se fue relajando poco a poco.

A la postre, sus sollozos cesaron y la tensión abandonó totalmente su cuerpo.

—Te he mojado la chaqueta.

—No te preocupes por eso.

Portia sorbió por la nariz.

—¿Tienes un pañuelo?

La soltó lo justo para sacarse un pañuelo del bolsillo y dárselo.

Ella le secó la chaqueta con el pañuelo antes de enjugarse los ojos y sonarse la nariz. Después, se guardó el arrugado trozo de tela en el bolsillo y lo miró a los ojos.

Sus pestañas seguían húmedas y sus enormes ojos azules brillaban. La expresión que vio en ellos...

Inclinó la cabeza y la besó. Al principio con gentileza, pero poco a poco la fue acercando a él; poco a poco fue profundizando la caricia hasta que la tuvo hechizada.

Hasta que dejó de pensar.

De pensar en el hecho de que llorar entre sus brazos era muy revelador; posiblemente más revelador y mucho más íntimo que yacer desnudos. Desde una perspectiva emocional, para ella lo era, pero no quería que pensara en eso.

Ni que pensara en lo que él sentía, en la inmensa alegría que lo embargaba porque le hubiera permitido verla expuesta y sin defensas. Verla como realmente era, sin máscaras; una mujer con un corazón tierno y dulce.

Un corazón que, por lo general, lo guardaba celosamente.

Un corazón que él deseaba.

Más que nada en la vida.

La noche cayó, y con ella una tensión expectante e incómoda. Tal y como había previsto, el señor Stokes no descubrió nada relevante. Ese hecho hizo que un manto pesimista se cerniera sobre la casa.

Ya no quedaban sonrisas con las que aligerar el ambiente. Nadie sugirió entretenerse con un poco de música. Las damas charlaban entre sus susurros apesadumbrados sobre naderías... Sobre cosas insustanciales que no importaban en lo más mínimo.

Cuando se reunió con las mujeres, acompañado de lord Netherfield y lord Glossup, Simon buscó a Portia y la llevó a la terraza. En el exterior, lejos del ambiente opresivo del salón, les costaba menos respirar y podían hablar sin tapujos.

Aunque en el exterior la temperatura no era más fresca, ya que el ambiente resultaba bochornoso y pesado por culpa de la tormenta que se acercaba.

Tras soltarse de su brazo, Portia se acercó a la balaustrada y colocó las dos manos sobre ella antes de clavar la vista en el jardín.

—¿Por qué matar a Dennis?

Simon se había detenido en mitad de la terraza y allí se quedó para darle algo de espacio.

—Posiblemente por el mismo motivo que lo intentó contigo. Sólo que Dennis no tuvo tanta suerte.

—Pero si Dennis sabía algo, ¿por qué no lo dijo? El señor Stokes lo interrogó, ¿no es así?

—Sí. Y tal vez dijera algo, pero a la persona equivocada.

Portia se giró con el ceño fruncido.

—¿Qué quieres decir?

La pregunta hizo que torciera el gesto.

—Cuando el señor Stokes le llevó las noticias a los gitanos, una de las mujeres le dijo que Dennis había estado dándole vueltas a algo. No dijo de qué se trataba... Según ella, podía ser algo que hubiera visto de vuelta al campamento después de enterarse de la muerte de Kitty.

Portia se giró de nuevo para contemplar la creciente oscuridad del jardín.

—No paro de darle vueltas al asunto, pero sigo sin recordar...

Él esperó. Al ver que no decía nada, retrocedió unos pasos, se metió las manos en los bolsillos y se apoyó contra la pared. Después, contempló cómo la noche se cernía sobre los árboles y los jardines, reclamándolos mientras los últimos rayos de sol se desvanecían.

Contempló a Portia y contuvo el impulso de acorralarla, de reclamarla, de encerrarla en una torre lejos del mundo y de cualquier mal. La sensación era conocida, pero mucho más poderosa que antes. Antes de que comprendiera qué era en realidad.

El viento se levantó y con él llegó el olor a tierra mojada. Al igual que él, Portia parecía contenta de estar allí fuera, dejándose empapar por la tranquilidad de la noche.

Esa misma mañana la había seguido a la distancia indicada por ella, preguntándose sobre qué quería pensar. Él mismo había estado pensando, y había deseado poseer la capacidad de impedirle que reflexionara sobre su relación

Porque cuando lo hacía... En fin, era molesto e inquietante. La idea de que Portia le diera demasiadas vueltas a su relación y se convenciera de que era demasiado peligrosa lo aterrorizaba.

Un miedo elocuente, una vulnerabilidad reveladora.

Él también lo sabía.

Tal vez, y de una vez por todas, empezara a comprenderlo.

Portia siempre había sido «ella», la única que sin pretenderlo le había dejado una huella en el corazón y en los sentidos por el mero hecho de existir. Siempre había sabido que era especial para él; pero dada su conocida actitud hacia los hombres (y en especial hacia los hombres como él), había ocultado la verdad y se había negado a reconocerla. Se había negado a reconocer en lo que podía llegar a convertirse si crecía; tal y como había sucedido.

Ya no podía seguir negándolo. Los últimos días lo habían despojado de todas sus máscaras, de todas sus defensas. Hasta dejar bien a la vista, al menos a sus propios ojos, lo que sentía por ella.

Portia aún no lo había visto, pero ya llegaría el momento.

Y lo que hiciera entonces, lo que decidiera entonces...

Se concentró en ella, en su delgada figura junto a la balaustrada. Sintió el acuciante impulso de reclamarla y mandar al infierno las consecuencias; de renunciar a la farsa de permitir que tomara la decisión de entregarse a él por propia voluntad. Un impulso que se adueñaba de él poco a poco y que se había intensificado a causa del peligro de los últimos días... No obstante, sabía que cualquier movimiento que hiciera en esa dirección equivaldría a una bofetada para ella.

Portia dejaría de confiar en él y se retraería.

Y la perdería.

El viento agitó su cabello azabache. La temperatura había bajado, ya que la lluvia se acercaba.

Se apartó de la pared y dio un paso hacia ella...

En ese momento, escuchó una especie de chirrido por encima de sus cabezas y levantó la vista.

Vio cómo una sombra se separaba del tejado.

Se abalanzó sobre Portia y la tiró al suelo, amortiguando el golpe con su propio cuerpo, pero interponiéndose entre ella y el objeto que caía.

Uno de los enormes maceteros que adornaban el antepecho del tejado se estrelló contra la terraza en el mismo lugar donde Portia había estado. Se hizo añicos con un ruido semejante a un cañonazo.

Uno de los fragmentos se le clavó en el brazo que había levantado para protegerla; sintió un dolor agudo y, luego, nada.

El silencio que siguió fue tan absoluto que el contraste resultó abrumador.

Alzó la vista, se percató del peligro y se apresuró a levantar a Portia.

En el interior, alguien gritó y se desató el caos. Lord Glossup y lord Netherfield aparecieron en las puertas de la terraza.

Les bastó un vistazo para comprender lo que había pasado.

—¡Por el amor de Dios! —exclamó lord Glossup al tiempo que se acercaba a ellos—. ¿Se encuentra bien, querida?

Portia asintió sin soltarle la chaqueta. Lord Glossup le dio unas desmañadas palmaditas en el hombro antes de bajar los escalones de la terraza. Una vez en el jardín, levantó la vista hacia el tejado.

—No veo a nadie desde aquí, pero mis ojos ya no son lo que eran.

Desde la puerta que daba al salón, lord Netherfield les hizo señas.

—¡Entrad!

Simon miró a Portia y sintió cómo se enderezaba justo antes de soltarse de sus brazos para cruzar la puerta.

En el salón, lady O golpeaba la alfombra con el bastón de manera insistente; su arrebolado rostro lucía una expresión alarmada.

—¿Adónde vamos a llegar? Eso me gustaría saber.

Blenkinsop asomó la cabeza por la puerta.

—¿Qué desea, milord?

Lord Netherfield le hizo un gesto con la mano.

—Busca al señor Stokes. Han atacado a la señorita Ashford.

—¡Válgame Dios! —Lady Calvin se quedó lívida.

La señora Buckstead se sentó a su lado y le cogió las manos.

—Vamos, vamos. La señorita Ashford está perfectamente.

Sentadas en el diván junto a su madre, las hermanas Hammond estallaron en lágrimas. Lady Hammond y Lucy Buckstead no se encontraban mucho mejor, pero hicieron cuanto pudieron para calmarlas. La señora Archer y lady Glossup estaban totalmente anonadadas.

Lord Netherfield miró a Blenkinsop cuando lord Glossup regresó al salón.

—No, dile al señor Stokes que vaya a la biblioteca. Lo esperaremos allí.

Y eso hicieron. Aunque no pudieron sacar nada en claro del incidente, por más que lo intentaron.

Con la ayuda del mayordomo, los criados contaron lo que sabían y ayudaron a establecer dónde se encontraban sus cuatro sospechosos en el momento del ataque. James y Desmond se habían marchado del salón, supuestamente a sus habitaciones; Henry estaba en la oficina del administrador; Ambrose se encontraba en el despacho, redactando unas cartas. Todos habían estado solos; por tanto, cualquiera podía haber sido el responsable del ataque.

El señor Stokes y lord Glossup subieron hasta el tejado. Cuando regresaron, el investigador confirmó que era un juego de niños llegar hasta allí arriba y que cualquier hombre en plenas facultades físicas podría haber empujado el macetero de piedra de su peana.

—Pesan bastante, pero no están fijados al suelo. —Miró a Simon y su ceño se acentuó—. Está sangrando.

Simon se miró el brazo. El fragmento de piedra le había desgarrado la chaqueta y la tela estaba manchada de sangre.

—Sólo es un arañazo. Ya no sangra.

Portia, que estaba sentada a su lado, se inclinó hacia él, lo cogió del brazo y tiró hasta ver la herida. Simon contuvo un suspiro y la dejó hacer, consciente de que si no se lo permitía, se pondría en pie para echarle un vistazo. Y estaba tan pálida que no quería que se levantara.

Al ver la herida, que a él le parecía insignificante, su palidez se intensificó y desvió la vista hacia el señor Stokes.

—Si no nos necesita para nada más, me gustaría retirarme —le dijo.

—Por supuesto. —El investigador le hizo una reverencia—. Si surge algo, ya hablaré con ustedes mañana.

El hombre lo miró a los ojos cuando se pusieron en pie.

Al adivinar que estaba a punto de decir lo evidente, que Portia no debería quedarse sola en ningún momento, Simon negó con la cabeza. No, Portia no iba a quedarse sola. Y tampoco necesitaba que le recordaran el motivo.

La tomó del brazo y la sacó de la biblioteca. Atravesaron el vestíbulo hasta llegar a la escalinata. Una vez allí, Portia inspiró hondo, se recogió las faldas y subió sin su ayuda.

Al llegar arriba, se soltó las faldas.

—Tenemos que limpiar esa herida. —Se dio la vuelta y se encaminó hacia su habitación.

Simon frunció el ceño, pero la siguió.

—No es nada. Ni siquiera siento el corte.

—Los cortes que no se sienten suelen acabar en gangrena. —Al llegar a su habitación, se giró para mirarlo—. Seguro que no te molestará que te la limpie y te aplique un bálsamo. Si no lo sientes, no te dolerá.

Se detuvo frente a ella para observar su rostro. En él se leían claramente su determinación, su terquedad... y su extrema palidez. Iba a dolerle, pero no como ella creía. Apretó los dientes y extendió la mano para abrir la puerta.

—Si insistes...

Portia insistió, como era de esperar, y él se vio obligado a someterse. Tuvo que sentarse desnudo de cintura para arriba en el filo de la cama mientras ella revoloteaba sin parar a su alrededor.

Desde su más tierna infancia había detestado que las mujeres revolotearan a su alrededor... Había detestado con toda su alma que le curaran las heridas. Tenía más de una cicatriz por esa causa, pero las cicatrices no le preocupaban en absoluto... En cambio, una mujer en esas circunstancias, sobre todo una concentrada en atenderlo con devoción, siempre lo había hecho.

Y seguía haciéndolo. Apretó los dientes, se tragó el orgullo y la dejó hacer.

A esas alturas seguía sintiéndose como un conquistador reducido a un impotente niño de seis años... Impotente cuando se enfrentaba a la necesidad femenina de cuidarlo. Y, en cierta forma, atrapado por dicha necesidad.

Se concentró en el rostro de Portia y contempló con estoicismo cómo limpiaba la herida, aplicaba un poco de bálsamo y le vendaba el corte; un corte que, por cierto, debía de ser más profundo de lo que él había creído. Cuando terminó de colocarle la gasa alrededor del brazo, clavó la vista en sus dedos: delgados, elegantes y ágiles, como ella.

Sintió que las emociones que hasta ese momento había estado conteniendo se apoderaban de él. Lo arrastraban.

Levantó la cabeza mientras revivía en su mente lo sucedido en la terraza y sus músculos se tensaron de forma involuntaria.

No la había perdido de vista ni un instante y aun así había estado a punto de perderla.

No bien Portia hubo terminado, se puso en pie y se acercó a la ventana. Lejos de ella. Lejos de la tentación de acabar con ese juego y reclamarla, de hacerla suya, de llevársela de allí a un lugar donde no corriera peligro.

Intentó recordar que había más de un modo de perderla.

Portia lo observó alejarse y se percató de la tensión que lo embargaba, del modo en que apretaba los puños. Entretanto, apartó la palangana y los lienzos que había usado para limpiar la herida. Una vez hecho, se detuvo junto a la cama para observarlo con detenimiento.

Simon estaba junto a la ventana con la vista clavada en el exterior, listo para entrar en acción pero contenido. Su fuerza de voluntad era un ente vivo que lo retenía, que lo constreñía. Esa tensión reprimida... ¿sería miedo o la reacción posterior al miedo? ¿O tal vez la reacción al peligro, al hecho de haberla visto a ella en peligro? Fuera lo que fuese, era palpable, vibraba a su alrededor y los afectaba a ambos.

Todo era culpa del asesino. El macetero había sido la gota que colmara el vaso. Antes había tenido miedo, había estado molesta, más de lo que creía, pero estaba empezando a enfadarse.

Ya era bastante horroroso que el rufián hubiera matado, no una, sino dos veces, pero lo que le estaba haciendo a ella... Mucho peor, lo que esa situación le estaba haciendo a Simon y a la relación que existía entre ellos... Jamás había permitido que se inmiscuyeran en su vida.

La irritación dio paso al fastidio y éste acabó creciendo hasta convertirse en ira. Su mal humor siempre había vencido al miedo. Se acercó a la ventana y se apoyó contra el marco. Lo miró.

—¿Qué pasa?

Simon la miró de reojo y meditó la respuesta; pero, por una vez, no intentó sortear la pregunta.

—Quiero que estés a salvo.

Analizó lo que leyó en su rostro, en sus ojos. Lo que escuchó en el timbre ronco de su voz.

—¿Por qué es tan importante mi seguridad? ¿Por qué siempre quieres protegerme?

—Porque sí. —Simon devolvió la vista hacia los jardines—. Siempre ha sido así.

—Lo sé. Pero ¿por qué?

Simon tenía los dientes apretados y, por un instante, creyó que no iba a responderle. Sin embargo, dijo en voz baja:

—Porque eres importante para mí. Porque... al protegerte, me protejo a mí mismo. A una parte de mí. —Las palabras, una confesión de un descubrimiento reciente, no le habían resultado fáciles de pronunciar.

Él giró la cabeza, la miró a los ojos y reflexionó claramente sobre lo que había dicho, aunque no modificó su declaración ni un ápice.

Sin apartar la vista de sus ojos, Portia cruzó los brazos a la altura del pecho.

—Pero ¿qué es lo que de verdad te preocupa? Sabes que te dejaré vigilarme, que te dejaré protegerme, que no voy a cometer una temeridad, así que no puede ser eso.

La renuencia de Simon era palpable, como un muro de luz parpadeante que poco a poco se fue desvaneciendo.

—Quiero que seas mía. —Su mandíbula se tensó aún más—. No quiero que esto se interponga entre nosotros. —Inspiró hondo y volvió a clavar la mirada en el exterior—. Quiero que me prometas que no esgrimirás en mi contra lo que pase aquí, lo que pase entre nosotros por culpa de esta situación. —Y volvió a mirarla a los ojos—. Que no lo añadirás a la balanza. Que no dejarás que influya en tu decisión.

Observó sus ojos y en ellos leyó el torbellino de emociones y el depredador al acecho. El poder, la poderosa fuerza, la atávica necesidad que refrenaba. La necesidad masculina de dominar, de imponer su férrea voluntad. Hacía falta mucho valor para ver todo eso, reconocerlo, saberse su presa y no salir huyendo.

Al mismo tiempo, toda esa fuerza contenida corroboraba su compromiso a adaptarse en la medida de lo posible, a defenderla incluso de sus propios instintos.

Sostuvo su mirada.

—No puedo prometértelo. Jamás podré cerrar los ojos y no verte como eres, ni verme a mí como no soy.

Tras una prolongada y tensa pausa, Simon replicó en un murmullo ronco:

—Confía en mí. Es lo único que te pido. Confía en mí.

No respondió, aún era demasiado pronto. Y ese «único» implicaba, precisamente, toda una vida.

A causa de su silencio, los brazos de Simon la buscaron y la amoldaron a su cuerpo. Inclinó la cabeza hacia ella.

—Cuando vayas a tomar tu decisión, recuerda esto.

Portia le echó los brazos al cuello para ofrecerle sus labios, para ofrecerle su boca..., una boca que le pertenecía para que la tomara como quisiera. En ese sentido ya le pertenecía, tan profundamente como su alma de conquistador ansiaba.

Simon aceptó su ofrenda, la rodeó con los brazos y se apoderó de su boca antes de pegar sus cuerpos en una muestra explícita de lo que estaba por llegar.

Ella no se apartó, no le escondió nada... Una vez más, en esa esfera ya no existían barreras entre ellos.

Al menos en lo que a ella se refería.

Él, sin embargo, sí se reservaba algo, sí le ocultaba una parte de sí mismo, su más profundo anhelo. Y lo supo mientras dejaba que la cogiera en brazos y la llevara a la cama; mientras le quitaba el vestido, la camisola, los escarpines y las medias, y la dejaba desnuda entre las sábanas. Mientras lo observaba desvestirse antes de meterse en la cama con ella para acariciarla con las manos y la lengua, embriagándola de placer. Lo supo mientras le separaba las piernas y la penetraba; mientras cabalgaban juntos por el ya conocido paraje de la pasión, por ese sensual valle de deseo que los transportaba a un nivel de intimidad más profundo en el que sus pieles sudorosas y enfebrecidas se rozaban, sus alientos jadeantes se mezclaban y sus cuerpos se movían desesperados para alcanzar el placer más sublime.

Simon le había pedido que confiara en él. Y en esa esfera lo hacía. Pero él aún no confiaba del todo en ella... Al menos, no lo suficiente como para mostrarle ese rinconcito de su ser.

Ya llegaría el día.

Cuando alcanzaron el brillante pináculo de placer a la vez y se lanzaron a la gloriosa vorágine, Portia comprendió que ya había tomado una decisión, que ya se había comprometido a encajar esa pieza del rompecabezas, última y vital, que Simon era para ella.

Para lograrlo, tendría que entregarse a él por completo. Tal y como él deseaba, de todas las formas que quisiera y, seguramente, de todas las formas que necesitara.

Ése era el precio a pagar para acceder al último rincón de su alma.

Cuando se relajó bajo su cuerpo y yacieron exhaustos en la cama, le colocó las manos en la espalda y lo apretó contra ella, encantada de sentir su peso, la fuerte musculatura que la mantenía aplastada contra el colchón, pero que, al mismo tiempo, la protegía, la hacía sentirse segura y resguardada como si de un valioso tesoro se tratara.

Deslizó las manos hacia arriba y enterró los dedos en sus sedosos mechones para acariciárselos. Miró su rostro, medio oculto en la penumbra. Deseó que hubiera vuelto a encender las velas, ya que le encantaba verlo así: saciado y satisfecho, tras haber alcanzado el clímax dentro de ella.

El hecho de saber que le había provocado ese estado encerraba cierto poder, un poder delicioso.

Giró la cabeza y le rozó la sien con los labios.

—Aún no te he dado las gracias por salvarme la vida.

Simon resopló. Pasado un momento, dijo:

—Más tarde.

Sonrió y se quedó recostada, consciente de que mientras yacieran juntos ni el miedo ni el asesino mancillarían su mundo; de que lo único que contaba en esos momentos era lo que tenían entre ellos.

El vínculo emocional, el placer físico..., el efímero deleite.

El amor.

Había estado ahí todo el tiempo, esperando a que lo vieran, lo comprendieran y lo abrazaran.

Lo miró. Se dio cuenta de que la observaba.

Se dio cuenta de que no tenía que contarle nada, porque ya lo sabía.

Se apretó contra él y dejó que sus labios se encontraran en un beso que lo decía todo. Simon le acariciaba una mejilla con la palma de una mano cuando el beso terminó.

Una vez más, se miraron a los ojos mientras esa mano iba descendiendo por su cuerpo hasta dejar atrás el hombro y llegar a una cadera. Allí se detuvo, para apretarla contra su cuerpo. Cerró los ojos. Se dispuso a dormir.

Un gesto muy sencillo que lo decía todo.

Ella cerró los ojos y aceptó la verdad.

—Tenemos un problema. —El señor Stokes estaba en el centro del mirador, frente a Portia, Simon y Charlie. Acababan de dejar el comedor matinal, desierto esa mañana, cuando se cruzaron en el vestíbulo y les pidió un momento de su tiempo—. El señor Archer y el señor Buckstead me han pedido permiso para llevarse a sus familias de aquí. Puedo retrasar su marcha un día, dos a lo sumo, pero no más. Aunque me temo que ése no es el verdadero problema. —Se detuvo un instante, como si estuviera decidiendo el mejor modo de continuar—. La verdad es que carecemos de pruebas y tenemos muy pocas posibilidades de atrapar al asesino. —Levantó la mano cuando Charlie hizo ademán de interrumpirlo—. Sí, sé que eso dificultará mucho las cosas para los Glossup, pero hay más.

El investigador miró a Simon. Portia hizo lo mismo y se dio cuenta de que, fuera lo que fuese a lo que se refería, Simon lo entendía. La miró mientras el señor Stokes continuaba.

—La señorita Ashford parece ser el único cabo suelto del asesino. Después del intento de asesinato de anoche, sabemos que aunque ella no sepa nada que pueda identificarlo, nuestro rufián está convencido de lo contrario. La víbora tal vez fuera un intento de asustarla para que se marchara, pero lo de anoche... fue una tentativa en toda regla. Para silenciarla, de la misma manera que silenció a Dennis.

Simon miró al investigador.

—Lo que quiere decir es que no se detendrá. Se sentirá obligado a perseguir a Portia más allá de los confines de Glossup Hall, durante toda su vida, allá donde vaya, hasta que ya no represente una amenaza para él. ¿Se refiere a eso?

El señor Stokes asintió con un seco gesto de cabeza.

—Quienquiera que sea cree que tiene mucho que perder si la deja marchar. Debe de temer que, en algún momento, recuerde algo; algo que sin duda lo señalará como el asesino.

Portia hizo un mohín.

—Me he devanado los sesos, pero no tengo la menor idea de lo que puede ser ese algo. De verdad que no.

—La creo —dijo el señor Stokes—. Aunque no importa. El asesino cree lo contrario, ahí está el quid de la cuestión.

Charlie, inusualmente serio, intervino en ese momento.

—Es muy difícil proteger a alguien que se mueve en los círculos de la alta sociedad. Hay miles de formas de provocar un accidente.

Los tres hombres la miraron. Portia había esperado sentir miedo; sin embargo y para su alivio, sólo se sintió irritada.

—No voy a dejar que... —dijo y se detuvo para gesticular—. Que me encierren y me vigilen durante lo que me queda de vida.

El investigador torció el gesto.

—Bueno, pues... ése precisamente es el problema.

Simon clavó de nuevo la vista en el hombre.

—No nos ha traído aquí para contarnos esto. Tiene un plan para sacar a la luz a nuestro asesino. ¿De qué se trata?

El señor Stokes asintió con la cabeza.

—Sí, he ideado un plan, pero no les va a gustar —dijo, mientras los observaba— a ninguno de los tres.

Se produjo una breve pausa.

—¿Funcionará? —preguntó Simon.

El hombre no titubeó.

—No me molestaría siquiera en sugerirlo si no creyera que tiene muchas posibilidades de éxito.

Charlie se inclinó hacia delante con los brazos apoyados sobre los muslos.

—¿Cuál es nuestro objetivo? ¿Desenmascarar al asesino?

—Sí.

—De manera que no sólo Portia estará a salvo, sino que también los Glossup, Winfield o Calvin (quienquiera que sea inocente) se verán libres de sospecha, ¿no?

El señor Stokes volvió a asentir.

—Todo saldrá a la luz, atraparemos al asesino y se hará justicia. Mejor aún, todo el mundo sabrá que se ha hecho justicia.

—Y ¿cuál es su plan? —preguntó Portia.

El investigador titubeó un instante antes de explicarse.

—Todo gira en torno al hecho de que usted, señorita Ashford, es nuestra única baza para hacer salir al asesino de su escondrijo.

Con toda deliberación, el hombre miró a Simon.

Él enfrentó su mirada largo rato con el rostro inescrutable; después, se reclinó en el sillón e hizo un gesto con la mano.

—Cuéntenos su plan, señor Stokes.

16

A ninguno le gustó el plan.

Pero los tres lo aceptaron.

No se les ocurría nada mejor y estaba claro que tenían que hacer algo. Se sentían en la obligación de intentarlo al menos, de hacer cuanto estuviera en sus manos para que funcionara, por más espantoso que fuera el papel que se veían obligados a interpretar.

Portia no estaba segura de a quién le gustaba menos, si a Simon, a Charlie o a ella misma. La charada implicaba que pisotearan todos los conceptos por los que se regían, las ideas que conformaban sus personalidades.

Miró a Charlie, que paseaba por el jardín a su lado.

—Le advierto que no sé cómo coquetear.

—Limítese a fingir que soy Simon. Compórtese como lo haría con él.

—Solíamos discutir todo el tiempo. Ahora ya no lo hacemos.

—Me acuerdo... ¿Por qué dejaron de hacerlo? —Parecía verdaderamente perplejo.

—No lo sé. —Tras meditar un instante, añadió—: Tampoco creo que Simon lo sepa.

Charlie la miró y cuando ella se limitó a devolverle la mirada sin decir nada, frunció el ceño.

—Vamos a tener que pensar en algo... No tenemos tiempo para que practique. ¿Cree que podría...? Bueno,

¿cree que podría imitar a Kitty? Sería justicia poética, desde luego, que fueran sus artimañas las que nos permitieran atrapar a su asesino.

La idea tenía cierto atractivo, sí.

—Puedo intentarlo... Como si estuviéramos jugando a las charadas. Puedo fingir ser ella.

—Sí, eso mismo.

Lo miró a los ojos con una sonrisa. Una sonrisa deslumbrante. Como si acabara de encontrar una edición incunable de algún texto esotérico que llevara años buscando... Algo que sabía de antemano que iba a disfrutar muchísimo.

La repentina incomodidad que vio en los ojos de Charlie le arrancó una carcajada.

—¡Vamos! Sabe que es una farsa.

Con una sonrisa aún más genuina, se colgó de su brazo y se inclinó hacia él antes de echar un vistazo por encima del hombro... Hacia Simon, que estaba en la terraza y los miraba un tanto ceñudo.

La sonrisa amenazó con abandonarla, pero no tardó en armarse de valor y ensancharla, tras lo cual se concentró con renovadas fuerzas en Charlie. Sin quererlo, había actuado como debía, había actuado tal y como lo hubiera hecho Kitty. Sabía perfectamente la imagen que estarían dando a las demás personas que se sentaban en la terraza o que paseaban por allí para disfrutar del aire vespertino.

Charlie inspiró hondo y le dio unas palmaditas en la mano.

—Bueno, vamos allá... ¿Le he contado ya la historia de lord Carnegie y su pareja de tordos?

Charlie interpretó su papel a la perfección y le contó una historieta tras otra a cada cual más ridícula, lo que la ayudó en gran medida a reír y apoyarse en su brazo, aparentando ser una coqueta decidida a poner celoso a Simon, aunque sin llegar al nivel de Kitty.

Decidida a crear una desavenencia entre ellos.

El señor Stokes también había interpretado su papel y había ejercido su autoridad hasta donde realmente podía, de modo que contaban con dos días más para obligar al asesino a salir a la luz, ese día y el siguiente. Una vez que comunicó a los invitados que podrían marcharse en dos días, el ambiente se relajó un tanto. El asunto del macetero que cayó del antepecho acabó como un mero accidente gracias a la ayuda de lord Netherfield y lord Glossup.

No obstante, ninguno de esos dos caballeros conocían su plan; sólo ellos tres y el investigador estaban al corriente. Tal y como el señor Stokes había comentado con tanto acierto, cuantas menos personas estuvieran al tanto, más real parecería. Y el objetivo de dicho plan era hacer creer al asesino que, a la noche siguiente, Simon ya habría dejado de vigilarla.

—No me cabe duda de que el asesino preferirá encargarse de usted aquí si es posible —había dicho el señor Stokes—. Nuestro objetivo es proporcionarle una oportunidad creíble, demasiado buena como para dejarla escapar.

Le había dado la razón y por ese motivo allí estaba ella, coqueteando (o intentándolo, al menos) con Charlie.

—Vamos. —Con la sonrisa pintada en el rostro, lo arrastró hacia el camino que llevaba al templete—. Estoy segura de que Kitty le habría apartado del grupo de haber podido.

—Probablemente. —Charlie se dejó arrastrar.

Estaban a punto de enfilar el camino cuando Portia echó la vista atrás, en dirección a la alta figura que había en la terraza. Cuando desvió los ojos hacia Charlie, se encontró con una mirada muy astuta.

—Es una suerte que no puedan verla, porque se le olvida la charada en cuanto le pone los ojos encima. Va a tener que esforzarse si quiere hacerle creer a la gente que la... irritación mutua que se profesan Simon y usted ha desaparecido.

Intentó fulminarlo con la mirada; pero, cuando vio la expresión de sus ojos, se echó a reír y se colgó de su brazo.

—¡Pero qué tonto es!

Charlie resopló.

—Lo que usted diga, pero tampoco hace falta sobre-actuar. Se supone que debe ser creíble.

Portia esbozó una sonrisa sincera. Levantó la barbilla y echó a andar por el sendero muy cerca de Charlie; tan cerca como si fuera del brazo de Simon.

En cuanto estuvieron a cubierto de las miradas de aquellos que estaban en la terraza, Charlie aprovechó el tiempo para contarle cómo incitar a los caballeros como él.

—Un buen truco es estar pendiente de cada palabra que diga... con los ojos bien abiertos. Como si estuviera hablando el mismísimo... —Gesticuló.

—¿Ovidio?

Charlie parpadeó, aturdido.

—La verdad es que estaba pensando en Byron o Shelley, pero si le gusta más Ovidio... —Frunció el ceño—. ¿Conoce Simon los gustos tan raros que tiene?

El comentario le arrancó una carcajada. Le dio un golpecito en el brazo como si estuvieran bromeando. Sin embargo, le lanzó una mirada furibunda. Cuando llegaron al templete, lo cogió de la mano y tiró de él escalones arriba.

—Vamos, quiero admirar el paisaje.

Caminaron sobre el suelo de mármol hasta llegar al extremo más alejado, desde donde contemplaron el distante valle.

Charlie estaba de pie justo detrás de ella, muy cerca. Pasado un instante, inclinó la cabeza para murmurarle al oído:

—¿Sabe? Nunca lo he entendido... Bien sabe Dios que es muy atractiva, pero... ¡Le pido por favor que no me saque los ojos después de esto! Pero es que... la idea de tomarme ciertas libertades con usted me da un miedo horroroso.

Portia volvió a reír con genuino entusiasmo. Miró por encima del hombro y se encontró con los ojos de Charlie, cuya expresión estaba a caballo entre la burla y la mortificación.

—No importa. Sin duda es culpa de Ovidio.

Escucharon pasos en el camino. Se giraron y se apartaron..., poniendo especial cuidado en aparecer un tanto culpables.

Simon acompañaba a Lucy Buckstead escalones arriba.

Portia se sintió reaccionar de inmediato, sintió que sus sentidos clamaban por Simon, centrándose en él como si fueran incapaces de percibir ninguna otra cosa cuando él estaba cerca. Charlie estaba mucho más cerca, pero no la afectaba de ese modo en absoluto. La mera presencia de Simon le había desbocado el corazón.

Al recordar el comentario de Charlie, compuso la expresión más desinteresada de la que fue capaz.

Lucy se dio cuenta y su sonrisa titubeó.

—¡Ay, lo siento! No queríamos interrumpir nada.

—Ni mucho menos —dijo Simon—. Aunque la discusión parecía fascinante. ¿De qué iba? —preguntó con evidente reprobación.

Ella respondió con una mirada de frío desdén.

—De Ovidio.

Simon torció el gesto.

—Debería haberlo sabido.

Le había proporcionado la oportunidad perfecta, consciente de que la aprovecharía. A pesar de saber que era una farsa, la mueca desdeñosa la hirió. Darle la espalda y cogerse del brazo de Charlie fue mucho más fácil de lo que había creído.

—Ya nos hemos cansado del paisaje. Les dejaremos solos para que ustedes lo disfruten.

Era evidente que la pobre Lucy estaba muy incómoda. Charlie, cuyo semblante había sido impasible aunque alerta durante la conversación, dejó escapar un largo suspiro cuando se pusieron en marcha de regreso a los jardines codo con codo. Clavó la vista al frente.

—No sé si puedo hacerlo.

—Tenemos que hacerlo. La alternativa es impensable —replicó ella, dándole un apretón en el brazo.

Llegaron al prado y desde allí se encaminaron hacia la terraza para reunirse con el resto de los invitados. Y continuaron su charada a lo largo de todo el día.

Tras haber dado ese primer paso, Portia hizo de tripas corazón y se obligó a tratar a Simon no sólo como solía hacer antes de la fiesta campestre, sino con muchísima más frialdad, con muchísimo más desdén. No fue fácil. No podía mirarlo a los ojos, de modo que mantuvo la mirada clavada en sus labios, fruncidos en una mueca muy cercana al desprecio.

La actitud de Simon (la frialdad que demostraba, la evidente desaprobación) la ayudó, pero también le hizo muchísimo daño.

A pesar de saber que era una farsa, estaban inmersos en ese mundo irreal. Y, en dicho mundo, su comportamiento no sólo los amenazaba a ambos, sino también a lo que había entre ellos.

Reaccionó ante esa amenaza, por ilusoria que fuera. Se le hizo un nudo en el pecho que se convirtió en un dolorcillo de lo más real. Cuando cayó la noche y todo el mundo se retiró a sus habitaciones, sentía que las defensas que la protegían del mundo exterior se estaban desmoronando a pasos agigantados.

Sin embargo, todos los invitados habían sido testigos; y, a juzgar por sus expresiones y sus gestos reprobatorios, se habían tragado la representación.

Eso, se aseguró mientras daba vueltas en el catre delante de la chimenea del dormitorio de lady O, era lo único que importaba.

Incluso lady O la había mirado con desaprobación; aunque no hizo comentario alguno, como si fuera demasiado lista como para dejarse engañar. Se limitó a observarla con esa perspicaz mirada suya.

En esos momentos roncaba en su cama.

Los relojes de la casa marcaron la hora. Las doce. Medianoche. Sin duda, el resto de los habitantes estaban acurrucados en sus camas, durmiendo plácidamente. Giró para ponerse de espaldas en el colchón y cerró los ojos, intentando imitarlos.

No podía. Era incapaz de aplacar el torbellino de emociones que la consumía.

Era irracional, emocional, pero muy, muy real.

Inspiró hondo y sintió cómo se le atascaba el aire en la garganta. Le dolía el pecho, y así había sido desde la escena del templete.

Contuvo un juramento y apartó las mantas para levantarse. Ya tenía preparado el vestido para el día siguiente y se lo puso en ese momento; se lo abrochó como pudo para disimular en caso de encontrarse con alguien, se puso los escarpines, se metió las medias en el bolsillo y, tras echarle un último vistazo a lady O, salió a hurtadillas de la habitación.

De pie junto a la ventana, en mangas de camisa y con una copa de *brandy* en la mano, Simon contemplaba el jardín mientras intentaba no pensar. Intentaba calmar el torbellino de sus pensamientos. Intentaba hacer caso omiso del depredador que llevaba dentro, y de sus miedos. Eran miedos infundados, lo sabía; aun así...

La puerta se abrió. Cuando se giró para ver quién era, se encontró con Portia, que cerró la puerta en silencio tras ella.

La vio erguir los hombros y clavar la mirada en él. Lo estudió un instante en la penumbra antes de atravesar la estancia. Se detuvo a unos pasos, intentando descifrar su expresión.

—No esperaba que estuvieras despierto.

La miró a la cara y presintió más que vio la súbita inseguridad que la consumía.

—No te esperaba... No creí que vinieras.

Titubeó apenas un momento; después, dejó la copa en el alféizar y extendió los brazos hacia ella... en el mismo instante en que Portia acortaba la distancia que los separaba.

La abrazó con fuerza y ella le rodeó el cuello con los brazos cuando sus labios se encontraron; un instante antes de que sus bocas se devoraran y sus cuerpos se amoldaran el uno al otro. Durante un largo minuto, ambos se entregaron al beso; era su salvación en un mundo súbitamente peligroso.

Portia suspiró cuando el beso terminó y él se separó un poco. Apoyó la cabeza en su hombro.

—Es horroroso... Espantoso. ¿Cómo lo hacía Kitty? Aunque sea una charada... —Se estremeció y levantó la cabeza para mirarlo a la cara—. Me revuelve el estómago.

El comentario le arrancó una carcajada seca y desabrida.

—A mi estómago tampoco le sienta muy bien nuestro pequeño drama.

Su cercanía física lo consolaba como ninguna otra cosa podría hacerlo: ese cuerpo esbelto y voluptuoso, cálido y vibrante entre sus brazos; sus pechos apretados contra el torso; la presión de su vientre contra su erección... Su entrega era tan palpable, estaba tan claro que era suya, que el depredador que llevaba dentro se relajó y comenzó a ronronear.

Le acarició la espalda y sonrió ante la rapidez de su respuesta.

—Será mejor que nos acostemos —le dijo.

—Humm... —Portia le devolvió la sonrisa y se puso de puntillas para besarlo—. Será lo mejor... Es la única manera de que durmamos un poco.

El comentario le arrancó una carcajada y comenzó a sentirse mejor. La opresión que había sentido durante todo el día se evaporó y por fin lo dejó libre para respirar, vivir y amar nuevo.

Libre para amar a Portia.

Dejó que lo llevara de la mano a la cama, la dejó establecer las reglas que quisiera. Le dio todo lo que deseaba y mucho más, aunque ignoraba si ella se había dado cuenta o no.

Si había averiguado, o deducido, que la amaba.

Ya no le importaba si lo sabía o no. Lo que sentía estaba allí sin más; era demasiado real, demasiado fuerte, y estaba demasiado enraizado en su ser como para negarlo.

En cuanto a ella... no estaría allí esa noche, no se entregaría a él en cuerpo y alma como lo estaba haciendo si no sintiera lo mismo en el fondo de su corazón. Volvió a preguntarse si sería consciente de la verdad que transmitían sus actos; y si estaría preparada para admitirla.

Él, desde luego, estaba preparado para ser paciente.

Desnudo y tendido de espaldas en la cama, la contempló mientras ella le hacía el amor, mientras utilizaba su cuerpo para acariciarlo y disfrutaba abiertamente de cada minuto del encuentro. Le tomó los pechos entre las manos y la instó a inclinarse para darse un festín con los labios. Cuando sintió que llegaba al clímax volvió a incorporarla a fin de observarla, convencido de que jamás había visto una imagen más maravillosa en toda su vida.

Sólo había una cosa mejor: cuando se desplomaba totalmente saciada y él giraba con ella en brazos para aprisionarla bajo su cuerpo antes de hundirse en ella hasta el fondo. En ese ardiente y húmedo cuerpo que se cerraba en torno a su miembro y comenzaba a moverse al compás de sus envites cada vez más rápidos y desenfrenados.

Y en un abrir y cerrar de ojos llegaron adonde querían llegar, a ese pináculo que había sido su meta.

El éxtasis los inundó, el placer los abrumó, nublándoles el sentido y dejando a su paso el acompasado latir de sus corazones.

Yacieron abrazados en un halo de calidez y durmieron plácidamente.

La separación fue difícil. Para ambos. Intentaron desentenderse de ese vínculo que los había unido mucho más de lo que habían previsto; un vínculo más valioso de lo que jamás creyeron posible.

Cuando Portia se marchó justo después del alba, sola después de una discusión entre murmullos que ella había ganado, permaneció sentado en la cama, rememorando las horas pasadas y meditando sobre lo que habían significado, tanto para él como para ella.

El tictac del reloj de la chimenea marcaba el paso del

tiempo. Cuando dieron las siete, suspiró. Con bastante renuencia y total deliberación, se guardó sus pensamientos en lo más hondo de su mente, donde estarían a salvo de todo lo que se verían obligados a decir. Porque estaban obligados a interpretar una obra.

Apartó las mantas y se levantó para vestirse.

Charlie ya se encontraba en el comedor matinal cuando él entró. También estaban allí Henry, James y su padre. Intercambió los saludos de rigor y desvió la vista hacia Charlie cuando se sentó junto a James.

Lucy Buckstead fue la siguiente en llegar y, a continuación, apareció Portia. Alegre y radiante. Sus sonrisas estuvieron dirigidas casi en exclusiva a Charlie.

A él no le prestó atención.

Se sentó junto a Charlie y al punto entabló una animada conversación con él sobre conocidos comunes de la ciudad.

Mientras los observaba con expresión dura e implacable, Simon se reclinó en su silla.

James lo miró antes de desviar la vista hacia la pareja. Tras un momento, carraspeó y le preguntó por sus caballos.

Estaban teniendo éxito, pero era el último día, de manera que debían aprovechar bien el tiempo. Durante toda la mañana, las pullas entre ellos se fueron afilando y la tirantez fue alcanzando cotas insospechadas.

James intentó alejar a Charlie; los tres comprendieron y agradecieron el gesto. Lamentablemente, no podían consentirlo.

Al percatarse de lo difícil que les resultaría a Charlie y a Simon rechazar la ayuda de su amigo, Portia levantó la barbilla en gesto altanero y lo desairó. En su fuero interno le pedía disculpas y rogaba que su charada diera frutos, para poder explicárselo todo después.

Cualquiera habría dicho que lo había abofeteado. Con expresión pétrea, James inclinó la cabeza y se marchó.

Los tres intercambiaron una mirada fugaz antes de tomar aire y continuar con la farsa.

Cada vez era más doloroso. Cuando llegó la hora del almuerzo, se sentía físicamente mal. Tenía los primeros síntomas de un dolor de cabeza, pero se negó a abandonar.

El señor Stokes no se dejaba ver. En todos los aspectos, era el día perfecto para llevar a cabo su plan. Debido a la muerte de Kitty, nadie esperaba que hubiera entretenimientos, ni siquiera un paseo a caballo ni una partida de cartas. Todos los invitados eran espectadores de excepción de su drama. Si representaban bien sus papeles, no había razón para creer que su plan fallara.

Se sentó de nuevo junto a Charlie, buscó su atención con una chispeante alegría y lo recompensó con su mejor sonrisa cuando la obtuvo.

Desde el otro extremo de la mesa, Simon, que guardaba silencio, los estaba observando con un creciente malhumor.

Ese aire de reacción reprimida, de insatisfacción contenida, tiñó el ambiente de la casa y resultó contagioso para todos los demás. Cuando soltó una carcajada ante una broma de Charlie, lady O abrió la boca..., sólo para volver a cerrarla. Después, clavó la vista en su plato y jugueteó con la comida. Cuando alzó la cabeza, la miró con expresión furibunda, pero no llegó a decir nada.

Tras dejar escapar el aire que había estado reteniendo, Portia buscó los ojos de Charlie, le hizo un gesto sutil y ambos continuaron.

Cuando el almuerzo llegó a su fin, sufría un palpitante dolor de cabeza. Lord Netherfield se levantó de golpe, atravesó a Charlie con una mirada muy seria y le pidió hablar a solas.

Charlie la miró, espantado. No habían previsto ninguna intervención externa, de modo que carecían de un plan de contingencia para ese caso.

Ella esbozó una sonrisa aún más deslumbrante.

—Ay, cuánto lo siento, pero el señor Hastings iba a acompañarme a dar un paseo por los jardines. —Se colgó del brazo de Charlie, odiando con todas sus fuerzas el papel que estaba interpretando.

Lord Netherfield la miró con expresión reprobatoria.

—Estoy seguro de que encontrará a otra persona que pueda acompañarla... ¿Tal vez una de las otras jóvenes?

Charlie le apretó el brazo.

Y a Portia le pareció que su sonrisa se torcía cuando replicó:

—Bueno, la verdad es que son bastante... jóvenes, ya me entiende usted...

Lord Netherfield parpadeó. Antes de que pudiera responder, lady O apareció de la nada y le dio un golpecito en el costado.

—Deja que se vayan. —Su voz era cortante y muy baja, cosa de lo más inusual—. Utiliza esa cabeza que Dios te ha dado, Granny. Están tramando algo. —Esos ojos negros se entrecerraron con un brillo complacido—. Están jugando con fuego; pero si eso es lo que hace falta, lo menos que podemos hacer es dejar que lo intenten sin complicarles las cosas.

—¡Caramba! —Por el rostro de lord Netherfield pasaron un sinfín de emociones..., como si se estuviera esforzando por encontrar la expresión adecuada mientras su mente asimilaba las palabras de lady O. Parpadeó—. Comprendo.

—Estupendo. —La anciana le dio unos golpecitos en el brazo—. Ofréceme tu brazo y acompáñame a la terraza. En fin, un par de cojos tomados del brazo, menuda pareja... Pero así dejaremos vía libre a los jóvenes —dijo con su habitual mirada maliciosa— y podremos ver qué resulta de todo esto.

Portia y Charlie se quedaron rezagados. Con una intensa sensación de alivio, dejaron que la pareja de ancianos los precediera hacia la terraza, conscientes de que Simon había presenciado el interludio desde el otro extremo de la estancia. A pesar de la distancia habían sentido parte de la tensión que se apoderó de él. Tras intercambiar una mirada, bajaron los escalones de acceso al jardín.

Pasearon sin rumbo fijo, pero no tardó en quedar patente que Charlie comenzaba a flaquear. Cuando respondió a una de sus bromas con un comentario anodino, se colgó de su brazo y se pegó aún más a él, consciente de que a pesar de la cercanía no había nada entre ellos salvo una creciente amistad y la confianza que nacía de un objetivo común. Con suerte, eso les bastaría para dar la apariencia de intimidad que necesitaba su charada. Siempre y cuando ninguno de los dos metiera la pata, claro...

Se inclinó hacia él y le murmuró:

—Vayamos al lago. Si no hay nadie por allí, podremos escondernos en el pinar y descansar un rato. Después de todo el esfuerzo que nos está costando, sería imperdonable que diéramos un paso en falso y lo echáramos todo a perder.

Charlie se enderezó.

—Buena idea. —Se encaminó hacia el sendero del lago. Se encogió de hombros de forma muy sutil—. Simon nos está observando... Lo presiento.

Portia lo miró. No lo había tomado por un hombre especialmente perceptivo.

—He supuesto que nos seguiría.

—Creo que podemos darlo por hecho.

El sombrío comentario de Charlie hizo que lo mirara con detenimiento. Y se diera cuenta de que...

—Esto le gusta tanto como a nosotros...

La mirada que le lanzó, con total tranquilidad ya que estaban a salvo de las miradas de los demás, fue cuanto menos hosca.

—Sé que puedo afirmar sin temor a equivocarme que esto me gusta bastante menos que a ustedes, y eso que los dos odian esta farsa.

Portia mantuvo una expresión ceñuda mientras caminaban por el estrecho sendero que llevaba al lago.

—¿No puede tratarme como a una de las mujeres casadas con las que de vez en cuando se relaciona?

—Es que ése es el problema. Para mí es como si estuviera casada, con la diferencia de que es la esposa de Simon. Y créame que es una diferencia enorme. No me agrada la idea de que me descuarticen miembro a miembro... Tengo por norma evitar a los maridos celosos.

—Pero Simon no es mi marido.

—¿De veras? —Charlie enarcó las cejas—. Cualquiera lo diría a juzgar por su comportamiento... O por el de usted, ya que estamos. Y créame cuando le digo que soy un experto en la materia. —Bajó la vista al suelo y ella aprovechó para sonreír. Tras una pausa, continuó—: De hecho, creo que ésa es la única razón por la que este plan puede funcionar. —Alzó la vista y frunció el ceño.

Dada la distancia que los separaba de la casa y a sabiendas de que estaban totalmente a solas en el prado, era bastante seguro hablar sin tapujos.

—¿De verdad cree que está funcionando?

Charlie le sonrió y le apartó de la cara un mechón de cabello que el viento le había descolocado; no debían olvidarse de mantener las apariencias.

—Henry estaba descompuesto... sólo de vernos. James se ha quitado de en medio después de lo de esta mañana, pero ha seguido observándonos. Desmond... Bueno, no habla mucho, pero con Winifred fuera de escena, ha tenido tiempo de sobra y desde luego que no deja de fruncir el ceño cada vez que nos mira.

—¿Fruncir el ceño? ¿No nos observa sin más?

—No, frunce el ceño —le aseguró Charlie—. Pero no tengo ni idea de lo que significa. No lo conozco muy bien.

—¿Y Ambrose?

Charlie torció el gesto.

—Se ha dado cuenta, sí, pero tampoco parece que nos haya estado prestando mucha atención. Es el único que ha conseguido algo en los últimos días. Ha estado aprovechando el tiempo para convencer al señor Buckstead de que apoye su candidatura. También al señor Archer, aunque el pobre no está para esas cosas.

Cuando llegaron al camino del lago, aminoraron el paso; después, una vez que estuvieron al amparo del pinar, le apretó el brazo a Charlie.

—Mire hacia atrás y dígame si ve a alguien.

Charlie se giró y observó los senderos que llevaban a la casa.

—Nadie, ni un alma. Ni siquiera Simon.

—Bien, vamos. —Se recogió las faldas y se internó por un camino secundario; Charlie la siguió de cerca—. Nos encontrará.

Y lo hizo, pero no antes de experimentar un momento de pánico absoluto. Había pensado que se dirigirían al mirador. Así que cuando llegó allí y lo encontró desierto...

Mientras deambulaba por el pinar, atisbó el vestido azul de Portia entre los árboles un poco más adelante. El nudo que tenía en el pecho se deshizo al punto. Inspiró hondo, mucho más relajado, y continuó su camino, aplastando a su paso las agujas secas de los pinos.

Lo que sintió al llegar al mirador y ver los sillones y el sofá vacíos... Apretó los dientes y se desentendió del recuerdo. Jamás había sido consciente de sentir celos, pero la corrosiva emoción que lo había atravesado... no podía ser ninguna otra cosa.

No. Estaba claro que no iba a ser fácil tenerlo como marido; tenía que admitir que Portia estaba en lo cierto en su afán de meditar el asunto antes de aceptar. Tenía la impresión de que lo conocía muchísimo mejor de lo que se conocía él mismo, sobre todo en lo referente a los aspectos más emocionales de su hipotético matrimonio, de su futura unión.

Se habían detenido en un claro. Charlie estaba recostado contra el tronco de un árbol y Portia en otro, frente a él, con la cabeza echada hacia atrás y los ojos cerrados.

Salió al claro, se detuvo en el centro y los fulminó a ambos con la mirada.

—¿Qué diantres estáis haciendo? —preguntó en voz baja y controlada.

Portia abrió un ojo y lo miró.

—Descansando. —Volvió a cerrar el ojo y se enderezó un poco—. Charlie estaba exhausto y a punto de cometer un desliz. Igual que yo. Necesitábamos un respiro.

La respuesta le hizo fruncir el ceño.

—¿Por qué aquí?

Portia suspiró, giró la cabeza y abrió los ojos. Lo recorrió con la mirada de pies a cabeza.

—Las agujas de los pinos. Te escuchamos llegar hace siglos. Nadie puede acercarse sin que nos demos cuenta.

Charlie se apartó del árbol.

—Ahora que estás despierta, ¿te importaría sentarte? —Con una reverencia exagerada, le indicó la pequeña elevación del terreno que había en uno de los bordes del claro. Al ver que ella lo miraba sin más, añadió con mordacidad—: Para que nosotros podamos hacer lo mismo.

Simon miró a Portia y, al ver la expresión atónita de su rostro, sonrió por primera vez desde que se separaran esa mañana. La cogió de la mano y la arrastró hasta el lugar.

—No está acostumbrada a que traten su delicada sensibilidad con tanto tiento. De hecho... —dijo y la miró a los ojos mientras la hacía girarse—. De hecho, no creo que lo apruebe.

Vio cómo su mirada se tornaba furibunda y atisbó a la antigua Portia. Levantó la barbilla y resopló, pero se sentó.

Ellos también lo hicieron, uno a cada lado, encantados de estar sentados sobre la hierba.

El tiempo fue pasando mientras ellos descansaban en relajado silencio, con la mirada perdida en los árboles y dejando que la paz del lugar los calmara. La absorbieron como si fuera una poción mágica que les diera fuerzas para lo que aún estaba por llegar.

El sol estaba ya poniéndose cuando Simon se movió. Charlie y Portia lo miraron.

Vio la falta de entusiasmo en sus rostros, pero también su resolución.

—Será mejor que ensayemos el último acto —dijo, torciendo el gesto.

El telón se alzó en el salón antes de la cena. Portia llegó tarde, mucho después que el resto de los invitados. Hizo una gran entrada ataviada con el vestido de seda verde oscuro. Se detuvo en el vano de la puerta y, con la cabeza en alto, contempló a los reunidos.

Su mirada se posó sobre Simon; una mirada fría y desdeñosa, teñida de una innegable furia. Brillaba con algo parecido a la burla. Acto seguido, sus ojos se desviaron hacia Charlie... y su frialdad se disolvió con una sonrisa.

Sin hacer caso de Simon ni de los demás, se acercó a él.

Charlie le devolvió la sonrisa, no sin antes echarle un rápido vistazo a Simon. De todos modos, le ofreció el brazo mientras ella se acercaba y logró transmitir a la concurrencia la impresión de que se estaba pensando mejor la idea de seguir el obvio juego, gracias al sutil cambio de postura cuando ella llegó a su lado (como si quisiera apartarse un poco de los presentes para obtener más privacidad) y a la ligera incomodidad que traslucieron sus aciones.

El obvio juego no era otro que el de herir a Simon. Aunque nadie sabía con certeza si dicho ataque estaba destinado a ponerlo celoso o a castigarlo por algún tipo de transgresión u omisión. De todos modos, a nadie se le escapaban sus intenciones.

Rió a carcajadas, lo aduló y lo mantuvo hechizado con su mirada. Flirteó con todas sus ganas. Simon y Charlie habían pasado una hora entera enseñándole trucos. Puesto que reconocía la experiencia de ambos en la materia, siguió sus instrucciones al pie de la letra.

Le parecía que estaba mal, y aun así... los dos habían insistido en que continuara con la charada.

Mientras charlaba con vivacidad, sonriendo a Desmond, que se había acercado a ella y a Ambrose, que se unió al grupo más tarde, no se separó ni un instante de Charlie, a quien tenía cogido del brazo.

Simon estaba al otro lado del salón con Lucy, Drusilla y James, aunque sus ojos apenas si se apartaban de ella. Su expresión sólo podía tildarse de tormentosa.

Su temperamento era terrible y se percibía nada más

conocerlo; no era necesario que lo demostrara. En ese momento, lo estaba controlando a sabiendas; y era como un ente con vida propia que crecía y se expandía mientras los observaba.

Winifred se acercó a ellos.

—Dígame, señorita Ashford, ¿regresará mañana a casa de su hermano?

Era sin duda el comentario más mordaz que Winifred haría acerca de esa conducta tan inapropiada. Portia se disculpó con ella en silencio mientras ensanchaba la sonrisa.

—La verdad es que... —comenzó, mirando a Charlie con una ceja levemente arqueada antes de volver a concentrarse en Winifred—. Bueno, tal vez me vaya a Londres unos días. Le echaré un vistazo a la casa de la ciudad y atenderé otros asuntos. Por supuesto —prosiguió, dejando bien claro que sus claras expectativas desmentían lo que iba a decir—, hay tan pocos entretenimientos en julio que sin duda me aburriré soberanamente... —Miró de nuevo a Charlie—. Usted también va a regresar a la ciudad, ¿verdad?

Las implicaciones de la pregunta eran evidentes. Winifred estaba tan anonadada que dejó escapar un jadeo y compuso una expresión desencantada. Desmond arqueó una ceja en sutil desaprobación. Ambrose se aburría sin más.

—Milady, la cena está servida.

Portia jamás había estado tan agradecida de escuchar esas palabras. A saber lo que los demás habrían dicho si el momento se hubiera alargado... A saber qué habría replicado Charlie y lo que ella se habría visto forzada a añadir en respuesta... Benditos fuesen los mayordomos, pensó.

Desmond le ofreció el brazo a Winifred, que lo miró durante un instante antes de alzar la vista hasta sus ojos y decidir de repente que aceptaba su compañía hasta el comedor. Portia los siguió del brazo de Charlie. Su mirada se posó sobre la pareja que los precedía mientras rezaba para que no fuera Desmond el asesino y Charlie se vio obligado a darle un apretón en los dedos para que recordara que debía interpretar su papel.

Aprovechó esa distracción para su causa. Cuando estuvieron en el comedor, miró a Charlie de reojo con expresión elocuente y traviesa.

—Es demasiado exigente.

La sonrisa que acompañó a esas palabras fue una clara invitación a que exigiera cuanto quisiese; cosa que comprendió la mayor parte de los invitados que se sentaban a la mesa.

Las Hammond habían recuperado parte de su habitual jovialidad; con la cercanía de su partida y ya olvidado el incidente del macetero, volvieron a reír y bromear con Oswald y Swanston. Un entretenimiento tan inocente que ponía aún más en evidencia su propio comportamiento.

Agradeció a lady Glossup que hubiera separado a las partes en conflicto, de modo que las oportunidades de escenas violentas quedaran reducidas al mínimo. Ella estaba sentada cerca de uno de los extremos de la mesa; Simon estaba en el centro del lado opuesto y Charlie estaba en el mismo lado que ella, pero tan lejos que ni siquiera podían intercambiar una mirada.

Con total tranquilidad y haciendo caso omiso de las miradas sombrías que le lanzaba Simon, se dispuso a entretener a las personas que tenía a cada lado, el señor Archer y el señor Buckstead, dos de los caballeros que no se daban cuenta de lo que estaba pasando.

Cuando las damas se levantaron, abandonó el salón con expresión relajada y contenta. Sin embargo, cuando llegó a la altura de Simon, que ya estaba de pie al igual que el resto de los caballeros, enfrentó su mirada con beligerancia y frialdad. La sostuvo. Con la misma deliberación, acarició con las yemas de los dedos los hombros de Charlie y le alborotó el pelo que le caía sobre la nuca cuando pasó tras él, tras lo cual correspondió a la expresión asesina de Simon con una sonrisa y salió del comedor con la cabeza en alto y paso vivo.

Fueron muy pocos los que no se percataron del intercambio.

Lady O entrecerró los ojos, pero no dijo nada. Se limitó a observar.

Las otras damas mayores la censuraron abiertamente, aunque poco podían hacer dadas las circunstancias. Flirtear, incluso de esa manera, jamás había sido un crimen para la alta sociedad. Sólo el recuerdo de Kitty hacía que su comportamiento les resultara peligroso.

De todos modos, no les dio más motivos para reprochar su conducta; se comportó con toda la normalidad de la que fue capaz, con su habitual elegancia, mientras esperaban a que los caballeros se reunieran con ellas. Esa noche, la última de la fiesta campestre, sería imperdonable que no aparecieran en el salón. Así que no tardarían mucho... y todos presenciarían la escena final.

A medida que fueron pasando los minutos, su nerviosismo aumentó. Intentó no pensar en lo que estaba a punto de suceder; sin embargo se le estaba formando un horrible nudo en el estómago.

A la postre, las puertas se abrieron y dejaron paso a los caballeros. Lord Glossup, con Henry a su lado, encabezaba la marcha. Simon era el siguiente, junto a James; sus ojos recorrieron a las damas hasta dar con ella.

Tal y como habían dispuesto, Charlie apareció un par de pasos detrás de él.

Ella lo miró abiertamente y dejó que su rostro reflejara un intenso placer al verlo. Mostrando una sonrisa deslumbrante, se alejó del diván y cruzó la estancia en dirección a él.

Simon se interpuso en su camino. La aferró por el codo y la obligó a mirarlo.

—Si me concedes unos minutos de tu tiempo...

Ni una pregunta ni una petición.

Portia reaccionó y su expresión se tensó. Intentó soltarse... y compuso una mueca de dolor cuando él la aferró con más fuerza, clavándole los dedos en el brazo. Levantó la cabeza y lo miró a los ojos... de forma tan beligerante, tan desafiante como requería el papel.

—Creo que no.

En ese momento la sintió físicamente. Sintió que la furia de Simon se desataba y caía sobre ella.

—¿En serio? —Hablaba con voz tranquila, pero su furia giraba descontrolada en torno a ellos—. Pues yo creo que vas a darte cuenta de que estás en un error.

Aunque conocía el libreto al que se ceñían, aunque sabía lo que iba a hacer Simon a continuación, se quedó estupefacta cuando la obligó a volverse hacia las ventanas y, con el brazo bien sujeto, tiró de ella para sacarla a la terraza.

Casi a rastras.

Se vio obligada a seguirlo antes de que acabara por tirar de ella sin disimulos. O tropezara y cayera al suelo. Jamás en su vida la habían obligado a hacer nada; la sensación de impotencia bastó para que su temperamento estallara. Sintió que le ardían las mejillas.

Simon abrió las puertas y la sacó a la terraza; después, tiró de ella sin muchos miramientos hasta alejarse del salón.

Aunque no tanto como para que no pudieran oírlos.

Habían acordado que una vez que empezaran no podían permitirse cambiar de idea y alejarse del libreto que habían escrito.

A la postre, Portia consiguió reunir el aire suficiente para hablar.

—¡¿Cómo te atreves!? —Una vez que estuvieron fuera de la vista de los demás, se detuvo y comenzó a forcejear.

Simon la soltó, no sin antes demostrar una fugaz indecisión... que sólo duró lo que tardó en relajar los dedos.

Lo enfrentó echando chispas por los ojos, estudió su mirada... y comprendió que estaba tan cerca de perder el control como ella misma.

—No te atrevas a mangonearme. —Retrocedió un paso... y recordó su libreto. Levantó la barbilla—. No soy tuya para que me des órdenes. No te pertenezco.

No habría creído posible que la expresión de Simon se endureciera más, pero así fue.

Dio un paso hacia ella, acortando la distancia que los

separaba. La miraba con los ojos entrecerrados y con una expresión tan hosca y fría que sintió que se le helaba el alma.

—Y yo ¿qué? —La furia reprimida de su voz le provocó un estremecimiento—. ¿Soy un juguete con el que puedes divertirte un tiempo para tirarlo después? ¿Soy un perrito al que regalarle tus favores y del que te deshaces con una patada cuando te aburres?

Al mirarlo a los ojos, su determinación flaqueó. Se le encogió el corazón al darse cuenta de que Simon estaba contándole sus verdaderos miedos; al darse cuenta de que, para él, esa charada reflejaba una realidad ante la que se sentía muy vulnerable...

El impulso, o más bien la necesidad, de tranquilizarlo estuvo a punto de destrozarla. Echó mano de toda su fuerza de voluntad para enfrentar su mirada, erguirse hasta un punto casi doloroso y replicarle con desdén:

—No es culpa mía que hayas malinterpretado las cosas, ni que tu inflado ego masculino sea incapaz de aceptar que no he caído rendida a tus pies. —Alzó la voz, y dejó que sonara desdeñosa y desafiante—. Jamás te he prometido nada.

—¡Ja! —Simon replicó con tono desabrido y evidente sarcasmo—. Tú y tus promesas... —La miró y dejó que sus ojos la recorrieran con insolencia de pies a cabeza. Una mueca desdeñosa asomó a sus labios—. No eres más que una zorra calientapollas.

Portia lo fulminó con la mirada antes de abofetearlo.

Aunque ésa había sido su intención, la reacción de Portia le resultó dolorosa e inesperada.

—Y tú no eres más que un idiota insensible. —La voz le temblaba a causa de la pasión contenida y se vio obligada a tomar una profunda bocanada de aire—. ¡No sé qué vi en ti! ¡Ni siquiera puedo creer que haya perdido el tiempo contigo! No quiero volverte a ver ni a hablar contigo en...

—Me encantará no volver a hablar contigo en la vida.

Portia sostuvo su mirada. Sus apasionados temperamentos restallaban en torno a ellos, adornando la escena, pero sin arrastrarlos. De todos modos, aunque estaban actuando...

La vio inspirar hondo con dificultad y enderezar los hombros, tras lo cual le lanzó una mirada arrogante.

—No tengo nada más que decirte. No quiero volver a verte en la vida. ¡En la vida!

Simon apretó los dientes.

—Te prometo de corazón que no me verás. —Masculló antes de añadir—: ¿Me devolverás el favor?

—Será un verdadero placer. ¡Adiós!

Portia giró sobre los talones y bajó a toda prisa los escalones de la terraza. Sus rápidas pisadas eran indicio más que suficiente del estado en el que se encontraba.

Simon aguantó la respiración mientras luchaba denodadamente contra el impulso de seguirla. Sabía que la luna proyectaba su sombra sobre las baldosas de la terraza y que cualquiera que estuviera observando desde el salón se daría cuenta de que se había marchado sola. De que él no la había seguido.

Observó desde la distancia cómo llegaba al prado y enfilaba el camino del lago.

En ese instante se giró y atravesó la terraza, pasando por delante de las puertas que daban al salón (que seguían entreabiertas tal y como él las había dejado). Sin mirar a su alrededor, echó a andar hacia los establos.

Suplicando durante todo el camino que le diera tiempo a llegar hasta ella antes de que lo hiciera el asesino.

Portia atravesó el prado de camino al lago como alma que llevara el diablo. Había imaginado que conseguiría fingir un estado alterado a causa del nerviosismo, pero el torbellino de emociones que bullía en su interior lo lograba de por sí.

«¿Calientapollas?» Eso no lo habían ensayado. Aunque habían previsto que ella lo abofeteara. Simon lo había hecho de forma deliberada; tal vez pudiera comprender sus motivos, pero no pensaba perdonárselo así como así. En el acaloramiento de la discusión, el insulto había escocido.

Todavía le ardían las mejillas. Mientras caminaba en dirección al lago, se llevó las manos a la cara e intentó con cierta premura aliviar el rubor.

Intentó por todos los medios recuperar el sentido, concentrarse en los motivos que la habían llevado hasta allí, en los motivos por los que había escenificado esa espantosa discusión.

El señor Stokes había señalado que el asesino sólo se acercaría a ella si creía que estaba sola. Sola en un lugar donde pudiera asesinarla y huir sin que nadie lo viera. Nadie la creería tan estúpida como para andar deambulando de noche por el bosque... a menos que tuviera una razón de peso.

Además, nadie creería que Simon se lo permitiera... a

menos que él también tuviera una razón de peso. A menos que, tal y como había dicho Charlie, un cataclismo le impidiera vigilarla.

Al parecer, esa costumbre, que jamás había intentado ocultar, no había pasado desapercibida para nadie.

Ni siquiera se le había pasado por la cabeza la interpretación que hacían los demás de esa actitud protectora hasta que Charlie lo mencionó.

Y se preguntó cómo había estado tan ciega, sabiendo lo que sabía en esos momentos.

De pronto, recordó que debía mantenerse alerta. Si tenían éxito, en esos instantes habría salido en su busca.

Tal y como habían señalado el señor Stokes y Charlie, también era de dominio público su predilección por el camino del lago, aunque habían elegido ese escenario por otros motivos. El camino quedaba bien a la vista, de modo que Charlie y el señor Stokes podían ocultarse en las cercanías para vigilarla. Simon se reuniría con ellos, por supuesto, pero para que nadie sospechara de su plan, tendría que llegar después de haber rodeado los establos.

Blenkinsop también montaba guardia, y era la única persona a la que le habían confiado su plan. Simon había querido diseminar un ejército de criados por los jardines con las órdenes de que se mantuvieran inmóviles entre las sombras; la única razón por la que no había insistido era la posibilidad de que el asesino se topara con alguno mientras la perseguía y todos sus esfuerzos acabaran así en saco roto.

No obstante, Blenkinsop era de fiar y, al igual que todos los buenos criados, casi invisible. Sería el encargado de montar guardia en la mansión y de seguir a cualquier caballero que se dirigiera al lago.

Cuando llegó al borde del prado y comenzó a bajar la pendiente hacia el lago, levantó la cabeza para observar el cielo e inspiró hondo.

El clima era lo único que, hasta ese momento, no había jugado a su favor. El cielo estaba cubierto de nubarrones que si bien no oscurecían la tarde por completo sí ayudaban a que la luz se desvaneciera antes de tiempo.

Caminaba como si estuviera muy furiosa, en absoluto calmada y alerta para sus adentros como había esperado, sino con los nervios a flor de piel y dando un respingo al menor ruido. Las emociones que habían aflorado durante la discusión no se habían calmado del todo y la sumían en un estado de intranquilidad.

Habían asumido que si caminaba deprisa, llegaría al lago antes que el asesino sin mayor inconveniente... Esperaba que no hubieran pasado por alto algún detalle, como que el asesino ya estuviera en el exterior, paseando por los jardines, y, por tanto, mucho más cerca...

Los arbustos que tenía por delante se agitaron. Se detuvo, temblorosa...

Apareció un hombre de la nada.

Estaba tan sorprendida que ni siquiera gritó.

Se llevó la mano a los labios y emitió un jadeo. Después inspiró hondo...

Y lo reconoció. Al igual que reconoció la expresión sorprendida de su rostro.

Arturo levantó ambas manos en un gesto tranquilizador y retrocedió un par de pasos.

—Mis disculpas, señorita. No quería asustarla.

Portia soltó el aire entre dientes. Y frunció el ceño.

—¿Qué hace aquí? —Mantuvo la voz baja—. La señora Glossup está muerta, ya lo sabe.

Arturo no se arredró, sino que frunció el ceño a su vez.

—He venido para ver a Rosie.

—¿A Rosie?

—La doncella. Somos... buenos amigos.

La respuesta la desconcertó.

—Usted... antes... ¿No venía para encontrarse con la señora Glossup?

Un rictus desdeñoso asomó a los labios del gitano.

—¿Esa *putain*? ¿Qué iba a querer de ella?

—¡Caray!

Revisó sus teorías para llegar a una nueva conclusión. Se dio cuenta de que Arturo seguía con el ceño fruncido, así que irguió los hombros y levantó la barbilla.

—Será mejor que se vaya. —Le hizo un gesto con la mano.

El ceño del gitano se acentuó.

—No debería estar aquí sola. Hay un asesino suelto. Y usted sí que lo sabe.

Justo lo que le hacía falta, otro hombre sobreprotector.

Arturo dio un paso hacia ella.

Levantó todavía más la barbilla y entrecerró los ojos.

—¡Márchese! —Señaló el estrecho sendero por el que había aparecido—. Si no lo hace, gritaré y le diré a todo el mundo que usted es el asesino.

El gitano se debatió entre ponerla a prueba o no, pero acabó por hacerse a un lado a regañadientes.

—Es una mujer muy agresiva.

—¡Porque estoy rodeada de hombres muy agresivos!

La cortante respuesta zanjó el asunto; Arturo se perdió entre los arbustos sin que su expresión se le aclarara del todo. Sus pisadas quedaron amortiguadas por la hierba.

Se hizo de nuevo el silencio. Tomó aire y siguió su camino lo más rápido que pudo. Las sombras parecían adquirir consistencia y volverse más densas. Dio un respingo con el corazón en la boca al ver algo..., pero después se dio cuenta de que sólo era eso, una sombra.

Con el corazón desbocado, llegó por fin a la pequeña elevación tras la que estaba el lago. Se detuvo para recuperar el aliento y clavó la vista en el agua, oscura, silenciosa y tranquila.

Agudizó el oído, pero sólo le llegó el suave murmullo de las hojas. La brisa no era lo bastante fuerte como para agitar la superficie del agua, de modo que el lago se asemejaba a un espejo negro, con la salvedad de que no reflejaba ninguna imagen.

A esas alturas apenas había luz; mientras bajaba la colina, deseó haberse puesto un vestido más claro, amarillo o celeste. Su vestido de seda verde oscuro se confundía con las sombras; sólo su rostro, los brazos, los hombros y el escote destacaban en la oscuridad.

Bajó la vista y dejó que el fino chal de seda que se había puesto sobre los hombros resbalara hasta los codos. No tenía sentido que se ocultara más de lo necesario. Al llegar a la orilla, enfiló el camino que bordeaba el lago en dirección contraria al mirador.

Tenía los nervios a flor de piel, listos para saltar al menor indicio de ataque. El señor Stokes y Charlie estaban apostados cerca; teniendo en cuenta el tiempo que había perdido con Arturo, Simon también debía de estar cerca.

El simple hecho de pensarlo le resultó reconfortante. Siguió caminando con presteza, pero fue aminorando el paso poco a poco, como haría en circunstancias normales a medida que la furia hubiera ido abandonándola.

Había dejado atrás el sendero que llevaba al pinar y aún estaba bastante lejos del mirador cuando los arbustos que se alineaban junto al camino se agitaron.

Le dio un vuelco el corazón. Se detuvo, escudriñó la oscuridad y esperó...

—Soy yo. Lo siento.

Charlie. Dejó escapar el aire con exasperación y clavó la vista en el suelo mientras se ajustaba el chal como si se hubiera enredado en un arbusto.

—¡Me ha dado un susto de muerte!

Ambos hablaban en susurros.

—Me toca vigilar esta parte, pero cuesta horrores esconderse por aquí. Voy a acercarme más a los pinos.

Portia frunció el ceño.

—Recuerde las agujas del suelo.

—Lo haré. Simon debe de estar cerca del mirador y el señor Stokes está cerca del sendero que lleva a la casa a través del pinar.

—Gracias. —Tras agitar el chal, levantó la cabeza y siguió caminando.

Respiró hondo para calmar sus destrozados nervios.

La brisa se había calmado. La noche parecía haberse detenido y guardaba un silencio expectante, como si también esperara el desarrollo de los acontecimientos.

Se detuvo al llegar al claro del mirador, como si estuviera meditando qué hacer a continuación, aunque no tuviera intención alguna de entrar, ya que sus leales paladines no la verían en el interior. Dio media vuelta y continuó.

Comenzó a pasearse como si estuviera pensando. Mantuvo la cabeza gacha, si bien observó en todo momento sus alrededores con disimulo. Tenía los sentidos alerta. Habían llegado a la conclusión de que el asesino intentaría estrangularla, ya que una pistola hacía demasiado ruido y era fácil de rastrear, y un cuchillo era demasiado sucio.

La verdad era que no se había detenido a reflexionar sobre la identidad del rufián; ni siquiera había pensado con cuál de los cuatro sospechosos se encontraría esa noche. Mientras caminaba y esperaba, tuvo tiempo de sobra y todos los motivos del mundo para hacerlo. No quería que fuera Henry ni tampoco James, sin embargo... Bueno, a juzgar por lo que sabía, si tuviera que elegir a uno, se decantaría por James.

En su cabeza, era a James a quien esperaba esa noche.

James poseía el coraje. La resolución. Cualidades que también había reconocido en Simon.

A sus ojos, James era el sospechoso más viable.

Desmond... Había aguantado durante mucho tiempo la interferencia de Kitty y la había evitado durante años hasta hacer de ello una estrategia. Le costaba trabajo imaginárselo en las garras de una furia asesina. Lo bastante furioso como para matar.

En cuanto a Ambrose... no se lo imaginaba haciendo nada impetuoso. Era un hombre envarado (en una ocasión escuchó a Charlie murmurar acerca de la parte de su anatomía en la que estaría incrustada dicha vara y estaba totalmente de acuerdo con él), muy cuidadoso con su conducta, muy calculador y tan centrado en su carrera política que la idea de que lo dominara una furia asesina por el hecho de que Kitty se le hubiera insinuado en público... era del todo increíble.

Tenía que ser James. A pesar de lo que sentían por él, sabía que si llegaba el caso, Simon y Charlie no harían nada para protegerlo. Les resultaría muy doloroso, pero se lo entregarían al señor Stokes en persona. Su código de honor así se lo exigiría.

Lo comprendía a la perfección; de hecho, lo comprendía mejor que muchos caballeros. Nadie hablaba ya de su hermano Edward, unos años menor que Luc. Muchas familias tenían a una manzana podrida entre sus filas; se limitaban a expulsarlas. A pesar de todo, esperaba que los Glossup no tuvieran que enfrentarse a semejante escándalo.

El sendero que llevaba a la casa apareció de pronto frente a ella. Casi había recorrido el perímetro del lago... y no se había topado con nadie. ¿Habría andado demasiado deprisa o quizás estaría el asesino esperándola entre las sombras del camino que llevaba a la mansión?

Al llegar al sendero, levantó la vista, escudriñó las sombras de la pendiente... y vio a un hombre en la parte superior, bajo un enorme rododendro. Lo vislumbró gracias al espeso follaje que tenía detrás de él.

Era Henry.

Estaba anonadada, sorprendida... Bajó la vista y siguió caminando como si no lo hubiera visto mientras su mente trabajaba a toda velocidad.

¿Había sido él? ¿Habría averiguado que Kitty intentaba presionar a James con el bebé tal y como ellos suponían? ¿Habría sido ésa la gota que colmara el vaso?

Aunque se sentía helada, siguió andando. Si era Henry, tendría que arreglárselas para que bajara hasta donde ella se encontraba, porque era el único modo de estar a salvo. Sin detenerse, prosiguió hacia el pinar acompañada por el frufrú de las faldas que se le arremolinaban entre las piernas; estaba a punto de perder los nervios y el control por el ansia de escuchar unas pisadas a su espalda...

Una figura emergió de uno de los senderos secundarios a unos metros de ella y esperó con tranquilidad a que llegara a su altura.

Ambrose. Lo reconoció al instante. ¡Maldición! ¡Iba a estropearlo todo! El hombre sonrió cuando ella se acercó;

se devanó los sesos en busca de una excusa, por tonta que fuera, para que se marchara.

—He oído su discusión con el señor Cynster. Aunque comprendo que necesite estar sola, no debería alejarse tanto.

¿Qué verían los hombres en ella que sentían el impulso de protegerla?

Hizo a un lado la irritación mientras se detenía junto a Ambrose y lo saludaba con un gesto de la cabeza.

—Le agradezco su preocupación, pero me gustaría estar sola.

La sonrisa del hombre adquirió un tinte ciertamente arrogante.

—Me temo mucho, querida, que no podemos permitirlo. —No intentó cogerla del brazo, pero sí se giró para caminar a su lado.

Con el ceño fruncido, Portia reanudó la marcha mientras intentaba decidir qué hacer a continuación. Tenía que librarse de él... ¿Debía decirle que habían planeado una trampa, que ella era el cebo y que él estaba interfiriendo? ¿Debía decirle que era bastante posible que el asesino estuviera observándolos de cerca?

La oscura linde del pinar se alzaba a su derecha. El lago, con sus mansas aguas, estaba a su izquierda. Ambrose caminaba entre la oscuridad de los altos pinos y ella. Según lo que le había dicho Charlie, acababan de dejar atrás al señor Stokes. La tentación de mirar en esa dirección, de comprobar si Henry había mordido el anzuelo y bajaba la colina, era fuerte, pero se resistió.

Llegaron al camino del pinar; continuó buscando frenéticamente una razón con la que enviar a Ambrose de vuelta a la casa utilizando esa ruta...

—Tengo que admitir, querida, que jamás la creí tan estúpida como Kitty.

Esas palabras, pronunciadas con la más absoluta serenidad, la hicieron volver al presente.

—¿Qué quiere decir con eso? —preguntó, girando la cabeza para mirarlo

—Caramba, pues que no la había tomado por una de esas necias que se divierten enfrentando a los hombres. Tratándolos como si fueran marionetas cuyos hilos maneja —respondió sin detenerse, con la vista clavada en el suelo, no en ella; su expresión, o lo que atisbaba de ella, parecía ensimismada—. Ése fue el estilo de la pobre Kitty hasta el final —prosiguió con el mismo tono sereno—. Se creía muy poderosa. —Sus labios se torcieron con una mueca irónica—. ¿Quién sabe? Es posible que tuviera algo de poder, pero jamás aprendió a utilizarlo. —En ese momento, la miró—. Creí que usted era diferente. Desde luego, creí que era más lista. —Cuando sus ojos se encontraron, sonrió—. Tampoco es que me queje, que conste.

Fue esa sonrisa la que la sacó de su estupor, la que le heló la sangre. La que la convenció de que paseaba al lado del asesino de Kitty, de que no habían sido ni Henry ni James...

—¿No? —Se detuvo y consiguió fruncir el ceño. No iba a dar un paso más hacia el pinar, hacia esa oscuridad impenetrable donde nadie los vería—. Dígame, si no ha venido a criticar (con bastante impertinencia, por cierto) mi comportamiento, ¿a qué ha venido?

Se dio la vuelta mientras hablaba y se colocó frente a él. El camino que habían recorrido quedó frente a ella y de ese modo podría ver al señor Stokes cuando saliera de su escondite sin que Ambrose lo hiciera.

El hombre seguía sonriendo.

—Es muy sencillo, querida. He venido a silenciarla de una vez por todas y a asegurarme de que el señor Cynster carga con las culpas. Está por aquí fuera, al igual que usted. Después de la escenita de la terraza... —Su aterradora sonrisa se ensanchó—. No habría podido planearlo mejor.

Ambrose levantó las manos, que hasta ese momento habían estado ocultas tras su espalda. En una de ellas vio un cordón de cortina de cuyo extremo colgaba una borla. Ambrose se apresuró a coger el otro extremo para tensarlo...

Y, sin pensárselo, ella lo cogió. Lo agarró con ambas manos y se colgó prácticamente de él.

Ambrose soltó un juramento mientras forcejeaba para desembarazarse de ella, pero no pudo. Era imposible que lo lograra sin deshacerse al mismo tiempo del cordón.

En ese instante, Portia vio la voluminosa sombra del señor Stokes, que salía de entre los arbustos y corría hacia ellos a espaldas de Ambrose.

Con un gruñido, éste soltó el cordón, desequilibrándola en el proceso. Al verla tambalearse, aprovechó la oportunidad y cogió uno de los extremos de su chal de seda.

Se lo echó por encima y le rodeó el cuello con él.

Portia no pensó, no tenía tiempo que perder. Metió una mano bajo el chal y, un instante antes de que Ambrose se apretara, se dejó caer contra él al tiempo que tiraba de la prenda hacia delante. Aprovechó el hueco que creó para agacharse.

Y zafarse del chal.

Acabó en cuclillas a los pies de su asaltante, al borde del lago. El señor Stokes se acercaba a la carrera. Ambrose estaba demasiado cerca, refunfuñando mientras retorcía el chal entre las manos.

Sin pensárselo, se tiró al lago.

Las oscuras aguas se cerraron sobre su cabeza. Ni siquiera en las orillas se hacía pie. El agua estaba fría pero no helada, ya que el sol estival la había calentado. Tampoco tenía que luchar contra la corriente, así que le resultó sencillo salir a la superficie y comenzar a nadar.

Mientras se alejaba de la orilla, atisbó el rostro estupefacto de Ambrose un instante antes de que escuchara al señor Stokes, antes de que lo viera, antes de que se diera cuenta...

Su rostro quedó demudado por la furia...

Ella siguió nadando. Tras ella escuchó un golpe y un gemido cuando el investigador chocó con Ambrose. No se detuvo y continuó alejándose de la orilla, luchando contra el impedimento que suponían sus faldas. Cuando hubo interpuesto una distancia segura, se giró.

Charlie también se acercaba a la carrera para echar una mano. Henry lo hacía mucho más despacio. Simon, cuya intención había sido la de ayudar al señor Stokes, se había detenido en el sendero, en el punto más cercano a ella. En esos momentos, estaba en la orilla. Observando. Listo para entrar en acción...

Charlie intentó agarrar a Ambrose cuando se unió a la pelea, pero éste luchaba como un poseso y logró liberarse...

Para tirarse al lago.

Con el corazón en la garganta, Portia se giró para seguir nadando y vio cómo Simon se tensaba...

Pero no se lanzó al agua.

Escuchó un chapoteo... No... Demasiados chapoteos. Echó un vistazo hacia atrás.

Y comprendió, al igual que el resto, que Ambrose había creído que el lago era puramente ornamental, que no era profundo... y que no sabía nadar. Al menos, no muy bien. Dio un par de brazadas y comenzó a hundirse.

Portia se giró del todo para no perder detalle...

El señor Stokes y Charlie estaban en la orilla con los brazos en jarras y resollando mientras observaban a un aterrado Ambrose que luchaba por mantenerse a flote.

Salió a la superficie escupiendo agua.

—¡Socorro! ¡Cabrones, me estoy ahogando! ¡Ayudadme!

Fue el señor Stokes quien contestó.

—¿Por qué deberíamos hacerlo?

—Porque me estoy ahogando... ¡Voy a morir!

—Tal y como yo lo veo, sería la mejor solución. Nos ahorraría un montón de quebraderos de cabeza.

Anonadada, Portia miró al investigador. Eso no bastaba, tenían que obtener una confesión de que era el asesino...

Claro que el señor Stokes sabía lo que se hacía.

Cuando Ambrose volvió a salir a la superficie, gritó:

—Muy bien. ¡Lo confieso! Yo lo hice. ¡Yo maté a esa puta!

—Se está refiriendo a la señora Glossup, ¿verdad?

—¡Sí, maldita sea! —Ambrose gritaba con toda su alma—. ¡Sacadme de aquí de una vez!

El señor Stokes miró primero a Charlie y después a Henry, quien se había acercado a ellos muy despacio y estaba atónito.

—¿Lo han escuchado?

Charlie asintió con la cabeza. Cuando Henry se dio cuenta de que el investigador también le hablaba a él, se apresuró a hacer lo mismo.

—Muy bien. —El señor Stokes miró a Ambrose—. Yo tampoco sé nadar. ¿Cómo lo sacamos?

Desde el lago, Portia les gritó la solución.

—Utilicen mi chal. —Estaba tirado en el suelo, justo donde Ambrose lo había dejado—. Hagan un nudo en cada extremo y enróllenlo para que, al tirarlo, llegue hasta él. Es de seda. Si no está rasgado, aguantará.

Esperó pacientemente mientras seguían sus instrucciones. En ese momento, escuchó que alguien mascullaba una orden desde la orilla.

—¡Ni se te ocurra acudir en su ayuda!

Por primera vez en horas, sonrió.

Por suerte, en cuanto estuvo seguro de que lo rescatarían, Ambrose se calmó lo suficiente para mantenerse a flote hasta que le lanzaron el chal. Una vez que lo hicieron, se lanzó hacia él y aferró el extremo anudado. El hecho de haber estado a punto de ahogarse sumado al pánico lo había dejado sin fuerzas. Mientras lo sacaban del agua, temblando como una hoja, Portia se giró y nadó hacia la orilla.

Donde Simon la esperaba.

Le resultó imposible interpretar su expresión mientras se acercaba. Sintió una oleada de alivio acompañada de algo que no supo identificar. Con una sonrisa, feliz de seguir viva, levantó las manos. Simon se las cogió y tiró de ella para ayudarla a subir.

No bien hubo puesto los pies en el suelo, la soltó y la estrechó entre sus brazos. La apretó contra su pecho con todas sus fuerzas. Y la besó, ajeno al hecho de que estaba empapada. Fue un beso rudo, apasionado, arrebatador y desesperado que le arrebató la razón.

Conociéndolo, eso era mucho mejor que el zarandeo que habría cabido esperar...

Cuando por fin levantó la cabeza y pudo mirarlo a los ojos, no necesitó pensar para interpretar la tensión que lo embargaba, para saber que había estado a un paso de perder el control.

—Estoy perfectamente —le aseguró, a fin de calmar el miedo que lo atenazaba, la vulnerabilidad que había descubierto hacía muy poco tiempo y de la que ella era la causante.

Simon resopló y parte de la tensión se esfumó.

—Si no recuerdo mal, el plan no incluía que te tiraras al lago.

Cuando aflojó el abrazo, se apartó de él, si bien la dejó ir a regañadientes. Se pasó las manos por el talle del vestido para escurrirlo antes de cogerse las faldas y retorcerlas a tal fin.

—Me pareció la vía de escape más lógica. —Mantuvo un tono sereno a propósito, como si estuvieran hablando de algo sin importancia.

—¿Qué habría pasado si hubiera sabido nadar? —masculló con la voz aún crispada y un tono reprobatorio—. No tenías ni idea de si sabía nadar o no.

Se enderezó y lo miró a los ojos.

—No tenía ni idea de lo que sabía hacer Ambrose, pero yo nado muy bien. —Enarcó un tanto las cejas y dejó que una sonrisilla asomara a sus labios—. Y tú lo haces aún mejor.

Simon sostuvo su mirada. Percibió cómo sopesaba su respuesta... Y, de pronto, cayó en la cuenta.

—Tú sabías que sé nadar, ¿verdad?

Él frunció los labios, que hasta ese momento habían estado muy apretados, y después soltó el aire.

—No —contestó con un susurro. Sin apartar los ojos de los suyos, añadió tras un breve titubeo—: Pero asumí que sabías nadar o no te habrías tirado al lago.

Leyó la expresión de su rostro, de sus ojos, y sonrió encantada cuando una embriagadora oleada de alegría se apoderó de ella. Bajó la vista al suelo, sonriendo.

—Eso es. —Tras colgarse de su brazo, se giró para ver lo que estaban haciendo los demás.

Simon seguía observando su rostro.

—¿Qué?

Le devolvió la mirada y sonrió con dulzura.

—Luego te lo explico.

Cuando ya hubiera saboreado el momento y hubiera encontrado las palabras para decirle cuánto le agradecía su autocontrol. Había aguardado en la orilla del lago, dispuesto a entrar en acción y protegerla; pero, al saber que ella podía salvarse solita, se había contenido y la había dejado hacer. No la había tratado como si fuera una inútil; no la había asfixiado con su afán protector. Se había comportado como si fuera una compañera con diferentes habilidades que él, pero con la capacidad necesaria para resolver la situación.

Había actuado justo cuando lo necesitaba, pero había resistido la tentación de hacerlo antes.

Podían tener un futuro juntos... Con el tiempo, con el roce, ese afán protector se convertiría en una respuesta más racional y meditada... que tendría en cuenta sus deseos.

La esperanza afloró en su interior y la llenó de una alegría que nada tenía que ver con los recientes acontecimientos.

Si bien dichos acontecimientos estaban en pleno desarrollo. Blenkinsop acababa de unirse al grupo del pinar. El mayordomo y el señor Stokes echaron a andar por el sendero, arrastrando a Ambrose con ellos. Los dejaron atrás cuando comenzaron a subir la suave pendiente. Ambrose tiritaba y tenía las manos atadas con su chal. Ni siquiera los miró.

Henry y Charlie los seguían muy de cerca, mientras éste le explicaba al primero todo lo que habían estado haciendo.

Henry se detuvo a su lado y le cogió las manos.

—Charlie aún no me lo ha contado todo, pero tengo entendido, querida, que le debemos muchísimo.

—Tonterías... Todos hemos echado una mano —replicó ella, ruborizándose.

—No son tonterías. Sin usted y su coraje, no habrían conseguido atrapar al asesino. —Su mirada se desvió hacia Simon y entre ellos pasó un mensaje profundamente masculino—. Y gracias a ti, Simon. —Extendió el brazo y le dio unas palmaditas en el hombro. Tras lo cual la miró... y cayó en la cuenta de que estaba ataviada con dos prendas de seda empapadas. Carraspeó y apartó la vista hacia la mansión—. Charlie y yo nos adelantaremos, pero usted no debería tardar en cambiarse. No es sensato andar mojado, ni siquiera en verano.

Charlie la miró con una sonrisa antes de inclinar la cabeza en dirección a Simon.

—¡Lo atrapamos!

Su evidente alegría por que todo se hubiera solucionado, por que hubieran demostrado la inocencia de James, Henry y Desmond, resultó contagiosa.

Ambos sonrieron. Henry y Charlie reanudaron su camino y ellos los siguieron, muy despacio. Cuando ascendieron la pendiente comenzó a soplar el viento y el roce sobre su piel mojada le provocó un escalofrío.

Simon se detuvo y se quitó la chaqueta para echársela por encima de los hombros. Ella sonrió, agradecida por el calor que irradiaba el forro de seda de la prenda, aunque la temperatura de la noche era de lo más agradable. Se cerró la chaqueta y lo miró a los ojos.

—Gracias.

—Servirá de momento —refunfuñó él.

Volvió a cogerla de la mano. Ella hizo ademán de seguir adelante, pero él la detuvo. La distancia que los separaba de los otros se incrementó.

Lo miró con las cejas arqueadas.

Simon estaba contemplando a Henry y Charlie. Inspiró hondo antes de hablar.

—Lo que sucedió en la terraza... Todo lo que dije. Te pido disculpas. No quise decir... —Gesticuló con la mano, como si quisiera borrar la horrible escena, y le echó un vistazo al rostro antes de apartar la mirada.

Portia se acercó, alzó la mano que tenía libre y lo obligó a girar el rostro para que la mirara.

Accedió a regañadientes.

Le giró el rostro hasta que pudo leer la expresión de sus ojos, hasta que percibió la vulnerabilidad que se empeñaba en ocultar. En justificar.

Al menos ya lo comprendía. Por fin. Y le llegaba al alma.

—Jamás sucederá. Créeme. —Jamás se aprovecharía de él para después darle la espalda. Jamás lo amaría para después abandonarlo.

Su tensa expresión no se suavizó.

—¿Es posible prometer algo así?

Lo miró a los ojos.

—Entre nosotros, sí.

En ese instante, le tocó a él leer su expresión, ver que hablaba con sinceridad. Respiró aliviado, y el movimiento le ensanchó el pecho. El cambio que se obró en él fue perceptible. Su actitud volvía a ser posesiva en lugar de protectora.

La rodeó con los brazos y la estrechó suavemente contra su cuerpo.

—Espera —lo detuvo, poniéndole una mano en el pecho—. No vayas tan deprisa.

Simon enarcó las cejas y ella casi pudo escuchar la protesta que le pasó por la cabeza. Se acomodó de nuevo entre sus brazos antes de hablar.

—Tenemos que terminar lo que hemos empezado. Tenemos que saber lo que realmente pasó para zanjar este asunto, para olvidarnos de Ambrose y de los asesinatos de una vez por todas. Después podremos hablar... —hizo una pausa para tomar aliento—. De nosotros.

Sin apartar la mirada de ella, Simon torció el gesto y la soltó.

—Muy bien. Terminemos con esto de una vez.

La cogió de la mano y juntos atravesaron el prado hasta la mansión.

Fue una escena tan siniestra como había previsto. Hubo alivio, pero no triunfo. Al rescatar a los Glossup, y también a los Archer, que habían estado en la cuerda floja a causa de su relación con Desmond, habían dejado que todo el peso recayera sobre los Calvin. Para mortificación de todos.

Simon entró con Portia en la biblioteca por las puertas de la terraza. Lo que vieron al llegar fue, sin duda, una de las peores pesadillas del señor Stokes. Intercambiaron una mirada, pero no estaba en su mano remediar la situación.

Las damas se habían rebelado. Se habían dado cuenta de que estaba pasando algo y habían tomado la biblioteca por asalto. Una vez que las hubieron puesto al corriente de los hechos fundamentales (que Ambrose había matado a Kitty), se acomodaron en los sillones y los sofás, y se negaron a marcharse.

Todo el mundo, literalmente, estaba allí, incluso dos criados. La única parte interesada que no estaba presente era Arturo; y a tenor de las expresiones anonadadas e incrédulas de los presentes, así como de lo que estaba por llegar, Simon sospechaba que el gitano estaría eternamente agradecido por haberse perdido semejante trago.

Ojalá pudiera decir lo mismo... Miró a Portia y supo, por la terca expresión de su rostro, que no consentiría que la mandaran a su habitación para cambiarse antes de conocer todas las respuestas. Tras sacar el sillón de detrás del escritorio principal, lo colocó junto al diván donde estaba lady O y la obligó a sentarse.

Lady O miró por el rabillo del ojo su vestido empapado.

—Sin duda alguna, también habrá alguna explicación para eso, ¿no?

El extraño deje de su voz, sumado a la expresión de sus ojos, les dejó bien claro que se había asustado mucho.

Portia extendió el brazo y cogió una de sus manos.

—No he corrido peligro alguno.

—¡No sé yo!

Lady O lanzó a Simon una mirada de lo más elocuente, como si le dijera que se ofendería muchísimo si no estaba a la altura de lo que había esperado de él.

Cosa que le recordó... Echó una mirada al señor Stokes, que estaba totalmente concentrado en asegurarle a lady Calvin que lo explicaría todo si le daba la oportunidad. De modo que aprovechó el momento para llamar a uno de los criados. Cuando éste se acercó, le soltó una retahíla de órdenes. El criado se alejó con una reverencia, sin duda encantado de poder comunicarles las últimas noticias al resto de la servidumbre.

—¡Damas y caballeros! —exclamó el señor Stokes desde el centro de la estancia con voz apremiante—. Ya que han insistido en quedarse, debo pedirles que guarden silencio mientras interrogo al señor Calvin. Si deseo la confirmación de algo en concreto, lo preguntaré.

El investigador esperó un momento. En cuanto las damas se acomodaron dispuestas a escuchar, soltó el aire y se giró hacia Ambrose, que estaba sentado con la cabeza gacha en una silla colocada bajo la araña central, de frente a la multitud congregada en la chimenea.

Estaba flanqueado por Blenkinsop y un fornido criado, que no se movían de su lado.

—Bien, señor Calvin, ya ha admitido delante de unos cuantos testigos que estranguló a la señora Glossup. ¿Podría detallarme cómo la asesinó?

Ambrose no levantó la cabeza. Continuó con los brazos apoyados en los muslos y la mirada fija en sus manos atadas.

—La estrangulé con el cordón de la cortina de esa ventana. —Señaló con la cabeza el ventanal más cercano al escritorio.

—¿Por qué?

—Porque esa estúpida no me dejaba tranquilo.

—¿A qué se refiere?

Ambrose debía de ser muy consciente de la presencia de su madre, que parecía haber sufrido un golpe mortal allí sentada en el diván con el rostro lívido, aferrada a las manos de lady Glossup y Drusilla, mientras lo miraba con una especie de súplica espantada. Como si se hubiera dado cuenta de que no tenía escapatoria, de que si lo contaba todo sin omitir detalle y sin mentir, el mal trago pasaría antes, inspiró hondo y confesó:

—Kitty y yo tuvimos... tuvimos una aventura a principios de año, en Londres. No era mi tipo, pero no paraba de perseguirme y yo necesitaba el apoyo del señor Archer. Me pareció un movimiento magistral. Prometió hablar con su padre a mi favor. Cuando llegó el verano y dejamos la ciudad, nos separamos. —Se encogió de hombros—. De manera bastante amigable. Habíamos acordado que asistiría a esta fiesta, pero, aparte de eso, parecía haberse olvidado de mí. O eso creí. —Se detuvo para tomar aire—. Cuando llegué a la mansión, su comportamiento había empeorado de forma considerable, pero parecía perseguir a James. Así que no me preocupé hasta que me pilló a solas una noche y me dijo que estaba embarazada. Al principio, no entendí cuál era el problema, pero ella no tardó en sacarme de mi error. ¡Me quedé espantado! —Incluso en ese momento, mientras contaba lo sucedido, la emoción quedaba patente en su voz—. Jamás se me pasó por la cabeza que Henry y ella... Bueno, jamás se me ocurrió que una mujer casada se comportara como ella a sabiendas de que ya no contaba con la protección de su matrimonio. —Se detuvo, como si estuviera experimentando de nuevo la misma sorpresa.

El señor Stokes, con el ceño fruncido, le preguntó:

—¿En qué medida contribuyó esa situación a su decisión de matarla?

Ambrose miró al hombre y meneó la cabeza.

—Muchísimas damas casadas tienen hijos que no son de sus maridos. No vi ningún problema hasta que Kitty me aseguró con vehemencia que no tendría ese niño bajo ninguna circunstancia y que recaía sobre mí la responsabilidad de arreglarlo todo para librarse de él, porque de otro modo diría a los cuatro vientos que era mío, se lo diría a su padre. Ése fue el ultimátum que me dio aquella noche.

Volvió a clavar la mirada en sus manos.

—No tenía ni idea de lo que hacer. Mi carrera política... Dar la imagen sólida que necesita un candidato a la Cámara Baja para ser elegido... Sólo necesitaba el apoyo del señor Archer. Y, una vez aquí, también me di cuenta de que lord Glossup y el señor Buckstead estaban dispuestos a apoyarme. Iba todo tan bien... Salvo por Kitty. —Su voz se tornó desabrida, pero no alzó la mirada—. No sabía cómo ayudarla... Si le soy sincero, ni siquiera sé si lo habría hecho de haberlo sabido. No es el tipo de requerimiento que una dama hace a su amante, la mayoría sabe cómo ocuparse de esos asuntos por sí mismas. Creí que le bastaría con preguntar. Estaba aquí, en el campo, seguro que hay un montón de criadas que saben de estas cosas... Estaba convencido de que se las apañaría. Era eso o que orquestara una reconciliación con Henry.

Entrelazó las manos y prosiguió:

—Cometí el error de decírselo tal cual. —Un escalofrío lo recorrió de pies a cabeza—. Dios, ¡cómo se lo tomó! Cualquiera habría dicho que le recomendé un traguito de cicuta. Comenzó a vociferar, enfurecida y sin darse cuenta de que alzaba cada vez más la voz. Intenté que se callara y me abofeteó. Empezó a gritar...

»Cogí el cordón de la cortina y se lo enrollé en el cuello... y apreté. —Hizo una pausa y la biblioteca quedó sumida en un silencio sepulcral. Un instante después, ladeó la cabeza y, con la mirada perdida, siguió recordando—. Fue sorprendentemente fácil... Kitty no era muy fuerte. Forcejeó un poco, intentó arañarme, sujetarme las manos, pero la inmovilicé hasta que dejó de luchar... Cuando la solté, cayó al suelo sin más.

Su tono de voz cambió.

—Fue entonces cuando me di cuenta de que la había matado. Me fui corriendo... a mi habitación. Lejos de aquí. Me serví una buena copa de *brandy*. Estaba tomando un sorbo cuando me di cuenta de que tenía la manga de la chaqueta desgarrada y de que le faltaba un trozo. Entonces recordé que de ahí me había agarrado Kitty... Comprendí... En fin, me acordé de que había visto el trozo de tela en su mano cuando yacía en el suelo. Era de cuadros... Yo era el único que llevaba una chaqueta de cuadros ese día.

»Salí corriendo de mi habitación. Estaba en la escalinata cuando la señorita Ashford gritó. El señor Cynster apareció como una exhalación, seguido del señor Hastings. Ya no podía hacer nada. Me quedé allí, a la espera de que me acusaran, pero... no pasó nada. —Tomó aire—. El señor Hastings salió de la biblioteca y cerró la puerta tras él. Levantó la cabeza y me miró. Comprendí que no me acusaba de nada. En cambio, me preguntó dónde estaban Henry y el mayordomo. Cuando se fue, me di cuenta de que todavía había esperanza, de que nadie había reparado en el trozo de tela. De que si pudiera cogerlo, estaría a salvo.

Se detuvo un instante.

—No tenía nada que perder. Bajé la escalinata. Henry y el mayordomo aparecieron corriendo y yo entré tras ellos en la biblioteca. La señorita Ashford y el señor Cynster estaban en el otro extremo de la estancia. Ella estaba muy afectada y él no prestaba atención a nada más. Ambos me vieron, pero ninguno reaccionó. Seguía llevando la misma chaqueta de cuadros, así que era imposible que hubieran visto el trozo de tela. Me acerqué al escritorio, justo detrás de Henry y el mayordomo. Estaban estupefactos, anonadados... Se limitaban a mirarla. Yo hice lo mismo, pero miré su mano derecha.

Levantó la cabeza.

—No había nada. No daba crédito a lo que veía. Tenía los dedos abiertos y la mano, laxa. Entonces me di cuenta de que le habían movido los brazos, de que no tenía la cabeza en la misma posición. Pensé en la señorita Ashford, deduje que había entrado en la biblioteca y que al ver a Kitty en el suelo había corrido hacia ella, la había tocado y le había frotado las manos... Todas esas estupideces que suelen hacer las mujeres. El trozo de tela era muy pequeño, apenas de unos centímetros de largo. Si se había caído de la mano de Kitty...

Su mirada descendió hasta las alfombras turcas que cubrían el suelo de la biblioteca.

—Marrón, verde y rojo. La chaqueta tenía los mismos colores que las alfombras. El trozo de tela se podría haber enredado en las faldas de la señorita Ashford, en sus enaguas o incluso en el bajo de un pantalón. Una vez lejos de las manos de Kitty, podría estar en cualquier sitio y habría costado mucho trabajo localizarlo. No podía arriesgarme a buscarlo a plena vista. Henry y el mayordomo seguían estupefactos, así que aproveché la oportunidad. Rodeé el escritorio y me agaché como si quisiera echar un vistazo más de cerca; hice que la manga de la chaqueta se enganchara en uno de los tiradores de los cajones y, cuando me levanté, se desgarró. Solté un juramento y me disculpé. Aunque Henry y el mayordomo estaban algo aturdidos, se dieron cuenta de lo que había pasado. Si más tarde se encontraba un trozo de tela de mi chaqueta, podría aducir ese momento como excusa.

Su mirada seguía perdida.

—Me sentí a salvo. Ya había salido de la biblioteca cuando se me ocurrió otra cosa: ¿y si alguien había encontrado el cuerpo de Kitty antes que la señorita Ashford y había cogido el trozo de tela? El problema era que no se me ocurría quién podría ser ese alguien. Cualquiera habría dado la voz de alarma y me habría denunciado..., cualquiera menos mi madre. Me había dicho que pasaría la tarde escribiendo unas cartas para no perder el contacto con las personas que me podían apoyar. Fui a su habitación. Estaba allí, escribiendo. No sabía nada del asesinato. Se lo conté y me marché.

Se detuvo, con la cabeza ligeramente ladeada, como si estuviera rememorando un momento extraño.

—Regresé a mi dormitorio y apuré el *brandy*. Empecé a pensar en los criados. No tenían motivos para estar en la biblioteca a esa hora del día, pero nunca se sabe qué se le puede ocurrir a un criado hacendoso. Así que decidí quemar la chaqueta. A nadie le extrañaría que me librara de ella después de habérmela rasgado. Una vez que la chaqueta estuviera destruida, si alguien intentaba chantajearme, siempre podría decir que el trozo de tela era similar pero no idéntico. ¿Cómo iban a estar seguros con los cuadros?

Se removió, inquieto.

—Me llevé la chaqueta al bosque y la quemé. El jardinero gitano me vio, pero no le di mucha importancia por aquel entonces. Estaba convencido de haber cubierto todas las posibilidades..., salvo que, como supuse al principio, el trozo de tela estuviera en la mano de Kitty cuando la señorita Ashford lo encontró, pero la fuerte impresión hubiera hecho que se olvidara de ello.

Bajó la vista y se llevó las manos atadas a la cara para frotarse la frente.

—No podía olvidar la imagen del trozo de tela en la mano de Kitty. La veía como si la tuviera delante de mí. Cuanto más pensaba en ello, más me convencía de que la señorita Ashford tenía que haberlo visto. Incluso con el trozo de tela desaparecido y la chaqueta destruida... Era posible que acabara por relacionar ambas cosas cuando se sosegara. Cualquier insinuación por su parte de que yo era el asesino y nadie me apoyaría. Una acusación de su parte arruinaría mi carrera en un abrir y cerrar de ojos. Me di cuenta de que no tenía la menor garantía de que siguiera sin recordar el detalle del trozo de tela cuando se recuperara de la impresión.

El señor Stokes intervino en ese momento.

—De modo que intentó darle un susto de muerte metiéndole una víbora en la cama.

Un coro de exclamaciones horrorizadas rompió el hechizo que había caído sobre los presentes. Para la mayoría de ellos, era la primera noticia que tenían de la víbora.

Con la vista clavada en las manos, Ambrose asintió con la cabeza.

—Me topé con la víbora de vuelta a la mansión. Aún tenía el saco en el que había metido la chaqueta. Creí que un nuevo susto la ofuscaría aún más o que incluso la instaría a marcharse... Pero no lo hizo. Y entonces llegó usted y me vi obligado a actuar con mucho más cuidado. Sin embargo, conforme iban pasando los días y nadie decía nada sobre el dichoso trozo de tela, comprendí que mis suposiciones eran ciertas: nadie se lo había llevado. Estaba allí cuando la señorita Ashford encontró a Kitty. —Levantó la cabeza y clavó los ojos en Portia—. ¿Lo recuerda ya? Debió de haberlo visto. Lo aferraba con la mano derecha.

Portia enfrentó su mirada, pero negó con la cabeza.

—No estaba allí cuando yo la encontré.

Ambrose adoptó una actitud un tanto arrogante.

—Estaba allí, seguro...

—¡Eres un idiota!

Semejante afirmación, hecha a voz en grito, sobresaltó a todo el mundo. E hizo que todas las miradas se volvieran hacia Drusilla, que hasta ese momento había estado sentada muy erguida junto a su madre. Tenía el rostro lívido, los ojos desorbitados y el cuerpo en tensión por una emoción muy poderosa.

Tenía los ojos clavados en su hermano.

—Tú... ¡imbécil! Portia no dijo nada... Lo habría hecho de haber visto ese trozo de tela. Tal vez estuviera ofuscada, pero no había perdido el sentido común.

Tan sorprendido como el resto, Ambrose se limitó a mirarla boquiabierto.

El señor Stokes fue el primero en recuperarse de la impresión.

—¿Qué sabe de ese trozo de tela, señorita Calvin?

La mirada de Drusilla se desvió hacia el investigador y su semblante se tornó aún más pálido.

—Yo...

Su rostro mostró todo lo que sentía. Acababa de comprender que...

Lady Calvin se llevó una mano a los labios para reprimir un grito. Lady Glossup le pasó un brazo por los hombros.

La señora Buckstead, sentada junto a Drusilla, se inclinó hacia ella.

—Debes decirnos todo lo que sabes, querida. No te queda otra alternativa.

Drusilla miró a la mujer, inspiró hondo y echó un vistazo al señor Stokes.

—Aquella tarde estaba paseando por los jardines. Entré en la casa a través de las puertas de la biblioteca. Vi a Kitty tirada en el suelo, con el trozo de tela en la mano. Lo reconocí al instante, por supuesto. Me di cuenta de que Ambrose había alcanzado su límite... —Se detuvo para humedecerse los labios—. Por la razón que fuese, la había matado. Si lo atrapaban... El escándalo, la vergüenza... acabaría con nuestra madre. Así que cogí el trozo de tela de manos de Kitty y me lo guardé. Escuché voces en el vestíbulo principal, eran el señor Cynster y Portia, así que salí de nuevo por las puertas de la terraza.

El señor Stokes la miró con severidad.

—¿Por qué no le dijo nada a nadie cuando comenzaron los ataques contra la señorita Ashford?

La mirada de Drusilla voló hasta su rostro. Se tambaleó un poco y su rostro se tornó ceniciento.

—¿Qué ataques? —Su voz sonaba débil y horrorizada—. No sabía nada de la víbora. —Después, miró a su hermano—. El macetero... Pero lo del macetero fue un accidente, ¿no?

El señor Stokes miró de nuevo a Ambrose.

—Es mejor que lo confiese todo.

—Tomé la costumbre de subir al tejado, para que nadie viera lo preocupado que estaba —explicó él—. Vi a la señorita Ashford en la terraza. Parecía estar sola... No vi al señor Cynster junto a la pared. Ya que estaba allí arriba... Fue muy sencillo. —De pronto, tomó una honda bocanada de aire y levantó la cabeza sin mirar a nadie en particular—. Tiene que entender que no me quedaba alternativa... No si quería conseguir un puesto en la Cámara Baja. Ése era mi objetivo y...

Se detuvo y bajó la cabeza. Apretó las manos con fuerza. El señor Stokes desvió la mirada hacia Drusilla, que observaba a su hermano con el rostro ceniciento.

Cuando miró al investigador, éste le preguntó:

—¿Por qué no le dijo a su hermano que había cogido el trozo de tela?

Ella se limitó a mirarlo durante largo rato. El hombre estaba a punto de repetir la pregunta cuando Drusilla desvió la vista hacia su hermano. Inspiró hondo y dijo:

—Lo odio, ¿sabe? No, es imposible que usted lo sepa. En casa sólo existe él. Ambrose. Él siempre lo ha recibido todo, para mí nunca ha habido nada. Lo único que importa es Ambrose. Incluso ahora. Quiero a mi madre, la he cuidado como una buena hija, me he quedado a su lado... Incluso cogí ese trozo de tela para protegerla. A ella, no a mi hermano. Jamás lo haría por él. —Había comenzado hablando en un susurro, pero a medida que se explicaba su voz se iba tornando más estridente y chillona—. Sin embargo, mi madre sólo piensa en Ambrose, incluso en este momento.

Mantuvo los ojos fijos en la cabeza gacha de su hermano.

—Él lo heredó todo de nuestro padre, yo no recibí nada. Hasta la propiedad de nuestra madre irá a parar a sus manos. Soy su huésped. Puede echarme cuando le venga en gana, y no crea que no lo sabe. Siempre se ha asegurado de que no lo olvide.

Su rostro quedó demudado por las emociones. La amargura y los celos, reprimidos durante años, habían aflorado y manaban de ella como un torrente.

—El trozo de tela... Cogerlo, guardarlo, era mi oportunidad para vengarme. No se lo dije porque quería que sintiera miedo, que sufriera, quería que supiera que estaba en las manos de alguien que podría destruirlo. —De repente, miró al investigador—. Por supuesto, tarde o temprano se lo habría dicho. En cuanto me recordara lo inútil que era, la acompañante tan sosa que sería para un hombre de su futura posición... —Se detuvo un momento antes de añadir—: Ni siquiera se me pasó por la cabeza que no supusiera... Le bastaba con pensar un poco para darse cuenta de que sólo nuestra madre o yo habríamos cogido el trozo de tela para protegerlo. Mi madre se lo habría dicho de inmediato. Al verlo guardar silencio, creí que había adivinado que lo tenía yo, pero que se cuidaba mucho de hablar del tema mientras estuviéramos aquí. —Enfrentó la mirada del señor Stokes—. Jamás se me ha ocurrido pensar que supuso que Portia lo había visto y que era tan tonta como para no recordarlo.

El silencio se apoderó de la estancia. Un silencio tan absoluto que se escuchaba el tictac del reloj que había en la repisa de la chimenea.

Drusilla tenía la vista clavada en el suelo. Ambrose estaba sentado con la cabeza gacha. La mirada de Lady Calvin se paseaba entre sus hijos, como si ya no los reconociera; después, enterró la cara entre las manos y se echó a llorar.

El sonido hizo que los demás salieran de la estupefacción en la que los había sumido semejante confesión. Todos se pusieron en movimiento. Charlie se levantó de su asiento como si fuera incapaz de seguir sentado, como si deseara marcharse de allí.

Lord Netherfield carraspeó antes de mirar al señor Stokes.

—Si me permite...

El hombre asintió con la cabeza.

El anciano miró a Ambrose.

—No ha dicho nada de Dennis, el gitano. ¿Por qué mató al muchacho?

Ambrose no levantó la cabeza.

—Me vio quemando la chaqueta. Después llegó el señor Stokes y comenzó a interrogar a todo el mundo. —Se retorció las manos y prosiguió—: No quise matar a Kitty, de verdad que no. Ella me obligó a hacerlo... No me pareció justo que matarla significara mi ruina. Sólo la señorita Ashford y ese gitano podrían... —Se detuvo un instante y barbotó una excusa infantil—: ¡Eran ellos o yo! ¡Se trataba de mi vida!

Lord Glossup se puso en pie; su rostro, por regla general afable, mostraba una patente repulsión.

—Señor Stokes, ¿tiene lo que necesita?

El aludido se enderezó.

—Desde luego, señor. Estoy seguro de que podemos...

Lord Glossup y el investigador se dispusieron a discutir los arreglos necesarios para retener a Ambrose. El resto de los presentes se marchó.

Al ver que las damas titubeaban, Lady O se puso en pie.

—Catherine, querida, creo que debemos retirarnos al salón. Un poco de té nos vendrá bien a todos. Estoy segura de que Drusilla quiere retirarse de inmediato a su habitación, pero creo que al resto nos sentará bien un tónico reconstituyente.

Portia se levantó, pero Simon la detuvo cogiéndola del brazo. Lady O los miró, comprendió al punto, y asintió con la cabeza.

—Por supuesto, tú subirás a darte un baño y a cambiarte de ropa. Cualquier otra cosa sería perjudicial para tu salud. Tu hermano no me perdonaría si te devuelvo a casa con un resfriado.

El ligero énfasis de sus palabras, el ligero brillo de sus astutos ojos negros, les dijo que estaba decidida a enviarla a casa con algo más.

Simon se limitó a inclinar la cabeza en respuesta a su mensaje. Lady O refunfuñó y salió de la biblioteca, seguida del resto de las damas. Lady Calvin necesitó apoyarse en lady Glossup y la señora Buckstead para caminar.

—Vamos. —Cogió a Portia del brazo y la condujo hasta las puertas del otro extremo de la biblioteca, desde las que llegarían antes a la escalinata.

El señor Stokes los interceptó.

—Una cosa más: aún tengo que considerar la posibilidad de presentar cargos contra la señorita Calvin.

Tanto Portia como él miraron a Drusilla, que seguía sentada en el diván, sola. Tenía los ojos clavados en su hermano; éste estaba inclinado hacia delante, con los brazos apoyados en las piernas y la vista clavada en sus manos.

Portia se estremeció y miró al señor Stokes.

—¡Los celos son algo horrible!

El señor Stokes, que enfrentó su mirada, asintió con la cabeza.

—No pretendía hacer daño a nadie. No me cabe duda de que ignoraba las tendencias homicidas de su hermano.

—No creo que sea necesario presentar cargos. —Portia levantó la cabeza—. Ya tiene bastante castigo con todo lo que ha confesado... No va a facilitarle la vida, ni mucho menos.

El investigador volvió a asentir antes de desviar la mirada hacia Simon.

Por su parte, él no se sentía tan dispuesto a mostrarse benévolo, pero comprendía que el origen de su reacción radicaba en el hecho de que había sido Portia la amenazada. Ella lo miró al ver que no decía nada... y fue entonces cuando supo que no le quedaba alternativa. Portia sería capaz de leer en él como un libro abierto si no controlaba sus impulsos. Asintió con un gesto brusco de cabeza.

—Nada de presentar cargos. No tiene sentido.

Portia esbozó una media sonrisa antes de concentrarse de nuevo en el señor Stokes.

Los tres se demoraron allí un momento, mirándose, aliviados, satisfechos. No había necesidad de expresar lo que sentían con palabras. El señor Stokes no pertenecía a su clase, pero habían forjado una especie de amistad. Y todos reconocían ese hecho.

Pasado un instante, el hombre carraspeó y apartó la mirada.

—Me marcharé con el señor Calvin al clarear el día. Es lo mejor. Así podrán retomar sus vidas lo antes posible. —Los miró de nuevo y les tendió la mano—. Gracias. Jamás lo habría atrapado sin su ayuda y la del señor Hastings. —Se dieron un apretón de manos—. Espero... —Se ruborizó, pero se obligó a continuar—. Espero que la charada no haya malogrado su relación.

Simon miró a Portia, quien, a su vez, sonrió al investigador.

—Las revelaciones fueron bastante interesantes... Creo que nos sobrepondremos. —Lo miró de soslayo.

Al sentirse expuesto, Simon intentó reprimir un gruñido y volvió a cogerla del brazo.

—Te espera un baño en tu habitación.

Tras intercambiar un último saludo, dejaron al señor Stokes en la biblioteca.

James y Charlie los esperaban en el vestíbulo.

—Gracias... a los dos —dijo James, con una sonrisa de oreja a oreja. Tomó a Portia de las manos—. Aún no sé toda la historia, pero aun así..., ¡ha sido usted muy valiente!

En esa ocasión, fue incapaz de contener el gruñido.

—¡Por el amor de Dios! ¡Sólo me faltaba que se le subiera a la cabeza! —exclamó.

James se echó a reír. Lo apartó de un codazo y reanudó la marcha hacia la planta superior.

—Ya nos pondremos al día luego —añadió James mientras ellos subían la escalinata.

Simon lo miró por encima del hombro.

—Mañana.

Y, con los dientes apretados, tiró de Portia.

18

Un criado los aguardaba en la planta superior para acompañarlos hasta la habitación que habían preparado, según sus órdenes. No era la habitación que había ocupado en un principio, por lo de la víbora; ni tampoco la de lady O, porque ya estaba demasiado atestada con el catre como para añadir también una bañera. Era una de las *suites* que rara vez se usaban, compuesta por un amplio dormitorio con una cama enorme y un gabinete privado.

La hizo pasar y descubrieron a dos doncellas que vertían en la bañera un par de humeantes cubos de agua. Había unos cuantos más junto a la chimenea.

—Deshazte de ellas —le dijo, mirándola directamente a los ojos.

Portia alzó una ceja con un gesto socarrón y esbozó una sonrisilla. Se quitó su chaqueta de los hombros y se la dio. Una de las doncellas se apresuró a ayudarla a desvestirse. Con la chaqueta en la mano, Simon se perdió por la puerta que comunicaba el dormitorio con el gabinete para esperar allí.

La chaqueta estaba empapada. La dejó sobre una silla y se acercó a la ventana. Clavó la mirada en las siluetas de los árboles e intentó no pensar, no demorarse en las emociones que el día había suscitado.

Intentó, en vano, refrenar la más poderosa de ellas; la emoción que ella y sólo ella lograba despertar. Una emoción que siempre se había cuidado mucho de ocultar, incluso a ojos de Portia. Incluso en ese momento.

Y que a lo largo de los últimos días había ido creciendo, se había hecho mucho más insistente.

Escuchó que la puerta del dormitorio se abría y se cerraba. Acto seguido, las pisadas de las doncellas resonaron en el pasillo hasta desvanecerse.

Respiró hondo, refrenó sus demonios y echó a andar hacia la puerta que comunicaba las dos estancias.

Cuando la abrió, confirmó que Portia estaba sola.

En la bañera. Enjabonándose el pelo.

Hizo acopio de valor antes de entrar y cerrar la puerta a su espalda. Se encaminó a la puerta principal y echó el pestillo. Frente al escritorio había una silla de patas torneadas. La cogió al pasar junto a ella y la llevó hasta la chimenea. La colocó con el respaldo frente a la bañera y se sentó a horcajadas.

Portia lo miró.

—Ya que estabas tan impaciente por despachar a las doncellas, supongo que estarás dispuesto a ocupar su lugar, ¿no?

Se obligó a no encogerse de hombros, a no reaccionar a la mirada especulativa de esos ojos azul cobalto. La bañera era demasiado pequeña.

—Lo que necesites...

Cruzó los brazos sobre el respaldo de la silla y dejó la frase en el aire mientras enfrentaba su mirada, dispuesto a observar.

Dispuesto a someterse a una calculada tortura.

Y ella lo torturó a placer enjabonándose con delicadeza los brazos y acariciándose esas larguísimas piernas de la forma más seductora. El agua la cubrió hasta la parte superior de los muslos cuando se alzó sobre las rodillas. El brillo de sus nalgas fue de lo más excitante, de modo que se vio obligado a cerrar los ojos y pensar en otra cosa.

Portia eligió ese preciso momento para pedirle que la ayudara a aclararse el pelo. Se puso en pie con todo el cuerpo en tensión, cogió un cubo y...

Ella lo miró a los ojos.

—Poco a poco. Necesito quitarme toda la espuma.

Se acercó a la bañera para verter el agua mientras ella se aclaraba el pelo y se lo retorcía. No se había dado cuenta de lo largo que lo tenía. Mojado, le llegaba hasta las caderas y su mirada se desvió hacia...

Tuvo que cerrar los ojos al instante. Con la mandíbula apretada y la vista clavada en su cabeza, le siguió vertiendo el agua mientras sujetaba el cubo con todas sus fuerzas.

Hasta que quedó vacío.

Portia se echó el pelo hacia atrás, aferró los bordes de la bañera y se puso en pie. El agua cayó en cascada por las caderas y los muslos.

Con la mente en blanco y la boca seca, Simon soltó el cubo y, sin mirar, alargó el brazo hacia las toallas apiladas sobre un taburete. Después de coger una, la sacudió para extenderla y la sostuvo al tiempo que se alejaba un poco para que ella pudiera salir de la bañera.

Portia cogió la toalla y se la llevó al pecho mientras sus ojos lo estudiaban.

Simon enfrentó su escrutinio con todo el estoicismo del que fue capaz, tras lo cual volvió a coger otra toalla..., con la que le cubrió la cabeza.

Escuchó una risilla sofocada.

Comenzó a secarle el pelo. Estaba tan húmedo que podría empapar la cama entera. Ella se dejó hacer al tiempo que se agachaba un poco y se giraba para secar su voluptuoso cuerpo y sus largas extremidades.

Una vez satisfecha, dejó caer la toalla, le quitó la que tenía en la mano y la arrojó al suelo. El corazón estuvo a punto de salírsele por la boca cuando se acercó y sus brazos la rodearon por iniciativa propia.

Ella le arrojó los brazos al cuello y alzó el rostro para que la besara.

La complació al instante. Se apoderó de sus labios y de su boca en cuanto se ofreció, y sintió cómo su control se resquebrajaba cuando ella se pegó contra su cuerpo.

Acababa de interrumpir el beso y de alzar la cabeza cuando se percató del brillo decidido de sus ojos.

—Quiero celebrarlo —dijo Portia con la vista clavada en sus labios. Se puso de puntillas y los rozó suavemente con los suyos—. Ahora.

—En la cama. —Esa mujer iba a ser su perdición. No le cabía la menor duda.

Como si hubiera captado algo en su tono de voz, ella ladeó la cabeza y lo observó con detenimiento antes de sonreír. Una sonrisa demasiado ladina, demasiado resuelta para su gusto.

—Con una condición —añadió ella con esa voz ronca y sensual que siempre lograba tensarle la entrepierna—. Esta vez lo quiero todo.

Sintió que algo se hacía añicos en su interior.

—¿Todo?

—Ajá —respondió con los ojos clavados en los suyos—. Todo..., incluyendo eso que te empeñas en ocultar.

Por primera vez en su vida, se sintió embriagado de deseo. Apretó la mandíbula y le dijo entre dientes:

—No sabes lo que estás diciendo.

Una ceja negra se arqueó con arrogancia... en flagrante desafío.

—¿De veras?

Su tono de voz era una tortura de por sí.

Antes de que pudiera contestarle, ella se giró entre sus brazos con la elegancia de una hurí, se amoldó a su cuerpo y le lanzó una mirada por encima del hombro. Mientras frotaba su trasero contra su dolorosa erección del modo más sugerente, lo miró a los ojos y esperó un instante antes de preguntarle:

—¿Estás seguro?

Ella lo sabía. Lo leyó en sus ojos, de un azul tan oscuro que prácticamente parecía negro. Quiso preguntarle cómo demonios lo sabía, pero su mente era incapaz de hilar dos palabras seguidas.

Era incapaz de pensar en otra cosa que no fuera la certeza de que, de algún modo, ella conocía su más profundo deseo. Y estaba dispuesta a satisfacerlo. Había accedido a satisfacerlo.

Cosa que le quedó bien clara cuando extendió una mano y, tras echar la cabeza hacia atrás, tiró de su rostro para besarlo. Se abrió a la invasión de su lengua y la acarició en respuesta con la suya. Lo exhortó a darse un festín. Cuando la obedeció, le apartó la mano de la mejilla. Acto seguido, le cogió las dos manos y se las llevó a los pechos.

Contuvo la respiración un instante cuando los apretó contra las palmas. El sonido que brotó de la garganta de Portia, sofocado en parte gracias al beso, le encendió la sangre en las venas. Se apartó de sus labios y, sin soltarle los pechos, musitó:

—¿Estás segura?

Ella bajó los párpados cuando comenzó a acariciar esas turgentes curvas con afán posesivo. Cuando los abrió, sus ojos resplandecían.

—Soy tuya. —Pronunció las palabras con voz segura y decidida—. Tómame como desees. —Sostuvo su mirada sin flaquear—. Quiero todo lo que puedas ofrecerme. Todos tus deseos, todos tus anhelos. Todo.

Su autocontrol se derrumbó en ese instante. La pasión rugió en sus venas, con más fuerza que nunca. La soltó y la giró entre sus brazos antes de inclinar la cabeza y atrapar sus labios para devorarla.

Lo que lo impulsaba no era deseo, ni lujuria, ni siquiera era pasión; era algo que surgía de la mezcla de esas tres cosas, pero que estaba imbuido de algo más. De un anhelo primitivo y desesperado. De algo que estaba enterrado bajo las capas de su fachada civilizada y cuya existencia pocas mujeres podrían adivinar.

Y que, por tanto, jamás habían tentado.

Jamás lo habían invitado a salir a la superficie.

Sin interrumpir el beso, la alzó del suelo y ella se aferró a su cuello con la misma desesperación que lo embargaba a él, con la misma avidez.

Fue retrocediendo con ella en brazos hasta que sus piernas se toparon con la cama. Echó mano de todas sus fuerzas para apartarla, dar la vuelta y arrojarla sobre la brillante colcha carmesí.

—Espera.

Portia aguardó tal y como había aterrizado, casi de costado, y supo que no tendría que esperar mucho. Lo observó mientras se desvestía y dejó que su mirada vagara por su rostro, deleitándose en los austeros rasgos mientras él arrojaba el chaleco a un lado. Tenía la expresión más adusta y tensa que le había visto jamás. La fuerza que exudaba su cuerpo, implícita en cada uno de sus movimientos, le resultó mucho más clara, más intensa. Mucho menos contenida.

La camisa siguió al chaleco. Se retiró hacia atrás un poco para disfrutar mejor de ese despliegue de piel desnuda y de músculos que se abultaban al menor movimiento, como cuando se agachó para quitarse las botas.

Se deshizo en un santiamén de los pantalones y de los calcetines. Y allí estuvo, desnudo y a todas luces excitado. Su mirada la atravesó y la recorrió de arriba abajo mientras se acercaba a la cama. Cuando estuvo cerca, extendió un brazo para acariciarle una pantorrilla. Siguió subiendo por la parte posterior de su muslo hasta que cerró la mano en torno a una nalga mientras que con la otra la instaba a ponerse de rodillas.

La miró a los ojos.

—Si quieres que me detenga, sólo tienes que decirlo.

Ella sostuvo su mirada; una mirada misteriosa y abrasadora... Y estuvo a punto de sonreír.

—Sabes que eso no va a pasar.

Sus miradas siguieron entrelazadas un instante más antes de que él cerrara los ojos y la ayudara a darse la vuelta.

A ponerse boca abajo.

Sintió cómo se hundía el colchón cuando Simon subió a la cama y se colocó tras ella. Cuando se inclinó, sintió el calor de su cuerpo que le abrasaba la cara posterior de los muslos y las nalgas como si fuera una lengua de fuego. La besó en la base de la espalda, justo sobre la hendidura que separaba sus glúteos.

Al instante, la agarró por las caderas, inmovilizándola mientras trazaba un húmedo reguero de besos ardientes por su espalda, como si de verdad tuviera intención de devorarla.

El áspero vello de su pecho le acarició la piel. Estaba envuelta en su calor a pesar de que sus cuerpos aún no se rozaban. Él había apoyado todo su peso en los brazos mientras seguía moviéndose sobre ella y la rodeaba como si fuera un poderoso animal que acabara de capturarla y estuviera decidido a poseerla.

Se estremeció en respuesta. Cerró los ojos un instante y saboreó la oleada de pasión que la invadió hasta engullirla. Echó un vistazo por encima del hombro cuando sintió que él le apartaba el pelo al llegar a la nuca.

Sus ojos se encontraron un instante cuando Simon alzó la cabeza. Después, se incorporó un poco, capturó sus piernas entre los muslos y le colocó las manos en las caderas. Desde allí fueron ascendiendo muy despacio por sus costados hasta que comenzó a acariciarle la parte inferior de los pechos con las yemas de los dedos. Cuando estuvo satisfecho, siguió hasta los brazos y fue descendiendo. Se detuvo al llegar a los codos.

—Extiende los brazos sobre la cama, por encima de la cabeza.

Le indicó cómo hacerlo y ella se lo permitió. Con la pérdida de ese apoyo, acabó tendida sobre la colcha. Sintió el roce de la seda en los pezones, endurecidos por el deseo.

Cuando le colocó las muñecas sobre los almohadones, la soltó.

—Déjalos así. No se te ocurra mover los brazos.

Una orden áspera e indiscutible. El corazón comenzó a latirle con fuerza y sus sentidos se pusieron en alerta cuando sus lentas y posesivas caricias regresaron, pero en sentido inverso. Lo sentía muy cerca, pero aparte del ocasional roce del vello del pecho, sólo la tocó con las manos y los labios.

Y con la mirada. Sentía su abrasadora mirada sobre ella, siguiendo el movimiento de sus manos a medida que descendía por su espalda, por su cintura y detenía los pulgares sobre los hoyuelos de la parte baja de su espalda.

Sintió un hormigueo y una extraña emoción.

Para su sorpresa, Simon se alejó y se incorporó. Le colocó las rodillas a ambos lados de las piernas... y la aferró por las caderas para alzarla poco a poco.

Hasta que quedó de rodillas frente a él.

Estaba a punto de incorporarse...

—Deja los brazos donde te he dicho.

El tono de su voz le provocó un escalofrío y le puso los nervios a flor de piel. Obedeció mucho antes de pensar en lo que estaba haciendo. Sin el uso de los brazos estaba indefensa y expuesta... con el trasero alzado.

Antes de que pudiera percatarse de la sumisión total que implicaba la postura, sintió una de sus manos en la espalda, en la cintura.

Inmovilizándola.

Justo cuando se dio cuenta de sus intenciones, su otra mano le acarició el trasero con audacia, siguiendo la hendidura hasta llegar a su húmeda e hinchada entrepierna, fácilmente accesible en esa postura.

La mantuvo así mientras la atormentaba con sus indagadoras caricias. Sin llegar a penetrarla. No mostró la menor compasión por sus ávidos sentidos. Al contrario, avivó su ansia hasta que sintió la piel en llamas, hasta que su respiración no fue más que un resuello entrecortado.

Hasta que comenzó a gemir.

El desvergonzado sonido la sobresaltó, pero sólo fue el primero de muchos. Simon la mantuvo inmóvil, negándole la satisfacción que la incesante estimulación demandaba. Negándole la posibilidad de satisfacer ese anhelo que crecía poco a poco en su interior y que amenazaba con consumirla.

Se mordió el labio inferior y cerró los ojos. Sólo podía mover la cabeza y eso hizo que el pelo cayera desordenado a su alrededor. Intentó contener los gemidos que brotaban de su garganta.

No pudo.

Así que gimió. Y volvió a hacerlo mientras alzaba las caderas, incrementando el sensual tormento.

Justo antes de que cediera del todo y le dijera abiertamente lo que quería, Simon se movió. La abrió con los dedos, guió la gruesa punta de su erección hasta su sexo y embistió con toda deliberación.

La penetró hasta el fondo con un solo envite que la dejó sin aliento.

La postura hizo que sintiera la penetración más completa que nunca.

La agarró por las caderas, afianzó las rodillas y se retiró un poco antes de volver a embestir. Todo ello sin apartar la mano que la inmovilizaba. Que la instaba a seguir en una postura suplicante ante él, ofreciéndole su cuerpo para su entera satisfacción.

Una ofrenda que él tomaba, aceptaba y degustaba con cada profundo, fuerte y magistral envite.

Le había asegurado que era suya y él le había tomado la palabra. Mientras la inmovilizaba y la poseía cada vez más rápido, con más ardor y frenesí, por fin comprendió lo que significaban esas palabras.

Y no vio motivo alguno para quejarse.

El fuego, las llamas y el amor estaban allí. A su alrededor, sobre ellos, en su interior. Se entregó a la emoción del momento y se lanzó al infierno.

Se rindió de buena gana.

Simon jadeó cuando sintió que Portia se tensaba a su alrededor. Cerró los ojos y se regodeó en la exquisita sensación que le provocaba el roce de ese firme trasero cada vez que se hundía en su abrasadora humedad. Una vez y otra y otra más.

Le apartó la mano de la espalda y la sostuvo por las caderas. La aferró con fuerza y la poseyó a placer, libre de las restricciones que lo habían encadenado hasta ese momento. Tomó todo lo que ella le había ofrecido.

La invitación más formidable que una mujer podía hacer: ofrecerse a un hombre para que la poseyera como quisiera.

El corazón le latía desbocado y amenazaba con estallarle mientras saciaba sus sentidos. Mientras sentía cómo el cuerpo de Portia respondía, paso a paso, exigiendo más. Igual que el suyo.

Le soltó las caderas y se inclinó sobre ella antes de pasarle las manos por los costados. Ascendió hasta llegar a sus pechos y los rodeó. Tenía los pezones endurecidos. Los acarició y pellizcó hasta que la escuchó gritar. Hasta que volvió a gemir.

Su cuerpo cobró vida bajo él. Comenzó a moverse al compás de sus caderas, saliendo al encuentro de cada embestida. Le apartó el pelo de la nuca con la nariz y le mordisqueó el cuello.

Cuando la sintió arquearse bajo él, le dio un lametón y ella estalló. Sus músculos lo apresaron con fuerza y los espasmos la sacudieron mientras seguía hundiéndose en ella, hasta lo más profundo de su alma.

Cerró los brazos alrededor de sus hombros y la inmovilizó mientras su cuerpo respondía a los espasmos de su clímax hundiéndose con más ardor en ella, ansioso de seguirla hasta esa gloriosa cumbre de deleite sensual que trascendía cualquier placer mundano y los arrojaba a un paradisíaco éxtasis.

A un vórtice de satisfacción inconmensurable. A la satisfacción más absoluta que había conocido jamás. La celebración que ella ansiaba los había llevado a una nueva dimensión, a un plano distinto.

No supo cuánto tiempo pasó antes de que reuniera las fuerzas y el sentido común suficientes para salir de ella, apartar la ropa de cama y dejarse caer sin soltarla sobre el colchón.

Permaneció tendido sin moverse, entregado al momento. Dejó que la paz y la certeza lo inundaran. La certeza más absoluta.

Ambos se quedaron dormidos.

Cuando despertó, descubrió que Portia yacía acurrucada contra él, dándole la espalda, y que él tenía uno de los brazos sobre su cintura.

Ella también estaba despierta. Lo supo por la tensión de su cuerpo, ya que no podía verle la cara.

Se apoyó en un codo y se inclinó sobre ella.

Portia ladeó la cabeza, lo miró y sonrió.

Aun a la luz de la luna, el resultado de esa sonrisa fue glorioso.

Portia alzó una mano, deseosa de acariciar una de sus mejillas. Sin dejar de sonreír, volvió a girar la cabeza sobre la almohada y se deleitó en la sensación de tenerlo detrás, con una evidente e inmensa erección.

Estaba inmóvil, pero aun así...

Su sonrisa se ensanchó. Extendió un brazo hacia él y tomó su miembro en la mano. Lo acarició mientras rememoraba ciertos detalles...

—Me acusaste de ser una calientapollas... ¿Lo dijiste en serio?

—Ni siquiera estaba seguro de que supieras lo que significaba —refunfuñó él.

Portia sonrió mientras recorría la punta de su erección con la yema del pulgar.

—A decir verdad, no es normal encontrársela así de repente en los textos de Ovidio, pero entiendo el significado de ciertas palabras de nueva acuñación.

—¿De nueva acuñación?

La respuesta era innecesaria, porque Simon no estaba pensando precisamente en palabras.

La mano que lo acariciaba se cerró en torno a él con más fuerza.

—No me has contestado —le reprochó.

Simon tomó aire. Hubo un breve silencio antes de que replicara:

—No lo eres en términos generales, pero sí específicamente.

Analizó un instante la respuesta mientras lo acariciaba a conciencia.

—¿Quieres decir que te excito?

En ese momento, fue ella la que se quedó sin aliento cuando Simon le alzó la pierna un poco y sus dedos la penetraron con maestría.

—Tu simple existencia me excita —dijo sin dejar de acariciarla.

La respuesta hizo que esbozara una sonrisa de oreja a oreja.

—¿Cómo es eso? —preguntó de nuevo sin aliento al tiempo que cambiaba la posición de las caderas y sentía que él se movía a su espalda.

—En cuanto te veo, sólo puedo pensar en hundirme en tu cuerpo. —Le acercó esa parte de su cuerpo que estaba siendo objeto de discusión—. Así.

Portia cerró los ojos mientras él la penetraba muy despacio. Se retiró antes de volver a permitirle que disfrutara a placer de su regreso. Contuvo el aliento mientras su cuerpo cobraba vida de repente. Al instante, logró tomar aire para afirmar con decisión:

—Creo que me gusta esto de ser una calientapollas, al menos específicamente hablando.

Simon se inclinó sobre ella para acariciarle el lóbulo de la oreja con los labios al tiempo que le pasaba el brazo bajo el suyo y cerraba la mano sobre un pecho. El gesto le informó de que, lejos de quejarse, a él también le encantaba que lo fuera.

Un poco más tarde..., bastante más tarde, yacían exhaustos en la cama. Estaba tendida sobre Simon, con la cabeza apoyada sobre su pecho, donde él la había colocado. Entretanto, él jugueteaba distraídamente con su pelo.

Poco después, tomó una honda bocanada de aire.

—Te quiero. Lo sabes, ¿verdad?

Ella tardó apenas un instante en responder.

—Sí. —Alzó la cabeza y le sonrió. Entrelazó las manos sobre su pecho y apoyó la barbilla en ellas mientras lo estudiaba.

El color azul cobalto de sus ojos había vuelto a oscurecerse y resplandecían en la oscuridad mientras los contemplaba, a la espera.

Su sonrisa, la de una mujer claramente satisfecha, se ensanchó.

—Yo también te quiero —confesó, aunque con el ceño fruncido—. Pero todavía no lo entiendo.

Simón titubeó un instante antes de replicar:

—No creo que el amor sea algo que necesitemos entender. —Bien sabía Dios que él no lo hacía.

El ceño de Portia se acentuó.

—Tal vez, pero no puedo dejar de pensar...

Deslizó las manos por su esbelta espalda mientras la interrumpía.

—¿Te ha dicho alguien alguna vez que piensas demasiado?

—Sí. Tú.

—Pues deja de pensar. —Sus manos bajaron un poco más y la acariciaron de forma muy sugerente.

Ella lo miró a los ojos y enarcó una ceja.

—Oblígame.

Sostuvo su mirada y confirmó que esas palabras eran, efectivamente, la invitación que él había escuchado. Esbozó una sonrisa... maliciosa.

—Será un placer.

Giró hasta quedar sobre ella y se dispuso a complacerla.

Portia no volvió a pensar con coherencia hasta bien entrado el día.

Tal vez ella no hubiera estado pensando, pero él sí. Había estado haciendo planes, aunque Portia todavía no lo supiera.

Cuando la vio llegar al comedor matinal, ya había convencido a lady O de que era imperativo que se la llevara, a Portia, no a lady O, a cierto lugar. Por fortuna, la susodicha llegó demasiado tarde como para escuchar el sitio concreto.

—Lo sabrás cuando lleguemos —fue todo lo que le dijo.

Con la mandíbula tensa y una expresión que ella ya conocía muy bien, Simon se dispuso a dar buena cuenta de un plato de jamón.

Decidió preguntarle a lady O.

La anciana desestimó la pregunta con un gesto de la mano antes incluso de haber acabado de formularla.

—Hazme caso: será mejor que lo dejes llevarte a la ciudad. No creo que te guste viajar despacio en mi carruaje, dando tumbos. No cuando tienes una opción mejor. —Sonrió... y sus ojos se iluminaron con ese brillo diabólico tan habitual en ella—. Si estuviera en tu lugar, yo no me lo pensaría.

Lo que la dejó sin más remedio que acceder.

Mientras daba buena cuenta del té y la tostada, observó a los comensales. La transformación era evidente. La mesa estaba presidida por un ambiente mucho más relajado. Todavía había cierta reserva en los ojos de algunos presentes, pero el alivio era inmenso y así lo confirmaban sus sonrisas.

Lady Calvin, por supuesto, no estaba presente. Al igual que las restantes damas de más edad, salvo lady O y lady Hammond.

—Lo está llevando muy mal, la pobrecilla —le confió lady Hammond—. Siempre ha soñado con ver a Ambrose en el Parlamento y ahora... verse obligada a enfrentar todo esto, además de todo lo que se ha revelado también acerca de Drusilla... Está totalmente hundida. Catherine le ha dicho que se quede un par de días más, al menos hasta que esté un poco más repuesta para viajar.

Drusilla tampoco estaba en la mesa del desayuno, como era de esperar.

No tardaron en reunirse en el vestíbulo principal para las despedidas. Los carruajes aguardaban a los invitados en el patio. Las Hammond fueron las primeras en marcharse y los Buckstead las siguieron de inmediato.

Portia se percató de que, a pesar de su opinión inicial,

James y Lucy estaban un poco apartados de la concurrencia. James acompañó a la muchacha hasta el carruaje y la ayudó a subir. En ese instante, decidió que invitaría a Lucy a alguna fiesta campestre en un futuro cercano... y a James también.

El único punto a decidir era el lugar donde se celebraría la fiesta en cuestión.

En ese instante lady O puso fin a la ronda de despedidas y, tomada del brazo de lord Netherfield, encabezó la marcha hacia los escalones. Simon y ella los siguieron a tiempo de escuchar cómo le decía al anciano:

—Unos días muy animados, Granny, pero hazme el favor de dejar los asesinatos a un lado la próxima vez. Son un poco excesivos para mi avanzada edad.

—Y para la mía, querida —refunfuñó el aludido—. Pero, al menos, ha servido para que estos jovenzuelos hayan demostrado su valía. —Les dedicó una sonrisa en la que estuvieron incluidos Charlie y James, que los seguían a cierta distancia—. Al parecer aún queda esperanza para las generaciones más jóvenes.

El resoplido que soltó lady O fue de lo más sarcástico.

—Muérdete la lengua. Lo único que les hace falta es que se les suban los halagos a la cabeza...

Charlie, que hizo un esfuerzo evidente por ocultar una sonrisa, se adelantó para ayudar a la anciana a subir al carruaje. Ella aceptó la ayuda con un despliegue de aplomo. Una vez sentada, los atravesó con la mirada.

—A vosotros dos os veré en Londres. No me decepcionéis.

Sus palabras sonaron como una advertencia para que se comportaran. Sin embargo, ambos interpretaron correctamente la naturaleza de la sugerencia.

Lord Netherfield sonrió y despidió a la anciana con la mano. Ellos lo imitaron y esperaron hasta que el carruaje enfiló el camino para dirigirse al tílburi de Simon, que los aguardaba con los caballos enganchados en el otro extremo del patio.

James y Charlie los siguieron. Mientras Simon examinaba la pareja de bayos con ojo crítico, James tomó a Portia de las manos.

—No voy a avergonzarla de nuevo dándole las gracias, pero espero que nos veamos en Londres este otoño. —Titubeó un instante antes de echar un vistazo hacia Simon—. En fin, Kitty había logrado que rechazara de plano la idea del matrimonio, pero ahora... —Alzó una ceja con gesto alegre, pero un tanto curioso—. Tal vez haya esperanza y deba reconsiderar mi postura.

Ella sonrió.

—De hecho, creo que debería hacerlo. —Se puso de puntillas y le dio un beso en la mejilla. Al instante, se giró hacia Charlie y lo miró con las cejas enarcadas.

Él también enfrentó su mirada con una sonrisa antes de parpadear. Sus ojos volaron hacia James.

—¡Ah, no! Ni hablar. Un soltero empedernido, ése soy yo... Demasiado superficial para cualquier dama con dos dedos de frente.

—Tonterías. —También lo besó en la mejilla—. Algún día de éstos, alguna dama con más de dos dedos de frente le calará. Y, entonces, ¿qué?

—Emigraré.

Todos estallaron en carcajadas.

James la ayudó a subir al tílburi.

—Y tú, ¿qué? —le preguntó a Simon cuando éste se acercó.

Antes de contestar, Simon la miró con expresión pensativa, tras lo cual le tendió la mano a su amigo.

—Pregúntamelo dentro de tres meses.

James se echó a reír y le estrechó la mano.

—Sospecho que sabré tu respuesta un poco antes.

Simon estrechó la mano de Charlie antes de sentarse. Agitó las riendas en cuanto estuvieron acomodados y se marcharon entre sonrisas y despedidas con la mano.

Portia se reclinó en el asiento para reflexionar. Su baúl y su sombrerera iban bien asegurados en el lugar que normalmente ocupaba Wilks, el cual viajaba con lady O. No había, por tanto, nada que suscitara sospechas en el hecho de que Simon la condujera a Londres. Ni el menor atisbo de escándalo en el hecho de que viajaran a solas en un carruaje descubierto. Iban siguiendo a lady O, que hacía las veces de carabina. Todo muy decoroso.

Salvo por el detalle de que Simon y ella no iban directamente a Londres, sino que antes se detendrían en algún otro lugar. Aunque no sabía dónde, ni mucho menos el porqué.

A pesar de saber de antemano que tomarían otro camino distinto al de la ciudad, le sorprendió que Simon hiciera girar a los caballos hacia el oeste, en dirección contraria a Ashmore, nada más transponer la verja de Glossup Hall.

—¿Al oeste del condado? —Se devanó los sesos intentando averiguar algo—. ¿Gabriel y Alathea? ¿O Lucifer y Phyllida?

Simon sonrió y meneó la cabeza.

—No conoces el lugar al que vamos. Nunca has estado en él. Y yo llevo años sin ir por allí.

—¿Habremos llegado para antes del atardecer?

—Mucho antes.

Decidió que lo mejor sería acomodarse en el asiento y contemplar el paisaje. Se dio cuenta de que el sentimiento que la embargaba era, ni más ni menos, que una increíble felicidad. Aun cuando no tuviera la menor idea de adónde la llevaba.

Tuvo que hacer el esfuerzo de contener una sonrisa. Sabía que si Simon se percataba, le exigiría una explicación. Aunque se le ocurriera una excusa apropiada, ése no era el momento ni el lugar.

La sencilla verdad era que no se imaginaba en la misma situación con otro hombre y tomándoselo tan alegremente.

Dejó que sus ojos vagaran hasta el rostro de Simon y lo observó un instante antes de clavar la vista al frente para que él no se diera cuenta de su escrutinio. Confiaba en él. Por completo. Y no sólo en el plano físico, aunque a esas alturas la verdad entre ellos estaba muy clara al respecto: le pertenecía en la misma medida que él a ella y, al parecer, así había sido siempre. Pero también confiaba en él en otros ámbitos.

Confiaba en su fuerza. Sabía que jamás la utilizaría en su contra, pero que siempre estaría ahí para protegerla. Confiaba en su lealtad, en su fuerza de voluntad y, sobre todo, confiaba en su corazón.

Sabía, en lo más profundo de su alma, que en esa vulnerabilidad que le había dejado ver, que había aceptado que ella debía ver, subyacía una promesa que perduraría toda la vida.

El amor. La fuente de toda confianza, la piedra angular del matrimonio.

Confianza, fuerza, seguridad... y amor.

Lo tenían todo.

Lo único que tenían que hacer era seguir adelante.

Adondequiera que él la estuviera llevando.

Arrellanada en el asiento y con la vista clavada al frente, decidió que estaba encantada de seguir el camino sin importar cuál fuera su destino.

Su destino era la población de Queen Charlton, en Somerset. Y, para ser más precisos, una casa solariega llamada Risby Grange. Simon hizo un alto en el pueblo y reservó una enorme habitación en la posada. Portia se aseguró de no quitarse los guantes en ningún momento, pero no detectó indicio alguno de que la posadera sospechara que no estaban casados.

Tal vez Charlie tuviera razón y su mutuo compromiso fuera patente a pesar de que no lo habían refrendado como mandaban los cánones.

Dejaron el equipaje en la posada y enfilaron un serpenteante camino. Era media tarde cuando pasaban bajo el arco de entrada de Risby Grange.

Simon detuvo el tílburi nada más traspasar la verja de la propiedad, junto a una casita. Ante ellos estaba la mansión, bañada por la luz del sol y plácidamente situada sobre la cresta de una suave loma. Su fachada de piedra gris, rematada en lo más alto por un antepecho almenado, estaba prácticamente cubierta por las plantas trepadoras y sus ventanas emplomadas parecían recibirlos con alegría.

Era una construcción antigua, sólida y muy bien conservada, aunque parecía estar deshabitada.

—¿Quién vive aquí? —le preguntó.

—En este momento, nadie aparte del guarda de la propiedad. —Simon dejó que los bayos prosiguieran por el camino con un suave trote—. Dudo mucho que esté por aquí ahora mismo. Tengo una llave.

Lo miró y aguardó una explicación, pero él no dijo nada más. Siguieron hasta dejar el tílburi en el prado más próximo a la entrada. Ambos se apearon de un salto. Tras atar las riendas a un árbol y comprobar que el freno estuviera echado, la tomó de la mano y atravesaron el patio en dirección a los escalones.

Una vez que llegaron a la puerta, tiró del cordón de la campanilla que había a la entrada. Escucharon cómo tintineaba en las profundidades de la mansión. Aguardaron un tiempo prudencial, pero nadie les abrió.

—El guarda es también el guardabosques, así que es probable que no esté. —Se sacó una enorme llave del bolsillo y la introdujo en la cerradura para abrir la puerta.

Él entró en primer lugar y echó un vistazo a su alrededor. Portia lo siguió, pisándole los talones.

Olvidó de inmediato todas las preguntas sobre el motivo de su presencia en el lugar a medida que la curiosidad la abandonaba. Dejó atrás el vestíbulo con sus paredes revestidas de madera y sus vidrieras de colores para ir de habitación en habitación, sin esperar siquiera a Simon.

Desde el exterior daba la impresión de que la mansión era muy extensa y el interior lo confirmaba. Había multitud de pasillos que llevaban a un sinfín de estancias. Otros pasillos partían de otros vestíbulos secundarios y se internaban en el corazón de la casa. Sin embargo, todas las habitaciones eran elegantes, acogedoras y estaban amuebladas con piezas antiguas muy bien conservadas. Las tapicerías y las cortinas eran preciosas y los objetos decorativos también eran antiguos. Algunos, por lo que alcanzó a ver, eran antiquísimas herencias familiares.

Todo estaba cubierto por una fina pátina de polvo, si bien el lugar no tenía ese típico olor mohoso de las casas que llevaban cerradas mucho tiempo. En cambio, parecía aguardar la llegada de un nuevo ocupante. Como si el dueño anterior se hubiera marchado poco tiempo atrás, pero se esperara en breve la llegada del nuevo. Era una casa pensada para llenarla de risas, amor y felicidad. Construida para que una numerosa familia habitara sus incontables estancias. Y eso flotaba en el ambiente de forma tan evidente que era casi tangible. Ésa era una casa que había visto crecer a muchas generaciones, que vivía y respiraba confiada en el futuro. Y que aguardaba ese futuro con ansia.

Portia conocía el lema de los Cynster: «Tener y retener.» Lo reconoció, así como el escudo de armas de la familia, en varios lugares: cojines, paneles de madera tallada, en una vidriera...

A la postre, subieron la escalinata y llegaron al grandioso salón de la planta superior. Se detuvo frente al ventanal situado justo sobre la puerta principal y se giró para mirar a Simon. Él estaba apoyado en el marco de la puerta, observándola.

—¿De quién es esta casa?

Él estudió su expresión antes de contestar.

—Mía.

Portia alzó las cejas y aguardó a que se explicara.

Él sonrió.

—Era de la tía abuela Clara. Como los demás ya estaban casados y tenían hogares propios, me la dejó en su testamento.

Portia ladeó la cabeza y lo observó con detenimiento.

—¿Por qué hemos venido?

Se enderezó y echó a andar hacia ella.

—Venía de camino aquí, pero hice un alto en la fiesta. —Se detuvo frente a ella, la tomó de la mano y la hizo girar de modo que pudiera contemplar la magnífica vista de los prados que se extendían hasta llegar a la verja de entrada—. Ya te lo he dicho. Hacía años que no venía. Mis recuerdos... No sabía hasta qué punto eran fiables. Quería confirmar que la mansión era tal cual la recordaba: una casa que clama por una esposa y una familia. —La miró mientras ella lo observaba—. Y mis recuerdos no me engañaban. Es una casa creada para ser el hogar de una familia.

Portia sostuvo su mirada.

—Cierto. ¿Y qué tenías planeado hacer una vez que confirmaras tus recuerdos?

Él esbozó una sonrisa fugaz.

—¿Tú qué crees? Pues buscar una esposa... —Se llevó su mano a los labios sin apartar la mirada de sus ojos—. Y formar una familia.

Ella parpadeó.

—Vaya. —Volvió a parpadear antes de apartar la vista en dirección al ventanal.

Sin soltarle la mano, él le preguntó:

—¿Qué pasa?

Hubo un breve silencio antes de que Portia contestara.

—¿Recuerdas cuando me encontraste en el mirador mientras hacía el voto de considerar a todos los caballeros adecuados? La razón por la que decidí hacerlo... Bueno, me di cuenta de que quería tener hijos. De que quería tener mi propia familia. Y, para lograrlo, necesitaba un marido. —Sonrió y lo miró a los ojos—. Claro que a lo que me refería en realidad era que estaba buscando a un caballero adecuado que complaciera todos mis deseos y me permitiera llevar las riendas de nuestra vida en común.

—No me cabe la menor duda —replicó él con evidente sarcasmo. Al ver que Portia no decía nada más y, en cambio, se limitaba a mirarlo como si lo estuviera viendo por primera vez, le preguntó con voz queda—: ¿Es por eso por lo que vas a casarte conmigo?

Todavía no había dicho que fuera a hacerlo, pero ambos sabían que sería así. Ya lo había decidido, aunque aún no se lo hubiera dicho con palabras. Sus ojos azul cobalto chispearon al percatarse de su treta antes de que su expresión se suavizara nuevamente. Esbozó una sonrisa.

—Lady O es de lo más sorprendente.

Simon comprendió que había perdido el hilo de la conversación.

—¿En qué sentido?

—Me dijo que el deseo de tener hijos podía ser una razón muy aceptable para considerar un futuro matrimonio, pero que no era motivo en sí mismo para casarse. Sin embargo, me aseguró que si seguía investigando, que si seguía considerando a los distintos caballeros con el matrimonio en mente, la razón correcta acabaría por presentarse sin más.

Entrelazó los dedos con los de Portia.

—¿Y ha sido así?

Ella lo miró a los ojos y esbozó una sonrisa serena.

—Sí. Te quiero y tú me quieres. Lady O, como siempre, tenía razón. No hay ningún otro motivo que sustente un matrimonio.

La estrechó entre sus brazos y sintió que sus cuerpos reaccionaban en cuanto se rozaron. No sólo en el plano sexual, sino también de un modo mucho más profundo, reconfortante e íntimo. Saboreó la sensación, saboreó la cercanía de Portia mientras ella le arrojaba los brazos al cuello y sentía entre sus manos la fuerza que animaba ese cuerpo esbelto; mientras veía en sus ojos una inteligencia igual a la suya.

—No va a ser fácil.

—Evidentemente, no. Y me niego a prometer que voy a ser una esposa agradable.

Simon sonrió.

—Ya eres bastante agradable. La palabra que buscas es «obediente», o tal vez «apacible»... y jamás has sido ninguna de las dos cosas.

—Tonterías. Lo soy cuando me conviene.

—Ahí está el problema.

—No pienso cambiar.

La miró a los ojos.

—No quiero que lo hagas. Si aceptas que yo tengo tantas posibilidades de cambiar como tú, podemos tomar ese acuerdo como punto de partida.

Portia sonrió. El suyo no sería el matrimonio que había deseado. Pero sí sería el que necesitaba.

—A pesar de nuestro pasado, hasta ahora nos hemos llevado bien. Si lo intentamos, ¿crees que podríamos conseguir que esto dure toda la vida?

—Si los dos lo intentamos, lo lograremos. —Hizo una pausa antes de añadir—: Después de todo, hemos encontrado la razón correcta.

—Sin duda —replicó ella antes de tirar de él para besarlo—. Estoy empezando a creer que hay algo de verdad en eso de que el amor puede con todo.

Simon se detuvo a escasos centímetros de sus labios.

—¿Hasta con nosotros?

Ella resopló con fastidio.

—Contigo, conmigo..., con los dos. Y ahora bésame.

Sonrió antes de obedecerla.

Había llegado al final de su viaje y había descubierto lo que buscaba. En brazos de Portia había descubierto su verdadero objetivo.